UKANAGAN UNIVERSITY COLLEGE
LIBRARY
BRITISH

RAYMOND CHANDLER

The Big Sleep
Farewell, My Lovely
The High Window

with an Introduction by
Diane Johnson

Alfred A. Knopf   New York   Toronto

255

THIS IS A BORZOI BOOK

PUBLISHED BY ALFRED A. KNOPF

First included in Everyman's Library, 2002
The Big Sleep Copyright © 1939 by Raymond Chandler
Copyright renewed 1966 by Mrs. Helga Greene
Farewell, My Lovely Copyright © 1940 by Raymond Chandler
Copyright renewed 1967 by Mrs. Helga Greene
The High Window Copyright © 1942 by Raymond Chandler
Copyright renewed 1969 by Mrs. Helga Greene
Introduction, Bibliography, and Chronology Copyright © 2002
by Everyman Publishers plc
Typography by Peter B. Willberg

All rights reserved under International and Pan-American Copyright
Conventions. Published in the United States by Alfred A. Knopf,
a division of Random House, Inc., New York, and simultaneously in
Canada by Random House of Canada Limited, Toronto. Distributed
by Random House, Inc., New York

www.randomhouse.com/everymans

ISBN 0-375-41501-7

Book Design by Barbara de Wilde and Carol Devine Carson

Printed and bound in Germany
by GGP Media, Pössneck

RAYMOND CHANDLER

CONTENTS

INTRODUCTION

Raymond Chandler is often called the greatest of the American hard-boiled detective-story writers. His only rival would be his acquaintance Dashiell Hammett, six years his junior but finished with writing by the time Chandler, at the age of fifty, was beginning. Chandler was by heritage and education British, though he was born in Chicago in 1888, and his father was an American, a hard-drinking engineer for the railroads, whom he never saw again after his parents divorced. Without money, his Anglo-Irish Quaker mother decided to take the seven-year-old Raymond back to her home in Ireland, and then to London, where they were supported by an uncle who saw to it that he got a good English education in 'public', that is, private schools, most importantly Dulwich College, which also produced such other notable writers as C. S. Forester and P. G. Wodehouse. Here he became truly British, read the classics and played rugby like other English schoolboys. Though he showed an aptitude for writing, he expected to go into the law.

This was not to be. When Raymond was sixteen, the generous uncle thought he had supported his sister Florence and her son long enough. Raymond was obliged to leave Dulwich College, and so was thrust rather abruptly into a harsh real world for which he had little practical training, with the obligation to support his mother. First of all, however, he toured the Continent, like many young Englishmen before him, spending some time in Paris and in Germany to complete his education. He then returned to England to take a civil service examination, where he came in third of 800 candidates, and was given a job in the Admiralty. This did not last, nor did a term of teaching at his old school. The restless young man moved to Bloomsbury, then the heart of literary London, wrote book reviews, and tried living by his pen, not without success; but a boy of no private means needed a serious job.

When he was twenty-four, he decided to put his unpromising literary career behind him and embarked for America to make his fortune, trying a variety of jobs in a variety of places from the midwest to California, learning bookkeeping and stringing tennis rackets among others. As his biographer Tom Hiney says, 'There is no doubt that the character of Philip Marlowe was fleshed out in these resolute, if friendless and moneyless months in Californian boarding houses.' But it would be some years before Chandler's great detective character Philip Marlowe saw the light of day. Chandler decided to settle permanently in Los Angeles, where he had landed a good job, and his mother came back to America to keep house for him. Unlike Dashiell Hammett, a Pinkerton detective, the more sheltered Chandler, with no real experience of crime and detection, worked as a business executive, and lived with his mother until he was over thirty-five.

The First World War was to change many things. Chandler joined the Canadian army, saying later that it felt more natural for him to wear a British uniform, and saw some action in Europe; it was in the trenches that he learned the details of blood and death that Marlowe would need to know. He was discharged in 1919 and, back in Los Angeles, planned to marry the love of his life, Cissy Pascal, a beautiful, twice-married woman seventeen years older than he, who pretended to be ten years younger than she was, and looked his own age. His mother, dying of cancer, opposed this peculiar marriage, so for a time Chandler, working as an executive in an oil company, supported both women in separate establishments. He and Cissy were married in 1924, after Florence's death, and they would be married, happily, it appeared, until she died more than thirty years later, when she was eighty-four and Chandler sixty-six. He would live only another four chaotic, troubled years.

By the end of the 1920s, a life-long problem, alcoholism, interrupted his career. Almost all the great American writers of the twenties and thirties were alcoholics – Chandler, Hammett, Faulkner, Fitzgerald, Hemingway – and the valorization of drinking is a striking feature in the literature of the period. Hardly a page goes by without somebody taking a drink in *The Sun Also Rises* and *The Big Sleep*. This was almost certainly in part a result of Prohibition, which was repealed in 1933, but not before it had altered the behavior of the nation, giving it bootleggers and speakeasies, and institutionalized hypocrisy: everybody drank and law enforcement winked. Heavy use of alcohol was tolerated and even fashionable, somehow linked with the prevailing atmosphere of gaiety, wisecracking and crime. Susceptible people like Hammett and Chandler were caught in the paradox of a debilitating habit that would also furnish them with material. Another paradox: Chandler's worsening bouts of drunkenness would get him fired from his executive job but propelled him into writing, the career he had always wanted anyhow.

The shock of being fired was salutary. Post-Depression America was in a period of self-help and individual striving. Even matchbooks advertised writing schools and vocabulary improvement techniques for people hoping to emerge from the pack. Chandler was forty-four, without a job, and with a bad drinking problem, but he had always been, and known himself to be, a good writer. After leaving school in London, he had published some poems, and it was as a poet that he saw himself, but now he signed up for a course in short-story writing. He left Los Angeles and Cissy, sobered up with the help of some army buddies in Seattle, went back to L.A. and Cissy, and learned, methodically and with great determination, how to write fiction. He studied the work of Erle Stanley Gardner, Hemingway, and the stories in a pulp magazine of detective fiction, *Black Mask*, in which his first story was published at the end of 1933.

Between 1933 and 1938, when he sat down to write his first novel, Chandler had written twenty-one *Black Mask* stories in which, under the guidance of its famous editor, Joseph Shaw, he polished the distinctive qualities of his later fiction. Here were the Marlowe prototypes, bad cops and good cops, Los Angeles and Bay City (Santa Monica) settings, the formula subjects of crime, sex, sadism and alcohol, a Chandleresque commitment to vivid minor characters, occasional passages of fine writing that hinted at his secret literary tastes, and a characteristic tone that hovers on the edge of satire. It is perhaps this tone that Ross Macdonald refers to when he says of Chandler that 'he writes like a slumming angel' – not quite the unmodified compliment it is sometimes taken for. One suspects that Chandler's Englishness accounts for the slightly patronizing detachment in Marlowe's tone when he describes the Los Angeles and Bay City underside, with its colorful new-world characters and rough manners. Capturing the American self-image, tough and self-deprecating, he also reflects a British impression of America, as a visitor struck by its brash color and the special cadence of the American language.

It is in *The Big Sleep* that he introduces his great creation, Philip Marlowe. Marlowe is partly generic hero – the high-principled loner characteristic of both cowboy and detective genres – and partly alter-ego, embodying Chandler's real attitudes and idealized projections of himself as a tough private detective, irresistible to women. Marlowe is an alcoholic bach-elor from California, an idealistic, misogynist and generally misanthropic ex-cop who despises women and yet retains a gentlemanly, protective feeling about them. Judging from the enthusiasm of the women he meets, he's good-looking, 'six feet of iron man [Chandler was just under six feet], one-ninety pounds stripped and with [his] face washed'. But like the cowboy heroes of the era, he almost always turns down female advances, which have only served to confirm his low impression of the morality of women in general. He has traces of chivalry – when he has to belabor old Mrs Morrison verbally, he feels bad about it: 'I don't like being rough with old ladies – even if they are lying gossips.' He goes out of his way to help Merle Davis and other nice girls. For himself, he prefers 'smooth, shiny girls, hard-boiled and loaded with sin', to nice girls, and most of the women he meets belong to the first category. He's tender-hearted enough to rescue a strug-gling beetle, and carefully carries it out of a high-rise to place it on a bush. He gets scared, has a sense of humor and of history, and sometimes indulges himself in flowery riffs of language: 'I'm afraid of death and despair ... of dark water and drowned men's faces and skulls with empty eye sockets. I'm afraid of dying, of being nothing, of not finding a man named Brunette.'

For a tough guy, he is also slightly hapless. He's not particularly lucky, is often caught off guard, is strangled, drugged and sapped. It may be revealing that Chandler himself wanted the comic actor Cary Grant to play the part of Marlowe in the movies, though he was delighted with Humphrey Bogart too. What is appealing about Marlowe is his rueful self-questioning, his ability to say that he's wrong or a chump. His life, lonesome and underpaid, has a dignity which he is careful to preserve. He throws Carmen Sternwood out of his room after she's showed up naked and called him a 'filthy name' when he won't sleep with her: 'this was the room I had to live in. It was all I had in the way of a home. In it was everything that was mine, that had any association for me, any past, anything that took the place of a family. Not much; a few books, pictures, radio, chessmen ...'

There are obvious sources in Chandler's own experience of several situations in *The Big Sleep*. Like Carmen Sternwood, Cissy had posed in the nude when young. She had also taken opium, though hardly to the extent of the pathological Carmen. Marlowe's alcohol problems mirrored Chandler's own, though when writing these three novels, he was still on the wagon (he would fall off when he went to Hollywood in 1943). Not that Marlowe considers that he has a problem, though he often regrets in the morning having taken that last drink, and his lurid dreams can resemble DTs: 'I was a pink-headed bug crawling up the side of the City Hall.' Chandler when drinking had both blackouts and DTs, and would eventually be hospitalized for alcohol-related health and mental ailments.

The Big Sleep, greatly admired by the perceptive publisher Alfred A Knopf, who had also brought out Hammett and James M. Cain (*The Postman Always Rings Twice*), was not taken seriously by critics, and sold fewer than thirteen thousand copies. People who did read it were often taken aback by the depiction of general depravity – porn pictures, dope, nymphomania, gambling, obsessions, rackets and crime rings, and the mention of unmentionables – the 'pouched ring of pale rubber' among the litter in a slum, for instance – though for modern readers, it is Marlowe's coolly equable tone about all this that constitutes the novel's charm. It would only come into its own after the film version with Humphrey Bogart appeared in 1946, though it was also published successfully in France and England.

His second novel, *Farewell, My Lovely*, published in May 1940, fared little better, but Chandler had begun to develop a following, including such fellow writers as Erle Stanley Gardner and S. J. Perelman. *Farewell, My Lovely* is an advance over even the very fine *Big Sleep*. The plot is similarly picaresque, with a similar double-twist ending, but here Chandler has Marlowe more firmly in control. Marlowe's qualities are also more confidently rendered: his rapid assessments of other characters, his idiosyncrasies – putting on his pajamas and going to bed when he's expecting both the villain Malloy, and a lady – his drinking habits, his sudden moods of liking or compassion for a down-and-out informer or minor thug, his innate fastidiousness, and above all a certain generosity of spirit, even trustfulness, beneath the surface cynicism, qualities that must have been a lot like Chandler's own.

His critical reputation continued to outpace his sales and readership. He rose to cult status in England following praise of his work by W. H. Auden and Somerset Maugham, and American critics eventually followed suit. One definition of art demands that the effort of the artist be somehow apparent, not in the sense of strain but of loving effort lavished on his medium, 'pains', as one critic called it, and it was this quality that attracted Edmund Wilson, who excepted Chandler from his general condemnation of detective stories. Chandler himself considered his writing to be art and wanted to make sure no one missed that – he included in his books both literary observations, as when Marlowe recognizes the source of the cocker spaniel Heathcliffe's name or alludes to Pepys's diaries, and just enough fancy writing to make the point. Despite his little barbs at modernist writers (he describes Hemingway as 'a guy that keeps saying the same thing over and over until you begin to believe it must be good'), he shares many of the same almost Deco aesthetic qualities of hard-edged stylization.

Chandler has nearly limitless powers of description, whether full-dress, as in his long portraits of the Sternwoods in *The Big Sleep*, or in his jewel-like little pictures of any minor character: 'a sloe-eyed lad in a blue mess jacket with bright buttons, a bright smile and a gangster mouth, handed the girls up from the taxi', or a clerk who has a 'washed-out blue smock, was thin on top as to hair, had fairly honest eyes and his chin would never hit a wall before he saw it'. Sometimes he tosses off a casual simile – 'Her eyes became narrow and almost black and as shallow as enamel on a cafeteria tray' – and sometimes contents himself with an offhand phrase: someone is 'drunker than a legion convention', another character is 'a ruthless permanent'. He never fails to render vivid, almost indelible, the least members of his panoply of sexy, predatory women, cops and underworld characters.

A modern, politically correct reader will be struck by the absolute lack of political correctness in Marlowe's world, and perhaps be startled by the embarrassingly crude ethnic and gender slurs. We have dinges and shines, dames and tramps, limp-wristed male cuties, 'short, dirty wops', 'greasy sensual Jews', and 'almost clean' Chinamen. The explanation for the language lies, no doubt, in verisimilitude; Marlowe and Chandler lived in a competitive, dangerous, and not overly polite post-Depression world. At best, it conveys Chandler's relish for vernacular speech, and especially American speech, in which he found a colorful pungency absent from the polite diction of Dulwich. But it also depicts an unusually hostile city of armed people ready to pull knives or take a swing at Marlowe unprovoked; whether that was the reality of the time, a reflex of Chandler's own world view, or an Englishman's appalled perception of a tough frontier, is not always clear.

Some critics have found *The High Window*, Chandler's third Marlowe novel, which he struggled to write over the next two years, a falling off from the first two. It is true that in the beginning of the book, the wisecracking Marlowe is irritatingly elliptical, the chip on his shoulder almost insurmountably present. Perhaps that was a result of Chandler's fatigue and growing restlessness, but the effect is to intensify the reader's impression of Marlowe's alienation and inner despair, qualities that serve to elevate him even farther above the cohort of tough detectives from which he sprang. The plot – Marlowe is hired to find a valuable coin – is as clever as usual, and infinitely clearer, the characters as vivid, the whole somehow a little closer to normal life than were the sinister underworld figures and nymphomaniac daughters in *The Big Sleep*. The characters are in general more sympathetic; though the reader somehow likes the grumpy Mrs Murdock more than Marlowe does, he draws us into sharing his liking for Phillips and Mr Morningstar, two characters who will be murdered, increasing the impact for the reader of their bloody fates.

The High Window was published in 1942, and, still tired and restless, Chandler rapidly wrote *The Lady in the Lake*, 1943. But he was spoiling for a change, so after the publication of this fourth Marlowe novel (see volume 2), he entered a new phase of his life, working for Hollywood, where he would make more money, gather more fame, go back to drinking with the legendary self-destructiveness that marked the careers of Hammett, Fitzgerald and Faulkner in Hollywood, and write only three more novels in the nearly twenty years that remained to him.

Diane Johnson

DIANE JOHNSON is the bestselling author of *Le Divorce*, which was a 1997 US National Book Award finalist, *Le Mariage*, *Persian Nights*, *Lying Low* and several other novels. She is also a travel writer, essayist and book reviewer. She wrote the screenplay for Stanley Kubrick's *The Shining*, and has written a biography of Dashiell Hammett.

SELECT BIBLIOGRAPHY

NOVELS
The Big Sleep. New York: Alfred A. Knopf, 1939; London: Hamish Hamilton, 1939.
Farewell, My Lovely. New York: Alfred A. Knopf, 1940; London: Hamish Hamilton, 1940.
The High Window. New York: Alfred A. Knopf, 1942; London: Hamish Hamilton, 1943.
The Lady in the Lake. New York: Alfred A. Knopf, 1943; London: Hamish Hamilton, 1944.
The Little Sister. London: Hamish Hamilton, 1949; Boston: Houghton Mifflin, 1949.
The Long Goodbye. London: Hamish Hamilton, 1953; Boston: Houghton Mifflin, 1954.
Playback. London: Hamish Hamilton, 1958; Boston: Houghton Mifflin, 1958.

STORIES
'Blackmailers Don't Shoot'. *Black Mask*, December 1933.
'Smart-Aleck Kill'. *Black Mask*, July 1934.
'Finger Man'. *Black Mask*, October 1934.
'Killer in the Rain'. *Black Mask*, January 1935.
'Nevada Gas'. *Black Mask*, June 1935.
'Spanish Blood'. *Black Mask*, November 1935.
'Guns at Cyrano's'. *Black Mask*, January 1936.
'The Man Who Liked Dogs'. *Black Mask*, March 1936.
'Noon Street Nemesis' (republished as 'Pickup on Noon Street'. *Detective Fiction Weekly*, May 30, 1936.
'Goldfish'. *Black Mask*, June 1936.
'The Curtain'. *Black Mask*, September 1936.
'Try the Girl'. *Black Mask*, January 1937.
'Mandarin's Jade'. *Dime Detective Magazine*, November 1937.
'Red Wind'. *Dime Detective Magazine*, January 1938.
'The King in Yellow'. *Dime Detective Magazine*, March 1938.
'Bay City Blues'. *Dime Detective Magazine*, June 1938.
'The Lady in the Lake'. *Dime Detective Magazine*, January 1939.
'Pearls Are a Nuisance'. *Dime Detective Magazine*, April 1939.
'Trouble Is My Business'. *Dime Detective Magazine*, August 1939.
'I'll Be Waiting'. *Saturday Evening Post*, October 14, 1939.

'The Bronze Door'. Unknown Magazine, November 1939.
'No Crime in the Mountains'. *Detective Story*, September 1941.
'Professor Bingo's Snuff'. *Park East*, June–August 1951; *Go*, June–July 1951.
'Marlowe Takes on the Syndicate'. *London Daily Mail*, April 6–10 1959, also published as 'Wrong Pidgeon'. *Manhunt*, February 1961. Reprinted as 'The Pencil'.

BIOGRAPHY
There are several biographies, including *The Life of Raymond Chandler* by Frank MacShane (Cape, 1976), *Raymond Chandler* by William Marling (Twayne, 1986) and Tom Hiney's *Raymond Chandler: An Authorized Biography* (Chatto & Windus, 1977; Grove Atlantic, 2001). *The Raymond Chandler Papers* (ed. Tom Hiney and Frank MacShane, Hamish Hamilton, 2000) includes letters, essays and stories. Miriam Gross's *The World of Raymond Chandler* (Weidenfeld & Nicolson, 1977) offers a pictorial biography and a lavishly illustrated study of the milieu of the Marlowe novels. Jerry Speir's *Raymond Chandler* (Ungar, 1981) contains a useful bibliography.

CHRONOLOGY

DATE	AUTHOR'S LIFE	LITERARY CONTEXT
1888	Raymond Thornton Chandler born 23 July in Chicago.	
1892		1892 James M. Cain born.
1894		1894 Dashiell Hammett born.
1895	Parents divorce. Moves to London with his mother.	1895 Twain: *Pudd'nhead Wilson.* Conan Doyle: *The Memoirs of Sherlock Holmes.* Hardy: *Jude the Obscure.*
1896		1896 Chekhov: *The Seagull.* Fitzgerald born.
1899		1899 Chopin: *The Awakening.* James: *The Awkward Age.* Hornung: *Raffles: The Amateur Cracksman.* Hemingway born. Nabokov born.
1900	Attends Dulwich College, as a day student (to 1904).	1900 Dreiser: *Sister Carrie.* Conrad: *Lord Jim.* Freud: *The Interpretation of Dreams.*
1901		1901 Mann: *Buddenbrooks.* Kipling: *Kim.*
1902		1902 Conan Doyle: *The Hound of the Baskervilles.* Steinbeck born.
1904		1904 James: *The Golden Bowl.* Chekhov dies.
1905–6	Attends language schools in France and Germany in preparation for British Civil Service examinations.	1905 Conan Doyle: *The Return of Sherlock Holmes.* 1906 Wharton: *The House of Mirth.* Beckett born.
1907	Returns to London. Works as a civil servant for the Admiralty.	1907 Conrad: *The Secret Agent.* Auden born.
1909–12	Resigns from Admiralty and works as a literary journalist, contributing poems, reviews, sketches and translations to *The Westminster Gazette* and *The Academy.*	1909 Stein: *Three Lives.* 1910 Forster: *Howards End.* Wells: *The History of Mr Polly.*

1888 The US becomes the leading manufacturing nation in the world.

1892 California earthquake disaster.
1894 Nicholas II becomes Tsar of Russia.
1895 Beginning of Freudian psychoanalysis.

1896 William McKinley elected US president. Klondike Gold Rush.

1899 Outbreak of Boer War. Alfred Hitchcock born.

1900 US population 76 million. US rail network just less than 200,000 miles. First International Socialist Congress in Paris. Planck's quantum theory.

1901 President McKinley assassinated. Succeeded by Theodore Roosevelt, in a progressive era in American politics. Marconi transmits message across the Atlantic. Death of Queen Victoria. Accession of Edward VII.

1904 War breaks out between Japan and Russia.

1905 Einstein's theory of relativity. General strikes, mutiny and incipient revolution in Russia.
1906 San Francisco earthquake.

1907 Cubist exhibition in Paris.

1909 First Ford Model T car.
1910 Death of Edward VII; accession of George V.

DATE	AUTHOR'S LIFE	LITERARY CONTEXT
1912	Returns to America, spends time in St Louis and Omaha, then settles in California. Does odd jobs, including working for a sporting goods firm and on a ranch.	1912 Dreiser: *The Financier*. Mann: *Death in Venice*.
1913–17	Enrols in night-school bookkeeping course and works as an accountant for the Los Angeles Creamery. His mother comes from England to live with him.	1913 Frost: *A Boy's Will*. Cather: *O Pioneers!* Lawrence: *Sons and Lovers*. 1914 Burroughs: *Tarzan of the Apes*. Joyce: *Dubliners*. 1915 Ford: *The Good Soldier*. Lawrence: *The Rainbow*. Kafka: *Metamorphosis*.
1917	Enlists in Canadian army, is assigned to 7th Batallion of Canadian Expeditionary Force, serves in trenches and is made sergeant.	1917 Conan Doyle: *His Last Bow*. Eliot: 'The Love Song of J. Alfred Prufrock'.
1918	In June is transferred to Royal Air Force.	1918 Cather: *My Ántonia*.
1919–22	Discharged and takes a job in a bank in San Francisco before returning to Los Angeles and working for *The Daily Express*. Has an affair with Cissy Pascal, who is seventeen years his senior and now gets a second divorce.	1919 *Black Mask*, pulp magazine, set up. Anderson: *Winesburg, Ohio*. Wodehouse: *My Man Jeeves*. 1920 Fitzgerald: *This Side of Paradise*. Lewis: *Main Street*. Wharton: *The Age of Innocence*. Pound: *Hugh Selwyn Mauberley*. Christie: *The Mysterious Affair at Styles* (first novel). 1921 Dos Passos: *Three Soldiers*. Lawrence: *Women in Love*. Pirandello: *Six Characters in Search of an Author*.
1922	Takes job with Dabney Oil Syndicate as bookkeeper and soon rises to Vice-President.	1922 Carroll John Daly creates the first hard-boiled detective in 'The False Burton Combs'. Eliot: *The Waste Land*. Joyce: *Ulysses*. Mansfield: *The Garden Party*. Hemingway: *In Our Time*.

CHRONOLOGY

DATE	AUTHOR'S LIFE	LITERARY CONTEXT
1923		
1924	Mother dies. Marries Cissy.	1924 Forster: *A Passage to India*. Ford: *Parade's End* (to 1928).
1925		1925 Dreiser: *An American Tragedy*. Fitzgerald: *The Great Gatsby*. Loos: *Gentlemen Prefer Blondes*. Stein: *The Making of Americans*. Dos Passos: *Manhattan Transfer*. Woolf: *Mrs Dalloway*. Kafka: *The Trial*.
1926		1926 Fitzgerald: *All the Sad Young Men*. Faulkner: *Soldier's Pay*. Hemingway: *The Sun Also Rises*. Christie: *The Murder of Roger Ackroyd*.
1927		1927 Cather: *Death Comes for the Archbishop*. Wilder: *The Bridge of San Luis Rey*. Woolf: *To the Lighthouse*. Conan Doyle: *The Case Book of Sherlock Holmes*. Proust: *Remembrance of Things Past*.
1928		1928 O'Neill: *Strange Interlude*. Lawrence: *Lady Chatterley's Lover*. Waugh: *Decline and Fall*.
1929		
1930		1930 Faulkner: *As I Lay Dying*. Hammett: *The Maltese Falcon*. Crane: *The Bridge*. Freud *Civilization and its Discontents*. Lawrence dies.
1931		1931 Hammett: *The Glass Key*.
1932	Sacked for drinking and absenteeism, goes to Seattle without Cissy but returns when he becomes ill.	1932 Caldwell: *Tobacco Road*. Erle Stanley Gardner: *The Case of the Velvet Claws* (first Perry Mason novel). Huxley: *Brave New World*. Crane dies.

CHRONOLOGY

1923 Calvin Coolidge elected president after Harding's death.
1924 Death of Lenin. First Labour government in UK.

1925 Al Capone is a powerful force in Chicago.
The 'Monkey Trial' in Dayton, Tennessee, finds for *Genesis*, signalling the
withdrawal of Southern culture into otherworldliness.

1926 Television invented by John Logie Baird. First liquid fuel rocket.
General strike in the UK.

1927 Lindbergh's solo Atlantic flight. Trotsky expelled from Communist
Party in USSR.

1928 First full-length film; first television broadcast; 13 million radios and
26 million cars in use in US. Herbert Hoover elected US president. Amelia
Earhart is the first woman to fly the Atlantic solo. Gershwin: *An American
in Paris.*
1929 Wall Street Crash on 24 October. Beginning of world depression.
US establishes Federal Loans. Museum of Modern Art in New York
founded. Land speed record set at 231 mph.
1930 US Unemployment at 13 million. US tariff raised. France begins
Maginot Line. Gandhi embarks on civil disobedience campaign in India.
Empire State Building opened.

1931 Al Capone found guilty of tax evasion and imprisoned. Britain
abandons Gold Standard. Invention of electric razor.
1932 Lindbergh's son kidnapped. Franklin D. Roosevelt elected US
president and inaugurates New Deal. Stock prices in US fall to 20% of
1929 value.

DATE	AUTHOR'S LIFE	LITERARY CONTEXT
1933	Studies Erle Stanley Gardner and other representatives of pulp fiction, and spends five months writing his first story, 'Blackmailers Don't Shoot', which is published by pulp detective magazine, *Black Mask*.	1933 Nathaniel West: *Miss Lonelyhearts*. Book burnings in Germany.
1934–39	Lives in and around Los Angeles, writing a total of twenty pulp stories for *Black Mask* and other magazines.	1934 Cain: *The Postman Always Rings Twice* (banned in Boston). Hammett: *The Thin Man*. Fitzgerald: *Tender is the Night*. Miller: *Tropic of Cancer*. Waugh: *A Handful of Dust*. Christie: *Murder on the Orient Express*. 1935 Wolfe: *Of Time and the River*. Lewis: *It Can't Happen Here*. 1936 Cain: *Double Indemnity*. Mitchell: *Gone with the Wind*. Dos Passos: *The Big Money*. Faulkner: *Absalom, Absalom!* Eliot: *Collected Poems*. Wodehouse: *Laughing Gas*. Lorca killed by Fascist militia in Spain. 1937 Hemingway: *To Have and Have Not*. Steinbeck: *Of Mice and Men*. Stevens: *The Man with the Blue Guitar*. Dos Passos: *U.S.A.* Erle Stanley Gardner: *The D.A. Calls it Murder* (first D.A. Douglas Selby novel). Christie: *Death on the Nile* C. S. Forester: *The Happy Return* (first Hornblower novel). 1938 Cummings: *Collected Poems*. Waugh: *Scoop*. Sartre: *Nausea*. Beckett: *Murphy*.
1939	Publishes his first full-length detective story, *The Big Sleep*.	1939 Joyce: *Finnegans Wake*. Steinbeck: *The Grapes of Wrath*.

CHRONOLOGY

1933 The Twenty-First Amendment, repealing Prohibition, ratified. Hitler appointed Chancellor in Germany. USSR recognized by US.

1934 Depth of Great Depression in US; half of the banks have failed. Al Capone sent to Alcatraz.

1935: Nuremberg Laws depriving Jews of rights and citizenship in Germany. Mussolini invades Abyssinia. Transcontinental air service begins in US. Gershwin: *Porgy and Bess*.
1936 Roosevelt re-elected by landslide. Spanish Civil War (to 1939). Abdication of King Edward VIII who wishes to marry the American divorcee Wallis Simpson. Hitler and Mussolini form Rome–Berlin axis. Stalin's Great Purge of Communist Party in Russia (to 1938).

1937 Japanese invasion of China. First jet engine and nylon stockings. In the US around 75 million visit the movies every week. Strikes against Republic Steel in Chicago: four strikers killed and forty-four injured.

1938 Germany annexes Austria; Munich crisis. Hitchcock: *The Lady Vanishes*.

1939 Nazi-Soviet Pact. Hitler invades Poland: World War II begins. First commercial transatlantic flights. Vivien Leigh and Clark Gable star in *Gone with the Wind*.

DATE	AUTHOR'S LIFE	LITERARY CONTEXT
1940–43	Continues with pulp writing and also publishes three full-length works: *Farewell, My Lovely* (1940), *The High Window* (1942) and *The Lady in the Lake* (1943).	1940 Hemingway: *For Whom the Bell Tolls*. Greene: *The Power and the Glory*. Fitzgerald dies. 1941 Fitzgerald: *The Last Tycoon* (posthumous). Cain: *Mildred Pierce*. Nabokov: *The Real Life of Sebastian Knight*. Brecht: *Mother Courage*. Woolf and Joyce die. 1942 Paul: *A Narrow Street*. Camus: *The Stranger*.
1943	Adapts James Cain's crime novel *Double Indemnity* with Billy Wilder for Paramount Studios.	
1944–46	Works for various film studios but is open about his dislike for the industry. Wins Edgar Allen Poe Award in 1946 (and again in 1956).	1944 Williams: *The Glass Menagerie*. Eliot: *Four Quartets*. 1945 Thurber: *The Thurber Carnival*. Orwell: *Animal Farm*. Waugh: *Brideshead Revisited*. Borges: *Fictions*. Dreiser dies.
1946	Moves to La Jolla and begins to detach himself from movie industry.	1946 Cain: *Past All Dishonor*. Goodis: *Dark Passage*.
1947		1947 Williams: *A Streetcar Named Desire*. Cain: *Butterfly*.
1948		1948 Mailer: *The Naked and the Dead*. Cain: *The Moth*. Eliot wins Nobel Prize.
1949	Publishes first post-Hollywood novel, *The Little Sister*. Works on *The Long Goodbye* (to 1952) as Cissy's health deteriorates.	1949 Miller: *Death of a Salesman*. Orwell: *Nineteen Eighty-Four*. Greene: *The Third Man*. Faulkner wins Nobel Prize.
1950	'The Simple Act of Murder' published. Works with Hitchcock on a film version of Patricia Highsmith's *Strangers on a Train*.	1950 Eliot: *The Cocktail Party*.

CHRONOLOGY

1940 France surrenders to Germany. The Battle of Britain. Trotsky assassinated in Mexico. Churchill prime minister in UK. Penicillin developed. Extraction of plutonium from uranium.

1941 Japanese attack Pearl Harbor. US enters war on 11 December. Hitler invades Russia. US introduces 'lease-lend' system of aid to Britain. Orson Welles: *Citizen Kane*. Irving Berlin: 'White Christmas'. Beginnings of 'bebop'.

1942 Rommel defeated at El Alamein. Build-up of American air force in Free China. World's first nuclear reactor constructed at Chicago University. 1943 Russians defeat Germans at Stalingrad. Allied armies victorious in North Africa. Allied invasion of Italy.

1944 Allied landings in Normandy; German retreat; liberation of Paris. Roosevelt elected for fourth term.

1945 Unconditional surrender of Germany and suicide of Hitler. Bombing of Hiroshima and Nagasaki. End of World War II. United Nations founded. Death of Roosevelt. Truman president of US. Attlee prime minister in UK.

1946 Churchill makes 'Iron Curtain' speech. Cold War begins. Film of *The Big Sleep* released with Humphrey Bogart and Lauren Bacall.

1947 India proclaimed independent. Marshall Plan (US aid for European post-war recovery).

1948 Jewish state of Israel comes into existence. Soviet blockade of West Berlin. Gandhi assassinated. Apartheid introduced in South Africa. Month-long strike of coal miners in US. Hitchcock: *Rope*.

1949 Chinese Revolution. North Atlantic Treaty signed in Washington. Orson Welles stars in *The Third Man*.

1950 Senator Joseph McCarthy accuses State Department of being riddled with Communists and begins period of Communist witch-hunts in US (to1954). Korean War begins (to 1953).

DATE	AUTHOR'S LIFE	LITERARY CONTEXT
1951		1951 Jones: *From Here to Eternity*. Salinger: *The Catcher in the Rye*. Frost: *Complete Poems*.
1952		1952 Beckett: *Waiting for Godot*. Ellison: *The Invisible Man*. O'Connor: *Wise Blood*. Steinbeck: *East of Eden*.
1953	*The Long Goodbye* published, cementing Chandler's literary standing among critics on both sides of the Atlantic.	1953 Bellow: *The Adventures of Augie March*. Faulkner: *Requiem for a Nun*. Williams: *Camino Real*. Fleming: *Casino Royale*.
1954	Cissy dies and Chandler attempts suicide shortly afterwards. Briefly admitted to a psychiatric hospital.	1954 Amis: *Lucky Jim*. Fleming: *Live and Let Die*. Hemingway wins Nobel Prize.
1955–57	Lives between La Jolla and Europe, mostly in hotels. Drinks heavily.	1955 Nabokov: *Lolita*. Williams: *Cat on a Hot Tin Roof*. Miller: *A View from the Bridge*. 1956 Highsmith: *The Talented Mr Ripley*. Goodis: *Shoot the Piano Player*. Osborne: *Look Back in Anger*. Fleming: *Diamonds are Forever*. 1957 Kerouac: *On the Road*. Nabokov: *Pnin*.
1958	Publishes *Playback*.	1958 Pasternak: *Doctor Zhivago*. Capote: *Breakfast at Tiffany's*.
1959	Dies in La Jolla on 26 March, aged seventy.	1959 Burroughs: *Naked Lunch*. Bellow: *Henderson the Rain King*. Grass: *The Tin Drum*.

CHRONOLOGY

THE BIG SLEEP

1

IT WAS ABOUT eleven o'clock in the morning, mid October, with the sun not shining and a look of hard wet rain in the clearness of the foothills. I was wearing my powder-blue suit, with dark blue shirt, tie and display handkerchief, black brogues, black wool socks with dark blue clocks on them. I was neat, clean, shaved and sober, and I didn't care who knew it. I was everything the well-dressed private detective ought to be. I was calling on four million dollars.

The main hallway of the Sternwood place was two stories high. Over the entrance doors, which would have let in a troop of Indian elephants, there was a broad stained-glass panel showing a knight in dark armor rescuing a lady who was tied to a tree and didn't have any clothes on but some very long and convenient hair. The knight had pushed the vizor of his helmet back to be sociable, and he was fiddling with the knots on the ropes that tied the lady to the tree and not getting anywhere. I stood there and thought that if I lived in the house, I would sooner or later have to climb up there and help him. He didn't seem to be really trying.

There were French doors at the back of the hall, beyond them a wide sweep of emerald grass to a white garage, in front of which a slim dark young chauffeur in shiny black leggings was dusting a maroon Packard convertible. Beyond the garage were some decorative trees trimmed as carefully as poodle dogs. Beyond them a large greenhouse with a domed roof. Then more trees and beyond everything the solid, uneven, comfortable line of the foothills.

On the east side of the hall a free staircase, tile-paved, rose to a gallery with a wrought-iron railing and another piece of stained-glass romance. Large hard chairs with rounded red plush seats were backed into the vacant spaces of the wall round about. They didn't look as if anybody had ever sat in them. In the middle of the west wall there was a big empty fireplace with a brass screen in four hinged panels, and over the fireplace a marble mantel with cupids at the corners. Above the mantel there was a large oil portrait, and above the portrait two bullet-torn or moth-eaten cavalry pennants crossed in a glass frame. The portrait was a stiffly posed job of an officer in full regimentals of about the time of the Mexican war. The officer had a neat black imperial, black mustachios, hot hard coal-black eyes, and the general look of a man it would pay to get along with. I thought this might be General Sternwood's grandfather. It could hardly be the General himself, even though I had heard he was pretty far gone in years to have a couple of daughters still in the dangerous twenties.

I was still staring at the hot black eyes when a door opened far back under the stairs. It wasn't the butler coming back. It was a girl.

She was twenty or so, small and delicately put together, but she looked durable. She wore pale blue slacks and they looked well on her. She walked as if she were floating. Her hair was a fine tawny wave cut much shorter than the current fashion of pageboy tresses curled in at the bottom. Her eyes were slate-gray, and had almost no expression when they looked at me. She came over near me and smiled with her mouth and she had little sharp predatory teeth, as white as fresh orange pith and as shiny as porcelain. They glistened between her thin too taut lips. Her face lacked color and didn't look too healthy.

"Tall, aren't you?" she said.

"I didn't mean to be."

4

Her eyes rounded. She was puzzled. She was thinking. I could see, even on that short acquaintance, that thinking was always going to be a bother to her.

"Handsome too," she said. "And I bet you know it."

I grunted.

"What's your name?"

"Reilly," I said. "Doghouse Reilly."

"That's a funny name." She bit her lip and turned her head a little and looked at me along her eyes. Then she lowered her lashes until they almost cuddled her cheeks and slowly raised them again, like a theater curtain. I was to get to know that trick. That was supposed to make me roll over on my back with all four paws in the air.

"Are you a prizefighter?" she asked, when I didn't.

"Not exactly. I'm a sleuth."

"A – a –" She tossed her head angrily, and the rich color of it glistened in the rather dim light of the big hall. "You're making fun of me."

"Uh-uh."

"What?"

"Get on with you," I said. "You heard me."

"You didn't say anything. You're just a big tease." She put a thumb up and bit it. It was a curiously shaped thumb, thin and narrow like an extra finger, with no curve in the first joint. She bit it and sucked it slowly, turning it around in her mouth like a baby with a comforter.

"You're awfully tall," she said. Then she giggled with secret merriment. Then she turned her body slowly and lithely, without lifting her feet. Her hands dropped limp at her sides. She tilted herself towards me on her toes. She fell straight back into my arms. I had to catch her or let her crack her head on the tessellated floor. I caught her under her arms and she went rubber-legged on me instantly. I had to hold her close to hold her up. When her head was against my chest she screwed it around and giggled at me.

5

"You're cute," she giggled. "I'm cute too."

I didn't say anything. So the butler chose that convenient moment to come back through the French doors and see me holding her.

It didn't seem to bother him. He was a tall, thin, silver man, sixty or close to it or a little past it. He had blue eyes as remote as eyes could be. His skin was smooth and bright and he moved like a man with very sound muscles. He walked slowly across the floor towards us and the girl jerked away from me. She flashed across the room to the foot of the stairs and went up them like a deer. She was gone before I could draw a long breath and let it out.

The butler said tonelessly: "The General will see you now, Mr. Marlowe."

I pushed my lower jaw up off my chest and nodded at him. "Who was that?"

"Miss Carmen Sternwood, sir."

"You ought to wean her. She looks old enough."

He looked at me with grave politeness and repeated what he had said.

2

WE WENT OUT at the French doors and along a smooth red-flagged path that skirted the far side of the lawn from the garage. The boyish-looking chauffeur had a big black and chromium sedan out now and was dusting that. The path took us along to the side of the greenhouse and the butler opened a door for me and stood aside. It opened into a sort of vestibule that was about as warm as a slow oven. He came in after me, shut the outer door, opened an inner door and we went through that. Then it was really hot. The air was thick, wet, steamy and larded with the cloying smell of tropical orchids in bloom. The glass walls and roof were heavily mist-ed and big drops of moisture splashed down on the plants. The light had an unreal greenish color, like light filtered through an aquarium tank. The plants filled the place, a forest of them, with nasty meaty leaves and stalks like the newly washed fingers of dead men. They smelled as overpowering as boiling alcohol under a blanket.

The butler did his best to get me through without being smacked in the face by the sodden leaves, and after a while we came to a clearing in the middle of the jungle, under the domed roof. Here, in a space of hexagonal flags, an old red Turkish rug was laid down and on the rug was a wheel chair, and in the wheel chair an old and obviously dying man watched us come with black eyes from which all fire had died long ago, but which still had the coal-black directness of the eyes in the portrait that hung above the mantel in the hall. The rest of his face was a leaden mask, with the bloodless lips and the sharp nose and the sunken temples and the outward-turning earlobes of approaching dissolution. His long narrow body was wrapped – in that heat – in a traveling rug and a faded red bathrobe. His thin clawlike hands were folded loosely on the rug, purple-nailed. A few locks of dry white hair clung to his scalp, like wild flowers fighting for life on a bare rock.

The butler stood in front of him and said: "This is Mr. Marlowe, General."

The old man didn't move or speak, or even nod. He just looked at me lifelessly. The butler pushed a damp wicker chair against the backs of my legs and I sat down. He took my hat with a deft scoop.

Then the old man dragged his voice up from the bottom of a well and said: "Brandy, Norris. How do you like your brandy, sir?"

"Any way at all," I said.

The butler went away among the abominable plants. The General spoke again, slowly, using his strength as carefully as an out-of-work show-girl uses her last good pair of stockings.

7

"I used to like mine with champagne. The champagne as cold as Valley Forge and about a third of a glass of brandy beneath it. You may take your coat off, sir. It's too hot in here for a man with blood in his veins."

I stood up and peeled off my coat and got a handkerchief out and mopped my face and neck and the backs of my wrists. St. Louis in August had nothing on that place. I sat down again and I felt automatically for a cigarette and then stopped. The old man caught the gesture and smiled faintly.

"You may smoke, sir. I like the smell of tobacco."

I lit the cigarette and blew a lungful at him and he sniffed at it like a terrier at a rathole. The faint smile pulled at the shadowed corners of his mouth.

"A nice state of affairs when a man has to indulge his vices by proxy," he said dryly. "You are looking at a very dull survival of a rather gaudy life, a cripple paralyzed in both legs and with only half of his lower belly. There's very little that I can eat and my sleep is so close to waking that it is hardly worth the name. I seem to exist largely on heat, like a newborn spider, and the orchids are an excuse for the heat. Do you like orchids?"

"Not particularly," I said.

The General half-closed his eyes. "They are nasty things. Their flesh is too much like the flesh of men. And their perfume has the rotten sweetness of a prostitute."

I stared at him with my mouth open. The soft wet heat was like a pall around us. The old man nodded, as if his neck was afraid of the weight of his head. Then the butler came pushing back through the jungle with a teawagon, mixed me a brandy and soda, swathed the copper ice bucket with a damp napkin, and went away softly among the orchids. A door opened and shut behind the jungle.

I sipped the drink. The old man licked his lips watching me, over and over again, drawing one lip slowly across the other with a funeral absorption, like an undertaker dry-washing his hands.

8

"Tell me about yourself, Mr. Marlowe. I suppose I have a right to ask?"

"Sure, but there's very little to tell. I'm thirty-three years old, went to college once and can still speak English if there's any demand for it. There isn't much in my trade. I worked for Mr. Wilde, the District Attorney, as an investigator once. His chief investigator, a man named Bernie Ohls, called me and told me you wanted to see me. I'm unmarried because I don't like policemen's wives."

"And a little bit of a cynic," the old man smiled. "You didn't like working for Wilde?"

"I was fired. For insubordination. I test very high on insubordination, General."

"I always did myself, sir. I'm glad to hear it. What do you know about my family?"

"I'm told you are a widower and have two young daughters, both pretty and both wild. One of them has been married three times, the last time to an ex-bootlegger who went in the trade by the name of Rusty Regan. That's all I heard, General."

"Did any of it strike you as peculiar?"

"The Rusty Regan part, maybe. But I always got along with bootleggers myself."

He smiled his faint economical smile. "It seems I do too. I'm very fond of Rusty. A big curly-headed Irishman from Clonmel, with sad eyes and a smile as wide as Wilshire Boulevard. The first time I saw him I thought he might be what you are probably thinking he was, an adventurer who happened to get himself wrapped up in some velvet."

"You must have liked him," I said. "You learned to talk the language."

He put his thin bloodless hands under the edge of the rug. I put my cigarette stub out and finished my drink.

"He was the breath of life to me – while he lasted. He spent hours with me, sweating like a pig, drinking brandy by the quart and telling me stories of the Irish revolution. He had been an officer in the I.R.A. He wasn't even legally in the United States. It was a ridiculous marriage of course, and it probably didn't last a month, as a marriage. I'm telling you the family secrets, Mr. Marlowe."

"They're still secrets," I said. "What happened to him?"

The old man looked at me woodenly. "He went away, a month ago. Abruptly, without a word to anyone. Without saying good-bye to me. That hurt a little, but he had been raised in a rough school. I'll hear from him one of these days. Meantime I am being blackmailed again."

I said: "Again?"

He brought his hands from under the rug with a brown envelope in them. "I should have been very sorry for anybody who tried to blackmail me while Rusty was around. A few months before he came – that is to say about nine or ten months ago – I paid a man named Joe Brody five thousand dollars to let my younger daughter Carmen alone."

"Ah," I said.

He moved his thin white eyebrows. "That means what?"

"Nothing," I said.

He went on staring at me, half frowning. Then he said: "Take this envelope and examine it. And help yourself to the brandy."

I took the envelope off his knees and sat down with it again. I wiped off the palms of my hands and turned it around. It was addressed to General Guy Sternwood, 3765 Alta Brea Crescent, West Hollywood, California. The address was in ink, in the slanted printing engineers use. The envelope was slit. I opened it up and took out a brown card and three slips of stiff paper. The card was of thin brown linen, printed in gold: "Mr. Arthur Gwynn Geiger." No address. Very small in the lower left-hand corner: "Rare Books and De Luxe Editions." I turned the card over. More of the slanted printing on the back. "Dear Sir: In spite of the legal uncollectibility of the enclosed, which frankly represent gambling debts, I assume you might wish them honored. Respectfully, A. G. Geiger."

I looked at the slips of stiffish white paper. They were promissory notes filled out in ink, dated on several dates early in the month before, September. "On Demand I promise to pay to Arthur Gwynn Geiger or Order the sum of One Thousand Dollars ($1000.00) without interest. Value Received. Carmen Sternwood."

The written part was in a sprawling moronic handwriting with a lot of fat curlicues and circles for dots. I mixed myself another drink and sipped it and put the exhibit aside.

"Your conclusions?" the General asked.

"I haven't any yet. Who is this Arthur Gwynn Geiger?"

"I haven't the faintest idea."

"What does Carmen say?"

"I haven't asked her. I don't intend to. If I did, she would suck her thumb and look coy."

I said: "I met her in the hall. She did that to me. Then she tried to sit in my lap."

Nothing changed in his expression. His clasped hands rested peacefully on the edge of the rug, and the heat, which made me feel like a New England boiled dinner, didn't seem to make him even warm.

"Do I have to be polite?" I asked. "Or can I just be natural?"

"I haven't noticed that you suffer from many inhibitions, Mr. Marlowe."

"Do the two girls run around together?"

"I think not. I think they go their separate and slightly divergent roads to perdition. Vivian is spoiled, exacting, smart and quite ruthless. Carmen is a child who likes to pull wings off flies. Neither of them has any more moral sense than a cat. Neither have I. No Sternwood ever had. Proceed."

"They're well educated, I suppose. They know what they're doing."

"Vivian went to good schools of the snob type and to college. Carmen went to half a dozen schools of greater and greater liberality, and ended up where she started. I presume they both had, and still have, all the usual vices. If I sound a little sinister as a parent, Mr. Marlowe, it is because my hold on life is too slight to include any Victorian hypocrisy." He leaned his head back and closed his eyes, then opened them again suddenly. "I need not add that a man who indulges in parenthood for the first time at the age of fifty-four deserves all he gets."

I sipped my drink and nodded. The pulse in his lean gray throat throbbed visibly and yet so slowly that it was hardly a pulse at all. An old man two-thirds dead and still determined to believe he could take it.

"Your conclusions?" he snapped suddenly.

"I'd pay him."

"Why?"

"It's a question of a little money against a lot of annoyance. There has to be something behind it. But nobody's going to break your heart, if it hasn't been done already. And it would take an awful lot of chiselers an awful lot of time to rob you of enough so that you'd even notice it."

"I have pride, sir," he said coldly.

"Somebody's counting on that. It's the easiest way to fool them. That or the police. Geiger can collect on these notes, unless you can show fraud. Instead of that he makes you a present of them and admits they are gambling debts, which gives you a defense, even if he had kept the notes. If he's a crook, he knows his onions, and if he's an honest man doing a little loan business on the side, he ought to have his money. Who was this Joe Brody you paid the five thousand dollars to?"

"Some kind of gambler. I hardly recall. Norris would know. My butler."

"Your daughters have money in their own right, General?"

"Vivian has, but not a great deal. Carmen is still a minor under her mother's will. I give them both generous allowances."

I said: "I can take this Geiger off your back, General, if that's what you want. Whoever he is and whatever he has. It may cost you a little money, besides what you pay me. And of course it won't get you anything. Sugaring them never does. You're already listed on their book of nice names."

"I see." He shrugged his wide sharp shoulders in the faded red bathrobe. "A moment ago you said pay him. Now you say it won't get me anything."

"I mean it might be cheaper and easier to stand for a certain amount of squeeze. That's all."

"I'm afraid I'm rather an impatient man, Mr. Marlowe. What are your charges?"

"I get twenty-five a day and expenses – when I'm lucky."

"I see. It seems reasonable enough for removing morbid growths from people's backs. Quite a delicate operation. You realize that, I hope. You'll make your operation as little of a shock to the patient as possible? There might be several of them, Mr. Marlowe."

I finished my second drink and wiped my lips and my face. The heat didn't get any less hot with the brandy in me. The General blinked at me and plucked at the edge of his rug.

"Can I make a deal with this guy, if I think he's within hooting distance of being on the level?"

"Yes. The matter is now in your hands. I never do things by halves."

"I'll take him out," I said. "He'll think a bridge fell on him."

"I'm sure you will. And now I must excuse myself. I am tired." He reached out and touched the bell on the arm of his chair. The cord was plugged into a black cable that wound along the side of the deep dark green boxes in which the orchids grew and festered. He closed his eyes, opened them again in a brief bright stare, and settled back among his cushions. The lids dropped again and he didn't pay any more attention to me.

I stood up and lifted my coat off the back of the damp wicker chair and went off with it among the orchids, opened the two doors and stood outside in the brisk October air getting myself some oxygen. The chauffeur over by the garage had gone away. The butler came along the red path with smooth light steps and his back as straight as an ironing board. I shrugged into my coat and watched him come.

He stopped about two feet from me and said gravely: "Mrs. Regan would like to see you before you leave, sir. And in the matter of money the General has instructed me to give you a check for whatever seems desirable."

"Instructed you how?"

He looked puzzled, then he smiled. "Ah, I see, sir. You are, of course, a detective. By the way he rang his bell."

"You write his checks?"

"I have that privilege."

"That ought to save you from a pauper's grave. No money now, thanks. What does Mrs. Regan want to see me about?"

His blue eyes gave me a smooth level look. "She has a misconception of the purpose of your visit, sir."

"Who told her anything about my visit?"

"Her windows command the greenhouse. She saw us go in. I was obliged to tell her who you were."

"I don't like that," I said.

His blue eyes frosted. "Are you attempting to tell me my duties, sir?"

"No. But I'm having a lot of fun trying to guess what they are."

We stared at each other for a moment. He gave me a blue glare and turned away.

3

THIS ROOM WAS too big, the ceiling was too high, the doors were too tall, and the white carpet that went from wall to wall looked like a fresh fall of snow at Lake Arrowhead. There were full-length mirrors and crystal doodads all over the place. The ivory furniture had chromium on it, and the enormous ivory drapes lay tumbled on the white carpet a yard from the windows. The white made the ivory look dirty and the ivory made the white look bled out. The windows stared towards the darkening foothills. It was going to rain soon. There was pressure in the air already.

I sat down on the edge of a deep soft chair and looked at Mrs. Regan. She was worth a stare. She was trouble. She was stretched out on a modernistic chaise-longue with her slippers off, so I stared at her legs in the sheerest silk stockings. They seemed to be arranged to stare at. They were visible to the knee and one of them well beyond. The knees were dimpled, not bony and sharp. The calves were beautiful, the ankles long and slim and with enough melodic line for a tone poem. She was tall and rangy and strong-looking. Her head was against an ivory satin cushion. Her hair was black and wiry and parted in the middle and she had the hot black eyes of the portrait in the hall. She had a good mouth and a good chin. There was a sulky droop to her lips and the lower lip was full.

She had a drink. She took a swallow from it and gave me a cool level stare over the rim of the glass.

"So you're a private detective," she said. "I didn't know they really existed, except in books. Or else they were greasy little men snooping around hotels."

There was nothing in that for me, so I let it drift with the current. She put her glass down on the flat arm of the chaise-longue and flashed an emerald and touched her hair. She said slowly: "How did you like Dad?"

"I liked him," I said.

"He liked Rusty. I suppose you know who Rusty is?"

"Uh-huh."

"Rusty was earthy and vulgar at times, but he was very real. And he was a lot of fun for Dad. Rusty shouldn't have gone off like that. Dad feels very badly about it, although he won't say so. Or did he?"

"He said something about it."

"You're not much of a gusher, are you, Mr. Marlowe? But he wants to find him, doesn't he?"

I stared at her politely through a pause. "Yes and no," I said.

"That's hardly an answer. Do you think you can find him?"

"I didn't say I was going to try. Why not try the Missing Persons Bureau? They have the organization. It's not a one-man job."

"Oh, Dad wouldn't hear of the police being brought into it." She looked at me smoothly across her glass again, emptied it, and rang a bell. A maid came into the room by a side door. She was a middle-aged woman with a long yellow gentle face, a long nose, no chin, large wet eyes. She looked like a nice old horse that had been turned out to pasture after long service. Mrs. Regan waved the empty glass at her and she mixed another drink and handed it to her and left the room, without a word, without a glance in my direction.

When the door shut Mrs. Regan said: "Well, how will you go about it then?"

"How and when did he skip out?"

"Didn't Dad tell you?"

I grinned at her with my head on one side. She flushed. Her hot black eyes looked mad. "I don't see what there is to be cagey about," she snapped. "And I don't like your manners."

"I'm not crazy about yours," I said. "I didn't ask to see you. You sent for me. I don't mind your ritzing me or drinking your lunch out of a Scotch bottle. I don't mind your showing me your legs. They're very swell legs and it's a pleasure to make their acquaintance. I don't mind if you don't like my manners. They're pretty bad. I grieve over them during the long winter evenings. But don't waste your time trying to cross-examine me."

She slammed her glass down so hard that it slopped over on an ivory cushion. She swung her legs to the floor and stood up with her eyes sparking fire and her nostrils wide. Her mouth was open and her bright teeth glared at me. Her knuckles were white.

"People don't talk like that to me," she said thickly.

I sat there and grinned at her. Very slowly she closed her mouth and looked down at the spilled liquor. She sat down on the edge of the chaise-longue and cupped her chin in one hand.

"My God, you big dark handsome brute! I ought to throw a Buick at you."

I snicked a match on my thumbnail and for once it lit. I puffed smoke into the air and waited.

"I loathe masterful men," she said. "I simply loathe them."

"Just what is it you're afraid of, Mrs. Regan?"

Her eyes whitened. Then they darkened until they seemed to be all pupil. Her nostrils looked pinched.

"That wasn't what he wanted with you at all," she said in a strained voice that still had shreds of anger clinging to it. "About Rusty. Was it?"

"Better ask him."

She flared up again. "Get out! Damn you, get out!"

I stood up. "Sit down!" she snapped. I sat down. I flicked a finger at my palm and waited.

"Please," she said. "Please. You could find Rusty – if Dad wanted you to."

That didn't work either. I nodded and asked: "When did he go?"

"One afternoon a month back. He just drove away in his car without saying a word. They found the car in a private garage somewhere."

"They?"

She got cunning. Her whole body seemed to go lax. Then she smiled at me winningly. "He didn't tell you then." Her voice was almost gleeful, as if she had outsmarted me. Maybe she had.

"He told me about Mr. Regan, yes. That's not what he wanted to see me about. Is that what you've been trying to get me to say?"

"I'm sure I don't care what you say."

I stood up again. "Then I'll be running along." She didn't speak. I went over to the tall white door I had come in at. When I looked back she had her lip between her teeth and was worrying it like a puppy at the fringe of a rug.

I went out, down the tile staircase to the hall, and the butler drifted out of somewhere with my hat in his hand. I put it on while he opened the door for me.

"You made a mistake," I said. "Mrs. Regan didn't want to see me."

He inclined his silver head and said politely: "I'm sorry, sir. I make many mistakes." He closed the door against my back.

I stood on the step breathing my cigarette smoke and looking down a succession of terraces with flowerbeds and trimmed trees to the high iron fence with gilt spears that hemmed in the estate. A winding driveway dropped down between retaining walls to the open iron gates. Beyond the fence the hill sloped for several miles. On this lower level faint and far off I could just barely see some of the old wooden derricks of the oilfield from which the Sternwoods had made their money. Most of the field was public park now, cleaned up and donated to the city by General Sternwood. But a little of it was still producing in groups of wells pumping five or six barrels a day. The Sternwoods, having moved up the hill, could no longer smell the stale sump water or the oil, but they could still look out of their front windows and see what had made them rich. If they wanted to. I didn't suppose they would want to.

I walked down a brick path from terrace to terrace, followed along inside the fence and so out of the gates to where I had left my car under a pepper tree on the street. Thunder was crackling in the foothills now and the sky above them was purple-black. It was going to rain hard. The air had the damp foretaste of rain. I put the top up on my convertible before I started downtown.

She had lovely legs. I would say that for her. They were a couple of pretty smooth citizens, she and her father. He was probably just trying me out; the job he had given me was a lawyer's job. Even if Mr. Arthur Gwynn Geiger, *Rare Books and De Luxe Editions*, turned out to be a blackmailer, it was still a lawyer's job. Unless there was a lot more to it than met the eye. At a casual glance I thought I might have a lot of fun finding out.

I drove down to the Hollywood public library and did a little superficial research in a stuffy volume called Famous First Editions. Half an hour of it made me need my lunch.

4

A. G. GEIGER'S place was a store frontage on the north side of the boulevard near Las Palmas. The entrance door was set far back in the middle and there was a copper trim on the windows, which were backed with Chinese screens, so I couldn't see into the store. There was a lot of oriental junk in the windows. I didn't know whether it was any good, not being a collector of antiques, except unpaid bills. The entrance door was plate glass, but I couldn't see much through that either, because the store was very dim. A building entrance adjoined it on one side and on the other was a glittering credit jewelry establishment. The jeweler stood in his entrance, teetering on his heels and looking bored, a tall handsome white-haired

Jew in lean dark clothes, with about nine carats of diamond on his right hand. A faint knowing smile curved his lips when I turned into Geiger's store. I let the door close softly behind me and walked on a thick blue rug that paved the floor from wall to wall. There were blue leather easy chairs with smoke stands beside them. A few sets of tooled leather bindings were set out on narrow polished tables, between book ends. There were more tooled bindings in glass cases on the walls. Nice-looking merchandise, the kind a rich promoter would buy by the yard and have somebody paste his bookplate in. At the back there was a grained wood partition with a door in the middle of it, shut. In the corner made by the partition and one wall a woman sat behind a small desk with a carved wooden lantern on it.

She got up slowly and swayed towards me in a tight black dress that didn't reflect any light. She had long thighs and she walked with a certain something I hadn't often seen in book-stores. She was an ash blonde with greenish eyes, beaded lashes, hair waved smoothly back from ears in which large jet buttons glittered. Her fingernails were silvered. In spite of her get-up she looked as if she would have a hall bedroom accent.

She approached me with enough sex appeal to stampede a businessmen's lunch and tilted her head to finger a stray, but not very stray, tendril of softly glowing hair. Her smile was tentative, but could be persuaded to be nice.

"Was it something?" she enquired.

I had my horn-rimmed sunglasses on. I put my voice high and let a bird twitter in it. "Would you happen to have a Ben Hur 1860?"

She didn't say: "Huh?" but she wanted to. She smiled bleakly. "A first edition?"

"Third," I said. "The one with the erratum on page 116."

"I'm afraid not – at the moment."

"How about a Chevalier Audubon 1840 – the full set, of course?"

"Er — not at the moment," she purred harshly. Her smile was now hanging by its teeth and eyebrows and wondering what it would hit when it dropped.

"You *do* sell books?" I said in my polite falsetto.

She looked me over. No smile now. Eyes medium to hard. Pose very straight and stiff. She waved silver fingernails at the glassed-in shelves. "What do they look like — grapefruit?" she enquired tartly.

"Oh, that sort of thing hardly interests me, you know. Probably has duplicate sets of steel engravings, tuppence colored and a penny plain. The usual vulgarity. No. I'm sorry. No."

"I see." She tried to jack the smile back up on her face. She was as sore as an alderman with the mumps. "Perhaps Mr. Geiger — but he's not in at the moment." Her eyes studied me carefully. She knew as much about rare books as I knew about handling a flea circus.

"He might be in later?"

"I'm afraid not until late."

"Too bad," I said. "Ah, too bad. I'll sit down and smoke a cigarette in one of these charming chairs. I have rather a blank afternoon. Nothing to think about but my trigonometry lesson."

"Yes," she said. "Ye-es, of course."

I stretched out in one and lit a cigarette with the round nickel lighter on the smoking stand. She still stood, holding her lower lip with her teeth, her eyes vaguely troubled. She nodded at last, turned slowly and walked back to her little desk in the corner. From behind the lamp she stared at me. I crossed my ankles and yawned. Her silver nails went out to the cradle phone on the desk, didn't touch it, dropped and began to tap on the desk.

Silence for about five minutes. The door opened and a tall hungry-looking bird with a cane and a big nose came in neatly, shut the door behind him against the pressure of the door closer, marched over to the corner and placed a wrapped parcel on the desk. He took a pinseal wallet with gold corners from his pocket and showed the blonde something. She pressed a button on the desk. The tall bird went to the door in the paneled partition and opened it barely enough to slip through.

I finished my cigarette and lit another. The minutes dragged by. Horns tooted and grunted on the boulevard. A big red interurban car grumbled past. A traffic light gonged. The blonde leaned on her elbow and cupped a hand over her eyes and stared at me behind it. The partition door opened and the tall bird with the cane slid out. He had another wrapped parcel, the shape of a large book. He went over to the desk and paid money. He left as he had come, walking on the balls of his feet, breathing with his mouth open, giving me a sharp side glance as he passed.

I got to my feet, tipped my hat to the blonde and went out after him. He walked west, swinging his cane in a small tight arc just above his right shoe. He was easy to follow. His coat was cut from a rather loud piece of horse robe with shoulders so wide that his neck stuck up out of it like a celery stalk and his head wobbled on it as he walked. We went a block and a half. At the Highland Avenue traffic signal I pulled up beside him and let him see me. He gave me a casual, then a suddenly sharpened side glance, and quickly turned away. We crossed Highland with the green light and made another block. He stretched his long legs and had twenty yards on me at the corner. He turned right. A hundred feet up the hill he stopped and hooked his cane over his arm and fumbled a leather cigarette case out of an inner pocket. He put a cigarette in his mouth, dropped his match, looked back when he picked it up, saw me watching him from the corner, and straightened up as if somebody had booted him from behind. He almost raised dust going up the block, walking with long gawky strides and jabbing his cane into the sidewalk. He turned left again. He had at least half a block on me when I reached the place where he had turned. He had me wheezing. This was a narrow tree-lined street with a retaining wall on one side and three bungalow courts on the other.

He was gone. I loafed along the block peering this way and that. At the second bungalow court I saw something. It was called "The La Baba," a quiet dim place with a double row of tree-shaded bungalows. The central walk was lined with Italian cypresses trimmed short and chunky, something the shape of the oil jars in Ali Baba and the Forty Thieves. Behind the third jar a loud-patterned sleeve edge moved.

I leaned against a pepper tree in the parkway and waited. The thunder in the foothills was rumbling again. The glare of lightning was reflected on piled-up black clouds off to the south. A few tentative raindrops splashed down on the sidewalk and made spots as large as nickels. The air was as still as the air in General Sternwood's orchid house.

The sleeve behind the tree showed again, then a big nose and one eye and some sandy hair without a hat on it. The eye stared at me. It disappeared. Its mate reappeared like a woodpecker on the other side of the tree. Five minutes went by. It got him. His type are half nerves. I heard a match strike and then whistling started. Then a dim shadow slipped along the grass to the next tree. Then he was out on the walk coming straight towards me, swinging the cane and whistling. A sour whistle with jitters in it. I stared vaguely up at the dark sky. He passed within ten feet of me and didn't give me a glance. He was safe now. He had ditched it.

I watched him out of sight and went up the central walk of the La Baba and parted the branches of the third cypress. I drew out a wrapped book and put it under my arm and went away from there. Nobody yelled at me.

5

BACK ON THE boulevard I went into a drugstore phone booth and looked up Mr. Arthur Gwynn Geiger's residence. He lived on Laverne Terrace, a hillside street off Laurel Canyon Boulevard. I dropped my nickel and dialed his number just for fun. Nobody answered. I turned to the classified section and noted a couple of bookstores within blocks of where I was.

The first I came to was on the north side, a large lower floor devoted to stationery and office supplies, a mass of books on the mezzanine. It didn't look the right place. I crossed the street and walked two blocks east to the other one. This was more like it, a narrowed cluttered little shop stacked with books from floor to ceiling and four or five browsers taking their time putting thumb marks on the new jackets. Nobody paid any attention to them. I shoved on back into the store, passed through a partition and found a small dark woman reading a law book at a desk.

I flipped my wallet open on her desk and let her look at the buzzer pinned to the flap. She looked at it, took her glasses off and leaned back in her chair. I put the wallet away. She had the fine-drawn face of an intelligent Jewess. She stared at me and said nothing.

I said: "Would you do me a favor, a very small favor?"

"I don't know. What is it?" She had a smoothly husky voice.

"You know Geiger's store across the street, two blocks west?"

"I think I may have passed it."

"It's a bookstore," I said. "Not your kind of a bookstore. You know darn well."

She curled her lip slightly and said nothing. "You know Geiger by sight?" I asked.

"I'm sorry. I don't know Mr. Geiger."

"Then you couldn't tell me what he looks like?"

Her lip curled some more. "Why should I?"

"No reason at all. If you don't want to, I can't make you."

She looked out through the partition door and leaned back again. "That was a sheriff's star, wasn't it?"

"Honorary deputy. Doesn't mean a thing. It's worth a dime cigar."

"I see." She reached for a pack of cigarettes and shook one loose and reached for it with her lips. I held a match for her. She thanked me, leaned back again and regarded me through smoke. She said carefully:

"You wish to know what he looks like and you don't want to interview him?"

"He's not there," I said.

"I presume he will be. After all, it's his store."

"I don't want to interview him just yet," I said.

She looked out through the open doorway again. I said: "Know anything about rare books?"

"You could try me."

"Would you have a Ben Hur, 1860, Third Edition, the one with the duplicated line on page 116?"

She pushed her yellow law book to one side and reached a fat volume up on the desk, leafed it through, found her page, and studied it. "Nobody would," she said without looking up. "There isn't one."

"Right."

"What in the world are you driving at?"

"The girl in Geiger's store didn't know that."

She looked up. "I see. You interest me. Rather vaguely."

"I'm a private dick on a case. Perhaps I ask too much. It didn't seem much to me somehow."

She blew a soft gray smoke ring and poked her finger through. It came to pieces in frail wisps. She spoke smoothly, indifferently. "In his early forties, I should judge. Medium height, fattish. Would weigh about a hundred and sixty pounds. Fat face, Charlie Chan moustache, thick soft neck. Soft all over. Well dressed, goes without a hat, affects a knowledge of antiques and hasn't any. Oh yes. His left eye is glass."

"You'd make a good cop," I said.

She put the reference book back on an open shelf at the end of her desk, and opened the law book in front of her again. "I hope not," she said. She put her glasses on.

I thanked her and left. The rain had started. I ran for it, with the wrapped book under my arm. My car was on a side street pointing at the boulevard almost opposite Geiger's store. I was well sprinkled before I got there. I tumbled into the car and ran both windows up and wiped my parcel off with my handkerchief. Then I opened it up.

I knew about what it would be, of course. A heavy book, well bound, handsomely printed in handset type on fine paper. Larded with full-page arty photographs. Photos and letterpress were alike of an indescribable filth. The book was not new. Dates were stamped on the front endpaper, in and out dates. A rent book. A lending library of elaborate smut.

I rewrapped the book and locked it up behind the seat. A racket like that, out in the open on the boulevard, seemed to mean plenty of protection. I sat there and poisoned myself with cigarette smoke and listened to the rain and thought about it.

6

RAIN FILLED THE gutters and splashed knee-high off the sidewalk. Big cops in slickers that shone like gun barrels had a lot of fun carrying giggling girls across the bad places. The rain drummed hard on the roof of the car and the burbank top began to leak. A pool of water formed on the floorboards for me to keep my feet in. It was too early in the fall for that kind of rain. I struggled into a trench coat and made a dash for the nearest drugstore and bought myself a pint of whiskey. Back in the car I used enough of it to keep warm and interested. I was long overparked, but the cops were too busy carrying girls and blowing whistles to bother about that.

In spite of the rain, or perhaps even because of it, there was business done at Geiger's. Very nice cars stopped in front and very nice-looking people went in and out with wrapped parcels. They were not all men.

He showed about four o'clock. A cream-colored coupe stopped in front of the store and I caught a glimpse of the fat face and the Charlie Chan moustache as he dodged out of it and into the store. He was hatless and wore a belted green leather raincoat. I couldn't see his glass eye at that distance. A tall and very good-looking kid in a jerkin came out of the store and rode the coupe off around the corner and came back walking, his glistening black hair plastered with rain.

Another hour went by. It got dark and the rain-clouded lights of the stores were soaked up by the black street. Street-car bells jangled crossly. At around five-fifteen the tall boy in the jerkin came out of Geiger's with an umbrella and went after the cream-colored coupe. When he had it in front Geiger came out and the tall boy held the umbrella over Geiger's bare head. He folded it, shook it off and handed it into the car. He dashed back into the store. I started my motor.

The coupe went west on the boulevard, which forced me to make a left turn and a lot of enemies, including a motor-man who stuck his head out into the rain to bawl me out. I was two blocks behind the coupe before I got in the groove. I hoped Geiger was on his way home. I caught sight of him two or three times and then made him turning north into Laurel Canyon Drive. Halfway up the grade he turned left and took a curving ribbon of wet concrete which was called Laverne Terrace. It was a narrow street with a high bank on one side and a scattering of cabin-like houses built down the slope on the other side, so that their roofs were not very much above road level. Their front windows were masked by hedges and shrubs. Sodden trees dripped all over the landscape.

Geiger had his lights on and I hadn't. I speeded up and passed him on a curve, picked a number off a house as I went by and turned at the end of the block. He had already stopped. His car lights were tilted in at the garage of a small house with a square box hedge so arranged that it masked the front door completely. I watched him come out of the garage with his umbrella up and go in through the hedge. He didn't act as if he expected anybody to be tailing him. Light went on in the house. I drifted down to the next house above it, which seemed empty but had no signs out. I parked, aired out the convertible, had a drink from my bottle, and sat. I didn't know what I was waiting for, but something told me to wait. Another army of sluggish minutes dragged by.

Two cars came up the hill and went over the crest. It seemed to be a very quiet street. At a little after six more bright lights bobbed through the driving rain. It was pitch black by then. A car dragged to a stop in front of Geiger's house. The filaments of its lights glowed dimly and died. The door opened and a woman got out. A small slim woman in a vagabond hat and a transparent raincoat. She went in through the box maze. A bell rang faintly, light through the rain, a closing door, silence.

I reached a flash out of my car pocket and went down-grade and looked at the car. It was a Packard convertible, maroon or dark brown. The left window was down. I felt for the license holder and poked light at it. The registration read: Carmen Sternwood, 3765 Alta Brea Crescent, West Hollywood. I went back to my car again and sat and sat. The top dripped on my knees and my stomach burned from the whiskey. No more cars came up the hill. No lights went on in the house before which I was parked. It seemed like a nice neighborhood to have bad habits in.

At seven-twenty a single flash of hard white light shot out of Geiger's house like a wave of summer lightning. As the darkness folded back on it and ate it up a thin tinkling scream echoed out and lost itself among the rain-drenched trees. I was out of the car and on my way before the echoes died.

There was no fear in the scream. It had a sound of half-pleasurable shock, an accent of drunkenness, an overtone of pure idiocy. It was a nasty sound. It made me think of men in white and barred windows and hard narrow cots with leather wrist and ankle straps fastened to them. The Geiger hideaway was perfectly silent again when I hit the gap in the hedge and dodged around the angle that masked the front door. There was an iron ring in a lion's mouth for a knocker. I reached for it, I had hold of it. At that exact instant, as if somebody had been waiting for the cue, three shots boomed in the house. There was a sound that might have been a long harsh sigh. Then a soft messy thump. And then rapid footsteps in the house – going away.

The door fronted on a narrow run, like a footbridge over a gully, that filled the gap between the house wall and the edge of the bank. There was no porch, no solid ground, no way to get around to the back. The back entrance was at the top of a flight of wooden steps that rose from the alley-like street below. I knew this because I heard a clatter of feet on the steps, going down. Then I heard the sudden roar of a starting car. It faded swiftly into the distance. I thought the sound was echoed by another car, but I wasn't sure. The house in front of me was as silent as a vault. There wasn't any hurry. What was in there was in there.

I straddled the fence at the side of the runway and leaned far out to the draped but unscreened French window and tried to look in at the crack where the drapes came together. I saw lamplight on a wall and one end of a bookcase. I got back on the runway and took all of it and some of the hedge and gave the front door the heavy shoulder. This was foolish. About the only part of a California house you can't put your foot through is the front door. All it did was hurt my shoulder and make me mad. I climbed over the railing again and kicked the French window in, used my hat for a glove and pulled out most of the lower small pane of glass. I could now reach in and draw a bolt that fastened the window to the sill. The rest was easy. There was no top bolt. The catch gave. I climbed in and pulled the drapes off my face.

Neither of the two people in the room paid any attention to the way I came in, although only one of them was dead.

7

IT WAS A wide room, the whole width of the house. It had a low beamed ceiling and brown plaster walls decked out with strips of Chinese embroidery and Chinese and Japanese prints in grained wood frames. There were low bookshelves, there was a thick pinkish Chinese rug in which a gopher could have spent a week without showing his nose above the nap. There were floor cushions, bits of odd silk tossed around, as if who-ever lived there had to have a piece he could reach out and thumb. There was a broad low divan of old rose tapestry. It had a wad of clothes on it, including lilac-colored silk underwear. There was a big carved lamp on a pedestal, two other stand-ing lamps with jade-green shades and long tassels. There was a black desk with carved gargoyles at the corners and behind it a yellow satin cushion on a polished black chair with carved arms and back. The room contained an odd assortment of odors, of which the most emphatic at the moment seemed to be the pungent aftermath of cordite and the sickish aroma of ether.

On a sort of low dais at one end of the room there was a high-backed teakwood chair in which Miss Carmen Sternwood was sitting on a fringed orange shawl. She was sitting very straight, with her hands on the arms of the chair, her knees close together, her body stiffly erect in the pose of an Egyptian goddess, her chin level, her small bright teeth shining between her parted lips. Her eyes were wide open.

The dark slate color of the iris had devoured the pupil. They were mad eyes. She seemed to be unconscious, but she didn't have the pose of unconsciousness. She looked as if, in her mind, she was doing something very important and making a fine job of it. Out of her mouth came a tinny chuckling noise which didn't change her expression or even move her lips.

She was wearing a pair of long jade earrings. They were nice earrings and had probably cost a couple of hundred dollars. She wasn't wearing anything else.

She had a beautiful body, small, lithe, compact, firm, rounded. Her skin in the lamplight had the shimmering luster of a pearl. Her legs didn't quite have the raffish grace of Mrs. Regan's legs, but they were very nice. I looked her over without either embarrassment or ruttishness. As a naked girl she was not there in that room at all. She was just a dope. To me she was always just a dope.

I stopped looking at her and looked at Geiger. He was on his back on the floor, beyond the fringe of the Chinese rug, in front of a thing that looked like a totem pole. It had a profile like an eagle and its wide round eye was a camera lens. The lens was aimed at the naked girl in the chair. There was a blackened flash bulb clipped to the side of the totem pole. Geiger was wearing Chinese slippers with thick felt soles, and his legs were in black satin pajamas and the upper part of him wore a Chinese embroidered coat, the front of which was mostly blood. His glass eye shone brightly up at me and was by far the most life-like thing about him. At a glance none of the three shots I heard had missed. He was very dead.

The flash bulb was the sheet lightning I had seen. The crazy scream was the doped and naked girl's reaction to it. The three shots had been somebody else's idea of how the proceedings might be given a new twist. The idea of the lad who had gone down the back steps and slammed into a car and raced away. I could see merit in his point of view.

A couple of fragile gold-veined glasses rested on a red lacquer tray on the end of the black desk, beside a pot-bellied flagon of brown liquid. I took the stopper out and sniffed at it. It smelled of ether and something else, possibly laudanum. I had never tried the mixture but it seemed to go pretty well with the Geiger menage.

I listened to the rain hitting the roof and the north windows. Beyond was no other sound, no cars, no siren, just the rain beating. I went over to the divan and peeled off my trench coat and pawed through the girl's clothes. There was a pale green rough wool dress of the pull-on type, with half sleeves. I thought I might be able to handle it. I decided to pass up her underclothes, not from feelings of delicacy, but because I couldn't see myself putting her pants on and snapping her brassiere. I took the dress over to the teak chair on the dais. Miss Sternwood smelled of ether also, at a distance of several feet. The tinny chuckling noise was still coming from her and a little froth oozed down her chin. I slapped her face. She blinked and stopped chuckling. I slapped her again.

"Come on," I said brightly. "Let's be nice. Let's get dressed."

She peered at me, her slaty eyes as empty as holes in a mask. "Gugutoterell," she said.

I slapped her around a little more. She didn't mind the slaps. They didn't bring her out of it. I set to work with the dress. She didn't mind that either. She let me hold her arms up and she spread her fingers out wide, as if that was cute. I got her hands through the sleeves, pulled the dress down over her back, and stood her up. She fell into my arms giggling. I set her back in the chair and got her stockings and shoes on her.

"Let's take a little walk," I said. "Let's take a nice little walk."

We took a little walk. Part of the time her earrings banged against my chest and part of the time we did the splits in unison, like adagio dancers. We walked over to Geiger's body and back. I had her look at him. She thought he was cute. She giggled and tried to tell me so, but she just bubbled. I walked her over to the divan and spread her out on it. She hiccuped twice, giggled a little and went to sleep. I stuffed her belongings into my pockets and went over behind the totem pole thing. The camera was there all right, set inside it, but there was no plateholder in the camera. I looked around on the floor, thinking he might have got it out before he was shot. No plateholder. I took hold of his limp chilling hand and rolled him a little. No plateholder. I didn't like this development.

I went into a hall at the back of the room and investigated the house. There was a bathroom on the right and a locked door, a kitchen at the back. The kitchen window had been jimmied. The screen was gone and the place where the hook had pulled out showed on the sill. The back door was unlocked. I left it unlocked and looked into a bedroom on the left side of the hall. It was neat, fussy, womanish. The bed had a flounced cover. There was perfume on the triple-mirrored dressing table, beside a handkerchief, some loose money, a man's brushes, a keyholder. A man's clothes were in the closet and a man's slippers under the flounced edge of the bed cover. Mr. Geiger's room. I took the keyholder back to the living room and went through the desk. There was a locked steel box in the deep drawer. I used one of the keys on it. There was nothing in it but a blue leather book with an index and a lot of writing in code, in the same slanting printing that had written to General Sternwood. I put the notebook in my pocket, wiped the steel box where I had touched it, locked the desk up, pocketed the keys, turned the gas logs off in the fireplace, wrapped myself in my coat and tried to rouse Miss Sternwood. It couldn't be done. I crammed her vagabond hat on her head and swathed her in her coat and carried her out to her car. I went back and put all the lights out and shut the front door, dug her keys out of her bag and started the

Packard. We went off down the hill without lights. It was less than ten minutes' drive to Alta Brea Crescent. Carmen spent them snoring and breathing ether in my face. I couldn't keep her head off my shoulder. It was all I could do to keep it out of my lap.

8

THERE WAS DIM light behind narrow leaded panes in the side door of the Sternwood mansion. I stopped the Packard under the porte-cochere and emptied my pockets out on the seat. The girl snored in the corner, her hat tilted rakishly over her nose, her hands hanging limp in the folds of the raincoat. I got out and rang the bell. Steps came slowly, as if from a long dreary distance. The door opened and the straight, silvery butler looked out at me. The light from the hall made a halo of his hair.

He said: "Good evening, sir," politely and looked past me at the Packard. His eyes came back to look at my eyes.

"Is Mrs. Regan in?"

"No, sir."

"The General is asleep, I hope?"

"Yes. The evening is his best time for sleeping."

"How about Mrs. Regan's maid?"

"Mathilda? She's here, sir."

"Better get her down here. The job needs the woman's touch. Take a look in the car and you'll see why."

He took a look in the car. He came back. "I see," he said. "I'll get Mathilda."

"Mathilda will do right by her," I said.

"We all try to do right by her," he said.

"I guess you have had practice," I said.

He let that one go. "Well, good-night," I said. "I'm leaving it in your hands."

"Very good, sir. May I call you a cab?"

"Positively," I said, "not. As a matter of fact I'm not here. You're just seeing things."

He smiled then. He gave me a duck of his head and I turned and walked down the driveway and out of the gates.

Ten blocks of that, winding down curved rain-swept streets, under the steady drip of trees, past lighted windows in big houses in ghostly enormous grounds, vague clusters of eaves and gables and lighted windows high on the hillside, remote and inaccessible, like witch houses in a forest. I came out at a service station glaring with wasted light, where a bored attendant in a white cap and a dark blue windbreaker sat hunched on a stool, inside the steamed glass, reading a paper. I started in, then kept going. I was as wet as I could get already. And on a night like that you can grow a beard waiting for a taxi. And taxi drivers remember.

I made it back to Geiger's house in something over half an hour of nimble walking. There was nobody there, no car on the street except my own car in front of the next house. It looked as dismal as a lost dog. I dug my bottle of rye out of it and poured half of what was left down my throat and got inside to light a cigarette. I smoked half of it, threw it away, got out again and went down to Geiger's. I unlocked the door and stepped into the still warm darkness and stood there, dripping quietly on the floor and listening to the rain. I groped to a lamp and lit it.

The first thing I noticed was that a couple of strips of embroidered silk were gone from the wall. I hadn't counted them, but the spaces of brown plaster stood out naked and obvious. I went a little farther and put another lamp on. I looked at the totem pole. At its foot, beyond the margin of the Chinese rug, on the bare floor another rug had been spread. It hadn't been there before. Geiger's body had. Geiger's body was gone.

That froze me. I pulled my lips back against my teeth and leered at the glass eye in the totem pole. I went through the house again. Everything was exactly as it had been. Geiger wasn't in his flounced bed or under it or in his closet. He wasn't in the kitchen or the bathroom. That left the locked door on the right of the hall. One of Geiger's keys fitted the lock. The room inside was interesting, but Geiger wasn't in it. It was interesting because it was so different from Geiger's room. It was a hard bare masculine bedroom with a polished wood floor, a couple of small throw rugs in an Indian design, two straight chairs, a bureau in dark grained wood with a man's toilet set and two black candles in foot-high brass candlesticks. The bed was narrow and looked hard and had a maroon batik cover. The room felt cold. I locked it up again, wiped the knob off with my handkerchief, and went back to the totem pole. I knelt down and squinted along the nap of the rug to the front door. I thought I could see two parallel grooves pointing that way, as though heels had dragged. Whoever had done it had meant business. Dead men are heavier than broken hearts.

It wasn't the law. They would have been there still, just about getting warmed up with their pieces of string and chalk and their cameras and dusting powders and their nickel cigars. They would have been very much there. It wasn't the killer. He had left too fast. He must have seen the girl. He couldn't be sure she was too batty to see him. He would be on his way to distant places. I couldn't guess the answer, but it was all right with me if somebody wanted Geiger missing instead of just murdered. It gave me a chance to find out if I could tell it leaving Carmen Sternwood out. I locked up again, choked my car to life and rode off home to a shower, dry clothes and a late dinner. After that I sat around in the apartment and drank too much hot toddy trying to crack the code in Geiger's blue indexed notebook. All I could be sure of was that it was a list of names and addresses, probably of the customers. There were over four hundred of them. That made it a nice racket, not to mention any blackmail angles, and there were probably plenty of those. Any name on the list might be a prospect as the killer. I didn't envy the police their job when it was handed to them.

I went to bed full of whiskey and frustration and dreamed about a man in a bloody Chinese coat who chased a naked girl with long jade earrings while I ran after them and tried to take a photograph with an empty camera.

9

THE NEXT MORNING was bright, clear and sunny. I woke up with a motorman's glove in my mouth, drank two cups of coffee and went through the morning papers. I didn't find any reference to Mr. Arthur Gwynn Geiger in either of them. I was shaking the wrinkles out of my damp suit when the phone rang. It was Bernie Ohls, the D.A.'s chief investigator, who had given me the lead to General Sternwood.

"Well, how's the boy?" he began. He sounded like a man who had slept well and didn't owe too much money.

"I've got a hangover," I said.

"Tsk, tsk." He laughed absently and then his voice became a shade too casual, a cagey cop voice. "Seen General Sternwood yet?"

"Uh-huh."

"Done anything for him?"

"Too much rain," I answered, if that was an answer.

"They seem to be a family things happen to. A big Buick belonging to one of them is washing about in the surf off Lido fish pier."

I held the telephone tight enough to crack it. I also held my breath.

"Yeah," Ohls said cheerfully. "A nice new Buick sedan all messed up with sand and sea water. . . . Oh, I almost forgot. There's a guy inside it."

I let my breath out so slowly that it hung on my lip. "Regan?" I asked.

"Huh? Who? Oh, you mean the ex-legger the eldest girl picked up and went and married. I never saw him. What would he be doing down there?"

"Quit stalling. What would anybody be doing down there?"

"I don't know, pal. I'm dropping down to look see. Want to go along?"

"Yes."

"Snap it up," he said. "I'll be in my hutch."

Shaved, dressed and lightly breakfasted I was at the Hall of Justice in less than an hour. I rode up to the seventh floor and went along to the group of small offices used by the D.A.'s men. Ohls' was no larger than the others, but he had it to himself. There was nothing on his desk but a blotter, a cheap pen set, his hat and one of his feet. He was a medium-sized blondish man with stiff white eyebrows, calm eyes and well-kept teeth. He looked like anybody you would pass on the street. I happened to know he had killed nine men – three of them when he was covered, or somebody thought he was.

He stood up and pocketed a flat tin of toy cigars called Entractes, jiggled the one in his mouth up and down and looked at me carefully along his nose, with his head thrown back.

"It's not Regan," he said. "I checked. Regan's a big guy, as tall as you and a shade heavier. This is a young kid."

I didn't say anything.

"What made Regan skip out?" Ohls asked. "You interested in that?"

"I don't think so," I said.

"When a guy out of the liquor traffic marries into a rich family and then waves good-bye to a pretty dame and a couple million legitimate bucks – that's enough to make even me think. I guess you thought that was a secret."

"Uh-huh."

"Okay, keep buttoned, kid. No hard feelings." He came around the desk tapping his pockets and reaching for his hat.

"I'm not looking for Regan," I said.

He fixed the lock on his door and we went down to the official parking lot and got into a small blue sedan. We drove out Sunset, using the siren once in a while to beat a signal. It was a crisp morning, with just enough snap in the air to make life seem simple and sweet, if you didn't have too much on your mind. I had.

It was thirty miles to Lido on the coast highway, the first ten of them through traffic. Ohls made the run in three quarters of an hour. At the end of that time we skidded to a stop in front of a faded stucco arch and I took my feet out of the floorboards and we got out. A long pier railed with white two-by-fours stretched seaward from the arch. A knot of people leaned out at the far end and a motorcycle officer stood under the arch keeping another group of people from going out on the pier. Cars were parked on both sides of the highway, the usual ghouls, of both sexes. Ohls showed the motorcycle officer his badge and we went out on the pier, into a loud fish smell which one night's hard rain hadn't even dented.

"There she is – on the power barge," Ohls said, pointing with one of his toy cigars.

A low black barge with a wheelhouse like a tug's was crouched against the pilings at the end of the pier. Something that glistened in the morning sunlight was on its deck, with hoist chains still around it, a large black and chromium car. The arm of the hoist had been swung back into position and lowered to deck level. Men stood around the car. We went down slippery steps to the deck.

Ohls said hello to a deputy in green khaki and a man in plain clothes. The barge crew of three men leaned against the front of the wheelhouse and chewed tobacco. One of them was rubbing at his wet hair with a dirty bath-towel. That would be the man who had gone down into the water to put the chains on.

We looked the car over. The front bumper was bent, one headlight smashed, the other bent up but the glass still unbroken. The radiator shell had a big dent in it, and the paint and nickel were scratched up all over the car. The upholstery was sodden and black. None of the tires seemed to be damaged.

The driver was still draped around the steering post with his head at an unnatural angle to his shoulders. He was a slim dark-haired kid who had been good-looking not so long ago. Now his face was bluish white and his eyes were a faint dull gleam under the lowered lids and his open mouth had sand in it. On the left side of his forehead there was a dull bruise that stood out against the whiteness of the skin.

Ohls backed away, made a noise in his throat and put a match to his little cigar. "What's the story?"

The uniformed man pointed up at the rubbernecks on the end of the pier. One of them was fingering a place where the white two-by-fours had been broken through in a wide space. The splintered wood showed yellow and clean, like fresh-cut pine.

"Went through there. Must have hit pretty hard. The rain stopped early down here, around nine p.m. The broken wood's dry inside. That puts it after the rain stopped. She fell in plenty of water not to be banged up worse, not more than half tide or she'd have drifted farther, and not more than half tide going out or she'd have crowded the piles. That makes it around ten last night. Maybe nine-thirty, not earlier. She shows under the water when the boys come down to fish this morning, so we get the barge to hoist her out and we find the dead guy."

The plainclothesman scuffed at the deck with the toe of his shoe. Ohls looked sideways along his eyes at me, and twitched his little cigar like a cigarette.

"Drunk?" he asked, of nobody in particular.

The man who had been toweling his head went over to the rail and cleared his throat in a loud hawk that made everybody look at him. "Got some sand," he said, and spat. "Not as much as the boy friend got – but some."

The uniformed man said: "Could have been drunk. Showing off all alone in the rain. Drunks will do anything."

"Drunk, hell," the plainclothesman said. "The hand throttle's set halfway down and the guy's been sapped on the side of the head. Ask me and I'll call it murder."

Ohls looked at the man with the towel. "What do you think, buddy?"

The man with the towel looked flattered. He grinned. "I say suicide, Mac. None of my business, but you ask me, I say suicide. First off the guy plowed an awful straight furrow down that pier. You can read his tread marks all the way nearly. That puts it after the rain like the Sheriff said. Then he hit the pier hard and clean or he don't go through and land right side up. More likely turned over a couple of times. So he had plenty of speed and hit the rail square. That's more than half-throttle. He could have done that with his hand falling and he could have hurt his head falling too."

Ohls said: "You got eyes, buddy. Frisked him?" he asked the deputy. The deputy looked at me, then at the crew against the wheelhouse. "Okay, save that," Ohls said.

A small man with glasses and a tired face and a black bag came down the steps from the pier. He picked out a fairly clean spot on the deck and put the bag down. Then he took his hat off and rubbed the back of his neck and stared out to sea, as if he didn't know where he was or what he had come for.

Ohls said: "There's your customer, Doc. Dove off the pier last night. Around nine to ten. That's all we know."

The small man looked in at the dead man morosely. He fingered the head, peered at the bruise on the temple, moved the head around with both hands, felt the man's ribs. He lifted a lax dead hand and stared at the fingernails. He let it fall and watched it fall. He stepped back and opened his bag and took out a printed pad of D.O.A. forms and began to write over a carbon.

"Broken neck's the apparent cause of death," he said, writing. "Which means there won't be much water in him. Which means he's due to start getting stiff pretty quick now he's out in the air. Better get him out of the car before he does. You won't like doing it after."

Ohls nodded. "How long dead, Doc?"

"I wouldn't know."

Ohls looked at him sharply and took the little cigar out of his mouth and looked at that sharply. "Pleased to know you, Doc. A coroner's man that can't guess within five minutes has me beat."

The little man grinned sourly and put his pad in his bag and clipped his pencil back on his vest. "If he ate dinner last night, I'll tell you – if I know what time he ate it. But not within five minutes."

"How would he get that bruise – falling?"

The little man looked at the bruise again. "I don't think so. That blow came from something covered. And it had already bled subcutaneously while he was alive."

"Blackjack, huh?"

"Very likely."

The little M.E.'s man nodded, picked his bag off the deck and went back up the steps to the pier. An ambulance was backing into position outside the stucco arch. Ohls looked at me and said: "Let's go. Hardly worth the ride, was it?"

We went back along the pier and got into Ohls' sedan again. He wrestled it around on the highway and drove back towards town along a three-lane highway washed clean by the rain, past low rolling hills of yellow-white sand terraced with pink moss. Seaward a few gulls wheeled and swooped over something in the surf and far out a white yacht looked as if it was hanging in the sky.

Ohls cocked his chin at me and said: "Know him?"

42

"Sure. The Sternwood chauffeur. I saw him dusting that very car out there yesterday."

"I don't want to crowd you, Marlowe. Just tell me, did the job have anything to do with him?"

"No. I don't even know his name."

"Owen Taylor. How do I know? Funny about that. About a year or so back we had him in the cooler on a Mann Act rap. It seems he run Sternwood's hotcha daughter, the young one, off to Yuma. The sister ran after them and brought them back and had Owen heaved into the icebox. Then next day she comes down to the D.A. and gets him to beg the kid off with the U. S. 'cutor. She says the kid meant to marry her sister and wanted to, only the sister can't see it. All *she* wanted was to kick a few high ones off the bar and have herself a party. So we let the kid go and then darned if they don't have him come back to work. And a little later we get the routine report on his prints from Washington, and he's got a prior back in Indiana, attempted hold-up six years ago. He got off with six months in the county jail, the very one Dillinger bust out of. We hand that to the Sternwoods and they keep him on just the same. What do you think of that?"

"They seem to be a screwy family," I said. "Do they know about last night?"

"No. I gotta go up against them now."

"Leave the old man out of it, if you can."

"Why?"

"He has enough troubles and he's sick."

"You mean Regan?"

I scowled. "I don't know anything about Regan, I told you. I'm not looking for Regan. Regan hasn't bothered anybody that I know of."

Ohls said: "Oh," and stared thoughtfully out to sea and the sedan nearly went off the road. For the rest of the drive back to town he hardly spoke. He dropped me off in Hollywood near the Chinese Theater and turned back west to Alta Brea

Crescent. I ate lunch at a counter and looked at an afternoon paper and couldn't find anything about Geiger in it.

After lunch I walked east on the boulevard to have another look at Geiger's store.

10

THE LEAN BLACK-EYED credit jeweler was standing in his entrance in the same position as the afternoon before. He gave me the same knowing look as I turned in. The store looked just the same. The same lamp glowed on the small desk in the corner and the same ash blonde in the same black suede-like dress got up from behind it and came towards me with the same tentative smile on her face.

"Was it −?" she said and stopped. Her silver nails twitched at her side. There was an overtone of strain in her smile. It wasn't a smile at all. It was a grimace. She just thought it was a smile.

"Back again," I chirped airily, and waved a cigarette. "Mr. Geiger in today?"

"I'm − I'm afraid not. No − I'm afraid not. Let me see − you wanted . . . ?"

I took my dark glasses off and tapped them delicately on the inside of my left wrist. If you can weigh a hundred and ninety pounds and look like a fairy, I was doing my best.

"That was just a stall about those first editions," I whispered. "I have to be careful. I've got something he'll want. Something he's wanted for a long time."

The silver fingernails touched the blond hair over one small jet-buttoned ear. "Oh, a salesman," she said. "Well − you might come in tomorrow. I think he'll be here tomorrow."

"Drop the veil," I said. "I'm in the business too."

Her eyes narrowed until they were a faint greenish glitter, like a forest pool far back in the shadow of trees. Her fingers clawed at her palm. She stared at me and chopped off a breath.

"Is he sick? I could go up to the house," I said impatiently. "I haven't got forever."

"You – a – you – a –" her throat jammed. I thought she was going to fall on her nose. Her whole body shivered and her face fell apart like a bride's pie crust. She put it together again slowly, as if lifting a great weight, by sheer will power. The smile came back, with a couple of corners badly bent.

"No," she breathed. "No. He's out of town. That – wouldn't be any use. Can't you – come in – tomorrow?"

I had my mouth open to say something when the partition door opened a foot. The tall dark handsome boy in the jerkin looked out, pale-faced and tight-lipped, saw me, shut the door quickly again, but not before I had seen on the floor behind him a lot of wooden boxes lined with newspapers and packed loosely with books. A man in very new overalls was fussing with them. Some of Geiger's stock was being moved out.

When the door shut I put my dark glasses on again and touched my hat. "Tomorrow, then. I'd like to give you a card, but you know how it is."

"Ye-es. I know how it is." She shivered a little more and made a faint sucking noise between her bright lips. I went out of the store and west on the boulevard to the corner and north on the street to the alley which ran behind the stores. A small black truck with wire sides and no lettering on it was backed up to Geiger's place. The man in the very new overalls was just heaving a box up on the tailboard. I went back to the boulevard and along the block next to Geiger's and found a taxi standing at a fireplug. A fresh-faced kid was reading a horror magazine behind the wheel. I leaned in and showed him a dollar: "Tail job?"

He looked me over. "Cop?"

"Private."

He grinned. "My meat, Jack." He tucked the magazine over his rear view mirror and I got into the cab. We went around the block and pulled up across from Geiger's alley, beside another fireplug.

There were about a dozen boxes on the truck when the man in overalls closed the screened doors and hooked the tailboard up and got in behind the wheel.

"Take him," I told my driver.

The man in overalls gunned his motor, shot a glance up and down the alley and ran away fast in the other direction. He turned left out of the alley. We did the same. I caught a glimpse of the truck turning east on Franklin and told my driver to close in a little. He didn't or couldn't do it. I saw the truck two blocks away when we got to Franklin. We had it in sight to Vine and across Vine and all the way to Western. We saw it twice after Western. There was a lot of traffic and the fresh-faced kid tailed from too far back. I was telling him about that without mincing words when the truck, now far ahead, turned north again. The street at which it turned was called Brittany Place. When we got to Brittany Place the truck had vanished.

The fresh-faced kid made comforting sounds at me through the panel and we went up the hill at four miles an hour looking for the truck behind bushes. Two blocks up, Brittany Place swung to the east and met Randall Place in a tongue of land on which there was a white apartment house with its front on Randall Place and its basement garage opening on Brittany. We were going past that and the fresh-faced kid was telling me the truck couldn't be far away when I looked through the arched entrance of the garage and saw it back in the dimness with its rear doors open again.

We went around to the front of the apartment house and I got out. There was nobody in the lobby, no switchboard. A wooden desk was pushed back against the wall beside a panel of gilt mailboxes. I looked the names over. A man named Joseph Brody had Apartment 405. A man named Joe Brody had received five thousand dollars from General Sternwood to stop

46

playing with Carmen and find some other little girl to play with. It could be the same Joe Brody. I felt like giving odds on it.

I went around an elbow of wall to the foot of tiled stairs and the shaft of the automatic elevator. The top of the elevator was level with the floor. There was a door beside the shaft lettered "Garage." I opened it and went down narrow steps to the basement. The automatic elevator was propped open and the man in new overalls was grunting hard as he stacked heavy boxes in it. I stood beside him and lit a cigarette and watched him. He didn't like my watching him.

After a while I said: "Watch the weight, bud. She's only tested for half a ton. Where's the stuff going?"

"Brody, four-o-five," he grunted. "Manager?"

"Yeah. Looks like a nice lot of loot."

He glared at me with pale white-rimmed eyes. "Books," he snarled. "A hundred pounds a box, easy, and me with a seventy-five pound back."

"Well, watch the weight," I said.

He got into the elevator with six boxes and shut the doors. I went back up the steps to the lobby and out to the street and the cab took me downtown again to my office building. I gave the fresh-faced kid too much money and he gave me a dog-eared business card which for once I didn't drop into the majolica jar of sand beside the elevator bank.

I had a room and a half on the seventh floor at the back. The half-room was an office split in two to make reception rooms. Mine had my name on it and nothing else, and that only on the reception room. I always left this unlocked, in case I had a client, and the client cared to sit down and wait.

I had a client.

11

SHE WORE BROWNISH speckled tweeds, a mannish shirt and tie, hand-carved walking shoes. Her stockings were just as sheer as the day before, but she wasn't showing as much of her legs. Her black hair was glossy under a brown Robin Hood hat that might have cost fifty dollars and looked as if you could have made it with one hand out of a desk blotter.

"Well, you *do* get up," she said, wrinkling her nose at the faded red settee, the two odd semi-easy chairs, the net curtains that needed laundering and the boy's size library table with the venerable magazines on it to give the place a professional touch. "I was beginning to think perhaps you worked in bed, like Marcel Proust."

"Who's he?" I put a cigarette in my mouth and stared at her. She looked a little pale and strained, but she looked like a girl who could function under a strain.

"A French writer, a connoisseur in degenerates. You wouldn't know him."

"Tut, tut," I said. "Come into my boudoir."

She stood up and said: "We didn't get along very well yesterday. Perhaps I was rude."

"We were both rude," I said. I unlocked the communicating door and held it for her. We went into the rest of my suite, which contained a rust-red carpet, not very young, five green filing cases, three of them full of California climate, an advertising calendar showing the Quints rolling around on a sky-blue floor, in pink dresses, with seal-brown hair and sharp black eyes as large as mammoth prunes. There were three near-walnut chairs, the usual desk with the usual blotter, pen set, ashtray and telephone, and the usual squeaky swivel chair behind it.

"You don't put on much of a front," she said, sitting down at the customer's side of the desk.

I went over to the mail slot and picked up six envelopes, two letters and four pieces of advertising matter. I hung my hat on the telephone and sat down.

"Neither do the Pinkertons," I said. "You can't make much money at this trade, if you're honest. If you have a front, you're making money – or expect to."

"Oh – are you honest?" she asked and opened her bag. She picked a cigarette out of a French enamel case, lit it with a pocket lighter, dropped case and lighter back into the bag and left the bag open.

"Painfully."

"How did you get into this slimy kind of business then?"

"How did you come to marry a bootlegger?"

"My God, let's not start quarreling again. I've been trying to get you on the phone all morning. Here and at your apartment."

"About Owen?"

Her face tightened sharply. Her voice was soft. "Poor Owen," she said. "So you know about that."

"A D.A.'s man took me down to Lido. He thought I might know something about it. But he knew much more than I did. He knew Owen wanted to marry your sister – once."

She puffed silently at her cigarette and considered me with steady black eyes. "Perhaps it wouldn't have been a bad idea," she said quietly. "He was in love with her. We don't find much of that in our circle."

"He had a police record."

She shrugged. She said negligently: "He didn't know the right people. That's all a police record means in this rotten crime-ridden country."

"I wouldn't go that far."

She peeled her right glove off and bit her index finger at the first joint, looking at me with steady eyes. "I didn't come to see you about Owen. Do you feel yet that you can tell me what my father wanted to see you about?"

"Not without his permission."

"Was it about Carmen?"

"I can't even say that." I finished filling a pipe and put a match to it. She watched the smoke for a moment. Then her hand went into her open bag and came out with a thick white envelope. She tossed it across the desk.

"You'd better look at it anyway," she said.

I picked it up. The address was typewritten to Mrs. Vivian Regan, 3765 Alta Brea Crescent, West Hollywood. Delivery had been by messenger service and the office stamp showed 8:35 a.m. as the time out. I opened the envelope and drew out the shiny 4¼ by 3¼ photo that was all there was inside.

It was Carmen sitting in Geiger's high-backed teakwood chair on the dais, in her earrings and her birthday suit. Her eyes looked even a little crazier than I remembered them. The back of the photo was blank. I put it back in the envelope.

"How much do they want?" I asked.

"Five thousand – for the negative and the rest of the prints. The deal has to be closed tonight, or they give the stuff to some scandal sheet."

"The demand came how?"

"A woman telephoned me, about half an hour after this thing was delivered."

"There's nothing in the scandal sheet angle. Juries convict without leaving the box on that stuff nowadays. What else is there?"

"Does there have to be something else?"

"Yes."

She stared at me, a little puzzled. "There is. The woman said there was a police jam connected with it and I'd better lay it on the line fast, or I'd be talking to my little sister through a wire screen."

"Better," I said. "What kind of jam?"

"I don't know."

"Where is Carmen now?"

"She's at home. She was sick last night. She's still in bed, I think."

"Did she go out last night?"

"No. I was out, but the servants say she wasn't. I was down at Las Olindas, playing roulette at Eddie Mars' Cypress Club. I lost my shirt."

"So you like roulette. You would."

She crossed her legs and lit another cigarette. "Yes. I like roulette. All the Sternwoods like losing games, like roulette and marrying men that walk out on them and riding steeplechases at fifty-eight years old and being rolled on by a jumper and crippled for life. The Sternwoods have money. All it has bought them is a rain check."

"What was Owen doing last night with your car?"

"Nobody knows. He took it without permission. We always let him take a car on his night off, but last night wasn't his night off." She made a wry mouth. "Do you think —?"

"He knew about this nude photo? How would I be able to say? I don't rule him out. Can you get five thousand in cash right away?"

"Not unless I tell Dad — or borrow it. I could probably borrow it from Eddie Mars. He ought to be generous with me, heaven knows."

"Better try that. You may need it in a hurry."

She leaned back and hung an arm over the back of the chair. "How about telling the police?"

"It's a good idea. But you won't do it."

"Won't I?"

"No. You have to protect your father and your sister. You don't know what the police might turn up. It might be something they couldn't sit on. Though they usually try in blackmail cases."

"Can you do anything?"

"I think I can. But I can't tell you why or how."

"I like you," she said suddenly. "You believe in miracles. Would you have a drink in the office?"

I unlocked my deep drawer and got out my office bottle and two pony glasses. I filled them and we drank. She snapped her bag shut and pushed her chair back.

"I'll get the five grand," she said. "I've been a good customer of Eddie Mars. There's another reason why he should be nice to me, which you may not know." She gave me one of those smiles the lips have forgotten before they reach the eyes. "Eddie's blonde wife is the lady Rusty ran away with."

I didn't say anything. She stared tightly at me and added: "That doesn't interest you?"

"It ought to make it easier to find him – if I was looking for him. You don't think he's in this mess, do you?"

She pushed her empty glass at me. "Give me another drink. You're the hardest guy to get anything out of. You don't even move your ears."

I filled the little glass. "You've got all you wanted out of me – a pretty good idea I'm not looking for your husband."

She put the drink down very quickly. It made her gasp – or gave her an opportunity to gasp. She let a breath out slowly.

"Rusty was no crook. If he had been, it wouldn't have been for nickels. He carried fifteen thousand dollars, in bills. He called it his mad money. He had it when I married him and he had it when he left me. No – Rusty's not in on any cheap blackmail racket."

She reached for the envelope and stood up. "I'll keep in touch with you," I said. "If you want to leave me a message, the phone girl at my apartment house will take care of it."

We walked over to the door. Tapping the white envelope against her knuckles, she said: "You still feel you can't tell me what Dad –"

"I'd have to see him first."

She took the photo out and stood looking at it, just inside the door. "She has a beautiful little body, hasn't she?"

"Uh-huh."

She leaned a little towards me. "You ought to see mine," she said gravely.

"Can it be arranged?"

She laughed suddenly and sharply and went halfway through the door, then turned her head to say coolly: "You're as cold-blooded a beast as I ever met, Marlowe. Or can I call you Phil?"

"Sure."

"You can call me Vivian."

"Thanks, Mrs. Regan."

"Oh, go to hell, Marlowe." She went on out and didn't look back.

I let the door shut and stood with my hand on it, staring at the hand. My face felt a little hot. I went back to the desk and put the whiskey away and rinsed out the two pony glasses and put them away.

I took my hat off the phone and called the D.A.'s office and asked for Bernie Ohls.

He was back in his cubbyhole. "Well, I let the old man alone," he said. "The butler said he or one of the girls would tell him. This Owen Taylor lived over the garage and I went through his stuff. Parents at Dubuque, Iowa. I wired the Chief of Police there to find out what they want done. The Sternwood family will pay for it."

"Suicide?" I asked.

"No can tell. He didn't leave any notes. He had no leave to take the car. Everybody was home last night but Mrs. Regan. She was down at Las Olindas with a playboy named Larry Cobb. I checked on that. I know a lad on one of the tables."

"You ought to stop some of that flash gambling," I said.

"With the syndicate we got in this county? Be your age, Marlowe. That sap mark on the boy's head bothers me. Sure you can't help me on this?"

I liked his putting it that way. It let me say no without actually lying. We said good-bye and I left the office, bought all three afternoon papers and rode a taxi down to the Hall of Justice to get my car out of the lot. There was nothing in any of the papers about Geiger. I took another look at his blue notebook, but the code was just as stubborn as it had been the night before.

12

THE TREES ON the upper side of Laverne Terrace had fresh
green leaves after the rain. In the cool afternoon sunlight
I could see the steep drop of the hill and the flight of steps
down which the killer had run after his three shots in the
darkness. Two small houses fronted on the street below. They
might or might not have heard the shots.

There was no activity in front of Geiger's house or anywhere along the block. The box hedge looked green and
peaceful and the shingles on the roof were still damp. I drove
past slowly, gnawing at an idea. I hadn't looked in the garage
the night before. Once Geiger's body slipped away I hadn't
really wanted to find it. It would force my hand. But dragging
him to the garage, to his own car and driving that off into one
of the hundred odd lonely canyons around Los Angeles would
be a good way to dispose of him for days or even for weeks.
That supposed two things: a key to his car and two in the party.
It would narrow the sector of search quite a lot, especially as
I had had his personal keys in my pocket when it happened.

I didn't get a chance to look at the garage. The doors were
shut and padlocked and something moved behind the hedge
as I drew level. A woman in a green and white check coat and
a small button of a hat on soft blond hair stepped out of the
maze and stood looking wild-eyed at my car, as if she hadn't
heard it come up the hill. Then she turned swiftly and dodged
back out of sight. It was Carmen Sternwood, of course.

I went on up the street and parked and walked back. In the
daylight it seemed an exposed and dangerous thing to do.
I went in through the hedge. She stood there straight and
silent against the locked front door. One hand went slowly up
to her teeth and her teeth bit at her funny thumb. There were
purple smears under her eyes and her face was gnawed white
by nerves.

She half smiled at me. She said: "Hello," in a thin, brittle voice. "Wha – what –?" That tailed off and she went back to the thumb.

"Remember me?" I said. "Doghouse Reilly, the man that grew too tall. Remember?"

She nodded and a quick jerky smile played across her face.

"Let's go in," I said. "I've got a key. Swell, huh?"

"Wha – wha –?"

I pushed her to one side and put the key in the door and opened it and pushed her in through it. I shut the door again and stood there sniffing. The place was horrible by daylight. The Chinese junk on the walls, the rug, the fussy lamps, the teakwood stuff, the sticky riot of colors, the totem pole, the flagon of ether and laudanum – all this in the daytime had a stealthy nastiness, like a fag party.

The girl and I stood looking at each other. She tried to keep a cute little smile on her face but her face was too tired to be bothered. It kept going blank on her. The smile would wash off like water off sand and her pale skin had a harsh granular texture under the stunned and stupid blankness of her eyes. A whitish tongue licked at the corners of her mouth. A pretty, spoiled and not very bright little girl who had gone very, very wrong, and nobody was doing anything about it. To hell with the rich. They made me sick. I rolled a cigarette in my fingers and pushed some books out of the way and sat on the end of the black desk. I lit my cigarette, puffed a plume of smoke and watched the thumb and tooth act for a while in silence. Carmen stood in front of me, like a bad girl in the principal's office.

"What are you doing here?" I asked her finally.

She picked at the cloth of her coat and didn't answer.

"How much do you remember of last night?"

She answered that – with a foxy glitter rising at the back of her eyes. "Remember what? I was sick last night. I was home." Her voice was a cautious throaty sound that just reached my ears.

"Like hell you were."

Her eyes flicked up and down very swiftly.

"Before you went home," I said. "Before I took you home. Here. In that chair" – I pointed to it – "on that orange shawl. You remember all right."

A slow flush crept up her throat. That was something. She could blush. A glint of white showed under the clogged gray irises. She chewed hard on her thumb.

"You – were the one?" she breathed.

"Me. How much of it stays with you?"

She said vaguely: "Are you the police?"

"No. I'm a friend of your father's."

"You're not the police?"

"No."

She let out a thin sigh. "Wha – what do you want?"

"Who killed him?"

Her shoulders jerked, but nothing more moved in her face. "Who else – knows?"

"About Geiger? I don't know. Not the police, or they'd be camping here. Maybe Joe Brody."

It was a stab in the dark but it got a yelp out of her. "Joe Brody! Him!"

Then we were both silent. I dragged at my cigarette and she ate her thumb.

"Don't get clever, for God's sake," I urged her. "This is a spot for a little old-fashioned simplicity. Did Brody kill him?"

"Kill who?"

"Oh, Christ," I said.

She looked hurt. Her chin came down an inch. "Yes," she said solemnly. "Joe did it."

"Why?"

"I don't know." She shook her head, persuading herself that she didn't know.

"Seen much of him lately?"

Her hands went down and made small white knots. "Just once or twice. I hate him."

"Then you know where he lives."

"Yes."

"And you don't like him any more?"

"I hate him!"

"Then you'd like him for the spot."

A little blank again. I was going too fast for her. It was hard not to. "Are you willing to tell the police it was Joe Brody?" I probed.

Sudden panic flamed all over her face. "If I can kill the nude photo angle, of course," I added soothingly.

She giggled. That gave me a nasty feeling. If she had screeched or wept or even nosedived to the floor in a dead faint, that would have been all right. She just giggled. It was suddenly a lot of fun. She had had her photo taken as Isis and somebody had swiped it and somebody had bumped Geiger off in front of her and she was drunker than a Legion convention, and it was suddenly a lot of nice clean fun. So she giggled. Very cute. The giggles got louder and ran around the corners of the room like rats behind the wainscoting. She started to go hysterical. I slid off the desk and stepped up close to her and gave her a smack on the side of the face.

"Just like last night," I said. "We're a scream together. Reilly and Sternwood, two stooges in search of a comedian."

The giggles stopped dead, but she didn't mind the slap any more than last night. Probably all her boy friends got around to slapping her sooner or later. I could understand how they might. I sat down on the end of the black desk again.

"Your name isn't Reilly," she said seriously. "It's Philip Marlowe. You're a private detective. Viv told me. She showed me your card." She smoothed the cheek I had slapped. She smiled at me, as if I was nice to be with.

"Well, you do remember," I said. "And you came back to look for that photo and you couldn't get into the house. Didn't you?"

Her chin ducked down and up. She worked the smile.

57

I was having the eye put on me. I was being brought into camp. I was going to yell "Yippee!" in a minute and ask her to go to Yuma.

"The photo's gone," I said. "I looked last night, before I took you home. Probably Brody took it with him. You're not kidding me about Brody?"

She shook her head earnestly.

"It's a pushover," I said. "You don't have to give it another thought. Don't tell a soul you were here, last night or today. Not even Vivian. Just forget you were here. Leave it to Reilly."

"Your name isn't —" she began, and then stopped and shook her head vigorously in agreement with what I had said or with what she had just thought of. Her eyes became narrow and almost black and as shallow as enamel on a cafeteria tray. She had had an idea. "I have to go home now," she said, as if we had been having a cup of tea.

"Sure."

I didn't move. She gave me another cute glance and went on towards the front door. She had her hand on the knob when we both heard a car coming. She looked at me with questions in her eyes. I shrugged. The car stopped, right in front of the house. Terror twisted her face. There were steps and the bell rang. Carmen stared back at me over her shoulder, her hand clutching the door knob, almost drooling with fear. The bell kept on ringing. Then the ringing stopped. A key tickled at the door and Carmen jumped away from it and stood frozen. The door swung open. A man stepped through it briskly and stopped dead, staring at us quietly, with complete composure.

13

HE WAS A gray man, all gray, except for his polished black shoes and two scarlet diamonds in his gray satin tie that looked like the diamonds on roulette layouts. His shirt was gray and his double-breasted suit of soft, beautifully cut flannel. Seeing Carmen he took a gray hat off and his hair underneath it was gray and as fine as if it had been sifted through gauze. His thick gray eyebrows had that indefinably sporty look. He had a long chin, a nose with a hook to it, thoughtful gray eyes that had a slanted look because the fold of skin over his upper lid came down over the corner of the lid itself.

He stood there politely, one hand touching the door at his back, the other holding the gray hat and flapping it gently against his thigh. He looked hard, not the hardness of the tough guy. More like the hardness of a well-weathered horseman. But he was no horseman. He was Eddie Mars.

He pushed the door shut behind him and put that hand in the lap-seamed pocket of his coat and left the thumb outside to glisten in the rather dim light of the room. He smiled at Carmen. He had a nice easy smile. She licked her lips and stared at him. The fear went out of her face. She smiled back.

"Excuse the casual entrance," he said. "The bell didn't seem to rouse anybody. Is Mr. Geiger around?"

I said: "No. We don't know just where he is. We found the door a little open. We stepped inside."

He nodded and touched his long chin with the brim of his hat. "You're friends of his, of course?"

"Just business acquaintances. We dropped by for a book."

"A book, eh?" He said that quickly and brightly and, I thought, a little slyly, as if he knew all about Geiger's books. Then he looked at Carmen again and shrugged.

I moved towards the door. "We'll trot along now," I said. I took hold of her arm. She was staring at Eddie Mars. She liked him.

"Any message – if Geiger comes back?" Eddie Mars asked gently.

"We won't bother you."

"That's too bad," he said, with too much meaning. His gray eyes twinkled and then hardened as I went past him to open

59

the door. He added in a casual tone: "The girl can dust. I'd like to talk to you a little, soldier."

I let go of her arm. I gave him a blank stare. "Kidder, eh?" he said nicely. "Don't waste it. I've got two boys outside in a car that always do just what I want them to."

Carmen made a sound at my side and bolted through the door. Her steps faded rapidly downhill. I hadn't seen her car, so she must have left it down below. I started to say: "What the hell – !"

"Oh, skip it," Eddie Mars sighed. "There's something wrong around here. I'm going to find out what it is. If you want to pick lead out of your belly, get in my way."

"Well, well," I said, "a tough guy."

"Only when necessary, soldier." He wasn't looking at me any more. He was walking around the room, frowning, not paying any attention to me. I looked out above the broken pane of the front window. The top of a car showed over the hedge. Its motor idled.

Eddie Mars found the purple flagon and the two gold-veined glasses on the desk. He sniffed at one of the glasses, then at the flagon. A disgusted smile wrinkled his lips. "The lousy pimp," he said tonelessly.

He looked at a couple of books, grunted, went on around the desk and stood in front of the little totem pole with the camera eye. He studied it, dropped his glance to the floor in front of it. He moved the small rug with his foot, then bent swiftly, his body tense. He went down on the floor with one gray knee. The desk hid him from me partly. There was a sharp exclamation and he came up again. His arm flashed under his coat and a black Luger appeared in his hand. He held it in long brown fingers, not pointing it at me, not pointing it at anything.

"Blood," he said. "Blood on the floor there, under the rug. Quite a lot of blood."

"Is that so?" I said, looking interested.

He slid into the chair behind the desk and hooked the mulberry-colored phone towards him and shifted the Luger to his left hand. He frowned sharply at the telephone, bringing his thick gray eyebrows close together and making a hard crease in the weathered skin at the top of his hooked nose. "I think we'll have some law," he said.

I went over and kicked at the rug that lay where Geiger had lain. "It's old blood," I said. "Dried blood."

"Just the same we'll have some law."

"Why not?" I said.

His eyes went narrow. The veneer had flaked off him, leaving a well-dressed hard boy with a Luger. He didn't like my agreeing with him.

"Just who the hell are you, soldier?"

"Marlowe is the name. I'm a sleuth."

"Never heard of you. Who's the girl?"

"Client. Geiger was trying to throw a loop on her with some blackmail. We came to talk it over. He wasn't here. The door being open we walked in to wait. Or did I tell you that?"

"Convenient," he said. "The door being open. When you didn't have a key."

"Yes. How come *you* had a key?"

"Is that any of your business, soldier?"

"I could make it my business."

He smiled tightly and pushed his hat back on his gray hair. "And I could make your business my business."

"You wouldn't like it. The pay's too small."

"All right, bright eyes. I own this house. Geiger is my tenant. Now what do you think of that?"

"You know such lovely people."

"I take them as they come. They come all kinds." He glanced down at the Luger, shrugged and tucked it back under his arm. "Got any good ideas, soldier?"

"Lots of them. Somebody gunned Geiger. Somebody got gunned by Geiger, who ran away. Or it was two other fellows.

61

Or Geiger was running a cult and made blood sacrifices in front of that totem pole. Or he had chicken for dinner and liked to kill his chickens in the front parlor."

The gray man scowled at me.

"I give up," I said. "Better call your friends downtown."

"I don't get it," he snapped. "I don't get your game here."

"Go ahead, call the buttons. You'll get a big reaction from it."

He thought that over without moving. His lips went back against his teeth. "I don't get that, either," he said tightly.

"Maybe it just isn't your day. I know you, Mr. Mars. The Cypress Club at Las Olindas. Flash gambling for flash people. The local law in your pocket and a well-greased line into L.A. In other words, protection. Geiger was in a racket that needed that too. Perhaps you spared him a little now and then, seeing he's your tenant."

His mouth became a hard white grimace. "Geiger was in what racket?"

"The smut book racket."

He stared at me for a long level minute. "Somebody got to him," he said softly. "You know something about it. He didn't show at the store today. They don't know where he is. He didn't answer the phone here. I came up to see about it. I find blood on the floor, under a rug. And you and a girl here."

"A little weak," I said. "But maybe you can sell the story to a willing buyer. You missed a little something, though. Somebody moved his books out of the store today – the nice books he rented out."

He snapped his fingers sharply and said: "I should have thought of that, soldier. You seem to get around. How do you figure it?"

"I think Geiger was rubbed. I think that is his blood. And the books being moved out gives a motive for hiding the body for a while. Somebody is taking over the racket and wants a little time to organize."

"They can't get away with it," Eddie Mars said grimly.

"Who says so? You and a couple of gunmen in your car outside? This is a big town now, Eddie. Some very tough people have checked in here lately. The penalty of growth."

"You talk too damned much," Eddie Mars said. He bared his teeth and whistled twice, sharply. A car door slammed outside and running steps came through the hedge. Mars flicked the Luger out again and pointed it at my chest. "Open the door."

The knob rattled and a voice called out. I didn't move. The muzzle of the Luger looked like the mouth of the Second Street tunnel, but I didn't move. Not being bullet proof is an idea I had had to get used to.

"Open it yourself, Eddie. Who the hell are you to give me orders? Be nice and I might help you out."

He came to his feet rigidly and moved around the end of the desk and over to the door. He opened it without taking his eyes off me. Two men tumbled into the room, reaching busily under their arms. One was an obvious pug, a good-looking pale-faced boy with a bad nose and one ear like a club steak. The other man was slim, blond, deadpan, with close-set eyes and no color in them.

Eddie Mars said: "See if this bird is wearing any iron."

The blond flicked a short-barreled gun out and stood pointing it at me. The pug sidled over flatfooted and felt my pockets with care. I turned around for him like a bored beauty modeling an evening gown.

"No gun," he said in a burry voice.

"Find out who he is."

The pug slipped a hand into my breast pocket and drew out my wallet. He flipped it open and studied the contents. "Name's Philip Marlowe, Eddie. Lives at the Hobart Arms on Franklin. Private license, deputy's badge and all. A shamus." He slipped the wallet back in my pocket, slapped my face lightly and turned away.

"Beat it," Eddie Mars said.

The two gunmen went out again and closed the door. There was the sound of them getting back into the car. They started its motor and kept it idling once more.

"All right. Talk," Eddie Mars snapped. The peaks of his eyebrows made sharp angles against his forehead.

"I'm not ready to give out. Killing Geiger to grab his racket would be a dumb trick and I'm not sure it happened that way, assuming he has been killed. But I'm sure that whoever got the books knows what's what, and I'm sure that the blonde lady down at his store is scared batty about something or other. And I have a guess who got the books."

"Who?"

"That's the part I'm not ready to give out. I've got a client, you know."

He wrinkled his nose. "That —" he chopped it off quickly.

"I expected you would know the girl," I said.

"Who got the books, soldier?"

"Not ready to talk, Eddie. Why should I?"

He put the Luger down on the desk and slapped it with his open palm. "This," he said. "And I might make it worth your while."

"That's the spirit. Leave the gun out of it. I can always hear the sound of money. How much are you clinking at me?"

"For doing what?"

"What did you want done?"

He slammed the desk hard. "Listen, soldier. I ask you a question and you ask me another. We're not getting anywhere. I want to know where Geiger is, for my own personal reasons. I didn't like his racket and I didn't protect him. I happen to own this house. I'm not so crazy about that right now. I can believe that whatever you know about all this is under glass, or there would be a flock of johns squeaking sole leather around this dump. You haven't got anything to sell. My guess is you need a little protection yourself. So cough up."

It was a good guess, but I wasn't going to let him know it. I lit a cigarette and blew the match out and flicked it at the glass eye of the totem pole. "You're right," I said. "If anything has happened to Geiger, I'll have to give what I have to the law. Which puts it in the public domain and doesn't leave me anything to sell. So with your permission I'll just drift."

His face whitened under the tan. He looked mean, fast and tough for a moment. He made a movement to lift the gun. I added casually: "By the way, how is Mrs. Mars these days?"

I thought for a moment I had kidded him a little too far. His hand jerked at the gun, shaking. His face was stretched out by hard muscles. "Beat it," he said quite softly. "I don't give a damn where you go or what you do when you get there. Only take a word of advice, soldier. Leave me out of your plans or you'll wish your name was Murphy and you lived in Limerick."

"Well, that's not so far from Clonmel," I said. "I hear you had a pal came from there."

He leaned down on the desk, frozen-eyed, unmoving. I went over to the door and opened it and looked back at him. His eyes had followed me, but his lean gray body had not moved. There was hate in his eyes. I went out and through the hedge and up the hill to my car and got into it. I turned it around and drove up over the crest. Nobody shot at me. After a few blocks I turned off, cut the motor and sat for a few moments. Nobody followed me either. I drove back into Hollywood.

14

IT WAS TEN minutes to five when I parked near the lobby entrance of the apartment house on Randall Place. A few windows were lit and radios were bleating at the dusk. I rode the automatic elevator up to the fourth floor and went along a wide hall carpeted in green and paneled in ivory. A cool breeze blew down the hall from the open screened door to the fire escape.

There was a small ivory pushbutton beside the door marked "405." I pushed it and waited what seemed a long time. Then the door opened noiselessly about a foot. There was a steady, furtive air in the way it opened. The man was long-legged, long-waisted, high-shouldered and he had dark brown eyes in a brown expressionless face that had learned to control its expressions long ago. Hair like steel wool grew far back on his head and gave him a great deal of domed brown forehead that might at a careless glance have seemed a dwelling place for brains. His somber eyes probed at me impersonally. His long thin brown fingers held the edge of the door. He said nothing.

I said: "Geiger?"

Nothing in the man's face changed that I could see. He brought a cigarette from behind the door and tucked it between his lips and drew a little smoke from it. The smoke came towards me in a lazy, contemptuous puff and behind it words in a cool, unhurried voice that had no more inflection than the voice of a faro dealer.

"You said what?"

"Geiger. Arthur Gwynn Geiger. The guy that has the books."

The man considered that without any haste. He glanced down at the tip of his cigarette. His other hand, the one that had been holding the door, dropped out of sight. His shoulder had a look as though his hidden hand might be making motions.

"Don't know anybody by that name," he said. "Does he live around here?"

I smiled. He didn't like the smile. His eyes got nasty. I said: "You're Joe Brody?"

The brown face hardened. "So what? Got a grift, brother – or just amusing yourself?"

"So you're Joe Brody," I said. "And you don't know any-body named Geiger. That's very funny."

"Yeah? You got a funny sense of humor maybe. Take it away and play on it somewhere else."

I leaned against the door and gave him a dreamy smile. "You got the books, Joe. I got the sucker list. We ought to talk things over."

He didn't shift his eyes from my face. There was a faint sound in the room behind him, as though a metal curtain ring clicked lightly on a metal rod. He glanced sideways into the room. He opened the door wider.

"Why not – if you think you've got something?" he said coolly. He stood aside from the door. I went past him into the room.

It was a cheerful room with good furniture and not too much of it. French windows in the end wall opened on a stone porch and looked across the dusk at the foothills. Near the windows a closed door in the west wall and near the entrance door another door in the same wall. This last had a plush cur-tain drawn across it on a thin brass rod below the lintel.

That left the east wall, in which there were no doors. There was a davenport backed against the middle of it, so I sat down on the davenport. Brody shut the door and walked crab-fash-ion to a tall oak desk studded with square nails. A cedarwood box with gilt hinges lay on the lowered leaf of the desk. He carried the box to an easy chair midway between the other two doors and sat down. I dropped my hat on the davenport and waited.

"Well, I'm listening," Brody said. He opened the cigar box and dropped his cigarette stub into a dish at his side. He put a long thin cigar in his mouth. "Cigar?" He tossed one at me through the air.

I reached for it. Brody took a gun out of the cigar box and pointed it at my nose. I looked at the gun. It was a black Police .38. I had no argument against it at the moment.

"Neat, huh?" Brody said. "Just kind of stand up a minute. Come forward just about two yards. You might grab a little air while you're doing that." His voice was the elaborately casual voice of the tough guy in pictures. Pictures have made them all like that.

"Tsk, tsk," I said, not moving at all. "Such a lot of guns around town and so few brains. You're the second guy I've met within hours who seems to think a gat in the hand means a world by the tail. Put it down and don't be silly, Joe."

His eyebrows came together and he pushed his chin at me. His eyes were mean.

"The other guy's name is Eddie Mars," I said. "Ever hear of him?"

"No." Brody kept the gun pointed at me.

"If he ever gets wise to where you were last night in the rain, he'll wipe you off the way a check raiser wipes a check."

"What would I be to Eddie Mars?" Brody asked coldly. But he lowered the gun to his knee.

"Not even a memory," I said.

We stared at each other. I didn't look at the pointed black slipper that showed under the plush curtain on the doorway to my left.

Brody said quietly: "Don't get me wrong. I'm not a tough guy – just careful. I don't know hell's first whisper about you. You might be a lifetaker for all I know."

"You're not careful enough," I said. "That play with Geiger's books was terrible."

He drew a long slow breath and let it out silently. Then he leaned back and crossed his long legs and held the Colt on his knee.

"Don't kid yourself I won't use this heat, if I have to," he said. "What's your story?"

"Have your friend with the pointed slippers come on in. She gets tired holding her breath."

Brody called out without moving his eyes off my stomach. "Come on in, Agnes."

The curtain swung aside and the green-eyed, thigh-swinging ash blonde from Geiger's store joined us in the room. She looked at me with a kind of mangled hatred. Her nostrils were pinched and her eyes had darkened a couple of shades. She looked very unhappy.

"I knew damn well you were trouble," she snapped at me. "I told Joe to watch his step."

"It's not his step, it's the back of his lap he ought to watch," I said.

"I suppose that's funny," the blonde squealed.

"It has been," I said. "But it probably isn't any more."

"Save the gags," Brody advised me. "Joe's watchin' his step plenty. Put some light on so I can see to pop this guy, if it works out that way."

The blonde snicked on a light in a big square standing lamp. She sank down into a chair beside the lamp and sat stiffly, as if her girdle was too tight. I put my cigar in my mouth and bit the end off. Brody's Colt took a close interest in me while I got matches out and lit the cigar. I tasted the smoke and said:

"The sucker list I spoke of is in code. I haven't cracked it yet, but there are about five hundred names. You got twelve boxes of books that I know of. You should have at least five hundred books. There'll be a bunch more out on loan, but say five hundred is the full crop, just to be cautious. If it's a good active list and you could run it even fifty per cent down the line, that would be one hundred and twenty-five thousand rentals. Your girl friend knows all about that. I'm only guessing. Put the average rental as low as you like, but it won't be less than a dollar. That merchandise costs money. At a dollar a rental you take one hundred and twenty-five grand and you still have your capital. I mean, you still have Geiger's capital. That's enough to spot a guy for."

The blonde yelped: "You're crazy, you goddam egg-headed – !"

Brody put his teeth sideways at her and snarled: "Pipe down, for Chrissake. Pipe down!"

She subsided into an outraged mixture of slow anguish and bottled fury. Her silvery nails scraped on her knees.

"It's no racket for bums," I told Brody almost affectionately. "It takes a smooth worker like you, Joe. You've got to get confidence and keep it. People who spend their money for second-hand sex jags are as nervous as dowagers who can't find the rest room. Personally I think the blackmail angles are a big mistake. I'm for shedding all that and sticking to legitimate sales and rentals."

Brody's dark brown stare moved up and down my face. His Colt went on hungering for my vital organs. "You're a funny guy," he said tonelessly. "Who has this lovely racket?"

"*You* have," I said. "Almost."

The blonde choked and clawed her ear. Brody didn't say anything. He just looked at me.

"What?" the blonde yelped. "You sit there and try to tell us Mr. Geiger ran that kind of business right down on the main drag? You're nuts!"

I leered at her politely. "Sure I do. Everybody knows the racket exists. Hollywood's made to order for it. If a thing like that has to exist, then right out on the street is where all practical coppers want it to exist. For the same reason they favor red light districts. They know where to flush the game when they want to."

"My God," the blonde wailed. "You let this cheesehead sit there and insult me, Joe? You with a gun in your hand and him holding nothing but a cigar and his thumb?"

"I like it," Brody said. "The guy's got good ideas. Shut your trap and keep it shut, or I'll slap it shut for you with this." He flicked the gun around in an increasingly negligent manner.

The blonde gasped and turned her face to the wall. Brody looked at me and said cunningly: "*How* have I got that lovely racket?"

"You shot Geiger to get it. Last night in the rain. It was dandy shooting weather. The trouble is he wasn't alone when you whiffed him. Either you didn't notice that, which seems unlikely, or you got the wind up and lammed. But you had nerve enough to take the plate out of his camera and you had nerve enough to come back later on and hide his corpse, so you could tidy up on the books before the law knew it had a murder to investigate."

"Yah," Brody said contemptuously. The Colt wobbled on his knee. His brown face was as hard as a piece of carved wood. "You take chances, mister. It's kind of goddamned lucky for you I *didn't* bop Geiger."

"You can step off for it just the same," I told him cheerfully. "You're made to order for the rap."

Brody's voice rustled. "Think you got me framed for it?"

"Positive."

"How come?"

"There's somebody who'll tell it that way. I told you there was a witness. Don't go simple on me, Joe."

He exploded then. "That goddamned little hot pants!" he yelled. "She would, god damn her! She would – just that!"

I leaned back and grinned at him. "Swell. I thought you had those nude photos of her."

He didn't say anything. The blonde didn't say anything. I let them chew on it. Brody's face cleared slowly, with a sort of grayish relief. He put his Colt down on the end table beside his chair but kept his right hand close to it. He knocked ash from his cigar on the carpet and stared at me with eyes that were a tight shine between narrowed lids.

"I guess you think I'm dumb," Brody said.

"Just average, for a grifter. Get the pictures."

"What pictures?"

I shook my head. "Wrong play, Joe. Innocence gets you nowhere. You were either there last night, or you got the nude photo from somebody that was there. You knew *she* was there, because you had your girl friend threaten Mrs. Regan with a police rap. The only ways you could know enough to do that would be by seeing what happened or by holding the photo and knowing where and when it was taken. Cough up and be sensible."

"I'd have to have a little dough," Brody said. He turned his head a little to look at the green-eyed blonde. Not now green-eyed and only superficially a blonde. She was as limp as a fresh-killed rabbit.

"No dough," I said.

He scowled bitterly. "How'd you get to me?"

I flicked my wallet out and let him look at my buzzer. "I was working on Geiger – for a client. I was outside last night, in the rain. I heard the shots. I crashed in. I didn't see the killer. I saw everything else."

"And kept your lip buttoned," Brody sneered.

I put my wallet away. "Yes," I admitted. "Up till now. Do I get the photos or not?"

"About these books," Brody said. "I don't get that."

"I tailed them here from Geiger's store. I have a witness."

"That punk kid?"

"What punk kid?"

He scowled again. "The kid that works at the store. He skipped out after the truck left. Agnes don't even know where he flops."

"That helps," I said, grinning at him. "That angle worried me a little. Either of you ever been in Geiger's house – before last night?"

"Not even last night," Brody said sharply. "So she says I gunned him, eh?"

"With the photos in hand I might be able to convince her she was wrong. There was a little drinking being done."

Brody sighed. "She hates my guts. I bounced her out. I got paid, sure, but I'd of had to do it anyway. She's too screwy for a simple guy like me." He cleared his throat. "How about a little dough? I'm down to nickels. Agnes and me gotta move on."

"Not from my client."

"Listen —"

"Get the pictures, Brody."

"Oh, hell," he said. "You win." He stood up and slipped the Colt into his side pocket. His left hand went up inside his coat. He was holding it there, his face twisted with disgust, when the door buzzer rang and kept on ringing.

15

HE DIDN'T LIKE that. His lower lip went in under his teeth, and his eyebrows drew down sharply at the corners. His whole face became sharp and foxy and mean.

The buzzer kept up its song. I didn't like it either. If the visitors should happen to be Eddie Mars and his boys, I might get chilled off just for being there. If it was the police, I was caught with nothing to give them but a smile and a promise. And if it was some of Brody's friends — supposing he had any — they might turn out to be tougher than he was.

The blonde didn't like it. She stood up in a surge and chipped at the air with one hand. Nerve tension made her face old and ugly.

Watching me, Brody jerked a small drawer in the desk and picked a bone-handled automatic out of it. He held it at the blonde. She slid over to him and took it, shaking.

"Sit down next to him," Brody snapped. "Hold it on him low down, away from the door. If he gets funny use your own judgment. We ain't licked yet, baby."

"Oh, Joe," the blonde wailed. She came over and sat next to me on the davenport and pointed the gun at my leg artery. I didn't like the jerky look in her eyes.

The door buzzer stopped humming and a quick impatient rapping on the wood followed it. Brody put his hand in his pocket, on his gun, and walked over to the door and opened it with his left hand. Carmen Sternwood pushed him back into the room by putting a little revolver against his lean brown lips.

Brody backed away from her with his mouth working and an expression of panic on his face. Carmen shut the door behind her and looked neither at me nor at Agnes. She stalked Brody carefully, her tongue sticking out a little between her teeth. Brody took both hands out of his pockets and gestured placatingly at her. His eyebrows designed themselves into an odd assortment of curves and angles. Agnes turned the gun away from me and swung it at Carmen. I shot my hand out and closed my fingers down hard over her hand and jammed my thumb on the safety catch. It was already on. I kept it on. There was a short silent tussle, to which neither Brody nor Carmen paid any attention whatever. I had the gun. Agnes breathed deeply and shivered the whole length of her body. Carmen's face had a bony scraped look and her breath hissed. Her voice said without tone:

"I want my pictures, Joe."

Brody swallowed and tried to grin. "Sure, kid, sure." He said it in a small flat voice that was as much like the voice he had used to me as a scooter is like a ten-ton truck.

Carmen said: "You shot Arthur Geiger. I saw you. I want my pictures." Brody turned green.

"Hey, wait a minute, Carmen," I yelped.

Blonde Agnes came to life with a rush. She ducked her head and sank her teeth in my right hand. I made more noises and shook her off.

"Listen, kid," Brody whined. "Listen a minute —"

The blonde spat at me and threw herself on my leg and tried to bite that. I cracked her on the head with the gun, not very hard, and tried to stand up. She rolled down my legs and wrapped her arms around them. I fell back on the davenport. The blonde was strong with the madness of love or fear, or a mixture of both, or maybe she was just strong.

Brody grabbed for the little revolver that was so close to his face. He missed. The gun made a sharp rapping noise that was not very loud. The bullet broke glass in a folded-back French window. Brody groaned horribly and fell down on the floor and jerked Carmen's feet from under her. She landed in a heap and the little revolver went skidding off into a corner. Brody jumped up on his knees and reached for his pocket.

I hit Agnes on the head with less delicacy than before, kicked her off my feet, and stood up. Brody flicked his eyes at me. I showed him the automatic. He stopped trying to get his hand into his pocket.

"Christ!" he whined. "Don't let her kill me!"

I began to laugh. I laughed like an idiot, without control. Blonde Agnes was sitting up on the floor with her hands flat on the carpet and her mouth wide open and a wick of metallic blond hair down over her right eye. Carmen was crawling on her hands and knees, still hissing. The metal of her little revolver glistened against the baseboard over in the corner. She crawled towards it relentlessly.

I waved my share of the guns at Brody and said: "Stay put. You're all right."

I stepped past the crawling girl and picked the gun up. She looked up at me and began to giggle. I put her gun in my pocket and patted her on the back. "Get up, angel. You look like a Pekinese."

I went over to Brody and put the automatic against his midriff and reached his Colt out of his side pocket. I now had all the guns that had been exposed to view. I stuffed them into my pockets and held my hand out to him.

"Give."

He nodded, licking his lips, his eyes still scared. He took a fat envelope out of his breast pocket and gave it to me. There was a developed plate in the envelope and five glossy prints.

"Sure these are all?"

He nodded again. I put the envelope in my own breast pocket and turned away. Agnes was back on the davenport, straightening her hair. Her eyes ate Carmen with a green distillation of hate. Carmen was up on her feet too, coming towards me with her hand out, still giggling and hissing. There was a little froth at the corners of her mouth. Her small white teeth glinted close to her lips.

"Can I have them now?" she asked me with a coy smile.

"I'll take care of them for you. Go on home."

"Home?"

I went to the door and looked out. The cool night breeze was blowing peacefully down the hall. No excited neighbors hung out of doorways. A small gun had gone off and broken a pane of glass, but noises like that don't mean much any more. I held the door open and jerked my head at Carmen. She came towards me, smiling uncertainly.

"Go on home and wait for me," I said soothingly.

She put her thumb up. Then she nodded and slipped past me into the hall. She touched my cheek with her fingers as she went by. "You'll take care of Carmen, won't you?" she cooed.

"Check."

"You're cute."

"What you see is nothing," I said. "I've got a Bali dancing girl tattooed on my right thigh."

Her eyes rounded. She said: "Naughty," and wagged a finger at me. Then she whispered: "Can I have my gun?"

"Not now. Later. I'll bring it to you."

She grabbed me suddenly around the neck and kissed me on the mouth. "I like you," she said. "Carmen likes you a lot." She ran off down the hall as gay as a thrush, waved at me from the stairs and ran down the stairs out of my sight.

I went back into Brody's apartment.

16

I WENT OVER to the folded-back French window and looked at the small broken pane in the upper part of it. The bullet from Carmen's gun had smashed the glass like a blow. It had not made a hole. There was a small hole in the plaster which a keen eye would find quickly enough. I pulled the drapes over the broken pane and took Carmen's gun out of my pocket. It was a Banker's Special, .22 caliber, hollow point cartridges. It had a pearl grip, and a small round silver plate set into the butt was engraved: "Carmen from Owen." She made saps of all of them.

I put the gun back in my pocket and sat down close to Brody and stared into his bleak brown eyes. A minute passed. The blonde adjusted her face by the aid of a pocket mirror. Brody fumbled around with a cigarette and jerked: "Satisfied?"

"So far. Why did you put the bite on Mrs. Regan instead of the old man?"

"Tapped the old man once. About six, seven months ago. I figure maybe he gets sore enough to call in some law."

"What made you think Mrs. Regan wouldn't tell him about it?"

He considered that with some care, smoking his cigarette and keeping his eyes on my face. Finally he said: "How well you know her?"

"I've met her twice. You must know her a lot better to take a chance on that squeeze with the photo."

"She skates around plenty. I figure maybe she has a couple of soft spots she don't want the old man to know about. I figure she can raise five grand easy."

"A little weak," I said. "But pass it. You're broke, eh?"

"I been shaking two nickels together for a month, trying to get them to mate."

"What you do for a living?"

"Insurance. I got desk room in Puss Walgreen's office, Fulwider Building, Western and Santa Monica."

"When you open up, you open up. The books here in your apartment?"

He snapped his teeth and waved a brown hand. Confidence was oozing back into his manner. "Hell, no. In storage."

"You had a man bring them here and then you had a storage outfit come and take them away again right afterwards?"

"Sure. I don't want them moved direct from Geiger's place, do I?"

"You're smart," I said admiringly. "Anything incriminating in the joint right now?"

He looked worried again. He shook his head sharply.

"That's fine," I told him. I looked across at Agnes. She had finished fixing her face and was staring at the wall, blank-eyed, hardly listening. Her face had the drowsiness which strain and shock induce, after their first incidence.

Brody flicked his eyes warily. "Well?"

"How'd you come by the photo?"

He scowled. "Listen, you got what you came after, got it plenty cheap. You done a nice neat job. Now go peddle it to your top man. I'm clean. I don't know nothing about any photo, do I, Agnes?"

The blonde opened her eyes and looked at him with vague but uncomplimentary speculation. "A half smart guy," she said with a tired sniff. "That's all I ever draw. Never once a guy that's smart all the way around the course. Never once."

I grinned at her. "Did I hurt your head much?"

"You and every other man I ever met."

I looked back at Brody. He was pinching his cigarette between his fingers, with a sort of twitch. His hand seemed to be shaking a little. His brown poker face was still smooth.

"We've got to agree on a story," I said. "For instance, Carmen wasn't here. That's very important. She wasn't here. That was a vision you saw."

"Huh!" Brody sneered. "If you say so, pal, and if —" he put his hand out palm up and cupped the fingers and rolled the thumb gently against the index and middle fingers.

I nodded. "We'll see. There might be a small contribution. You won't count it in grands, though. Now where did you get the picture?"

"A guy slipped it to me."

"Uh-huh. A guy you just passed in the street. You wouldn't know him again. You never saw him before."

Brody yawned. "It dropped out of his pocket," he leered.

"Uh-huh. Got an alibi for last night, poker pan?"

"Sure. I was right here. Agnes was with me. Okay, Agnes?"

"I'm beginning to feel sorry for you again," I said.

His eyes flicked wide and his mouth hung loose, the cigarette balanced on his lower lip.

"You think you're smart and you're so goddamned dumb," I told him. "Even if you don't dance off up in Quentin, you have such a bleak long lonely time ahead of you."

His cigarette jerked and dropped ash on his vest.

"Thinking about how smart you are," I said.

"Take the air," he growled suddenly. "Dust. I got enough chinning with you. Beat it."

"Okay." I stood up and went over to the tall oak desk and took his two guns out of my pockets, laid them side by side on the blotter so that the barrels were exactly parallel. I reached my hat off the floor beside the davenport and started for the door.

Brody yelped: "Hey!"

I turned and waited. His cigarette was jiggling like a doll on a coiled spring. "Everything's smooth, ain't it?" he asked.

"Why, sure. This is a free country. You don't have to stay out of jail, if you don't want to. That is, if you're a citizen. Are you a citizen?"

He just stared at me, jiggling the cigarette. The blonde Agnes turned her head slowly and stared at me along the same

79

level. Their glances contained almost the exact same blend of foxiness, doubt and frustrated anger. Agnes reached her silvery nails up abruptly and yanked a hair out of her head and broke it between her fingers, with a bitter jerk.

Brody said tightly: "You're not going to any cops, brother. Not if it's the Sternwoods you're working for. I've got too much stuff on that family. You got your pictures and you got your hush. Go and peddle your papers."

"Make your mind up," I said. "You told me to dust, I was on my way out, you hollered at me and I stopped, and now I'm on my way out again. Is that what you want?"

"You ain't got anything on me," Brody said.

"Just a couple of murders. Small change in your circle."

He didn't jump more than an inch, but it looked like a foot. The white cornea showed all around the tobacco-colored iris of his eyes. The brown skin of his face took on a greenish tinge in the lamplight.

Blonde Agnes let out a low animal wail and buried her head in a cushion on the end of the davenport. I stood there and admired the long line of her thighs.

Brody moistened his lips slowly and said: "Sit down, pal. Maybe I have a little more for you. What's that crack about two murders mean?"

I leaned against the door. "Where were you last night about seven-thirty, Joe?"

His mouth drooped sulkily and he stared down at the floor. "I was watching a guy, a guy who had a nice racket I figured he needed a partner in. Geiger. I was watching him now and then to see had he any tough connections. I figure he has friends or he don't work the racket as open as he does. But they don't go to his house. Only dames."

"You didn't watch hard enough," I said. "Go on."

"I'm there last night on the street below Geiger's house. It's raining hard and I'm buttoned up in my coupe and I don't see anything. There's a car in front of Geiger's and another car a little way up the hill. That's why I stay down below. There's a big Buick parked down where I am and after a while I go over and take a gander into it. It's registered to Vivian Regan. Nothing happens, so I scram. That's all." He waved his cigarette. His eyes crawled up and down my face.

"Could be," I said. "Know where that Buick is now?"

"Why would I?"

"In the Sheriff's garage. It was lifted out of twelve feet of water off Lido fish pier this a.m. There was a dead man in it. He had been sapped and the car pointed out the pier and the hand throttle pulled down."

Brody was breathing hard. One of his feet tapped restlessly. "Jesus, guy, you can't pin that one on me," he said thickly.

"Why not? This Buick was down back of Geiger's according to you. Well, Mrs. Regan didn't have it out. Her chauffeur, a lad named Owen Taylor, had it out. He went over to Geiger's place to have words with him, because Owen Taylor was sweet on Carmen, and he didn't like the kind of games Geiger was playing with her. He let himself in the back way with a jimmy and a gun and he caught Geiger taking a photo of Carmen without any clothes on. So his gun went off, as guns will, and Geiger fell down dead and Owen ran away, but not without the photo negative Geiger had just taken. So you ran after him and took the photo from him. How else would you have got hold of it?"

Brody licked his lips. "Yeah," he said. "But that don't make me knock him off. Sure, I heard the shots and saw this killer come slamming down the back steps into the Buick and off. I took out after him. He hit the bottom of the canyon and went west on Sunset. Beyond Beverly Hills he skidded off the road and had to stop and I came up and played copper. He had a gun but his nerve was bad and I sapped him down. So I went through his clothes and found out who he was and I lifted the plateholder, just out of curiosity. I was wondering what it was all about and getting my neck wet when he came out of it all of a sudden and knocked me off the car. He was out of sight when I picked myself up. That's the last I saw of him."

"How did you know it was Geiger he shot?" I asked gruffly.

Brody shrugged. "I figure it was, but I can be wrong. When I had the plate developed and saw what was on it, I was pretty damn sure. And when Geiger didn't come down to the store this morning and didn't answer his phone I was plenty sure. So I figure it's a good time to move his books out and make a quick touch on the Sternwoods for travel money and blow for a while."

I nodded. "That seems reasonable. Maybe you didn't murder anybody at that. Where did you hide Geiger's body?"

He jumped his eyebrows. Then he grinned. "Nix, nix. Skip it. You think I'd go back there and handle him, not knowing when a couple carloads of law would come tearing around the corner? Nix."

"Somebody hid the body," I said.

Brody shrugged. The grin stayed on his face. He didn't believe me. While he was still not believing me the door buzzer started to ring again. Brody stood up sharply, hard-eyed. He glanced over at his guns on the desk.

"So she's back again," he growled.

"If she is, she doesn't have her gun," I comforted him. "Don't you have any other friends?"

"Just about one," he growled. "I got enough of this puss in the corner game." He marched to the desk and took the Colt. He held it down at his side and went to the door. He put his left hand to the knob and twisted it and opened the door a foot and leaned into the opening, holding the gun tight against his thigh.

A voice said: "Brody?"

Brody said something I didn't hear. The two quick reports were muffled. The gun must have been pressed tight against

Brody's body. He tilted forward against the door and the weight of his body pushed it shut with a bang. He slid down the wood. His feet pushed the carpet away behind him. His left hand dropped off the knob and the arm slapped the floor with a thud. His head was wedged against the door. He didn't move. The Colt clung to his right hand.

I jumped across the room and rolled him enough to get the door open and crowd through. A woman peered out of a door almost opposite. Her face was full of fright and she pointed along the hall with a clawlike hand.

I raced down the hall and heard thumping feet going down the tile steps and went down after the sound. At the lobby level the front door was closing itself quietly and running feet slapped the sidewalk outside. I made the door before it was shut, clawed it open again and charged out.

A tall hatless figure in a leather jerkin was running diagonally across the street between the parked cars. The figure turned and flame spurted from it. Two heavy hammers hit the stucco wall beside me. The figure ran on, dodged between two cars, vanished.

A man came up beside me and barked: "What happened?"

"Shooting going on," I said.

"Jesus!" He scuttled into the apartment house.

I walked quickly down the sidewalk to my car and got in and started it. I pulled out from the curb and drove down the hill, not fast. No other car started up on the other side of the street. I thought I heard steps, but I wasn't sure about that. I rode down the hill a block and a half, turned at the intersection and started back up. The sound of a muted whistling came to me faintly along the sidewalk. Then steps. I double parked and slid out between two cars and went down low. I took Carmen's little revolver out of my pocket.

The sound of the steps grew louder, and the whistling went on cheerfully. In a moment the jerkin showed. I stepped out between the two cars and said: "Got a match, buddy?"

The boy spun towards me and his right hand darted up to go inside the jerkin. His eyes were a wet shine in the glow of the round electroliers. Moist dark eyes shaped like almonds, and a pallid handsome face with wavy black hair growing low on the forehead in two points. A very handsome boy indeed, the boy from Geiger's store.

He stood there looking at me silently, his right hand on the edge of the jerkin, but not inside it yet. I held the little revolver down at my side.

"You must have thought a lot of that queen," I said.

"Go — yourself," the boy said softly, motionless between the parked cars and the five-foot retaining wall on the inside of the sidewalk.

A siren wailed distantly coming up the long hill. The boy's head jerked towards the sound. I stepped in close and put my gun into his jerkin.

"Me or the cops?" I asked him.

His head rolled a little sideways as if I had slapped his face. "Who are you?" he snarled.

"Friend of Geiger's."

"Get away from me, you son of a bitch."

"This is a small gun, kid. I'll give it you through the navel and it will take three months to get you well enough to walk. But you'll get well. So you can walk to the nice new gas chamber up in Quentin."

He said: "Go — yourself." His hand moved inside the jerkin. I pressed harder on his stomach. He let out a long soft sigh, took his hand away from the jerkin and let it fall limp at his side. His wide shoulders sagged. "What you want?" he whispered.

I reached inside the jerkin and plucked out the automatic. "Get into my car, kid."

He stepped past me and I crowded him from behind. He got into the car.

"Under the wheel, kid. You drive."

84

He slid under the wheel and I got into the car beside him. I said: "Let the prowl car pass up the hill. They'll think we moved over when we heard the siren. Then turn her down hill and we'll go home."

I put Carmen's gun away and leaned the automatic against the boy's ribs. I looked back through the window. The whine of the siren was very loud now. Two red lights swelled in the middle of the street. They grew larger and blended into one and the car rushed by in a wild flurry of sound.

"Let's go," I said.

The boy swung the car and started off down the hill.

"Let's go home," I said. "To Laverne Terrace."

His smooth lips twitched. He swung the car west on Franklin. "You're a simple-minded lad. What's your name?"

"Carol Lundgren," he said lifelessly.

"You shot the wrong guy, Carol. Joe Brody didn't kill your queen."

He spoke three words to me and kept on driving.

17

A MOON HALF gone from the full glowed through a ring of mist among the high branches of the eucalyptus trees on Laverne Terrace. A radio sounded loudly from a house low down the hill. The boy swung the car over to the box hedge in front of Geiger's house, killed the motor and sat looking straight before him with both hands on the wheel. No light showed through Geiger's hedge.

I said: "Anybody home, son?"

"You ought to know."

"How would I know?"

"Go — yourself."

"That's how people get false teeth."

He showed me his in a tight grin. Then he kicked the door open and got out. I scuttled out after him. He stood with his fists on his hips, looking silently at the house above the top of the hedge.

"All right," I said. "You have a key. Let's go on in."

"Who said I had a key?"

"Don't kid me, son. The fag gave you one. You've got a nice clean manly little room in there. He shooed you out and locked it up when he had lady visitors. He was like Caesar, a husband to women and a wife to men. Think I can't figure people like him and you out?"

I still held his automatic more or less pointed at him, but he swung on me just the same. It caught me flush on the chin. I backstepped fast enough to keep from falling, but I took plenty of the punch. It was meant to be a hard one, but a pansy has no iron in his bones, whatever he looks like.

I threw the gun down at the kid's feet and said: "Maybe you need this."

He stooped for it like a flash. There was nothing slow about his movements. I sank a fist in the side of his neck. He toppled over sideways, clawing for the gun and not reaching it. I picked it up again and threw it in the car. The boy came up on all fours, leering with his eyes too wide open. He coughed and shook his head.

"You don't want to fight," I told him. "You're giving away too much weight."

He wanted to fight. He shot at me like a plane from a catapult, reaching for my knees in a diving tackle. I sidestepped and reached for his neck and took it into chancery. He scraped the dirt hard and got his feet under him enough to use his hands on me where it hurt. I twisted him around and heaved him a little higher. I took hold of my right wrist with my left hand and turned my right hipbone into him and for a moment it was a balance of weights. We seemed to hang there in the misty moonlight, two grotesque creatures whose feet scraped on the road and whose breath panted with effort.

I had my right forearm against his windpipe now and all the strength of both arms in it. His feet began a frenetic shuffle and he wasn't panting any more. He was iron-bound. His left foot sprawled off to one side and the knee went slack. I held on half a minute longer. He sagged on my arm, an enormous weight I could hardly hold up. Then I let go. He sprawled at my feet, out cold. I went to the car and got a pair of handcuffs out of the glove compartment and twisted his wrists behind him and snapped them on. I lifted him by the armpits and managed to drag him in behind the hedge, out of sight from the street. I went back to the car and moved it a hundred feet up the hill and locked it.

He was still out when I got back. I unlocked the door, dragged him into the house, shut the door. He was beginning to gasp now. I switched a lamp on. His eyes fluttered open and focused on me slowly.

I bent down, keeping out of the way of his knees and said: "Keep quiet or you'll get the same and more of it. Just lie quiet and hold your breath. Hold it until you can't hold it any longer and then tell yourself that you have to breathe, that you're black in the face, that your eyeballs are popping out, and that you're going to breathe right now, but that you're sitting strapped in the chair in the clean little gas chamber up in San Quentin and when you take that breath you're fighting with all your soul not to take it, it won't be air you'll get, it will be cyanide fumes. And that's what they call humane execution in our state now."

"Go — yourself," he said with a soft stricken sigh.

"You're going to cop a plea, brother, don't ever think you're not. And you're going to say just what we want you to say and nothing we don't want you to say."

"Go — yourself."

"Say that again and I'll put a pillow under your head."

His mouth twitched. I left him lying on the floor with his wrists shackled behind him and his cheek pressed into the rug and an animal brightness in his visible eye. I put on another lamp and stepped into the hallway at the back of the living room. Geiger's bedroom didn't seem to have been touched. I opened the door, not locked now, of the bedroom across the hall from it. There was a dim flickering light in the room and a smell of sandalwood. Two cones of incense ash stood side by side on a small brass tray on the bureau. The light came from the two tall black candles in the foot-high candlesticks. They were standing on straight-backed chairs, one on either side of the bed.

Geiger lay on the bed. The two missing strips of Chinese tapestry made a St. Andrew's Cross over the middle of his body, hiding the blood-smeared front of his Chinese coat. Below the cross his black-pajama'd legs lay stiff and straight. His feet were in the slippers with thick white felt soles. Above the cross his arms were crossed at the wrists and his hands lay flat against his shoulders, palms down, fingers close together and stretched out evenly. His mouth was closed and his Charlie Chan moustache was as unreal as a toupee. His broad nose was pinched and white. His eyes were almost closed, but not entirely. The faint glitter of his glass eye caught the light and winked at me.

I didn't touch him. I didn't go very near him. He would be as cold as ice and as stiff as a board.

The black candles guttered in the draft from the open door. Drops of black wax crawled down their sides. The air of the room was poisonous and unreal. I went out and shut the door again and went back to the living room. The boy hadn't moved. I stood still, listening for sirens. It was all a question of how soon Agnes talked and what she said. If she talked about Geiger, the police would be there any minute. But she might not talk for hours. She might even have got away.

I looked down at the boy. "Want to sit up, son?"

He closed his eye and pretended to go to sleep. I went over to the desk and scooped up the mulberry-colored phone and dialed Bernie Ohls' office. He had left to go home at six o'clock. I dialed the number of his home. He was there.

"This is Marlowe," I said. "Did your boys find a revolver on Owen Taylor this morning?"

I could hear him clearing his throat and then I could hear him trying to keep the surprise out of his voice. "That would come under the heading of police business," he said.

"If they did, it had three empty shells in it."

"How the hell did you know that?" Ohls asked quietly.

"Come over to 7244 Laverne Terrace, off Laurel Canyon Boulevard. I'll show you where the slugs went."

"Just like that, huh?"

"Just like that."

Ohls said: "Look out the window and you'll see me coming round the corner. I thought you acted a little cagey on that one."

"Cagey is no word for it," I said.

18

OHLS STOOD LOOKING down at the boy. The boy sat on the couch leaning sideways against the wall. Ohls looked at him silently, his pale eyebrows bristling and stiff and round like the little vegetable brushes the Fuller Brush man gives away.

He asked the boy: "Do you admit shooting Brody?"

The boy said his favorite three words in a muffled voice.

Ohls sighed and looked at me. I said: "He doesn't have to admit that. I have his gun."

Ohls said: "I wish to Christ I had a dollar for every time I've had that said to me. What's funny about it?"

"It's not meant to be funny," I said.

"Well, that's something," Ohls said. He turned away. "I've called Wilde. We'll go over and see him and take this punk.

He can ride with me and you can follow on behind in case he tries to kick me in the face."

"How do you like what's in the bedroom?"

"I like it fine," Ohls said. "I'm kind of glad that Taylor kid went off the pier. I'd hate to have to help send him to the deathhouse for rubbing that skunk."

I went back into the small bedroom and blew out the black candles and let them smoke. When I got back to the living room Ohls had the boy up on his feet. The boy stood glaring at him with sharp black eyes in a face as hard and white as cold mutton fat.

"Let's go," Ohls said and took him by the arm as if he didn't like touching him. I put the lamps out and followed them out of the house. We got into our cars and I followed Ohls' twin tail-lights down the long curving hill. I hoped this would be my last trip to Laverne Terrace.

Taggart Wilde, the District Attorney, lived at the corner of Fourth and Lafayette Park, in a white frame house the size of a carbarn, with a red sandstone porte-cochere built on to one side and a couple of acres of soft rolling lawn in front. It was one of those solid old-fashioned houses which it used to be the thing to move bodily to new locations as the city grew westward. Wilde came of an old Los Angeles family and had probably been born in the house when it was on West Adams or Figueroa or St. James Park.

There were two cars in the driveway already, a big private sedan and a police car with a uniformed chauffeur who leaned smoking against his rear fender and admired the moon. Ohls went over and spoke to him and the chauffeur looked in at the boy in Ohls' car.

We went up to the house and rang the bell. A slick-haired blond man opened the door and led us down the hall and through a huge sunken living room crowded with heavy dark furniture and along another hall on the far side of it. He knocked at a door and stepped inside, then held the door wide and we went into a paneled study with an open French door at the end and a view of dark garden and mysterious trees. A smell of wet earth and flowers came in at the window. There were large dim oils on the walls, easy chairs, books, a smell of good cigar smoke which blended with the smell of wet earth and flowers.

Taggart Wilde sat behind a desk, a middle-aged plump man with clear blue eyes that managed to have a friendly expression without really having any expression at all. He had a cup of black coffee in front of him and he held a dappled thin cigar between the neat careful fingers of his left hand. Another man sat at the corner of the desk in a blue leather chair, a cold-eyed hatchet-faced man, as lean as a rake and as hard as the manager of a loan office. His neat well-kept face looked as if it had been shaved within the hour. He wore a well-pressed brown suit and there was a black pearl in his tie. He had the long nervous fingers of a man with a quick brain. He looked ready for a fight.

Ohls pulled a chair up and sat down and said: "Evening, Cronjager. Meet Phil Marlowe, a private eye who's in a jam." Ohls grinned.

Cronjager looked at me without nodding. He looked me over as if he was looking at a photograph. Then he nodded his chin about an inch. Wilde said: "Sit down, Marlowe. I'll try to handle Captain Cronjager, but you know how it is. This is a big city now."

I sat down and lit a cigarette. Ohls looked at Cronjager and asked: "What did you get on the Randall Place killing?"

The hatchet-faced man pulled one of his fingers until the knuckle cracked. He spoke without looking up. "A stiff, two slugs in him. Two guns that hadn't been fired. Down on the street we got a blonde trying to start a car that didn't belong to her. Hers was right next to it, the same model. She acted rattled so the boys brought her in and she spilled. She was in there when this guy Brody got it. Claims she didn't see the killer."

"That all?" Ohls asked.

Cronjager raised his eyebrows a little. "Only happened about an hour ago. What did you expect – moving pictures of the killing?"

"Maybe a description of the killer," Ohls said.

"A tall guy in a leather jerkin – if you call that a description."

"He's outside in my heap," Ohls said. "Handcuffed. Marlowe put the arm on him for you. Here's his gun." Ohls took the boy's automatic out of his pocket and laid it on a corner of Wilde's desk. Cronjager looked at the gun but didn't reach for it.

Wilde chuckled. He was leaning back and puffing his dappled cigar without letting go of it. He bent forward to sip from his coffee cup. He took a silk handkerchief from the breast pocket of the dinner jacket he was wearing and touched his lips with it and tucked it away again.

"There's a couple more deaths involved," Ohls said, pinching the soft flesh at the end of his chin.

Cronjager stiffened visibly. His surly eyes became points of steely light.

Ohls said: "You heard about a car being lifted out of the Pacific Ocean off Lido pier this a.m. with a dead guy in it?"

Cronjager said: "No," and kept on looking nasty.

"The dead guy in the car was chauffeur to a rich family," Ohls said. "The family was being blackmailed on account of one of the daughters. Mr. Wilde recommended Marlowe to the family, through me. Marlowe played it kind of close to the vest."

"I love private dicks that play murders close to the vest," Cronjager snarled. "You don't have to be so goddamned coy about it."

"Yeah," Ohls said. "I don't have to be so goddamned coy about it. It's not so goddamned often I get a chance to be coy with a city copper. I spend most of my time telling them where to put their feet so they won't break an ankle."

Cronjager whitened around the corners of his sharp nose. His breath made a soft hissing sound in the quiet room. He said very quietly: "You haven't had to tell any of *my* men where to put their feet, smart guy."

"We'll see about that," Ohls said. "This chauffeur I spoke of that's drowned off Lido shot a guy last night in your territory. A guy named Geiger who ran a dirty book racket in a store on Hollywood Boulevard. Geiger was living with the punk I got outside in my car. I mean living with him, if you get the idea."

Cronjager was staring at him levelly now. "That sounds like it might grow up to be a dirty story," he said.

"It's my experience most police stories are," Ohls growled and turned to me, his eyebrows bristling. "You're on the air, Marlowe. Give it to him."

I gave it to him.

I left out two things, not knowing just why, at the moment, I left out one of them. I left out Carmen's visit to Brody's apartment and Eddie Mars' visit to Geiger's in the afternoon. I told the rest of it just as it happened.

Cronjager never took his eyes off my face and no expression of any kind crossed his as I talked. At the end of it he was perfectly silent for a long minute. Wilde was silent, sipping his coffee, puffing gently at his dappled cigar. Ohls stared at one of his thumbs.

Cronjager leaned slowly back in his chair and crossed one ankle over his knee and rubbed the ankle bone with his thin nervous hand. His lean face wore a harsh frown. He said with deadly politeness:

"So all you did was not report a murder that happened last night and then spend today foxing around so that this kid of Geiger's could commit a second murder this evening."

"That's all," I said. "I was in a pretty tough spot. I guess I did wrong, but I wanted to protect my client and I hadn't any reason to think the boy would go running for Brody."

"That kind of thinking is police business, Marlowe. If Geiger's death had been reported last night, the books could never have been moved from the store to Brody's apartment. The kid wouldn't have been led to Brody and wouldn't have killed him. Say Brody was living on borrowed time. His kind usually are. But a life is a life."

"Right," I said. "Tell that to your coppers next time they shoot down some scared petty larceny crook running away up an alley with a stolen spare."

Wilde put both his hands down on his desk with a solid smack. "That's enough of that," he snapped. "What makes you so sure, Marlowe, that this Taylor boy shot Geiger? Even if the gun that killed Geiger was found on Taylor's body or in the car, it doesn't absolutely follow that he was the killer. The gun might have been planted – say by Brody, the actual killer."

"It's physically possible," I said, "but morally impossible. It assumes too much coincidence and too much that's out of character for Brody and his girl, and out of character for what he was trying to do. I talked to Brody for a long time. He was a crook, but not a killer type. He had two guns, but he wasn't wearing either of them. He was trying to find a way to cut in on Geiger's racket, which naturally he knew all about from the girl. He says he was watching Geiger off and on to see if he had any tough backers. I believe him. To suppose he killed Geiger in order to get his books, then scrammed with the nude photo Geiger had just taken of Carmen Sternwood, then planted the gun on Owen Taylor and pushed Taylor into the ocean off Lido, is to suppose a hell of a lot too much. Taylor had the motive, jealous rage, and the opportunity to kill Geiger. He was out in one of the family cars without per-mission. He killed Geiger right in front of the girl, which Brody would never have done, even if he had been a killer. I can't see anybody with a purely commercial interest in Geiger doing that. But Taylor would have done it. The nude photo business was just what would have made him do it."

Wilde chuckled and looked along his eyes at Cronjager. Cronjager cleared his throat with a snort. Wilde asked: "What's this business about hiding the body? I don't see the point of that."

I said: "The kid hasn't told us, but he must have done it. Brody wouldn't have gone into the house after Geiger was shot. The boy must have got home when I was away taking Carmen to her house. He was afraid of the police, of course, being what he is, and he probably thought it a good idea to have the body hidden until he had removed his effects from the house. He dragged it out of the front door, judging by the marks on the rug, and very likely put it in the garage. Then he packed up whatever belongings he had there and took them away. And later on, sometime in the night and before the body stiffened, he had a revulsion of feeling and thought he hadn't treated his dead friend very nicely. So he went back and laid him out on the bed. That's all guessing, of course."

Wilde nodded. "Then this morning he goes down to the store as if nothing had happened and keeps his eyes open. And when Brody moved the books out he found out where they were going and assumed that whoever got them had killed Geiger just for that purpose. He may even have known more about Brody and the girl than they suspected. What do you think, Ohls?"

Ohls said: "We'll find out – but that doesn't help Cronjager's troubles. What's eating him is all this happened last night and he's only just been rung in on it."

Cronjager said sourly: "I think I can find some way to deal with that angle too." He looked at me sharply and immediately looked away again.

Wilde waved his cigar and said: "Let's see the exhibits, Marlowe." I emptied my pockets and put the catch on his desk: the three notes and Geiger's card to General Sternwood, Carmen's photos, and the blue notebook with the code list of names and addresses. I had already given Geiger's keys to Ohls.

Wilde looked at what I gave him, puffing gently at his cigar. Ohls lit one of his own toy cigars and blew smoke peacefully at the ceiling. Cronjager leaned on the desk and looked at what I had given Wilde.

Wilde tapped the three notes signed by Carmen and said: "I guess these were just a come-on. If General Sternwood paid them, it would be through fear of something worse. Then Geiger would have tightened the screws. Do you know what he was afraid of?" He was looking at me.

I shook my head.

"Have you told your story complete in all relevant details?"

"I left out a couple of personal matters. I intend to keep on leaving them out, Mr. Wilde."

Cronjager said: "Hah!" and snorted with deep feeling.

"Why?" Wilde asked quietly.

"Because my client is entitled to that protection, short of anything but a Grand Jury. I have a license to operate as a private detective. I suppose that word 'private' has some meaning. The Hollywood Division has two murders on its hands, both solved. They have both killers. They have the motive, the instrument in each case. The blackmail angle has got to be suppressed, as far as the names of the parties are concerned."

"Why?" Wilde asked again.

"That's okay," Cronjager said dryly. "We're glad to stooge for a shamus of his standing."

I said: "I'll show you." I got up and went back out of the house to my car and got the book from Geiger's store out of it. The uniformed police driver was standing besides Ohls' car. The boy was inside it, leaning back sideways in the corner.

"Has he said anything?" I asked.

"He made a suggestion," the copper said and spat. "I'm letting it ride."

I went back into the house, put the book on Wilde's desk and opened up the wrappings. Cronjager was using a telephone on the end of the desk. He hung up and sat down as I came in.

Wilde looked through the book, wooden-faced, closed it and pushed it towards Cronjager. Cronjager opened it, looked at a page or two, shut it quickly. A couple of red spots the size of half dollars showed on his cheekbones.

I said: "Look at the stamped dates on the front endpaper."

Cronjager opened the book again and looked at them. "Well?"

"If necessary," I said, "I'll testify under oath that that book came from Geiger's store. The blonde, Agnes, will admit what kind of business the store did. It's obvious to anybody with eyes that that store is just a front for something. But the Hollywood police allowed it to operate, for their own reasons. I dare say the Grand Jury would like to know what those reasons are."

Wilde grinned. He said: "Grand Juries do ask those embarrassing questions sometimes – in a rather vain effort to find out just why cities are run as they are run."

Cronjager stood up suddenly and put his hat on. "I'm one against three here," he snapped. "I'm a homicide man. If this Geiger was running indecent literature, that's no skin off my nose. But I'm ready to admit it won't help my division any to have it washed over in the papers. What do you birds want?"

Wilde looked at Ohls. Ohls said calmly: "I want to turn a prisoner over to you. Let's go."

He stood up. Cronjager looked at him fiercely and stalked out of the room. Ohls went after him. The door closed again. Wilde tapped on his desk and stared at me with his clear blue eyes.

"You ought to understand how any copper would feel about a cover-up like this," he said. "You'll have to make statements of all of it – at least for the files. I think it may be possible to keep the two killings separate and to keep General Sternwood's name out of both of them. Do you know why I'm not tearing your ear off?"

"No. I expected to get both ears torn off."

"What are you getting for it all?"

"Twenty-five dollars a day and expenses."

"That would make fifty dollars and a little gasoline so far."

"About that."

He put his head on one side and rubbed the back of his left little finger along the lower edge of his chin.

"And for that amount of money you're willing to get yourself in Dutch with half the law enforcement of this county?"

"I don't like it," I said. "But what the hell am I to do? I'm on a case. I'm selling what I have to sell to make a living. What little guts and intelligence the Lord gave me and a willingness to get pushed around in order to protect a client. It's against my principles to tell as much as I've told tonight, without consulting the General. As for the cover-up, I've been in police business myself, as you know. They come a dime a dozen in any big city. Cops get very large and emphatic when an outsider tries to hide anything, but they do the same things themselves every other day, to oblige their friends or anybody with a little pull. And I'm not through. I'm still on the case. I'd do the same thing again, if I had to."

"Providing Cronjager doesn't get your license," Wilde grinned. "You said you held back a couple of personal matters. Of what import?"

"I'm still on the case," I said, and stared straight into his eyes.

Wilde smiled at me. He had the frank daring smile of an Irishman. "Let me tell you something, son. My father was a close friend of old Sternwood. I've done all my office permits – and maybe a good deal more – to save the old man from grief. But in the long run it can't be done. Those girls of his are bound certain to hook up with something that can't be hushed, especially that little blonde brat. They ought not to be running around loose. I blame the old man for that. I guess he doesn't realize what the world is today. And there's another thing I might mention while we're talking man to man and I don't have to growl at you. I'll bet a dollar to a Canadian dime that the General's afraid his son-in-law, the ex-bootlegger, is mixed up in this somewhere, and what he really hoped you would find out is that he isn't. What do you think of that?"

"Regan didn't sound like a blackmailer, what I heard of him. He had a soft spot where he was and he walked out on it."

Wilde snorted. "The softness of that spot neither you nor I could judge. If he was a certain sort of man, it would not have been so very soft. Did the General tell you he was looking for Regan?"

"He told me he wished he knew where he was and that he was all right. He liked Regan and was hurt the way he bounced off without telling the old man good-bye."

Wilde leaned back and frowned. "I see," he said in a changed voice. His hand moved the stuff on his desk around, laid Geiger's blue notebook to one side and pushed the other exhibits towards me. "You may as well take these," he said. "I've no further use for them."

19

IT WAS CLOSE to eleven when I put my car away and walked around to the front of the Hobart Arms. The plate-glass door was put on the lock at ten, so I had to get my keys out. Inside, in the square barren lobby, a man put a green evening paper down beside a potted palm and flicked a cigarette butt into the tub the palm grew in. He stood up and waved his hat at me and said: "The boss wants to talk to you. You sure keep your friends waiting, pal."

I stood still and looked at his flattened nose and club steak ear. "What about?"

"What do you care? Just keep your nose clean and everything will be jake." His hand hovered near the upper buttonhole of his open coat.

"I smell of policemen," I said. "I'm too tired to talk, too tired to eat, too tired to think. But if you think I'm not too tired to take orders from Eddie Mars – try getting your gat out before I shoot your good ear off."

"Nuts. You ain't got no gun." He stared at me levelly. His dark wiry brows closed in together and his mouth made a downward curve.

"That was then," I told him. "I'm not always naked."

He waved his left hand. "Okay. You win. I wasn't told to blast anybody. You'll hear from him."

"Too late will be too soon," I said, and turned slowly as he passed me on his way to the door. He opened it and went out without looking back. I grinned at my own foolishness, went along to the elevator and upstairs to the apartment. I took Carmen's little gun out of my pocket and laughed at it. Then I cleaned it thoroughly, oiled it, wrapped it in a piece of canton flannel and locked it up. I made myself a drink and was drinking it when the phone rang. I sat down beside the table on which it stood.

"So you're tough tonight," Eddie Mars' voice said.

"Big, fast, tough and full of prickles. What can I do for you?"

"Cops over there – you know where. You keep me out of it?"

"Why should I?"

"I'm nice to be nice to, soldier. I'm not nice not to be nice to."

"Listen hard and you'll hear my teeth chattering."

He laughed dryly. "Did you – or did you?"

"I did. I'm damned if I know why. I guess it was just complicated enough without you."

"Thanks, soldier. Who gunned him?"

"Read it in the paper tomorrow – maybe."

"I want to know now."

"Do you get everything you want?"

"No. Is that an answer, soldier?"

"Somebody you never heard of gunned him. Let it go at that."

"If that's on the level, someday I may be able to do you a favor."

"Hang up and let me go to bed."

He laughed again. "You're looking for Rusty Regan, aren't you?"

"A lot of people seem to think I am, but I'm not."

"If you were, I could give you an idea. Drop in and see me down at the beach. Any time. Glad to see you."

"Maybe."

"Be seeing you then." The phone clicked and I sat holding it with a savage patience. Then I dialed the Sternwoods' number and heard it ring four or five times and then the butler's suave voice saying: "General Sternwood's residence."

"This is Marlowe. Remember me? I met you about a hundred years ago – or was it yesterday?"

"Yes, Mr. Marlowe. I remember, of course."

"Is Mrs. Regan home?"

"Yes, I believe so. Would you –"

I cut in on him with a sudden change of mind. "No. You give her the message. Tell her I have the pictures, all of them, and that everything is all right."

"Yes . . . yes. . . ." The voice seemed to shake a little. "You have the pictures – all of them – and everything is all right. . . . Yes, sir. I may say – thank you very much, sir."

The phone rang back in five minutes. I had finished my drink and it made me feel as if I could eat the dinner I had forgotten all about; I went out leaving the telephone ringing. It was ringing when I came back. It rang at intervals until half-past twelve. At that time I put my lights out and opened the windows up and muffled the phone bell with a piece of paper and went to bed. I had a bellyful of the Sternwood family.

I read all three of the morning papers over my eggs and bacon the next morning. Their accounts of the affair came as close to the truth as newspaper stories usually come – as close as Mars is to Saturn. None of the three connected Owen Taylor, driver of the Lido Pier Suicide Car, with the Laurel Canyon Exotic Bungalow Slaying. None of them mentioned the Sternwoods, Bernie Ohls or me. Owen Taylor was "chauffeur to a wealthy family." Captain Cronjager of the Hollywood Division got all the credit for solving the two slayings in his district, which were supposed to arise out of a dispute over the proceeds from a wire service maintained by one Geiger in the back of the bookstore on Hollywood Boulevard. Brody had shot Geiger and Carol Lundgren had shot Brody in revenge. Police were holding Carol Lundgren in custody. He had confessed. He had a bad record – probably in high school. Police were also holding one Agnes Lozelle, Geiger's secretary, as a material witness.

It was a nice write-up. It gave the impression that Geiger had been killed the night before, that Brody had been killed about an hour later, and that Captain Cronjager had solved both murders while lighting a cigarette. The suicide of Taylor made Page One of Section II. There was a photo of the sedan on the deck of the power lighter, with the license plate blacked out, and something covered with a cloth lying on the deck beside the running board. Owen Taylor had been despondent and in poor health. His family lived in Dubuque, and his body would be shipped there. There would be no inquest.

20

CAPTAIN GREGORY OF the Missing Persons Bureau laid my card down on his wide flat desk and arranged it so that its edges exactly paralleled the edges of the desk. He studied it with his head on one side, grunted, swung around in his swivel chair and looked out of his window at the barred top floor of the Hall of Justice half a block away. He was a burly man with tired eyes and the slow deliberate movements of a night watchman. His voice was toneless, flat and uninterested.

"Private dick, eh?" he said, not looking at me at all, but looking out of his window. Smoke wisped from the blackened bowl of a briar that hung on his eye tooth. "What can I do for you?"

"I'm working for General Guy Sternwood, 3765 Alta Brea Crescent, West Hollywood."

Captain Gregory blew a little smoke from the corner of his mouth without removing the pipe. "On what?"

"Not exactly on what you're working on, but I'm interested. I thought you could help me."

"Help you on what?"

"General Sternwood's a rich man," I said. "He's an old friend of the D.A.'s father. If he wants to hire a full-time boy to run errands for him, that's no reflection on the police. It's just a luxury he is able to afford himself."

"What makes you think I'm doing anything for him?"

I didn't answer that. He swung around slowly and heavily in his swivel chair and put his large feet flat on the bare linoleum that covered his floor. His office had the musty smell of years of routine. He stared at me bleakly.

"I don't want to waste your time, Captain," I said and pushed my chair back – about four inches.

He didn't move. He kept on staring at me out of his washed-out tired eyes. "You know the D.A.?"

"I've met him. I worked for him once. I know Bernie Ohls, his chief investigator, pretty well."

Captain Gregory reached for a phone and mumbled into it: "Get me Ohls at the D.A.'s office."

He sat holding the phone down on its cradle. Moments passed. Smoke drifted from his pipe. His eyes were heavy and motionless like his hand. The bell tinkled and he reached for my card with his left hand. "Ohls? . . . Al Gregory at headquarters. A guy named Philip Marlowe is in my office. His card says he's a private investigator. He wants information from me. . . . Yeah? What does he look like? . . . Okay, thanks."

He dropped the phone and took his pipe out of his mouth and tamped the tobacco with the brass cap of a heavy pencil. He did it carefully and solemnly, as if that was as important as anything he would have to do that day. He leaned back and stared at me some more.

"What you want?"

"An idea of what progress you're making, if any."

He thought that over. "Regan?" he asked finally.

"Sure."

"Know him?"

"I never saw him. I hear he's a good-looking Irishman in his late thirties, that he was once in the liquor racket, that he married General Sternwood's older daughter and that they didn't click. I'm told he disappeared about a month back."

"Sternwood oughta think himself lucky instead of hiring private talent to beat around in the tall grass."

"The General took a big fancy to him. Such things happen. The old man is crippled and lonely. Regan used to sit around with him and keep him company."

"What you think you can do that we can't do?"

"Nothing at all, in so far as finding Regan goes. But there's a rather mysterious blackmail angle. I want to make sure Regan isn't involved. Knowing where he is or isn't might help."

"Brother, I'd like to help you, but I don't know where he is. He pulled down the curtain and that's that."

"Pretty hard to do against your organization, isn't it, Captain?"

"Yeah – but it can be done – for a while." He touched a bell button on the side of his desk. A middle-aged woman put her head in at a side door. "Get me the file on Terence Regan, Abba."

The door closed. Captain Gregory and I looked at each other in some more heavy silence. The door opened again and the woman put a tabbed green file on his desk. Captain Gregory nodded her out, put a pair of heavy horn-rimmed glasses on his veined nose and turned the papers in the file over slowly. I rolled a cigarette around in my fingers.

"He blew on the sixteenth of September," he said. "The only thing important about that is it was the chauffeur's day off and nobody saw Regan take his car out. It was late afternoon, though. We found the car four days later in a garage belonging to a ritzy bungalow court place near the Sunset Towers. A garage man reported it to the stolen car detail, said it didn't belong there. The place is called the Casa de Oro. There's an angle to that I'll tell you about in a minute. We couldn't find out anything about who put the car in there. We print the car but don't find any prints that are on file anywhere. The car in that garage don't jibe with foul play, although there's a reason to suspect foul play. It jibes with something else I'll tell you about in a minute."

I said: "That jibes with Eddie Mars' wife being on the missing list."

He looked annoyed. "Yeah. We investigate the tenants and find she's living there. Left about the time Regan did, within two days anyway. A guy who sounds a bit like Regan had been seen with her, but we don't get a positive identification. It's goddamned funny in this police racket how an old woman can look out of a window and see a guy running and pick him out of a line-up six months later, but we can show hotel help a clear photo and they just can't be sure."

"That's one of the qualifications for good hotel help," I said.

"Yeah. Eddie Mars and his wife didn't live together, but they were friendly, Eddie says. Here's some of the possibilities. First off Regan carried fifteen grand, packed it in his clothes all the time. Real money, they tell me. Not just a top card and a bunch of hay. That's a lot of jack but this Regan might be the boy to have it around so he could take it out and look at it when somebody was looking at him. Then again maybe he wouldn't give a damn. His wife says he never made a nickel off of old man Sternwood except room and board and a Packard one-twenty his wife gave him. Tie that for an ex-legger in the rich gravy."

"It beats me," I said.

"Well, here we are with a guy who ducks out and has fifteen grand in his pants and folks know it. Well, that's money. I might duck out myself, if I had fifteen grand, and me with two kids in high school. So the first thought is somebody rolls him for it and rolls him too hard, so they have to take him out in the desert and plant him among the cactuses. But I don't like that too well. Regan carried a gat and had plenty of experience using it, and not just in a greasy-faced liquor mob. I understand he commanded a whole brigade in the Irish troubles back in 1922 or whenever it was. A guy like that wouldn't be white meat to a heister. Then, his car being in that garage makes whoever rolled him know he was sweet on Eddie Mars' wife, which he was, I guess, but it ain't something every poolroom bum would know."

"Got a photo?" I asked.

"Him, not her. That's funny too. There's a lot of funny angles to this case. Here." He pushed a shiny print across the desk and I looked at an Irish face that was more sad than merry and more reserved than brash. Not the face of a tough guy and not the face of a man who could be pushed around much by anybody. Straight dark brows with strong bone under them. A forehead wide rather than high, a mat of dark clustering hair, a thin short nose, a wide mouth. A chin that had strong lines but was small for the mouth. A face that looked a little taut, the face of a man who would move fast and play for keeps. I passed the print back. I would know that face, if I saw it.

Captain Gregory knocked his pipe out and refilled it and tamped the tobacco down with his thumb. He lit it, blew smoke and began to talk again.

"Well, there could be people who would know he was sweet on Eddie Mars' frau. Besides Eddie himself. For a wonder *he* knew it. But he don't seem to give a damn. We check him pretty thoroughly around that time. Of course Eddie wouldn't have knocked him off out of jealousy. The set-up would point to him too obvious."

"It depends how smart he is," I said. "He might try the double bluff."

Captain Gregory shook his head. "If he's smart enough to get by in his racket, he's too smart for that. I get your idea. He pulls the dumb play because he thinks we wouldn't expect him to pull the dumb play. From a police angle that's wrong. Because he'd have us in his hair so much it would interfere with his business. *You* might think a dumb play would be smart. I might think so. The rank and file wouldn't. They'd make his life miserable. I've ruled it out. If I'm wrong, you can prove it on me and I'll eat my chair cushion. Till then I'm leaving Eddie in the clear. Jealousy is a bad motive for his type. Top-flight racketeers have business brains. They learn to do things that are good policy and let their personal feelings take care of themselves. I'm leaving that out."

"What are you leaving in?"

"The dame and Regan himself. Nobody else. She was a blonde then, but she won't be now. We don't find her car, so they probably left in it. They had a long start on us – fourteen days. Except for that car of Regan's I don't figure we'd have got the case at all. Of course I'm used to them that way, especially in good-class families. And of course everything I've done has had to be under the hat."

He leaned back and thumped the arms of his chair with the heels of his large heavy hands.

"I don't see nothing to do but wait," he said. "We've got

readers out, but it's too soon to look for results. Regan had fifteen grand we know of. The girl had some, maybe a lot in rocks. But they'll run out of dough some day. Regan will cash a check, drop a marker, write a letter. They're in a strange town and they've got new names, but they've got the same old appetites. They got to get back in the fiscal system."

"What did the girl do before she married Eddie Mars?"

"Torcher."

"Can't you get any old professional photos?"

"No. Eddie must of had some, but he won't loosen up. He wants her let alone. I can't make him. He's got friends in town, or he wouldn't be what he is." He grunted. "Any of this do you any good?"

I said: "You'll never find either of them. The Pacific Ocean is too close."

"What I said about my chair cushion still goes. We'll find him. It may take time. It could take a year or two."

"General Sternwood may not live that long," I said.

"We've done all we could, brother. If he wants to put out a reward and spend some money, we might get results. The city don't give me the kind of money it takes." His large eyes peered at me and his scratchy eyebrows moved. "You serious about thinking Eddie put them both down?"

I laughed. "No. I was just kidding. I think what you think, Captain. That Regan ran away with a woman who meant more to him than a rich wife he didn't get along with. Besides, she isn't rich yet."

"You met her, I suppose?"

"Yes. She'd make a jazzy week-end, but she'd be wearing for a steady diet."

He grunted and I thanked him for his time and information and left. A gray Plymouth sedan tailed me away from the City Hall. I gave it a chance to catch up with me on a quiet street. It refused the offer, so I shook it off and went about my business.

21

I DIDN'T GO near the Sternwood family. I went back to the office and sat in my swivel chair and tried to catch up on my foot-dangling. There was a gusty wind blowing in at the windows and the soot from the oil burners of the hotel next door was down-drafted into the room and rolling across the top of the desk like tumbleweed drifting across a vacant lot. I was thinking about going out to lunch and that life was pretty flat and that it would probably be just as flat if I took a drink and that taking a drink all alone at that time of day wouldn't be any fun anyway. I was thinking this when Norris called up. In his carefully polite manner he said that General Sternwood was not feeling very well and that certain items in the newspaper had been read to him and he assumed that my investigation was now completed.

"Yes, as regards Geiger," I said. "I didn't shoot him, you know."

"The General didn't suppose you did, Mr. Marlowe."

"Does the General know anything about those photographs Mrs. Regan was worrying about?"

"No, sir. Decidedly not."

"Did you know what the General gave me?"

"Yes, sir. Three notes and a card, I believe."

"Right. I'll return them. As to the photos I think I'd better just destroy them."

"Very good, sir. Mrs. Regan tried to reach you a number of times last night —"

"I was out getting drunk," I said.

"Yes. Very necessary, sir, I'm sure. The General has instructed me to send you a check for five hundred dollars. Will that be satisfactory?"

"More than generous," I said.

"And I presume we may now consider the incident closed?"

"Oh sure. Tight as a vault with a busted time lock."

"Thank you, sir. I am sure we all appreciate it. When the General is feeling a little better – possibly tomorrow – he would like to thank you in person."

"Fine," I said. "I'll come out and drink some more of his brandy, maybe with champagne."

"I shall see that some is properly iced," the old boy said, almost with a smirk in his voice.

That was that. We said good-bye and hung up. The coffee shop smell from next door came in at the windows with the soot but failed to make me hungry. So I got out my office bottle and took the drink and let my self-respect ride its own race.

I counted it up on my fingers. Rusty Regan had run away from a lot of money and a handsome wife to go wandering with a vague blonde who was more or less married to a racketeer named Eddie Mars. He had gone suddenly without good-byes and there might be any number of reasons for that. The General had been too proud, or, at the first interview he gave me, too careful, to tell me the Missing Persons Bureau had the matter in hand. The Missing Persons people were dead on their feet on it and evidently didn't think it worth bothering over. Regan had done what he had done and that was his business. I agreed with Captain Gregory that Eddie Mars would have been very unlikely to involve himself in a double murder just because another man had gone to town with the blonde he was not even living with. It might have annoyed him, but business is business, and you have to hold your teeth clamped around Hollywood to keep from chewing on stray blondes. If there had been a lot of money involved, that would be different. But fifteen grand wouldn't be a lot of money to Eddie Mars. He was no two-bit chiseler like Brody.

Geiger was dead and Carmen would have to find some other shady character to drink exotic blends of hootch with.

I didn't suppose she would have any trouble. All she would have to do would be to stand on the corner for five minutes and look coy. I hoped that the next grifter who dropped the hook on her would play her a little more smoothly, a little more for the long haul rather than the quick touch.

Mrs. Regan knew Eddie Mars well enough to borrow money from him. That was natural, if she played roulette and was a good loser. Any gambling house owner would lend a good client money in a pinch. Apart from this they had an added bond of interest in Regan. He was her husband and he had gone off with Eddie Mars' wife.

Carol Lundgren, the boy killer with the limited vocabulary, was out of circulation for a long, long time, even if they didn't strap him in a chair over a bucket of acid. They wouldn't, because he would take a plea and save the county money. They all do when they don't have the price of a big lawyer. Agnes Lozelle was in custody as a material witness. They wouldn't need her for that, if Carol took a plea, and if he pleaded guilty on arraignment, they would turn her loose. They wouldn't want to open up any angles on Geiger's business, apart from which they had nothing on her.

That left me. I had concealed a murder and suppressed evidence for twenty-four hours, but I was still at large and had a five-hundred-dollar check coming. The smart thing for me to do was to take another drink and forget the whole mess.

That being the obviously smart thing to do, I called Eddie Mars and told him I was coming down to Las Olindas that evening to talk to him. That was how smart I was.

I got down there about nine, under a hard high October moon that lost itself in the top layers of a beach fog. The Cypress Club was at the far end of the town, a rambling frame mansion that had once been the summer residence of a rich man named De Cazens, and later had been a hotel. It was now a big dark outwardly shabby place in a thick grove of wind-twisted Monterey cypresses, which gave it its name. It had enormous scrolled porches, turrets all over the place, stained-glass trims around the big windows, big empty stables at the back, a general air of nostalgic decay. Eddie Mars had left the outside much as he had found it, instead of making it over to look like an MGM set. I left my car on a street with sputtering arc lights and walked into the grounds along a damp gravel path to the main entrance. A doorman in a double-breasted guard's coat let me into a huge dim silent lobby from which a white oak staircase curved majestically up to the darkness of an upper floor. I checked my hat and coat and waited, listening to music and confused voices behind heavy double doors. They seemed a long way off, and not quite of the same world as the building itself. Then the slim pasty-faced blond man who had been with Eddie Mars and the pug at Geiger's place came through a door under the staircase, smiled at me bleakly and took me back with him along a carpeted hall to the boss's office.

This was a square room with a deep old bay window and a stone fireplace in which a fire of juniper logs burned lazily. It was wainscoted in walnut and had a frieze of faded damask above the paneling. The ceiling was high and remote. There was a smell of cold sea.

Eddie Mars' dark sheenless desk didn't belong in the room, but neither did anything made after 1900. His carpet had a Florida suntan. There was a bartop radio in the corner and a Sèvres china tea set on a copper tray beside a samovar. I wondered who that was for. There was a door in the corner that had a time lock on it.

Eddie Mars grinned at me sociably and shook hands and moved his chin at the vault. "I'm a pushover for a heist mob here except for that thing," he said cheerfully. "The local johns drop in every morning and watch me open it. I have an arrangement with them."

"You hinted you had something for me," I said. "What is it?"

"What's your hurry? Have a drink and sit down."

"No hurry at all. You and I haven't anything to talk about but business."

"You'll have the drink and like it," he said. He mixed a couple and put mine down beside a red leather chair and stood crosslegged against the desk himself, one hand in the side pocket of his midnight-blue dinner jacket, the thumb outside and the nail glistening. In dinner clothes he looked a little harder than in gray flannel, but he still looked like a horseman. We drank and nodded at each other.

"Ever been here before?" he asked.

"During prohibition. I don't get any kick out of gambling."

"Not with money," he smiled. "You ought to look in tonight. One of your friends is outside betting the wheels. I hear she's doing pretty well. Vivian Regan."

I sipped my drink and took one of his monogrammed cigarettes.

"I kind of liked the way you handled that yesterday," he said. "You made me sore at the time but I could see afterwards how right you were. You and I ought to get along. How much do I owe you?"

"For doing what?"

"Still careful, eh? I have my pipe line into headquarters, or I wouldn't be here. I get them the way they happen, not the way you read them in the papers." He showed me his large white teeth.

"How much have you got?" I asked.

"You're not talking money?"

"Information was the way I understood it."

"Information about what?"

"You have a short memory, Regan."

"Oh, that." He waved his glistening nails in the quiet light from one of those bronze lamps that shoot a beam at the ceiling. "I hear you got the information already. I felt I owed you a fee. I'm used to paying for nice treatment."

"I didn't drive down here to make a touch. I get paid for what I do. Not much by your standards, but I make out. One customer at a time is a good rule. You didn't bump Regan off, did you?"

"No. Did you think I did?"

"I wouldn't put it past you."

He laughed. "You're kidding."

I laughed. "Sure, I'm kidding. I never saw Regan, but I saw his photo. You haven't got the men for the work. And while we're on that subject don't send me any more gun punks with orders. I might get hysterical and blow one down."

He looked through his glass at the fire, set it down on the end of the desk and wiped his lips with a sheer lawn handkerchief.

"You talk a good game," he said. "But I dare say you can break a hundred and ten. You're not really interested in Regan, are you?"

"No, not professionally. I haven't been asked to be. But I know somebody who would like to know where he is."

"She doesn't give a damn," he said.

"I mean her father."

He wiped his lips again and looked at the handkerchief almost as if he expected to find blood on it. He drew his thick gray eyebrows close together and fingered the side of his weatherbeaten nose.

"Geiger was trying to blackmail the General," I said. "The General wouldn't say so, but I figure he was at least half scared Regan might be behind it."

Eddie Mars laughed. "Uh-uh. Geiger worked that one on everybody. It was strictly his own idea. He'd get notes from people that looked legal – were legal, I dare say, except that he wouldn't have dared sue on them. He'd present the notes, with a nice flourish, leaving himself empty-handed. If he drew an ace, he had a prospect that scared and he went to work. If he didn't draw an ace, he just dropped the whole thing."

"Clever guy," I said. "He dropped it all right. Dropped it and fell on it. How come *you* know all this?"

He shrugged impatiently. "I wish to Christ I didn't know half the stuff that's brought to me. Knowing other people's business is the worst investment a man can make in my circle. Then if it was just Geiger you were after, you're washed up on that angle."

"Washed up and paid off."

"I'm sorry about that. I wish old Sternwood would hire himself a soldier like you on a straight salary, to keep those girls of his home at least a few nights a week."

"Why?"

His mouth looked sulky. "They're plain trouble. Take the dark one. She's a pain in the neck around here. If she loses, she plunges and I end up with a fistful of paper which nobody will discount at any price. She has no money of her own except an allowance and what's in the old man's will is a secret. If she wins, she takes my money home with her."

"You get it back the next night," I said.

"I get some of it back. But over a period of time I'm loser."

He looked earnestly at me, as if that was important to me. I wondered why he thought it necessary to tell me at all. I yawned and finished my drink.

"I'm going out and look the joint over," I said.

"Yes, do." He pointed to a door near the vault door. "That leads to a door behind the tables."

"I'd rather go in the way the suckers enter."

"Okay. As you please. We're friends, aren't we, soldier?"

"Sure." I stood up and we shook hands.

"Maybe I can do you a real favor some day," he said. "You got it all from Gregory this time."

"So you own a piece of him too."

"Oh not that bad. We're just friends."

I stared at him for a moment, then went over to the door I had come in at. I looked back at him when I had it open.

"You don't have anybody tailing me around in a gray Plymouth sedan, do you?"

His eyes widened sharply. He looked jarred. "Hell, no. Why should I?"

"I couldn't imagine," I said, and went on out. I thought his surprise looked genuine enough to be believed. I thought he even looked a little worried. I couldn't think of any reason for that.

22

IT WAS ABOUT ten-thirty when the little yellow-sashed Mexican orchestra got tired of playing a low-voiced, prettied-up rhumba that nobody was dancing to. The gourd player rubbed his finger tips together as if they were sore and got a cigarette into his mouth almost with the same movement. The other four, with a timed simultaneous stoop, reached under their chairs for glasses from which they sipped, smacking their lips and flashing their eyes. Tequila, their manner said. It was probably mineral water. The pretense was as wasted as the music. Nobody was looking at them.

The room had been a ballroom once and Eddie Mars had changed it only as much as his business compelled him. No chromium glitter, no indirect lighting from behind angular cornices, no fused glass pictures, or chairs in violent leather and polished metal tubing, none of the pseudomodernistic circus of the typical Hollywood night trap. The light was from heavy crystal chandeliers and the rose-damask panels of the wall were still the same rose damask, a little faded by time and darkened by dust, that had been matched long ago against the parquetry floor, of which only a small glass-smooth space in front of the little Mexican orchestra showed bare. The rest was covered by a heavy old-rose carpeting that must have cost plenty. The parquetry was made of a dozen kinds of hard-wood, from Burma teak through half a dozen shades of oak and ruddy wood that looked like mahogany, and fading out to the hard pale wild lilac of the California hills, all laid in elaborate patterns, with the accuracy of a transit.

It was still a beautiful room and now there was roulette in it instead of measured, old-fashioned dancing. There were three tables close to the far wall. A low bronze railing joined them and made a fence around the croupiers. All three tables were working, but the crowd was at the middle one. I could see Vivian Regan's black head close to it, from across the room where I was leaning against the bar and turning a small glass of bacardi around on the mahogany.

The bartender leaned beside me watching the cluster of well-dressed people at the middle table. "She's pickin' 'em tonight, right on the nose," he said. "That tall black-headed frail."

"Who is she?"

"I wouldn't know her name. She comes here a lot though."

"The hell you wouldn't know her name."

"I just work here, mister," he said without any animosity. "She's all alone too. The guy was with her passed out. They took him out to his car."

"I'll take her home," I said.

"The hell you will. Well, I wish you luck anyways. Should I gentle up that bacardi or do you like it the way it is?"

"I like it the way it is as well as I like it at all," I said.

"Me, I'd just as leave drink croup medicine," he said.

The crowd parted and two men in evening clothes pushed their way out and I saw the back of her neck and her bare shoulders in the opening. She wore a low-cut dress of dull green velvet. It looked too dressy for the occasion. The crowd closed and hid all but her black head. The two men came across the room and leaned against the bar and asked for Scotch and soda. One of them was flushed and excited. He was mopping his face with a black-bordered handkerchief. The double satin stripes down the side of his trousers were wide enough for tire tracks.

"Boy, I never saw such a run," he said in a jittery voice. "Eight wins and two stand-offs in a row on that red. That's roulette, boy, that's roulette."

"It gives me the itch," the other one said. "She's betting a grand at a crack. She can't lose." They put their beaks in their drinks, gurgled swiftly and went back.

"So wise the little men are," the barkeep drawled. "A grand a crack, huh. I saw an old horseface in Havana once —"

The noise swelled over at the middle table and a chiseled foreign voice rose above it saying: "If you will just be patient a moment, madam. The table cannot cover your bet. Mr. Mars will be here in a moment."

I left my bacardi and padded across the carpet. The little orchestra started to play a tango, rather loud. No one was dancing or intending to dance. I moved through a scattering of people in dinner clothes and full evening dress and sports clothes and business suits to the end table at the left. It had gone dead. Two croupiers stood behind it with their heads together and their eyes sideways. One moved a rake back and forth aimlessly over the empty layout. They were both staring at Vivian Regan.

Her long lashes twitched and her face looked unnaturally white. She was at the middle table, exactly opposite the wheel. There was a disordered pile of money and chips in front of her. It looked like a lot of money. She spoke to the croupier with a cool, insolent, ill-tempered drawl.

"What kind of a cheap outfit is this, I'd like to know. Get busy and spin that wheel, highpockets. I want one more play and I'm playing table stakes. You take it away fast enough I've noticed, but when it comes to dishing it out you start to whine."

The croupier smiled a cold polite smile that had looked at thousands of boors and millions of fools. His tall dark disinterested manner was flawless. He said gravely: "The table cannot cover your bet, madam. You have over sixteen thousand dollars there."

"It's your money," the girl jeered. "Don't you want it back?"

A man beside her tried to tell her something. She turned swiftly and spat something at him and he faded back into the crowd red-faced. A door opened in the paneling at the far end of the enclosed place made by the bronze railing. Eddie Mars came through the door with a set indifferent smile on his face, his hands thrust into the pockets of his dinner jacket, both thumbnails glistening outside. He seemed to like that pose. He strolled behind the croupiers and stopped at the corner of the middle table. He spoke with lazy calm, less politely than the croupier.

"Something the matter, Mrs. Regan?"

She turned her face to him with a sort of lunge. I saw the curve of her cheek stiffen, as if with an almost unbearable inner tautness. She didn't answer him.

Eddie Mars said gravely: "If you're not playing any more, you must let me send someone home with you."

The girl flushed. Her cheekbones stood out white in her face. Then she laughed off-key. She said bitterly:

"One more play, Eddie. Everything I have on the red. I like red. It's the color of blood."

Eddie Mars smiled faintly, then nodded and reached into his inner breast pocket. He drew out a large pinseal wallet with gold corners and tossed it carelessly along the table to the croupier. "Cover her bet in even thousands," he said, "if no one objects to this turn of the wheel being just for the lady."

No one objected. Vivian Regan leaned down and pushed all her winnings savagely with both hands on to the large red diamond on the layout.

The croupier leaned over the table without haste. He counted and stacked her money and chips, placed all but a few chips and bills in a neat pile and pushed the rest back off the layout with his rake. He opened Eddie Mars' wallet and drew out two flat packets of thousand-dollar bills. He broke one, counted six bills out, added them to the unbroken packet, put the four loose bills in the wallet and laid it aside as carelessly as if it had been a packet of matches. Eddie Mars didn't touch the wallet. Nobody moved except the croupier. He spun the wheel left-handed and sent the ivory ball skittering along the upper edge with a casual flirt of his wrist. Then he drew his hands back and folded his arms.

Vivian's lips parted slowly until her teeth caught the light and glittered like knives. The ball drifted lazily down the slope of the wheel and bounced on the chromium ridges above the numbers. After a long time and then very suddenly motion left it with a dry click. The wheel slowed, carrying the ball around with it. The croupier didn't unfold his arms until the wheel had entirely ceased to revolve.

"The red wins," he said formally, without interest. The little ivory ball lay in Red 25, the third number from the Double Zero. Vivian Regan put her head back and laughed triumphantly.

The croupier lifted his rake and slowly pushed the stack of thousand-dollar bills across the layout, added them to the stake, pushed everything slowly out of the field of play.

Eddie Mars smiled, put his wallet back in his pocket, turned on his heel and left the room through the door in the paneling.

A dozen people let their breath out at the same time and broke for the bar. I broke with them and got to the far end of the room before Vivian had gathered up her winnings and turned away from the table. I went out into the large quiet lobby, got my hat and coat from the check girl, dropped a quarter in her tray and went out on the porch. The doorman loomed up beside me and said: "Can I get your car for you, sir?"

I said: "I'm just going for a walk."

The scrollwork along the edge of the porch was wet with the fog. The fog dripped from the Monterey cypresses that shadowed off into nothing towards the cliff above the ocean. You could see a scant dozen feet in any direction. I went down the porch steps and drifted off through the trees, following an indistinct path until I could hear the wash of the surf licking at the fog, low down at the bottom of the cliff. There wasn't a gleam of light anywhere. I could see a dozen trees clearly at one time, another dozen dimly, then nothing at all but the fog. I circled to the left and drifted back towards the gravel path that went around to the stables where they parked the cars. When I could make out the outlines of the house I stopped. A little in front of me I had heard a man cough.

My steps hadn't made any sound on the soft moist turf. The man coughed again, then stifled the cough with a handkerchief or a sleeve. While he was still doing that I moved forward closer to him. I made him out, a vague shadow close to the path. Something made me step behind a tree and crouch down. The man turned his head. His face should have been a white blur when he did that. It wasn't. It remained dark. There was a mask over it.

I waited, behind the tree.

23

LIGHT STEPS, THE steps of a woman, came along the invisible pathway and the man in front of me moved forward and seemed to lean against the fog. I couldn't see the woman, then I could see her indistinctly. The arrogant carriage of her head seemed familiar. The man stepped out very quickly. The two figures blended in the fog, seemed to be part of the fog. There was dead silence for a moment. Then the man said:

"This is a gun, lady. Gentle now. Sound carries in the fog. Just hand me the bag."

The girl didn't make a sound. I moved forward a step. Quite suddenly I could see the foggy fuzz on the man's hat brim. The girl stood motionless. Then her breathing began to make a rasping sound, like a small file on soft wood.

"Yell," the man said, "and I'll cut you in half."

She didn't yell. She didn't move. There was a movement from him, and a dry chuckle. "It better be in here," he said. A catch clicked and a fumbling sound came to me. The man turned and came towards my tree. When he had taken three or four steps he chuckled again. The chuckle was something out of my own memories. I reached a pipe out of my pocket and held it like a gun.

I called out softly: "Hi, Lanny."

The man stopped dead and started to bring his hand up. I said: "No. I told you never to do that, Lanny. You're covered."

Nothing moved. The girl back on the path didn't move. I didn't move. Lanny didn't move.

"Put the bag down between your feet, kid," I told him. "Slow and easy."

He bent down. I jumped out and reached him still bent over. He straightened up against me breathing hard. His hands were empty.

"Tell me I can't get away with it," I said. I leaned against him and took the gun out of his overcoat pocket. "Somebody's always giving me guns," I told him. "I'm weighted down with them till I walk all crooked. Beat it."

Our breaths met and mingled, our eyes were like the eyes of two tomcats on a wall. I stepped back.

"On your way, Lanny. No hard feelings. You keep it quiet and I keep it quiet. Okay?"

"Okay," he said thickly.

The fog swallowed him. The faint sound of his steps and then nothing. I picked the bag up and felt in it and went towards the path. She still stood there motionless, a gray fur coat held tight around her throat with an ungloved hand on which a ring made a faint glitter. She wore no hat. Her dark parted hair was part of the darkness of the night. Her eyes too.

"Nice work, Marlowe. Are you my bodyguard now?" Her voice had a harsh note.

"Looks that way. Here's the bag."

She took it. I said: "Have you a car with you?"

She laughed. "I came with a man. What are you doing here?"

"Eddie Mars wanted to see me."

"I didn't know you knew him. Why?"

"I don't mind telling you. He thought I was looking for somebody he thought had run away with his wife."

"Were you?"

"No."

"Then what did you come for?"

"To find out why he thought I was looking for somebody he thought had run away with his wife."

"Did you find out?"

"No."

"You leak information like a radio announcer," she said. "I suppose it's none of my business – even if the man was my husband. I thought you weren't interested in that."

"People keep throwing it at me."

She clicked her teeth in annoyance. The incident of the masked man with the gun seemed to have made no impression on her at all. "Well, take me to the garage," she said. "I have to look in at my escort."

We walked along the path and around a corner of the building and there was light ahead, then around another corner and came to a bright enclosed stable yard lit with two floodlights. It was still paved with brick and still sloped down to a grating in the middle. Cars glistened and a man in a brown smock got up off a stool and came forward.

"Is my boy friend still blotto?" Vivian asked him carelessly.

"I'm afraid he is, miss. I put a rug over him and run the windows up. He's okay, I guess. Just kind of resting."

We went over to a big Cadillac and the man in the smock pulled the rear door open. On the wide back seat, loosely arranged, covered to the chin with a plaid robe, a man lay snoring with his mouth open. He seemed to be a big blond man who would hold a lot of liquor.

"Meet Mr. Larry Cobb," Vivian said. "Mister Cobb – Mister Marlowe."

I grunted.

"Mr. Cobb was my escort," she said. "Such a nice escort, Mr. Cobb. So attentive. You should see him sober. *I* should see him sober. Somebody should see him sober. I mean, just for the record. So it could become a part of history, that brief flashing moment, soon buried in time, but never forgotten – when Larry Cobb was sober."

"Yeah," I said.

"I've even thought of marrying him," she went on in a high strained voice, as if the shock of the stick-up was just beginning to get to her. "At odd times when nothing pleasant would come into my mind. We all have those spells. Lots of money, you know. A yacht, a place on Long Island, a place at Newport, a place at Bermuda, places dotted here and there all over the world probably – just a good Scotch bottle apart. And to Mr. Cobb a bottle of Scotch is not very far."

"Yeah," I said. "Does he have a driver to take him home?"

"Don't say 'yeah.' It's common." She looked at me with arched eyebrows. The man in the smock was chewing his lower lip hard. "Oh, undoubtedly a whole platoon of drivers. They probably do squads right in front of the garage every morning, buttons shining, harness gleaming, white gloves immaculate – a sort of West Point elegance about them."

"Well, where the hell is this driver?" I asked.

"He drove hisself tonight," the man in the smock said, almost apologetically. "I could call his home and have somebody come down for him."

Vivian turned around and smiled at him as if he had just presented her with a diamond tiara. "That would be lovely," she said. "Would you do that? I really wouldn't want

Mr. Cobb to die like that – with his mouth open. Someone might think he had died of thirst."

The man in the smock said: "Not if they sniffed him, miss."

She opened her bag and grabbed a handful of paper money and pushed it at him. "You'll take care of him, I'm sure."

"Jeeze," the man said, pop-eyed. "I sure will, miss."

"Regan is the name," she said sweetly. "Mrs. Regan. You'll probably see me again. Haven't been here long, have you?"

"No'm." His hands were doing frantic things with the fistful of money he was holding.

"You'll get to love it here," she said. She took hold of my arm. "Let's ride in your car, Marlowe."

"It's outside on the street."

"Quite all right with me, Marlowe. I love a nice walk in the fog. You meet such interesting people."

"Oh, nuts," I said.

She held on to my arm and began to shake. She held me hard all the way to the car. She had stopped shaking by the time we reached it. I drove down a curving lane of trees on the blind side of the house. The lane opened on De Cazens Boulevard, the main drag of Las Olindas. We passed under the ancient sputtering arc lights and after a while there was a town, buildings, dead-looking stores, a service station with a light over a nightbell, and at last a drugstore that was still open.

"You better have a drink," I said.

She moved her chin, a point of paleness in the corner of the seat. I turned diagonally into the curb and parked. "A little black coffee and a smattering of rye would go well," I said.

"I could get as drunk as two sailors and love it."

I held the door for her and she got out close to me, brushing my cheek with her hair. We went into the drugstore. I bought a pint of rye at the liquor counter and carried it over to the stools and set it down on the cracked marble counter.

"Two coffees," I said. "Black, strong and made this year."

"You can't drink liquor in here," the clerk said. He had a washed-out blue smock, was thin on top as to hair, had fairly honest eyes and his chin would never hit a wall before he saw it.

Vivian Regan reached into her bag for a pack of cigarettes and shook a couple loose just like a man. She held them towards me.

"It's against the law to drink liquor in here," the clerk said.

I lit the cigarettes and didn't pay any attention to him. He drew two cups of coffee from a tarnished nickel urn and set them in front of us. He looked at the bottle of rye, muttered under his breath and said wearily: "Okay, I'll watch the street while you pour it."

He went and stood at the display window with his back to us and his ears hanging out.

"My heart's in my mouth doing this," I said, and unscrewed the top of the whiskey bottle and loaded the coffee. "The law enforcement in this town is terrific. All through prohibition Eddie Mars' place was a night club and they had two uniformed men in the lobby every night – to see that the guests didn't bring their own liquor instead of buying it from the house."

The clerk turned suddenly and walked back behind the counter and went in behind the little glass window of the prescription room.

We sipped our loaded coffee. I looked at Vivian's face in the mirror back of the coffee urn. It was taut, pale, beautiful and wild. Her lips were red and harsh.

"You have wicked eyes," I said. "What's Eddie Mars got on you?"

She looked at me in the mirror. "I took plenty away from him tonight at roulette – starting with five grand I borrowed from him yesterday and didn't have to use."

"That might make him sore. You think he sent that loogan after you?"

"What's a loogan?"

"A guy with a gun."

"Are you a loogan?"

"Sure," I laughed. "But strictly speaking a loogan is on the wrong side of the fence."

"I often wonder if there is a wrong side."

"We're losing the subject. What has Eddie Mars got on you?"

"You mean a hold on me of some sort?"

"Yes."

Her lip curled. "Wittier, please, Marlowe. Much wittier."

"How's the General? I don't pretend to be witty."

"Not too well. He didn't get up today. You could at least stop questioning me."

"I remember a time when I thought the same about you. How much does the General know?"

"He probably knows everything."

"Norris would tell him?"

"No. Wilde, the District Attorney, was out to see him. Did you burn those pictures?"

"Sure. You worry about your little sister, don't you – from time to time."

"I think she's all I do worry about. I worry about Dad in a way, to keep things from him."

"He hasn't many illusions," I said, "but I suppose he still has pride."

"We're his blood. That's the hell of it." She stared at me in the mirror with deep, distant eyes. "I don't want him to die despising his own blood. It was always wild blood, but it wasn't always rotten blood."

"Is it now?"

"I guess you think so."

"Not yours. You're just playing the part."

She looked down. I sipped some more coffee and lit another cigarette for us. "So you shoot people," she said quietly. "You're a killer."

"Me? How?"

"The papers and the police fixed it up nicely. But I don't believe everything I read."

"Oh, you think I accounted for Geiger – or Brody – or both of them."

She didn't say anything. "I didn't have to," I said. "I might have, I suppose, and got away with it. Neither of them would have hesitated to throw lead at me."

"That makes you just a killer at heart, like all cops."

"Oh, nuts."

"One of those dark deadly quiet men who have no more feelings than a butcher has for slaughtered meat. I knew it the first time I saw you."

"You've got enough shady friends to know different."

"They're all soft compared to you."

"Thanks, lady. You're no English muffin yourself."

"Let's get out of this rotten little town."

I paid the check, put the bottle of rye in my pocket, and we left. The clerk still didn't like me.

We drove away from Las Olindas through a series of little dank beach towns with shack-like houses built down on the sand close to the rumble of the surf and larger houses built back on the slopes behind. A yellow window shone here and there, but most of the houses were dark. A smell of kelp came in off the water and lay on the fog. The tires sang on the moist concrete of the boulevard. The world was a wet emptiness.

We were close to Del Rey before she spoke to me for the first time since we left the drugstore. Her voice had a muffled sound, as if something was throbbing deep under it.

"Drive down by the Del Rey beach club. I want to look at the water. It's the next street on the left."

There was a winking yellow light at the intersection. I turned the car and slid down a slope with a high bluff on one side, interurban tracks to the right, a low straggle of lights far off beyond the tracks, and then very far off a glitter of pier lights and a haze in the sky over a city. That way the fog was almost gone. The road crossed the tracks where they turned to run under the bluff, then reached a paved strip of waterfront highway that bordered an open and uncluttered beach. Cars were parked along the sidewalk, facing out to sea, dark. The lights of the beach club were a few hundred yards away.

I braked the car against the curb and switched the head-lights off and sat with my hands on the wheel. Under the thinning fog the surf curled and creamed, almost without sound, like a thought trying to form itself on the edge of consciousness.

"Move closer," she said almost thickly.

I moved out from under the wheel into the middle of the seat. She turned her body a little away from me as if to peer out of the window. Then she let herself fall backwards, with-out a sound, into my arms. Her head almost struck the wheel. Her eyes were closed, her face was dim. Then I saw that her eyes opened and flickered, the shine of them visible even in the darkness.

"Hold me close, you beast," she said.

I put my arms around her loosely at first. Her hair had a harsh feeling against my face. I tightened my arms and lifted her up. I brought her face slowly up to my face. Her eyelids were flickering rapidly, like moth wings.

I kissed her tightly and quickly. Then a long slow clinging kiss. Her lips opened under mine. Her body began to shake in my arms.

"Killer," she said softly, her breath going into my mouth.

I strained her against me until the shivering of her body was almost shaking mine. I kept on kissing her. After a long time she pulled her head away enough to say: "Where do you live?"

"Hobart Arms. Franklin near Kenmore."

"I've never seen it."

"Want to?"

"Yes," she breathed.

"What has Eddie Mars got on you?"

Her body stiffened in my arms and her breath made a harsh sound. Her head pulled back until her eyes, wide open, ringed with white, were staring at me.

"So that's the way it is," she said in a soft dull voice.

"That's the way it is. Kissing is nice, but your father didn't hire me to sleep with you."

"You son of a bitch," she said calmly, without moving.

I laughed in her face. "Don't think I'm an icicle," I said. "I'm not blind or without senses. I have warm blood like the next guy. You're easy to take – too damned easy. What has Eddie Mars got on you?"

"If you say that again, I'll scream."

"Go ahead and scream."

She jerked away and pulled herself upright, far back in the corner of the car.

"Men have been shot for little things like that, Marlowe."

"Men have been shot for practically nothing. The first time we met I told you I was a detective. Get it through your lovely head. I work at it, lady. I don't play at it."

She fumbled in her bag and got a handkerchief out and bit on it, her head turned away from me. The tearing sound of the handkerchief came to me. She tore it with her teeth, slowly, time after time.

"What makes you think he has anything on me?" she whispered, her voice muffled by the handkerchief.

"He lets you win a lot of money and sends a gunpoke around to take it back for him. You're not more than mildly surprised. You didn't even thank me for saving it for you. I think the whole thing was just some kind of an act. If I wanted to flatter myself, I'd say it was at least partly for my benefit."

"You think he can win or lose as he pleases."

"Sure. On even money bets, four times out of five."

"Do I have to tell you I loathe your guts, Mister Detective?"

"You don't owe me anything. I'm paid off."

She tossed the shredded handkerchief out of the car window. "You have a lovely way with women."

"I liked kissing you."

"You kept your head beautifully. That's so flattering. Should I congratulate you, or my father?"

"I liked kissing you."

Her voice became an icy drawl. "Take me away from here, if you will be so kind. I'm quite sure I'd like to go home."

"You won't be a sister to me?"

"If I had a razor, I'd cut your throat – just to see what ran out of it."

"Caterpillar blood," I said.

I started the car and turned it and drove back across the interurban tracks to the highway and so on into town and up to West Hollywood. She didn't speak to me. She hardly moved all the way back. I drove through the gates and up the sunken driveway to the porte-cochere of the big house. She jerked the car door open and was out of it before it had quite stopped. She didn't speak even then. I watched her back as she stood against the door after ringing the bell. The door opened and Norris looked out. She pushed past him quickly and was gone. The door banged shut and I was sitting there looking at it.

I turned back down the driveway and home.

24

THE APARTMENT HOUSE lobby was empty this time. No gunman waiting under the potted palm to give me orders. I took the automatic elevator up to my floor and walked along the hallway to the tune of a muted radio behind a door. I needed a drink and was in a hurry to get one. I didn't switch the light on inside the door. I made straight for the kitchen-ette and brought up short in three or four feet. Something was wrong. Something on the air, a scent. The shades were down at the windows and the street light leaking in at the sides made a dim light in the room. I stood still and listened. The scent on the air was a perfume, a heavy cloying perfume.

There was no sound, no sound at all. Then my eyes adjusted themselves more to the darkness and I saw there was something across the floor in front of me that shouldn't have been there. I backed, reached the wall switch with my thumb and flicked the light on.

The bed was down. Something in it giggled. A blond head was pressed into my pillow. Two bare arms curved up and the hands belonging to them were clasped on top of the blond head. Carmen Sternwood lay on her back, in my bed, giggling at me. The tawny wave of her hair was spread out on the pil-low as if by a careful and artificial hand. Her slaty eyes peered at me and had the effect, as usual, of peering from behind a barrel. She smiled. Her small sharp teeth glinted.

"Cute, aren't I?" she said.

I said harshly: "Cute as a Filipino on Saturday night."

I went over to a floor lamp and pulled the switch, went back to put off the ceiling light, and went across the room again to the chessboard on a card table under the lamp. There was a problem laid out on the board, a six-mover. I couldn't solve it, like a lot of my problems. I reached down and moved a knight, then pulled my hat and coat off and threw them somewhere. All this time the soft giggling went on from the bed, that sound that made me think of rats behind a wains-coting in an old house.

"I bet you can't even guess how I got in."

I dug a cigarette out and looked at her with bleak eyes. "I bet I can. You came through the keyhole, just like Peter Pan."

"Who's he?"

"Oh, a fellow I used to know around the poolroom."

She giggled. "You're cute, aren't you?" she said.

I began to say: "About that thumb —" but she was ahead of me. I didn't have to remind her. She took her right hand from behind her head and started sucking the thumb and eyeing me with very round and naughty eyes.

"I'm all undressed," she said, after I had smoked and stared at her for a minute.

"By God," I said, "it was right at the back of my mind. I was groping for it. I almost had it, when you spoke. In another minute I'd have said 'I bet you're all undressed.' I always wear my rubbers in bed myself, in case I wake up with a bad conscience and have to sneak away from it."

"You're cute." She rolled her head a little, kittenishly. Then she took her left hand from under her head and took hold of the covers, paused dramatically, and swept them aside. She was undressed all right. She lay there on the bed in the lamplight, as naked and glistening as a pearl. The Sternwood girls were giving me both barrels that night.

I pulled a shred of tobacco off the edge of my lower lip.

"That's nice," I said. "But I've already seen it all. Remember? I'm the guy that keeps finding you without any clothes on."

She giggled some more and covered herself up again.

"Well, how *did* you get in?" I asked her.

"The manager let me in. I showed him your card. I'd stolen it from Vivian. I told him you told me to come here and wait for you. I was — I was mysterious." She glowed with delight.

"Neat," I said. "Managers are like that. Now I know how you got in tell me how you're going to go out."

She giggled. "Not going — not for a long time. . . . I like it here. You're cute."

"Listen," I pointed my cigarette at her. "Don't make me dress you again. I'm tired. I appreciate all you're offering me. It's just more than I could possibly take. Doghouse Reilly never let a pal down that way. I'm your friend. I won't let you

133

down – in spite of yourself. You and I have to keep on being friends, and this isn't the way to do it. Now will you dress like a nice little girl?"

She shook her head from side to side.

"Listen," I plowed on, "you don't really care anything about me. You're just showing how naughty you can be. But you don't have to show me. I knew it already. I'm the guy that found –"

"Put the light out," she giggled.

I threw my cigarette on the floor and stamped on it. I took a handkerchief out and wiped the palms of my hands. I tried it once more.

"It isn't on account of the neighbors," I told her. "They don't really care a lot. There's a lot of stray broads in any apartment house and one more won't make the building rock. It's a question of professional pride. You know – professional pride. I'm working for your father. He's a sick man, very frail, very helpless. He sort of trusts me not to pull any stunts. Won't you please get dressed, Carmen?"

"Your name isn't Doghouse Reilly," she said. "It's Philip Marlowe. You can't fool me."

I looked down at the chessboard. The move with the knight was wrong. I put it back where I had moved it from. Knights had no meaning in this game. It wasn't a game for knights.

I looked at her again. She lay still now, her face pale against the pillow, her eyes large and dark and empty as rain barrels in a drought. One of her small five-fingered thumbless hands picked at the cover restlessly. There was a vague glimmer of doubt starting to get born in her somewhere. She didn't know about it yet. It's so hard for women – even nice women – to realize that their bodies are not irresistible.

I said: "I'm going out in the kitchen and mix a drink. Want one?"

"Uh-huh." Dark silent mystified eyes stared at me solemnly, the doubt growing larger in them, creeping into them noiselessly, like a cat in long grass stalking a young blackbird.

"If you're dressed when I get back, you'll get the drink. Okay?"

Her teeth parted and a faint hissing noise came out of her mouth. She didn't answer me. I went out to the kitchenette and got out some Scotch and fizzwater and mixed a couple of highballs. I didn't have anything really exciting to drink, like nitroglycerin or distilled tiger's breath. She hadn't moved when I got back with the glasses. The hissing had stopped. Her eyes were dead again. Her lips started to smile at me. Then she sat up suddenly and threw all the covers off her body and reached.

"Gimme."

"When you're dressed. Not *until* you're dressed."

I put the two glasses down on the card table and sat down myself and lit another cigarette. "Go ahead. I won't watch you."

I looked away. Then I was aware of the hissing noise very sudden and sharp. It startled me into looking at her again. She sat there naked, propped on her hands, her mouth open a little, her face like scraped bone. The hissing noise came tearing out of her mouth as if she had nothing to do with it. There was something behind her eyes, blank as they were, that I had never seen in a woman's eyes.

Then her lips moved very slowly and carefully, as if they were artificial lips and had to be manipulated with springs.

She called me a filthy name.

I didn't mind that. I didn't mind what she called me, what anybody called me. But this was the room I had to live in. It was all I had in the way of a home. In it was everything that was mine, that had any association for me, any past, anything that took the place of a family. Not much; a few books, pictures, radio, chessmen, old letters, stuff like that. Nothing. Such as they were they had all my memories.

I couldn't stand her in that room any longer. What she called me only reminded me of that.

I said carefully: "I'll give you three minutes to get dressed and out of here. If you're not out by then, I'll throw you out – by force. Just the way you are, naked. And I'll throw your clothes after you into the hall. Now – get started."

Her teeth chattered and the hissing noise was sharp and animal. She swung her feet to the floor and reached for her clothes on a chair beside the bed. She dressed. I watched her. She dressed with stiff awkward fingers – for a woman – but quickly at that. She was dressed in a little over two minutes. I timed it.

She stood there beside the bed, holding a green bag tight against a fur-trimmed coat. She wore a rakish green hat crooked on her head. She stood there for a moment and hissed at me, her face still like scraped bone, her eyes still empty and yet full of some jungle emotion. Then she walked quickly to the door and opened it and went out, without speaking, without looking back. I heard the elevator lurch into motion and move in the shaft.

I walked to the windows and pulled the shades up and opened the windows wide. The night air came drifting in with a kind of stale sweetness that still remembered auto-mobile exhausts and the streets of the city. I reached for my drink and drank it slowly. The apartment house door closed itself down below me. Steps tinkled on the quiet sidewalk. A car started up not far away. It rushed off into the night with a rough clashing of gears. I went back to the bed and looked down at it. The imprint of her head was still in the pillow, of her small corrupt body still on the sheets.

I put my empty glass down and tore the bed to pieces savagely.

25

IT WAS RAINING again the next morning, a slanting gray rain like a swung curtain of crystal beads. I got up feeling sluggish and tired and stood looking out of the windows, with a dark harsh taste of Sternwoods still in my mouth. I was as empty of life as a scarecrow's pockets. I went out to the kitchenette and drank two cups of black coffee. You can have a hangover from other things than alcohol. I had one from women. Women made me sick.

I shaved and showered and dressed and got my raincoat out and went downstairs and looked out of the front door. Across the street, a hundred feet up, a gray Plymouth sedan was parked. It was the same one that had tried to trail me around the day before, the same one that I had asked Eddie Mars about. There might be a cop in it, if a cop had that much time on his hands and wanted to waste it following me around. Or it might be a smoothie in the detective business trying to get a noseful of somebody else's case in order to chisel a way into it. Or it might be the Bishop of Bermuda disapproving of my night life.

I went out back and got my convertible from the garage and drove it around front past the gray Plymouth. There was a small man in it, alone. He started up after me. He worked better in the rain. He stayed close enough so that I couldn't make a short block and leave that before he entered it, and he stayed back far enough so that other cars were between us most of the time. I drove down to the boulevard and parked in the lot next to my building and came out of there with my raincoat collar up and my hat brim low and the raindrops tapping icily at my face in between. The Plymouth was across the way at a fireplug. I walked down to the intersection and crossed with the green light and walked back, close to the edge of the sidewalk and the parked cars. The Plymouth hadn't moved. Nobody got out of it. I reached it and jerked open the door on the curb side.

A small bright-eyed man was pressed back into the corner behind the wheel. I stood and looked in at him, the rain thumping my back. His eyes blinked behind the swirling smoke of a cigarette. His hands tapped restlessly on the thin wheel.

I said: "Can't you make your mind up?"

He swallowed and the cigarette bobbed between his lips. "I don't think I know you," he said, in a tight little voice.

"Marlowe's the name. The guy you've been trying to follow around for a couple of days."

"I ain't following anybody, doc."

"This jalopy is. Maybe you can't control it. Have it your own way. I'm now going to eat breakfast in the coffee shop across the street, orange juice, bacon and eggs, toast, honey, three or four cups of coffee and a toothpick. I am then going up to my office, which is on the seventh floor of the building right opposite you. If you have anything that's worrying you beyond endurance, drop up and chew it over. I'll only be oiling my machine gun."

I left him blinking and walked away. Twenty minutes later I was airing the scrubwoman's Soirée d'Amour out of my office and opening up a thick rough envelope addressed in a fine old-fashioned pointed handwriting. The envelope contained a brief formal note and a large mauve check for five hundred dollars, payable to Philip Marlowe and signed, Guy de Brisay Sternwood, by Vincent Norris. That made it a nice morning. I was making out a bank slip when the buzzer told me somebody had entered my two by four reception room. It was the little man from the Plymouth.

"Fine," I said. "Come in and shed your coat."

He slid past me carefully as I held the door, as carefully as though he feared I might plant a kick in his minute buttocks. We sat down and faced each other across the desk. He was a very small man, not more than five feet three and would hardly weigh as much as a butcher's thumb. He had tight brilliant eyes that wanted to look hard, and looked as hard as oysters on the half shell. He wore a double-breasted dark gray suit that was too wide in the shoulders and had too much lapel. Over this, open, an Irish tweed coat with some badly worn spots. A lot of foulard tie bulged out and was rainspotted above his crossed lapels.

"Maybe you know me," he said. "I'm Harry Jones."

I said I didn't know him. I pushed a flat tin of cigarettes at him. His small neat fingers speared one like a trout taking the fly. He lit it with the desk lighter and waved his hand.

"I been around," he said. "Know the boys and such. Used to do a little liquor-running down from Hueneme Point. A tough racket, brother. Riding the scout car with a gun in your lap and a wad on your hip that would choke a coal chute. Plenty of times we paid off four sets of law before we hit Beverly Hills. A tough racket."

"Terrible," I said.

He leaned back and blew smoke at the ceiling from the small tight corner of his small tight mouth.

"Maybe you don't believe me," he said.

"Maybe I don't," I said. "And maybe I do. And then again maybe I haven't bothered to make my mind up. Just what is the build-up supposed to do to me?"

"Nothing," he said tartly.

"You've been following me around for a couple of days," I said. "Like a fellow trying to pick up a girl and lacking the last inch of nerve. Maybe you're selling insurance. Maybe you knew a fellow called Joe Brody. That's a lot of maybes, but I have a lot on hand in my business."

His eyes bulged and his lower lip almost fell in his lap. "Christ, how'd you know that?" he snapped.

"I'm psychic. Shake your business up and pour it. I haven't got all day."

The brightness of his eyes almost disappeared between the suddenly narrowed lids. There was silence. The rain pounded down on the flat tarred roof over the Mansion House lobby below my windows. His eyes opened a little, shined again, and his voice was full of thought.

"I was trying to get a line on you, sure," he said. "I've got something to sell – cheap, for a couple of C notes. How'd you tie me to Joe?"

I opened a letter and read it. It offered me a six months' correspondence course in fingerprinting at a special professional discount. I dropped it into the waste basket and looked at the little man again. "Don't mind me. I was just guessing. You're not a cop. You don't belong to Eddie Mars' outfit. I asked him last night. I couldn't think of anybody else but Joe Brody's friends who would be that much interested in me."

"Jesus," he said and licked his lower lip. His face had turned white as paper when I mentioned Eddie Mars. His mouth drooped open and his cigarette hung to the corner of it by some magic, as if it had grown there. "Aw, you're kidding me," he said at last, with the sort of smile the operating room sees.

"All right. I'm kidding you." I opened another letter. This one wanted to send me a daily newsletter from Washington, all inside stuff, straight from the cookhouse. "I suppose Agnes is loose," I added.

"Yeah. She sent me. You interested?"

"Well – she's a blonde."

"Nuts. You made a crack when you were up there that night – the night Joe got squibbed off. Something about Brody must have known something good about the Sternwoods or he wouldn't have taken the chance on that picture he sent them."

"Uh-huh. So he had? What was it?"

"That's what the two hundred bucks pays for."

I dropped some more fan mail into the basket and lit myself a fresh cigarette.

"We gotta get out of town," he said. "Agnes is a nice girl. You can't hold that stuff on her. It's not so easy for a dame to get by these days."

"She's too big for you," I said. "She'll roll on you and smother you."

"That's kind of a dirty crack, brother," he said with something that was near enough to dignity to make me stare at him.

I said: "You're right. I've been meeting the wrong kind of people lately. Let's cut out the gabble and get down to cases. What have you got for the money?"

"Would you pay for it?"

"If it does what?"

"If it helps you find Rusty Regan."

"I'm not looking for Rusty Regan."

"Says you. Want to hear it or not?"

"Go ahead and chirp. I'll pay for anything I use. Two C notes buys a lot of information in my circle."

"Eddie Mars had Regan bumped off," he said calmly, and leaned back as if he had just been made a vice-president.

I waved a hand in the direction of the door. "I wouldn't even argue with you," I said. "I wouldn't waste the oxygen. On your way, small size."

He leaned across the desk, white lines at the corners of his mouth. He snubbed his cigarette out carefully, over and over again, without looking at it. From behind a communicating door came the sound of a typewriter clacking monotonously to the bell, to the shift, line after line.

"I'm not kidding," he said.

"Beat it. Don't bother me. I have work to do."

"No you don't," he said sharply. "I ain't that easy. I came here to speak my piece and I'm speaking it. I knew Rusty myself. Not well, well enough to say 'How's a boy?' and he'd answer me or he wouldn't, according to how he felt. A nice guy though. I always liked him. He was sweet on a singer named Mona Grant. Then she changed her name to Mars. Rusty got sore and married a rich dame that hung around the joints like she couldn't sleep well at home. You know all about her, tall, dark, enough looks for a Derby winner, but the type would put a lot of pressure on a guy. High-strung. Rusty wouldn't get along with her. But Jesus, he'd get along with her old man's dough, wouldn't he? That's what you think. This Regan was a cockeyed sort of buzzard. He had long-range eyes. He was looking over into the next valley all the time. He wasn't scarcely around where he was. I don't think he gave a damn about dough. And coming from me, brother, that's a compliment."

The little man wasn't so dumb after all. A three for a quarter grifter wouldn't even think such thoughts, much less know how to express them.

I said: "So he ran away."

"He started to run away, maybe. With this girl Mona. She wasn't living with Eddie Mars, didn't like his rackets. Especially the side lines, like blackmail, bent cars, hideouts for hot boys from the east, and so on. The talk was Regan told Eddie one night, right out in the open, that if he ever messed Mona up in any criminal rap, he'd be around to see him."

"Most of this is on the record, Harry," I said. "You can't expect money for that."

"I'm coming to what isn't. So Regan blew. I used to see him every afternoon in Vardi's drinking Irish whiskey and staring at the wall. He don't talk much any more. He'd give me a bet now and then, which was what I was there for, to pick up bets for Puss Walgreen."

"I thought he was in the insurance business."

"That's what it says on the door. I guess he'd sell you insurance at that, if you tramped on him. Well, about the middle of September I don't see Regan any more. I don't notice it right away. You know how it is. A guy's there and you see him and then he ain't there and you don't not see him until something makes you think of it. What makes me think about it is I hear a guy say laughing that Eddie Mars' woman lammed out with Rusty Regan and Mars is acting like he was best man, instead of being sore. So I tell Joe Brody and Joe was smart."

"Like hell he was," I said.

"Not copper smart, but still smart. He's out for the dough. He gets to figuring could he get a line somehow on the two lovebirds he could maybe collect twice – once from Eddie Mars and once from Regan's wife. Joe knew the family a little."

"Five grand worth," I said. "He nicked them for that a while back."

"Yeah?" Harry Jones looked mildly surprised. "Agnes ought to of told me that. There's a frail for you. Always holding out. Well, Joe and me watch the papers and we don't see anything, so we know old Sternwood has a blanket on it. Then one day I see Lash Canino in Vardi's. Know him?"

I shook my head.

"There's a boy that is tough like some guys think they are tough. He does a job for Eddie Mars when Mars needs him – trouble-shooting. He'd bump a guy off between drinks. When Mars don't need him he don't go near him. And he don't stay in L.A. Well it might be something and it might not. Maybe they got a line on Regan and Mars has just been sitting back with a smile on his puss, waiting for the chance. Then again it might be something else entirely. Anyway I tell Joe and Joe gets on Canino's tail. He can tail. Me, I'm no good at it. I'm giving that one away. No charge. And Joe tails Canino out to the Sternwood place and Canino parks outside the estate and a car come up beside him with a girl in it. They talk for a while and Joe thinks the girl passes something over, like maybe dough. The girl beats it. It's Regan's wife. Okay, she knows Canino and Canino knows Mars. So Joe figures Canino knows something about Regan and is trying to squeeze a little on the side for himself. Canino blows and Joe loses him. End of Act One."

"What does this Canino look like?"

"Short, heavy set, brown hair, brown eyes, and always wears brown clothes and a brown hat. Even wears a brown suede raincoat. Drives a brown coupe. Everything brown for Mr. Canino."

143

"Let's have Act Two," I said.

"Without some dough that's all."

"I don't see two hundred bucks in it. Mrs. Regan married an ex-bootlegger out of the joints. She'd know other people of his sort. She knows Eddie Mars well. If she thought anything had happened to Regan, Eddie would be the very man she'd go to, and Canino might be the man Eddie would pick to handle the assignment. Is that all you have?"

"Would you give the two hundred to know where Eddie's wife is?" the little man asked calmly.

He had all my attention now. I almost cracked the arms of my chair leaning on them.

"Even if she was alone?" Harry Jones added in a soft, rather sinister tone. "Even if she never run away with Regan at all, and was being kept now about forty miles from L.A. in a hideout – so the law would keep on thinking she had dusted with him? Would you pay two hundred bucks for that, shamus?"

I licked my lips. They tasted dry and salty. "I think I would," I said. "Where?"

"Agnes found her," he said grimly. "Just by a lucky break. Saw her out riding and managed to tail her home. Agnes will tell you where that is – when she's holding the money in her hand."

I made a hard face at him. "You could tell the coppers for nothing, Harry. They have some good wreckers down at Central these days. If they killed you trying, they still have Agnes."

"Let 'em try," he said. "I ain't so brittle."

"Agnes must have something I didn't notice."

"She's a grifter, shamus. I'm a grifter. We're all grifters. So we sell each other out for a nickel. Okay. See can you make me." He reached for another of my cigarettes, placed it neatly between his lips and lit it with a match the way I do myself, missing twice on his thumbnail and then using his foot. He puffed evenly and stared at me level-eyed, a funny little hard guy I could have thrown from home plate to second base.

144

A small man in a big man's world. There was something I liked about him.

"I haven't pulled anything in here," he said steadily. "I come in talking two C's. That's still the price. I come because I thought I'd get a take it or leave it, one right gee to another. Now you're waving cops at me. You oughta be ashamed of yourself."

I said: "You'll get the two hundred – for that information. I have to get the money myself first."

He stood up and nodded and pulled his worn little Irish tweed coat tight around his chest. "That's okay. After dark is better anyway. It's a leery job – buckin' guys like Eddie Mars. But a guy has to eat. The book's been pretty dull lately. I think the big boys have told Puss Walgreen to move on. Suppose you come over there to the office, Fulwider Building, Western and Santa Monica, four-twenty-eight at the back. You bring the money, I'll take you to Agnes."

"Can't you tell me yourself? I've seen Agnes."

"I promised her," he said simply. He buttoned his overcoat, cocked his hat jauntily, nodded again and strolled to the door. He went out. His steps died along the hall.

I went down to the bank and deposited my five-hundred-dollar check and drew out two hundred in currency. I went upstairs again and sat in my chair thinking about Harry Jones and his story. It seemed a little too pat. It had the austere simplicity of fiction rather than the tangled woof of fact. Captain Gregory ought to have been able to find Mona Mars, if she was that close to his beat. Supposing, that is, he had tried.

I thought about it most of the day. Nobody came into the office. Nobody called me on the phone. It kept on raining.

26

AT SEVEN THE rain had stopped for a breathing spell, but the gutters were still flooded. On Santa Monica the water was level with the sidewalk and a thin film of it washed over the top of the curbing. A traffic cop in shining black rubber from boots to cap sloshed through the flood on his way from the shelter of a sodden awning. My rubber heels slithered on the sidewalk as I turned into the narrow lobby of the Fulwider Building. A single drop light burned far back, beyond an open, once gilt elevator. There was a tarnished and well-missed spittoon on a gnawed rubber mat. A case of false teeth hung on the mustard-colored wall like a fuse box in a screen porch. I shook the rain off my hat and looked at the building directory beside the case of teeth. Numbers with names and numbers without names. Plenty of vacancies or plenty of tenants who wished to remain anonymous. Painless dentists, shyster detective agencies, small sick businesses that had crawled there to die, mail order schools that would teach you how to become a railroad clerk or a radio technician or a screen writer — if the postal inspectors didn't catch up with them first. A nasty building. A building in which the smell of stale cigar butts would be the cleanest odor.

An old man dozed in the elevator, on a ramshackle stool, with a burst-out cushion under him. His mouth was open, his veined temples glistened in the weak light. He wore a blue uniform coat that fitted him the way a stall fits a horse. Under that gray trousers with frayed cuffs, white cotton socks and black kid shoes, one of which was slit across a bunion. On the stool he slept miserably, waiting for a customer. I went past him softly, the clandestine air of the building prompting me, found the fire door and pulled it open. The fire stairs hadn't been swept in a month. Bums had slept on them, eaten on them, left crusts and fragments of greasy newspaper, matches, a gutted imitation-leather pocketbook. In a shadowy angle against the scribbled wall a pouched ring of pale rubber had fallen and had not been disturbed. A very nice building.

I came out at the fourth floor sniffing for air. The hallway had the same dirty spittoon and frayed mat, the same mustard walls, the same memories of low tide. I went down the line and turned a corner. The name: "L. D. Walgreen – Insurance," showed on a dark pebbled glass door, on a second dark door, on a third behind which there was a light. One of the dark doors said: "Entrance."

A glass transom was open above the lighted door. Through it the sharp bird-like voice of Harry Jones spoke, saying:

"Canino? . . . Yeah, I've seen you around somewhere. Sure."

I froze. The other voice spoke. It had a heavy purr, like a small dynamo behind a brick wall. It said: "I thought you would." There was a vaguely sinister note in that voice.

A chair scraped on linoleum, steps sounded, the transom above me squeaked shut. A shadow melted from behind the pebbled glass.

I went back to the first of the three doors marked with the name Walgreen. I tried it cautiously. It was locked. It moved in a loose frame, an old door fitted many years past, made of half-seasoned wood and shrunken now. I reached my wallet out and slipped the thick hard window of celluloid from over my driver's license. A burglar's tool the law had forgotten to proscribe. I put my gloves on, leaned softly and lovingly against the door and pushed the knob hard away from the frame. I pushed the celluloid plate into the wide crack and felt for the slope of the spring lock. There was a dry click, like a small icicle breaking. I hung there motionless, like a lazy fish in the water. Nothing happened inside. I turned the knob and pushed the door back into darkness. I shut it behind me as carefully as I had opened it.

The lighted oblong of an uncurtained window faced me, cut by the angle of a desk. On the desk a hooded typewriter took form, then the metal knob of a communicating door. This was unlocked. I passed into the second of the three offices. Rain rattled suddenly against the closed window. Under its noise I crossed the room. A tight fan of light spread from an inch opening of the door into the lighted office. Everything very convenient. I walked like a cat on a mantel and reached the hinged side of the door, put an eye to the crack and saw nothing but light against the angle of the wood.

The purring voice was now saying quite pleasantly: "Sure, a guy could sit on his fanny and crab what another guy done if he knows what it's all about. So you go to see this peeper. Well, that was your mistake. Eddie don't like it. The peeper told Eddie some guy in a gray Plymouth was tailing him. Eddie naturally wants to know who and why, see."

Harry Jones laughed lightly. "What makes it his business?"

"That don't get you no place."

"You know why I went to the peeper. I already told you. Account of Joe Brody's girl. She has to blow and she's shatting on her uppers. She figures the peeper can get her some dough. I don't have any."

The purring voice said gently: "Dough for what? Peepers don't give that stuff out to punks."

"He could raise it. He knows rich people." Harry Jones laughed, a brave little laugh.

"Don't fuss with me, little man." The purring voice had an edge, like sand in the bearings.

"Okay, okay. You know the dope on Brody's bump-off. That screwy kid done it all right, but the night it happened this Marlowe was right there in the room."

"That's known, little man. He told it to the law."

"Yeah – here's what isn't. Brody was trying to peddle a nudist photo of the young Sternwood girl. Marlowe got wise to him. While they were arguing about it the young Sternwood girl dropped around herself – with a gat. She took a shot at Brody. She lets one fly and breaks a window. Only the peeper didn't tell the coppers about that. And Agnes didn't neither. She figures it's railroad fare for her not to."

"This ain't got anything to do with Eddie?"

"Show me how."

"Where's this Agnes at?"

"Nothing doing."

"You tell me, little man. Here, or in the back room where the boys pitch dimes against the wall."

"She's my girl now, Canino. I don't put my girl in the middle for anybody."

A silence followed. I listened to the rain lashing the windows. The smell of cigarette smoke came through the crack of the door. I wanted to cough. I bit hard on a handkerchief.

The purring voice said, still gentle: "From what I hear this blonde broad was just a shill for Geiger. I'll talk it over with Eddie. How much you tap the peeper for?"

"Two centuries."

"Get it?"

Harry Jones laughed again. "I'm seeing him tomorrow. I have hopes."

"Where's Agnes?"

"Listen —"

"Where's Agnes?"

Silence.

"Look at it, little man."

I didn't move. I wasn't wearing a gun. I didn't have to see through the crack of the door to know that a gun was what the purring voice was inviting Harry Jones to look at. But I didn't think Mr. Canino would do anything with his gun beyond showing it. I waited.

"I'm looking at it," Harry Jones said, his voice squeezed tight as if it could hardly get past his teeth. "And I don't see anything I didn't see before. Go ahead and blast and see what it gets you."

"A Chicago overcoat is what it would get *you*, little man."

Silence.

"Where's Agnes?"

Harry Jones sighed. "Okay," he said wearily. "She's in an apartment house at 28 Court Street, up on Bunker Hill.

Apartment 301. I guess I'm yellow all right. Why should I front for that twist?"

"No reason. You got good sense. You and me'll go out and talk to her. All I want is to find out is she dummying up on you, kid. If it's the way you say it is, everything is jakeloo. You can put the bite on the peeper and be on your way. No hard feelings?"

"No," Harry Jones said. "No hard feelings, Canino."

"Fine. Let's dip the bill. Got a glass?" The purring voice was now as false as an usherette's eyelashes and as slippery as a watermelon seed. A drawer was pulled open. Something jarred on wood. A chair squeaked. A scuffing sound on the floor. "This is bond stuff," the purring voice said.

There was a gurgling sound. "Moths in your ermine, as the ladies say."

Harry Jones said softly: "Success."

I heard a sharp cough. Then a violent retching. There was a small thud on the floor, as if a thick glass had fallen. My fingers curled against my raincoat.

The purring voice said gently: "You ain't sick from just one drink, are you, pal?"

Harry Jones didn't answer. There was labored breathing for a short moment. Then thick silence folded down. Then a chair scraped.

"So long, little man," said Mr. Canino.

Steps, a click, the wedge of light died at my feet, a door opened and closed quietly. The steps faded, leisurely and assured.

I stirred around the edge of the door and pulled it wide and looked into blackness relieved by the dim shine of a window. The corner of a desk glittered faintly. A hunched shape took form in a chair behind it. In the close air there was a heavy clogged smell, almost a perfume. I went across to the corridor door and listened. I heard the distant clang of the elevator.

I found the light switch and light glowed in a dusty glass bowl hanging from the ceiling by three brass chains. Harry Jones looked at me across the desk, his eyes wide open, his face frozen in a tight spasm, the skin bluish. His small dark head was tilted to one side. He sat upright against the back of the chair.

A street-car bell clanged at an almost infinite distance and the sound came buffeted by innumerable walls. A brown half pint of whiskey stood on the desk with the cap off. Harry Jones' glass glinted against a castor of the desk. The second glass was gone.

I breathed shallowly, from the top of my lungs, and bent above the bottle. Behind the charred smell of the bourbon another odor lurked, faintly, the odor of bitter almonds. Harry Jones dying had vomited on his coat. That made it cyanide.

I walked around him carefully and lifted a phone book from a hook on the wooden frame of the window. I let it fall again, reached the telephone as far as it would go from the little dead man. I dialed information. The voice answered.

"Can you give me the phone number of Apartment 301, 28 Court Street?"

"One moment, please." The voice came to me borne on the smell of bitter almonds. A silence. "The number is Wentworth two-five-two-eight. It is listed under Glendower Apartments."

I thanked the voice and dialed the number. The bell rang three times, then the line opened. A radio blared along the wire and was muted. A burly male voice said: "Hello."

"Is Agnes there?"

"No Agnes here, buddy. What number you want?"

"Wentworth two-five-two-eight."

"Right number, wrong gal. Ain't that a shame?" The voice cackled.

I hung up and reached for the phone book again and looked up the Wentworth Apartments. I dialed the manager's number. I had a blurred vision of Mr. Canino driving fast through rain to another appointment with death.

"Glendower Apartments. Mr. Schiff speaking."

"This is Wallis, Police Identification Bureau. Is there a girl named Agnes Lozelle registered in your place?"

"Who did you say you were?"

I told him again.

"If you give me your number, I'll –"

"Cut the comedy," I said sharply, "I'm in a hurry. Is there or isn't there?"

"No. There isn't." The voice was as stiff as a breadstick.

"Is there a tall blonde with green eyes registered in the flop?"

"Say, this isn't any flop –"

"Oh, can it, *can it* !" I rapped at him in a police voice. "You want me to send the vice squad over there and shake the joint down? I know all about Bunker Hill apartment houses, mister. Especially the ones that have phone numbers listed for each apartment."

"Hey, take it easy, officer. I'll co-operate. There's a couple of blondes here, sure. Where isn't there? I hadn't noticed their eyes much. Would yours be alone?"

"Alone, or with a little chap about five feet three, a hundred and ten, sharp black eyes, wears a double-breasted dark gray suit and Irish tweed overcoat, gray hat. My information is Apartment 301, but all I get there is the big razzoo."

"Oh, she ain't there. There's a couple of car salesmen living in three-o-one."

"Thanks, I'll drop around."

"Make it quiet, won't you? Come to my place, direct?"

"Much obliged, Mr. Schiff." I hung up.

I wiped sweat off my face. I walked to the far corner of the office and stood with my face to the wall, patted it with a hand. I turned around slowly and looked across at little Harry Jones grimacing in his chair.

"Well, you fooled him, Harry," I said out loud, in a voice that sounded queer to me. "You lied to him and you drank your cyanide like a little gentleman. You died like a poisoned rat, Harry, but you're no rat to me."

I had to search him. It was a nasty job. His pockets yielded nothing about Agnes, nothing that I wanted at all. I didn't think they would, but I had to be sure. Mr. Canino might be back. Mr. Canino would be the kind of self-confident gentleman who would not mind returning to the scene of his crime.

I put the light out and started to open the door. The phone bell rang jarringly down on the baseboard. I listened to it, my jaw muscles drawn into a knot, aching. Then I shut the door and put the light on again and went across to it.

"Yeah?"

A woman's voice. Her voice. "Is Harry around?"

"Not for a minute, Agnes."

She waited a while on that. Then she said slowly: "Who's talking?"

"Marlowe, the guy that's trouble to you."

"Where is he?" sharply.

"I came over to give him two hundred bucks in return for certain information. The offer holds. I have the money. Where are you?"

"Didn't he tell you?"

"No."

"Perhaps you'd better ask him. Where is he?"

"I can't ask him. Do you know a man named Canino?"

Her gasp came as clearly as though she had been beside me.

"Do you want the two C's or not?" I asked.

"I – I want it pretty bad, mister."

"All right then. Tell me where to bring it."

"I – I –" Her voice trailed off and came back with a panic rush. "Where's Harry?"

"Got scared and blew. Meet me somewhere – anywhere at all – I have the money."

"I don't believe you – about Harry. It's a trap."

"Oh stuff. I could have had Harry hauled in long ago. There isn't anything to make a trap for. Canino got a line on Harry somehow and he blew. I want quiet, you want quiet, Harry wants quiet." Harry already had it. Nobody could take it away from him. "You don't think I'd stooge for Eddie Mars, do you, angel?"

"No-o, I guess not. Not that. I'll meet you in half an hour. Beside Bullocks Wilshire, the east entrance to the parking lot."

"Right," I said.

I dropped the phone in its cradle. The wave of almond odor flooded me again, and the sour smell of vomit. The little dead man sat silent in his chair, beyond fear, beyond change.

I left the office. Nothing moved in the dingy corridor. No pebbled glass door had light behind it. I went down the fire stairs to the second floor and from there looked down at the lighted roof of the elevator cage. I pressed the button. Slowly the car lurched into motion. I ran down the stairs again. The car was above me when I walked out of the building.

It was raining hard again. I walked into it with the heavy drops slapping my face. When one of them touched my tongue I knew that my mouth was open and the ache at the side of my jaws told me it was open wide and strained back, mimicking the rictus of death carved upon the face of Harry Jones.

27

"GIVE ME THE MONEY."

The motor of the gray Plymouth throbbed under her voice and the rain pounded above it. The violet light at the top of Bullock's green-tinged tower was far above us, serene and withdrawn from the dark, dripping city. Her black-gloved hand reached out and I put the bills in it. She bent over to count them under the dim light of the dash. A bag clicked open, clicked shut. She let a spent breath die on her lips. She leaned towards me.

"I'm leaving, copper. I'm on my way. This is a getaway stake and God how I need it. What happened to Harry?"

"I told you he ran away. Canino got wise to him somehow. Forget Harry. I've paid and I want my information."

"You'll get it. Joe and I were out riding Foothill Boulevard Sunday before last. It was late and the lights coming up and the usual mess of cars. We passed a brown coupe and I saw the girl who was driving it. There was a man beside her, a dark short man. The girl was a blonde. I'd seen her before. She was Eddie Mars' wife. The guy was Canino. You wouldn't forget either of them, if you ever saw them. Joe tailed the coupe from in front. He was good at that. Canino, the watchdog, was taking her out for air. A mile or so east of Realito a road turns towards the foothills. That's orange country to the south but to the north it's as bare as hell's back yard and smack up against the hills there's a cyanide plant where they make the stuff for fumigation. Just off the highway there's a small garage and paintshop run by a gee named Art Huck. Hot car drop, likely. There's a frame house beyond this, and beyond the house nothing but the foothills and the bare stone outcrop and the cyanide plant a couple of miles on. That's the place where she's holed up. They turned off on this road and Joe swung around and went back and we saw the car turn off the road where the frame house was. We sat there half an hour looking through the cars going by. Nobody came back out. When it was quite dark Joe sneaked up there and took a look. He said there were lights in the house and a radio was going and just the one car out in front, the coupe. So we beat it."

She stopped talking and I listened to the swish of tires on Wilshire. I said: "They might have shifted quarters since then but that's what you have to sell – that's what you have to sell. Sure you knew her?"

"If you ever see her, you won't make a mistake the second time. Good-bye, copper, and wish me luck. I got a raw deal."

"Like hell you did," I said, and walked away across the street to my own car.

The gray Plymouth moved forward, gathered speed, and darted around the corner onto Sunset Place. The sound of its motor died, and with it blonde Agnes wiped herself off the slate for good, so far as I was concerned. Three men dead, Geiger, Brody and Harry Jones, and the woman went riding off in the rain with my two hundred in her bag and not a mark on her. I kicked my starter and drove on downtown to eat. I ate a good dinner. Forty miles in the rain is a hike, and I hoped to make it a round trip.

I drove north across the river, on into Pasadena, through Pasadena and almost at once I was in orange groves. The tumbling rain was solid white spray in the headlights. The windshield wiper could hardly keep the glass clear enough to see through. But not even the drenched darkness could hide the flawless lines of the orange trees wheeling away like endless spokes into the night.

Cars passed with a tearing hiss and a wave of dirty spray. The highway jerked through a little town that was all packing houses and sheds, and railway sidings nuzzling them. The groves thinned out and dropped away to the south and the road climbed and it was cold and to the north the black foothills crouched closer and sent a bitter wind whipping down their flanks. Then faintly out of the dark two yellow vapor lights glowed high up in the air and a neon sign between them said: "Welcome to Realito."

Frame houses were spaced far back from a wide main street, then a sudden knot of stores, the lights of a drugstore behind fogged glass, the fly-cluster of cars in front of the movie theater, a dark bank on a corner with a clock sticking out over the sidewalk and a group of people standing in the rain looking at its windows, as if they were some kind of a show. I went on. Empty fields closed in again.

Fate stage-managed the whole thing. Beyond Realito, just about a mile beyond, the highway took a curve and the rain fooled me and I went too close to the shoulder. My right front tire let go with an angry hiss. Before I could stop the right rear went with it. I jammed the car to a stop, half on the pavement, half on the shoulder, got out and flashed a spotlight around. I had two flats and one spare. The flat butt of a heavy galvanized tack stared at me from the front tire.

The edge of the pavement was littered with them. They had been swept off, but not far enough off.

I snapped the flash off and stood there breathing rain and looking up a side road at a yellow light. It seemed to come from a skylight. The skylight could belong to a garage, the garage could be run by a man named Art Huck, and there could be a frame house next door to it. I tucked my chin down in my collar and started towards it, then went back to unstrap the license holder from the steering post and put it in my pocket. I leaned lower under the wheel. Behind a weighted flap, directly under my right leg as I sat in the car, there was a hidden compartment. There were two guns in it. One belonged to Eddie Mars' boy Lanny and one belonged to me. I took Lanny's. It would have had more practice than mine. I stuck it nose down in an inside pocket and started up the side road.

The garage was a hundred yards from the highway. It showed the highway a blank side wall. I played the flash on it quickly. "Art Huck – Auto Repairs and Painting." I chuckled, then Harry Jones' face rose up in front of me, and I stopped chuckling. The garage doors were shut, but there was an edge of light under them and a thread of light where the halves met. I went on past. The frame house was there, light in two front windows, shades down. It was set well back from the road, behind a thin clump of trees. A car stood on the gravel drive in front. It was dark, indistinct, but it would be a brown coupe and it would belong to Mr. Canino. It squatted there peacefully in front of the narrow wooden porch.

He would let her take it out for a spin once in a while, and sit beside her, probably with a gun handy. The girl Rusty Regan ought to have married, that Eddie Mars couldn't keep, the girl that hadn't run away with Regan. Nice Mr. Canino.

I trudged back to the garage and banged on the wooden door with the butt of my flash. There was a hung instant of silence, as heavy as thunder. The light inside went out. I stood there grinning and licking the rain off my lip. I clicked the spot on the middle of the doors. I grinned at the circle of white. I was where I wanted to be.

A voice spoke through the door, a surly voice: "What you want?"

"Open up. I've got two flats back on the highway and only one spare. I need help."

"Sorry, mister. We're closed up. Realito's a mile west. Better try there."

I didn't like that. I kicked the door hard. I kept on kicking it. Another voice made itself heard, a purring voice, like a small dynamo behind a wall. I liked this voice. It said: "A wise guy, huh? Open up, Art."

A bolt squealed and half of the door bent inward. My flash burned briefly on a gaunt face. Then something that glittered swept down and knocked the flash out of my hand. A gun had peaked at me. I dropped low where the flash burned on the wet ground and picked it up.

The surly voice said: "Kill that spot, bo. Folks get hurt that way."

I snapped the flash off and straightened. Light went on inside the garage, outlined a tall man in coveralls. He backed away from the open door and kept a gun leveled at me.

"Step inside and shut the door, stranger. We'll see what we can do."

I stepped inside, and shut the door behind my back. I looked at the gaunt man, but not at the other man who was shadowy over by a workbench, silent. The breath of the garage was sweet and sinister with the smell of hot pyroxylin paint.

"Ain't you got no sense?" the gaunt man chided me. "A bank job was pulled at Realito this noon."

"Pardon," I said, remembering the people staring at the bank in the rain. "I didn't pull it. I'm a stranger here."

"Well, there was," he said morosely. "Some say it was a couple of punk kids and they got 'em cornered back here in the hills."

"It's a nice night for hiding," I said. "I suppose they threw tacks out. I got some of them. I thought you just needed the business."

"You didn't ever get socked in the kisser, did you?" the gaunt man asked me briefly.

"Not by anybody your weight."

The purring voice from over in the shadows said: "Cut out the heavy menace, Art. This guy's in a jam. You run a garage, don't you?"

"Thanks," I said, and didn't look at him even then.

"Okay, okay," the man in the coveralls grumbled. He tucked his gun through a flap in his clothes and bit a knuckle, staring at me moodily over it. The smell of the pyroxylin paint was as sickening as ether. Over in the corner, under a drop light, there was a big new-looking sedan with a paint gun lying on its fender.

I looked at the man by the workbench now. He was short and thick-bodied with strong shoulders. He had a cool face and cool dark eyes. He wore a belted brown suede raincoat that was heavily spotted with rain. His brown hat was tilted rakishly. He leaned his back against the workbench and looked me over without haste, without interest, as if he was looking at a slab of cold meat. Perhaps he thought of people that way.

He moved his dark eyes up and down slowly and then glanced at his fingernails one by one, holding them up against the light and studying them with care, as Hollywood has taught it should be done. He spoke around a cigarette.

"Got two flats, huh? That's tough. They swept them tacks, I thought."

"I skidded a little on the curve."

"Stranger in town you said?"

"Traveling through. On the way to L.A. How far is it?"

"Forty miles. Seems longer this weather. Where from, stranger?"

"Santa Rosa."

"Come the long way, eh? Tahoe and Lone Pine?"

"Not Tahoe. Reno and Carson City."

"Still the long way." A fleeting smile curved his lips.

"Any law against it?" I asked him.

"Huh? No, sure not. Guess you think we're nosey. Just on account of that heist back there. Take a jack and get his flats, Art."

"I'm busy," the gaunt man growled. "I've got work to do. I got this spray job. And it's raining, you might have noticed."

The man in brown said pleasantly: "Too damp for a good spray job, Art. Get moving."

I said: "They're front and rear, on the right side. You could use the spare for one spot, if you're busy."

"Take two jacks, Art," the brown man said.

"Now, listen —" Art began to bluster.

The brown man moved his eyes, looked at Art with a soft quiet-eyed stare, lowered them again almost shyly. He didn't speak. Art rocked as if a gust of wind had hit him. He stamped over to the corner and put a rubber coat over his coveralls, a sou'wester on his head. He grabbed a socket wrench and a hand jack and wheeled a dolly jack over to the doors.

He went out silently, leaving the door yawning. The rain blustered in. The man in brown strolled over and shut it and strolled back to the workbench and put his hips exactly where they had been before. I could have taken him then. We were alone. He didn't know who I was. He looked at me lightly and threw his cigarette on the cement floor and stamped on it without looking down.

"I bet you could use a drink," he said. "Wet the inside and even up." He reached a bottle from the workbench behind him and set it on the edge and set two glasses beside it. He poured a stiff jolt into each and held one out.

Walking like a dummy I went over and took it. The memory of the rain was still cold on my face. The smell of hot paint drugged the close air of the garage.

"That Art," the brown man said. "He's like all mechanics. Always got his face in a job he ought to have done last week. Business trip?"

I sniffed my drink delicately. It had the right smell. I watched him drink some of his before I swallowed mine. I rolled it around on my tongue. There was no cyanide in it. I emptied the little glass and put it down beside him and moved away.

"Partly," I said. I walked over to the half-painted sedan with the big metal paint gun lying along its fender. The rain hit the flat roof hard. Art was out in it, cursing.

The brown man looked at the big car. "Just a panel job, to start with," he said casually, his purring voice still softer from the drink. "But the guy had dough and his driver needed a few bucks. You know the racket."

I said: "There's only one that's older." My lips felt dry. I didn't want to talk. I lit a cigarette. I wanted my tires fixed. The minutes passed on tiptoe. The brown man and I were two strangers chance-met, looking at each other across a little dead man named Harry Jones. Only the brown man didn't know that yet.

Feet crunched outside and the door was pushed open. The light hit pencils of rain and made silver wires of them. Art trundled two muddy flats in sullenly, kicked the door shut, let one of the flats fall over on its side. He looked at me savagely.

"You sure pick spots for a jack to stand on," he snarled.

The brown man laughed and took a rolled cylinder of nickels out of his pocket and tossed it up and down on the palm of his hand.

"Don't crab so much," he said dryly. "Fix those flats."

"I'm fixin' them, ain't I?"

"Well, don't make a song about it."

"Yah!" Art peeled his rubber coat and sou'wester off and threw them away from him. He heaved one tire up on a spreader and tore the rim loose viciously. He had the tube out and cold-patched in nothing flat. Still scowling, he strode over to the wall beside me and grabbed an air hose, put enough air into the tube to give it body and let the nozzle of the air hose smack against the whitewashed wall.

I stood watching the roll of wrapped coins dance in Canino's hand. The moment of crouched intensity had left me. I turned my head and watched the gaunt mechanic beside me toss the air-stiffened tube up and catch it with his hands wide, one on each side of the tube. He looked it over sourly, glanced at a big galvanized tub of dirty water in the corner and grunted.

The teamwork must have been very nice. I saw no signal, no glance of meaning, no gesture that might have a special import. The gaunt man had the stiffened tube high in the air, staring at it. He half turned his body, took one long quick step, and slammed it down over my head and shoulders, a perfect ringer.

He jumped behind me and leaned hard on the rubber. His weight dragged on my chest, pinned my upper arms tight to my sides. I could move my hands, but I couldn't reach the gun in my pocket.

The brown man came almost dancing towards me across the floor. His hand tightened over the roll of nickels. He came up to me without sound, without expression. I bent forward and tried to heave Art off his feet.

The fist with the weighted tube inside it went through my spread hands like a stone through a cloud of dust. I had the stunned moment of shock when the lights danced and the visible world went out of focus but was still there. He hit me again. There was no sensation in my head. The bright glare got brighter. There was nothing but hard aching white light. Then there was darkness in which something red wriggled like a germ under a microscope. Then there was nothing bright or wriggling, just darkness and emptiness and a rushing wind and a falling as of great trees.

28

IT SEEMED THERE was a woman and she was sitting near a lamp, which was where she belonged, in a good light. Another light shone hard on my face, so I closed my eyes again and tried to look at her through the lashes. She was so platinumed that her hair shone like a silver fruit bowl. She wore a green knitted dress with a broad white collar turned over it. There was a sharp-angled glossy bag at her feet. She was smoking and a glass of amber fluid was tall and pale at her elbow.

I moved my head a little, carefully. It hurt, but not more than I expected. I was trussed like a turkey ready for the oven. Handcuffs held my wrists behind me and a rope went from them to my ankles and then over the end of the brown davenport on which I was sprawled. The rope dropped out of sight over the davenport. I moved enough to make sure it was tied down.

I stopped these furtive movements and opened my eyes again and said: "Hello."

The woman withdrew her gaze from some distant mountain

peak. Her small firm chin turned slowly. Her eyes were the blue of mountain lakes. Overhead the rain still pounded, with a remote sound, as if it was somebody else's rain.

"How do you feel?" It was a smooth silvery voice that matched her hair. It had a tiny tinkle in it, like bells in a doll's house. I thought that was silly as soon as I thought of it.

"Great," I said. "Somebody built a filling station on my jaw."

"What did you expect, Mr. Marlowe – orchids?"

"Just a plain pine box," I said. "Don't bother with bronze or silver handles. And don't scatter my ashes over the blue Pacific. I like the worms better. Did you know that worms are of both sexes and that any worm can love any other worm?"

"You're a little light-headed," she said, with a grave stare.

"Would you mind moving this light?"

She got up and went behind the davenport. The light went off. The dimness was a benison.

"I don't think you're so dangerous," she said. She was tall rather than short, but no bean-pole. She was slim, but not a dried crust. She went back to her chair.

"So you know my name."

"You slept well. They had plenty of time to go through your pockets. They did everything but embalm you. So you're a detective."

"Is that all they have on me?"

She was silent. Smoke floated dimly from the cigarette. She moved it in the air. Her hand was small and had shape, not the usual bony garden tool you see on women nowadays.

"What time is it?" I asked.

She looked sideways at her wrist, beyond the spiral of smoke, at the edge of the grave luster of the lamplight. "Ten-seventeen. You have a date?"

"I wouldn't be surprised. Is this the house next to Art Huck's garage?"

"Yes."

"What are the boys doing – digging a grave?"

"They had to go somewhere."

"You mean they left you here alone?"

Her head turned slowly again. She smiled. "You don't look dangerous."

"I thought they were keeping you a prisoner."

It didn't seem to startle her. It even slightly amused her. "What made you think that?"

"I know who you are."

Her very blue eyes flashed so sharply that I could almost see the sweep of their glance, like the sweep of a sword. Her mouth tightened. But her voice didn't change.

"Then I'm afraid you're in a bad spot. And I hate killing."

"And you Eddie Mars' wife? Shame on you."

She didn't like that. She glared at me. I grinned. "Unless you can unlock these bracelets, which I'd advise you not to do, you might spare me a little of that drink you're neglecting."

She brought the glass over. Bubbles rose in it like false hopes. She bent over me. Her breath was as delicate as the eyes of a fawn. I gulped from the glass. She took it away from my mouth and watched some of the liquid run down my neck.

She bent over me again. Blood began to move around in me, like a prospective tenant looking over a house.

"Your face looks like a collision mat," she said.

"Make the most of it. It won't last long even this good."

She swung her head sharply and listened. For an instant her face was pale. The sounds were only the rain drifting against the walls. She went back across the room and stood with her side to me, bent forward a little, looking down at the floor.

"Why did you come here and stick your neck out?" she asked quietly. "Eddie wasn't doing you any harm. You know perfectly well that if I hadn't hid out here, the police would have been certain Eddie murdered Rusty Regan."

"He did," I said.

She didn't move, didn't change position an inch. Her breath made a harsh quick sound. I looked around the room.

Two doors, both in the same wall, one half open. A carpet of red and tan squares, blue curtains at the windows, a wallpaper with bright green pine trees on it. The furniture looked as if it had come from one of those places that advertise on bus benches. Gay, but full of resistance.

She said softly: "Eddie didn't do anything to him. I haven't seen Rusty in months. Eddie's not that sort of man."

"You left his bed and board. You were living alone. People at the place where you lived identified Regan's photo."

"That's a lie," she said coldly.

I tried to remember whether Captain Gregory had said that or not. My head was too fuzzy. I couldn't be sure.

"And it's none of your business," she added.

"The whole thing is my business. I'm hired to find out."

"Eddie's not that sort of man."

"Oh, you like racketeers."

"As long as people will gamble there will be places for them to gamble."

"That's just protective thinking. Once outside the law you're all the way outside. You think he's just a gambler. I think he's a pornographer, a blackmailer, a hot car broker, a killer by remote control, and a suborner of crooked cops. He's whatever looks good to him, whatever has the cabbage pinned to it. Don't try to sell me on any high-souled racketeers. They don't come in that pattern."

"He's not a killer." Her nostrils flared.

"Not personally. He has Canino. Canino killed a man tonight, a harmless little guy who was trying to help somebody out. I almost saw him killed."

She laughed wearily.

"All right," I growled. "Don't believe it. If Eddie is such a nice guy, I'd like to get to talk to him without Canino around. You know what Canino will do — beat my teeth out and then kick me in the stomach for mumbling."

She put her head back and stood there thoughtful and withdrawn, thinking something out.

"I thought platinum hair was out of style," I bored on, just to keep sound alive in the room, just to keep from listening.

"It's a wig, silly. While mine grows out." She reached up and yanked it off. Her own hair was clipped short all over, like a boy's. She put the wig back on.

"Who did that to you?"

She looked surprised. "I had it done. Why?"

"Yes. Why?"

"Why, to show Eddie I was willing to do what he wanted me to do – hide out. That he didn't need to have me guarded. I wouldn't let him down. I love him."

"Good grief," I groaned. "And you have me right here in the room with you."

She turned a hand over and stared at it. Then abruptly she walked out of the room. She came back with a kitchen knife. She bent and sawed at my rope.

"Canino has the key to the handcuffs," she breathed. "I can't do anything about those."

She stepped back, breathing rapidly. She had cut the rope at every knot.

"You're a kick," she said. "Kidding with every breath – the spot you're in."

"I thought Eddie wasn't a killer."

She turned away quickly and went back to her chair by the lamp and sat down and put her face in her hands. I swung my feet to the floor and stood up. I tottered around, stiff-legged. The nerve on the left side of my face was jumping in all its branches. I took a step. I could still walk. I could run, if I had to.

"I guess you mean me to go," I said.

She nodded without lifting her head.

"You'd better go with me – if you want to keep on living."

"Don't waste time. He'll be back any minute."

"Light a cigarette for me."

I stood beside her, touching her knees. She came to her feet with a sudden lurch. Our eyes were only inches apart.

"Hello, Silver-Wig," I said softly.

She stepped back, around the chair, and swept a package of cigarettes up off the table. She jabbed one loose and pushed it roughly into my mouth. Her hand was shaking. She snapped a small green leather lighter and held it to the cigarette. I drew in the smoke, staring into her lake-blue eyes. While she was still close to me I said:

"A little bird named Harry Jones led me to you. A little bird that used to hop in and out of cocktail bars picking up horse bets for crumbs. Picking up information too. This little bird picked up an idea about Canino. One way and another he and his friends found out where you were. He came to me to sell the information because he knew – how he knew is a long story – that I was working for General Sternwood. I got his information, but Canino got the little bird. He's a dead little bird now, with his feathers ruffled and his neck limp and a pearl of blood on his beak. Canino killed him. But Eddie Mars wouldn't do that, would he, Silver-Wig? He never killed anybody. He just hires it done."

"Get out," she said harshly. "Get out of here quick."

Her hand clutched in midair on the green lighter. The fingers strained. The knuckles were as white as snow.

"But Canino doesn't know I know that," I said. "About the little bird. All he knows is I'm nosing around."

Then she laughed. It was almost a racking laugh. It shook her as the wind shakes a tree. I thought there was puzzlement in it, not exactly surprise, but as if a new idea had been added to something already known and it didn't fit. Then I thought that was too much to get out of a laugh.

"It's very funny," she said breathlessly. "Very funny, because, you see – I still love him. Women –" She began to laugh again.

I listened hard, my head throbbing. Just the rain still. "Let's go," I said. "Fast."

She took two steps back and her face set hard. "Get out, you! Get out! You can walk to Realito. You can make it – and you can keep your mouth shut – for an hour or two at least. You owe me that much."

"Let's go," I said. "Got a gun, Silver-Wig?"

"You know I'm not going. You know that. Please, please get out of here quickly."

I stepped up close to her, almost pressing against her. "You're going to stay here after turning me loose? Wait for that killer to come back so you can say so sorry? A man who kills like swatting a fly. Not much. You're going with me, Silver-Wig."

"No."

"Suppose," I said thinly, "your handsome husband *did* kill Regan? Or suppose Canino did, without Eddie's knowing it. Just suppose. How long will *you* last, after turning me loose?"

"I'm not afraid of Canino. I'm still his boss's wife."

"Eddie's a handful of mush," I snarled. "Canino would take him with a teaspoon. He'll take him the way the cat took the canary. A handful of mush. The only time a girl like you goes for a wrong gee is when he's a handful of mush."

"Get out!" she almost spit at me.

"Okay." I turned away from her and moved out through the half-open door into a dark hallway. Then she rushed after me and pushed past to the front door and opened it. She peered out into the wet blackness and listened. She motioned me forward.

"Good-bye," she said under her breath. "Good luck in everything but one thing. Eddie didn't kill Rusty Regan. You'll find him alive and well somewhere, when he wants to be found."

I leaned against her and pressed her against the wall with my body. I pushed my mouth against her face. I talked to her that way.

"There's no hurry. All this was arranged in advance, rehearsed to the last detail, timed to the split second. Just like a radio program. No hurry at all. Kiss me, Silver-Wig."

Her face under my mouth was like ice. She put her hands up and took hold of my head and kissed me hard on the lips. Her lips were like ice, too.

I went out through the door and it closed behind me, without sound, and the rain blew in under the porch, not as cold as her lips.

29

THE GARAGE NEXT door was dark. I crossed the gravel drive and a patch of sodden lawn. The road ran with small rivulets of water. It gurgled down a ditch on the far side. I had no hat. That must have fallen in the garage. Canino hadn't bothered to give it back to me. He hadn't thought I would need it any more. I imagined him driving back jauntily through the rain, alone, having left the gaunt and sulky Art and the probably stolen sedan in a safe place. She loved Eddie Mars and she was hiding to protect him. So he would find her there when he came back, calm beside the light and the untasted drink, and me tied up on the davenport. He would carry her stuff out to the car and go through the house carefully to make sure nothing incriminating was left. He would tell her to go out and wait. She wouldn't hear a shot. A blackjack is just as effective at short range. He would tell her he had left me tied up and I would get loose after a while. He would think she was that dumb. Nice Mr. Canino.

The raincoat was open in front and I couldn't button it, being handcuffed. The skirts flapped against my legs like the wings of a large and tired bird. I came to the highway. Cars went by in a wide swirl of water illuminated by headlights. The tearing noise of their tires died swiftly. I found my convertible where I had left it, both tires fixed and mounted, so it could be driven away, if necessary. They thought of everything. I got into it and leaned down sideways under the wheel and fumbled aside the flap of leather that covered the pocket.

I got the other gun, stuffed it up under my coat and started back. The world was small, shut in, black. A private world for Canino and me.

Halfway there the headlights nearly caught me. They turned swiftly off the highway and I slid down the bank into the wet ditch and flopped there breathing water. The car hummed by without slowing. I lifted my head, heard the rasp of its tires as it left the road and took the gravel of the drive-way. The motor died, the lights died, a door slammed. I didn't hear the house door shut, but a fringe of light trickled through the clump of trees, as though a shade had been moved aside from a window, or the light had been put on in the hall.

I came back to the soggy grass plot and sloshed across it. The car was between me and the house, the gun was down at my side, pulled as far around as I could get it, without pulling my left arm out by the roots. The car was dark, empty, warm. Water gurgled pleasantly in the radiator. I peered in at the door. The keys hung on the dash. Canino was very sure of himself. I went around the car and walked carefully across the gravel to the window and listened. I couldn't hear any voices, any sound but the swift bong-bong of the raindrops hitting the metal elbows at the bottom of the rain gutters.

I kept on listening. No loud voices, everything quiet and refined. He would be purring at her and she would be telling him she had let me go and I had promised to let them get away. He wouldn't believe me, as I wouldn't believe him. So he wouldn't be in there long. He would be on his way and take her with him. All I had to do was wait for him to come out.

I couldn't do it. I shifted the gun to my left hand and leaned down to scoop up a handful of gravel. I tossed it against the screen of the window. It was a feeble effort. Very little of it reached the glass above the screen, but the loose rattle of that little was like a dam bursting.

I ran back to the car and got on the running board behind it. The house had already gone dark. That was all. I dropped quietly on the running board and waited. No soap. Canino was too cagey.

I straightened up and got into the car backwards, fumbled around for the ignition key and turned it. I reached with my foot, but the starter button had to be on the dash. I found it at last, pulled it and the starter ground. The warm motor caught at once. It purred softly, contentedly. I got out of the car again and crouched down by the rear wheels.

I was shivering now but I knew Canino wouldn't like that last effect. He needed that car badly. A darkened window slid down inch by inch, only some shifting of light on the glass showing it moved. Flame spouted from it abruptly, the blended roar of three swift shots. Glass starred in the coupe. I yelled with agony. The yell went off into a wailing groan. The groan became a wet gurgle, choked with blood. I let the gurgle die sickeningly, one choked gasp. It was nice work. I liked it. Canino liked it very much. I heard him laugh. It was a large booming laugh, not at all like the purr of his speaking voice.

Then silence for a little while, except for the rain and the quietly throbbing motor of the car. Then the house door crawled open, a deeper blackness in the black night. A figure showed in it cautiously, something white around the neck. It was her collar. She came out on the porch stiffly, a wooden woman. I caught the pale shine of her silver wig. Canino came crouched methodically behind her. It was so deadly it was almost funny.

She came down the steps. Now I could see the white stiffness of her face. She started towards the car. A bulwark of defense for Canino, in case I could still spit in his eye. Her voice spoke through the lisp of the rain, saying slowly, without any tone: "I can't see a thing, Lash. The windows are misted."

He grunted something and the girl's body jerked hard, as though he had jammed a gun into her back. She came on again and drew near the lightless car. I could see him behind her now, his hat, a side of his face, the bulk of his shoulder. The girl stopped rigid and screamed. A beautiful thin tearing scream that rocked me like a left hook.

"I can see him!" she screamed. "Through the window. Behind the wheel, Lash!"

He fell for it like a bucket of lead. He knocked her roughly to one side and jumped forward, throwing his hand up. Three more spurts of flame cut the darkness. More glass scarred. One bullet went on through and smacked into a tree on my side. A ricochet whined off into the distance. But the motor went quietly on.

He was low down, crouched against the gloom, his face a grayness without form that seemed to come back slowly after the glare of the shots. If it was a revolver he had, it might be empty. It might not. He had fired six times, but he might have reloaded inside the house. I hoped he had. I didn't want him with an empty gun. But it might be an automatic.

I said: "Finished?"

He whirled at me. Perhaps it would have been nice to allow him another shot or two, just like a gentleman of the old school. But his gun was still up and I couldn't wait any longer. Not long enough to be a gentleman of the old school. I shot him four times, the Colt straining against my ribs. The gun jumped out of his hand as if it had been kicked. He reached both his hands for his stomach. I could hear them smack hard against his body. He fell like that, straight forward, holding himself together with his broad hands. He fell face down in the wet gravel. And after that there wasn't a sound from him.

Silver-Wig didn't make a sound either. She stood rigid, with the rain swirling at her. I walked around Canino and kicked his gun, without any purpose. Then I walked after it and bent over sideways and picked it up. That put me close beside her. She spoke moodily, as if she was talking to herself.

"I — I was afraid you'd come back."

I said: "We had a date. I told you it was all arranged." I began to laugh like a loon.

Then she was bending down over him, touching him. And after a little while she stood up with a small key on a thin chain.

She said bitterly: "Did you have to kill him?"

I stopped laughing as suddenly as I had started. She went behind me and unlocked the handcuffs.

"Yes," she said softly. "I suppose you did."

30

THIS WAS ANOTHER day and the sun was shining again.

Captain Gregory of the Missing Persons Bureau looked heavily out of his office window at the barred upper floor of the Hall of Justice, white and clean after the rain. Then he turned ponderously in his swivel chair and tamped his pipe with a heat-scarred thumb and stared at me bleakly.

"So you got yourself in another jam."

"Oh, you heard about it."

"Brother, I sit here all day on my fanny and I don't look as if I had a brain in my head. But you'd be surprised what I hear. Shooting this Canino was all right I guess, but I don't figure the homicide boys pinned any medals on you."

"There's been a lot of killing going on around me," I said. "I haven't been getting my share of it."

He smiled patiently. "Who told you this girl out there was Eddie Mars' wife?"

I told him. He listened carefully and yawned. He tapped his gold-studded mouth with a palm like a tray. "I guess you figure I ought to of found her."

"That's a fair deduction."

"Maybe I knew," he said. "Maybe I thought if Eddie and his woman wanted to play a little game like that, it would be smart – or as smart as I ever get – to let them think they were getting away with it. And then again maybe you think I was letting Eddie get away with it for more personal reasons." He held his big hand out and revolved the thumb against the index and second fingers.

"No," I said. "I didn't really think that. Not even when Eddie seemed to know all about our talk here the other day."

He raised his eyebrows as if raising them was an effort, a trick he was out of practice on. It furrowed his whole forehead and when it smoothed out it was full of white lines that turned reddish as I watched them.

"I'm a copper," he said. "Just a plain ordinary copper. Reasonably honest. As honest as you could expect a man to be in a world where it's out of style. That's mainly why I asked you to come in this morning. I'd like you to believe that. Being a copper I like to see the law win. I'd like to see the flashy well-dressed mugs like Eddie Mars spoiling their manicures in the rock quarry at Folsom, alongside of the poor little slum-bred hard guys that got knocked over on their first caper and never had a break since. That's what I'd like. You and me both lived too long to think I'm likely to see it happen. Not in this town, not in any town half this size, in any part of this wide, green and beautiful U.S.A. We just don't run our country that way."

I didn't say anything. He blew smoke with a backward jerk of his head, looked at the mouthpiece of his pipe and went on:

"But that don't mean I think Eddie Mars bumped off Regan or had any reason to or would have done it if he had. I just figured maybe he knows something about it, and maybe sooner or later something will sneak out into the open. Hiding his wife out at Realito was childish, but it's the kind of childishness a smart monkey thinks is smart. I had him in here last night, after the D.A. got through with him. He admitted the whole thing. He said he knew Canino as a reliable protection guy and that's what he had him for. He didn't know anything about his hobbies or want to. He didn't know Harry Jones. He didn't know Joe Brody. He did know Geiger, of course, but claims he didn't know about his racket. I guess you heard all that."

"Yes."

"You played it smart down there at Realito, brother. Not trying to cover up. We keep a file on unidentified bullets nowadays. Someday you might use that gun again. Then you'd be over a barrel."

"I played it smart," I said, and leered at him.

He knocked his pipe out and stared down at it broodingly. "What happened to the girl?" he asked, not looking up.

"I don't know. They didn't hold her. We made statements, three sets of them, for Wilde, for the Sheriff's office, for the Homicide Bureau. They turned her loose. I haven't seen her since. I don't expect to."

"Kind of a nice girl, they say. Wouldn't be one to play dirty games."

"Kind of a nice girl," I said.

Captain Gregory sighed and rumpled his mousy hair. "There's just one more thing," he said almost gently. "You look like a nice guy, but you play too rough. If you really want to help the Sternwood family – leave 'em alone."

"I think you're right, Captain."

"How do you feel?"

"Swell," I said. "I was standing on various pieces of carpet most of the night, being balled out. Before that I got soaked to the skin and beaten up. I'm in perfect condition."

"What the hell did you expect, brother?"

"Nothing else." I stood up and grinned at him and started for the door. When I had almost reached it he cleared his throat suddenly and said in a harsh voice: "I'm wasting my breath, huh? You still think you can find Regan."

I turned around and looked him straight in the eyes. "No, I don't think I can find Regan. I'm not even going to try. Does that suit you?"

He nodded slowly. Then he shrugged. "I don't know what the hell I even said that for. Good luck, Marlowe. Drop around any time."

"Thanks, Captain."

I went down out of the City Hall and got my car from the parking lot and drove home to the Hobart Arms. I lay down on the bed with my coat off and stared at the ceiling and listened to the traffic sounds on the street outside and watched the sun move slowly across a corner of the ceiling. I tried to go to sleep, but sleep didn't come. I got up and took a drink, although it was the wrong time of day, and lay down again. I still couldn't go to sleep. My brain ticked like a clock. I sat up on the side of the bed and stuffed a pipe and said out loud:

"That old buzzard knows something."

The pipe tasted as bitter as lye. I put it aside and lay down again. My mind drifted through waves of false memory, in which I seemed to do the same thing over and over again, go to the same places, meet the same people, say the same words to them, over and over again, and yet each time it seemed real, like something actually happening, and for the first time. I was driving hard along the highway through the rain, with Silver-Wig in the corner of the car, saying nothing, so that by the time we reached Los Angeles we seemed to be utter strangers again. I was getting out at an all night drugstore and phoning Bernie Ohls that I had killed a man at Realito and was on my way over to Wilde's house with Eddie Mars' wife, who had seen me do it. I was pushing the car along the silent, rain-polished streets to Lafayette Park and up under the porte-cochere of Wilde's big frame house and the porch light was already on, Ohls having telephoned ahead that I was coming. I was in Wilde's study and he was behind his desk in a flowered dressing-gown and a tight hard face and a dappled cigar moved in his fingers and up to the bitter smile on his lips. Ohls was there and a slim gray scholarly man from the Sheriff's office who looked and talked more like a professor of economics than a cop. I was telling the story and they were listening quietly and Silver-Wig sat in a shadow with her hands folded in her lap, looking at nobody. There was a lot of telephoning. There were two men from the Homicide Bureau who looked at me as if I was some kind of strange beast escaped from a traveling circus. I was driving again, with one of them beside me, to the Fulwider Building. We were there in the room where Harry Jones was still in the chair behind the desk, the twisted stiffness of his dead face and the sour-sweet smell in the room. There was a medical examiner, very young and husky, with red bristles on his neck. There was a finger-print man fussing around and I was telling him not to forget the latch of the transom. (He found Canino's thumb print on it, the only print the brown man had left to back up my story.)

I was back again at Wilde's house, signing a typewritten statement his secretary had run off in another room. Then the door opened and Eddie Mars came in and an abrupt smile flashed to his face when he saw Silver-Wig, and he said: "Hello, sugar," and she didn't look at him or answer him. Eddie Mars fresh and cheerful, in a dark business suit, with a fringed white scarf hanging outside his tweed overcoat. Then they were gone, everybody was gone out of the room but myself and Wilde, and Wilde was saying in a cold, angry voice: "This is the last time, Marlowe. The next fast one you pull I'll throw you to the lions, no matter whose heart it breaks."

It was like that, over and over again, lying on the bed and watching the patch of sunlight slide down the corner of the wall. Then the phone rang, and it was Norris, the Sternwood butler, with his usual untouchable voice.

"Mr. Marlowe? I telephoned your office without success, so I took the liberty of trying to reach you at home."

"I was out most of the night," I said. "I haven't been down."

"Yes, sir. The General would like to see you this morning, Mr. Marlowe, if it's convenient."

"Half an hour or so," I said. "How is he?"

"He's in bed, sir, but not doing badly."

"Wait till he sees me," I said, and hung up.

I shaved, changed clothes and started for the door. Then I went back and got Carmen's little pearl-handled revolver and dropped it into my pocket. The sunlight was so bright that it danced. I got to the Sternwood place in twenty minutes and drove up under the arch at the side door. It was eleven-fifteen. The birds in the ornamental trees were crazy with song after the rain, the terraced lawns were as green as the Irish flag, and the whole estate looked as though it had been made about ten minutes before. I rang the bell. It was five days since I had rung it for the first time. It felt like a year.

A maid opened the door and led me along a side hall to the main hallway and left me there, saying Mr. Norris would be down in a moment. The main hallway looked just the same. The portrait over the mantel had the same hot black eyes and the knight in the stained-glass window still wasn't getting anywhere untying the naked damsel from the tree.

In a few minutes Norris appeared, and he hadn't changed either. His acid-blue eyes were as remote as ever, his grayish-pink skin looked healthy and rested, and he moved as if he was twenty years younger than he really was. I was the one who felt the weight of the years.

We went up the tiled staircase and turned the opposite way from Vivian's room. With each step the house seemed to grow larger and more silent. We reached a massive old door that looked as if it had come out of a church. Norris opened it softly and looked in. Then he stood aside and I went in past him across what seemed to be about a quarter of a mile of carpet to a huge canopied bed like the one Henry the Eighth died in.

General Sternwood was propped up on pillows. His bloodless hands were clasped on top of the sheet. They looked gray against it. His black eyes were still full of fight and the rest of his face still looked like the face of a corpse.

"Sit down, Mr. Marlowe." His voice sounded weary and a little stiff.

I pulled a chair close to him and sat down. All the windows were shut tight. The room was sunless at that hour. Awnings cut off what glare there might be from the sky. The air had the faint sweetish smell of old age.

He stared at me silently for a long minute. He moved a hand, as if to prove to himself that he could still move it, then folded it back over the other. He said lifelessly:

"I didn't ask you to look for my son-in-law, Mr. Marlowe."

"You wanted me to, though."

"I didn't ask you to. You assume a great deal. I usually ask for what I want."

I didn't say anything.

"You have been paid," he went on coldly. "The money is of no consequence one way or the other. I merely feel that you have, no doubt unintentionally, betrayed a trust."

He closed his eyes on that. I said: "Is that all you wanted to see me about?"

He opened his eyes again, very slowly, as though the lids were made of lead. "I suppose you are angry at that remark," he said.

I shook my head. "You have an advantage over me, General. It's an advantage I wouldn't want to take away from you, not a hair of it. It's not much, considering what you have to put up with. You can say anything you like to me and I wouldn't think of getting angry. I'd like to offer you your money back. It may mean nothing to you. It might mean something to me."

"What does it mean to you?"

"It means I have refused payment for an unsatisfactory job. That's all."

"Do you do many unsatisfactory jobs?"

"A few. Everyone does."

"Why did you go to see Captain Gregory?"

I leaned back and hung an arm over the back of the chair. I studied his face. It told me nothing. I didn't know the answer to his question – no satisfactory answer.

I said: "I was convinced you put those Geiger notes up to me chiefly as a test, and that you were a little afraid Regan might somehow be involved in an attempt to blackmail you. I didn't know anything about Regan then. It wasn't until I talked to Captain Gregory that I realized Regan wasn't that sort of guy in all probability."

"That is scarcely answering my question."

I nodded. "No. That is scarcely answering your question. I guess I just don't like to admit that I played a hunch. The morning I was here, after I left you out in the orchid house, Mrs. Regan sent for me. She seemed to assume I was hired to look for her husband and she didn't seem to like it. She let drop however that 'they' had found his car in a certain garage. The 'they' could only be the police. Consequently the police must know something about it. If they did, the Missing Persons Bureau would be the department that would have the case. I didn't know whether you had reported it, of course, or somebody else, or whether they had found the car through somebody reporting it abandoned in a garage. But I know cops, and I knew that if they got that much, they would get a little more – especially as your driver happened to have a police record. I didn't know how much more they would get. That started me thinking about the Missing Persons Bureau. What convinced me was something in Mr. Wilde's manner the night we had the conference over at his house about Geiger and so on. We were alone for a minute and he asked me whether you had told me you were looking for Regan. I said you had told me you wished you knew where he was and that he was all right. Wilde pulled his lip in and looked funny. I knew just as plainly as though he had said it that by 'looking for Regan' he meant using the machinery of the law to look for him. Even then I tried to go up against Captain

Gregory in such a way that I wouldn't tell him anything he didn't know already."

"And you allowed Captain Gregory to think I had employed you to find Rusty?"

"Yeah. I guess I did – when I was sure he had the case."

He closed his eyes. They twitched a little. He spoke with them closed. "And do you consider that ethical?"

"Yes," I said. "I do."

The eyes opened again. The piercing blackness of them was startling coming suddenly out of that dead face. "Perhaps I don't understand," he said.

"Maybe you don't. The head of a Missing Persons Bureau isn't a talker. He wouldn't be in that office if he was. This one is a very smart cagey guy who tries, with a lot of success at first, to give the impression he's a middle-aged hack fed up with his job. The game I play is not spillikins. There's always a large element of bluff connected with it. Whatever I might say to a cop, he would be apt to discount it. And to *that* cop it wouldn't make much difference what I said. When you hire a boy in my line of work it isn't like hiring a window-washer and showing him eight windows and saying: 'Wash those and you're through.' *You* don't know what I have to go through or over or under to do your job for you. I do it my way. I do my best to protect you and I may break a few rules, but I break them in your favor. The client comes first, unless he's crooked. Even then all I do is hand the job back to him and keep my mouth shut. After all you didn't tell me *not* to go to Captain Gregory."

"That would have been rather difficult," he said with a faint smile.

"Well, what have I done wrong? Your man Norris seemed to think when Geiger was eliminated the case was over. I don't see it that way. Geiger's method of approach puzzled me and still does. I'm not Sherlock Holmes or Philo Vance. I don't expect to go over ground the police have covered and pick up a broken pen point and build a case from it. If you think there is anybody in the detective business making a living doing that sort of thing, you don't know much about cops. It's not things like that they overlook, if they overlook anything. I'm not saying they often overlook anything when they're really allowed to work. But if they do, it's apt to be something looser and vaguer, like a man of Geiger's type sending you his evidence of debt and asking you to pay like a gentleman – Geiger, a man in a shady racket, in a vulnerable position, protected by a racketeer and having at least some negative protection from some of the police. Why did he do that? Because he wanted to find out if there was anything putting pressure on you. If there was, you would pay him. If not, you would ignore him and wait for his next move. But there was something putting a pressure on you. Regan. You were afraid he was not what he had appeared to be, that he had stayed around and been nice to you just long enough to find out how to play games with your bank account."

He started to say something but I interrupted him. "Even at that it wasn't your money you cared about. It wasn't even your daughters. You've more or less written them off. It's that you're still too proud to be played for a sucker – and you really liked Regan."

There was a silence. Then the General said quietly: "You talk too damn much, Marlowe. Am I to understand you are still trying to solve that puzzle?"

"No. I've quit. I've been warned off. The boys think I play too rough. That's why I thought I should give you back your money – because it isn't a completed job by my standards."

He smiled. "Quit, nothing," he said. "I'll pay you another thousand dollars to find Rusty. He doesn't have to come back. I don't even have to know where he is. A man has a right to live his own life. I don't blame him for walking out on my daughter, nor even for going so abruptly. It was probably a sudden impulse. I want to know that he is all right wherever he is. I want to know it from him directly, and if he should happen to need money, I should want him to have that also. Am I clear?"

I said: "Yes, General."

He rested a little while, lax on the bed, his eyes closed and dark-lidded, his mouth tight and bloodless. He was used up. He was pretty nearly licked. He opened his eyes again and tried to grin at me.

"I guess I'm a sentimental old goat," he said. "And no soldier at all. I took a fancy to that boy. He seemed pretty clean to me. I must be a little too vain about my judgment of character. Find him for me, Marlowe. Just find him."

"I'll try," I said. "You'd better rest now. I've talked your arm off."

I got up quickly and walked across the wide floor and out. He had his eyes shut again before I opened the door. His hands lay limp on the sheet. He looked a lot more like a dead man than most dead men look. I shut the door quietly and went back along the upper hall and down the stairs.

31

THE BUTLER APPEARED with my hat. I put it on and said: "What do you think of him?"

"He's not as weak as he looks, sir."

"If he was, he'd be ready for burial. What did this Regan fellow have that bored into him so?"

The butler looked at me levelly and yet with a queer lack of expression. "Youth, sir," he said. "And the soldier's eye."

"Like yours," I said.

"If I may say so, sir, not unlike yours."

"Thanks. How are the ladies this morning?"

He shrugged politely.

"Just what I thought," I said, and he opened the door for me.

I stood outside on the step and looked down the vistas of grassed terraces and trimmed trees and flowerbeds to the tall metal railing at the bottom of the gardens. I saw Carmen about halfway down, sitting on a stone bench, with her head between her hands, looking forlorn and alone.

I went down the red brick steps that led from terrace to terrace. I was quite close before she heard me. She jumped up and whirled like a cat. She wore the light blue slacks she had worn the first time I saw her. Her blond hair was the same loose tawny wave. Her face was white. Red spots flared in her cheeks as she looked at me. Her eyes were slaty.

"Bored?" I said.

She smiled slowly, rather shyly, then nodded quickly. Then she whispered: "You're not mad at me?"

"I thought you were mad at me."

She put her thumb up and giggled. "I'm not." When she giggled I didn't like her any more. I looked around. A target hung on a tree about thirty feet away, with some darts sticking to it. There were three or four more on the stone bench where she had been sitting.

"For people with money you and your sister don't seem to have much fun," I said.

She looked at me under her long lashes. This was the look that was supposed to make me roll over on my back. I said: "You like throwing those darts?"

"Uh-huh."

"That reminds me of something." I looked back towards the house. By moving about three feet I made a tree hide me from it. I took her little pearl-handled gun out of my pocket. "I brought you back your artillery. I cleaned it and loaded it up. Take my tip – don't shoot it at people, unless you get to be a better shot. Remember?"

Her face went paler and her thin thumb dropped. She looked at me, then at the gun I was holding. There was a fascination in her eyes. "Yes," she said, and nodded. Then suddenly: "Teach me to shoot."

"Huh?"

"Teach me how to shoot. I'd like that."

"Here? It's against the law."

She came close to me and took the gun out of my hand, cuddled her hand around the butt. Then she tucked it quickly inside her slacks, almost with a furtive movement, and looked around.

"I know where," she said in a secret voice. "Down by some of the old wells." She pointed off down the hill. "Teach me?"

I looked into her slaty blue eyes. I might as well have looked at a couple of bottle-tops. "All right. Give me back the gun until I see if the place looks all right."

She smiled and made a mouth, then handed it back with a secret naughty air, as if she was giving me a key to her room. We walked up the steps and around to my car. The gardens seemed deserted. The sunshine was as empty as a headwaiter's smile. We got into the car and I drove down the sunken driveway and out through the gates.

"Where's Vivian?" I asked.

"Not up yet." She giggled.

I drove on down the hill through the quiet opulent streets with their faces washed by the rain, bore east to La Brea, then south. We reached the place she meant in about ten minutes.

"In there." She leaned out of the window and pointed.

It was a narrow dirt road, not much more than a track, like the entrance to some foothill ranch. A wide five-barred gate was folded back against a stump and looked as if it hadn't been shut in years. The road was fringed with tall eucalyptus trees and deeply rutted. Trucks had used it. It was empty and sunny now, but not yet dusty. The rain had been too hard and too recent. I followed the ruts along and the noise of city traffic grew curiously and quickly faint, as if this were not in the city at all, but far away in a daydream land. Then the oil-stained, motionless walking-beam of a squat wooden derrick stuck up over a branch. I could see the rusty old steel cable that connected this walking-beam with a half a dozen others. The beams didn't move, probably hadn't moved for a year. The wells were no longer pumping. There was a pile of rusted pipe, a loading platform that sagged at one end, half a dozen empty oil drums lying in a ragged pile. There was the stagnant, oil-scummed water of an old sump iridescent in the sunlight.

"Are they going to make a park of all this?" I asked.

She dipped her chin down and gleamed at me.

"It's about time. The smell of that sump would poison a herd of goats. This the place you had in mind?"

"Uh-huh. Like it?"

"It's beautiful." I pulled up beside the loading platform. We got out. I listened. The hum of the traffic was a distant web of sound, like the buzzing of bees. The place was as lonely as a churchyard. Even after the rain the tall eucalyptus trees still looked dusty. They always look dusty. A branch broken off by the wind had fallen over the edge of the sump and the flat leathery leaves dangled in the water.

I walked around the sump and looked into the pump-house. There was some junk in it, nothing that looked like recent activity. Outside a big wooden bull wheel was tilted against the wall. It looked like a good place all right.

I went back to the car. The girl stood beside it preening her hair and holding it out in the sun. "Gimme," she said, and held her hand out.

I took the gun out and put it in her palm. I bent down and picked up a rusty can.

"Take it easy now," I said. "It's loaded in all five. I'll go over and set this can in that square opening in the middle of that big wooden wheel. See?" I pointed. She ducked her head, delighted. "That's about thirty feet. Don't start shooting until I get back beside you. Okay?"

"Okay," she giggled.

I went back around the sump and set the can up in the middle of the bull wheel. It made a swell target. If she missed the can, which she was certain to do, she would probably hit the wheel. That would stop a small slug completely. However, she wasn't going to hit even that.

I went back towards her around the sump. When I was about ten feet from her, at the edge of the sump, she showed me all her sharp little teeth and brought the gun up and started to hiss.

I stopped dead, the sump water stagnant and stinking at my back.

"Stand there, you son of a bitch," she said.

The gun pointed at my chest. Her hand seemed to be quite steady. The hissing sound grew louder and her face had the scraped bone look. Aged, deteriorated, become animal, and not a nice animal.

I laughed at her. I started to walk towards her. I saw her small finger tighten on the trigger and grow white at the tip. I was about six feet away from her when she started to shoot.

The sound of the gun made a sharp slap, without body, a brittle crack in the sunlight. I didn't see any smoke. I stopped again and grinned at her.

She fired twice more, very quickly. I don't think any of the shots would have missed. There were five in the little gun. She had fired four. I rushed her.

I didn't want the last one in my face, so I swerved to one side. She gave it to me quite carefully, not worried at all. I think I felt the hot breath of the powder blast a little.

I straightened up. "My, but you're cute," I said.

Her hand holding the empty gun began to shake violently. The gun fell out of it. Her mouth began to shake. Her whole face went to pieces. Then her head screwed up towards her left ear and froth showed on her lips. Her breath made a whining sound. She swayed.

I caught her as she fell. She was already unconscious. I pried her teeth open with both hands and stuffed a wadded handkerchief in between them. It took all my strength to do it. I lifted her up and got her into the car, then went back for the gun and dropped it into my pocket. I climbed in under the wheel, backed the car and drove back the way we had come along the rutted road, out of the gateway, back up the hill and so home.

Carmen lay crumpled in the corner of the car, without motion. I was halfway up the drive to the house before she stirred. Then her eyes suddenly opened wide and wild. She sat up.

"What happened?" she gasped.

"Nothing. Why?"

"Oh, yes it did," she giggled. "I wet myself."

"They always do," I said.

She looked at me with a sudden sick speculation and began to moan.

32

THE GENTLE-EYED, horse-faced maid let me into the long gray and white upstairs sitting room with the ivory drapes tumbled extravagantly on the floor and the white carpet from wall to wall. A screen star's boudoir, a place of charm and seduction, artificial as a wooden leg. It was empty at the moment. The door closed behind me with the unnatural softness of a hospital door. A breakfast table on wheels stood by the chaise-longue. Its silver glittered. There were cigarette ashes in the coffee cup. I sat down and waited.

It seemed a long time before the door opened again and Vivian came in. She was in oyster-white lounging pajamas trimmed with white fur, cut as flowingly as a summer sea frothing on the beach of some small and exclusive island.

She went past me in long smooth strides and sat down on the edge of the chaise-longue. There was a cigarette in her lips, at the corner of her mouth. Her nails today were copper red from quick to tip, without half moons.

"So you're just a brute after all," she said quietly, staring at me. "An utter callous brute. You killed a man last night. Never mind how I heard it. I heard it. And now you have to come out here and frighten my kid sister into a fit."

I didn't say a word. She began to fidget. She moved over to a slipper chair and put her head back against a white cushion that lay along the back of the chair against the wall. She blew pale gray smoke upwards and watched it float towards the ceiling and come apart in wisps that were for a little while distinguishable from the air and then melted and were nothing. Then very slowly she lowered her eyes and gave me a cool hard glance.

"I don't understand you," she said. "I'm thankful as hell one of us kept his head the night before last. It's bad enough to have a bootlegger in my past. Why don't you for Christ's sake say something?"

"How is she?"

"Oh, she's all right, I suppose. Fast asleep. She always goes to sleep. What did you do to her?"

"Not a thing. I came out of the house after seeing your father and she was out in front. She had been throwing darts at a target on a tree. I went down to speak to her because I had something that belonged to her. A little revolver Owen Taylor gave her once. She took it over to Brody's place the other evening, the evening he was killed. I had to take it away from her there. I didn't mention it, so perhaps you didn't know it."

The black Sternwood eyes got large and empty. It was her turn not to say anything.

"She was pleased to get her little gun back and she wanted me to teach her how to shoot and she wanted to show me the old oil wells down the hill where your family made some of its money. So we went down there and the place was pretty creepy, all rusted metal and old wood and silent wells and greasy scummy sumps. Maybe that upset her. I guess you've been there yourself. It was kind of eerie."

"Yes – it is." It was a small breathless voice now.

"So we went in there and I stuck a can up in a bull wheel for her to pop at. She threw a wingding. Looked like a mild epileptic fit to me."

"Yes." The same minute voice. "She has them once in a while. Is that all you wanted to see me about?"

"I guess you still wouldn't tell me what Eddie Mars has on you."

"Nothing at all. And I'm getting a little tired of that question," she said coldly.

"Do you know a man named Canino?"

She drew her fine black brows together in thought. "Vaguely. I seem to remember the name."

"Eddie Mars' trigger man. A tough hombre, they said. I guess he was. Without a little help from a lady I'd be where he is – in the morgue."

"The ladies seem to –" She stopped dead and whitened. "I can't joke about it," she said simply.

"I'm not joking, and if I seem to talk in circles, it just seems that way. It all ties together – everything. Geiger and his cute little blackmail tricks, Brody and his pictures, Eddie Mars and his roulette tables, Canino and the girl Rusty Regan didn't run away with. It all ties together."

"I'm afraid I don't even know what you're talking about."

"Suppose you did – it would be something like this. Geiger got his hooks into your sister, which isn't very difficult, and got some notes from her and tried to blackmail your father with them, in a nice way. Eddie Mars was behind Geiger, protecting him and using him for a cat's-paw. Your father sent for me instead of paying up, which showed he wasn't scared about anything. Eddie Mars wanted to know that. He had something on you and he wanted to know if he had it on the General too. If he had, he could collect a lot of money in a hurry. If not, he would have to wait until you got your share of the family fortune, and in the meantime be satisfied with whatever spare cash he could take away from you across the roulette table. Geiger was killed by Owen Taylor, who was in love with your silly little sister and didn't like the kind of games Geiger played with her. That didn't mean anything to Eddie. He was playing a deeper game than Geiger knew anything about, or than Brody knew anything about, or anybody except you and Eddie and a tough guy named Canino. Your husband disappeared and Eddie, knowing everybody knew there had been bad blood between him and Regan, hid his wife out at Realito and put Canino to guard her, so that it would look as if she had run away with Regan. He even got Regan's car into the garage of the place where Mona Mars had been living. But that sounds a little silly taken merely as an attempt to divert suspicion that Eddie had killed your husband or had him killed. It isn't so silly, really. He had another motive. He was playing for a million or so. He knew where Regan had gone and why and he didn't want the police to have to find out. He wanted them to have an explanation of the disappearance that would keep them satisfied. Am I boring you?"

"You tire me," she said in a dead, exhausted voice. "God, how you tire me!"

"I'm sorry. I'm not just fooling around trying to be clever. Your father offered me a thousand dollars this morning to find Regan. That's a lot of money to me, but I can't do it."

Her mouth jumped open. Her breath was suddenly strained and harsh. "Give me a cigarette," she said thickly. "Why?" The pulse in her throat had begun to throb.

I gave her a cigarette and lit a match and held it for her. She drew in a lungful of smoke and let it out raggedly and then the cigarette seemed to be forgotten between her fingers. She never drew on it again.

"Well, the Missing Persons Bureau can't find him," I said. "It's not so easy. What they can't do it's not likely that I can do."

"Oh." There was a shade of relief in her voice.

"That's one reason. The Missing Persons people think he just disappeared on purpose, pulled down the curtain, as they call it. They don't think Eddie Mars did away with him."

"Who said anybody did away with him?"

"We're coming to it," I said.

For a brief instant her face seemed to come to pieces, to become merely a set of features without form or control. Her mouth looked like the prelude to a scream. But only for an instant. The Sternwood blood had to be good for something more than her black eyes and her recklessness.

I stood up and took the smoking cigarette from between her fingers and killed it in an ashtray. Then I took Carmen's little gun out of my pocket and laid it carefully, with exaggerated care, on her white satin knee. I balanced it there, and stepped back with my head on one side like a window-dresser getting the effect of a new twist of a scarf around a dummy's neck.

I sat down again. She didn't move. Her eyes came down millimeter by millimeter and looked at the gun.

"It's harmless," I said. "All five chambers empty. She fired them all. She fired them all at me."

The pulse jumped wildly in her throat. Her voice tried to say something and couldn't. She swallowed.

"From a distance of five or six feet," I said. "Cute little thing, isn't she? Too bad I had loaded the gun with blanks." I grinned nastily. "I had a hunch about what she would do – if she got the chance."

She brought her voice back from a long way off. "You're a horrible man," she said. "Horrible."

"Yeah. You're her big sister. What are you going to do about it?"

"You can't prove a word of it."

"Can't prove what?"

"That she fired at you. You said you were down there around the wells with her, alone. You can't prove a word of what you say."

"Oh that," I said. "I wasn't thinking of trying. I was thinking of another time – when the shells in the little gun had bullets in them."

Her eyes were pools of darkness, much emptier than darkness.

"I was thinking of the day Regan disappeared," I said. "Late in the afternoon. When he took her down to those old wells to teach her to shoot and put up a can somewhere and told her to pop at it and stood near her while she shot. And she didn't shoot at the can. She turned the gun and shot him, just the way she tried to shoot me today, and for the same reason."

She moved a little and the gun slid off her knee and fell to the floor. It was one of the loudest sounds I ever heard. Her eyes were riveted on my face. Her voice was a stretched whisper of agony. "Carmen! . . . Merciful God, Carmen! . . . Why?"

"Do I really have to tell you why she shot at me?"

"Yes." Her eyes were still terrible. "I'm – I'm afraid you do."

"Night before last when I got home she was in my apartment. She'd kidded the manager into letting her in to wait for me. She was in my bed – naked. I threw her out on her ear. I guess maybe Regan did the same thing to her sometime. But you can't do that to Carmen."

She drew her lips back and made a half-hearted attempt to lick them. It made her, for a brief instant, look like a frightened child. The lines of her cheeks sharpened and her hand went up slowly like an artificial hand worked by wires and its fingers closed slowly and stiffly around the white fur at her collar. They drew the fur tight against her throat. After that she just sat staring.

"Money," she croaked. "I suppose you want money."

"How much money?" I tried not to sneer.

"Fifteen thousand dollars?"

I nodded. "That would be about right. That would be the established fee. That was what he had in his pockets when she

194

shot him. That would be what Mr. Canino got for disposing of the body when you went to Eddie Mars for help. But that would be small change to what Eddie expects to collect one of these days, wouldn't it?"

"You son of a bitch!" she said.

"Uh-huh. I'm a very smart guy. I haven't a feeling or a scruple in the world. All I have the itch for is money. I am so money greedy that for twenty-five bucks a day and expenses, mostly gasoline and whiskey, I do my thinking myself, what there is of it; I risk my whole future, the hatred of the cops and of Eddie Mars and his pals, I dodge bullets and eat saps, and say thank you very much, if you have any more trouble, I hope you'll think of me, I'll just leave one of my cards in case anything comes up. I do all this for twenty-five bucks a day – and maybe just a little to protect what little pride a broken and sick old man has left in his blood, in the thought that his blood is not poison, and that although his two little girls are a trifle wild, as many nice girls are these days, they are not per-verts or killers. And that makes me a son of a bitch. All right. I don't care anything about that. I've been called that by peo-ple of all sizes and shapes, including your little sister. She called me worse than that for not getting into bed with her. I got five hundred dollars from your father, which I didn't ask for, but he can afford to give it to me. I can get another thousand for finding Mr. Rusty Regan, if I could find him. Now you offer me fifteen grand. That makes me a big shot. With fifteen grand I could own a home and a new car and four suits of clothes. I might even take a vacation without worrying about losing a case. That's fine. What are you offering it to me for? Can I go on being a son of a bitch, or do I have to become a gentleman, like that lush that passed out in his car the other night?"

She was as silent as a stone woman.

"All right," I went on heavily. "Will you take her away? Somewhere far off from here where they can handle her type, where they will keep guns and knives and fancy drinks away from her? Hell, she might even get herself cured, you know. It's been done."

She got up and walked slowly to the windows. The drapes lay in heavy ivory folds beside her feet. She stood among the folds and looked out, towards the quiet darkish foothills. She stood motionless, almost blending into the drapes. Her hands hung loose at her sides. Utterly motionless hands. She turned and came back along the room and walked past me blindly. When she was behind me she caught her breath sharply and spoke.

"He's in the sump," she said. "A horrible decayed thing. I did it. I did just what you said. I went to Eddie Mars. She came home and told me about it, just like a child. She's not normal. I knew the police would get it all out of her. In a little while she would even brag about it. And if dad knew, he would call them instantly and tell them the whole story. And sometime in that night he would die. It's not his dying – it's what he would be thinking just before he died. Rusty wasn't a bad fellow. I didn't love him. He was all right, I guess. He just didn't mean anything to me, one way or another, alive or dead, compared with keeping it from dad."

"So you let her run around loose," I said, "getting into other jams."

"I was playing for time. Just for time. I played the wrong way, of course. I thought she might even forget it herself. I've heard they do forget what happens in those fits. Maybe she has forgotten it. I knew Eddie Mars would bleed me white, but I didn't care. I had to have help and I could only get it from somebody like him. . . . There have been times when I hardly believed it all myself. And other times when I had to get drunk quickly – whatever time of day it was. Awfully damn quickly."

"You'll take her away," I said. "And do that awfully damn quickly."

She still had her back to me. She said softly now: "What about you?"

"Nothing about me. I'm leaving. I'll give you three days. If you're gone by then – okay. If you're not, out it comes. And don't think I don't mean that."

She turned suddenly. "I don't know what to say to you. I don't know how to begin."

"Yeah. Get her out of here and see that she's watched every minute. Promise?"

"I promise. Eddie –"

"Forget Eddie. I'll go see him after I get some rest. I'll handle Eddie."

"He'll try to kill you."

"Yeah," I said. "His best boy couldn't. I'll take a chance on the others. Does Norris know?"

"He'll never tell."

"I thought he knew."

I went quickly away from her down the room and out and down the tiled staircase to the front hall. I didn't see anybody when I left. I found my hat alone this time. Outside the bright gardens had a haunted look, as though small wild eyes were watching me from behind the bushes, as though the sunshine itself had a mysterious something in its light. I got into my car and drove off down the hill.

What did it matter where you lay once you were dead? In a dirty sump or in a marble tower on top of a high hill? You were dead, you were sleeping the big sleep, you were not bothered by things like that. Oil and water were the same as wind and air to you. You just slept the big sleep, not caring about the nastiness of how you died or where you fell. Me, I was part of the nastiness now. Far more a part of it than Rusty Regan was. But the old man didn't have to be. He could lie quiet in his canopied bed, with his bloodless hands folded on the sheet, waiting. His heart was a brief, uncertain murmur. His thoughts were as gray as ashes. And in a little while he too, like Rusty Regan, would be sleeping the big sleep.

On the way downtown I stopped at a bar and had a couple of double Scotches. They didn't do me any good. All they did was make me think of Silver-Wig, and I never saw her again.

FAREWELL, MY LOVELY

1

IT WAS ONE of the mixed blocks over on Central Avenue, the blocks that are not yet all Negro. I had just come out of a three-chair barber shop where an agency thought a relief barber named Dimitrios Aleidis might be working. It was a small matter. His wife said she was willing to spend a little money to have him come home.

I never found him, but Mrs. Aleidis never paid me any money either.

It was a warm day, almost the end of March, and I stood outside the barber shop looking up at the jutting neon sign of a second floor dine and dice emporium called Florian's. A man was looking up at the sign too. He was looking up at the dusty windows with a sort of ecstatic fixity of expression, like a hunky immigrant catching his first sight of the Statue of Liberty. He was a big man but not more than six feet five inches tall and not wider than a beer truck. He was about ten feet away from me. His arms hung loose at his sides and a for-gotten cigar smoked behind his enormous fingers.

Slim quiet Negroes passed up and down the street and stared at him with darting side glances. He was worth looking at. He wore a shaggy borsalino hat, a rough gray sports coat with white golf balls on it for buttons, a brown shirt, a yellow tie, pleated gray flannel slacks and alligator shoes with white explosions on the toes. From his outer breast pocket cascaded a show handkerchief of the same brilliant yellow as his tie. There were a couple of colored feathers tucked into the band of his hat, but he didn't really need them. Even on Central Avenue, not the quietest dressed street in the world, he looked about as inconspicuous as a tarantula on a slice of angel food.

His skin was pale and he needed a shave. He would always need a shave. He had curly black hair and heavy eyebrows that almost met over his thick nose. His ears were small and neat for a man of that size and his eyes had a shine close to tears that gray eyes often seem to have. He stood like a statue, and after a long time he smiled.

He moved slowly across the sidewalk to the double swinging doors which shut off the stairs to the second floor. He pushed them open, cast a cool expressionless glance up and down the street, and moved inside. If he had been a smaller man and more quietly dressed, I might have thought he was going to pull a stick-up. But not in those clothes, and not with that hat, and that frame.

The doors swung back outwards and almost settled to a stop. Before they had entirely stopped moving they opened again, violently, outwards. Something sailed across the sidewalk and landed in the gutter between two parked cars. It landed on its hands and knees and made a high keening noise like a cornered rat. It got up slowly, retrieved a hat and stepped back onto the sidewalk. It was a thin, narrow-shouldered brown youth in a lilac colored suit and a carnation. It had slick black hair. It kept its mouth open and whined for a moment. People stared at it vaguely. Then it settled its hat jauntily, sidled over to the wall and walked silently splay-footed off along the block.

Silence. Traffic resumed. I walked along to the double doors and stood in front of them. They were motionless now. It wasn't any of my business. So I pushed them open and looked in.

A hand I could have sat in came out of the dimness and took hold of my shoulder and squashed it to a pulp. Then the hand moved me through the doors and casually lifted me up a step. The large face looked at me. A deep soft voice said to me, quietly:

"Smokes in here, huh? Tie that for me, pal."

It was dark in there. It was quiet. From up above came vague sounds of humanity, but we were alone on the stairs. The big man stared at me solemnly and went on wrecking my shoulder with his hand.

"A dinge," he said. "I just thrown him out. You seen me throw him out?"

He let go of my shoulder. The bone didn't seem to be broken, but the arm was numb.

"It's that kind of a place," I said, rubbing my shoulder. "What did you expect?"

"Don't say that, pal," the big man purred softly, like four tigers after dinner. "Velma used to work here. Little Velma."

He reached for my shoulder again. I tried to dodge him but he was as fast as a cat. He began to chew my muscles up some more with his iron fingers.

"Yeah," he said. "Little Velma. I ain't seen her in eight years. You say this here is a dinge joint?"

I croaked that it was.

He lifted me up two more steps. I wrenched myself loose and tried for a little elbow room. I wasn't wearing a gun. Looking for Dimitrios Aleidis hadn't seemed to require it. I doubted if it would do me any good. The big man would probably take it away from me and eat it.

"Go on up and see for yourself," I said, trying to keep the agony out of my voice.

He let go of me again. He looked at me with a sort of sadness in his gray eyes. "I'm feelin' good," he said. "I wouldn't want anybody to fuss with me. Let's you and me go on up and maybe nibble a couple."

"They won't serve you. I told you it's a colored joint."

"I ain't seen Velma in eight years," he said in his deep sad voice. "Eight long years since I said good-bye. She ain't wrote to me in six. But she'll have a reason. She used to work here. Cute she was. Let's you and me go on up, huh?"

"All right," I yelled. "I'll go up with you. Just lay off carrying me. Let me walk. I'm fine. I'm all grown up. I go to the bathroom alone and everything. Just don't carry me."

"Little Velma used to work here," he said gently. He wasn't listening to me.

We went on up the stairs. He let me walk. My shoulder ached. The back of my neck was wet.

2

TWO MORE SWING doors closed off the head of the stairs from whatever was beyond. The big man pushed them open lightly with his thumbs and we went into the room. It was a long narrow room, not very clean, not very bright, not very cheerful. In the corner a group of Negroes chanted and chattered in the cone of light over a crap table. There was a bar against the right hand wall. The rest of the room was mostly small round tables. There were a few customers, men and women, all Negroes.

The chanting at the crap table stopped dead and the light over it jerked out. There was a sudden silence as heavy as a water-logged boat. Eyes looked at us, chestnut colored eyes, set in faces that ranged from gray to deep black. Heads turned slowly and the eyes in them glistened and stared in the dead alien silence of another race.

A large, thick-necked Negro was leaning against the end of the bar with pink garters on his shirt sleeves and pink and white suspenders crossing his broad back. He had bouncer written all over him. He put his lifted foot down slowly and turned slowly and stared at us, spreading his feet gently and moving a broad tongue along his lips. He had a battered face that looked as if it had been hit by everything but the bucket of a dragline. It was scarred, flattened, thickened, checkered, and welted. It was a face that had nothing to fear. Everything had been done to it that anybody could think of.

The short crinkled hair had a touch of gray. One ear had lost the lobe.

The Negro was heavy and wide. He had big heavy legs and they looked a little bowed, which is unusual in a Negro. He moved his tongue some more and smiled and moved his body. He came towards us in a loose fighter's crouch. The big man waited for him silently.

The Negro with the pink garters on his arms put a massive brown hand against the big man's chest. Large as it was, the hand looked like a stud. The big man didn't move. The bouncer smiled gently.

"No white folks, brother. Jes' fo' the colored people. I'se sorry."

The big man moved his small sad gray eyes and looked around the room. His cheeks flushed a little. "Shine box," he said angrily, under his breath. He raised his voice. "Where's Velma at?" he asked the bouncer.

The bouncer didn't quite laugh. He studied the big man's clothes, his brown shirt and yellow tie, his rough gray coat and the white golf balls on it. He moved his thick head around delicately and studied all this from various angles. He looked down at the alligator shoes. He chuckled lightly. He seemed amused. I felt a little sorry for him. He spoke softly again.

"Velma, you says? No Velma heah, brother. No hooch, no gals, no nothing. Jes' the scram, white boy, jes' the scram."

"Velma used to work here," the big man said. He spoke almost dreamily, as if he was all by himself, out in the woods, picking johnny-jump-ups. I got my handkerchief out and wiped the back of my neck again.

The bouncer laughed suddenly. "Shuah," he said, throwing a quick look back over his shoulder at his public. "Velma used to work heah. But Velma don't work heah no mo'. She done reti'ed. Haw, haw."

"Kind of take your goddamned mitt off my shirt," the big man said.

The bouncer frowned. He was not used to being talked to like that. He took his hand off the shirt and doubled it into a fist about the size and color of a large eggplant. He had his job, his reputation for toughness, his public esteem to consider. He considered them for a second and made a mistake. He swung the fist very hard and short with a sudden outward jerk of the elbow and hit the big man on the side of the jaw. A soft sigh went around the room.

It was a good punch. The shoulder dropped and the body swung behind it. There was a lot of weight in that punch and the man who landed it had had plenty of practice. The big man didn't move his head more than an inch. He didn't try to block the punch. He took it, shook himself lightly, made a quiet sound in his throat and took hold of the bouncer by the throat.

The bouncer tried to knee him in the groin. The big man turned him in the air and slid his gaudy shoes apart on the scaly linoleum that covered the floor. He bent the bouncer backwards and shifted his right hand to the bouncer's belt. The belt broke like a piece of butcher's string. The big man put his enormous hands flat against the bouncer's spine and heaved. He threw him clear across the room, spinning and staggering and flailing with his arms. Three men jumped out of the way. The bouncer went over with a table and smacked into the baseboard with a crash that must have been heard in Denver. His legs twitched. Then he lay still.

"Some guys," the big man said, "has got wrong ideas about when to get tough." He turned to me. "Yeah," he said. "Let's you and me nibble one."

We went over to the bar. The customers, by ones and twos and threes, became quiet shadows that drifted soundless across the floor, soundless through the doors at the head of the stairs. Soundless as shadows on the grass. They didn't even let the doors swing.

We leaned against the bar. "Whiskey sour," the big man said. "Call yours."

"Whiskey sour," I said.

We had whiskey sours.

The big man licked his whiskey sour impassively down the side of the thick squat glass. He stared solemnly at the barman, a thin, worried-looking Negro in a white coat who moved as if his feet hurt him.

"*You* know where Velma is?"

"Velma, you says?" the barman whined. "I ain't seen her 'round heah lately. Not right lately, nossuh."

"How long you been here?"

"Let's see," the barman put his towel down and wrinkled his forehead and started to count on his fingers. "'Bout ten months, I reckon. 'Bout a yeah. 'Bout —"

"Make your mind up," the big man said.

The barman goggled and his Adam's apple flopped around like a headless chicken.

"How long's this coop been a dinge joint?" the big man demanded gruffly.

"Says which?"

The big man made a fist into which his whiskey sour glass melted almost out of sight.

"Five years anyway," I said. "This fellow wouldn't know anything about a white girl named Velma. Nobody here would."

The big man looked at me as if I had just hatched out. His whiskey sour hadn't seemed to improve his temper.

"Who the hell asked you to stick your face in?" he asked me.

I smiled. I made it a big warm friendly smile. "I'm the fellow that came in with you. Remember?"

He grinned back then, a flat white grin without meaning. "Whiskey sour," he told the barman. "Shake them fleas outa your pants. Service."

The barman scuttled around, rolling the whites of his eyes. I put my back against the bar and looked at the room. It was

207

now empty, save for the barman, the big man and myself, and the bouncer crushed over against the wall. The bouncer was moving. He was moving slowly as if with great pain and effort. He was crawling softly along the baseboard like a fly with one wing. He was moving behind the tables, wearily, a man suddenly old, suddenly disillusioned. I watched him move. The barman put down two more whiskey sours. I turned to the bar. The big man glanced casually over at the crawling bouncer and then paid no further attention to him.

"There ain't nothing left of the joint," he complained. "They was a little stage and band and cute little rooms where a guy could have fun. Velma did some warbling. A redhead she was. Cute as lace pants. We was to of been married when they hung the frame on me."

I took my second whiskey sour. I was beginning to have enough of the adventure. "What frame?" I asked.

"Where you figure I been them eight years I said about?"

"Catching butterflies."

He prodded his chest with a forefinger like a banana. "In the caboose. Malloy is the name. They call me Moose Malloy, on account of I'm large. The Great Bend bank job. Forty grand. Solo job. Ain't that something?"

"You going to spend it now?"

He gave me a sharp look. There was a noise behind us. The bouncer was on his feet again, weaving a little. He had his hand on the knob of a dark door over behind the crap table. He got the door open, half fell through. The door clattered shut. A lock clicked.

"Where's that go?" Moose Malloy demanded.

The barman's eyes floated in his head, focused with diffi-culty on the door through which the bouncer had stumbled.

"Tha – tha's Mistah Montgomery's office, suh. He's the boss. He's got his office back there."

"He might know," the big man said. He drank his drink at a gulp. "He better not crack wise neither. Two more of the same."

He crossed the room slowly, lightfooted, without a care in the world. His enormous back hid the door. It was locked. He shook it and a piece of the panel flew off to one side. He went through and shut the door behind him.

There was silence. I looked at the barman. The barman looked at me. His eyes became thoughtful. He polished the counter and sighed and leaned down with his right arm.

I reached across the counter and took hold of the arm. It was thin, brittle. I held it and smiled at him.

"What you got down there, bo?"

He licked his lips. He leaned on my arm, and said nothing. Grayness invaded his shining face.

"This guy is tough," I said. "And he's liable to go mean. Drinks do that to him. He's looking for a girl he used to know. This place used to be a white establishment. Get the idea?"

The barman licked his lips.

"He's been away a long time," I said. "Eight years. He doesn't seem to realize how long that is, although I'd expect him to think it a life time. He thinks the people here should know where his girl is. Get the idea?"

The barman said slowly: "I thought you was with him."

"I couldn't help myself. He asked me a question down below and then dragged me up. I never saw him before. But I didn't feel like being thrown over any houses. What you got down there?"

"Got me a sawed-off," the barman said.

"Tsk. That's illegal," I whispered. "Listen, you and I are together. Got anything else?"

"Got me a gat," the barman said. "In a cigar box. Leggo my arm."

"That's fine," I said. "Now move along a bit. Easy now. Sideways. This isn't the time to pull the artillery."

"Says you," the barman sneered, putting his tired weight against my arm. "Says —"

He stopped. His eyes rolled. His head jerked.

There was a dull flat sound at the back of the place, behind the closed door beyond the crap table. It might have been a slammed door. I didn't think it was. The barman didn't think so either.

The barman froze. His mouth drooled. I listened. No other sound. I started quickly for the end of the counter. I had listened too long.

The door at the back opened with a bang and Moose Malloy came through it with a smooth heavy lunge and stopped dead, his feet planted and a wide pale grin on his face.

A Colt Army .45 looked like a toy pistol in his hand.

"Don't nobody try to fancy pants," he said cozily. "Freeze the mitts on the bar."

The barman and I put our hands on the bar.

Moose Malloy looked the room over with a raking glance. His grin was taut, nailed on. He shifted his feet and moved silently across the room. He looked like a man who could take a bank single-handed – even in those clothes.

He came to the bar. "Rise up, nigger," he said softly. The barman put his hands high in the air. The big man stepped to my back and prowled me over carefully with his left hand. His breath was hot on my neck. It went away.

"Mister Montgomery didn't know where Velma was neither," he said. "He tried to tell me – with this." His hard hand patted the gun. I turned slowly and looked at him. "Yeah," he said. "You'll know me. You ain't forgetting me, pal. Just tell them johns not to get careless is all." He waggled the gun. "Well so long, punks. I gotta catch a street car."

He started towards the head of the stairs.

"You didn't pay for the drinks," I said.

He stopped and looked at me carefully.

"Maybe you got something there," he said, "but I wouldn't squeeze it too hard."

He moved on, slipped through the double doors, and his steps sounded remotely going down the stairs.

The barman stooped. I jumped around behind the counter and jostled him out of the way. A sawed-off shotgun lay under a towel on a shelf under the bar. Beside it was a cigar box. In the cigar box was a .38 automatic. I took both of them. The barman pressed back against the tier of glasses behind the bar.

I went back around the end of the bar and across the room to the gaping door behind the crap table. There was a hallway behind it, L-shaped, almost lightless. The bouncer lay sprawled on its floor unconscious, with a knife in his hand. I leaned down and pulled the knife loose and threw it down a back stairway. The bouncer breathed stertorously and his hand was limp.

I stepped over him and opened a door marked "Office" in flaked black paint.

There was a small scarred desk close to a partly boarded-up window. The torso of a man was bolt upright in the chair. The chair had a high back which just reached to the nape of the man's neck. His head was folded back over the high back of the chair so that his nose pointed at the boarded-up window. Just folded, like a handkerchief or a hinge.

A drawer of the desk was open at the man's right. Inside it was a newspaper with a smear of oil in the middle. The gun would have come from there. It had probably seemed like a good idea at the time, but the position of Mr. Montgomery's head proved that the idea had been wrong.

There was a telephone on the desk. I laid the sawed-off shotgun down and went over to lock the door before I called the police. I felt safer that way and Mr. Montgomery didn't seem to mind.

When the prowl car boys stamped up the stairs, the bouncer and the barman had disappeared and I had the place to myself.

3

A MAN NAMED Nulty got the case, a lean-jawed sourpuss with long yellow hands which he kept folded over his kneecaps most of the time he talked to me. He was a detective-lieutenant attached to the 77th Street Division and we talked in a bare room with two small desks against opposite walls and room to move between them, if two people didn't try it at once. Dirty brown linoleum covered the floor and the smell of old cigar butts hung in the air. Nulty's shirt was frayed and his coat sleeves had been turned in at the cuffs. He looked poor enough to be honest, but he didn't look like a man who could deal with Moose Malloy.

He lit half of a cigar and threw the match on the floor, where a lot of company was waiting for it. His voice said bitterly:

"Shines. Another shine killing. That's what I rate after eighteen years in this man's police department. No pix, no space, not even four lines in the want-ad section."

I didn't say anything. He picked my card up and read it again and threw it down.

"Philip Marlowe, Private Investigator. One of those guys, huh? Jesus, you look tough enough. What was you doing all that time?"

"All what time?"

"All the time this Malloy was twisting the neck of this smoke."

"Oh, that happened in another room," I said. "Malloy hadn't promised me he was going to break anybody's neck."

"Ride me," Nulty said bitterly. "Okay, go ahead and ride me. Everybody else does. What's another one matter? Poor old Nulty. Let's go on up and throw a couple of nifties at him. Always good for a laugh, Nulty is."

"I'm not trying to ride anybody," I said. "That's the way it happened – in another room."

"Oh, sure," Nulty said through a fan of rank cigar smoke. "I was down there and saw, didn't I? Don't you pack no rod?"

"Not on that kind of a job."

"What kind of a job?"

"I was looking for a barber who had run away from his wife. She thought he could be persuaded to come home."

"You mean a dinge?"

"No, a Greek."

"Okay," Nulty said and spit into his wastebasket. "Okay. You met the big guy how?"

"I told you already. I just happened to be there. He threw a Negro out of the doors of Florian's and I unwisely poked my head in to see what was happening. So he took me upstairs."

"You mean he stuck you up?"

"No, he didn't have the gun then. At least, he didn't show one. He took the gun away from Montgomery, probably. He just picked me up. I'm kind of cute sometimes."

"I wouldn't know," Nulty said. "You seem to pick up awful easy."

"All right," I said. "Why argue? I've seen the guy and you haven't. He could wear you or me for a watch charm. I didn't know he had killed anybody until after he left. I heard a shot, but I got the idea somebody had got scared and shot at Malloy and then Malloy took the gun away from whoever did it."

"And why would you get an idea like that?" Nulty asked almost suavely. "He used a gun to take that bank, didn't he?"

"Consider the kind of clothes he was wearing. He didn't go there to kill anybody; not dressed like that. He went there to look for this girl named Velma that had been his girl before he was pinched for the bank job. She worked there at Florian's or whatever place was there when it was still a white joint. He was pinched there. You'll get him all right."

"Sure," Nulty said. "With that size and them clothes. Easy."

"He might have another suit," I said. "And a car and a hide-out and money and friends. But you'll get him."

Nulty spit in the wastebasket again. "I'll get him," he said, "about the time I get my third set of teeth. How many guys is put on it? One. Listen, you know why? No space. One time there was five smokes carved Harlem sunsets on each other down on East Eighty-four. One of them was cold already. There was blood on the furniture, blood on the walls, blood even on the ceiling. I go down and outside the house a guy that works on the *Chronicle*, a newshawk, is coming off the porch and getting into his car. He makes a face at us and says, 'Aw, hell, shines,' and gets in his heap and goes away. Don't even go in the house."

"Maybe he's a parole breaker," I said. "You'd get some co-operation on that. But pick him up nice or he'll knock off a brace of prowlies for you. Then you'll get space."

"And I wouldn't have the case no more neither," Nulty sneered.

The phone rang on his desk. He listened to it and smiled sorrowfully. He hung up and scribbled on a pad and there was a faint gleam in his eyes, a light far back in a dusty corridor.

"Hell, they got him. That was Records. Got his prints, mug and everything. Jesus, that's a little something anyway." He read from his pad. "Jesus, this is a man. Six five and one-half, two hundred sixty-four pounds, without his necktie. Jesus, that's a boy. Well, the hell with him. They got him on the air now. Probably at the end of the hot car list. Ain't nothing to do but just wait." He threw his cigar into a spittoon.

"Try looking for the girl," I said. "Velma. Malloy will be looking for her. That's what started it all. Try Velma."

"You try her," Nulty said. "I ain't been in a joy house in twenty years."

I stood up. "Okay," I said, and started for the door.

"Hey, wait a minute," Nulty said. "I was only kidding. You ain't awful busy, are you?"

I rolled a cigarette around in my fingers and looked at him and waited by the door.

"I mean you got time to sort of take a gander around for this dame. That's a good idea you had there. You might pick something up. You can work under glass."

"What's in it for me?"

He spread his yellow hands sadly. His smile was as cunning as a broken mousetrap. "You been in jams with us boys before. Don't tell me no. I heard different. Next time it ain't doing you any harm to have a pal."

"What good is it going to do me?"

"Listen," Nulty urged. "I'm just a quiet guy. But any guy in the department can do you a lot of good."

"Is this for love – or are you paying anything in money?"

"No money," Nulty said, and wrinkled his sad yellow nose. "But I'm needing a little credit bad. Since the last shake-up, things is really tough. I wouldn't forget it, pal. Not ever."

I looked at my watch. "Okay, if I think of anything, it's yours. And when you get the mug, I'll identify it for you. After lunch." We shook hands and I went down the mud-colored hall and stairway to the front of the building and my car.

It was two hours since Moose Malloy had left Florian's with the Army Colt in his hand. I ate lunch at a drugstore, bought a pint of bourbon, and drove eastward to Central Avenue and north on Central again. The hunch I had was as vague as the heat waves that danced above the sidewalk.

Nothing made it my business except curiosity. But strictly speaking, I hadn't had any business in a month. Even a no-charge job was a change.

4

FLORIAN'S WAS CLOSED up, of course. An obvious plain-clothesman sat in front of it in a car, reading a paper with one eye. I didn't know why they bothered. Nobody there knew anything about Moose Malloy. The bouncer and the barman had not been found. Nobody on the block knew anything about them, for talking purposes.

I drove past slowly and parked around the corner and sat looking at a Negro hotel which was diagonally across the block from Florian's and beyond the nearest intersection. It was called the Hotel Sans Souci. I got out and walked back across the intersection and went into it. Two rows of hard empty chairs stared at each other across a strip of tan fiber carpet. A desk was back in the dimness and behind the desk a baldheaded man had his eyes shut and his soft brown hands clasped peacefully on the desk in front of him. He dozed, or appeared to. He wore an Ascot tie that looked as if it had been tied about the year 1880. The green stone in his stickpin was not quite as large as an apple. His large loose chin was folded down gently on the tie, and his folded hands were peaceful and clean, with manicured nails, and gray halfmoons in the purple of the nails.

A metal embossed sign at his elbow said: "This Hotel is Under the Protection of The International Consolidated Agencies, Ltd. Inc."

When the peaceful brown man opened one eye at me thoughtfully I pointed at the sign.

"H.P.D. man checking up. Any trouble here?"

H.P.D. means Hotel Protective Department, which is the department of a large agency that looks after check bouncers and people who move out by the back stairs leaving unpaid bills and second-hand suitcases full of bricks.

"Trouble, brother," the clerk said in a high sonorous voice, "is something we is fresh out of." He lowered his voice four or five notches and added: "What was the name again?"

"Marlowe. Philip Marlowe —"

"A nice name, brother. Clean and cheerful. You're looking right well today." He lowered his voice again. "But you ain't no H.P.D. man. Ain't seen one in years." He unfolded his hands and pointed languidly at the sign. "I acquired that second-hand, brother, just for the effect."

"Okay," I said. I leaned on the counter and started to spin a half dollar on the bare, scarred wood of the counter.

"Heard what happened over at Florian's this morning?"

"Brother, I forgit." Both his eyes were open now and he was watching the blur of light made by the spinning coin.

"The boss got bumped off," I said. "Man named Montgomery. Somebody broke his neck."

"May the Lawd receive his soul, brother." Down went the voice again. "Cop?"

"Private – on a confidential lay. And I know a man who can keep things confidential when I see one."

He studied me, then closed his eyes and thought. He reopened them cautiously and stared at the spinning coin. He couldn't resist looking at it.

"Who done it?" he asked softly. "Who fixed Sam?"

"A tough guy out of the jailhouse got sore because it wasn't a white joint. It used to be, it seems. Maybe you remember?"

He said nothing. The coin fell over with a light ringing whirr and lay still.

"Call your play," I said. "I'll read you a chapter of the Bible or buy you a drink. Say which."

"Brother, I kind of like to read my Bible in the seclusion of my family." His eyes were bright, toadlike, steady.

"Maybe you've just had lunch," I said.

"Lunch," he said, "is something a man of my shape and disposition aims to do without." Down went the voice. "Come 'round this here side of the desk."

I went around and drew the flat pint of bonded bourbon out of my pocket and put it on the shelf. I went back to the front of the desk. He bent over and examined it. He looked satisfied.

"Brother, this don't buy you nothing at all," he said. "But I is pleased to take a light snifter in your company."

He opened the bottle, put two small glasses on the desk and quietly poured each full to the brim. He lifted one, sniffed it carefully, and poured it down his throat with his little finger lifted.

He tasted it, thought about it, nodded and said: "This come out of the correct bottle, brother. In what manner can I be of service to you? There ain't a crack in the sidewalk 'round here I don't know by its first name. Yessuh, this liquor has been keepin' the right company." He refilled his glass.

I told him what had happened at Florian's and why. He stared at me solemnly and shook his bald head.

"A nice quiet place Sam run too," he said. "Ain't nobody been knifed there in a month."

"When Florian's was a white joint some six or eight years ago or less, what was the name of it?"

"Electric signs come kind of high, brother."

I nodded. "I thought it might have had the same name. Malloy would probably have said something if the name had been changed. But who ran it?"

"I'm a mite surprised at you, brother. The name of that pore sinner was Florian. Mike Florian —"

"And what happened to Mike Florian?"

The Negro spread his gentle brown hands. His voice was sonorous and sad. "Daid, brother. Gathered to the Lawd. Nineteen hundred and thirty-four, maybe thirty-five. I ain't precise on that. A wasted life, brother, and a case of pickled kidneys, I heard say. The ungodly man drops like a polled steer, brother, but mercy waits for him up yonder." His voice went down to the business level. "Damn if I know why."

"Who did he leave behind him? Pour another drink."

He corked the bottle firmly and pushed it across the counter. "Two is all, brother — before sundown. I thank you. Your method of approach is soothin' to a man's dignity. . . . Left a widow. Name of Jessie."

"What happened to her?"

"The pursuit of knowledge, brother, is the askin' of many questions. I ain't heard. Try the phone book."

There was a booth in the dark corner of the lobby. I went over and shut the door far enough to put the light on.

I looked up the name in the chained and battered book. No Florian in it at all. I went back to the desk.

"No soap," I said.

The Negro bent regretfully and heaved a city directory up on top of the desk and pushed it towards me. He closed his eyes. He was getting bored. There was a Jessie Florian, Widow, in the book. She lived at 1644 West 54th Place. I wondered what I had been using for brains all my life.

I wrote the address down on a piece of paper and pushed the directory back across the desk. The Negro put it back where he had found it, shook hands with me, then folded his hands on the desk exactly where they had been when I came in. His eyes drooped slowly and he appeared to fall asleep.

The incident for him was over. Halfway to the door I shot a glance back at him. His eyes were closed and he breathed softly and regularly, blowing a little with his lips at the end of each breath. His bald head shone.

I went out of the Hotel Sans Souci and crossed the street to my car. It looked too easy. It looked much too easy.

5

1644 WEST 54TH Place was a dried-out brown house with a dried-out brown lawn in front of it. There was a large bare patch around a tough-looking palm tree. On the porch stood one lonely wooden rocker, and the afternoon breeze made the unpruned shoots of last year's poinsettias tap-tap against the cracked stucco wall. A line of stiff yellowish half-washed clothes jittered on a rusty wire in the side yard.

I drove on a quarter block, parked my car across the street and walked back.

The bell didn't work so I rapped on the wooden margin of the screen door. Slow steps shuffled and the door opened and I was looking into dimness at a blowsy woman who was blowing her nose as she opened the door. Her face was gray and puffy. She had weedy hair of that vague color which is neither brown nor blond, that hasn't enough life in it to be ginger, and isn't clean enough to be gray. Her body was thick in a shapeless outing flannel bathrobe many moons past color and design. It was just something around her body. Her toes were large and obvious in a pair of man's slippers of scuffed brown leather.

I said: "Mrs. Florian? Mrs. Jessie Florian?"

"Uh-huh," the voice dragged itself out of her throat like a sick man getting out of bed.

"You are the Mrs. Florian whose husband once ran a place of entertainment on Central Avenue? Mike Florian?"

She thumbed a wick of hair past her large ear. Her eyes glittered with surprise. Her heavy clogged voice said:

"Wha–what? My goodness sakes alive. Mike's been gone these five years. Who did you say you was?"

The screen door was still shut and hooked.

"I'm a detective," I said. "I'd like a little information."

She stared at me a long dreary minute. Then with effort she unhooked the door and turned away from it.

"Come on in then. I ain't had time to get cleaned up yet," she whined. "Cops, huh?"

I stepped through the door and hooked the screen again. A large handsome cabinet radio droned to the left of the door in the corner of the room. It was the only decent piece of furniture the place had. It looked brand new. Everything else was junk – dirty overstuffed pieces, a wooden rocker that matched the one on the porch, a square arch into a dining room with a stained table, finger marks all over the swing door to the kitchen beyond. A couple of frayed lamps with once gaudy shades that were now as gay as superannuated streetwalkers.

The woman sat down in the rocker and flopped her slippers and looked at me. I looked at the radio and sat down on the end of a davenport. She saw me looking at it. A bogus heartiness, as weak as a Chinaman's tea, moved into her face and voice. "All the comp'ny I got," she said. Then she tittered. "Mike ain't done nothing new, has he? I don't get cops calling on me much."

Her titter contained a loose alcoholic overtone. I leaned back against something hard, felt for it and brought up an empty quart gin bottle. The woman tittered again.

"A joke that was," she said. "But I hope to Christ they's enough cheap blondes where he is. He never got enough of them here."

"I was thinking more about a redhead," I said.

"I guess he could use a few of them too." Her eyes, it seemed to me, were not so vague now. "I don't call to mind. Any special redhead?"

"Yes. A girl named Velma. I don't know what last name she used except that it wouldn't be her real one. I'm trying to trace her for her folks. Your place on Central is a colored place now, although they haven't changed the name, and of course the people there never heard of her. So I thought of you."

"Her folks taken their time getting around to it – looking for her," the woman said thoughtfully.

"There's a little money involved. Not much. I guess they have to get her in order to touch it. Money sharpens the memory."

"So does liquor," the woman said. "Kind of hot today, ain't it? You said you was a copper though." Cunning eyes, steady attentive face. The feet in the man's slippers didn't move.

I held up the dead soldier and shook it. Then I threw it to one side and reached back on my hip for the pint of bond bourbon the Negro hotel clerk and I had barely tapped. I held it out on my knee. The woman's eyes became fixed in an incredulous stare. Then suspicion climbed all over her face, like a kitten, but not so playfully.

"You ain't no copper," she said softly. "No copper ever bought a drink of that stuff. What's the gag, mister?"

She blew her nose again, on one of the dirtiest handkerchiefs I ever saw. Her eyes stayed on the bottle. Suspicion fought with thirst, and thirst was winning. It always does.

"This Velma was an entertainer, a singer. You wouldn't know her? I don't suppose you went there much."

Seaweed colored eyes stayed on the bottle. A coated tongue coiled on her lips.

"Man, that's liquor," she sighed. "I don't give a damn who you are. Just hold it careful, mister. This ain't no time to drop anything."

She got up and waddled out of the room and came back with two thick smeared glasses.

"No fixin's. Just what you brought is all," she said.

I poured her a slug that would have made me float over a wall. She reached for it hungrily and put it down her throat like an aspirin tablet and looked at the bottle. I poured her another and a smaller one for me. She took it over to her rocker. Her eyes had turned two shades browner already.

"Man, this stuff dies painless with me," she said and sat down. "It never knows what hit it. What was we talkin' about?"

"A redhaired girl named Velma who used to work in your place on Central Avenue."

"Yeah." She used her second drink. I went over and stood the bottle on an end beside her. She reached for it. "Yeah. Who you say you was?"

I took out a card and gave it to her. She read it with her tongue and lips, dropped it on a table beside her and set her empty glass on it.

"Oh, a private guy. You ain't said that, mister." She waggled a finger at me with gay reproach. "But your liquor says you're an all right guy at that. Here's to crime." She poured a third drink for herself and drank it down.

I sat down and rolled a cigarette around in my fingers and waited. She either knew something or she didn't. If she knew something, she either would tell me or she wouldn't. It was that simple.

"Cute little redhead," she said slowly and thickly. "Yeah, I remember her. Song and dance. Nice legs and generous with

222

'em. She went off somewheres. How would I know what them tramps do?"

"Well, I didn't really think you would know," I said. "But it was natural to come and ask you, Mrs. Florian. Help yourself to the whiskey – I could run out for more when we need it."

"You ain't drinkin'," she said suddenly.

I put my hand around my glass and swallowed what was in it slowly enough to make it seem more than it was.

"Where's her folks at?" she asked suddenly.

"What does that matter?"

"Okay," she sneered. "All cops is the same. Okay, handsome. A guy that buys me a drink is a pal." She reached for the bottle and set up Number 4. "I shouldn't ought to barber with you. But when I like a guy, the ceiling's the limit." She simpered. She was as cute as a washtub. "Hold on to your chair and don't step on no snakes," she said. "I got me an idea."

She got up out of the rocker, sneezed, almost lost the bathrobe, slapped it back against her stomach and stared at me coldly.

"No peekin'," she said, and went out of the room again, hitting the door frame with her shoulder.

I heard her fumbling steps going into the back part of the house.

The poinsettia shoots tap-tapped dully against the front wall. The clothes line creaked vaguely at the side of the house. The ice cream peddler went by ringing his bell. The big new handsome radio in the corner whispered of dancing and love with a deep soft throbbing note like the catch in a torch singer's voice.

Then from the back of the house there were various types of crashing sounds. A chair seemed to fall over backwards, a bureau drawer was pulled out too far and crashed to the floor, there was fumbling and thudding and muttered thick language. Then the slow click of a lock and the squeak of a trunk top going up. More fumbling and banging. A tray landed on the floor. I got up from the davenport and sneaked into the dining room and from that into a short hall. I looked around the edge of an open door.

She was in there swaying in front of the trunk, making grabs at what was in it, and then throwing her hair back over her forehead with anger. She was drunker than she thought. She leaned down and steadied herself on the trunk and coughed and sighed. Then she went down on her thick knees and plunged both hands into the trunk and groped.

They came up holding something unsteadily. A thick package tied with faded pink tape. Slowly, clumsily, she undid the tape. She slipped an envelope out of the package and leaned down again to thrust the envelope out of sight into the right-hand side of the trunk. She retied the tape with fumbling fingers.

I sneaked back the way I had come and sat down on the davenport. Breathing stertorous noises, the woman came back into the living room and stood swaying in the doorway with the tape-tied package.

She grinned at me triumphantly, tossed the package and it fell somewhere near my feet. She waddled back to the rocker and sat down and reached for the whiskey.

I picked the package off the floor and untied the faded pink tape.

"Look 'em over," the woman grunted. "Photos. Newspaper stills. Not that them tramps ever got in no newspapers except by way of the police blotter. People from the joint they are. They're all the bastard left me – them and his old clothes."

I leafed through the bunch of shiny photographs of men and women in professional poses. The men had sharp foxy faces and racetrack clothes or eccentric clownlike makeup. Hoofers and comics from the filling station circuit. Not many of them would ever get west of Main Street. You would find them in tanktown vaudeville acts, cleaned up, or down in the cheap burlesque houses, as dirty as the law allowed and once in a while just enough dirtier for a raid and a noisy police court trial, and then back in their shows again, grinning, sadistically filthy and as rank as the smell of stale sweat. The women had good legs and displayed their inside curves more than Will Hays would have liked. But their faces were as threadbare as a bookkeeper's office coat. Blondes, brunettes, large cowlike eyes with a peasant dullness in them. Small sharp eyes with urchin greed in them. One or two of the faces obviously vicious. One or two of them might have had red hair. You couldn't tell from the photographs. I looked them over casually, without interest and tied the tape again.

"I wouldn't know any of these," I said. "Why am I looking at them?"

She leered over the bottle her right hand was grappling with unsteadily. "Ain't you looking for Velma?"

"Is she one of these?"

Thick cunning played on her face, had no fun there and went somewhere else. "Ain't you got a photo of her – from her folks?"

"No."

That troubled her. Every girl has a photo somewhere, if it's only in short dresses with a bow in her hair. I should have had it.

"I ain't beginnin' to like you again," the woman said almost quietly.

I stood up with my glass and went over and put it down beside hers on the end table.

"Pour me a drink before you kill the bottle."

She reached for the glass and I turned and walked swiftly through the square arch into the dining room, into the hall, into the cluttered bedroom with the open trunk and the spilled tray. A voice shouted behind me. I plunged ahead down into the right side of the trunk, felt an envelope and brought it up swiftly.

She was out of her chair when I got back to the living room, but she had only taken two or three steps. Her eyes had a peculiar glassiness. A murderous glassiness.

"Sit down," I snarled at her deliberately. "You're not dealing with a simple-minded lug like Moose Malloy this time."

It was a shot more or less in the dark, and it didn't hit anything. She blinked twice and tried to lift her nose with her upper lip. Some dirty teeth showed in a rabbit leer.

"Moose? The Moose? What about him?" she gulped.

"He's loose," I said. "Out of jail. He's wandering, with a forty-five gun in his hand. He killed a nigger over on Central this morning because he wouldn't tell him where Velma was. Now he's looking for the fink that turned him up eight years ago."

A white look smeared the woman's face. She pushed the bottle against her lips and gurgled at it. Some of the whiskey ran down her chin.

"And the cops are looking for *him*," she said and laughed. "Cops. Yah!"

A lovely old woman. I liked being with her. I liked getting her drunk for my own sordid purposes. I was a swell guy. I enjoyed being me. You find almost anything under your hand in my business, but I was beginning to be a little sick at my stomach.

I opened the envelope my hand was clutching and drew out a glazed still. It was like the others but it was different, much nicer. The girl wore a Pierrot costume from the waist up. Under the white conical hat with a black pompon on the top, her fluffed out hair had a dark tinge that might have been red. The face was in profile but the visible eye seemed to have gaiety in it. I wouldn't say the face was lovely and unspoiled, I'm not that good at faces. But it was pretty. People had been nice to that face, or nice enough for their circle. Yet it was a very ordinary face and its prettiness was strictly assembly line. You would see a dozen faces like it on a city block in the noon hour.

Below the waist the photo was mostly legs and very nice legs at that. It was signed across the lower right-hand corner: "Always yours – Velma Valento."

I held it up in front of the Florian woman, out of her reach. She lunged but came short.

"Why hide it?" I asked.

She made no sound except thick breathing. I slipped the photo back into the envelope and the envelope into my pocket.

"Why hide it?" I asked again. "What makes it different from the others? Where is she?"

"She's dead," the woman said. "She was a good kid, but she's dead, copper. Beat it."

The tawny mangled brows worked up and down. Her hand opened and the whiskey bottle slid to the carpet and began to gurgle. I bent to pick it up. She tried to kick me in the face. I stepped away from her.

"And that still doesn't say why you hid it," I told her. "When did she die? How?"

"I am a poor sick old woman," she grunted. "Get away from me, you son of a bitch."

I stood there looking at her, not saying anything, not thinking of anything particular to say. I stepped over to her side after a moment and put the flat bottle, now almost empty, on the table at her side.

She was staring down at the carpet. The radio droned pleasantly in the corner. A car went by outside. A fly buzzed in a window. After a long time she moved one lip over the other and spoke to the floor, a meaningless jumble of words from which nothing emerged. Then she laughed and threw her head back and drooled. Then her right hand reached for the bottle and it rattled against her teeth as she drained it. When it was empty she held it up and shook it and threw it at me. It went off in the corner somewhere, skidding along the carpet and bringing up with a thud against the baseboard.

She leered at me once more, then her eyes closed and she began to snore.

It might have been an act, but I didn't care. Suddenly I had enough of the scene, too much of it, far too much of it.

I picked my hat off the davenport and went over to the door and opened it and went out past the screen. The radio still droned in the corner and the woman still snored gently in her chair. I threw a quick look back at her before I closed the door, then shut it, opened it again silently and looked again.

Her eyes were still shut but something gleamed below the lids. I went down the steps, along the cracked walk to the street.

In the next house a window curtain was drawn aside and a narrow intent face was close to the glass, peering, an old woman's face with white hair and a sharp nose.

Old Nosey checking up on the neighbors. There's always at least one like her to the block. I waved a hand at her. The curtain fell.

I went back to my car and got into it and drove back to the 77th Street Division, and climbed upstairs to Nulty's smelly little cubbyhole of an office on the second floor.

6

NULTY DIDN'T SEEM to have moved. He sat in his chair in the same attitude of sour patience. But there were two more cigar stubs in his ashtray and the floor was a little thicker in burnt matches.

I sat down at the vacant desk and Nulty turned over a photo that was lying face down on his desk and handed it to me. It was a police mug, front and profile, with a fingerprint classification underneath. It was Malloy all right, taken in a strong light, and looking as if he had no more eyebrows than a French roll.

"That's the boy." I passed it back.

"We got a wire from Oregon State pen on him," Nulty said. "All time served except his copper. Things look better. We got him cornered. A prowl car was talking to a conductor the end of the Seventh Street line. The conductor mentioned a guy that size, looking like that. He got off Third and Alexandria. What he'll do is break into some big house where the folks are away. Lots of 'em there, old-fashioned places too far downtown now and hard to rent. He'll break in one and we got him bottled. What you been doing?"

"Was he wearing a fancy hat and white golf balls on his jacket?"

Nulty frowned and twisted his hands on his kneecaps. "No, a blue suit. Maybe brown."

"Sure it wasn't a sarong?"

"Huh? Oh yeah, funny. Remind me to laugh on my day off."

I said: "That wasn't the Moose. He wouldn't ride a street car. He had money. Look at the clothes he was wearing. He couldn't wear stock sizes. They must have been made to order."

"Okay, ride me," Nulty scowled. "What you been doing?"

"What you ought to have done. This place called Florian's was under the same name when it was a white night trap. I talked to a Negro hotelman who knows the neighborhood. The sign was expensive so the shines just went on using it when they took over. The man's name was Mike Florian. He's dead some years, but his widow is still around. She lives at 1644 West 54th Place. Her name is Jessie Florian. She's not in the phone book, but she is in the city directory."

"Well, what do I do – date her up?" Nulty asked.

"I did it for you. I took in a pint of bourbon with me. She's a charming middle-aged lady with a face like a bucket of mud and if she has washed her hair since Coolidge's second term, I'll eat my spare tire, rim and all."

"Skip the wisecracks," Nulty said.

"I asked Mrs. Florian about Velma. You remember, Mr. Nulty, the redhead named Velma that Moose Malloy was looking for? I'm not tiring you, am I, Mr. Nulty?"

"What you sore about?"

"You wouldn't understand. Mrs. Florian said she didn't remember Velma. Her home is very shabby except for a new radio, worth seventy or eighty dollars."

"You ain't told me why that's something I should start screaming about."

"Mrs. Florian – Jessie to me – said her husband left her nothing but his old clothes and a bunch of stills of the gang who worked at his joint from time to time. I plied her with liquor and she is a girl who will take a drink if she has to knock you down to get the bottle. After the third or fourth she went into her modest bedroom and threw things around and dug the bunch of stills out of the bottom of an old trunk. But I was watching her without her knowing it and she slipped one out of the packet and hid it. So after a while I snuck in there and grabbed it."

I reached into my pocket and laid the Pierrot girl on his desk. He lifted it and stared at it and his lips quirked at the corners.

"Cute," he said. "Cute enough. I could of used a piece of that once. Haw, haw. Velma Valento, huh? What happened to this doll?"

"Mrs. Florian says she died – but that hardly explains why she hid the photo."

"It don't do at that. Why did she hide it?"

"She wouldn't tell me. In the end, after I told her about the Moose being out, she seemed to take a dislike to me. That seems impossible, doesn't it?"

"Go on," Nulty said.

"That's all. I've told you the facts and given you the exhibit. If you can't get somewhere on this set-up, nothing I could say would help."

"Where would I get? It's still a shine killing. Wait'll we get the Moose. Hell, it's eight years since he saw the girl unless she visited him in the pen."

"All right," I said. "But don't forget he's looking for her and he's a man who would bear down. By the way, he was in for a bank job. That means a reward. Who got it?"

"I don't know," Nulty said. "Maybe I could find out. Why?"

"Somebody turned him up. Maybe he knows who. That would be another job he would give time to." I stood up. "Well, good-bye and good luck."

"You walking out on me?"

I went over to the door. "I have to go home and take a bath and gargle my throat and get my nails manicured."

"You ain't sick, are you?"

"Just dirty," I said. "Very, very dirty."

"Well, what's your hurry? Sit down a minute." He leaned back and hooked his thumbs in his vest, which made him look a little more like a cop, but didn't make him look any more magnetic.

"No hurry," I said. "No hurry at all. There's nothing more I can do. Apparently this Velma is dead, if Mrs. Florian is telling the truth — and I don't at the moment know of any reason why she should lie about it. That was all I was interested in."

"Yeah," Nulty said suspiciously — from force of habit.

"And you have Moose Malloy all sewed up anyway, and that's that. So I'll just run on home now and go about the business of trying to earn a living."

"We might miss out on the Moose," Nulty said. "Guys get away once in a while. Even big guys." His eyes were suspicious also, insofar as they contained any expression at all. "How much she slip you?"

"What?"

"How much this old lady slip you to lay off?"

"Lay off what?"

231

"Whatever it is you're layin' off from now on." He moved his thumbs from his armholes and placed them together in front of his vest and pushed them against each other. He smiled.

"Oh, for Christ's sake," I said, and went out of the office, leaving his mouth open.

When I was about a yard from the door, I went back and opened it again quietly and looked in. He was sitting in the same position, pushing his thumbs at each other. But he wasn't smiling any more. He looked worried. His mouth was still open.

He didn't move or look up. I didn't know whether he heard me or not. I shut the door again and went away.

7

THEY HAD REMBRANDT on the calendar that year, a rather smeary self-portrait due to imperfectly registered color plate. It showed him holding a smeared palette with a dirty thumb and wearing a tam-o'-shanter which wasn't any too clean either. His other hand held a brush poised in the air, as if he might be going to do a little work after a while, if somebody made a down payment. His face was aging, saggy, full of the disgust of life and the thickening effects of liquor. But it had a hard cheerfulness that I liked, and the eyes were as bright as drops of dew.

I was looking at him across my office desk at about four-thirty when the phone rang and I heard a cool, supercilious voice that sounded as if it thought it was pretty good. It said drawlingly, after I had answered:

"You are Philip Marlowe, a private detective?"

"Check."

"Oh – you mean, yes. You have been recommended to me as a man who can be trusted to keep his mouth shut. I should like you to come to my house at seven o'clock this evening. We can discuss a matter. My name is Lindsay Marriott and

I live at 4212 Cabrillo Street, Montemar Vista. Do you know where that is?"

"I know where Montemar Vista is, Mr. Marriott."

"Yes. Well, Cabrillo Street is rather hard to find. The streets down here are all laid out in a pattern of interesting but intricate curves. I should suggest that you walk up the steps from the sidewalk cafe. If you do that, Cabrillo is the third street you come to and my house is the only one on the block. At seven then?"

"What is the nature of the employment, Mr. Marriott?"

"I should prefer not to discuss that over the phone."

"Can't you give me some idea? Montemar Vista is quite a distance."

"I shall be glad to pay your expenses, if we don't agree. Are you particular about the nature of the employment?"

"Not as long as it's legitimate."

The voice grew icicles. "I should not have called you, if it were not."

A Harvard boy. Nice use of the subjunctive mood. The end of my foot itched, but my bank account was still trying to crawl under a duck. I put honey into my voice and said: "Many thanks for calling me, Mr. Marriott. I'll be there."

He hung up and that was that. I thought Mr. Rembrandt had a faint sneer on his face. I got the office bottle out of the deep drawer of the desk and took a short drink. That took the sneer out of Mr. Rembrandt in a hurry.

A wedge of sunlight slipped over the edge of the desk and fell noiselessly to the carpet. Traffic lights bong-bonged outside on the boulevard, interurban cars pounded by, a typewriter clacked monotonously in the lawyer's office beyond the party wall. I had filled and lit a pipe when the telephone rang again.

It was Nulty this time. His voice sounded full of baked potato. "Well, I guess I ain't quite bright at that," he said, when he knew who he was talking to. "I miss one. Malloy went to see that Florian dame."

233

I held the phone tight enough to crack it. My upper lip suddenly felt a little cold. "Go on. I thought you had him cornered."

"Was some other guy. Malloy ain't around there at all. We get a call from some old window-peeker on West Fifty-four. Two guys was to see the Florian dame. Number one parked the other side of the street and acted kind of cagey. Looked the dump over good before he went in. Was in about an hour. Six feet, dark hair, medium heavy built. Come out quiet."

"He had liquor on his breath too," I said.

"Oh, sure. That was you, wasn't it? Well, Number two was the Moose. Guy in loud clothes as big as a house. He come in a car too but the old lady don't get the license, can't read the number that far off. This was about a hour after you was there, she says. He goes in fast and is in about five minutes only. Just before he gets back in his car he takes a big gat out and spins the chamber. I guess that's what the old lady saw he done. That's why she calls up. She don't hear no shots though, inside the house."

"That must have been a big disappointment," I said.

"Yeah. A nifty. Remind me to laugh on my day off. The old lady misses one too. The prowl boys go down there and don't get no answer on the door, so they walk in, the front door not being locked. Nobody's dead on the floor. Nobody's home. The Florian dame has skipped out. So they stop by next door and tell the old lady and she's sore as a boil on account of she didn't see the Florian dame go out. So they report back and go on about the job. So about an hour, maybe hour and a half after that, the old lady phones in again and says Mrs. Florian is home again. So they give the call to me and I ask her what makes that important and she hangs up in my face."

Nulty paused to collect a little breath and wait for my comments. I didn't have any. After a moment he went on grumbling.

"What you make of it?"

"Nothing much. The Moose would be likely to go by there, of course. He must have known Mrs. Florian pretty well. Naturally he wouldn't stick around very long. He would be afraid the law might be wise to Mrs. Florian."

"What I figure," Nulty said calmly. "Maybe I should go over and see her – kind of find out where she went to."

"That's a good idea," I said. "If you can get somebody to lift you out of your chair."

"Huh? Oh, another nifty. It don't make a lot of difference any more now though. I guess I won't bother."

"All right," I said. "Let's have it whatever it is."

He chuckled. "We got Malloy all lined up. We really got him this time. We make him at Girard, headed north in a rented hack. He gassed up there and the service station kid recognized him from the description we broadcast a while back. He said everything jibed except Malloy had changed to a dark suit. We got county and state law on it. If he goes on north we get him at the Ventura line, and if he slides over to the Ridge Route, he had to stop at Castaic for his check ticket. If he don't stop, they phone ahead and block the road. We don't want no cops shot up, if we can help it. That sound good?"

"It sounds all right," I said. "If it really is Malloy, and if he does exactly what you expect him to do."

Nulty cleared his throat carefully. "Yeah. What you doing on it – just in case?"

"Nothing. Why should I be doing anything on it?"

"You got along pretty good with that Florian dame. Maybe she would have some more ideas."

"All you need to find out is a full bottle," I said.

"You handled her real nice. Maybe you ought to kind of spend a little more time on her."

"I thought this was a police job."

"Oh sure. Was your idea about the girl though."

"That seems to be out – unless the Florian is lying about it."

"Dames lie about anything – just for practice," Nulty said grimly. "You ain't real busy, huh?"

"I've got a job to do. It came in since I saw you. A job where I get paid. I'm sorry."

"Walking out, huh?"

"I wouldn't put it that way. I just have to work to earn a living."

"Okay, pal. If that's the way you feel about it, okay."

"I don't feel any way about it," I almost yelled. "I just don't have time to stooge for you or any other cop."

"Okay, get sore," Nulty said, and hung up.

I held the dead phone and snarled into it: "Seventeen hundred and fifty cops in this town and they want me to do their leg work for them."

I dropped the phone into its cradle and took another drink from the office bottle.

After a while I went down to the lobby of the building to buy an evening paper. Nulty was right in one thing at least. The Montgomery killing hadn't even made the want-ad section so far.

I left the office again in time for an early dinner.

8

I GOT DOWN to Montemar Vista as the light began to fade, but there was still a fine sparkle on the water and the surf was breaking far out in long smooth curves. A group of pelicans was flying bomber formation just under the creaming lip of the waves. A lonely yacht was taking in toward the yacht harbor at Bay City. Beyond it the huge emptiness of the Pacific was purple-gray.

Montemar Vista was a few dozen houses of various sizes and shapes hanging by their teeth and eyebrows to a spur of mountain and looking as if a good sneeze would drop them down among the box lunches on the beach.

Above the beach the highway ran under a wide concrete arch which was in fact a pedestrian bridge. From the inner end of this a flight of concrete steps with a thick galvanized handrail on one side ran straight as a ruler up the side of the mountain. Beyond the arch the sidewalk cafe my client had spoken of was bright and cheerful inside, but the iron-legged tile-topped tables outside under the striped awning were empty save for a single dark woman in slacks who smoked and stared moodily out to sea, with a bottle of beer in front of her. A fox terrier was using one of the iron chairs for a lamppost. She chided the dog absently as I drove past and gave the sidewalk cafe my business to the extent of using its parking space.

I walked back through the arch and started up the steps. It was a nice walk if you liked grunting. There were two hundred and eighty steps up to Cabrillo Street. They were drifted over with windblown sand and the handrail was as cold and wet as a toad's belly.

When I reached the top the sparkle had gone from the water and a seagull with a broken trailing leg was twisting against the offsea breeze. I sat down on the damp cold top step and shook the sand out of my shoes and waited for my pulse to come down into the low hundreds. When I was breathing more or less normally again I shook my shirt loose from my back and went along to the lighted house which was the only one within yelling distance of the steps.

It was a nice little house with a salt-tarnished spiral of staircase going up to the front door and an imitation coachlamp for a porchlight. The garage was underneath and to one side. Its door was lifted up and rolled back and the light of the porchlamp shone obliquely on a huge black battleship of a car with chromium trimmings, a coyote tail tied to the Winged Victory on the radiator cap and engraved initials where the emblem should be. The car had a right-hand drive and looked as if had cost more than the house.

I went up the spiral steps, looked for a bell, and used a knocker in the shape of a tiger's head. Its clatter was swallowed in the early evening fog. I heard no steps in the house. My damp shirt felt like an icepack on my back. The door opened silently, and I was looking at a tall blond man in a white flannel suit with a violet satin scarf around his neck.

There was a cornflower in the lapel of his white coat and his pale blue eyes looked faded out by comparison. The violet scarf was loose enough to show that he wore no tie and that he had a thick, soft brown neck, like the neck of a strong woman. His features were a little on the heavy side, but handsome, he had an inch more of height than I had, which made him six feet one. His blond hair was arranged, by art or nature, in three precise blond ledges which reminded me of steps, so that I didn't like them. I wouldn't have liked them anyway. Apart from all this he had the general appearance of a lad who would wear a white flannel suit with a violet scarf around his neck and a cornflower in his lapel.

He cleared his throat lightly and looked past my shoulder at the darkening sea. His cool supercilious voice said: "Yes?"

"Seven o'clock," I said. "On the dot."

"Oh yes. Let me see, your name is −" He paused and frowned in the effort of memory. The effect was as phony as the pedigree of a used car. I let him work at it for a minute, then I said:

"Philip Marlowe. The same as it was this afternoon."

He gave me a quick darting frown, as if perhaps something ought to be done about that. Then he stepped back and said coldly:

"Ah yes. Quite so. Come in, Marlowe. My house boy is away this evening."

He opened the door wide with a fingertip, as though opening the door himself dirtied him a little.

I went in past him and smelled perfume. He closed the door. The entrance put us on a low balcony with a metal

238

railing that ran around three sides of a big studio living room. The fourth side contained a big fireplace and two doors. A fire was crackling in the fireplace. The balcony was lined with bookshelves and there were pieces of glazed metallic looking bits of sculpture on pedestals.

We went down three steps to the main part of the living room. The carpet almost tickled my ankles. There was a concert grand piano, closed down. On one corner of it stood a tall silver vase on a strip of peach-colored velvet, and a single yellow rose in the vase. There was plenty of nice soft furniture, a great many floor cushions, some with golden tassels and some just naked. It was a nice room, if you didn't get rough. There was a wide damask covered divan in a shadowy corner, like a casting couch. It was the kind of room where people sit with their feet in their laps and sip absinthe through lumps of sugar and talk with high affected voices and sometimes just squeak. It was a room where anything could happen except work.

Mr. Lindsay Marriott arranged himself in the curve of the grand piano, leaned over to sniff at the yellow rose, then opened a French enamel cigarette case and lit a long brown cigarette with a gold tip. I sat down on a pink chair and hoped I wouldn't leave a mark on it. I lit a Camel, blew smoke through my nose and looked at a piece of black shiny metal on a stand. It showed a full, smooth curve with a shallow fold in it and two protuberances on the curve. I stared at it. Marriott saw me staring at it.

"An interesting bit," he said negligently. "I picked it up just the other day. Asta Dial's *Spirit of Dawn*."

"I thought it was Klopstein's *Two Warts on a Fanny*," I said.

Mr. Lindsay Marriott's face looked as if he had swallowed a bee. He smoothed it out with an effort.

"You have a somewhat peculiar sense of humor," he said.

"Not peculiar," I said. "Just uninhibited."

"Yes," he said very coldly. "Yes – of course. I've no doubt... Well, what I wished to see you about is, as a matter of fact, a very slight matter indeed. Hardly worth bringing you down here for. I am meeting a couple of men tonight and paying them some money. I thought I might as well have someone with me. You carry a gun?"

"At times. Yes," I said. I looked at the dimple in his broad, fleshy chin. You could have lost a marble in it.

"I shan't want you to carry that. Nothing of that sort at all. This is a purely business transaction."

"I hardly ever shoot anybody," I said. "A matter of blackmail?"

He frowned. "Certainly not. I'm not in the habit of giving people grounds for blackmail."

"It happens to the nicest people. I might say particularly to the nicest people."

He waved his cigarette. His aquamarine eyes had a faintly thoughtful expression, but his lips smiled. The kind of smile that goes with a silk noose.

He blew some more smoke and tilted his head back. This accentuated the soft firm lines of his throat. His eyes came down slowly and studied me.

"I'm meeting these men – most probably – in a rather lonely place. I don't know where yet. I expect a call giving me the particulars. I have to be ready to leave at once. It won't be very far away from here. That's the understanding."

"You've been making this deal some time?"

"Three or four days, as a matter of fact."

"You left your bodyguard problem until pretty late."

He thought that over. He snicked some dark ash from his cigarette. "That's true. I had some difficulty making my mind up. It would be better for me to go alone, although nothing has been said definitely about my having someone with me. On the other hand I'm not much of a hero."

"They know you by sight, of course?"

"I – I'm not sure. I shall be carrying a large amount of money and it is not my money. I'm acting for a friend.

I shouldn't feel justified in letting it out of my possession, of course."

I snubbed out my cigarette and leaned back in the pink chair and twiddled my thumbs. "How much money – and what for?"

"Well, really –" it was a fairly nice smile now, but I still didn't like it.

"I can't go into that."

"You just want me to go along and hold your hat?"

His hand jerked again and some ash fell off on his white cuff. He shook it off and stared down at the place where it had been.

"I'm afraid I don't like your manner," he said, using the edge of his voice.

"I've had complaints about it," I said. "But nothing seems to do any good. Let's look at this job a little. You want a body-guard, but he can't wear a gun. You want a helper, but he isn't supposed to know what he's supposed to do. You want me to risk my neck without knowing why or what for or what the risk is. What are you offering for all this?"

"I hadn't really got around to thinking about it." His cheekbones were dusky red.

"Do you suppose you could get around to thinking about it?"

He leaned forward gracefully and smiled between his teeth. "How would you like a swift punch on the nose?"

I grinned and stood up and put my hat on. I started across the carpet towards the front door, but not very fast.

His voice snapped at my back. "I'm offering you a hundred dollars for a few hours of your time. If that isn't enough, say so. There's no risk. Some jewels were taken from a friend of mine in a holdup – and I'm buying them back. Sit down and don't be so touchy."

I went back to the pink chair and sat down again.

"All right," I said. "Let's hear about it."

We stared at each other for all of ten seconds. "Have you ever heard of Fei Tsui jade?" he asked slowly, and lit another of his dark cigarettes.

"No."

"It's the only really valuable kind. Other kinds are valuable to some extent for the material, but chiefly for the workmanship on them. Fei Tsui is valuable in itself. All known deposits were exhausted hundreds of years ago. A friend of mine owns a necklace of sixty beads of about six carats each, intricately carved. Worthy eighty or ninety thousand dollars. The Chinese government has a very slightly larger one valued at a hundred and twenty-five thousand. My friend's necklace was taken in a holdup a few nights ago. I was present, but quite helpless. I had driven my friend to an evening party and later to the Trocadero and we were on our way back to her home from there. A car brushed the left front fender and stopped, as I thought, to apologize. Instead of that it was a very quick and very neat holdup. Either three or four men, I really saw only two, but I'm sure another stayed in the car behind the wheel, and I thought I saw a glimpse of still a fourth at the rear window. My friend was wearing the jade necklace. They took that and two rings and a bracelet. The one who seemed to be the leader looked the things over without any apparent hurry under a small flashlight. Then he handed one of the rings back and said that would give us an idea what kind of people we were dealing with and to wait for a phone call before reporting to the police or the insurance company. So we obeyed their instructions. There's plenty of that sort of thing going on, of course. You keep the affair to yourself and pay ransom, or you never see your jewels again. If they're fully insured, perhaps you don't mind, but if they happen to be rare pieces, you would rather pay ransom."

I nodded. "And this jade necklace is something that can't be picked up every day."

He slid a finger along the polished surface of the piano with a dreamy expression, as if touching smooth things pleased him.

"Very much so. It's irreplaceable. She shouldn't have worn it out – ever. But she's a reckless sort of woman. The other things were good but ordinary."

"Uh-huh. How much are you paying?"

"Eight thousand dollars. It's dirt cheap. But if my friend couldn't get another like it, these thugs couldn't very easily dispose of it either. It's probably known to every one in the trade, all over the country."

"This friend of yours – does she have a name?"

"I'd prefer not to mention it at the moment."

"What are the arrangements?"

He looked at me along his pale eyes. I thought he seemed a bit scared, but I didn't know him very well. Maybe it was a hangover. The hand that held the dark cigarette couldn't keep still.

"We have been negotiating by telephone for several days – through me. Everything is settled except the time and place of meeting. It is to be sometime tonight. I shall presently be getting a call to tell me of that. It will not be very far away, they say, and I must be prepared to leave at once. I suppose that is so that no plant could be arranged. With the police, I mean."

"Uh-huh. Is the money marked? I suppose it *is* money?"

"Currency, of course. Twenty-dollar bills. No, why should it be marked?"

"It can be done so that it takes black light to detect it. No reason – except that the cops like to break up these gangs – if they can get any co-operation. Some of the money might turn up on some lad with a record."

He wrinkled his brow thoughtfully. "I'm afraid I don't know what black light is."

"Ultra-violet. It makes certain metallic inks glisten in the dark. I could get it done for you."

"I'm afraid there isn't time for that now," he said shortly.

"That's one of the things that worries me."

"Why?"

"Why you only called me this afternoon. Why you picked on me. Who told you about me?"

He laughed. His laugh was rather boyish, but not a very young boy. "Well, as a matter of fact I'll have to confess I merely picked your name at random out of the phone book. You see I hadn't intended to have anyone go with me. Then this afternoon I got to thinking why not."

I lit another of my squashed cigarettes and watched his throat muscles. "What's the plan?"

He spread his hands. "Simply to go where I am told, hand over the package of money, and receive back the jade necklace."

"Uh-huh."

"You seem fond of that expression."

"What expression?"

"Uh-huh."

"Where will I be – in the back of the car?"

"I suppose so. It's a big car. You could easily hide in the back of it."

"Listen," I said slowly. "You plan to go out with me hidden in your car to a destination you are to get over the phone some time tonight. You will have eight grand in currency on you and with that you are supposed to buy back a jade necklace worth ten or twelve times that much. What you will probably get will be a package you won't be allowed to open – providing you get anything at all. It's just as likely they will simply take your money, count it over in some other place, and mail you the necklace, if they feel bighearted. There's nothing to prevent them double-crossing you. Certainly nothing I could do would stop them. These are heist guys. They're tough. They might even knock you on the head – not hard – just enough to delay you while they go on their way."

"Well, as a matter of fact, I'm a little afraid of something like that," he said quietly, and his eyes twitched. "I suppose that's really why I wanted somebody with me."

"Did they put a flash on you when they pulled the stickup?"

He shook his head, no.

"No matter. They've had a dozen chances to look you over since. They probably knew all about you before that anyway. These jobs are cased. They're cased the way a dentist cases your tooth for a gold inlay. You go out with this dame much?"

"Well – not infrequently," he said stiffly.

"Married?"

"Look here," he snapped. "Suppose we leave the lady out of this entirely."

"Okay," I said. "But the more I know the fewer cups I break. I ought to walk away from this job, Marriott. I really ought. If the boys want to play ball, you don't need me. If they don't want to play ball, I can't do anything about it."

"All I want is your company," he said quickly.

I shrugged and spread my hands. "Okay – but I drive the car and carry the money – and you do the hiding in the back. We're about the same height. If there's any question, we'll just tell them the truth. Nothing to lose by it."

"No." He bit his lip.

"I'm getting a hundred dollars for doing nothing. If anybody gets conked, it ought to be me."

He frowned and shook his head, but after quite a long time his face cleared slowly and he smiled.

"Very well," he said slowly. "I don't suppose it matters much. We'll be together. Would you care for a spot of brandy?"

"Uh-huh. And you might bring me my hundred bucks. I like to feel money."

He moved away like a dancer, his body almost motionless from the waist up.

The phone rang as he was on his way out. It was in a little alcove off the living room proper, cut into the balcony. It wasn't the call we were thinking about though. He sounded too affectionate.

He danced back after a while with a bottle of Five-Star Martell and five nice crisp twenty-dollar bills. That made it a nice evening – so far.

9

THE HOUSE WAS very still. Far off there was a sound which might have been beating surf or cars zooming along a highway, or wind in pine trees. It was the sea, of course, breaking far down below. I sat there and listened to it and thought long, careful thoughts.

The phone rang four times within the next hour and a half. The big one came at eight minutes past ten. Marriott talked briefly, in a very low voice, cradled the instrument without a sound and stood up with a sort of hushed movement. His face looked drawn. He had changed to dark clothes now. He walked silently back into the room and poured himself a stiff drink in a brandy glass. He held it against the light a moment with a queer unhappy smile, swirled it once quickly and tilted his head back to pour it down his throat.

"Well – we're all set, Marlowe. Ready?"

"That's all I've been all evening. Where do we go?"

"A place called Purissima Canyon."

"I never heard of it."

"I'll get a map." He got one and spread it out quickly and the light blinked in his brassy hair as he bent over it. Then he pointed with his finger. The place was one of the many canyons off the foothill boulevard that turns into town from the coast highway north of Bay City. I had a vague idea where it was, but no more. It seemed to be at the end of a street called Camino de la Costa.

"It will be not more than twelve minutes from here," Marriott said quickly. "We'd better get moving. We only have twenty minutes to play with."

He handed me a light colored overcoat which made me a fine target. It fitted pretty well. I wore my own hat. I had a gun under my arm, but I hadn't told him about that.

While I put the coat on, he went on talking in a light nervous voice and dancing on his hands the thick manila envelope with the eight grand in it.

"Purissima Canyon has a sort of level shelf at the inner end of it, they say. This is walled off from the road by a white fence of four-by-fours, but you can just squeeze by. A dirt road winds down into a little hollow and we are to wait there without lights. There are no houses around."

"We?"

"Well, I mean 'I' – theoretically."

"Oh."

He handed me the manila envelope and I opened it up and looked at what was inside. It was money all right, a huge wad of currency. I didn't count it. I snapped the rubber around again and stuffed the packet down inside my overcoat. It almost caved in a rib.

We went to the door and Marriott switched off all the lights. He opened the front door cautiously and peered out at the foggy air. We went out and down the salt-tarnished spiral stairway to the street level and the garage.

It was a little foggy, the way it always is down there at night. I had to start up the windshield wiper for a while.

The big foreign car drove itself, but I held the wheel for the sake of appearances.

For two minutes we figure-eighted back and forth across the face of the mountain and then popped out right beside the sidewalk cafe. I could understand now why Mariott had told me to walk up the steps. I could have driven about in those curving, twisting streets for hours without making any more yardage than an angleworm in a bait can.

On the highway the lights of the streaming cars made an almost solid beam in both directions. The big cornpoppers were rolling north growling as they went and festooned all over with green and yellow overhang lights. Three minutes of that and we turned inland, by a big service station, and wound along the flank of the foothills. It got quiet. There was loneliness and the smell of kelp and the smell of wild sage from the hills. A yellow window hung here and there, all by itself, like the last orange. Cars passed, spraying the pavement with cold white light, then growled off into the darkness again. Wisps of fog chased the stars down the sky.

Marriott leaned forward from the dark rear seat and said:

"Those lights off to the right are the Belvedere Beach Club. The next canyon is Las Pulgas and the next after that Purissima. We turn right at the top of the second rise." His voice was hushed and taut.

I grunted and kept on driving. "Keep your head down," I said over my shoulder. "We may be watched all the way. This car sticks out like spats at an Iowa picnic. Could be the boys don't like your being twins."

We went down into a hollow at the inward end of a canyon and then up on the high ground and after a little while down again and up again. Then Marriott's tight voice said in my ear:

"Next street on the right. The house with the square turret. Turn beside that."

"You didn't help them pick this place out, did you?"

"Hardly," he said, and laughed grimly. "I just happen to know these canyons pretty well."

I swung the car to the right past a big corner house with a square white turret topped with round tiles. The headlights sprayed for an instant on a street sign that read: Camino de la Costa. We slid down a broad avenue lined with unfinished electroliers and weed-grown sidewalks. Some realtor's dream had turned into a hangover there. Crickets chirped and bullfrogs whooped in the darkness behind the overgrown sidewalks. Marriott's car was that silent.

There was a house to a block, then a house to two blocks, then no houses at all. A vague window or two was still lighted, but the people around there seemed to go to bed with the chickens. Then the paved avenue ended abruptly in a dirt road packed as hard as concrete in dry weather. The dirt road narrowed and dropped slowly downhill between walls of brush. The lights of the Belvedere Beach Club hung in the air to the right and far ahead there was a gleam of moving water. The acrid smell of the sage filled the night. Then a white-painted barrier loomed across the dirt road and Marriott spoke at my shoulder again.

"I don't think you can get past it," he said. "The space doesn't look wide enough."

I cut the noiseless motor, dimmed the lights and sat there, listening. Nothing. I switched the lights off altogether and got out of the car. The crickets stopped chirping. For a little while the silence was so complete that I could hear the sound of tires on the highway at the bottom of the cliffs, a mile away. Then one by one the crickets started up again until the night was full of them.

"Sit tight. I'm going down there and have a look-see," I whispered into the back of the car.

I touched the gun butt inside my coat and walked forward. There was more room between the brush and the end of the white barrier than there had seemed to be from the car. Someone had hacked the brush away and there were car marks in the dirt. Probably kids going down there to neck on warm nights. I went on past the barrier. The road dropped and curved. Below was darkness and a vague far-off sea-sound. And the lights of cars on the highway. I went on. The road ended in a shallow bowl entirely surrounded by brush. It was empty. There seemed to be no way into it but the way I had come. I stood there in the silence and listened.

Minute passed slowly after minute, but I kept on waiting for some new sound. None came. I seemed to have that hollow entirely to myself.

I looked across to the lighted beach club. From its upper windows a man with a good night glass could probably cover this spot fairly well. He could see a car come and go, see who got out of it, whether there was a group of men or just one. Sitting in a dark room with a good night glass you can see a lot more detail than you would think possible.

I turned to go back up the hill. From the base of a bush a cricket chirped loud enough to make me jump. I went on up around the curve and past the white barricade. Still nothing. The black car stood dimly shining against a grayness which was neither darkness nor light. I went over to it and put a foot on the running board beside the driver's seat.

"Looks like a tryout," I said under my breath, but loud enough for Marriott to hear me from the back of the car. "Just to see if you obey orders."

There was a vague movement behind but he didn't answer. I went on trying to see something besides bushes.

Whoever it was had a nice easy shot at the back of my head. Afterwards I thought I might have heard the swish of a sap. Maybe you always think that – afterwards.

10

"FOUR MINUTES," THE voice said. "Five, possibly six. They must have moved quick and quiet. He didn't even let out a yell."

I opened my eyes and looked fuzzily at a cold star. I was lying on my back. I felt sick.

The voice said: "It could have been a little longer. Maybe even eight minutes altogether. They must have been in the brush, right where the car stopped. The guy scared easily. They must have thrown a small light in his face and he passed out – just from panic. The pansy."

There was silence. I got up on one knee. Pains shot from the back of my head clear to my ankles.

"Then one of them got into the car," the voice said, "and waited for you to come back. The others hid again. They must have figured he would be afraid to come alone. Or something in his voice made them suspicious, when they talked to him on the phone."

I balanced myself woozily on the flat of my hands, listening.

"Yeah, that was about how it was," the voice said.

It was my voice. I was talking to myself, coming out of it. I was trying to figure the thing out subconsciously.

"Shut up, you dimwit," I said, and stopped talking to myself.

Far off the purl of motors, nearer the chirp of crickets, the peculiar long drawn ee-ee-ee of tree frogs. I didn't think I was going to like those sounds any more.

I lifted a hand off the ground and tried to shake the sticky sage ooze off it, then rubbed it on the side of my coat. Nice work, for a hundred dollars. The hand jumped at the inside pocket of the overcoat. No manila envelope, naturally. The hand jumped inside my own suit coat. My wallet was still there. I wondered if my hundred was still in it. Probably not. Something felt heavy against my left ribs. The gun in the shoulder holster.

That was a nice touch. They left me my gun. A nice touch of something or other – like closing a man's eyes after you knife him.

I felt the back of my head. My hat was still on. I took it off, not without discomfort, and felt the head underneath. Good old head, I'd had it a long time. It was a little soft now, a little pulpy, and more than a little tender. But a pretty light sapping at that. The hat had helped. I could still use the head. I could use it another year anyway.

I put my right hand back on the ground and took the left off and swiveled it around until I could see my watch. The illuminated dial showed 10.56, as nearly as I could focus on it.

The call had come at 10.08. Marriott had talked maybe two minutes. Another four had got us out of the house. Time passes very slowly when you are actually doing something. I mean, you can go through a lot of movements in very few minutes. Is that what I mean? What the hell do I care what I mean? Okay, better men than me have meant less. Okay, what I mean is, that would be 10.15, say. The place was about twelve minutes away. 10.27. I get out, walk down in the hollow, spend at the most eight minutes fooling around and come on back up to get my head treated. 10.35. Give me a minute to fall down and hit the ground with my face. The reason I hit it with my face, I got my chin scraped. It hurts. It feels scraped. That way I know it's scraped. No, I can't see it. I don't have to see it. It's my chin and I know whether it's scraped or not. Maybe you want to make something of it. Okay, shut up and let me think. What with? . . .

The watch showed 10.56 p.m. That meant I had been out for twenty minutes.

Twenty minutes' sleep. Just a nice doze. In that time I had muffed a job and lost eight thousand dollars. Well, why not? In twenty minutes you can sink a battleship, down three or four planes, hold a double execution. You can die, get married, get fired and find a new job, have a tooth pulled, have your tonsils out. In twenty minutes you can even get up in the morning. You can get a glass of water at a night club – maybe.

Twenty minutes' sleep. That's a long time. Especially on a cold night, out in the open. I began to shiver.

I was still on my knees. The smell of the sage was beginning to bother me. The sticky ooze from which wild bees get their honey. Honey was sweet, much too sweet. My stomach took a whirl. I clamped my teeth tight and just managed to keep it down my throat. Cold sweat stood out in lumps on my forehead, but I shivered just the same. I got up on one foot, then on both feet, straightened up, wobbling a little. I felt like an amputated leg.

I turned slowly. The car was gone. The dirt road stretched empty, back up the shallow hill towards the paved street, the end of Camino de la Costa. To the left the barrier of white-painted four-by-fours stood out against the darkness. Beyond the low wall of brush the pale glow in the sky would be the lights of Bay City. And over farther to the right and near by were the lights of the Belvedere Club.

I went over where the car had stood and got a fountain pen flash unclipped from my pocket and poked the little light down at the ground. The soil was red loam, very hard in dry weather, but the weather was not bone dry. There was a little fog in the air, and enough of the moisture had settled on the surface of the ground to show where the car had stood. I could see, very faint, the tread marks of the heavy ten-ply Vogue tires. I put the light on them and bent over and the pain made my head dizzy. I started to follow the tracks. They went straight ahead for a dozen feet, then swung over to the left. They didn't turn. They went towards the gap at the left-hand end of the white barricade. Then I lost them.

I went over to the barricade and shone the little light on the brush. Fresh-broken twigs. I went through the gap, on down the curving road. The ground was still softer here. More marks of the heavy tires. I went on down, rounded the curve and was at the edge of the hollow closed in by brush.

It was there all right, the chromium and glossy paint shining a little even in the dark, and the red reflector glass of the tail-lights shining back at the pencil flash. It was there, silent, lightless, all the doors shut. I went towards it slowly, gritting my teeth at every step. I opened one of the rear doors and put the beam of the flash inside. Empty. The front was empty too. The ignition was off. The key hung in the lock on a thin chain. No torn upholstery, no scarred glass, no blood, no bodies. Everything neat and orderly. I shut the doors and circled the car slowly, looking for a sign and not finding any.

A sound froze me.

A motor throbbed above the rim of the brush. I didn't jump more than a foot. The flash in my hand went out. A gun slid into my hand all by itself. Then headlight beams tilted up towards the sky, then tilted down again. The motor sounded like a small car. It had that contented sound that comes with moisture in the air.

The lights tilted down still more and got brighter. A car was coming down the curve of the dirt road. It came two-thirds of the way and then stopped. A spotlight clicked on and swung out to the side, held there for a long moment, went out again. The car came down the hill. I slipped the gun out of my pocket and crouched behind the motor of Marriott's car.

A small coupe of no particular shape or color slid into the hollow and turned so that its headlights raked the sedan from one end to the other. I got my head down in a hurry. The lights swept above me like a sword. The coupe stopped. The motor died. The headlights died. Silence. Then a door opened and a light foot touched the ground. More silence. Even the crickets were silent. Then a beam of light cut the darkness low down, parallel to the ground and only a few inches above it. The beam swept, and there was no way I could get my ankles out of it quickly enough. The beam stopped on my feet. Silence. The beam came up and raked the top of the hood again.

Then a laugh. It was a girl's laugh. Strained, taut as a mandolin wire. A strange sound in that place. The white beam shot under the car again and settled on my feet.

The voice said, not quite shrilly: "All right, you. Come out of there with your hands up and very damned empty. You're covered."

I didn't move.

The light wavered a little, as though the hand that held it wavered. It swept slowly along the hood once more. The voice stabbed at me again.

"Listen, stranger. I'm holding a ten shot automatic. I can shoot straight. Both your feet are vulnerable. What do you bid?"

"Put it up – or I'll blow it out of your hand!" I snarled. My voice sounded like somebody tearing slats off a chicken coop.

"Oh – a hard-boiled gentleman." There was a quaver in the voice, a nice little quaver. Then it hardened again. "Coming out? I'll count three. Look at the odds I'm giving you – twelve fat cylinders, maybe sixteen. But your feet will hurt. And ankle bones take years and years to get well and sometimes they never do really –"

I straightened up slowly and looked into the beam of the flashlight.

"I talk too much when I'm scared too," I said.

"Don't – don't move another inch! Who are you?"

I moved around the front of the car towards her. When I was six feet from the slim dark figure behind the flash I stopped. The flash glared at me steadily.

"You stay right there," the girl snapped angrily, after I had stopped. "Who are you?"

"Let's see your gun."

She held it forward into the light. It was pointed at my stomach. It was a little gun, it looked like a small Colt vest pocket automatic.

"Oh, that," I said. "That toy. It doesn't either hold ten shots. It holds six. It's just a little bitty gun, a butterfly gun. They shoot butterflies with them. Shame on you for telling a deliberate lie like that."

"Are you crazy?"

"Me? I've been sapped by a holdup man. I might be a little goofy."

"Is that – is that your car?"

"No."

"Who are you?"

255

"What were you looking at back there with your spot-light?"

"I get it. You ask the answers. He-man stuff. I was looking at a man."

"Does he have blond hair in waves?"

"Not now," she said quietly. "He might have had – once."

That jarred me. Somehow I hadn't expected it. "I didn't see him," I said lamely. "I was following the tire marks with a flashlight down the hill. Is he badly hurt?" I went another step towards her. The little gun jumped at me and the flash held steady.

"Take it easy," she said quietly. "Very easy. Your friend is dead."

I didn't say anything for a moment. Then I said: "All right, let's go look at him."

"Let's stand right here and not move and you tell me who you are and what happened." The voice was crisp. It was not afraid. It meant what it said.

"Marlowe. Philip Marlowe. An investigator. Private."

"That's who you are – if it's true. Prove it."

"I'm going to take my wallet out."

"I don't think so. Just leave your hands where they happen to be. We'll skip the proof for the time being. What's your story?"

"This man may not be dead."

"He's dead all right. With his brains on his face. The story, mister. Make it fast."

"As I said – he may not be dead. We'll go look at him." I moved one foot forward.

"Move and I'll drill you!" she snapped.

I moved the other foot forward. The flash jumped about a little. I think she took a step back.

"You take some awful chances, mister," she said quietly. "All right, go on ahead and I'll follow. You look like a sick man. If it hadn't been for that –"

"You'd have shot me. I've been sapped. It always makes me a little dark under the eyes."

"A nice sense of humor – like a morgue attendant," she almost wailed.

I turned away from the light and immediately it shone on the ground in front of me. I walked past the little coupe, an ordinary little car, clean and shiny under the misty starlight. I went on, up the dirt road, around the curve. The steps were close behind me and the flashlight guided me. There was no sound anywhere now except our steps and the girl's breathing. I didn't hear mine.

11

HALFWAY UP THE slope I looked off to the right and saw his foot. She swung the light. Then I saw all of him. I ought to have seen him as I came down, but I had been bent over, peering at the ground with the fountain pen flash, trying to read tire marks by a light the size of a quarter.

"Give me the flash," I said and reached back.

She put it into my hand, without a word. I went down on a knee. The ground felt cold and damp through the cloth.

He lay smeared to the ground, on his back, at the base of a bush, in that bag-of-clothes position that always means the same thing. His face was a face I had never seen before. His hair was dark with blood, the beautiful blond ledges were tangled with blood and some thick grayish ooze, like primeval slime.

The girl behind me breathed hard, but she didn't speak. I held the light on his face. He had been beaten to a pulp. One of his hands was flung out in a frozen gesture, the fingers curled. His overcoat was half twisted under him, as though he had rolled as he fell. His legs were crossed. There was a trickle as black as dirty oil at the corner of his mouth.

"Hold the flash on him," I said, passing it back to her. "If it doesn't make you sick."

She took it and held it without a word, as steady as an old homicide veteran. I got my fountain pen flash out again and started to go through his pockets, trying not to move him.

"You shouldn't do that," she said tensely. "You shouldn't touch him until the police come."

"That's right," I said. "And the prowl car boys are not supposed to touch him until the K-car men come and they're not supposed to touch him until the coroner's examiner sees him and the photographers have photographed him and the fingerprint man has taken his prints. And do you know how long all that is liable to take out here? A couple of hours."

"All right," she said. "I suppose you're always right. I guess you must be that kind of person. Somebody must have hated him to smash his head in like that."

"I don't suppose it was personal," I growled. "Some people just like to smash heads."

"Seeing that I don't know what it's all about, I couldn't guess," she said tartly.

I went through his clothes. He had loose silver and bills in one trouser pocket, a tooled leather keycase in the other, also a small knife. His left hip pocket yielded a small billfold with more currency, insurance cards, a driver's license, a couple of receipts. In his coat loose match folders, a gold pencil clipped to a pocket, two thin cambric handkerchiefs as fine and white as dry powdered snow. Then the enamel cigarette case from which I had seen him take his brown gold-tipped cigarettes. They were South American, from Montevideo. And in the other inside pocket a second cigarette case I hadn't seen before. It was made of embroidered silk, a dragon on each side, a frame of imitation tortoise-shell so thin it was hardly there at all. I tickled the catch open and looked in at three oversized Russian cigarettes under the band of elastic. I pinched one. They felt old and dry and loose. They had hollow mouthpieces.

"He smoked the others," I said over my shoulder. "These must have been for a lady friend. He would be a lad who would have a lot of lady friends."

The girl was bent over, breathing on my neck now. "Didn't you know him?"

"I only met him tonight. He hired me for a bodyguard."

"Some bodyguard."

I didn't say anything to that.

"I'm sorry," she almost whispered. "Of course I don't know the circumstances. Do you suppose those could be jujus? Can I look?"

I passed the embroidered case back to her.

"I knew a guy once who smoked jujus," she said. "Three highballs and three sticks of tea and it took a pipe wrench to get him off the chandelier."

"Hold the light steady."

There was a rustling pause. Then she spoke again.

"I'm sorry." She handed the case down again and I slipped it back in his pocket. That seemed to be all. All it proved was that he hadn't been cleaned out.

I stood up and took my wallet out. The five twenties were still in it.

"High-class boys," I said. "They only took the large money."

The flash was drooping to the ground. I put my wallet away again, clipped my own small flash to my pocket and reached suddenly for the little gun she was still holding in the same hand with the flashlight. She dropped the flashlight, but I got the gun. She stepped back quickly and I reached down for the light. I put it on her face for a moment, then snapped it off.

"You didn't have to be rough," she said, putting her hands down into the pockets of a long rough coat with flaring shoulders. "I didn't think you killed him."

I liked the cool quiet of her voice. I liked her nerve. We stood in the darkness, face to face, not saying anything for a moment. I could see the blush and light in the sky.

I put the light on her face and she blinked. It was a small neat vibrant face with large eyes. A face with bone under the skin, fine drawn like a Cremona violin. A very nice face.

"Your hair's red," I said. "You look Irish."

"And my name's Riordan. So what? Put that light out. It's not red, it's auburn."

I put it out. "What's your first name?"

"Anne. And don't call me Annie."

"What are you doing around here?"

"Sometimes at night I go riding. Just restless. I live alone. I'm an orphan. I know all this neighborhood like a book. I just happened to be riding along and noticed a light flickering down in the hollow. It seemed a little cold for young love. And they don't use lights, do they?"

"I never did. You take some awful chances, Miss Riordan."

"I think I said the same about you. I had a gun. I wasn't afraid. There's no law against going down there."

"Uh-huh. Only the law of self preservation. Here. It's not my night to be clever. I suppose you have a permit for the gun." I held it out to her, butt first.

She took it and tucked it down into her pocket. "Strange how curious people can be, isn't it? I write a little. Feature articles."

"Any money in it?"

"Very damned little. What were you looking for – in his pockets?"

"Nothing in particular. I'm a great guy to snoop around. We had eight thousand dollars to buy back some stolen jewelry for a lady. We got hijacked. Why they killed him I don't know. He didn't strike me as a fellow who would put up much of a fight. And I didn't hear a fight. I was down in the hollow when he was jumped. He was in the car, up above. We were supposed to drive down into the hollow but there didn't seem to be room for the car without scratching it up. So I went down there on foot and while I was down there they must have stuck him up. Then one of them got into the car and dry-gulched me. I thought he was still in the car, of course."

"That doesn't make you so terribly dumb," she said.

"There was something wrong with the job from the start. I could feel it. But I needed the money. Now I have to go to the cops and eat dirt. Will you drive me to Montemar Vista? I left my car there. He lived there."

"Sure. But shouldn't somebody stay with him? You could take my car — or I could go call the cops."

I looked at the dial of my watch. The faintly glowing hands said that it was getting towards midnight.

"No."

"Why not?"

"I don't know why not. I just feel it that way. I'll play it alone."

She said nothing. We went back down the hill and got into her little car and she started it and jockeyed it around without lights and drove it back up the hill and eased it past the barrier. A block away she sprang the lights on.

My head ached. We didn't speak until we came level with the first house on the paved part of the street. Then she said:

"You need a drink. Why not go back to my house and have one? You can phone the law from there. They have to come from West Los Angeles anyway. There's nothing up here but a fire station."

"Just keep on going down to the coast. I'll play it solo."

"But why? I'm not afraid of them. My story might help you."

"I don't want any help. I've got to think. I want to be by myself for a while."

"I — okay," she said.

She made a vague sound in her throat and turned on to the boulevard. We came to the service station at the coast highway and turned north to Montemar Vista and the sidewalk cafe there. It was lit up like a luxury liner. The girl pulled over on to the shoulder and I got out and stood holding the door.

I fumbled a card out of my wallet and passed it in to her. "Some day you may need a strong back," I said. "Let me know. But don't call me if it's brain work."

She tapped the card on the wheel and said slowly: "You'll find me in the Bay City phone book. 819 Twenty-fifth Street. Come around and pin a putty medal on me for minding my own business. I think you're still woozy from that crack on the head."

She swung her car swiftly around on the highway and I watched its twin tail-lights fade into the dark.

I walked past the arch and the sidewalk cafe into the parking space and got into my car. A bar was right in front of me and I was shaking again. But it seemed smarter to walk into the West Los Angeles police station the way I did twenty minutes later, as cold as a frog and as green as the back of a new dollar bill.

12

IT WAS AN HOUR and a half later. The body had been taken away, the ground gone over, and I had told my story three or four times. We sat, four of us, in the day captain's room at the West Los Angeles station. The building was quiet except for a drunk in a cell who kept giving the Australian bush call while he waited to go downtown for sunrise court.

A hard white light inside a glass reflector shone down on the flat topped table on which were spread the things that had come from Lindsay Marriott's pockets, things now that seemed as dead and homeless as their owner. The man across the table from me was named Randall and he was from Central Homicide in Los Angeles. He was a thin quiet man of fifty with smooth creamy gray hair, cold eyes, a distant manner. He wore a dark red tie with black spots on it and the spots kept dancing in front of my eyes. Behind him, beyond the cone of light two beefy men lounged like bodyguards, each of them watching one of my ears.

I fumbled a cigarette around in my fingers and lit it and didn't like the taste of it. I sat watching it burn between my fingers. I felt about eighty years old and slipping fast.

Randall said coldly: "The oftener you tell this story the sillier it sounds. This man Marriott had been negotiating for days, no doubt, about this payoff and then just a few hours before the final meeting he calls up a perfect stranger and hires him to go with him as a bodyguard."

"Not exactly as a bodyguard," I said. "I didn't even tell him I had a gun. Just for company."

"Where did he hear of you?"

"First he said a mutual friend. Then that he just picked my name out of the book."

Randall poked gently among the stuff on the table and detached a white card with an air of touching something not quite clean. He pushed it along the wood.

"He had your card. Your business card."

I glanced at the card. It had come out of his billfold, together with a number of other cards I hadn't bothered to examine back there in the hollow of Purissima Canyon. It was one of my cards all right. It looked rather dirty at that, for a man like Marriott. There was a round smear across one corner.

"Sure," I said. "I hand those out whenever I get a chance. Naturally."

"Marriott let you carry the money," Randall said. "Eight thousand dollars. He was rather a trusting soul."

I drew on my cigarette and blew the smoke towards the ceiling. The light hurt my eyes. The back of my head ached.

"I don't have the eight thousand dollars," I said. "Sorry."

"No. You wouldn't be here, if you had the money. Or would you?" There was a cold sneer on his face now, but it looked artificial.

"I'd do a lot for eight thousand dollars," I said. "But if I wanted to kill a man with a sap, I'd only hit him twice at the most – on the back of the head."

He nodded slightly. One of the dicks behind him spit into the wastebasket.

"That's one of the puzzling features. It looks like an amateur job, but of course it might be meant to look like an amateur job. The money was not Marriott's, was it?"

"I don't know. I got the impression not, but that was just an impression. He wouldn't tell me who the lady in the case was."

"We don't know anything about Marriott – yet," Randall said slowly. "I suppose it's at least possible he meant to steal the eight thousand himself."

"Huh?" I felt surprised. I probably looked surprised. Nothing changed in Randall's smooth face.

"Did you count the money?"

"Of course not. He just gave me a package. There was money in it and it looked like a lot. He said it was eight grand. Why would he want to steal it from me when he already had it before I came on the scene?"

Randall looked at a corner of the ceiling and drew his mouth down at the corners. He shrugged.

"Go back a bit," he said. "Somebody had stuck up Marriott and a lady and taken this jade necklace and stuff and had later offered to sell it back for what seems like a pretty small amount, in view of its supposed value. Marriott was to handle the payoff. He thought of handling it alone and we don't know whether the other parties made a point of that or whether it was mentioned. Usually in cases like that they are rather fussy. But Marriott evidently decided it was all right to have you along. Both of you figured you were dealing with an organized gang and that they would play ball within the limits of their trade. Marriott was scared. That would be natural enough. He wanted company. You were the company. But you are a complete stranger to him, just a name on a card handed to him by some unknown party, said by him to be a mutual friend. Then at the last minute Marriott decides to have you carry the money and do the talking while he hides in the car. You say that was your idea, but he may have been hoping you would suggest it, and if you didn't suggest it, he would have had the idea himself."

"He didn't like the idea at first," I said.

Randall shrugged again. "He pretended not to like the idea – but he gave in. So finally he gets a call and off you go to the place he describes. All this is coming from Marriott. None of it is known to you independently. When you get there, there seems to be nobody about. You are supposed to drive down into that hollow, but it doesn't look to be room enough for the big car. It wasn't, as a matter of fact, because the car was pretty badly scratched on the left side. So you get out and walk down into the hollow, see and hear nothing, wait a few minutes, come back to the car and then somebody in the car socks you on the back of the head. Now suppose Marriott wanted that money and wanted to make you the fall guy – wouldn't he have acted just the way he did?"

"It's a swell theory," I said. "Marriott socked me, took the money, then he got sorry and beat his brains out, after first burying the money under a bush."

Randall looked at me woodenly. "He had an accomplice of course. Both of you were supposed to be knocked out, and the accomplice would beat it with the money. Only the accomplice double-crossed Marriott by killing him. He didn't have to kill you because you didn't know him."

I looked at him with admiration and ground out my cigarette stub in a wooden tray that had once had a glass lining in it but hadn't any more.

"It fits the facts – so far as we know them," Randall said calmly. "It's no sillier than any other theory we could think up at the moment."

"It doesn't fit one fact – that I was socked from the car,

does it? That would make me suspect Marriott of having socked me — other things being equal. Although I didn't suspect him after he was killed."

"The way you were socked fits best of all," Randall said. "You didn't tell Marriott you had a gun, but he may have seen the bulge under your arm or at least suspected you had a gun. In that case he would want to hit you when you suspected nothing. And you wouldn't suspect anything from the back of the car."

"Okay," I said. "You win. It's a good theory, always supposing the money was not Marriott's and that he wanted to steal it and that he had an accomplice. So his plan is that we both wake up with bumps on our heads and the money is gone and we say so sorry and I go home and forget all about it. Is that how it ends? I mean is that how he expected it to end? It had to look good to him too, didn't it?"

Randall smiled wryly. "I don't like it myself. I was just trying it out. It fits the facts — as far as I know them, which is not far."

"We don't know enough to even start theorizing," I said. "Why not assume he was telling the truth and that he perhaps recognized one of the stick-up men?"

"You say you heard no struggle, no cry?"

"No. But he could have been grabbed quickly, by the throat. Or he could have been too scared to cry out when they jumped him. Say they were watching from the bushes and saw me go down the hill. I went some distance, you know. A good hundred feet. They go over to look into the car and see Marriott. Somebody sticks a gun in his face and makes him get out — quietly. Then he's sapped down. But something he says, or some way he looks, makes them think he has recognized somebody."

"In the dark?"

"Yes," I said. "It must have been something like that. Some voices stay in your mind. Even in the dark people are recognized."

Randall shook his head. "If this was an organized gang of jewel thieves, they wouldn't kill without a lot of provocation." He stopped suddenly and his eyes got a glazed look. He closed his mouth very slowly, very tight. He had an idea. "Hijack," he said.

I nodded. "I think that's an idea."

"There's another thing," he said. "How did you get here?"

"I drove my car."

"Where was your car?"

"Down at Montemar Vista, in the parking lot by the sidewalk cafe."

He looked at me very thoughtfully. The two dicks behind him looked at me suspiciously. The drunk in the cells tried to yodel, but his voice cracked and that discouraged him. He began to cry.

"I walked back to the highway," I said. "I flagged a car. A girl was driving it alone. She stopped and took me down."

"Some girl," Randall said. "It was late at night, on a lonely road, and she stopped."

"Yeah. Some of them will do that. I didn't get to know her, but she seemed nice." I stared at them, knowing they didn't believe me and wondering why I was lying about it.

"It was a small car," I said. "A Chevvy coupe. I didn't get the license number."

"Haw, he didn't get the license number," one of the dicks said and spat into the wastebasket again.

Randall leaned forward and stared at me carefully. "If you're holding anything back with the idea of working on this case yourself to make yourself a little publicity, I'd forget it, Marlowe. I don't like all the points in your story and I'm going to give you the night to think it over. Tomorrow I'll probably ask you for a sworn statement. In the meantime let me give you a tip. This is a murder and a police job and we wouldn't want your help, even if it was good. All we want from you is facts. Get me?"

"Sure. Can I go home now? I don't feel any too well."

"You can go home now." His eyes were icy.

I got up and started towards the door in a dead silence. When I had gone four steps Randall cleared his throat and said carelessly:

"Oh, one small point. Did you notice what kind of cig-arettes Marriott smoked?"

I turned. "Yes. Brown ones. South American, in a French enamel case."

He leaned forward and pushed the embroidered silk case out of the pile of junk on the table and then pulled it towards him.

"Ever see this one before?"

"Sure. I was just looking at it."

"I mean, earlier this evening."

"I believe I did," I said. "Lying around somewhere. Why?"

"You didn't search the body?"

"Okay," I said. "Yes, I looked through his pockets. That was in one of them. I'm sorry. Just professional curiosity. I didn't disturb anything. After all he was my client."

Randall took hold of the embroidered case with both hands and opened it. He sat looking into it. It was empty. The three cigarettes were gone.

I bit hard on my teeth and kept the tired look on my face. It was not easy.

"Did you see him smoke a cigarette out of this?"

"No."

Randall nodded coolly. "It's empty as you see. But it was in his pocket just the same. There's a little dust in it. I'm going to have it examined under a microscope. I'm not sure, but I have an idea it's marihuana."

I said: "If he had any of those, I should think he would have smoked a couple tonight. He needed something to cheer him up."

Randall closed the case carefully and pushed it away.

268

"That's all," he said. "And keep your nose clean."

I went out.

The fog had cleared off outside and the stars were as bright as artificial stars of chromium on a sky of black velvet. I drove fast. I needed a drink badly and the bars were closed.

13

I GOT UP at nine, drank three cups of black coffee, bathed the back of my head with ice-water and read the two morning papers that had been thrown against the apartment door. There was a paragraph and a bit about Moose Malloy, in Part II, but Nulty didn't get his name mentioned. There was nothing about Lindsay Marriott, unless it was on the society page.

I dressed and ate two soft-boiled eggs and drank a fourth cup of coffee and looked myself over in the mirror. I still looked a little shadowy under the eyes. I had the door open to leave when the phone rang.

It was Nulty. He sounded mean.

"Marlowe?"

"Yeah. Did you get him?"

"Oh sure. We got him." He stopped to snarl. "On the Ventura line, like I said. Boy, did we have fun! Six foot six, built like a coffer dam, on his way to Frisco to see the Fair. He had five quarts of hooch in the front seat of the rent car, and he was drinking out of another one as he rode along, doing a quiet seventy. All we had to go up against him with was two county cops with guns and blackjacks."

He paused and I turned over a few witty sayings in my mind, but none of them seemed amusing at the moment. Nulty went on:

"So he done exercises with the cops and when they was tired enough to go to sleep, he pulled one side off their car, threw the radio into the ditch, opened a fresh bottle of hooch, and went to sleep hisself. After a while the boys snapped out of it and bounced blackjacks off his head for about ten minutes before he noticed it. When he began to get sore they got handcuffs on him. It was easy. We got him in the icebox now, drunk driving, drunk in auto, assaulting police officer in performance of duty, two counts, malicious damage to official property, attempted escape from custody, assault less than mayhem, disturbing the peace, and parking on a state highway. Fun, ain't it?"

"What's the gag?" I asked. "You didn't tell me all that just to gloat."

"It was the wrong guy," Nulty said savagely. "This bird is named Stoyanoffsky and he lives in Hemet and he just got through working as a sandhog on the San Jack tunnel. Got a wife and four kids. Boy, is she sore. What you doing on Malloy?"

"Nothing. I have a headache."

"Any time you get a little free time –"

"I don't think so," I said. "Thanks just the same. When is the inquest on the nigger coming up?"

"Why bother?" Nulty sneered, and hung up.

I drove down to Hollywood Boulevard and put my car in the parking space beside the building and rode up to my floor. I opened the door of the little reception room which I always left unlocked, in case I had a client and the client wanted to wait.

Miss Anne Riordan looked up from a magazine and smiled at me.

She was wearing a tobacco brown suit with a high-necked white sweater inside it. Her hair by daylight was pure auburn and on it she wore a hat with a crown the size of a whiskey glass and a brim you could have wrapped the week's laundry in. She wore it at an angle of approximately forty-five degrees, so that the edge of the brim just missed her shoulder. In spite of that it looked smart. Perhaps because of that.

She was about twenty-eight years old. She had a rather narrow forehead of more height than is considered elegant.

Her nose was small and inquisitive, her upper lip a shade too long and her mouth more than a shade too wide. Her eyes were gray-blue with flecks of gold in them. She had a nice smile. She looked as if she had slept well. It was a nice face, a face you get to like. Pretty, but not so pretty that you would have to wear brass knuckles every time you took it out.

"I didn't know just what your office hours were," she said. "So I waited. I gather that your secretary is not here today."

"I don't have a secretary."

I went across and unlocked the inner door, then switched on the buzzer that rang on the outer door. "Let's go into my private thinking parlor."

She passed in front of me with a vague scent of very dry sandalwood and stood looking at the five green filing cases, the shabby rust-red rug, the half-dusted furniture, and the not too clean net curtains.

"I should think you would want somebody to answer the phone," she said. "And once in a while to send your curtains to the cleaners."

"I'll send them out come St. Swithin's Day. Have a chair. I might miss a few unimportant jobs. And a lot of leg art. I save money."

"I see," she said demurely, and placed a large suede bag carefully on the corner of the glass-topped desk. She leaned back and took one of my cigarettes. I burned my finger with a paper match lighting it for her.

She blew a fan of smoke and smiled through it. Nice teeth, rather large.

"You probably didn't expect to see me again so soon. How is your head?"

"Poorly. No, I didn't."

"Were the police nice to you?"

"About the way they always are."

"I'm not keeping you from anything important, am I?"

"No."

"All the same I don't think you're very pleased to see me."

I filled a pipe and reached for the packet of paper matches. I lit the pipe carefully. She watched that with approval. Pipe smokers were solid men. She was going to be disappointed in me.

"I tried to leave you out of it," I said. "I don't know why exactly. It's no business of mine any more anyhow. I ate my dirt last night and banged myself to sleep with a bottle and now it's a police case: I've been warned to leave it alone."

"The reason you left me out of it," she said calmly, "was that you didn't think the police would believe just mere idle curiosity took me down into that hollow last night. They would suspect some guilty reason and hammer at me until I was a wreck."

"How do you know I didn't think the same thing?"

"Cops are just people," she said irrelevantly.

"They start out that way, I've heard."

"Oh – cynical this morning." She looked around the office with an idle but raking glance. "Do you do pretty well in here? I mean financially? I mean, do you make a lot of money – with this kind of furniture?"

I grunted.

"Or should I try minding my own business and not asking impertinent questions?"

"Would it work, if you tried it?"

"Now we're both doing it. Tell me, why did you cover up for me last night? Was it on account of I have reddish hair and a beautiful figure?"

I didn't say anything.

"Let's try this one," she said cheerfully. "Would you like to know who that jade necklace belonged to?"

I could feel my face getting stiff. I thought hard but I couldn't remember for sure. And then suddenly I could. I hadn't said a word to her about a jade necklace.

I reached for the matches and relit my pipe. "Not very much," I said. "Why?"

"Because I know."

"Uh-huh."

"What do you do when you get real talkative – wiggle your toes?"

"All right," I growled. "You came here to tell me. Go ahead and tell me."

Her blue eyes widened and for a moment I thought they looked a little moist. She took her lower lip between her teeth and held it that way while she stared down at the desk. Then she shrugged and let go of her lip and smiled at me candidly.

"Oh I know I'm just a damned inquisitive wench. But there's a strain of bloodhound in me. My father was a cop. His name was Cliff Riordan and he was police chief of Bay City for seven years. I suppose that's what's the matter."

"I seem to remember. What happened to him?"

"He was fired. It broke his heart. A mob of gamblers headed by a man named Laird Brunette elected themselves a mayor. So they put Dad in charge of the Bureau of Records and Identification, which in Bay City is about the size of a tea-bag. So Dad quit and pottered around for a couple of years and then died. And Mother died soon after him. So I've been alone for two years."

"I'm sorry," I said.

She ground out her cigarette. It had no lipstick on it. "The only reason I'm boring you with this is that it makes it easy for me to get along with policemen. I suppose I ought to have told you last night. So this morning I found out who had charge of the case and went to see him. He was a little sore at you at first."

"That's all right," I said. "If I had told him the truth on all points, he still wouldn't have believed me. All he will do is chew one of my ears off."

She looked hurt. I got up and opened the other window. The noise of the traffic from the boulevard came in in waves, like nausea. I felt lousy. I opened the deep drawer of the desk and got the office bottle out and poured myself a drink.

Miss Riordan watched me with disapproval. I was no longer a solid man. She didn't say anything. I drank the drink and put the bottle away again and sat down.

"You didn't offer me one," she said coolly.

"Sorry. It's only eleven o'clock or less. I didn't think you looked the type."

Her eyes crinkled at the corners. "Is that a compliment?"

"In my circle, yes."

She thought that over. It didn't mean anything to her. It didn't mean anything to me either when I thought it over. But the drink made me feel a lot better.

She leaned forward and scraped her gloves slowly across the glass of the desk. "You wouldn't want to hire an assistant, would you? Not if it only cost you a kind word now and then?"

"No."

She nodded. "I thought probably you wouldn't. I'd better just give you my information and go on home."

I didn't say anything. I lit my pipe again. It makes you look thoughtful when you are not thinking.

"First of all, it occurred to me that a jade necklace like that would be a museum piece and would be well known," she said.

I held the match in the air, still burning and watching the flame crawl close to my fingers. Then I blew it out softly and dropped it in the tray and said:

"I didn't say anything to you about a jade necklace."

"No, but Lieutenant Randall did."

"Somebody ought to sew buttons on his face."

"He knew my father. I promised not to tell."

"You're telling me."

"You knew already, silly."

Her hand suddenly flew up as if it was going to fly to her mouth, but it only rose halfway and then fell back slowly and her eyes widened. It was a good act, but I knew something else about her that spoiled it.

"You *did* know, didn't you?" She breathed the words, hushedly.

"I thought it was diamonds. A bracelet, a pair of earrings, a pendant, three rings, one of the rings with emeralds too."

"Not funny," she said. "Not even fast."

"Fei Tsui jade. Very rare. Carved beads about six carats apiece, sixty of them. Worth eighty thousand dollars."

"You have such nice brown eyes," she said. "And you think you're tough."

"Well, who does it belong to and how did you find out?"

"I found out very simply. I thought the best jeweler in town would probably know, so I went and asked the manager of Block's. I told him I was a writer and wanted to do an article on rare jade – you know the line."

"So he believed your red hair and your beautiful figure."

She flushed clear to the temples. "Well, he told me any-way. It belongs to a rich lady who lives in Bay City, in an estate on the canyon. Mrs. Lewin Lockridge Grayle. Her husband is an investment banker or something, enormously rich, worth about twenty million. He used to own a radio station in Beverly Hills, Station KFDK, and Mrs. Grayle used to work there. He married her five years ago. She's a ravish-ing blonde. Mr. Grayle is elderly, liverish, stays home and takes calomel while Mrs. Grayle goes places and has a good time."

"This manager of Block's," I said. "He's a fellow that gets around."

"Oh, I didn't get all that from him, silly. Just about the necklace. The rest I got from Giddy Gertie Arbogast."

I reached into the deep drawer and brought the office bottle up again.

"You're not going to turn out to be one of those drunken detectives, are you?" she asked anxiously.

"Why not? They always solve their cases and they never even sweat. Get on with the story."

"Giddy Gertie is the society editor of the *Chronicle*. I've known him for years. He weighs two hundred and wears a Hitler mustache. He got out his morgue file on the Grayles. Look."

She reached into her bag and slid a photograph across the desk, a five-by-three glazed still.

It was a blonde. A blonde to make a bishop kick a hole in a stained glass window. She was wearing street clothes that looked black and white, and a hat to match and she was a little haughty, but not too much. Whatever you needed, wherever you happened to be – she had it. About thirty years old.

I poured a fast drink and burned my throat getting it down. "Take it away," I said. "I'll start jumping."

"Why, I got it for you. You'll want to see her, won't you?"

I looked at it again. Then I slid it under the blotter. "How about tonight at eleven?"

"Listen, this isn't just a bunch of gag lines, Mr. Marlowe. I called her up. She'll see you. On business."

"It may start out that way."

She made an impatient gesture, so I stopped fooling around and got my battle-scarred frown back on my face. "What will she see me about?"

"Her necklace, of course. It was like this. I called her up and had a lot of trouble getting to talk to her, of course, but finally I did. Then I gave her the song and dance I had given the nice man at Block's and it didn't take. She sounded as if she had a hangover. She said something about talking to her secretary, but I managed to keep her on the phone and ask her if it was true she had a Fei Tsui jade necklace. After a while she said, yes. I asked if I might see it. She said, what for? I said my piece over again and it didn't take any better than the first time. I could hear her yawning and bawling somebody outside the mouthpiece for putting me on. Then

I said I was working for Philip Marlowe. She said 'So what?' Just like that."

"Incredible. But all the society dames talk like tramps nowadays."

"I wouldn't know," Miss Riordan said sweetly. "Probably some of them *are* tramps. So I asked her if she had a phone with no extension and she said what business was it of mine. But the funny thing was she hadn't hung up on me."

"She had the jade on her mind and she didn't know what you were leading up to. And she may have heard from Randall already."

Miss Riordan shook her head. "No. I called him later and he didn't know who owned the necklace until I told him. He was quite surprised that I had found out."

"He'll get used to you," I said. "He'll probably have to. What then?"

"So I said to Mrs. Grayle: 'You'd still like it back, wouldn't you?' Just like that. I didn't know any other way to say it. I had to say something that would jar her a bit. It did. She gave me another number in a hurry. And I called that and I said I'd like to see her. She seemed surprised. So I had to tell her the story. She didn't like it. But she had been wondering why she hadn't heard from Marriott. I guess she thought he had gone south with the money or something. So I'm to see her at two o'clock. Then I'll tell her about you and how nice and discreet you are and how you would be a good man to help her get it back, if there's any chance and so on. She's already interested."

I didn't say anything. I just stared at her. She looked hurt. "What's the matter? Did I do right?"

"Can't you get it through your head that this is a police case now and that I've been warned to stay off it?"

"Mrs. Grayle has a perfect right to employ you, if she wants to."

"To do what?"

She snapped and unsnapped her bag impatiently. "Oh, my goodness − a woman like that − with her looks − can't you see −" She stopped and bit her lip. "What kind of man was Marriott?"

"I hardly knew him. I thought he was a bit of a pansy. I didn't like him very well."

"Was he a man who would be attractive to women?"

"Some women. Others would want to spit."

"Well, it looks as if he might have been attractive to Mrs. Grayle. She went out with him."

"She probably goes out with a hundred men. There's very little chance to get the necklace now."

"Why?"

I got up and walked to the end of the office and slapped the wall with the flat of my hand, hard. The clacking typewriter on the other side stopped for a moment, and then went on. I looked down through the open window into the shaft between my building and the Mansion House Hotel. The coffee shop smell was strong enough to build a garage on. I went back to my desk, dropped the bottle of whiskey back into the drawer, shut the drawer and sat down again. I lit my pipe for the eighth or ninth time and looked carefully across the half-dusted glass to Miss Riordan's grave and honest little face.

You could get to like that face a lot. Glamoured up blondes were a dime a dozen, but that was a face that would wear. I smiled at it.

"Listen, Anne. Killing Marriott was a dumb mistake. The gang behind this holdup would never pull anything like that. What must have happened was that some glowed-up runt they took along for a gun-holder lost his head. Marriott made a false move and some punk beat him down and it was done so quickly nothing could be done to prevent it. Here is an organized mob with inside information on jewels and the movements of the women that wear them. They ask

278

moderate returns and they would play ball. But here also is a back alley murder that doesn't fit at all. My idea is that whoever did it is a dead man hours ago, with weights on his ankles, deep in the Pacific Ocean. And either the jade went down with him or else they have some idea of its real value and they have cached it away in a place where it will stay for a long time – maybe for years before they dare bring it out again. Or, if the gang is big enough, it may show up on the other side of the world. The eight thousand they asked seems pretty low if they really know the value of the jade. But it would be hard to sell. I'm sure of one thing. They never meant to murder anybody."

Anne Riordan was listening to me with her lips slightly parted and a rapt expression on her face, as if she was looking at the Dalai Lhama.

She closed her mouth slowly and nodded once. "You're wonderful," she said softly. "But you're nuts."

She stood up and gathered her bag to her. "Will you go to see her or won't you?"

"Randall can't stop me – if it comes from her."

"All right. I'm going to see another society editor and get some more dope on the Grayles if I can. About her love life. She would have one, wouldn't she?"

The face framed in auburn hair was wistful.

"Who hasn't?" I sneered.

"I never had. Not really."

I reached up and shut my mouth with my hand. She gave me a sharp look and moved towards the door.

"You've forgotten something," I said.

She stopped and turned. "What?" She looked all over the top of the desk.

"You know damn well what."

She came back to the desk and leaned across it earnestly. "Why would they kill the man that killed Marriott, if they don't go in for murder?"

"Because he would be the type that would get picked up sometime and would talk – when they took his dope away from him. I mean they wouldn't kill a customer."

"What makes you so sure the killer took dope?"

"I'm not sure. I just said that. Most punks do."

"Oh." She straightened up and nodded and smiled. "I guess you mean these," she said and reached quickly into her bag and laid a small tissue bag package on the desk.

I reached for it, pulled a rubber band off it carefully and opened up the paper. On it lay three long thick Russian cigarettes with paper mouthpieces. I looked at her and didn't say anything.

"I know I shouldn't have taken them," she said almost breathlessly. "But I knew they were jujus. They usually come in plain papers but lately around Bay City they have been putting them out like this. I've seen several. I thought it was kind of mean for the poor man to be found dead with marihuana cigarettes in his pocket."

"You ought to have taken the case too," I said quietly. "There was dust in it. And it being empty was suspicious."

"I couldn't – with you there. I – I almost went back and did. But I didn't quite have the courage. Did it get you in wrong?"

"No," I lied. "Why should it?"

"I'm glad of that," she said wistfully.

"Why didn't you throw them away?"

She thought about it, her bag clutched to her side, her wide-brimmed absurd hat tilted so that it hid one eye.

"I guess it must be because I'm a cop's daughter," she said at last. "You just don't throw away evidence." Her smile was frail and guilty and her cheeks were flushed. I shrugged.

"Well –" the word hung in the air, like smoke in a closed room. Her lips stayed parted after saying it. I let it hang. The flush on her face deepened.

"I'm horribly sorry. I shouldn't have done it."

I passed that too.

She went very quickly to the door and out.

14

I POKED AT one of the long Russian cigarettes with a finger, then laid them in a neat row, side by side and squeaked my chair. You just don't throw away evidence. So they were evidence. Evidence of what? That a man occasionally smoked a stick of tea, a man who looked as if any touch of the exotic would appeal to him. On the other hand lots of tough guys smoked marihuana, also lots of band musicians and high school kids, and nice girls who had given up trying. American hashish. A weed that would grow anywhere. Unlawful to cultivate now. That meant a lot in a country as big as the U.S.A.

I sat there and puffed my pipe and listened to the clacking typewriter behind the wall of my office and the bong-bong of the traffic lights changing on Hollywood Boulevard and spring rustling in the air, like a paper bag blowing along a concrete sidewalk.

They were pretty big cigarettes, but a lot of Russians are, and marihuana is a coarse leaf. Indian hemp. American hashish. Evidence. God, what hats the women wear. My head ached. Nuts.

I got my penknife out and opened the small sharp blade, the one I didn't clean my pipe with, and reached for one of them. That's what a police chemist would do. Slit one down the middle and examine the stuff under a microscope, to start with. There might just happen to be something unusual about it. Not very likely, but what the hell, he was paid by the month.

I slit one down the middle. The mouthpiece part was pretty tough to slit. Okay, I was a tough guy, I slit it anyway. See if you can stop me.

Out of the mouthpiece shiny segments of rolled thin cardboard partly straightened themselves and had printing on them. I sat up straight and pawed for them. I tried to spread them out on the desk in order, but they slid around on the desk. I grabbed another of the cigarettes and squinted inside the mouthpiece. Then I went to work with the blade of the pocket knife in a different way. I pinched the cigarette down to the place where the mouthpieces began. The paper was thin all the way, you could feel the grain of what was underneath. So I cut the mouthpiece off carefully and then still more carefully cut through the mouthpiece longways, but only just enough. It opened out and there was another card underneath, rolled up, not touched this time.

I spread it out fondly. It was a man's calling card. Thin pale ivory, just off white. Engraved on that were delicately shaded words. In the lower left-hand corner a Stillwood Heights telephone number. In the lower right-hand corner the legend, "By Appointment Only." In the middle, a little larger, but still discreet: "Jules Amthor." Below, a little smaller: "Psychic Consultant."

I took hold of the third cigarette. This time, with a lot of difficulty, I teased the card out without cutting anything. It was the same. I put it back where it had been.

I looked at my watch, put my pipe in an ashtray, and then had to look at my watch again to see what time it was. I rolled the two cut cigarettes and the cut card in part of the tissue paper, the one that was complete with card inside in another part of the tissue paper and locked both little packages away in my desk.

I sat looking at the card. Jules Amthor, Psychic Consultant, By Appointment Only, Stillwood Heights phone number, no address. Three like that rolled inside three sticks of tea, in a Chinese or Japanese silk cigarette case with an imitation tortoise-shell frame, a trade article that might have cost thirty-five to seventy-five cents in any Oriental store, Hooey

Phooey Sing – Long Sing Tung, that kind of place, where a nice-mannered Jap hisses at you, laughing heartily when you say that the Moon of Arabia incense smells like the girls in Frisco Sadie's back parlor.

And all this in the pocket of a man who was very dead, and who had another and genuinely expensive cigarette case containing cigarettes which he actually smoked.

He must have forgotten it. It didn't make sense. Perhaps it hadn't belonged to him at all. Perhaps he had picked it up in a hotel lobby. Forgotten he had it on him. Forgotten to turn it in. Jules Amthor, Psychic Consultant.

The phone rang and I answered it absently. The voice had the cool hardness of a cop who thinks he is good. It was Randall. He didn't bark. He was the icy type.

"So you didn't know who that girl was last night? And she picked you up on the boulevard and you walked over to there. Nice lying, Marlowe."

"Maybe you have a daughter and you wouldn't like news cameramen jumping out of bushes and popping flashbulbs in her face."

"You lied to me."

"It was a pleasure."

He was silent a moment, as if deciding something. "We'll let that pass," he said. "I've seen her. She came in and told me her story. She's the daughter of a man I knew and respected, as it happens."

"She told you," I said, "and you told her."

"I told her a little," he said coldly. "For a reason. I'm calling you for the same reason. This investigation is going to be undercover. We have a chance to break this jewel gang and we're going to do it."

"Oh, it's a gang murder this morning. Okay."

"By the way, that was marihuana dust in that funny cigarette case – the one with the dragons on it. Sure you didn't see him smoke one out of it?"

"Quite sure. In my presence he smoked only the others. But he wasn't in my presence all the time."

"I see. Well, that's all. Remember what I told you last night. Don't try getting ideas about this case. All we want from you is silence. Otherwise –"

He paused. I yawned into the mouthpiece.

"I heard that," he snapped. "Perhaps you think I'm not in a position to make that stick. I am. One false move out of you and you'll be locked up as a material witness."

"You mean the papers are not to get the case?"

"They'll get the murder – but they won't know what's behind it."

"Neither do you," I said.

"I've warned you twice now," he said. "The third time is out."

"You're doing a lot of talking," I said, "for a guy that holds cards."

I got the phone hung in my face for that. Okay, the hell with him, let him work at it.

I walked around the office a little to cool off, bought myself a short drink, looked at my watch again and didn't see what time it was, and sat down at the desk once more.

Jules Amthor, Psychic Consultant. Consultations by Appointment Only. Give him enough time and pay him enough money and he'll cure anything from a jaded husband to a grasshopper plague. He would be an expert in frustrated love affairs, women who slept alone and didn't like it, wandering boys and girls who didn't write home, sell the property now or hold it for another year, will this part hurt me with my public or make me seem more versatile? Men would sneak in on him too, big strong guys that roared like lions around their offices and were all cold mush under their vests. But mostly it would be women, fat women that panted and thin women that burned, old women that dreamed and young women that thought they might have Electra complexes, women of all sizes, shapes and ages, but with one thing in common – money. No Thursdays at the County Hospital for Mr. Jules Amthor. Cash on the line for him. Rich bitches who had to be dunned for their milk bills would pay him right now.

A fakeloo artist, a hoopla spreader, and a lad who had his card rolled up inside sticks of tea, found on a dead man.

This was going to be good. I reached for the phone and asked the O-operator for the Stillwood Heights number.

15

A WOMAN'S VOICE answered, a dry, husky-sounding foreign voice: "'Allo."

"May I talk to Mr. Amthor?"

"Ah no. I regret. I am ver-ry sor-ry. Amthor never speaks upon the telephone. I am hees secretary. Weel I take the message?"

"What's the address out there? I want to see him."

"Ah, you weesh to consult Amthor professionally? He weel be ver-ry pleased. But he ees ver-ry beesy. When you weesh to see him?"

"Right away. Sometime today."

"Ah," the voice regretted, "that cannot be. The next week per'aps. I weel look at the book."

"Look," I said, "never mind the book. You 'ave the pencil?"

"But certainly I 'ave the pencil. I –"

"Take this down. My name is Philip Marlowe. My address is 615 Cahuenga Building, Hollywood. That's on Hollywood Boulevard near Ivar. My phone number is Glenview 7537." I spelled the hard ones and waited.

"Yes, Meester Marlowe. I 'ave that."

"I want to see Mr. Amthor about a man named Marriott." I spelled that too. "It is very urgent. It is a matter of life and death. I want to see him fast. F-a-s-t – fast. Sudden, in other words. Am I clear?"

"You talk ver-ry strange," the foreign voice said.

"No." I took hold of the phone standard and shook it. "I feel fine. I always talk like that. This is a very queer business. Mr. Amthor will positively want to see me. I'm a private detective. But I don't want to go to the police until I've seen him."

"Ah," the voice got as cool as a cafeteria dinner. "You are of the police, no?"

"Listen," I said. "I am of the police, no. I am a private detective. Confidential. But it is very urgent just the same. You call me back, no? You 'ave the telephone number, yes?"

"Si. I 'ave the telephone number. Meester Marriott – he ees sick?"

"Well, he's not up and around," I said. "So you know him?"

"But no. You say a matter of life and death. Amthor he cure many people –"

"This is one time he flops," I said. "I'll be waiting for a call."

I hung up and lunged for the office bottle. I felt as if I had been through a meat grinder. Ten minutes passed. The phone rang. The voice said:

"Amthor he weel see you at six o'clock."

"That's fine. What's the address?"

"He weel send a car."

"I have a car of my own. Just give me –"

"He weel send a car," the voice said coldly, and the phone clicked in my ear.

I looked at my watch once more. It was more than time for lunch. My stomach burned from the last drink. I wasn't hungry. I lit a cigarette. It tasted like a plumber's handkerchief. I nodded across the office at Mr. Rembrandt, then I reached for my hat and went out. I was halfway to the elevator before the thought hit me. It hit me without any reason or sense, like a dropped brick. I stopped and leaned against the marbled wall and pushed my hat around on my head and suddenly I laughed.

A girl passing me on the way from the elevators back to her work turned and gave me one of those looks which are supposed to make your spine feel like a run in a stocking. I waved my hand at her and went back to my office and grabbed the phone. I called up a man I knew who worked on the Lot Books of a title company.

"Can you find a property by the address alone?" I asked him.

"Sure. We have a cross-index. What is it?"

"1644 West 54th Place. I'd like to know a little something about the condition of the title."

"I'd better call you back. What's that number?"

He called back in about three minutes.

"Get your pencil out," he said. "It's Lot 8 of Block 11 of Caraday's Addition to the Maplewood Tract Number 4. The owner of record, subject to certain things, is Jessie Pierce Florian, widow."

"Yeah. What things?"

"Second half taxes, two ten-year street improvement bonds, one storm drain assessment bond also ten year, none of these delinquent, also a first trust deed of $2600."

"You mean one of those things where they can sell you out on ten minutes' notice?"

"Not quite that quick, but a lot quicker than a mortgage. There's nothing unusual about it except the amount. It's high for that neighborhood, unless it's a new house."

"It's a very old house and in bad repair," I said. "I'd say fifteen hundred would buy the place."

"Then it's distinctly unusual, because the refinancing was done only four years ago."

"Okay, who holds it? Some investment company?"

"No. An individual. Man named Lindsay Marriott, a single man. Okay?"

I forget what I said to him or what thanks I made. They probably sounded like words. I sat there, just staring at the wall.

My stomach suddenly felt fine. I was hungry. I went down to the Mansion House Coffee Shop and ate lunch and got my car out of the parking lot next to my building.

I drove south and east, towards West 54th Place. I didn't carry any liquor with me this time.

16

THE BLOCK LOOKED just as it had looked the day before. The street was empty except for an ice truck, two Fords in drive-ways, and a swirl of dust going around a corner. I drove slowly past No. 1644 and parked farther along and studied the houses on either side of mine. I walked back and stopped in front of it, looking at the tough palm tree and the drab unwatered scrap of lawn. The house seemed empty, but probably wasn't. It just had that look. The lonely rocker on the front porch stood just where it had stood yesterday. There was a throw-away paper on the walk. I picked it up and slapped it against my leg and then I saw the curtain move next door, in the near front window.

Old Nosey again. I yawned and tilted my hat down. A sharp nose almost flattened itself against the inside of the glass. White hair above it, and eyes that were just eyes from where I stood. I strolled along the sidewalk and the eyes watched me. I turned in towards her house. I climbed the wooden steps and rang the bell.

The door snapped open as if it had been on a spring. She was a tall old bird with a chin like a rabbit. Seen from close her eyes were as sharp as lights on still water. I took my hat off.

"Are you the lady who called the police about Mrs. Florian?"

She stared at me coolly and missed nothing about me, probably not even the mole on my right shoulder blade.

"I ain't sayin' I am, young man, and I ain't sayin' I ain't. Who are you?" It was a high twangy voice, made for talking over an eight party line.

"I'm a detective."

"Land's sakes. Why didn't you say so? What's she done now? I ain't seen a thing and I ain't missed a minute. Henry done all the goin' to the store for me. Ain't been a sound out of there."

She snapped the screen door unhooked and drew me in. The hall smelled of furniture oil. It had a lot of dark furniture that had once been in good style. Stuff with inlaid panels and scollops at the corners. We went into a front room that had cotton lace antimacassars pinned on everything you could stick a pin into.

"Say, didn't I see you before?" she asked suddenly, a note of suspicion crawling around in her voice. "Sure enough I did. You was the man that —"

"That's right. And I'm still a detective. Who's Henry?"

"Oh, he's just a little colored boy that does errands for me. Well, what you want, young man?" She patted a clean red and white apron and gave me the beady eye. She clicked her store teeth a couple of times for practice.

"Did the officers come here yesterday after they went to Mrs. Florian's house?"

"What officers?"

"The uniformed officers," I said patiently.

"Yes, they was here a minute. They didn't know nothing."

"Describe the big man to me — the one that had a gun and made you call up."

She described him with complete accuracy. It was Malloy all right.

"What kind of car did he drive?"

"A little car. He couldn't hardly get into it."

"That's all you can say? This man's a murderer!"

Her mouth gaped, but her eyes were pleased. "Land's sakes, I wish I could tell you, young man. But I never knew much about cars. Murder, eh? Folks ain't safe a minute in this town. When I come here twenty-two years ago we didn't lock our doors hardly. Now it's gangsters and crooked police and politicians fightin' each other with machine guns, so I've heard. Scandalous is what it is, young man."

"Yeah. What do you know about Mrs. Florian?"

The small mouth puckered. "She ain't neighborly. Plays her radio loud late nights. Sings. She don't talk to anybody." She leaned forward a little. "I'm not positive, but my opinion is she drinks liquor."

"She have many visitors?"

"She don't have no visitors at all."

"You'd know, of course, Mrs. –"

"Mrs. Morrison. Land's sakes, yes. What else have I got to do but look out of the windows?"

"I bet it's fun. Mrs. Florian has lived here a long time?"

"About ten years, I reckon. Had a husband once. Looked like a bad one to me. He died." She paused and thought. "I guess he died natural," she added. "I never heard different."

"Left her money?"

Her eyes receded and her chin followed them. She sniffed hard. "You been drinkin' liquor," she said coldly.

"I just had a tooth out. The dentist gave it to me."

"I don't hold with it."

"It's bad stuff, except for medicine," I said.

"I don't hold with it for medicine neither."

"I think you're right," I said. "Did he leave her money? Her husband?"

"I wouldn't know." Her mouth was the size of a prune and as smooth. I had lost out.

"Has anybody at all been there since the officers?"

"Ain't seen."

"Thank you very much, Mrs. Morrison. I won't trouble you any more now. You've been very kind and helpful."

I walked out of the room and opened the door. She followed me and cleared her throat and clicked her teeth a couple more times.

"What number should I call?" she asked, relenting a little.

"University 4-5000. Ask for Lieutenant Nulty. What does she live on – relief?"

"This ain't a relief neighborhood," she said coldly.

"I bet that side piece was the admiration of Sioux Falls once," I said, gazing at a carved sideboard that was in the hall because the dining room was too small for it. It had curved ends, thin carved legs, was inlaid all over, and had a painted basket of fruit on the front.

"Mason City," she said softly. "Yessir, we had a nice home once, me and George. Best there was."

I opened the screen door and stepped through it and thanked her again. She was smiling now. Her smile was as sharp as her eyes.

"Gets a registered letter first of every month," she said suddenly.

I turned and waited. She leaned towards me. "I see the mailman go up to the door and get her to sign. First day of every month. Dresses up then and goes out. Don't come home till all hours. Sings half the night. Times I could have called the police it was so loud."

I patted the thin malicious arm.

"You're one in a thousand, Mrs. Morrison," I said. I put my hat on, tipped it to her and left. Halfway down the walk I thought of something and swung back. She was still standing inside the screen door, with the house door open behind her. I went back up on the steps.

"Tomorrow's the first," I said. "First of April. April Fool's Day. Be sure to notice whether she gets her registered letter, will you, Mrs. Morrison?"

The eyes gleamed at me. She began to laugh – a high-pitched old woman's laugh. "April Fool's Day," she tittered. "Maybe she won't get it."

I left her laughing. The sound was like a hen having hiccups.

17

NOBODY ANSWERED MY ring or knock next door. I tried again. The screen door wasn't hooked. I tried the house door. It was unlocked. I stepped inside.

Nothing was changed, not even the smell of gin. There were still no bodies on the floor. A dirty glass stood on the small table beside the chair where Mrs. Florian had sat yesterday. The radio was turned off. I went over to the davenport and felt down behind the cushions. The same dead soldier and another one with him now.

I called out. No answer. Then I thought I heard a long slow unhappy breathing that was half groaning. I went through the arch and sneaked into the little hallway. The bedroom door was partly open and the groaning sound came from behind it. I stuck my head in and looked.

Mrs. Florian was in bed. She was lying flat on her back with a cotton comforter pulled up to her chin. One of the little fluffballs on the comforter was almost in her mouth. Her long yellow face was slack, half dead. Her dirty hair straggled on the pillow. Her eyes opened slowly and at me with no expression. The room had a sickening smell of sleep, liquor and dirty clothes. A sixty-nine cent alarm clock ticked on the peeling gray-white paint of the bureau. It ticked loud enough to shake the walls. Above it a mirror showed a distorted view of the woman's face. The trunk from which she had taken the photos was still open.

I said: "Good afternoon, Mrs. Florian. Are you sick?"

She worked her lips together slowly, rubbed one over the other, then slid a tongue out and moistened them and worked her jaws. Her voice came from her mouth sounding like a worn-out phonograph record. Her eyes showed recognition now, but not pleasure.

"You get him?"

"The Moose?"

"Sure."

"Not yet. Soon, I hope."

She screwed her eyes up and then snapped them open as if trying to get rid of a film over them.

"You ought to keep your house locked up," I said. "He might come back."

"You think I'm scared of the Moose, huh?"

"You acted like it when I was talking to you yesterday."

She thought about that. Thinking was weary work. "Got any liquor?"

"No, I didn't bring any today, Mrs. Florian. I was a little low on cash."

"Gin's cheap. It hits."

"I might go out for some in a little while. So you're not afraid of Malloy?"

"Why would I be?"

"Okay, you're not. What *are* you afraid of?"

Light snapped into her eyes, held for a moment, and faded out again. "Aw beat it. You coppers give me an ache in the fanny."

I said nothing. I leaned against the door frame and put a cigarette in my mouth and tried to jerk it up far enough to hit my nose with it. This is harder than it looks.

"Coppers," she said slowly, as if talking to herself, "will never catch that boy. He's good and he's got dough and he's got friends. You're wasting your time, copper."

"Just the routine," I said. "It was practically a self-defense anyway. Where would he be?"

She snickered and wiped her mouth on the cotton comforter.

"Soap now," she said. "Soft stuff. Copper-smart. You guys still think it gets you something."

"I liked the Moose," I said.

Interest flickered in her eyes. "You know him?"

"I was with him yesterday – when he killed the nigger over on Central."

She opened her mouth wide and laughed her head off without making any more sound than you would make cracking a breadstick. Tears ran out of her eyes and down her face.

"A big strong guy," I said. "Soft-hearted in spots too. Wanted his Velma pretty bad."

The eyes veiled. "Thought it was her folks was looking for her," she said softly.

"They are. But she's dead, you said. Nothing there. Where did she die?"

"Dalhart, Texas. Got a cold and went to the chest and off she went."

"You were there?"

"Hell, no. I just heard."

"Oh. Who told you, Mrs. Florian?"

"Some hoofer. I forget the name right now. Maybe a good stiff drink might help some. I feel like Death Valley."

"And you look like a dead mule," I thought, but didn't say it out loud. "There's just one more thing," I said, "then I'll maybe run out for some gin. I looked up the title to your house, I don't know just why."

She was rigid under the bedclothes, like a wooden woman. Even her eyelids were frozen half down over the clogged iris of her eyes. Her breath stilled.

"There's a rather large trust deed on it," I said. "Considering the low value of property around here. It's held by a man named Lindsay Marriott."

Her eyes blinked rapidly, but nothing else moved. She stared.

"I used to work for him," she said at last. "I used to be a servant in his family. He kind of takes care of me a little."

I took the unlighted cigarette out of my mouth and looked at it aimlessly and stuck it back in.

"Yesterday afternoon, a few hours after I saw you, Mr. Marriott called me up at my office. He offered me a job."

"What kind of job?" Her voice croaked now, badly.

I shrugged. "I can't tell you that. Confidential. I went to see him last night."

"You're a clever son of a bitch," she said thickly and moved a hand under the bedclothes.

I stared at her and said nothing.

"Copper-smart," she sneered.

I ran a hand up and down the door frame. It felt slimy. Just touching it made me want to take a bath.

"Well, that's all," I said smoothly. "I was just wondering how come. Might be nothing at all. Just a coincidence. It just looked as if it might mean something."

"Copper-smart," she said emptily. "Not a real copper at that. Just a cheap shamus."

"I suppose so," I said. "Well, good-bye, Mrs. Florian. By the way, I don't think you'll get a registered letter tomorrow morning."

She threw the bedclothes aside and jerked upright with her eyes blazing. Something glittered in her right hand. A small revolver, a Banker's Special. It was old and worn, but looked business-like.

"Tell it," she snarled. "Tell it fast."

I looked at the gun and the gun looked at me. Not too steadily. The hand behind it began to shake, but the eyes still blazed. Saliva bubbled at the corners of her mouth.

"You and I could work together," I said.

The gun and her jaw dropped at the same time. I was inches from the door. While the gun was still dropping, I slid through it and beyond the opening.

"Think it over," I called back.

There was no sound, no sound of any kind.

I went fast back through the hall and dining room and out of the house. My back felt queer as I went down the walk. The muscles crawled.

295

Nothing happened. I went along the street and got into my car and drove away from there.

The last day of March and hot enough for summer. I felt like taking my coat off as I drove. In front of the 77th Street Station, two prowl car men were scowling at a bent front fender. I went in through the swing doors and found a uniformed lieutenant behind the railing looking over the charge sheet. I asked him if Nulty was upstairs. He said he thought he was, was I a friend of his. I said yes. He said okay, go on up, so I went up the worn stairs and along the corridor and knocked at the door. The voice yelled and I went in.

He was picking his teeth, sitting in one chair with his feet on the other. He was looking at his left thumb, holding it up in front of his eyes and at arm's length. The thumb looked all right to me, but Nulty's stare was gloomy, as if he thought it wouldn't get well.

He lowered it to his thigh and swung his feet to the floor and looked at me instead of at his thumb. He wore a dark gray suit and a mangled cigar end was waiting on the desk for him to get through with the toothpick.

I turned the felt seat cover that lay on the other chair with its straps not fastened to anything, sat down, and put a cigarette in my face.

"You," Nulty said, and looked at his toothpick, to see if it was chewed enough.

"Any luck?"

"Malloy? I ain't on it any more."

"Who is?"

"Nobody ain't. Why? The guy's lammed. We got him on the teletype and they got readers out. Hell, he'll be in Mexico long gone."

"Well, all he did was kill a Negro," I said. "I guess that's only a misdemeanor."

"You still interested? I thought you was workin'?" His pale eyes moved damply over my face.

"I had a job last night, but it didn't last. Have you still got that Pierrot photo?"

He reached around and pawed under his blotter. He held it out. It still looked pretty. I stared at the face.

"This is really mine," I said. "If you don't need it for the file, I'd like to keep it."

"Should be in the file, I guess," Nulty said. "I forgot about it. Okay, keep it under your hat. I passed the file in."

I put the photo in my breast pocket and stood up. "Well, I guess that's all," I said, a little too airily.

"I smell something," Nulty said coldly.

I looked at the piece of rope on the edge of his desk. His eyes followed my look. He threw the toothpick on the floor and stuck the chewed cigar in his mouth.

"Not this either," he said.

"It's a vague hunch. If it grows more solid, I won't forget you."

"Things is tough. I need a break, pal."

"A man who works as hard as you deserves one," I said.

He struck a match on his thumbnail, looked pleased because it caught the first time, and started inhaling smoke from the cigar.

"I'm laughing," Nulty said sadly, as I went out.

The hall was quiet, the whole building was quiet. Down in front the prowl car men were still looking at their bent fender. I drove back to Hollywood.

The phone was ringing as I stepped into the office. I leaned down over the desk and said, "Yes?"

"Am I addressing Mr. Philip Marlowe?"

"Yes, this is Marlowe."

"This is Mrs. Grayle's residence. Mrs. Lewin Lockridge Grayle. Mrs. Grayle would like to see you here as soon as convenient."

"Where?"

"The address is Number 862 Aster Drive, in Bay City. May I say you will arrive within the hour?"

"Are you Mr. Grayle?"

"Certainly not, sir. I am the butler."

"That's me you hear ringing the door bell," I said.

18

IT WAS CLOSE TO the ocean and you could feel the ocean in the air but you couldn't see water from the front of the place. Aster Drive had a long smooth curve there and the houses on the inland side were just nice houses, but on the canyon side they were great silent estates, with twelve foot walls and wrought-iron gates and ornamental hedges; and inside, if you could get inside, a special brand of sunshine, very quiet, put up in noise-proof containers just for the upper classes.

A man in a dark blue Russian tunic and shiny black puttees and flaring breeches stood in the half-open gates. He was a dark, good-looking lad, with plenty of shoulders and shiny smooth hair and the peak on his rakish cap made a soft shadow over his eyes. He had a cigarette in the corner of his mouth and he held his head tilted a little, as if he liked to keep the smoke out of his nose. One hand had a smooth black gauntlet on it and the other was bare. There was a heavy ring on his third finger.

There was no number in sight, but this should be 862. I stopped my car and leaned out and asked him. It took him a long time to answer. He had to look me over very carefully. Also the car I was driving. He came over to me and as he came he carelessly dropped his ungloved hand towards his hip. It was the kind of carelessness that was meant to be noticed.

He stopped a couple of feet away from my car and looked me over again.

"I'm looking for the Grayle residence," I said.

"This is it. Nobody in."

"I'm expected."

He nodded. His eyes gleamed like water. "Name?"

298

"Philip Marlowe."

"Wait there." He strolled, without hurry, over to the gates and unlocked an iron door set into one of the massive pillars. There was a telephone inside. He spoke briefly into it, snapped the door shut, and came back to me.

"You have some identification?"

I let him look at the license on the steering post. "That doesn't prove anything," he said. "How do I know it's your car?"

I pulled the key out of the ignition and threw the door open and got out. That put me about a foot from him. He had nice breath. Haig and Haig at least.

"You've been at the sideboy again," I said.

He smiled. His eyes measured me. I said:

"Listen, I'll talk to the butler over that phone and he'll know my voice. Will that pass me in or do I have to ride on your back?"

"I just work here," he said softly. "If I didn't —" he let the rest hang in the air, and kept on smiling.

"You're a nice lad," I said and patted his shoulder. "Dartmouth or Dannemora?"

"Christ," he said. "Why didn't you say you were a cop?"

We both grinned. He waved his hand and I went in through the half-open gate. The drive curved and tall molded hedges of dark green completely screened it from the street and from the house. Through a green gate I saw a Jap gardener at work weeding a huge lawn. He was pulling a piece of weed out of the vast velvet expanse and sneering at it the way Jap gardeners do. Then the tall hedge closed in again and I didn't see anything more for a hundred feet. Then the hedge ended in a wide circle in which half a dozen cars were parked.

One of them was a small coupe. There were a couple of very nice two-tone Buicks of the latest model, good enough to go for the mail in. There was a black limousine, with dull nickel louvres and hubcaps the size of bicycle wheels. There was a long sport phaeton with the top down. A short very wide all-weather concrete driveway led from these to the side entrance of the house.

Off to the left, beyond the parking space there was a sunken garden with a fountain at each of the four corners. The entrance was barred by a wrought-iron gate with a flying Cupid in the middle. There were busts on light pillars and a stone seat with crouching griffins at each end. There was an oblong pool with stone waterlilies in it and a big stone bull-frog sitting on one of the leaves. Still farther a rose colonnade led to a thing like an altar, hedged in at both sides, yet not so completely but that the sun lay in an arabesque along the steps of the altar. And far over to the left there was a wild garden, not very large, with a sundial in the corner near an angle of wall that was built to look like a ruin. And there were flowers. There were a million flowers.

The house itself was not so much. It was smaller than Buckingham Palace, rather gray for California, and probably had fewer windows than the Chrysler Building.

I sneaked over to the side entrance and pressed a bell and somewhere a set of chimes made a deep mellow sound like church bells.

A man in a striped vest and gilt buttons opened the door, bowed, took my hat and was through for the day. Behind him in dimness, a man in striped knife-edge pants and a black coat and wing collar with gray striped tie leaned his gray head forward about half an inch and said: "Mr. Marlowe? If you will come this way, please —"

We went down a hall. It was a very quiet hall. Not a fly buzzed in it. The floor was covered with Oriental rugs and there were paintings along the walls. We turned a corner and there was more hall. A French window showed a gleam of blue water far off and I remembered almost with a shock that we were near the Pacific Ocean and that this house was on the edge of one of the canyons.

The butler reached a door and opened it against voices and stood aside and I went in. It was a nice room with large chesterfields and lounging chairs done in pale yellow leather arranged around a fireplace in front of which, on the glossy but not slippery floor, lay a rug as thin as silk and as old as Aesop's aunt. A jet of flowers glistened in a corner, another on a low table, the walls were of dull painted parchment, there was comfort, space, coziness, a dash of the very modern and a dash of the very old, and three people sitting in a sudden silence watching me cross the floor.

One of them was Anne Riordan, looking just as I had seen her last, except that she was holding a glass of amber fluid in her hand. One was a tall thin sad-faced man with a stony chin and deep eyes and no color in his face but an unhealthy yellow. He was a good sixty, or rather a bad sixty. He wore a dark business suit, a red carnation, and looked subdued.

The third was the blonde. She was dressed to go out, in a pale greenish blue. I didn't pay much attention to her clothes. They were what the guy designed for her and she would go to the right man. The effect was to make her look very young and to make her lapis lazuli eyes look very blue. Her hair was of the gold of old paintings and had been fussed with just enough but not too much. She had a full set of curves which nobody had been able to improve on. The dress was rather plain except for a clasp of diamonds at the throat. Her hands were not small, but they had shape, and the nails were the usual jarring note – almost magenta. She was giving me one of her smiles. She looked as if she smiled easily, but her eyes had a still look, as if they thought slowly and carefully. And her mouth was sensual.

"So nice of you to come," she said. "This is my husband. Mix Mr. Marlowe a drink, honey."

Mr. Grayle shook hands with me. His hand was cold and a little moist. His eyes were sad. He mixed a Scotch and soda and handed it to me.

Then he sat down in a corner and was silent. I drank half of the drink and grinned at Miss Riordan. She looked at me with a sort of absent expression, as if she had another clue.

"Do you think you can do anything for us?" the blonde asked slowly, looking down into her glass. "If you think you can, I'd be delighted. But the loss is rather small compared with having any more fuss with gangsters and awful people."

"I don't know very much about it really," I said.

"Oh, I hope you can." She gave me a smile I could feel in my hip pocket.

I drank the other half of my drink. I began to feel rested. Mrs. Grayle rang a bell set into the arm of the leather chester-field and a footman came in. She half pointed to the tray. He looked around and mixed two drinks. Miss Riordan was still playing cute with the same one and apparently Mr. Grayle didn't drink. The footman went out.

Mrs. Grayle and I held our glasses. Mrs. Grayle crossed her legs, a little carelessly.

"I don't know whether I can do anything," I said. "I doubt it. What is there to go on?"

"I'm sure you can." She gave me another smile. "How far did Lin Marriott take you into his confidence?"

She looked sideways at Miss Riordan. Miss Riordan just couldn't catch the look. She kept right on sitting. She looked sideways the other way. Mrs. Grayle looked at her husband. "Do you have to bother with this, honey?"

Mr. Grayle stood up and said he was very glad to have met me and that he would go and lie down for a while. He didn't feel very well. He hoped I would excuse him. He was so polite I wanted to carry him out of the room just to show my appreciation.

He left. He closed the door softly, as if he was afraid to wake a sleeper. Mrs. Grayle looked at the door for a moment and then put the smile back on her face and looked at me.

"Miss Riordan is in your complete confidence, of course."

"Nobody's in my complete confidence, Mrs. Grayle. She happens to know about this case – what there is to know."

"Yes." She drank a sip or two, then finished her glass at a swallow and set it aside.

"To hell with this polite drinking," she said suddenly. "Let's get together on this. You're a very good-looking man to be in your sort of racket."

"It's a smelly business," I said.

"I didn't quite mean that. Is there any money in it – or is that impertinent?"

"There's not much money in it. There's a lot of grief. But there's a lot of fun too. And there's always a chance of a big case."

"How does one get to be a private detective? You don't mind my sizing you up a little? And push that table over here, will you? So I can reach the drinks."

I got up and pushed the huge silver tray on a stand across the glossy floor to her side. She made two more drinks. I still had half of my second.

"Most of us are ex-cops," I said. "I worked for the D.A. for a while. I got fired."

She smiled nicely. "Not for incompetence, I'm sure."

"No, for talking back. Have you had any more phone calls?"

"Well –" She looked at Anne Riordan. She waited. Her look said things.

Anne Riordan stood up. She carried her glass, still full, over to the tray and set it down. "You probably won't run short," she said. "But if you do – and thanks very much for talking to me, Mrs. Grayle. I won't use anything. You have my word for it."

"Heavens, you're not leaving," Mrs. Grayle said with a smile.

Anne Riordan took her lower lip between her teeth and held it there for a moment as if making up her mind whether to bite it off and spit it out or leave it on a while longer.

"Sorry, afraid I'll have to. I don't work for Mr. Marlowe, you know. Just a friend. Good-bye, Mrs. Grayle."

The blonde gleamed at her. "I hope you'll drop in again soon. Any time." She pressed the bell twice. That got the butler. He held the door open.

Miss Riordan went out quickly and the door closed. For quite a while after it closed, Mrs. Grayle stared at it with a faint smile. "It's much better this way, don't you think?" she said after an interval of silence. I nodded. "You're probably wondering how she knows so much if she's just a friend," I said. "She's a curious little girl. Some of it she dug out herself, like who you were and who owned the jade necklace. Some of it just happened. She came by last night to that dell where Marriott was killed. She was out riding. She happened to see a light and came down there."

"Oh." Mrs. Grayle lifted a glass quickly and made a face. "It's horrible to think of. Poor Lin. He was rather a heel. Most of one's friends are. But to die like that is awful." She shuddered. Her eyes got large and dark.

"So it's all right about Miss Riordan. She won't talk. Her father was chief of police here for a long time," I said.

"Yes. So she told me. You're not drinking."

"I'm doing what *I* call drinking."

"You and I should get along. Did Lin – Mr. Marriott – tell you how the holdup happened?"

"Between here and the Trocadero somewhere. He didn't say exactly. Three or four men."

She nodded her golden gleaming head. "Yes. You know there was something rather funny about that holdup. They gave me back one of my rings, rather a nice one, too."

"He told me that."

"Then again I hardly ever wore the jade. After all, it's a museum piece, probably not many like it in the world, a very rare type of jade. Yet they snapped at it. I wouldn't expect them to think it had any value much, would you?"

"They'd know you wouldn't wear it otherwise. Who knew about its value?"

She thought. It was nice to watch her thinking. She still had her legs crossed, and still carelessly.

"All sorts of people, I suppose."

"But they didn't know you would be wearing it that night? Who knew that?"

She shrugged her pale blue shoulders. I tried to keep my eyes where they belonged.

"My maid. But she's had a hundred chances. And I trust her –"

"Why?"

"I don't know. I just trust some people. I trust you."

"Did you trust Marriott?"

Her face got a little hard. Her eyes a little watchful. "Not in some things. In others, yes. There are degrees." She had a nice way of talking, cool, half-cynical, and yet not hard-boiled. She rounded her words well.

"All right – besides the maid. The chauffeur?"

She shook her head, no. "Lin drove me that night, in his own car. I don't think George was around at all. Wasn't it Thursday?"

"I wasn't there. Marriott said four or five days before in telling me about it. Thursday would have been an even week from last night."

"Well, it was Thursday." She reached for my glass and her fingers touched mine a little, and were soft to the touch. "George gets Thursday evening off. That's the usual day, you know." She poured a fat slug of mellow-looking Scotch into my glass and squirted in some fizz-water. It was the kind of liquor you think you can drink forever, and all you do is get reckless. She gave herself the same treatment.

"Lin told you my name?" she asked softly, the eyes still watchful.

"He was careful not to."

"Then he probably misled you a little about the time. Let's see what we have. Maid and chauffeur out. Out of consideration as accomplices, I mean."

"They're not out by me."

"Well, at least I'm trying," she laughed. "Then there's Newton, the butler. He might have seen it on my neck that night. But it hangs down rather low and I was wearing a white fox evening wrap; no, I don't think he could have seen it."

"I bet you looked a dream," I said.

"You're not getting a little tight, are you?"

"I've been known to be soberer."

She put her head back and went off into a peal of laughter. I have only known four women in my life who could do that and still look beautiful. She was one of them.

"Newton is okay," I said. "His type don't run with hoodlums. That's just guessing, though. How about the footman?"

She thought and remembered, then shook her head. "He didn't see me."

"Anybody ask you to wear the jade?"

Her eyes instantly got more guarded. "You're not fooling me a damn bit," she said.

She reached for my glass to refill it. I let her have it, even though it still had an inch to go. I studied the lovely lines of her neck.

When she had filled the glasses and we were playing with them again I said, "Let's get the record straight and then I'll tell you something. Describe the evening."

She looked at her wrist watch, drawing a full length sleeve back to do it. "I ought to be –"

"Let him wait."

Her eyes flashed at that. I liked them that way. "There's such a thing as being just a little too frank," she said.

"Not in my business. Describe the evening. Or have me thrown out on my ear. One or the other. Make your lovely mind up."

"You'd better sit over here beside me."

"I've been thinking that a long time," I said. "Ever since you crossed your legs, to be exact."

She pulled her dress down. "These damn things are always up around your neck."

I sat beside her on the yellow leather chesterfield. "Aren't you a pretty fast worker?" she asked quietly.

I didn't answer her.

"Do you do much of this sort of thing?" she asked with a sidelong look.

"Practically none. I'm a Tibetan monk, in my spare time."

"Only you don't have any spare time."

"Let's focus," I said. "Let's get what's left of our minds – or mine – on the problem. How much are you going to pay me?"

"Oh, that's the problem. I thought you were going to get my necklace back. Or try to."

"I have to work in my own way. This way." I took a long drink and it nearly stood me on my head. I swallowed a little air.

"And investigate a murder," I said.

"That has nothing to do with it. I mean that's a police affair, isn't it?"

"Yeah – only the poor guy paid me a hundred bucks to take care of him – and I didn't. Makes me feel guilty. Makes me want to cry. Shall I cry?"

"Have a drink." She poured us some more Scotch. It didn't seem to affect her any more than water affects Boulder Dam.

"Well, where have we got to?" I said, trying to hold my glass so that the whiskey would stay inside it. "No maid, no chauffeur, no butler, no footman. We'll be doing our own laundry next. How did the holdup happen? Your version might have a few details Marriott didn't give me."

She leaned forward and cupped her chin in her hand. She looked serious without looking silly-serious.

"We went to a party in Brentwood Heights. Then Lin suggested we run over to the Troc for a few drinks and a few dances. So we did. They were doing some work on Sunset and it was very dusty. So coming back Lin dropped down to Santa Monica. That took us past a shabby looking hotel called the Hotel Indio, which I happened to notice for some silly meaningless reason. Across the street from it was a beer joint and a car was parked in front of that."

"Only one car – in front of a beer joint?"

"Yes. Only one. It was a very dingy place. Well, this car started up and followed us and of course I thought nothing of that either. There was no reason to. Then before we got to where Santa Monica turns into Arguello Boulevard, Lin said, 'Let's go over the other road' and turned up some curving residential street. Then all of a sudden a car rushed by us and grazed the fender and then pulled over to stop. A man in an overcoat and scarf and hat low on his face came back to apologize. It was a white scarf bunched out and it drew my eyes. It was about all I really saw of him except that he was tall and thin. As soon as he got close – and I remembered afterwards that he didn't walk in our headlights at all –"

"That's natural. Nobody likes to look into headlights. Have a drink. My treat this time."

She was leaning forward, her fine eyebrows – not daubs of paint – drawn together in a frown of thought. I made two drinks. She went on:

"As soon as he got close to the side where Lin was sitting he jerked the scarf up over his nose and a gun was shining at us. 'Stickup,' he said. 'Be very quiet and everything will be jake.' Then another man came over on the other side."

"In Beverly Hills," I said, "the best policed four square miles in California."

She shrugged. "It happened just the same. They asked for my jewelry and bag. The man with the scarf did. The one on my side never spoke at all. I passed the things across Lin and the man gave me back my bag and one ring. He said to hold off calling the police and insurance people for a while. They would make us a nice smooth easy deal. He said they found it easier to work on a straight percentage. He seemed to have all the time in the world. He said they could work through the insurance people, if they had to, but that meant cutting in a shyster, and they preferred not to. He sounded like a man with some education."

"It might have been Dressed-Up Eddie," I said. "Only he got bumped off in Chicago."

She shrugged. We had a drink. She went on.

"Then they left and we went home and I told Lin to keep quiet about it. The next day I got a call. We have two phones, one with extensions and one in my bedroom with no extensions. The call was on this. It's not listed, of course."

I nodded. "They can buy the number for a few dollars. It's done all the time. Some movie people have to change their numbers every month."

We had a drink.

"I told the man calling to take it up with Lin and he would represent me and if they were not too unreasonable, we might deal. He said okay, and from then on I guess they just stalled long enough to watch us a little. Finally, as you know, we agreed on eight thousand dollars and so forth."

"Could you recognize any of them?"

"Of course not."

"Randall know all this?"

"Of course. Do we have to talk about it any more? It bores me." She gave me the lovely smile.

"Did he make any comment?"

She yawned. "Probably. I forget."

I sat with my empty glass in my hand and thought. She took it away from me and started to fill it again.

I took the refilled glass out of her hand and transferred it to my left and took hold of her left hand with my right. It felt smooth and soft and warm and comforting. It squeezed mine. The muscles in it were strong. She was a well built woman, and no paper flower.

"I think he had an idea," she said. "But he didn't say what it was."

"Anybody would have an idea out of all that," I said.

She turned her head slowly and looked at me. Then she nodded. "You can't miss it, can you?"

"How long have you known him?"

"Oh, years. He used to be an announcer at the station my husband owned. KFDK. That's where I met him. That's where I met my husband too."

"I knew that. But Marriott lived as if he had money. Not riches, but comfortable money."

"He came into some and quit radio business."

"Do you know for a fact he came into money – or was that just something he said?"

She shrugged. She squeezed my hand.

"Or it may not have been very much money and he may have gone through it pretty fast." I squeezed her hand back. "Did he borrow from you?"

"You're a little old-fashioned, aren't you?" She looked down at the hand I was holding.

"I'm still working. And your Scotch is so good it keeps me half-sober. Not that I'd have to be drunk –"

"Yes." She drew her hand out of mine and rubbed it. "You must have quite a clutch – in your spare time. Lin Marriott was a high-class blackmailer, of course. That's obvious. He lived on women."

"He had something on you?"

"Should I tell you?"

"It probably wouldn't be wise."

She laughed. "I will, anyhow. I got a little tight at his house once and passed out. I seldom do. He took some photos of me – with my clothes up to my neck."

"The dirty dog," I said. "Have you got any of them handy?"

She slapped my wrist. She said softly:

"What's your name?"

"Phil. What's yours?"

"Helen. Kiss me."

She fell softly across my lap and I bent down over her face and began to browse on it. She worked her eyelashes and made butterfly kisses on my cheeks. When I got to her mouth it was half-open and burning and her tongue was a darting snake between her teeth.

The door opened and Mr. Grayle stepped quietly into the room. I was holding her and didn't have a chance to let go. I lifted my face and looked at him. I felt as cold as Finnegan's feet, the day they buried him.

The blonde in my arms didn't move, didn't even close her lips. She had a half-dreamy, half-sarcastic expression on her face.

Mr. Grayle cleared his throat slightly and said: "I beg your pardon, I'm sure," and went quietly out of the room. There was an infinite sadness in his eyes.

I pushed her away and stood up and got my handkerchief out and mopped my face.

She lay as I had left her, half sideways along the davenport, the skin showing in a generous sweep above one stocking.

"Who was that?" she asked thickly.

"Mr. Grayle."

"Forget him."

I went away from her and sat down in the chair I had sat in when I first came into the room.

After a moment she straightened herself out and sat up and looked at me steadily.

"It's all right. He understands. What the hell can he expect?"

"I guess he knows."

"Well, I tell you it's all right. Isn't that enough? He's a sick man. What the hell – "

311

"Don't go shrill on me. I don't like shrill women."

She opened a bag lying beside her and took out a small handkerchief and wiped her lips, then looked at her face in the mirror.

"I guess you're right," she said. "Just too much Scotch. Tonight at the Belvedere Club. Ten o'clock." She wasn't looking at me. Her breath was fast.

"Is that a good place?"

"Laird Brunette owns it. I know him pretty well."

"Right," I said. I was still cold. I felt nasty, as if I had picked a poor man's pocket.

She got a lipstick out and touched her lips very lightly and then looked at me along her eyes. She tossed the mirror. I caught it and looked at my face. I worked at it with my handkerchief and stood up to give her back the mirror.

She was leaning back, showing all her throat, looking at me lazily down her eyes.

"What's the matter?"

"Nothing. Ten o'clock at the Belvedere Club. Don't be too magnificent. All I have is a dinner suit. In the bar?"

She nodded, her eyes still lazy.

I went across the room and out, without looking back. The footman met me in the hall and gave me my hat, looking like the Great Stone Face.

19

I WALKED DOWN the curving driveway and lost myself in the shadow of the tall trimmed hedges and came to the gates. Another man was holding the fort now, a husky in plainclothes, an obvious bodyguard. He let me out with a nod.

A horn tooted. Miss Riordan's coupe was drawn up behind my car. I went over there and looked in at her. She looked cool and sarcastic.

She sat there with her hands on the wheel, gloved and slim. She smiled.

"I waited. I suppose it was none of my business. What did you think of her?"

"I bet she snaps a mean garter."

"Do you always have to say things like that?" She flushed bitterly. "Sometimes I hate men. Old men, young men, football players, opera tenors, smart millionaires, beautiful men who are gigolos and almost-heels who are – private detectives."

I grinned at her sadly. "I know I talk too smart. It's in the air nowadays. Who told you he was a gigolo?"

"Who?"

"Don't be obtuse. Marriott."

"Oh, it was a cinch guess. I'm sorry. I don't mean to be nasty. I guess you can snap her garter any time you want to, without much of a struggle. But there's one thing you can be sure of – you're a late comer to the show."

The wide curving street dozed peacefully in the sun. A beautifully painted panel truck slid noiselessly to a stop before a house across the street, then backed a little and went up the driveway to a side entrance. On the side of the panel truck was painted the legend: "Bay City Infant Service."

Anne Riordan leaned towards me, her gray-blue eyes hurt and clouded. Her slightly too long upper lip pouted and then pressed back against her teeth. She made a sharp little sound with her breath.

"Probably you'd like me to mind my own business, is that it? And not have ideas you don't have first. I thought I was helping a little."

"I don't need any help. The police don't want any from me. There's nothing I can do for Mrs. Grayle. She has a yarn about a beer parlor where a car started from and followed them, but what does that amount to? It was a crummy dive on Santa Monica. This was a high-class mob. There was somebody in it that could even tell Fei Tsui jade when he saw it."

"If he wasn't tipped off."

"There's that too," I said, and fumbled a cigarette out of a package. "Either way there's nothing for me in it."

"Not even about psychics?"

I stared rather blankly. "Psychics?"

"My God," she said softly. "And I thought you were a detective."

"There's a hush on part of this," I said. "I've got to watch my step. This Grayle packs a lot of dough in his pants. And law is where you buy it in this town. Look at the funny way the cops are acting. No build-up, no newspaper handout, no chance for the innocent stranger to step in with the trifling clue that turns out to be all important. Nothing but silence and warnings to me to lay off. I don't like it at all."

"You got most of the lipstick off," Anne Riordan said. "I mentioned psychics. Well, good-bye. It was nice to know you – in a way."

She pressed her starter button and jammed her gears in and was gone in a swirl of dust.

I watched her go. When she was gone I looked across the street. The man from the panel truck that said Bay City Infant Service came out of the side door of the house dressed in a uniform so white and stiff and gleaming that it made me feel clean just to look at it. He was carrying a carton of some sort. He got into his panel truck and drove away.

I figured he had just changed a diaper.

I got into my own car and looked at my watch before starting up. It was almost five.

The Scotch, as good enough Scotch will, stayed with me all the way back to Hollywood. I took the red lights as they came.

"There's a nice little girl," I told myself out loud, in the car, "for a guy that's interested in a nice little girl." Nobody said anything. "But I'm not," I said. Nobody said anything to that either. "Ten o'clock at the Belvedere Club," I said. Somebody said: "Phooey."

It sounded like my voice.

It was a quarter to six when I reached my office again. The building was very quiet. The typewriter beyond the party wall was stilled. I lit a pipe and sat down to wait.

20

THE INDIAN SMELLED. He smelled clear across the little reception room when the buzzer sounded and I opened the door between to see who it was. He stood just inside the corridor door looking as if he had been cast in bronze. He was a big man from the waist up and he had a big chest. He looked like a bum.

He wore a brown suit of which the coat was too small for his shoulders and his trousers were probably a little tight at the waist. His hat was at least two sizes too small and had been perspired in freely by somebody it fitted better than it fitted him. He wore it about where a house wears a wind vane. His collar had the snug fit of a horse-collar and was of about the same shade of dirty brown. A tie dangled outside his buttoned jacket, a black tie which had been tied with a pair of pliers in a knot the size of a pea. Around his bare and magnificent throat, above the dirty collar, he wore a wide piece of black ribbon, like an old woman trying to freshen up her neck.

He had a big flat face and a highbridged fleshy nose that looked as hard as the prow of a cruiser. He had lidless eyes, drooping jowls, the shoulders of a blacksmith and the short and apparently awkward legs of a chimpanzee. I found out later that they were only short.

If he had been cleaned up a little and dressed in a white nightgown, he would have looked like a very wicked Roman senator.

His smell was the earthy smell of primitive man, and not the slimy dirt of cities.

"Huh," he said. "Come quick. Come now."

I backed into my office and wiggled my finger at him and he followed me making as much noise as a fly makes walking on the wall. I sat down behind my desk and squeaked my swivel chair professionally and pointed to the customer's chair on the other side. He didn't sit down. His small black eyes were hostile.

"Come where?" I said.

"Huh. Me Second Planting. Me Hollywood Indian."

"Have a chair, Mr. Planting."

He snorted and his nostrils got very wide. They had been wide enough for mouseholes to start with.

"Name Second Planting. Name no Mister Planting."

"What can I do for you?"

He lifted his voice and began to intone in a deep-chested sonorous boom. "He say come quick. Great white father say come quick. He say me bring you in fiery chariot. He say –"

"Yeah. Cut out the pig Latin," I said. "I'm no schoolmarm at the snake dances."

"Nuts," the Indian said.

We sneered at each other across the desk for a moment. He sneered better than I did. Then he removed his hat with massive disgust and turned it upside down. He rolled a finger around under the sweatband. That turned the sweatband up into view, and it had not been misnamed. He removed a paper clip from the edge and threw a fold of tissue paper on the desk. He pointed at it angrily, with a well-chewed fingernail. His lank hair had a shelf around it, high up, from the too-tight hat.

I unfolded the piece of tissue paper and found a card inside. The card was no news to me. There had been three exactly like it in the mouthpieces of three Russian-appearing cigarettes.

I played with my pipe, stared at the Indian and tried to ride him with my stare. He looked as nervous as a brick wall.

"Okay, what does he want?"

"He want you come quick. Come now. Come in fiery – "

"Nuts," I said.

The Indian liked that. He closed his mouth slowly and winked an eye solemnly and then almost grinned.

"Also it will cost him a hundred bucks as a retainer," I added, trying to look as if that was a nickel.

"Huh?" Suspicious again. Stick to basic English.

"Hundred dollars," I said. "Iron men. Fish. Bucks to the number of one hundred. Me no money, me no come. Savvy?" I began to count a hundred with both hands.

"Huh. Big shot," the Indian sneered.

He worked under his greasy hatband and threw another fold of tissue paper on the desk. I took it and unwound it. It contained a brand new hundred dollar bill.

The Indian put his hat back on his head without bothering to tuck the hatband back in place. It looked only slightly more comic that way. I sat staring at the hundred dollar bill, with my mouth open.

"Psychic is right," I said at last. "A guy that smart I'm afraid of."

"Not got all day," the Indian remarked, conversationally.

I opened my desk and took out a Colt .38 automatic of the type known as Super Match. I hadn't worn it to visit Mrs. Lewin Lockridge Grayle. I stripped my coat off and strapped the leather harness on and tucked the automatic down inside it and strapped the lower strap and put my coat back on again.

This meant as much to the Indian as if I had scratched my neck.

"Gottum car," he said. "Big car."

"I don't like big cars any more," I said. "I gottum own car."

"You come my car," the Indian said threateningly.

"I come your car," I said.

I locked the desk and office up, switched the buzzer off and went out, leaving the reception room door unlocked as usual.

We went along the hall and down in the elevator. The Indian smelled. Even the elevator operator noticed it.

21

THE CAR WAS a dark blue seven-passenger sedan, a Packard of the latest model, custom-built. It was the kind of car you wear your rope pearls in. It was parked by a fire-hydrant and a dark foreign-looking chauffeur with a face of carved wood was behind the wheel. The interior was upholstered in quilted gray chenille. The Indian put me in the back. Sitting there alone I felt like a high-class corpse, laid out by an undertaker with a lot of good taste.

The Indian got in beside the chauffeur and the car turned in the middle of the block and a cop across the street said: "Hey," weakly, as if he didn't mean it, and then bent down quickly to tie his shoe.

We went west, dropped over to Sunset and slid fast and noiseless along that. The Indian sat motionless beside the chauffeur. An occasional whiff of his personality drifted back to me. The driver looked as if he was half asleep but he passed the fast boys in the convertible sedans as though they were being towed. They turned on all the green lights for him. Some drivers are like that. He never missed one.

We curved through the bright mile or two of the Strip, past the antique shops with famous screen names on them, past the windows full of point lace and ancient pewter, past the gleaming new nightclubs with famous chefs and equally famous gambling rooms, run by polished graduates of the Purple Gang, past the Georgian-Colonial vogue, now old hat, past the handsome modernistic buildings in which the Hollywood flesh-peddlers never stop talking money, past a drive-in lunch which somehow didn't belong, even though the girls wore white silk blouses and drum majorettes' shakos and nothing below the hips but glazed kid Hessian boots. Past all this and down a wide smooth curve to the bridle path of Beverly Hills and lights to the south, all colors of the spectrum and crystal clear in an evening without fog, past the shadowed mansions up on the hills to the north, past Beverly Hills altogether and up into the twisting foothill boulevard and the sudden cool dusk and the drift of wind from the sea.

It had been a warm afternoon, but the heat was gone. We whipped past a distant cluster of lighted buildings and an endless series of lighted mansions, not too close to the road. We dipped down to skirt a huge green polo field with another equally huge practice field beside it, soared again to the top of a hill and swung mountainward up a steep hillroad of clean concrete that passed orange groves, some rich man's pet because this is not orange country, and then little by little the lighted windows of the millionaires' homes were gone and the road narrowed and this was Stillwood Heights.

The smell of sage drifted up from a canyon and made me think of a dead man and a moonless sky. Straggly stucco houses were molded flat to the side of the hill, like bas-reliefs. Then there were no more houses, just the still dark foothills with an early star or two above them, and the concrete ribbon of road and a sheer drop on one side into a tangle of scrub oak and manzanita where sometimes you can hear the call of the quails if you stop and keep still and wait. On the other side of the road was a raw clay bank at the edge of which a few unbeatable wild flowers hung on like naughty children that won't go to bed.

Then the road twisted into a hairpin turn and the big tires scratched over loose stones, and the car tore less soundlessly up a long driveway lined with the wild geraniums. At the top of this, faintly lighted, lonely as a lighthouse, stood an eyrie, an eagle's nest, an angular building of stucco and glass brick, raw and modernistic and yet not ugly and altogether a swell place for a psychic consultant to hang out his shingle. Nobody would be able to hear any screams.

The car turned beside the house and a light flicked on over a black door set into the heavy wall. The Indian climbed out grunting and opened the rear door of the car. The chauffeur lit a cigarette with an electric lighter and a harsh smell of tobacco came back to me softly in the evening. I got out.

We went over to the black door. It opened of itself, slowly, almost with menace. Beyond it a narrow hallway probed back into the house. Light glowed from the glass brick walls.

The Indian growled. "Huh. You go in, big shot."

"After you, Mr. Planting."

He scowled and went in and the door closed after us as silently and mysteriously as it had opened. At the end of the narrow hallway we squeezed into a little elevator and the Indian closed the door and pressed a button. We rose softly, without sound. Such smelling as the Indian had done before was a mooncast shadow to what he was doing now.

The elevator stopped, the door opened. There was light and I stepped out into a turret room where the day was still trying to be remembered. There were windows all around it. Far off the sea flickered. Darkness prowled slowly on the hills. There were paneled walls where there were no windows, and rugs on the floor with the soft colors of old Persians, and there was a reception desk that looked as if it had been made of carvings stolen from an ancient church. And behind the desk a woman sat and smiled at me, a dry tight withered smile that would turn to powder if you touched it.

She had sleek coiled hair and a dark, thin, wasted Asiatic face. There were heavy colored stones in her ears and heavy rings on her fingers, including a moonstone and an emerald in a silver setting that may have been a real emerald but somehow managed to look as phony as a dime store slave bracelet. And her hands were dry and dark and not young and not fit for rings.

She spoke. The voice was familiar. "Ah, Meester Marlowe, so ver-ry good of you to come. Amthor he weel be so ver-ry pleased."

I laid the hundred dollar bill the Indian had given me down on the desk. I looked behind me. The Indian had gone down again in the elevator.

"Sorry. It was a nice thought, but I can't take this."

"Amthor he – he weesh to employ you, is it not?" She smiled again. Her lips rustled like tissue paper.

"I'd have to find out what the job is first."

She nodded and got up slowly from behind the desk. She swished before me in a tight dress that fitted her like a mermaid's skin and showed that she had a good figure if you like them four sizes bigger below the waist.

"I weel conduct you," she said.

She pressed a button in the paneling and a door slid open noiselessly. There was a milky glow beyond it. I looked back at her smile before I went through. It was older than Egypt now. The door slid silently shut behind me.

There was nobody in the room.

It was octagonal, draped in black velvet from floor to ceiling, with a high remote black ceiling that may have been of velvet too. In the middle of a coal black lusterless rug stood an octagonal white table, just large enough for two pairs of elbows and in the middle of it a milk white globe on a black stand. The light came from this. How, I couldn't see. On either side of the table there was a white octagonal stool which was a smaller edition of the table. Over against one wall there was one more such stool. There were no windows. There was nothing else in the room, nothing at all. On the walls there was not even a light fixture. If there were other doors, I didn't see them. I looked back at the one by which I had come in. I couldn't see that either.

I stood there for perhaps fifteen seconds with the faint obscure feeling of being watched. There was probably a peephole somewhere, but I couldn't spot it. I gave up trying. I listened to my breath. The room was so still that I could hear it going through my nose, softly, like little curtains rustling.

Then an invisible door on the far side of the room slid open and a man stepped through and the door closed behind him. The man walked straight to the table with his head down and sat on one of the octagonal stools and made a sweeping motion with one of the most beautiful hands I have ever seen.

"Please be seated. Opposite me. Do not smoke and do not fidget. Try to relax, completely. Now how may I serve you?"

I sat down, got a cigarette into my mouth and rolled it along my lips without lighting it. I looked him over. He was thin, tall and straight as a steel rod. He had the palest finest white hair I ever saw. It could have been strained through silk gauze. His skin was as fresh as a rose petal. He might have been thirty-five or sixty-five. He was ageless. His hair was brushed straight back from as good a profile as Barrymore ever had. His eyebrows were coal black, like the walls and ceiling and floor. His eyes were deep, far too deep. They were the depthless drugged eyes of the somnambulist. They were like a well I read about once. It was nine hundred years old, in an old castle. You could drop a stone into it and wait. You could listen and wait and then you would give up waiting and laugh and then just as you were ready to turn away a faint, minute splash would come back up to you from the bottom of that well, so tiny, so remote that you could hardly believe a well like that possible.

His eyes were deep like that. And they were also eyes without expression, without soul, eyes that could watch lions tear a man to pieces and never change, that could watch a man impaled and screaming in the hot sun with his eyelids cut off.

He wore a double-breasted black business suit that had been cut by an artist. He stared vaguely at my fingers.

"Please do not fidget," he said. "It breaks the waves, disturbs my concentration."

"It makes the ice melt, the butter run and the cat squawk," I said.

322

He smiled the faintest smile in the world. "You didn't come here to be impertinent, I'm sure."

"You seem to forget why I did come. By the way, I gave that hundred dollar bill back to your secretary. I came, as you may recall, about some cigarettes. Russian cigarettes filled with marihuana. With your card rolled in the hollow mouthpieces."

"You wish to find out why that happened?"

"Yeah. I ought to be paying you the hundred dollars."

"That will not be necessary. The answer is simple. There are things I do not know. This is one of them."

For a moment I almost believed him. His face was as smooth as an angel's wing.

"Then why send me a hundred dollars – and a tough Indian that stinks – and a car? By the way, does the Indian have to stink? If he's working for you, couldn't you sort of get him to take a bath?"

"He is a natural medium. They are rare – like diamonds, and like diamonds, are sometimes found in dirty places. I understand you are a private detective?"

"Yes."

"I think you are a very stupid person. You look stupid. You are in a stupid business. And you came here on a stupid mission."

"I get it," I said. "I'm stupid. It sank in after a while."

"And I think I need not detain you any longer."

"You're not detaining me," I said. "I'm detaining you. I want to know why those cards were in those cigarettes."

He shrugged the smallest shrug that could be shrugged. "My cards are available to anybody. I do not give my friends marihuana cigarettes. Your question remains stupid."

"I wonder if this would brighten it up any. The cigarettes were in a cheap Chinese or Japanese case of imitation tortoiseshell. Ever see anything like that?"

"No. Not that I recall."

"I can brighten it up a little more. The case was in the pocket of a man named Lindsay Marriott. Ever hear of him?"

He thought. "Yes. I tried at one time to treat him for camera shyness. He was trying to get into pictures. It was a waste of time. Pictures did not want him."

"I can guess that," I said. "He would photograph like Isadora Duncan. I've still got the big one left. Why did you send me the C-note?"

"My dear Mr. Marlowe," he said coldly, "I am no fool. I am in a very sensitive profession. I am a quack. That is to say I do things which the doctors in their small frightened selfish guild cannot accomplish. I am in danger at all times – from people like you. I merely wish to estimate the danger before dealing with it."

"Pretty trivial in my case, huh?"

"It hardly exists," he said politely and made a peculiar motion with his left hand which made my eyes jump at it. Then he put it down very slowly on the white table and looked at it. Then he raised his depthless eyes again and folded his arms.

"Your hearing –"

"I smell it now," I said. "I wasn't thinking of him."

I turned my head to the left. The Indian was sitting on the third white stool against the black velvet.

He had some kind of a white smock on him over his other clothes. He was sitting without a movement, his eyes closed, his head bent forward a little, as if he had been asleep for an hour. His dark strong face was full of shadows.

I looked back at Amthor. He was smiling his minute smile.

"I bet that makes the dowagers shed their false teeth," I said. "What does he do for real money – sit on your knee and sing French songs?"

He made an impatient gesture. "Get to the point, please."

"Last night Marriott hired me to go with him on an expedition that involved paying some money to some crooks at a spot they picked. I got knocked on the head. When I came out of it Marriott had been murdered."

Nothing changed much in Amthor's face. He didn't scream or run up the walls. But for him the reaction was sharp. He unfolded his arms and refolded them the other way. His mouth looked grim. Then he sat like a stone lion outside the Public Library.

"The cigarettes were found on him," I said.

He looked at me coolly. "But not by the police, I take it. Since the police have not been here."

"Correct."

"The hundred dollars," he said very softly, "was hardly enough."

"That depends what you expect to buy with it."

"You have these cigarettes with you?"

"One of them. But they don't prove anything. As you said, anybody could get your cards. I'm just wondering why they were where they were. Any ideas?"

"How well did you know Mr. Marriott?" he asked softly.

"Not at all. But I had ideas about him. They were so obvious they stuck out."

Amthor tapped lightly on the white table. The Indian still slept with his chin on his huge chest, his heavy-lidded eyes tight shut.

"By the way, did you ever meet a Mrs. Grayle, a wealthy lady who lives in Bay City?"

He nodded absently. "Yes, I treated her centers of speech. She had a very slight impediment."

"You did a sweet job on her," I said. "She talks as good as I do now."

That failed to amuse him. He still tapped on the table. I listened to the taps. Something about them I didn't like. They sounded like a code. He stopped, folded his arms again and leaned back against the air.

"What I like about this job everybody knows everybody," I said. "Mrs. Grayle knew Marriott too."

"How did you find that out?" he asked slowly.

I didn't say anything.

"You will have to tell the police – about those cigarettes," he said.

I shrugged.

"You are wondering why I do not have you thrown out," Amthor said pleasantly. "Second Planting could break your neck like a celery stalk. I am wondering myself. You seem to have some sort of theory. Blackmail I do not pay. It buys nothing – and I have many friends. But naturally there are certain elements which would like to show me in a bad light. Psychiatrists, sex specialists, neurologists, nasty little men with rubber hammers and shelves loaded with the literature of aberrations. And of course they are all – doctors. While I am still a – quack. What is your theory?"

I tried to stare him down, but it couldn't be done. I felt myself licking my lips.

He shrugged lightly. "I can't blame you for wanting to keep it to yourself. This is a matter that I must give thought to. Perhaps you are a much more intelligent man than I thought. I also make mistakes. In the meantime –" He leaned forward and put a hand on each side of the milky globe.

"I think Marriott was a blackmailer of women," I said. "And finger man for a jewel mob. But who told him what women to cultivate – so that he would know their comings and goings, get intimate with them, make love to them, make them load up with the ice and take them out, and then slip to a phone and tell the boys where to operate?"

"That," Amthor said carefully, "is your picture of Marriott – and of me. I am slightly disgusted."

I leaned forward until my face was not more than a foot from his. "You're in a racket. Dress it up all you please and it's still a racket. And it wasn't just the cards, Amthor. As you say, anybody could get those. It wasn't the marihuana. You wouldn't be in a cheap line like that – not with your chances. But on the back of each card there is a blank space. And on blank spaces, or even on written ones, there is sometimes invisible writing."

He smiled bleakly, but I hardly saw it. His hands moved over the milky bowl.

The light went out. The room was as black as Carry Nation's bonnet.

22

I KICKED MY stool back and stood up and jerked the gun out of the holster under my arm. But it was no good. My coat was buttoned and I was too slow. I'd have been too slow anyway, if it came to shooting anybody.

There was a soundless rush of air and an earthy smell. In the complete darkness the Indian hit me from behind and pinned my arms to my sides. He started to lift me. I could have got the gun out still and fanned the room with blind shots, but I was a long way from friends. It didn't seem as if there was any point in it.

I let go of the gun and took hold of his wrists. They were greasy and hard to hold. The Indian breathed gutturally and set me down with a jar that lifted the top of my head. He had my wrists now, instead of me having his. He twisted them behind me fast and a knee like a corner stone went into my back. He bent me. I can be bent. I'm not the City Hall. He bent me.

I tried to yell, for no reason at all. Breath panted in my throat and couldn't get out. The Indian threw me sideways and got a body scissors on me as I fell. He had me in a barrel. His hands went to my neck. Sometimes I wake up in the night. I feel them there and I smell the smell of him. I feel the breath fighting and losing and the greasy fingers digging in. Then I get up and take a drink and turn the radio on.

I was just about gone when the light flared on again, blood red, on account of the blood in my eyeballs and at the back of

327

them. A face floated around and a hand pawed me delicately, but the other hands stayed on my throat.

A voice said softly, "Let him breathe – a little."

The fingers slackened. I wrenched loose from them. Something that glinted hit me on the side of the jaw.

The voice said softly: "Get him on his feet."

The Indian got me on my feet. He pulled me back against the wall, holding me by both twisted wrists.

"Amateur," the voice said softly and the shiny thing that was as hard and bitter as death hit me again, across the face. Something warm trickled. I licked at it and tasted iron and salt.

A hand explored my wallet. A hand explored all my pockets. The cigarette in tissue paper came out and was unwrapped. It went somewhere in the haze that was in front of me.

"There were three cigarettes?" the voice said gently, and the shining thing hit my jaw again.

"Three," I gulped.

"Just where did you say the others were?"

"In my desk – at the office."

The shiny thing hit me again. "You are probably lying – but I can find out." Keys shone with funny little red lights in front of me. The voice said: "Choke him a little more."

The iron fingers went into my throat. I was strained back against him, against the smell of him and the hard muscles of his stomach. I reached up and took one of his fingers and tried to twist it.

The voice said softly: "Amazing. He's learning."

The glinting thing swayed through the air again. It smacked my jaw, the thing that had once been my jaw.

"Let him go. He's tame," the voice said.

The heavy strong arms dropped away and I swayed forward and took a step and steadied myself. Amthor stood smiling very slightly, almost dreamily in front of me. He held my gun in his delicate, lovely hand. He held it pointed at my chest.

"I could teach you," he said in his soft voice. "But to what purpose? A dirty little man in a dirty little world. One spot of brightness on you and you would still be that. Is it not so?" He smiled, so beautifully.

I swung at his smile with everything I had left.

It wasn't so bad considering. He reeled and blood came out of both his nostrils. Then he caught himself and straightened up and lifted the gun again.

"Sit down, my child," he said softly. "I have visitors coming. I am so glad you hit me. It helps a great deal."

I felt for the white stool and sat down and put my head down on the white table beside the milky globe which was now shining again softly. I stared at it sideways, my face on the table. The light fascinated me. Nice light, nice soft light.

Behind me and around me there was nothing but silence.

I think I went to sleep, just like that, with a bloody face on the table, and a thin beautiful devil with my gun in his hand watching me and smiling.

23

"ALL RIGHT," THE big one said. "You can quit stalling now."

I opened my eyes and sat up.

"Out in the other room, pally."

I stood up, still dreamy. We went somewhere, through a door. Then I saw where it was – the reception room with the windows all around. It was black dark now outside.

The woman with the wrong rings sat at her desk. A man stood beside her.

"Sit here, pally."

He pushed me down. It was a nice chair, straight but comfortable but I wasn't in the mood for it. The woman behind the desk had a notebook open and was reading out loud from it. A short elderly man with a deadpan expression and a gray mustache was listening to her.

Amthor was standing by a window, with his back to the room, looking out at the placid line of the ocean, far off, beyond the pier lights, beyond the world. He looked at it as if he loved it. He half turned his head to look at me once, and I could see that the blood had been washed off his face, but his nose wasn't the nose I had first met, not by two sizes. That made me grin, cracked lips and all.

"You got fun, pally?"

I looked at what made the sound, what was in front of me and what had helped me get where I was. He was a wind-blown blossom of some two hundred pounds with freckled teeth and the mellow voice of a circus barker. He was tough, fast and he ate red meat. Nobody could push him around. He was the kind of cop who spits on his blackjack every night instead of saying his prayers. But he had humorous eyes.

He stood in front of me splay-legged, holding my open wallet in his hand, making scratches on the leather with his right thumbnail, as if he just liked to spoil things. Little things, if they were all he had. But probably faces would give him more fun.

"Peeper, huh, pally? From the big bad burg, huh? Little spot of blackmail, huh?"

His hat was on the back of his head. He had dusty brown hair darkened by sweat on his forehead. His humorous eyes were flecked with red veins.

My throat felt as though it had been through a mangle. I reached up and felt it. That Indian. He had fingers like pieces of tool steel.

The dark woman stopped reading out of her notebook and closed it. The elderly smallish man with the gray mustache nodded and came over to stand behind the one who was talking to me.

"Cops?" I asked, rubbing my chin.

"What do *you* think, pally?"

Policeman's humor. The small one had a cast in one eye, and it looked half blind.

330

"Not L.A.," I said, looking at him. "That eye would retire him in Los Angeles."

The big man handed me my wallet. I looked through it. I had all the money still. All the cards. It had everything that belonged in it. I was surprised.

"Say something, pally," the big one said. "Something that would make us get fond of you."

"Give me back my gun."

He leaned forward a little and thought. I could see him thinking. It hurt his corns. "Oh, you want your gun, pally?" He looked sideways at the one with the gray mustache. "He wants his gun," he told him. He looked at me again. "And what would you want your gun for, pally?"

"I want to shoot an Indian."

"Oh, you want to shoot an Indian, pally."

"Yeah – just one Indian, pop."

He looked at the one with the mustache again. "This guy is very tough," he told him. "He wants to shoot an Indian."

"Listen, Hemingway, don't repeat everything I say," I said.

"I think the guy is nuts," the big one said. "He just called me Hemingway. Do you think he is nuts?"

The one with the mustache bit a cigar and said nothing. The tall beautiful man at the window turned slowly and said softly: "I think possibly he is a little unbalanced."

"I can't think of any reason why he should call me Hemingway," the big one said. "My name ain't Hemingway."

The older man said: "I didn't see a gun."

They looked at Amthor. Amthor said: "It's inside. I have it. I'll give it to you, Mr. Blane."

The big man leaned down from his hips and bent his knees a little and breathed in my face. "What for did you call me Hemingway, pally?"

"There are ladies present."

He straightened up again. "You see." He looked at the one with the mustache. The one with the mustache nodded and then turned and walked away, across the room. The sliding door opened. He went in and Amthor followed him.

There was silence. The dark woman looked down at the top of her desk and frowned. The big man looked at my right eyebrow and slowly shook his head from side to side, wonderingly.

The door opened again and the man with the mustache came back. He picked a hat up from somewhere and handed it to me. He took my gun out of his pocket and handed it to me. I knew by the weight it was empty. I tucked it under my arm and stood up.

The big man said: "Let's go, pally. Away from here. I think maybe a little air will help you to get straightened out."

"Okay, Hemingway."

"He's doing that again," the big man said sadly. "Calling me Hemingway on account of there are ladies present. Would you think that would be some kind of dirty crack in his book?"

The man with the mustache said, "Hurry up."

The big man took me by the arm and we went over to the little elevator. It came up. We got into it.

24

AT THE BOTTOM of the shaft we got out and walked along the narrow hallway and out of the black door. It was crisp clear air outside, high enough to be above the drift of foggy spray from the ocean. I breathed deeply.

The big man still had hold of my arm. There was a car standing there, a plain dark sedan, with private plates.

The big man opened the front door and complained: "It ain't really up to your class, pally. But a little air will set you up fine. Would that be all right with you? We wouldn't want to do anything that you wouldn't like us to do, pally."

"Where's the Indian?"

He shook his head a little and pushed me into the car. I got into the right side of the front seat. "Oh, yeah, the Indian," he said. "You got to shoot him with a bow and arrow. That's the law. We got him in the back of the car."

I looked in the back of the car. It was empty.

"Hell, he ain't there," the big one said. "Somebody must of glommed him off. You can't leave nothing in an unlocked car any more."

"Hurry up," the man with the mustache said, and got into the back seat. Hemingway went around and pushed his hard stomach behind the wheel. He started the car. We turned and drifted off down the driveway lined with wild geraniums. A cold wind lifted off the sea. The stars were too far off. They said nothing.

We reached the bottom of the drive and turned out onto the concrete mountain road and drifted without haste along that.

"How come you don't have a car with you, pally?"

"Amthor sent for me."

"Why would that be, pally?"

"It must have been he wanted to see me."

"This guy is good," Hemingway said. "He figures things out." He spit out of the side of the car and made a turn nicely and let the car ride its motor down the hill. "He says you called him up on the phone and tried to put the bite on him. So he figures he better have a look-see what kind of guy he is doing business with — if he is doing business. So he sends his own car."

"On account of he knows he is going to call some cops he knows and I won't need mine to get home with," I said. "Okay, Hemingway."

"Yeah, that again. Okay. Well he has a dictaphone under his table and his secretary takes it all down and when we come she reads it back to Mr. Blane here."

I turned and looked at Mr. Blane. He was smoking a cigar, peacefully, as though he had his slippers on. He didn't look at me.

"Like hell she did," I said. "More likely a stock bunch of notes they had all fixed up for a case like that."

"Maybe you would like to tell us why you wanted to see this guy," Hemingway suggested politely.

"You mean while I still have part of my face?"

"Aw, we ain't those kind of boys at all," he said, with a large gesture.

"You know Amthor pretty well, don't you, Hemingway?"

"Mr. Blane kind of knows him. Me, I just do what the orders is."

"Who the hell is Mr. Blane?"

"That's the gentleman in the back seat."

"And besides being in the back seat who the hell is he?"

"Why, Jesus, everybody knows Mr. Blane."

"All right," I said, suddenly feeling very weary.

There was a little more silence, more curves, more winding ribbons of concrete, more darkness, and more pain.

The big man said: "Now that we are all between pals and no ladies present we really don't give so much time to why you went back up there, but this Hemingway stuff is what really has me down."

"A gag," I said. "An old, old gag."

"Who is this Hemingway person at all?"

"A guy that keeps saying the same thing over and over until you begin to believe it must be good."

"That must take a hell of a long time," the big man said. "For a private dick you certainly have a wandering kind of mind. Are you still wearing your own teeth?"

"Yeah, with a few plugs in them."

"Well, you certainly have been lucky, pally."

The man in the back seat said: "This is all right. Turn right at the next."

"Check."

Hemingway swung the sedan into a narrow dirt road that edged along the flank of a mountain. We drove along that about a mile. The smell of the sage became over-powering.

"Here," the man in the back seat said.

Hemingway stopped the car and set the brake. He leaned across me and opened the door.

"Well, it's nice to have met you, pally. But don't come back. Anyways not on business. Out."

"I walk home from here?"

The man in the back seat said: "Hurry up."

"Yeah, you walk home from here, pally. Will that be all right with you?"

"Sure, it will give me time to think a few things out. For instance you boys are not L.A. cops. But one of you is a cop, maybe both of you. I'd say you are Bay City cops. I'm wondering why you were out of your territory."

"Ain't that going to be kind of hard to prove, pally?"

"Good night, Hemingway."

He didn't answer. Neither of them spoke. I started to get out of the car and put my foot on the running board and leaned forward, still a little dizzy.

The man in the back seat made a sudden flashing movement that I sensed rather than saw. A pool of darkness opened at my feet and was far, far deeper than the blackest night.

I dived into it. It had no bottom.

25

THE ROOM WAS full of smoke.

The smoke hung straight up in the air, in thin lines, straight up and down like a curtain of small clear beads. Two windows seemed to be open in an end wall, but the smoke didn't move. I had never seen the room before. There were bars across the windows.

I was dull, without thought. I felt as if I had slept for a year. But the smoke bothered me. I lay on my back and thought about it. After a long time I took a deep breath that hurt my lungs.

I yelled: "Fire!"

That made me laugh. I didn't know what was funny about it but I began to laugh. I lay there on the bed and laughed. I didn't like the sound of the laugh. It was the laugh of a nut.

The one yell was enough. Steps thumped rapidly outside the room and a key was jammed into a lock and the door swung open. A man jumped in sideways and shut the door after him. His right hand reached toward his hip.

He was a short thick man in a white coat. His eyes had a queer look, black and flat. There were bulbs of gray skin at the outer corners of them.

I turned my head on the hard pillow and yawned.

"Don't count that one, Jack. It slipped out," I said.

He stood there scowling, his right hand hovering towards his right hip. Greenish malignant face and flat black eyes and gray white skin and nose that seemed just a shell.

"Maybe you want some more strait-jacket," he sneered.

"I'm fine, Jack. Just fine. Had a long nap. Dreamed a little, I guess. Where am I?"

"Where you belong."

"Seems like a nice place," I said. "Nice people, nice atmosphere. I guess I'll have me a short nap again."

"Better be just that," he snarled.

He went out. The door shut. The lock clicked. The steps growled into nothing.

He hadn't done the smoke any good. It still hung there in the middle of the room, all across the room. Like a curtain. It didn't dissolve, didn't float off, didn't move. There was air in the room, and I could feel it on my face. But the smoke couldn't feel it. It was a gray web woven by a thousand spiders. I wondered how they had got them to work together.

Cotton flannel pajamas. The kind they have in the County Hospital. No front, not a stitch more than is essential. Coarse, rough material. The neck chafed my throat. My throat was still sore. I began to remember things. I reached up and felt the throat muscles. They were still sore. Just one Indian, pop. Okay, Hemingway. So you want to be a detective? Earn good money. Nine easy lessons. We provide badge. For fifty cents extra we send you a truss.

The throat felt sore but the fingers feeling it didn't feel anything. They might just as well have been a bunch of bananas. I looked at them. They looked like fingers. No good. Mail order fingers. They must have come with the badge and the truss. And the diploma.

It was night. The world outside the windows was a black world. A glass porcelain bowl hung from the middle of the ceiling on three brass chains. There was light in it. It had little colored lumps around the edge, orange and blue alternately. I stared at them. I was tired of the smoke. As I stared they began to open up like little portholes and heads popped out. Tiny beads, but alive, heads like the heads of small dolls, but alive. There was a man in a yachting cap with a Johnny Walker nose and a fluffy blonde in a picture hat and a thin man with a crooked bow tie. He looked like a waiter in a beachtown flytrap. He opened his lips and sneered: "Would you like your steak rare or medium, sir?"

I closed my eyes tight and winked them hard and when I opened them again it was just a sham porcelain bowl on three brass chains.

But the smoke still hung motionless in the moving air.

I took hold of the corner of a rough sheet and wiped the sweat off my face with the numb fingers the correspondence school had sent me after the nine easy lessons, one half in advance, Box Two Million Four Hundred and Sixty Eight Thousand Nine Hundred and Twenty Four, Cedar City, Iowa. Nuts. Completely nuts.

I sat up on the bed and after a while I could reach the floor with my feet. They were bare and they had pins and needles in them. Notions counter on the left, madam. Extra large safety pins on the right. The feet began to feel the floor. I stood up. Too far up. I crouched over, breathing hard, and held the side of the bed and a voice that seemed to come from under the bed said over and over again: "You've got the dt's . . . you've got the dt's . . . you've got the dt's."

I started to walk, wobbling like a drunk. There was a bottle of whiskey on a small white enamel table between the two barred windows. It looked like a good shape. It looked about half full. I walked towards it. There are a lot of nice people in the world, in spite. You can crab over the morning paper and kick the shins of the guy in the next seat at the movies and feel mean and discouraged and sneer at the politicians, but there are a lot of nice people in the world just the same. Take the guy that left that half bottle of whiskey there. He had a heart as big as one of Mae West's hips.

I reached it and put both my half-numb hands down on it and hauled it up to my mouth, sweating as if I was lifting one end of the Golden Gate Bridge.

I took a long untidy drink. I put the bottle down again, with infinite care. I tried to lick underneath my chin.

The whiskey had a funny taste. While I was realizing that it had a funny taste I saw a washbowl jammed into the corner of the wall. I made it. I just made it. I vomited. Dizzy Dean never threw anything harder.

Time passed – an agony of nausea and staggering and dazedness and clinging to the edge of the bowl and making animal sounds for help.

It passed. I staggered back to the bed and lay down on my back again and lay there panting, watching the smoke. The smoke wasn't quite so clear. Not quite so real. Maybe it was just something back of my eyes. And then quite suddenly it wasn't there at all and the light from the porcelain ceiling fixture etched the room sharply.

I sat up again. There was a heavy wooden chair against the wall near the door. There was another door besides the door the man in the white coat had come in at. A closet door, probably. It might even have my clothes in it. The floor was covered with green and gray linoleum in squares. The walls were painted white. A clean room. The bed on which I sat was a narrow iron hospital bed, lower than they usually are, and there were thick leather straps with buckles attached to the sides, about where a man's wrists and ankles would be.

It was a swell room – to get out of.

I had feeling all over my body now, soreness in my head and throat and in my arm. I couldn't remember about the arm. I rolled up the sleeve of the cotton pajama thing and looked at it fuzzily. It was covered with pin pricks on the skin all the way from the elbow to the shoulder. Around each was a small discolored patch, about the size of a quarter.

Dope. I had been shot full of dope to keep me quiet. Perhaps scopolamine too, to make me talk. Too much dope for the time. I was having the French fits coming out of it. Some do, some don't. It all depends how you are put together. Dope.

That accounted for the smoke and the little heads around the edge of the ceiling light and the voices and the screwy thoughts and the straps and bars and the numb fingers and feet. The whiskey was probably part of somebody's forty-eight-hour liquor cure. They had just left it around so that I wouldn't miss anything.

I stood up and almost hit the opposite wall with my stomach. That made me lie down and breathe very gently for quite a long time. I was tingling all over now and sweating. I could feel little drops of sweat form on my forehead and then slide slowly and carefully down the side of my nose to the corner of my mouth. My tongue licked at them foolishly.

I sat up once more and planted my feet on the floor and stood up.

"Okay, Marlowe," I said between my teeth. "You're a tough

339

guy. Six feet of iron man. One hundred and ninety pounds stripped and with your face washed. Hard muscles and no glass jaw. You can take it. You've been sapped down twice, had your throat choked and been beaten half silly on the jaw with a gun barrel. You've been shot full of hop and kept under it until you're as crazy as two waltzing mice. And what does all that amount to? Routine. Now let's see you do something really tough, like putting your pants on."

I lay down on the bed again.

Time passed again. I don't know how long. I had no watch. They don't make that kind of time in watches anyway.

I sat up. This was getting to be stale. I stood up and started to walk. No fun walking. Makes your heart jump like a nervous cat. Better lie down and go back to sleep. Better take it easy for a while. You're in bad shape, pally. Okay, Hemingway, I'm weak. I couldn't knock over a flower vase. I couldn't break a fingernail.

Nothing doing. I'm walking. I'm tough. I'm getting out of here.

I lay down on the bed again.

The fourth time was a little better. I got across the room and back twice. I went over to the washbowl and rinsed it out and leaned on it and drank water out of the palm of my hand. I kept it down. I waited a little and drank more. Much better.

I walked. I walked. I walked.

Half an hour of walking and my knees were shaking but my head was clear. I drank more water, a lot of water. I almost cried into the bowl while I was drinking it.

I walked back to the bed. It was a lovely bed. It was made of roseleaves. It was the most beautiful bed in the world. They had got it from Carole Lombard. It was too soft for her. It was worth the rest of my life to lie down in it for two minutes. Beautiful soft bed, beautiful sleep, beautiful eyes closing and lashes falling and the gentle sound of breathing and darkness and rest sunk in deep pillows. . . .

I walked.

They built the Pyramids and got tired of them and pulled them down and ground the stone up to make concrete for Boulder Dam and they built that and brought the water to the Sunny Southland and used it to have a flood with.

I walked all through it. I couldn't be bothered.

I stopped walking. I was ready to talk to somebody.

26

THE CLOSET DOOR was locked. The heavy chair was too heavy for me. It was meant to be. I stripped the sheets and pad off the bed and dragged the mattress to one side. There was a mesh spring underneath fastened top and bottom by coil springs of black enameled metal about nine inches long. I went to work on one of them. It was the hardest work I ever did. Ten minutes later I had two bleeding fingers and a loose spring. I swung it. It had a nice balance. It was heavy. It had a whip to it.

And when this was all done I looked across at the whiskey bottle and it would have done just as well, and I had forgotten all about it.

I drank some more water. I rested a little, sitting on the side of the bare springs. Then I went over to the door and put my mouth against the hinge side and yelled:

"Fire! Fire! Fire!"

It was a short wait and a pleasant one. He came running hard along the hallway outside and his key jammed viciously into the lock and twisted hard.

The door jumped open. I was flat against the wall on the opening side. He had the sap out this time, a nice little tool about five inches long, covered with woven brown leather. His eyes popped at the stripped bed and then began to swing around.

I giggled and socked him. I laid the coil spring on the side of his head and he stumbled forward. I followed him down to

341

his knees. I hit him twice more. He made a moaning sound. I took the sap out of his limp hand. He whined.

I used my knee on his face. It hurt my knee. He didn't tell me whether it hurt his face. While he was still groaning I knocked him cold with the sap.

I got the key from the outside of the door and locked it from the inside and went through him. He had more keys. One of them fitted my closet. In it my clothes hung. I went through my pockets. The money was gone from my wallet. I went back to the man with the white coat. He had too much money for his job. I took what I had started with and heaved him on to the bed and strapped him wrist and ankle and stuffed half a yard of sheet into his mouth. He had a smashed nose. I waited long enough to make sure he could breathe through it.

I was sorry for him. A simple hardworking little guy trying to hold his job down and get his weekly pay check. Maybe with a wife and kids. Too bad. And all he had to help him was a sap. It didn't seem fair. I put the doped whiskey down where he could reach it, if his hands hadn't been strapped.

I patted his shoulder. I almost cried over him.

All my clothes, even my gun harness and gun, but no shells in the gun, hung in the closet. I dressed with fumbling fingers, yawning a great deal.

The man on the bed rested. I left him there and locked him in.

Outside was a wide silent hallway with three closed doors. No sounds came from behind any of them. A wine-colored carpet crept down the middle and was as silent as the rest of the house. At the end there was a jog in the hall and then another hall at right angles and the head of a big old-fashioned staircase with white oak banisters. It curved graciously down into the dim hall below. Two stained glass inner doors ended the lower hall. It was tessellated and thick rugs lay on it. A crack of light seeped past the edge of an almost closed door. But no sound at all.

An old house, built as once they built them and don't build them any more. Standing probably on a quiet street with a rose arbor at the side and plenty of flowers in front. Gracious and cool and quiet in the bright California sun. And inside it who cares, but don't let them scream too loud.

I had my foot out to go down the stairs when I heard a man cough. That jerked me around and I saw there was a half-open door along the other hallway at the end. I tiptoed along the runner. I waited, close to the partly open door, but not in it. A wedge of light lay at my feet on the carpet. The man coughed again. It was a deep cough, from a deep chest. It sounded peaceful and at ease. It was none of my business. My business was to get out of there. But any man whose door could be open in that house interested me. He would be a man of position, worth tipping your hat to. I sneaked a little into the wedge of light. A newspaper rustled.

I could see part of a room and it was furnished like a room, not like a cell. There was a dark bureau with a hat on it and some magazines. Windows with lace curtains, a good carpet.

Bed springs creaked heavily. A big guy, like his cough. I reached out fingertips and pushed the door an inch or two. Nothing happened. Nothing ever was slower than my head craning in. I saw the room now, the bed, and the man on it, the ashtray heaped with stubs that overflowed on to a night table and from that to the carpet. A dozen mangled news-papers all over the bed. One of them in a pair of huge hands before a huge face. I saw the hair above the edge of the green paper. Dark, curly – black even – and plenty of it. A line of white skin under it. The paper moved a little more and I didn't breathe and the man on the bed didn't look up.

He needed a shave. He would always need a shave. I had seen him before, over on Central Avenue, in a Negro dive called Florian's. I had seen him in a old suit with white golf balls on the coat and a whiskey sour in his hand. And I had seen him with an Army Colt looking like a toy in his fist, stepping softly through a broken door. I had seen some of his work and it was the kind of work that stays done.

He coughed again and rolled his buttocks on the bed and yawned bitterly and reached sideways for a frayed pack of cigarettes on the night table. One of them went into his mouth. Light flared at the end of his thumb. Smoke came out of his nose.

"Ah," he said, and the paper went up in front of his face again.

I left him there and went back along the side hall. Mr. Moose Malloy seemed to be in very good hands. I went back to the stairs and down.

A voice murmured behind the almost closed door. I waited for the answering voice. None. It was a telephone conversation. I went over close to the door and listened. It was a low voice, a mere murmur. Nothing carried that meant anything. There was finally a dry clicking sound.

Silence continued inside the room after that.

This was the time to leave, to go far away. So I pushed the door open and stepped quietly in.

27

IT WAS AN OFFICE, not small, not large, with a neat professional look. A glass-doored bookcase with heavy books inside. A first aid cabinet on the wall. A white enamel and glass sterilizing cabinet with a lot of hypodermic needles and syringes inside it being cooked. A wide flat desk with a blotter on it, a bronze paper cutter, a pen set, an appointment book, very little else, except the elbows of a man who sat brooding, with his face in his hands.

Between the spread yellow fingers I saw hair the color of wet brown sand, so smooth that it appeared to be painted on his skull. I took three more steps and his eyes must have looked beyond the desk and seen my shoes move. His head

344

came up and he looked at me. Sunken colorless eyes in a parchment-like face. He unclasped his hands and leaned back slowly and looked at me with no expression at all.

Then he spread his hands with a sort of helpless but disapproving gesture and when they came to rest again, one of them was very close to the corner of the desk.

I took two steps more and showed him the blackjack. His index and second finger still moved towards the corner of the desk.

"The buzzer," I said, "won't buy you anything tonight. I put your tough boy to sleep."

His eyes got sleepy. "You have been a very sick man, sir. A very sick man. I can't recommend your being up and about yet."

I said: "The right hand." I snapped the blackjack at it. It coiled into itself like a wounded snake.

I went around the desk grinning without there being anything to grin at. He had a gun in the drawer of course. They always have a gun in the drawer and they always get it too late, if they get it at all. I took it out. It was a .38 automatic, a standard model not as good as mine, but I could use its ammunition. There didn't seem to be any in the drawer. I started to break the magazine out of his.

He moved vaguely, his eyes still sunken and sad.

"Maybe you've got another buzzer under the carpet," I said. "Maybe it rings in the Chief's office down at headquarters. Don't use it. Just for an hour I'm a very tough guy. Anybody comes in that door is walking into a coffin."

"There is no buzzer under the carpet," he said. His voice had the slightest possible foreign accent.

I got his magazine out and my empty one and changed them. I ejected the shell that was in the chamber of his gun and let it lie. I jacked one up into the chamber of mine and went back to the other side of the desk again.

There was a spring lock on the door. I backed towards it

345

and pushed it shut and heard the lock click. There was also a bolt. I turned that.

I went back to the desk and sat in a chair. It took my last ounce of strength.

"Whiskey," I said.

He began to move his hands around.

"Whiskey," I said.

He went to the medicine cabinet and got a flat bottle with a green revenue stamp on it and a glass.

"Two glasses," I said. "I tried your whiskey once. I damn near hit Catalina Island with it."

He brought two small glasses and broke the seal and filled the two glasses.

"You first," I said.

He smiled faintly and raised one of the glasses.

"Your health, sir – what remains of it." He drank. I drank. I reached for the bottle and stood it near me and waited for the heat to get to my heart. My heart began to pound, but it was back up in my chest again, not hanging on a shoelace.

"I had a nightmare," I said. "Silly idea. I dreamed I was tied to a cot and shot full of dope and locked in a barred room. I got very weak. I slept. I had no food. I was a sick man. I was knocked on the head and brought into a place where they did that to me. They took a lot of trouble. I'm not that important."

He said nothing. He watched me. There was a remote speculation in his eyes, as if he wondered how long I would live.

"I woke up and the room was full of smoke," I said. "It was just a hallucination, irritation of the optic nerve or whatever a guy like you would call it. Instead of pink snakes I had smoke. So I yelled and a toughie in a white coat came in and showed me a blackjack. It took me a long time to get ready to take it away from him. I got his keys and my clothes and even took my money out of his pocket. So here I am. All cured. What were you saying?"

346

"I made no remark," he said.

"Remarks want you to make them," I said. "They have their tongues hanging out waiting to be said. This thing here –" I waved the blackjack lightly, "is a persuader. I had to borrow it from a guy."

"Please give it to me at once," he said with a smile you would get to love. It was like the executioner's smile when he comes to your cell to measure you for the drop. A little friendly, a little paternal, and a little cautious at the same time. You would get to love it if there was any way you could live long enough.

I dropped the blackjack into his palm, his left palm.

"Now the gun, please," he said softly. "You have been a very sick man, Mr. Marlowe. I think I shall have to insist that you go back to bed."

I stared at him.

"I am Dr. Sonderborg," he said, "and I don't want any nonsense."

He laid the blackjack down on the desk in front of him. His smile was as stiff as a frozen fish. His long fingers made movements like dying butterflies.

"The gun, please," he said softly. "I advise strongly –"

"What time is it, warden?"

He looked mildly surprised. I had my wrist watch on now, but it had run down.

"It is almost midnight. Why?"

"What day is it?"

"Why, my dear sir – Sunday evening, of course."

I steadied myself on the desk and tried to think and held the gun close enough to him so that he might try and grab it.

"That's over forty-eight hours. No wonder I had fits. Who brought me here?"

He stared at me and his left hand began to edge towards the gun. He belonged to the Wandering Hand Society. The girls would have had a time with him.

"Don't make me get tough," I whined. "Don't make me lose my beautiful manners and my flawless English. Just tell me how I got here."

He had courage. He grabbed for the gun. It wasn't where he grabbed. I sat back and put it in my lap.

He reddened and grabbed for the whiskey and poured himself another drink and downed it fast. He drew a deep breath and shuddered. He didn't like the taste of liquor. Dopers never do.

"You will be arrested at once, if you leave here," he said sharply. "You were properly committed by an officer of the law —"

"Officers of the law can't do it."

That jarred him, a little. His yellowish face began to work.

"Shake it up and pour it," I said. "Who put me in here, why and how? I'm in a wild mood tonight. I want to go dance in the foam. I hear the banshees calling. I haven't shot a man in a week. Speak out, Dr. Fell. Pluck the antique viol, let the soft music float."

"You are suffering from narcotic poisoning," he said coldly. "You very nearly died. I had to give you digitalis three times. You fought, you screamed, you had to be restrained." His words were coming so fast they were leap-frogging themselves. "If you leave my hospital in this condition, you will get into serious trouble."

"Did you say you were a doctor — a medical doctor?"

"Certainly. I am Dr. Sonderborg, as I told you."

"You don't scream and fight from narcotic poisoning, doc. You just lie in a coma. Try again. And skim it. All I want is the cream. Who put me in your private funny house?"

"But —"

"But me no buts. I'll make a sop of you. I'll drown you in a butt of Malmsey wine. I wish I had a butt of Malmsey wine myself to drown in. Shakespeare. He knew his liquor too. Let's have a little of our medicine." I reached for his glass and poured us a couple more. "Get on with it, Karloff."

"The police put you in here."

"What police?"

"The Bay City police naturally." His restless yellow fingers twisted his glass. "This is Bay City."

"Oh. Did this police have a name?"

"A Sergeant Galbraith, I believe. Not a regular patrol car officer. He and another officer found you wandering outside the house in a dazed condition on Friday night. They brought you in because this place was close. I thought you were an addict who had taken an overdose. But perhaps I was wrong."

"It's a good story. I couldn't prove it wrong. But why keep me here?"

He spread his restless hands. "I have told you again and again that you were a very sick man and still are. What would you expect me to do?"

"I must owe you some money then."

He shrugged. "Naturally. Two hundred dollars."

I pushed my chair back a little. "Dirt cheap. Try and get it."

"If you leave here," he said sharply, "you will be arrested at once."

I leaned back over the desk and breathed in his face. "Not just for going out of here, Karloff. Open that wall safe."

He stood up in a smooth lunge. "This has gone quite far enough."

"You won't open it?"

"I most certainly will not open it."

"This is a gun I'm holding."

He smiled, narrowly and bitterly.

"It's an awful big safe," I said. "New too. This is a fine gun. You won't open it?"

Nothing changed in his face.

"Damn it," I said. "When you have a gun in your hand, people are supposed to do anything you tell them to. It doesn't work, does it?"

He smiled. His smile held a sadistic pleasure. I was slipping back. I was going to collapse.

I staggered at the desk and he waited, his lips parted softly.

I stood leaning there for a long moment, staring into his eyes. Then I grinned. The smile fell off his face like a soiled rag. Sweat stood out on his forehead.

"So long," I said. "I leave you to dirtier hands than mine."

I backed to the door and opened it and went out.

The front doors were unlocked. There was a roofed porch. The garden hummed with flowers. There was a white picket fence and a gate. The house was on a corner. It was a cool, moist night, no moon.

The sign on the corner said Descanso Street. Houses were lighted down the block. I listened for sirens. None came. The other sign said Twenty-third Street. I plowed over to Twenty-fifth Street and started towards the eight-hundred block. No. 819 was Anne Riordan's number. Sanctuary.

I had walked a long time before I realized that I was still holding the gun in my hand. And I had heard no sirens.

I kept on walking. The air did me good, but the whiskey was dying, and it writhed as it died. The block had fir trees along it, and brick houses, and looked like Capitol Hill in Seattle more than Southern California.

There was a light still in No. 819. It had a white porte-cochere, very tiny, pressed against a tall cypress hedge. There were rose bushes in front of the house. I went up the walk. I listened before I pushed the bell. Still no sirens wailing. The bell chimed and after a little while a voice croaked through one of those electrical contraptions that let you talk with your front door locked.

"What is it, please?"

"Marlowe."

Maybe her breath caught, maybe the electrical thing just made that sound being shut off.

The door opened wide and Miss Anne Riordan stood

there in a pale green slack suit looking at me. Her eyes went wide and scared. Her face under the glare of the porchlight was suddenly pale.

"My God," she wailed. "You look like Hamlet's father!"

28

THE LIVING ROOM had a tan figured rug, white and rose chairs, a black marble fireplace with very tall brass andirons, high bookcases built back into the walls, and rough cream drapes against the lowered venetian blinds.

There was nothing womanish in the room except a full length mirror with a clear sweep of floor in front of it.

I was half-sitting and half-lying in a deep chair with my legs on a footstool. I had had two cups of black coffee, then I had had a drink, then I had had two soft-boiled eggs and a slice of toast broken into them, then some more black coffee with brandy laced in it. I had had all this in the breakfast room, but I couldn't remember what it looked like any more. It was too long ago.

I was in good shape again. I was almost sober and my stomach was bunting towards third base instead of trying for the centerfield flagpole.

Anne Riordan sat opposite me, leaning forward, her neat chin cupped in her neat hand, her eyes dark and shadowy under the fluffed out reddish-brown hair. There was a pencil stuck through her hair. She looked worried. I had told her some of it, but not all. Especially about Moose Malloy I had not told her.

"I thought you were drunk," she said. "I thought you had to be drunk before you came to see me. I thought you had been out with that blonde. I thought – I don't know what I thought."

"I bet you didn't get all this writing," I said, looking around. "Not even if you got paid for what you thought you thought."

"And my dad didn't get it grafting on the cops either," she said. "Like that fat slob they have for chief of police nowadays."

"It's none of my business," I said.

She said: "We had some lots at Del Rey. Just sand lots they suckered him for. And they turned out to be oil lots."

I nodded and drank out of the nice crystal glass I was holding. What was in it had a nice warm taste.

"A fellow could settle down here," I said. "Move right in. Everything set for him."

"If he was that kind of fellow. And anybody wanted him to," she said.

"No butler," I said. "That makes it tough."

She flushed. "But you – you'd rather get your head beaten to a pulp and your arm riddled with dope needles and your chin used for a backboard in a basketball game. God knows there's enough of it."

I didn't say anything. I was too tired.

"At least," she said, "you had the brains to look in those mouthpieces. The way you talked over on Aster Drive I thought you had missed the whole thing."

"Those cards don't mean anything."

Her eyes snapped at me. "You sit there and tell me that after the man had you beaten up by a couple of crooked policemen and thrown in a two-day liquor cure to teach you to mind your own business? Why the thing stands out so far you could break off a yard of it and still have enough left for a baseball bat."

"I ought to have said that one," I said. "Just my style. Crude. What sticks out?"

"That this elegant psychic person is nothing but a high-class mobster. He picks the prospects and milks the minds and then tells the rough boys to go out and get the jewels."

"You really think that?"

She stared at me. I finished my glass and got my weak look on my face again. She ignored it.

"Of course I think it," she said. "And so do you."

"I think it's a little more complicated than that."

Her smile was cozy and acid at the same time. "I beg your pardon. I forgot for the moment you were a detective. It *would* have to be complicated, wouldn't it? I suppose there's a sort of indecency about a simple case."

"It's more complicated than that," I said.

"All right. I'm listening."

"I don't know. I just think so. Can I have one more drink?"

She stood up. "You know, you'll have to taste water some-time, just for the hell of it." She came over and took my glass. "This is going to be the last." She went out of the room and somewhere ice cubes tinkled and I closed my eyes and lis-tened to the small unimportant sounds. I had no business coming here. If they knew as much about me as I suspected, they might come here looking. That would be a mess.

She came back with the glass and her fingers cold from holding the cold glass touched mine and I held them for a moment and then let them go slowly as you let go of a dream when you wake with the sun in your face and have been in an enchanted valley.

She flushed and went back to her chair and sat down and made a lot of business of arranging herself in it.

She lit a cigarette, watching me drink.

"Amthor's a pretty ruthless sort of lad," I said. "But I don't somehow see him as the brain guy of a jewel mob. Perhaps I'm wrong. If he was and he thought I had something on him, I don't think I'd have got out of that dope hospital alive. But he's a man who has things to fear. He didn't get really tough until I began to babble about invisible writing."

She looked at me evenly. "Was there some?"

I grinned. "If there was, I didn't read it."

"That's a funny way to hide nasty remarks about a person, don't you think? In the mouthpieces of cigarettes. Suppose they were never found."

"I think the point is that Marriott feared something and that if anything happened to him, the cards *would* be found. The police would go over anything in his pockets with a fine toothcomb. That's what bothers me. If Amthor's a crook, nothing would have been left to find."

"You mean if Amthor murdered him – or had him murdered? But what Marriott knew about Amthor may not have had any direct connection with the murder."

I leaned back and pressed my back into the chair and finished my drink and made believe I was thinking that over. I nodded.

"But the jewel robbery had a connection with the murder. And we're assuming Amthor had a connection with the jewel robbery."

Her eyes were a little sly. "I bet you feel awful," she said. "Wouldn't you like to go to bed?"

"Here?"

She flushed to the roots of her hair. Her chin stuck out. "That was the idea. I'm not a child. Who the devil cares what I do or when or how?"

I put my glass aside and stood up. "One of my rare moments of delicacy is coming over me," I said. "Will you drive me to a taxi stand, if you're not too tired?"

"You damned sap," she said angrily. "You've been beaten to a pulp and shot full of God knows how many kinds of narcotics and I suppose all you need is a night's sleep to get up bright and early and start out being a detective again."

"I thought I'd sleep a little late."

"You ought to be in a hospital, you damn fool!"

I shuddered. "Listen," I said. "I'm not very clear-headed tonight and I don't think I ought to linger around here too long. I haven't a thing on any of these people that I could prove, but they seem to dislike me. Whatever I might say would be my word against the law, and the law in this town seems to be pretty rotten."

354

"It's a nice town," she said sharply, a little breathlessly. "You can't judge −"

"Okay, it's a nice town. So is Chicago. You could live there a long time and not see a Tommy gun. Sure, it's a nice town. It's probably no crookeder than Los Angeles. But you can only buy a piece of a big city. You can buy a town this size all complete, with the original box and tissue paper. That's the difference. And that makes me want out."

She stood up and pushed her chin at me. "You'll go to bed now and right here. I have a spare bedroom and you can turn right in and −"

"Promise to lock your door?"

She flushed and bit her lip. "Sometimes I think you're a world-beater," she said, "and sometimes I think you're the worst heel I ever met."

"On either count would you run me over to where I can get a taxi?"

"You'll stay here," she snapped. "You're not fit. You're a sick man."

"I'm not too sick to have my brain picked," I said nastily.

She ran out of the room so fast she almost tripped over the two steps from the living room up to the hall. She came back in nothing flat with a long flannel coat on over her slack suit and no hat and her reddish hair looking as mad as her face. She opened a side door and threw it away from her, bounced through it and her steps clattered on the driveway. A garage door made a faint sound lifting. A car door opened and slammed shut again. The starter ground and the motor caught and the lights flared past the open French door of the living room.

I picked my hat out of a chair and switched off a couple of lamps and saw that the French door had a Yale lock. I looked back a moment before I closed the door. It was a nice room. It would be a nice room to wear slippers in.

I shut the door and the little car slid up beside me and I went around behind it to get in.

She drove me all the way home, tight-lipped, angry. She drove like a fury. When I got out in front of my apartment house she said good night in a frosty voice and swirled the little car in the middle of the street and was gone before I could get my keys out of my pocket.

They locked the lobby door at eleven. I unlocked it and passed into the always musty lobby and along to the stairs and the elevator. I rode up to my floor. Bleak light shone along it. Milk bottles stood in front of service doors. The red fire door loomed at the back. It had an open screen that let in a lazy trickle of air that never quite swept the cooking smell out. I was home in a sleeping world, a world as harmless as a sleeping cat.

I unlocked the door of my apartment and went in and sniffed the smell of it, just standing there, against the door for a little while before I put the light on. A homely smell, a smell of dust and tobacco smoke, the smell of a world where men live, and keep on living.

I undressed and went to bed. I had nightmares and woke out of them sweating. But in the morning I was a well man again.

29

I WAS SITTING on the side of my bed in my pajamas, thinking about getting up, but not yet committed. I didn't feel very well, but I didn't feel as sick as I ought to, not as sick as I would feel if I had a salaried job. My head hurt and felt large and hot and my tongue was dry and had gravel on it and my throat was stiff and my jaw was not untender. But I had had worse mornings.

It was a gray morning with high fog, not yet warm but likely to be. I heaved up off the bed and rubbed the pit of my stomach where it was sore from vomiting. My left foot felt fine. It didn't have an ache in it. So I had to kick the corner of the bed with it.

I was still swearing when there was a sharp tap at the door, the kind of bossy knock that makes you want to open the door two inches, emit the succulent raspberry and slam it again.

I opened it a little wider than two inches. Detective-Lieutenant Randall stood there, in a brown gabardine suit, with a pork pie lightweight felt on his head, very neat and clean and solemn and with a nasty look in his eye.

He pushed the door lightly and I stepped away from it. He came in and closed it and looked around. "I've been looking for you for two days," he said. He didn't look at me. His eyes measured the room.

"I've been sick."

He walked around with a light springy step, his creamy gray hair shining, his hat under his arm now, his hands in his pockets. He wasn't a very big man for a cop. He took one hand out of his pocket and placed the hat carefully on top of some magazines.

"Not here," he said.

"In a hospital."

"Which hospital?"

"A pet hospital."

He jerked as if I had slapped his face. Dull color showed behind his skin.

"A little early in the day, isn't it – for that sort of thing?"

I didn't say anything. I lit a cigarette. I took one draw on it and sat down on the bed again, quickly.

"No cure for lads like you, is there?" he said. "Except to throw you in the sneezer."

"I've been a sick man and I haven't had my morning coffee. You can't expect a very high grade of wit."

"I told you not to work on this case."

"You're not God. You're not even Jesus Christ." I took another drag on the cigarette. Somewhere down inside me felt raw, but I liked it a little better.

"You'd be amazed how much trouble I could make you."

"Probably."

"Do you know why I haven't done it so far?"

"Yeah."

"Why?" He was leaning over a little, sharp as a terrier, with that stony look in his eyes they all get sooner or later.

"You couldn't find me."

He leaned back and rocked on his heels. His face shone a little. "I thought you were going to say something else," he said. "And if you said it, I was going to smack you on the button."

"Twenty million dollars wouldn't scare you. But you might get orders."

He breathed hard, with his mouth a little open. Very slowly he got a package of cigarettes out of his pocket and tore the wrapper. His fingers were trembling a little. He put a cigarette between his lips and went over to my magazine table for a match folder. He lit the cigarette carefully, put the match in the ashtray and not on the floor, and inhaled.

"I gave you some advice over the telephone the other day," he said. "Thursday."

"Friday."

"Yes — Friday. It didn't take. I can understand why. But I didn't know at that time you had been holding out evidence. I was just recommending a line of action that seemed like a good idea in this case."

"What evidence?"

He stared at me silently.

"Will you have some coffee?" I asked. "It might make you human."

"No."

"I will." I stood up and started for the kitchenette.

"Sit down," Randall snapped. "I'm far from through."

I kept on going out to the kitchenette, ran some water into the kettle and put it on the stove. I took a drink of cold water from the faucet, then another. I came back with a third glass in my hand to stand in the doorway and look at him. He hadn't moved. The veil of his smoke was almost a solid thing to one side of him. He was looking at the floor.

"Why was it wrong to go to Mrs. Grayle when she sent for me?" I asked.

"I wasn't talking about that."

"Yeah, but you were just before."

"She didn't send for you." His eyes lifted and had the stony look still. And the flush still dyed his sharp cheekbones. "You forced yourself on her and talked about scandal and practically blackmailed yourself into a job."

"Funny. As I remember it, we didn't even talk job. I didn't think there was anything in her story. I mean, anything to get my teeth into. Nowhere to start. And of course I supposed she had already told it to you."

"She had. That beer joint on Santa Monica is a crook hide-out. But that doesn't mean anything. I couldn't get a thing there. The hotel across the street smells too. Nobody we want. Cheap punks."

"She tell you I forced myself on her?"

He dropped his eyes a little. "No."

I grinned. "Have some coffee?"

"No."

I went back into the kitchenette and made the coffee and waited for it to drip. Randall followed me out this time and stood in the doorway himself.

"This jewel gang has been working in Hollywood and around for a good ten years to my knowledge," he said. "They went too far this time. They killed a man. I think I know why."

"Well, if it's a gang job and you break it, that will be the first gang murder solved since I lived in the town. And I could name and describe at least a dozen."

"It's nice of you to say that, Marlowe."

359

"Correct me if I'm wrong."

"Damn it," he said irritably. "You're not wrong. There were a couple solved for the record, but they were just rappers. Some punk took it for the high pillow."

"Yeah. Coffee?"

"If I drink some, will you talk to me decently, man to man, without wise-cracking?"

"I'll try. I don't promise to spill all my ideas."

"I can do without those," he said acidly.

"That's a nice suit you're wearing."

The flush dyed his face again. "This suit cost twenty-seven-fifty," he snapped.

"Oh Christ, a sensitive cop," I said, and went back to the stove.

"That smells good. How do you make it?"

I poured. "French drip. Coarse ground coffee. No filter papers." I got the sugar from the closet and the cream from the refrigerator. We sat down on opposite sides of the nook.

"Was that a gag, about your being sick, in a hospital?"

"No gag. I ran into a little trouble – down in Bay City. They took me in. Not the cooler, a private dope and liquor cure."

His eyes got distant. "Bay City, eh? You like it the hard way, don't you, Marlowe?"

"It's not that I like it the hard way. It's that I get it that way. But nothing like this before. I've been sapped twice, the second time by a police officer or a man who looked like one and claimed to be one. I've been beaten with my own gun and choked by a tough Indian. I've been thrown unconscious into this dope hospital and kept there locked up and part of the time probably strapped down. And I couldn't prove any of it, except that I actually do have quite a nice collection of bruises and my left arm has been needled plenty."

He stared hard at the corner of the table. "In Bay City," he said slowly.

"The name's like a song. A song in a dirty bathtub."

"What were you doing down there?"

"I didn't go down there. These cops took me over the line. I went to see a guy in Stillwood Heights. That's in L.A."

"A man named Jules Amthor," he said quietly. "Why did you swipe those cigarettes?"

I looked into my cup. The damned little fool. "It looked funny, him – Marriott – having that extra case. With reefers in it. It seems they make them up like Russian cigarettes down in Bay City with hollow mouthpieces and the Romanoff arms and everything."

He pushed his empty cup at me and I refilled it. His eyes were going over my face line by line, corpuscle by corpuscle, like Sherlock Holmes with his magnifying glass or Thorndyke with his pocket lens.

"You ought to have told me," he said bitterly. He sipped and wiped his lips with one of those fringed things they give you in apartment houses for napkins. "But you didn't swipe them. The girl told me."

"Aw well, hell," I said. "A guy never gets to do anything in this country any more. Always women."

"She likes you," Randall said, like a polite FBI man in a movie, a little sad, but very manly. "Her old man was as straight a cop as ever lost a job. She had no business taking those things. She likes you."

"She's a nice girl. Not my type."

"You don't like them nice?" He had another cigarette going. The smoke was being fanned away from his face by his hand.

"I like smooth shiny girls, hardboiled and loaded with sin."

"They take you to the cleaners," Randall said indifferently.

"Sure. Where else have I ever been? What do you call this session?"

He smiled his first smile of the day. He probably allowed himself four.

"I'm not getting much out of you," he said.

"I'll give you a theory, but you are probably way ahead of me on it. This Marriott was a blackmailer of women, because Mrs. Grayle just about told me so. But he was something else. He was the finger man for the jewel mob. The society finger, the boy who would cultivate the victim and set the stage. He would cultivate women he could take out, get to know them pretty well. Take this holdup a week from Thursday. It smells. If Marriott hadn't been driving the car, or hadn't taken Mrs. Grayle to the Troc or hadn't gone home the way he did, past that beer parlor, the holdup couldn't have been brought off."

"The chauffeur could have been driving," Randall said reasonably. "But that wouldn't have changed things much. Chauffeurs are not getting themselves pushed in the face with lead bullets by holdup men – for ninety a month. But there couldn't be many stickups with Marriott alone with women or things would get talked about."

"The whole point of this kind of racket is that things are not talked about," I said. "In consideration for that the stuff is sold back cheap."

Randall leaned back and shook his head. "You'll have to do better than that to interest me. Women talk about anything. It would get around that this Marriott was a kind of tricky guy to go out with."

"It probably did. That's why they knocked him off."

Randall stared at me woodenly. His spoon was stirring air in an empty cup. I reached over and he waved the pot aside. "Go on with that one," he said.

"They used him up. His usefulness was exhausted. It was about time for him to get talked about a little, as you suggest. But you don't quit in those rackets and you don't get your time. So this last holdup was just that for him – the last. Look, they really asked very little for the jade considering its value. And Marriott handled the contact. But all the same Marriott was scared. At the last moment he thought he had better not go alone. And he figured a little trick that if anything did

362

happen to him, something on him would point to a man, a man quite ruthless and clever enough to be the brains of that sort of mob, and a man in an unusual position to get information about rich women. It was a childish sort of trick but it did actually work."

Randall shook his head. "A gang would have stripped him, perhaps even have taken the body out to sea and dumped it."

"No. They wanted the job to look amateurish. They wanted to stay in business. They probably have another finger lined up," I said.

Randall still shook his head. "The man these cigarettes pointed to is not the type. He has a good racket of his own. I've inquired. What did you think of him?"

His eyes were too blank, much too blank. I said: "He looked pretty damned deadly to me. And there's no such thing as too much money, is there? And after all his psychic racket is a temporary racket for any one place. He has a vogue and everybody goes to him and after a while the vogue dies down and the business is licking its shoes. That is, if he's a psychic and nothing else. Just like movie stars. Give him five years. He could work it that long. But give him a couple of ways to use the information he must get out of these women and he's going to make a killing."

"I'll look him up more thoroughly," Randall said with the blank look. "But right now I'm more interested in Marriott. Let's go back farther – much farther. To how you got to know him."

"He just called me up. Picked my name out of the phone book. He said so, at any rate."

"He had your card."

I looked surprised. "Sure. I'd forgotten that."

"Did you ever wonder why he picked *your* name – ignoring that matter of your short memory?"

I stared at him across the top of my coffee cup. I was beginning to like him. He had a lot behind his vest besides his shirt.

"So that's what you really came up for?" I said.

He nodded. "The rest, you know, is just talk." He smiled politely at me and waited.

I poured some more coffee.

Randall leaned over sideways and looked along the cream-colored surface of the table. "A little dust," he said absently, then straightened up and looked me in the eye. "Perhaps I ought to go at this in a little different way," he said. "For instance, I think your hunch about Marriott is probably right. There's twenty-three grand in currency in his safe-deposit box – which we had a hell of a time to locate, by the way. There are also some pretty fair bonds and a trust deed to a property on West Fifty-fourth Place."

He picked a spoon up and rapped it lightly on the edge of his saucer and smiled. "That interest you?" he asked mildly. "The number was 1644 West Fifty-fourth Place."

"Yeah," I said thickly.

"Oh, there was quite a bit of jewelry in Marriott's box too – pretty good stuff. But I don't think he stole it. I think it was very likely given to him. That's one up for you. He was afraid to sell it – on account of the association of thought in his own mind."

I nodded. "He'd feel as if it was stolen."

"Yes. Now that trust deed didn't interest me at all at first, but here's how it works. It's what we fellows are up against in police work. We get all the homicide and doubtful death reports from outlying districts. We're supposed to read them the same day. That's a rule, like you shouldn't search without a warrant or frisk a guy for a gun without reasonable grounds. But we break rules. We have to. I didn't get around to some of the reports until this morning. Then I read one about a killing of a Negro on Central, last Thursday. By a tough ex-con called Moose Malloy. And there was an identifying witness. And sink my putt, if you weren't the witness."

He smiled, softly, his third smile. "Like it?"

"I'm listening."

"This was only this morning, understand. So I looked at the name of the man making the report and I knew him, Nulty. So I knew the case was a flop. Nulty is the kind of guy – well, were you ever up at Crestline?"

"Yeah."

"Well, up near Crestline there's a place where a bunch of old box cars have been made into cabins. I have a cabin up there myself, but not a box car. These box cars were brought up on trucks, believe it or not, and there they stand without any wheels. Now Nulty is the kind of guy who would make a swell brakeman on one of those box cars."

"That's not nice," I said. "A fellow officer."

"So I called Nulty up and he hemmed and hawed around and spit a few times and then he said you had an idea about some girl called Velma something or other that Malloy was sweet on a long time ago and you went to see the widow of the guy that used to own the dive where the killing happened when it was a white joint, and where Malloy and the girl both worked at that time. And her address was 1644 West Fifty-fourth Place, the place Marriott had the trust deed on."

"Yes?"

"So I just thought that was enough coincidence for one morning," Randall said. "And here I am. And so far I've been pretty nice about it."

"The trouble is," I said, "it looks like more than it is. This Velma girl is dead, according to Mrs. Florian. I have her photo."

I went into the living room and reached into my suit-coat and my hand was in midair when it began to feel funny and empty. But they hadn't even taken the photos. I got them out and took them to the kitchen and tossed the Pierrot girl down in front of Randall. He studied it carefully.

"Nobody I ever saw," he said. "That another one?"

"No, this is a newspaper still of Mrs. Grayle. Anne Riordan got it."

He looked at it and nodded. "For twenty million, I'd marry her myself."

"There's something I ought to tell you," I said. "Last night I was so damn mad I had crazy ideas about going down there and trying to bust it alone. This hospital is at Twenty-third and Descanso in Bay City. It's run by a man named Sonderborg who says he's a doctor. He's running a crook hideout on the side. I saw Moose Malloy there last night. In a room."

Randall sat very still, looking at me. "Sure?"

"You couldn't mistake him. He's a big guy, enormous. He doesn't look like anybody you ever saw."

He sat looking at me, without moving. Then very slowly he moved out from under the table and stood up.

"Let's go see this Florian woman."

"How about Malloy?"

He sat down again. "Tell me the whole thing, carefully."

I told him. He listened without taking his eyes off my face. I don't think he even winked. He breathed with his mouth slightly open. His body didn't move. His fingers tapped gently on the edge of the table. When I had finished he said:

"This Dr. Sonderborg – what did he look like?"

"Like a doper, and probably a dope peddler." I described him to Randall as well as I could.

He went quietly into the other room and sat down at the telephone. He dialed his number and spoke quietly for a long time. Then he came back. I had just finished making more coffee and boiling a couple of eggs and making two slices of toast and buttering them. I sat down to eat.

Randall sat down opposite me and leaned his chin in his hand. "I'm having a state narcotics man go down there with a fake complaint and ask to look around. He may get some ideas. He won't get Malloy. Malloy was out of there ten minutes after you left last night. That's one thing you can bet on."

"Why not the Bay City cops?" I put salt on my eggs.

Randall said nothing. When I looked up at him his face was red and uncomfortable.

"For a cop," I said, "you're the most sensitive guy I ever met."

"Hurry up with that eating. We have to go."

"I have to shower and shave and dress after this."

"Couldn't you just go in your pajamas?" he asked acidly.

"So the town is as crooked as all that?" I said.

"It's Laird Brunette's town. They say he put up thirty grand to elect a mayor."

"The fellow that owns the Belvedere Club?"

"And the two gambling boats."

"But it's in our county," I said.

He looked down at his clean, shiny fingernails.

"We'll stop by your office and get those other two reefers," he said. "If they're still there." He snapped his fingers. "If you'll lend me your keys, I'll do it while you get shaved and dressed."

"We'll go together," I said. "I might have some mail."

He nodded and after a moment sat down and lit another cigarette. I shaved and dressed and we left in Randall's car.

I had some mail, but it wasn't worth reading. The two cut up cigarettes in the desk drawer had not been touched. The office had no look of having been searched.

Randall took the two Russian cigarettes and sniffed at the tobacco and put them away in his pocket.

"He got one card from you," he mused. "There couldn't have been anything on the back of that, so he didn't bother about the others. I guess Amthor is not very much afraid – just thought you were trying to pull something. Let's go."

30

OLD NOSEY POKED her nose an inch outside the front door, sniffed carefully as if there might be an early violet blooming, looked up and down the street with a raking glance, and nodded her white head. Randall and I took our hats off. In that neighborhood that probably ranked you with Valentino. She seemed to remember me.

"Good morning, Mrs. Morrison," I said. "Can we step inside a minute? This is Lieutenant Randall from Headquarters."

"Land's sakes, I'm all flustered. I got a big ironing to do," she said.

"We won't keep you a minute."

She stood back from the door and we slipped past her into her hallway with the side piece from Mason City or wherever it was and from that into the neat living room with the lace curtains at the windows. A smell of ironing came from the back of the house. She shut the door in between as carefully as if it was made of short pie crust.

She had a blue and white apron on this morning. Her eyes were just as sharp and her chin hadn't grown any.

She parked herself about a foot from me and pushed her face forward and looked into my eyes.

"She didn't get it."

I looked wise. I nodded my head and looked at Randall and Randall nodded his head. He went to a window and looked at the side of Mrs. Florian's house. He came back softly, holding his pork pie under his arm, debonair as a French count in a college play.

"She didn't get it," I said.

"Nope, she didn't. Saturday was the first. April Fool's Day. He! He!" She stopped and was about to wipe her eyes with her apron when she remembered it was a rubber apron. That soured her a little. Her mouth got the pruny look.

"When the mailman come by and he didn't go up her walk she run out and called to him. He shook his head and went on. She went back in. She slammed the door so hard I figured a window'd break. Like she was mad."

"I swan," I said.

Old Nosey said to Randall sharply: "Let me see your

badge, young man. This young man had a whiskey breath on him t'other day. I ain't never rightly trusted him."

Randall took a gold and blue enamel badge out of his pocket and showed it to her.

"Looks like real police all right," she admitted. "Well, ain't nothing happened over Sunday. She went out for liquor. Come back with two square bottles."

"Gin," I said. "That just gives you an idea. Nice folks don't drink gin."

"Nice folks don't drink no liquor at all," Old Nosey said pointedly.

"Yeah," I said. "Come Monday, that being today, and the mailman went by again. This time she was really sore."

"Kind of smart guesser, ain't you, young man? Can't wait for folks to get their mouth open hardly."

"I'm sorry, Mrs. Morrison. This is an important matter to us —"

"This here young man don't seem to have no trouble keepin' his mouth in place."

"He's married," I said. "He's had practice."

Her face turned a shade of violet that reminded me, unpleasantly, of cyanosis. "Get out of my house afore I call the police!" she shouted.

"There is a police officer standing before you, madam," Randall said shortly. "You are in no danger."

"That's right there is," she admitted. The violet tint began to fade from her face. "I don't take to this man."

"You have company, madam. Mrs. Florian didn't get her registered letter today either — is that it?"

"No." Her voice was sharp and short. Her eyes were furtive. She began to talk rapidly, too rapidly. "People was there last night. I didn't even see them. Folks took me to the picture show. Just as we got back — no, just after they driven off — a car went away from next door. Fast without any lights. I didn't see the number."

She gave me a sharp sidelong look from her furtive eyes. I wondered why they were furtive. I wandered to the window and lifted the lace curtain. An official blue-gray uniform was nearing the house. The man wearing it wore a heavy leather bag over his shoulder and had a vizored cap.

I turned away from the window, grinning.

"You're slipping," I told her rudely. "You'll be playing shortstop in a Class C league next year."

"That's not smart," Randall said coldly.

"Take a look out of the window."

He did and his face hardened. He stood quite still looking at Mrs. Morrison. He was waiting for something, a sound like nothing else on earth. It came in a moment.

It was the sound of something being pushed into the front door mail slot. It might have been a handbill, but it wasn't. There were steps going back down the walk, then along the street, and Randall went to the window again. The mailman didn't stop at Mrs. Florian's house. He went on, his blue-gray back even and calm under the heavy leather pouch.

Randall turned his head and asked with deadly politeness: "How many mail deliveries a morning are there in this district, Mrs. Morrison?"

She tried to face it out. "Just the one," she said sharply – "one mornings and one afternoons."

Her eyes darted this way and that. The rabbit chin was trembling on the edge of something. Her hands clutched at the rubber frill that bordered the blue and white apron.

"The morning delivery just went by," Randall said dreamily. "Registered mail comes by the regular mailman?"

"She always got it Special Delivery," the old voice cracked.

"Oh. But on Saturday she ran out and spoke to the mailman when he didn't stop at her house. And you said nothing about Special Delivery."

It was nice to watch him working – on somebody else.

Her mouth opened wide and her teeth had the nice shiny look that comes from standing all night in a glass of solution. Then suddenly she made a squawking noise and threw the apron over her head and ran out of the room.

He watched the door through which she had gone. It was beyond the arch. He smiled. It was a rather tired smile.

"Neat, and not a bit gaudy," I said. "Next time you play the tough part. I don't like being rough with old ladies – even if they are lying gossips."

He went on smiling. "Same old story." He shrugged. "Police work. Phooey. She started with facts, as she knew facts. But they didn't come fast enough or seem exciting enough. So she tried a little lily-gilding."

He turned and we went out into the hall. A faint noise of sobbing came from the back of the house. For some patient man, long dead, that had been the weapon of final defeat, probably. To me it was just an old woman sobbing, but nothing to be pleased about.

We went quietly out of the house, shut the front door quietly and made sure that the screen door didn't bang. Randall put his hat on and sighed. Then he shrugged, spreading his cool well-kept hands out far from his body. There was a thin sound of sobbing still audible, back in the house.

The mailman's back was two houses down the street.

"Police work," Randall said quietly, under his breath, and twisted his mouth.

We walked across the space to the next house. Mrs. Florian hadn't even taken the wash in. It still jittered, stiff and yellowish on the wire line in the side yard. We went up on the steps and rang the bell. No answer. We knocked. No answer.

"It was unlocked last time," I said.

He tried the door, carefully screening the movement with his body. It was locked this time. We went down off the porch and walked around the house on the side away from Old Nosey. The back porch had a hooked screen. Randall knocked on that. Nothing happened. He came back off the two almost paintless wooden steps and went along the disused and overgrown driveway and opened up a wooden garage. The doors creaked. The garage was full of nothing. There were a few battered old-fashioned trunks not worth breaking up for firewood. Rusted gardening tools, old cans, plenty of those, in cartons. On each side of the doors, in the angle of the wall a nice fat black widow spider sat in its casual untidy web. Randall picked up a piece of wood and killed them absently. He shut the garage up again, walked back along the weedy drive to the front and up the steps of the house on the other side from Old Nosey. Nobody answered his ring or knock.

He came back slowly, looking across the street over his shoulder.

"Back door's easiest," he said. "The old hen next door won't do anything about it now. She's done too much lying."

He went up the two back steps and slid a knife blade neatly into the crack of the door and lifted the hook. That put us in the screen porch. It was full of cans and some of the cans were full of flies.

"Jesus, what a way to live!" he said.

The back door was easy. A five-cent skeleton key turned the lock. But there was a bolt.

"This jars me," I said. "I guess she's beat it. She wouldn't lock up like this. She's too sloppy."

"Your hat's older than mine," Randall said. He looked at the glass panel in the back door. "Lend it to me to push the glass in. Or shall we do a neat job?"

"Kick it in. Who cares around here?"

"Here goes."

He stepped back and lunged at the lock with his leg parallel to the floor. Something cracked idly and the door gave a few inches. We heaved it open and picked a piece of jagged cast metal off the linoleum and laid it politely on the woodstone drainboard, beside about nine empty gin bottles.

Flies buzzed against the closed windows of the kitchen. The place reeked. Randall stood in the middle of the floor, giving it the careful eye.

Then he walked softly through the swing door without touching it except low down with his toe and using that to push it far enough back so that it stayed open. The living room was much as I had remembered it. The radio was off.

"That's a nice radio," Randall said. "Cost money. If it's paid for. Here's something."

He went down on one knee and looked along the carpet. Then he went to the side of the radio and moved a loose cord with his foot. The plug came into view. He bent and studied the knobs on the radio front.

"Yeah," he said. "Smooth and rather large. Pretty smart, that. You don't get prints on a light cord, do you?"

"Shove it in and see if it's turned on."

He reached around and shoved it into the plug in the baseboard. The light went on at once. We waited. The thing hummed for a while and then suddenly a heavy volume of sound began to pour out of the speaker. Randall jumped at the cord and yanked it loose again. The sound was snapped off sharp.

When he straightened his eyes were full of light.

We went swiftly into the bedroom. Mrs. Jessie Pierce Florian lay diagonally across the bed, in a rumpled cotton house dress, with her head close to one end of the footboard. The corner post of the bed was smeared darkly with something the flies liked.

She had been dead long enough.

Randall didn't touch her. He stared down at her for a long time and then looked at me with a wolfish baring of his teeth.

"Brains on her face," he said. "That seems to be the theme song of this case. Only this was done with just a pair of hands. But Jesus what a pair of hands. Look at the neck bruises, the spacing of the finger marks."

"You look at them," I said. I turned away. "Poor old Nulty. It's not just a shine killing any more."

31

A SHINY BLACK bug with a pink head and pink spots on it crawled slowly along the polished top of Randall's desk and waved a couple of feelers around, as if testing the breeze for a takeoff. It wobbled a little as it crawled, like an old woman carrying too many parcels. A nameless dick sat at another desk and kept talking into an old-fashioned hushaphone telephone mouthpiece, so that his voice sounded like someone whispering in a tunnel. He talked with his eyes half closed, a big scarred hand on the desk in front of him holding a burning cigarette between the knuckles of the first and second fingers.

The bug reached the end of Randall's desk and marched straight off into the air. It fell on its back on the floor, waved a few thin worn legs in the air feebly and then played dead. Nobody cared, so it began waving the legs again and finally struggled over on its face. It trundled slowly off into a corner towards nothing, going nowhere.

The police loudspeaker box on the wall put out a bulletin about a holdup on San Pedro south of Forty-fourth. The holdup was a middle-aged man wearing a dark gray suit and gray felt hat. He was last seen running east on Forty-fourth and then dodging between two houses. "Approach carefully," the announcer said. "This suspect is armed with a .32 caliber revolver and has just held up the proprietor of a Greek restaurant at Number 3966 South San Pedro."

A flat click and the announcer went off the air and another one came on and started to read a hot car list, in a slow monotonous voice that repeated everything twice.

The door opened and Randall came in with a sheaf of letter size typewritten sheets. He walked briskly across the room and sat down across the desk from me and pushed some papers at me.

"Sign four copies," he said.

I signed four copies.

The pink bug reached a corner of the room and put feelers out for a good spot to take off from. It seemed a little discouraged. It went along the baseboard towards another corner. I lit a cigarette and the dick at the hushaphone abruptly got up and went out of the office.

Randall leaned back in his chair, looking just the same as ever, just as cool, just as smooth, just as ready to be nasty or nice as the occasion required.

"I'm telling you a few things," he said, "just so you won't go having any more brainstorms. Just so you won't go master-minding all over the landscape any more. Just so maybe for Christ's sake you will let this one lay."

I waited.

"No prints in the dump," he said. "You know which dump I mean. The cord was jerked to turn the radio off, but she turned it up herself probably. That's pretty obvious. Drunks like loud radios. If you have gloves on to do a killing and you turn up the radio to drown shots or something, you can turn it off the same way. But that wasn't the way it was done. And that woman's neck is broken. She was dead before the guy started to smack her head around. Now why did he start to smack her head around?"

"I'm just listening."

Randall frowned. "He probably didn't know he'd broken her neck. He was sore at her," he said. "Deduction." He smiled sourly.

I blew some smoke and waved it away from my face.

"Well, why was he sore at her? There was a grand reward paid the time he was picked up at Florian's for the bank job in Oregon. It was paid to a shyster who is dead since, but the Florians likely got some of it. Malloy may have suspected that.

Maybe he actually knew it. And maybe he was just trying to shake it out of her."

I nodded. It sounded worth a nod. Randall went on:

"He took hold of her neck just once and his fingers didn't slip. If we get him, we might be able to prove by the spacing of the marks that his hands did it. Maybe not. The doc figures it happened last night, fairly early. Motion picture time, anyway. So far we don't tie Malloy to the house last night, not by any neighbors. But it certainly looks like Malloy."

"Yeah," I said. "Malloy all right. He probably didn't mean to kill her, though. He's just too strong."

"That won't help him any," Randall said grimly.

"I suppose not. I just make the point that Malloy does not appear to me to be a killer type. Kill if cornered – but not for pleasure or money – and not women."

"Is that an important point?" he asked dryly.

"Maybe you know enough to know what's important. And what isn't. I don't."

He stared at me long enough for a police announcer to have time to put out another bulletin about the holdup of the Greek restaurant on South San Pedro. The suspect was now in custody. It turned out later that he was a fourteen-year-old Mexican armed with a water-pistol. So much for eye-witnesses.

Randall waited until the announcer stopped and went on:

"We got friendly this morning. Let's stay that way. Go home and lie down and have a good rest. You look pretty peaked. Just let me and the police department handle the Marriott killing and find Moose Malloy and so on."

"I got paid on the Marriott business," I said. "I fell down on the job. Mrs. Grayle has hired me. What do you want me to do – retire and live on my fat?"

He stared at me again. "I know. I'm human. They give you guys licenses, which must mean they expect you to do something with them besides hang them on the wall in your office. On the other hand any acting-captain with a grouch can break you."

"Not with the Grayles behind me."

He studied it. He hated to admit I could be even half right. So he frowned and tapped his desk.

"Just so we understand each other," he said after a pause. "If you crab this case, you'll be in a jam. It may be a jam you can wriggle out of this time. I don't know. But little by little you will build up a body of hostility in this department that will make it damn hard for you to do any work."

"Every private dick faces that every day of his life – unless he's just a divorce man."

"You can't work on murders."

"You've said your piece. I heard you say it. I don't expect to go out and accomplish things a big police department can't accomplish. If I have any small private notions, they are just that – small and private."

He leaned slowly across the desk. His thin restless fingers tap-tapped, like the poinsettia shoots tapping against Mrs. Jessie Florian's front wall. His creamy gray hair shone. His cool steady eyes were on mine.

"Let's go on," he said. "With what there is to tell. Amthor's away on a trip. His wife – and secretary – doesn't know or won't say where. The Indian has also disappeared. Will you sign a complaint against these people?"

"No. I couldn't make it stick."

He looked relieved. "The wife says she never heard of you. As to these two Bay City cops, if that's what they were – that's out of my hands. I'd rather not have the thing any more complicated than it is. One thing I feel pretty sure of – Amthor had nothing to do with Marriott's death. The cigarettes with his card in them were just a plant."

"Doc Sonderborg?"

He spread his hands. "The whole shebang skipped. Men from the D.A.'s office went down there on the quiet. No contact with Bay City at all. The house is locked up and empty. They got in, of course. Some hasty attempt had been made to clean up, but there are prints – plenty of them. It will take a week to work out what we have. There's a wall safe they're working on now. Probably had dope in it – and other things. My guess is that Sonderborg will have a record, not local, somewhere else, for abortion, or treating gunshot wounds or altering finger tips or for illegal use of dope. If it comes under Federal statutes, we'll get a lot of help."

"He said he was a medical doctor," I said.

Randall shrugged. "May have been once. May never have been convicted. There's a guy practicing medicine near Palm Springs right now who was indicted as a dope peddler in Hollywood five years ago. He was as guilty as hell – but the protection worked. He got off. Anything else worrying you?"

"What do you know about Brunette – for telling?"

"Brunette's a gambler. He's making plenty. He's making it an easy way."

"All right," I said, and started to get up. "That sounds reasonable. But it doesn't bring us any nearer to this jewel heist gang that killed Marriott."

"I can't tell you everything, Marlowe."

"I don't expect it," I said. "By the way, Jessie Florian told me – the second time I saw her – that she had been a servant in Marriott's family once. That was why he was sending her money. Anything to support that?"

"Yes. Letters in his safety-deposit box from her thanking him and saying the same thing." He looked as if he was going to lose his temper. "Now will you for God's sake go home and mind your own business?"

"Nice of him to take such care of the letters, wasn't it?"

He lifted his eyes until their glance rested on the top of my head. Then he lowered the lids until half the iris was covered. He looked at me like that for a long ten seconds. Then he smiled. He was doing an awful lot of smiling that day. Using up a whole week's supply.

"I have a theory about that," he said. "It's crazy, but it's human nature. Marriott was by the circumstances of his life a threatened man. All crooks are gamblers, more or less, and all gamblers are superstitious – more or less. I think Jessie Florian was Marriott's lucky piece. As long as he took care of her, nothing would happen to him."

I turned my head and looked for the pink-headed bug. He had tried two corners of the room now and was moving off disconsolately towards a third. I went over and picked him up in my handkerchief and carried him back to the desk.

"Look," I said. "This room is eighteen floors above ground. And this little bug climbs all the way up here just to make a friend. Me. *My* lucky piece." I folded the bug carefully into the soft part of the handkerchief and tucked the handkerchief into my pocket. Randall was pie-eyed. His mouth moved, but nothing came out of it.

"I wonder whose lucky piece Marriott was," I said.

"Not yours, pal." His voice was acid – cold acid.

"Perhaps not yours either." My voice was just a voice. I went out of the room and shut the door.

I rode the express elevator down to the Spring Street entrance and walked out on the front porch of City Hall and down some steps and over to the flower beds. I put the pink bug down carefully behind a bush.

I wondered, in the taxi going home, how long it would take him to make the Homicide Bureau again.

I got my car out of the garage at the back of the apartment house and ate some lunch in Hollywood before I started down to Bay City. It was a beautiful cool sunny afternoon down at the beach. I left Arguello Boulevard at Third Street and drove over to the City Hall.

32

IT WAS A cheap looking building for so prosperous a town. It looked more like something out of the Bible belt. Bums sat unmolested in a long row on the retaining wall that kept the front lawn – now mostly Bermuda grass – from falling into the street. The building was of three stories and had an old belfry at the top, and the bell still hanging in the belfry. They had probably rung it for the volunteer fire brigade back in the good old chaw-and-spit days.

The cracked walk and the front steps led to open double doors in which a knot of obvious city hall fixers hung around waiting for something to happen so they could make something else out of it. They all had the well-fed stomachs, the careful eyes, the nice clothes and the reach-me-down manners. They gave me about four inches to get in.

Inside was a long dark hallway that had been mopped the day McKinley was inaugurated. A wooden sign pointed out the police department Information Desk. A uniformed man dozed behind a pint-sized PBX set into the end of a scarred wooden counter. A plainclothesman with his coat off and his hog's leg looking like a fire plug against his ribs took one eye off his evening paper, bonged a spittoon ten feet away from him, yawned, and said the Chief's office was upstairs at the back.

The second floor was lighter and cleaner, but that didn't mean that it was clean and light. A door on the ocean side, almost at the end of the hall, was lettered: John Wax, Chief of Police. Enter.

Inside there was a low wooden railing and a uniformed man behind it working a typewriter with two fingers and one thumb. He took my card, yawned, said he would see, and managed to drag himself through a mahogany door marked John Wax, Chief of Police. Private. He came back and held the door in the railing for me.

I went on in and shut the door of the inner office. It was cool and large and had windows on three sides. A stained wood desk was set far back like Mussolini's, so that you had to walk across an expanse of blue carpet to get to it, and while you were doing that you would be getting the beady eye.

I walked to the desk. A tilted embossed sign on it read: John Wax, Chief of Police. I figured I might be able to remember the name. I looked at the man behind the desk. No straw was sticking to his hair.

He was a hammered-down heavyweight, with short pink hair and a pink scalp glistening through it. He had small, hungry, heavy-lidded eyes, as restless as fleas. He wore a suit of fawn-colored flannel, a coffee-colored shirt and tie, a diamond ring, a diamond-studded lodge pin in his lapel, and the required three stiff points of handkerchief coming up a little more than the required three inches from his outside breast pocket.

One of his plump hands was holding my card. He read it, turned it over and read the back, which was blank, read the front again, put it down on his desk and laid on it a paper-weight in the shape of a bronze monkey, as if he was making sure he wouldn't lose it.

He pushed a pink paw at me. When I gave it back to him, he motioned to a chair.

"Sit down, Mr. Marlowe. I see you are in our business more or less. What can I do for you?"

"A little trouble, Chief. You can straighten it out for me in a minute, if you care to."

"Trouble," he said softly. "A little trouble."

He turned in his chair and crossed his thick legs and gazed thoughtfully towards one of his pairs of windows. That let me see handspun lisle socks and English brogues that looked as if they had been pickled in port wine. Counting what I couldn't see and not counting his wallet he had half a grand on him. I figured his wife had money.

"Trouble," he said, still softly, "is something our little city don't know much about, Mr. Marlowe. Our city is small but very, very clean. I look out of my western windows and I see the Pacific Ocean. Nothing cleaner than that, is there?" He didn't mention the two gambling ships that were hull down on the brass waves just beyond the three-mile limit.

Neither did I. "That's right, Chief," I said.

He threw his chest a couple of inches farther. "I look out of my northern windows and I see the busy bustle of Arguello Boulevard and the lovely California foothills, and in the near foreground one of the nicest little business sections a man could want to know. I look out of my southern windows, which I am looking out of right now, and I see the finest little yacht harbor in the world, for a small yacht harbor. I don't have no eastern windows, but if I did have, I would see a residential section that would make your mouth water. No, sir, trouble is a thing we don't have a lot of on hand in our little town."

"I guess I brought mine with me, Chief. Some of it at least. Do you have a man working for you named Galbraith, a plainclothes sergeant?"

"Why yes, I believe I do," he said, bringing his eyes around. "What about him?"

"Do you have a man working for you that goes like this?" I described the other man, the one who said very little, was short, had a mustache and hit me with a blackjack. "He goes around with Galbraith, very likely. Somebody called him Mr. Blane, but that sounded like a phony."

"Quite on the contrary," the fat Chief said as stiffly as a fat man can say anything. "He is my Chief of Detectives. Captain Blane."

"Could I see these two guys in your office?"

He picked my card up and read it again. He laid it down. He waved a soft glistening hand.

"Not without a better reason than you have given me so far," he said suavely.

"I didn't think I could, Chief. Do you happen to know of a man named Jules Amthor? He calls himself a psychic adviser. He lives at the top of a hill in Stillwood Heights."

"No. And Stillwood Heights is not in my territory," the Chief said. His eyes now were the eyes of a man who has other thoughts.

"That's what makes it funny," I said. "You see, I went to call on Mr. Amthor in connection with a client of mine. Mr. Amthor got the idea I was blackmailing him. Probably guys in his line of business get that idea rather easily. He had a tough Indian bodyguard I couldn't handle. So the Indian held me and Amthor beat me up with my own gun. Then he sent for a couple of cops. They happened to be Galbraith and Mr. Blane. Could this interest you at all?"

Chief Wax flapped his hands on his desk top very gently. He folded his eyes almost shut, but not quite. The cool gleam of his eyes shone between the thick lids and it shone straight at me. He sat very still, as if listening. Then he opened his eyes and smiled.

"And what happened then?" he inquired, polite as a bouncer at the Stork Club.

"They went through me, took me away in their car, dumped me out on the side of a mountain and socked me with a sap as I got out."

He nodded, as if what I had said was the most natural thing in the world. "And this was in Stillwood Heights," he said softly.

"Yeah."

"You know what I think you are?" He leaned a little over the desk, but not far, on account of his stomach being in the way.

"A liar," I said.

"The door is there," he said, pointing to it with the little finger of his left hand.

I didn't move. I kept on looking at him. When he started to get mad enough to push his buzzer I said: "Let's not both make the same mistake. You think I'm a small time private dick trying to push ten times his own weight, trying to make a charge against a police officer that, even if it was true, the officer would take damn good care couldn't be proved. Not at all. I'm not making any complaints. I think the mistake was natural. I want to square myself with Amthor and I want your man Galbraith to help me do it. Mister Blane needn't bother. Galbraith will be enough. And I'm not here without backing. I have important people behind me."

"How far behind?" the Chief asked and chuckled wittily.

"How far is 862 Aster Drive, where Mr. Merwin Lockridge Grayle lives?"

His face changed so completely that it was as if another man sat in his chair. "Mrs. Grayle happens to be my client," I said.

"Lock the doors," he said. "You're a younger man than I am. Turn the bolt knobs. We'll make a friendly start on this thing. You have an honest face, Marlowe."

I got up and locked the doors. When I got back to the desk along the blue carpet, the Chief had a nice looking bottle out and two glasses. He tossed a handful of cardamom seeds on his blotter and filled both glasses.

We drank. He cracked a few cardamom seeds and we chewed them silently, looking into each other's eyes.

"That tasted right," he said. He refilled the glasses. It was my turn to crack the cardamom seeds. He swept the shells off his blotter to the floor and smiled and leaned back.

"Now let's have it," he said. "Has this job you are doing for Mrs. Grayle anything to do with Amthor?"

"There's a connection. Better check that I'm telling you the truth, though."

"There's that," he said and reached for his phone. Then he took a small book out of his vest and looked up a number. "Campaign contributors," he said and winked. "The Mayor is very insistent that all courtesies be extended. Yes, here it is." He put the book away and dialed.

He had the same trouble with the butler that I had. It made his ears get red. Finally he got her. His ears stayed red. She must have been pretty sharp with him. "She wants to talk to you," he said and pushed the phone across his broad desk.

"This is Phil," I said, winking naughtily at the Chief.

There was a cool provocative laugh. "What are you doing with that fat slob?"

"There's a little drinking being done."

"Do you have to do it with him?"

"At the moment, yes. Business. I said, is there anything new? I guess you know what I mean."

"No. Are you aware, my good fellow, that you stood me up for an hour the other night? Did I strike you as the kind of girl that lets that sorts of thing happen to her?"

"I ran into trouble. How about tonight?"

"Let me see — tonight is — what day of the week is it for heaven's sake?"

"I'd better call you," I said. "I may not be able to make it. This is Friday."

"Liar." The soft husky laugh came again. "It's Monday. Same time, same place — and no fooling this time?"

"I'd better call you."

"You'd better be there."

"I can't be sure. Let me call you."

"Hard to get? I see. Perhaps I'm a fool to bother."

"As a matter of fact you are."

"Why?"

"I'm a poor man, but I pay my own way. And it's not quite as soft a way as you would like."

"Damn you, if you're not there —"

"I said I'd call you."

She sighed. "All men are the same."

"So are all women — after the first nine."

She damned me and hung up. The Chief's eyes popped so far out of his head they looked as if they were on stilts.

He filled both glasses with a shaking hand and pushed one at me.

"So it's like that," he said very thoughtfully.

"Her husband doesn't care," I said, "so don't make a note of it."

He looked hurt as he drank his drink. He cracked the car-damom seeds very slowly, very thoughtfully. We drank to each other's baby blue eyes. Regretfully the Chief put the bottle and glasses out of sight and snapped a switch on his call box.

"Have Galbraith come up, if he's in the building. If not, try and get in touch with him for me."

I got up and unlocked the doors and sat down again. We didn't wait long. The side door was tapped on, the Chief called out, and Hemingway stepped into the room.

He walked solidly over to the desk and stopped at the end of it and looked at Chief Wax with the proper expression of tough humility.

"Meet Mr. Philip Marlowe," the Chief said genially. "A private dick from L.A."

Hemingway turned enough to look at me. If he had ever seen me before, nothing in his face showed it. He put a hand out and I put a hand out and he looked at the Chief again.

"Mr. Marlowe has a rather curious story," the Chief said, cunning, like Richelieu behind the arras. "About a man named Amthor who has a place in Stillwood Heights. He's some sort of crystal-gazer. It seems Marlowe went to see him and you and Blane happened in about the same time and there was an argument of some kind. I forget the details." He looked out of his windows with the expression of a man forgetting details.

"Some mistake," Hemingway said. "I never saw this man before."

"There was a mistake, as a matter of fact," the Chief said dreamily. "Rather trifling, but still a mistake. Mr. Marlowe thinks it of slight importance."

Hemingway looked at me again. His face still looked like a stone face.

"In fact he's not even interested in the mistake," the Chief dreamed on. "But he is interested in going to call on this man Amthor who lives in Stillwood Heights. He would like some-one with him. I thought of you. He would like someone who

386

would see that he got a square deal. It seems that Mr. Amthor has a very tough Indian bodyguard and Mr. Marlowe is a little inclined to doubt his ability to handle the situation without help. Do you think you could find out where this Amthor lives?"

"Yeah," Hemingway said. "But Stillwood Heights is over the line, Chief. This just a personal favor to a friend of yours?"

"You might put it that way," the Chief said, looking at his left thumb. "We wouldn't want to do anything not strictly legal, of course."

"Yeah," Hemingway said. "No." He coughed. "When do we go?"

The Chief looked at me benevolently. "Now would be okay," I said. "If it suits Mr. Galbraith."

"I do what I'm told," Hemingway said.

The Chief looked him over, feature by feature. He combed him and brushed him with his eyes. "How is Captain Blane today?" he inquired, munching on a cardamom seed.

"Bad shape. Bust appendix," Hemingway said. "Pretty critical."

The Chief shook his head sadly. Then he got hold of the arms of his chair and dragged himself to his feet. He pushed a pink paw across his desk.

"Galbraith will take good care of you, Marlowe. You can rely on that."

"Well, you've certainly been obliging, Chief," I said. "I certainly don't know how to thank you."

"Pshaw! No thanks necessary. Always glad to oblige a friend of a friend, so to speak." He winked at me. Hemingway studied the wink but he didn't say what he added it up to.

We went out, with the Chief's polite murmurs almost carrying us down the office. The door closed. Hemingway looked up and down the hall and then he looked at me.

"You played that one smart, baby," he said. "You must have got something we wasn't told about."

33

THE CAR DRIFTED quietly along a quiet street of homes. Arching pepper trees almost met above it to form a green tunnel. The sun twinkled through their upper branches and their narrow light leaves. A sign at the corner said it was Eighteenth Street.

Hemingway was driving and I sat beside him. He drove very slowly, his face heavy with thought.

"How much you tell him?" he asked, making up his mind.

"I told him you and Blane went over there and took me away and tossed me out of the car and socked me on the back of the head. I didn't tell him the rest."

"Not about Twenty-third and Descanso, huh?"

"No."

"Why not?"

"I thought maybe I could get more co-operation from you if I didn't."

"That's a thought. You really want to go over to Stillwood Heights, or was that just a stall?"

"Just a stall. What I really want is for you to tell me why you put me in that funnyhouse and why I was kept there?"

Hemingway thought. He thought so hard his cheek muscles made little knots under his grayish skin.

"That Blane," he said. "That sawed-off hunk of shin meat. I didn't mean for him to sap you. I didn't mean for you to walk home neither, not really. It was just an act, on account of we are friends with this swami guy and we kind of keep people from bothering him. You'd be surprised what a lot of people would try to bother him."

"Amazed," I said.

He turned his head. His gray eyes were lumps of ice. Then he looked again through the dusty windshield and did some more thinking.

"Them old cops get sap-hungry once in a while," he said. "They just got to crack a head. Jesus, was I scared. You dropped like a sack of cement. I told Blane plenty. Then we run you over to Sonderborg's place on account of it was a little closer and he was a nice guy and would take care of you."

"Does Amthor know you took me there?"

"Hell, no. It was our idea."

"On account of Sonderborg is such a nice guy and he would take care of me. And no kickback. No chance for a doctor to back up a complaint if I made one. Not that a complaint would have much chance in this sweet little town, if I did make it."

"You going to get tough?" Hemingway asked thoughtfully.

"Not me," I said. "And for once in your life neither are you. Because your job is hanging by a thread. You looked in the Chief's eyes and you saw that. I didn't go in there without credentials, not this trip."

"Okay," Hemingway said and spat out of the window. "I didn't have any idea of getting tough in the first place except just the routine big mouth. What next?"

"Is Blane really sick?"

Hemingway nodded, but somehow failed to look sad. "Sure is. Pain in the gut day before yesterday and it bust on him before they could get his appendix out. He's got a chance – but not too good."

"We'd certainly hate to lose him," I said. "A fellow like that is an asset to any police force."

Hemingway chewed that one over and spat it out of the car window.

"Okay, next question," he sighed.

"You told me why you took me to Sonderborg's place. You didn't tell me why he kept me there over forty-eight hours, locked up and shot full of dope."

Hemingway braked the car softly over beside the curb. He

put his large hands on the lower part of the wheel side by side and gently rubbed the thumbs together.

"I wouldn't have an idea," he said in a far-off voice.

"I had papers on me showing I had a private license," I said. "Keys, some money, a couple of photographs. If he didn't know you boys pretty well, he might think the crack on the head was just a gag to get into his place and look around. But I figure he knows you boys too well for that. So I'm puzzled."

"Stay puzzled, pally. It's a lot safer."

"So it is," I said. "But there's no satisfaction in it."

"You got the L.A. law behind you on this?"

"On this what?"

"On this thinking about Sonderborg."

"Not exactly."

"That don't mean yes or no."

"I'm not that important," I said. "The L.A. law can come in here any time they feel like it – two thirds of them anyway. The Sheriff's boys and the D.A.'s boys. I have a friend in the D.A.'s office. I worked there once. His name is Bernie Ohls. He's Chief Investigator."

"You give it to him?"

"No. I haven't spoken to him in a month."

"Thinking about giving it to him?"

"Not if it interferes with a job I'm doing."

"Private job?"

"Yes."

"Okay, what is it you want?"

"What's Sonderborg's real racket?"

Hemingway took his hands off the wheel and spat out of the window. "We're on a nice street here, ain't we? Nice homes, nice gardens, nice climate. You hear a lot about crooked cops, or do you?"

"Once in a while," I said.

"Okay, how many cops do you find living on a street even

390

as good as this, with nice lawns and flowers? I'd know four or five, all vice squad boys. They get all the gravy. Cops like me live in itty-bitty frame houses on the wrong side of town. Want to see where I live?"

"What would it prove?"

"Listen, pally," the big man said seriously. "You got me on a string, but it could break. Cops don't go crooked for money. Not always, not even often. They get caught in the system. They get you where they have you do what is told them or else. And the guy that sits back there in the nice big corner office, with the nice suit and the nice liquor breath he thinks chewing on them seeds makes smell like violets, only it don't – he ain't giving the orders either. You get me?"

"What kind of a man is the Mayor?"

"What kind of guy is a mayor anywhere? A politician. You think he gives the orders? Nuts. You know what's the matter with this country, baby?"

"Too much frozen capital, I heard."

"A guy can't stay honest if he wants to," Hemingway said. "That's what's the matter with this country. He gets chiseled out of his pants if he does. You gotta play the game dirty or you don't eat. A lot of bastards think all we need is ninety thousand FBI men in clean collars and brief cases. Nuts. The percentage would get them just the way it does the rest of us. You know what I think? I think we gotta make this little world all over again. Now take Moral Rearmament. There you've got something. M.R.A. There you've got something, baby."

"If Bay City is a sample of how it works, I'll take aspirin," I said.

"You could get too smart," Hemingway said softly. "You might not think it, but it could be. You could get so smart you couldn't think about anything but bein' smart. Me, I'm just a dumb cop. I take orders. I got a wife and two kids and I do what the big shots say. Blane could tell you things. Me, I'm ignorant."

"Sure Blane has appendicitis? Sure he didn't just shoot himself in the stomach for meanness?"

"Don't be that way," Hemingway complained and slapped his hands up and down on the wheel. "Try and think nice about people."

"About Blane?"

"He's human – just like the rest of us," Hemingway said. "He's a sinner – but he's human."

"What's Sonderborg's racket?"

"Okay, I was just telling you. Maybe I'm wrong. I had you figured for a guy that could be sold a nice idea."

"You don't know what his racket is," I said.

Hemingway took his handkerchief out and wiped his face with it. "Buddy, I hate to admit it," he said. "But you ought to know damn well that if I knew or Blane knew Sonderborg had a racket, either we wouldn't of dumped you in there or you wouldn't ever have come out, not walking. I'm talking about a real bad racket, naturally. Not fluff stuff like telling old women's fortunes out of a crystal ball."

"I don't think I was meant to come out walking," I said. "There's a drug called scopolamine, truth serum, that sometimes makes people talk without their knowing it. It's not sure fire, any more than hypnotism is. But it sometimes works. I think I was being milked in there to find out what I knew. But there are only three ways Sonderborg could have known that there was anything for me to know that might hurt him. Amthor might have told him, or Moose Malloy might have mentioned to him that I went to see Jessie Florian, or he might have thought putting me in there was a police gag."

Hemingway stared at me sadly. "I can't even see your dust," he said. "Who the hell is Moose Malloy?"

"A big hunk that killed a man over on Central Avenue a few days ago. He's on your teletype, if you ever read it. And you probably have a reader of him by now."

"So what?"

"So Sonderborg was hiding him. I saw him there, on a bed reading newspapers, the night I snuck out."

"How'd you get out? Wasn't you locked in?"

"I crocked the orderly with a bed spring. I was lucky."

"This big guy see you?"

"No."

Hemingway kicked the car away from the curb and a solid grin settled on his face. "Let's go collect," he said. "It figures. It figures swell. Sonderborg was hiding hot boys. If they had dough, that is. His set-up was perfect for it. Good money, too."

He kicked the car into motion and whirled around a corner.

"Hell, I thought he sold reefers," he said disgustedly. "With the right protection behind him. But hell, that's a small time racket. A peanut grift."

"Ever hear of the numbers racket? That's a small time racket too – if you're just looking at one piece of it."

Hemingway turned another corner sharply and shook his heavy head. "Right. And pin ball games and bingo houses and horse parlors. But add them all up and give one guy control and it makes sense."

"What guy?"

He went wooden on me again. His mouth shut hard and I could see his teeth were biting at each other inside it. We were on Descanso Street and going east. It was a quiet street even in late afternoon. As we got towards Twenty-third, it became in some vague manner less quiet. Two men were studying a palm tree as if figuring out how to move it. A car was parked near Dr. Sonderborg's place, but nothing showed in it. Halfway down the block a man was reading water meters.

The house was a cheerful spot by daylight. Tea rose begonias made a solid pale mass under the front windows and pansies a blur of color around the base of a white acacia in bloom. A scarlet climbing rose was just opening its buds on a fan-shaped trellis. There was a bed of winter sweet peas and a bronze-green humming bird prodding in them delicately. The house looked like the home of a well-to-do elderly couple who liked to garden. The late afternoon sun on it had a hushed and menacing stillness.

Hemingway slid slowly past the house and a tight little smile tugged at the corners of his mouth. His nose sniffed. He turned the next corner, and looked in his rear view mirror and stepped up the speed of the car.

After three blocks he braked at the side of the street again and turned to give me a hard level stare.

"L.A. law," he said. "One of the guys by the palm tree is called Donnelly. I know him. They got the house covered. So you didn't tell your pal downtown, huh?"

"I said I didn't."

"The Chief'll love this," Hemingway snarled. "They come down here and raid a joint and don't even stop by to say hello."

I said nothing.

"They catch this Moose Malloy?"

I shook my head. "Not so far as I know."

"How the hell far do you know, buddy?" he asked very softly.

"Not far enough. Is there any connection between Amthor and Sonderborg?"

"Not that I know of."

"Who runs this town?"

Silence.

"I heard a gambler named Laird Brunette put up thirty grand to elect the Mayor. I heard he owns the Belvedere Club and both the gambling ships out on the water."

"Might be," Hemingway said politely.

"Where can Brunette be found?"

"Why ask me, baby?"

"Where would you make for if you lost your hideout in this town?"

"Mexico."

I laughed. "Okay, will you do me a big favor?"

"Glad to."

"Drive me back downtown."

He started the car away from the curb and tooled it neatly along a shadowed street towards the ocean. The car reached the City Hall and slid around into the police parking zone and I got out.

"Come round and see me some time," Hemingway said. "I'll likely be cleaning spittoons."

He put his big hand out. "No hard feelings?"

"M.R.A.," I said and shook the hand.

He grinned all over. He called me back when I started to walk away. He looked carefully in all directions and leaned his mouth close to my ear.

"Them gambling ships are supposed to be out beyond city and state jurisdiction," he said. "Panama registry. If it was me that was —" he stopped dead, and his bleak eyes began to worry.

"I get it," I said. "I had the same sort of idea. I don't know why I bothered so much to get you to have it with me. But it wouldn't work — not for just one man."

He nodded, and then he smiled. "M.R.A.," he said.

34

I LAY ON my back on a bed in a waterfront hotel and waited for it to get dark. It was a small front room with a hard bed and a mattress slightly thicker than the cotton blanket that covered it. A spring underneath me was broken and stuck into the left side of my back. I lay there and let it prod me.

The reflection of a red neon light glared on the ceiling. When it made the whole room red it would be dark enough to go out. Outside cars honked along the alley they called the Speedway. Feet slithered on the sidewalks below my window.

395

There was a murmur and mutter of coming and going in the air. The air that seeped in through the rusted screens smelled of stale frying fat. Far off a voice of the kind that could be heard far off was shouting: "Get hungry, folks. Get hungry. Nice hot doggies here. Get hungry."

It got darker. I thought; and thought in my mind moved with a kind of sluggish stealthiness, as if it was being watched by bitter and sadistic eyes. I thought of dead eyes looking at a moonless sky, with black blood at the corners of the mouths beneath them. I thought of nasty old women beaten to death against the posts of their dirty beds. I thought of a man with bright blond hair who was afraid and didn't quite know what he was afraid of, who was sensitive enough to know that something was wrong, and too vain or too dull to guess what it was that was wrong. I thought of beautiful rich women who could be had. I thought of nice slim curious girls who lived alone and could be had too, in a different way. I thought of cops, tough cops that could be greased and yet were not by any means all bad, like Hemingway. Fat prosperous cops with Chamber of Commerce voices, like Chief Wax. Slim, smart and deadly cops like Randall, who for all their smartness and deadliness were not free to do a clean job in a clean way. I thought of sour old goats like Nulty who had given up trying. I thought of Indians and psychics and dope doctors.

I thought of lots of things. It got darker. The glare of the red neon sign spread farther and farther across the ceiling. I sat up on the bed and put my feet on the floor and rubbed the back of my neck.

I got up on my feet and went over to the bowl in the corner and threw cold water on my face. After a little while I felt a little better, but very little. I needed a drink, I needed a lot of life insurance, I needed a vacation, I needed a home in the country. What I had was a coat, a hat and a gun. I put them on and went out of the room.

There was no elevator. The hallways smelled and the stairs had grimed rails. I went down them, threw the key on the desk and said I was through. A clerk with a wart on his left eyelid nodded and a Mexican bellhop in a frayed uniform coat came forward from behind the dustiest rubber plant in California to take my bags. I didn't have any bags, so being a Mexican, he opened the door for me and smiled politely just the same.

Outside the narrow street fumed, the sidewalks swarmed with fat stomachs. Across the street a bingo parlor was going full blast and beside it a couple of sailors with girls were coming out of a photographer's shop where they had probably been having their photos taken riding on camels. The voice of the hot dog merchant split the dusk like an axe. A big blue bus blared down the street to the little circle where the street car used to turn on a turntable. I walked that way.

After a while there was a faint smell of ocean. Not very much, but as if they had kept this much just to remind people this had once been a clean open beach where the waves came in and creamed and the wind blew and you could smell something besides hot fat and cold sweat.

The little sidewalk car came trundling along the wide concrete walk. I got on it and rode to the end of the line and got off and sat on a bench where it was quiet and cold and there was a big brown heap of kelp almost at my feet. Out to sea they had turned the lights on in the gambling boats. I got back on the sidewalk car the next time it came and rode back almost to where I had left the hotel. If anybody was tailing me, he was doing it without moving. I didn't think there was. In that clean little city there wouldn't be enough crime for the dicks to be very good shadows.

The black piers glittered their length and then disappeared into the dark background of night and water. You could still smell hot fat, but you could smell the ocean too. The hot dog man droned on:

"Get hungry, folks, get hungry. Nice hot doggies. Get - hungry."

I spotted him in a white barbecue stand tickling wienies with a long fork. He was doing a good business even that early in the year. I had to wait some time to get him alone.

"What's the name of the one farthest out?" I asked, pointing with my nose.

"*Montecito*." He gave me the level steady look.

"Could a guy with reasonable dough have himself a time there?"

"What kind of a time?"

I laughed, sneeringly, very tough.

"Hot doggies," he chanted. "Nice hot doggies, folks." He dropped his voice. "Women?"

"Nix. I was figuring on a room with a nice sea breeze and good food and nobody to bother me. Kind of vacation."

He moved away. "I can't hear a word you say," he said, and then went into his chant.

He did some more business. I didn't know why I bothered with him. He just had that kind of face. A young couple in shorts came up and bought hot dogs and strolled away with the boy's arm around the girl's brassiere and each eating the other's hot dog.

The man slid a yard towards me and eyed me over. "Right now I should be whistling Roses of Picardy," he said, and paused. "That would cost you," he said.

"How much?"

"Fifty. Not less. Unless they want you for something."

"This used to be a good town," I said. "A cool-off town."

"Thought it still was," he drawled. "But why ask me?"

"I haven't an idea," I said. I threw a dollar bill on his counter. "Put it in the baby's bank," I said. "Or whistle Roses of Picardy."

He snapped the bill, folded it longways, folded it across and folded it again. He laid it on the counter and tucked his middle finger behind his thumb and snapped. The folded bill hit me lightly in the chest and fell noiselessly to the ground. I bent and picked it up and turned quickly. But nobody was behind me that looked like a dick.

I leaned against the counter and laid the dollar bill on it again. "People don't throw money at me," I said. "They hand it to me. Do you mind?"

He took the bill, unfolded it, spread it out and wiped it off with his apron. He punched his cash-register and dropped the bill into the drawer.

"They say money don't stink," he said. "I sometimes wonder."

I didn't say anything. Some more customers did business with him and went away. The night was cooling fast.

"I wouldn't try the *Royal Crown*," the man said. "That's for good little squirrels, that stick to their nuts. You look like dick to me, but that's your angle. I hope you swim good."

I left him, wondering why I had gone to him in the first place. Play the hunch. Play the hunch and get stung. In a little while you wake up with your mouth full of hunches. You can't order a cup of coffee without shutting your eyes and stabbing the menu. Play the hunch.

I walked around and tried to see if anybody walked behind me in any particular way. Then I sought out a restaurant that didn't smell of frying grease and found one with a purple neon sign and a cocktail bar behind a reed curtain. A male cutie with henna'd hair drooped at a bungalow grand piano and tickled the keys lasciviously and sang Stairway to the Stars in a voice with half the steps missing.

I gobbled a dry martini and hurried back through the reed curtain to the dining room.

The eighty-five-cent dinner tasted like a discarded mail bag and was served to me by a waiter who looked as if he would slug me for a quarter, cut my throat for six bits, and bury me at sea in a barrel of concrete for a dollar and a half, plus sales tax.

35

IT WAS A long ride for a quarter. The water taxi, an old launch painted up and glassed in for three-quarters of its length, slid through the anchored yachts and around the wide pile of stone which was the end of the breakwater. The swell hit us without warning and bounced the boat like a cork. But there was plenty of room to be sick that early in the evening. All the company I had was three couples and the man who drove the boat, a tough-looking citizen who sat a little on his left hip on account of having a black leather hip-holster inside his right hip pocket. The three couples began to chew each other's faces as soon as we left the shore.

I stared back at the lights of Bay City and tried not to bear down too hard on my dinner. Scattered points of light drew together and became a jeweled bracelet laid out in the show window of the night. Then the brightness faded and they were a soft orange glow appearing and disappearing over the edge of the swell. It was a long smooth even swell with no whitecaps, and just the right amount of heave to make me glad I hadn't pickled my dinner in bar whiskey. The taxi slid up and down the swell now with a sinister smoothness, like a cobra dancing. There was cold in the air, the wet cold that sailors never get out of their joints. The red neon pencils that outlined the *Royal Crown* faded off to the left and dimmed in the gliding gray ghosts of the sea, then shone out again, as bright as new marbles.

We gave this one a wide berth. It looked nice from a long way off. A faint music came over the water and music over the water can never be anything but lovely. The *Royal Crown* seemed to ride as steady as a pier on its four hawsers. Its landing stage was lit up like a theater marquee. Then all this faded into remoteness and another, older, smaller boat began to sneak out of the night towards us. It was not much to look at. A converted seagoing freighter with scummed and rusted plates, the superstructure cut down to the boat deck level, and above that two stumpy masts just high enough for a radio antenna. There was light on the *Montecito* also and music floated across the wet dark sea. The spooning couples took their teeth out of each other's necks and stared at the ship and giggled.

The taxi swept around in a wide curve, careened just enough to give the passengers a thrill, and eased up to the hemp fenders along the stage. The taxi's motor idled and backfired in the fog. A lazy searchlight beam swept a circle about fifty yards out from the ship.

The taximan hooked to the stage and a sloe-eyed lad in a blue mess jacket with bright buttons, a bright smile and a gangster mouth, handed the girls up from the taxi. I was last. The casual neat way he looked me over told me something about him. The casual neat way he bumped my shoulder clip told me more.

"Nix," he said softly. "Nix."

He had a smoothly husky voice, a hard Harry straining himself through a silk handkerchief. He jerked his chin at the taximan. The taximan dropped a short loop over a bitt, turned his wheel a little, and climbed out on the stage. He stepped behind me.

"No gats on the boat, laddy. Sorry and all that rot," Mess-jacket purred.

"I could check it. It's just part of my clothes. I'm a fellow who wants to see Brunette, on business."

He seemed mildly amused. "Never heard of him," he smiled. "On your way, bo."

The taximan hooked a wrist through my right arm.

"I want to see Brunette," I said. My voice sounded weak and frail, like an old lady's voice.

"Let's not argue," the sloe-eyed lad said. "We're not in Bay City now, not even in California, and by some good opinions not even in the U.S.A. Beat it."

"Back in the boat," the taximan growled behind me. "I owe you a quarter. Let's go."

I got back into the boat. Mess-jacket looked at me with his silent sleek smile. I watched it until it was no longer a smile, no longer a face, no longer anything but a dark figure against the landing lights. I watched it and hungered. The way back seemed longer. I didn't speak to the taximan and he didn't speak to me. As I got off at the wharf he handed me a quarter.

"Some other night," he said wearily, "when we got more room to bounce you."

Half a dozen customers waiting to get in stared at me, hearing him. I went past them, past the door of the little waiting room on the float, towards the shallow steps at the landward end.

A big redheaded roughneck in dirty sneakers and tarry pants and what was left of a torn blue sailor's jersey and a streak of black down the side of his face straightened from the railing and bumped into me casually.

I stopped. He looked too big. He had three inches on me and thirty pounds. But it was getting to be time for me to put my fist into somebody's teeth even if all I got for it was a wooden arm.

The light was dim and mostly behind him. "What's the matter, pardner?" he drawled. "No soap on the hell ship?"

"Go darn your shirt," I told him. "Your belly is sticking out."

"Could be worse," he said. "The gat's kind of bulgy under the light suit at that."

"What pulls your nose into it?"

"Jesus, nothing at all. Just curiosity. No offense, pal."

"Well, get the hell out of my way then."

402

"Sure. I'm just resting here."

He smiled a slow tired smile. His voice was soft, dreamy, so delicate for a big man that it was startling. It made me think of another soft-voiced big man I had strangely liked.

"You got the wrong approach," he said sadly. "Just call me Red."

"Step aside, Red. The best people make mistakes. I feel one crawling up my back."

He looked thoughtfully this way and that. He had me angled into a corner of the shelter on the float. We seemed to be more or less alone.

"You want on the *Monty*? Can be done. If you got a reason."

People in gay clothes and gay faces went past us and got into the taxi. I waited for them to pass.

"How much is the reason?"

"Fifty bucks. Ten more if you bleed in my boat."

I started around him.

"Twenty-five," he said softly. "Fifteen if you come back with friends."

"I don't have any friends," I said, and walked away. He didn't try to stop me.

I turned right along the cement walk down which the little electric cars come and go, trundling like baby carriages and blowing little horns that wouldn't startle an expectant mother. At the foot of the first pier there was a flaring bingo parlor, jammed full of people already. I went into it and stood against the wall behind the players, where a lot of other people stood and waited for a place to sit down.

I watched a few numbers go up on the electric indicator, listened to the table men call them off, tried to spot the house players and couldn't, and turned to leave.

A large blueness that smelled of tar took shape beside me. "Not got the dough – or just tight with it?" the gentle voice asked in my ear.

I looked at him again. He had the eyes you never see, that you only read about. Violet eyes. Almost purple. Eyes like a girl, a lovely girl. His skin was as soft as silk. Lightly reddened, but it would never tan. It was too delicate. He was bigger than Hemingway and younger, by many years. He was not as big as Moose Malloy, but he looked very fast on his feet. His hair was that shade of red that glints with gold. But except for the eyes he had a plain farmer face, with no stagy kind of handsomeness.

"What's your racket?" he asked. "Private eye?"

"Why do I have to tell you?" I snarled.

"I kind of thought that was it," he said. "Twenty-five too high? No expense account?"

"No."

He sighed. "It was a bum idea I had anyway," he said. "They'll tear you to pieces out there."

"I wouldn't be surprised. What's *your* racket?"

"A dollar here, a dollar there. I was on the cops once. They broke me."

"Why tell me?"

He looked surprised. "It's true."

"You must have been leveling."

He smiled faintly.

"Know a man named Brunette?"

The faint smile stayed on his face. Three bingoes were made in a row. They worked fast in there. A tall beak-faced man with sallow sunken cheeks and a wrinkled suit stepped close to us and leaned against the wall and didn't look at us. Red leaned gently towards him and asked: "Is there something we could tell you, pardner?"

The tall beak-faced man grinned and moved away. Red grinned and shook the building leaning against the wall again.

"I've met a man who could take you," I said.

"I wish there was more," he said gravely. "A big guy costs money. Things ain't scaled for him. He costs to feed, to put clothes on, and he can't sleep with his feet in the bed. Here's how it works. You might not think this is a good place to talk, but it is. Any finks drift along I'll know them and the rest of the crowd is watching those numbers and nothing else. I got a boat with an under-water by-pass. That is, I can borrow one. There's a pier down the line without lights. I know a loading port on the *Monty* I can open. I take a load out there once in a while. There ain't many guys below decks."

"They have a searchlight and lookouts," I said.

"We can make it."

I got my wallet out and slipped a twenty and a five against my stomach and folded them small. The purple eyes watched me without seeming to.

"One way?"

"Fifteen was the word."

"The market took a spurt."

A tarry hand swallowed the bills. He moved silently away. He faded into the hot darkness outside the doors. The beak-nosed man materialized at my left side and said quietly:

"I think I know that fellow in sailor clothes. Friend of yours? I think I seen him before."

I straightened away from the wall and walked away from him without speaking, out of the doors, then left, watching a high head that moved along from electrolier to electrolier a hundred feet ahead of me. After a couple of minutes I turned into a space between two concession shacks. The beak-nosed man appeared, strolling with his eyes on the ground. I stepped out to his side.

"Good evening," I said. "May I guess your weight for a quarter?" I leaned against him. There was a gun under the wrinkled coat.

His eyes looked at me without emotion. "Am I goin' to have to pinch you, son? I'm posted along this stretch to maintain law and order."

"Who's dismaintaining it right now?"

"Your friend had a familiar look to me."

"He ought to. He's a cop."

"Aw hell," the beak-nosed man said patiently. "That's where I seen him. Good night to you."

He turned and strolled back the way he had come. The tall head was out of sight now. It didn't worry me. Nothing about that lad would ever worry me.

I walked on slowly.

36

BEYOND THE ELECTROLIERS, beyond the beat and toot of the small sidewalk cars, beyond the smell of hot fat and pop-corn and the shrill children and the barkers in the peep shows, beyond everything but the smell of the ocean and the suddenly clear line of the shore and the creaming fall of the waves into the pebbled spume. I walked almost alone now. The noises died behind me, the hot dishonest light became a fumbling glare. Then the lightless finger of a black pier jutted seaward into the dark. This would be the one. I turned to go out on it.

Red stood up from a box against the beginning of the piles and spoke upwards to me. "Right," he said. "You go on out to the seasteps. I gotta go and get her and warm her up."

"Waterfront cop followed me. That guy in the bingo par-lor. I had to stop and speak to him."

"Olson. Pickpocket detail. He's good too. Except once in a while he will lift a leather and plant it, to keep up his arrest record. That's being a shade too good, or isn't it?"

"For Bay City I'd say just about right. Let's get going. I'm getting the wind up. I don't want to blow this fog away. It doesn't look much but it would help a lot."

"It'll last enough to fool a searchlight," Red said. "They got Tommy guns on that boat deck. You go on out the pier. I'll be along."

He melted into the dark and I went out onto the dark boards, slipping on fish-slimed planking. There was a low dirty railing at the far end. A couple leaned in a corner. They went away, the man swearing.

For ten minutes I listened to the water slapping the piles. A night bird whirred in the dark, the faint grayness of a wing cut across my vision and disappeared. A plane droned high in the ceiling. Then far off a motor barked and roared and kept on roaring like half a dozen truck engines. After a while the sound eased and dropped, then suddenly there was no sound at all.

More minutes passed. I went back to the seasteps and moved down them as cautiously as a cat on a wet floor. A dark shape slid out of the night and something thudded. A voice said: "All set. Get in."

I got into the boat and sat beside him under the screen. The boat slid out over the water. There was no sound from its exhaust now but an angry bubbling along both sides of the shell. Once more the lights of Bay City became something distantly luminous beyond the rise and fall of alien waves. Once more the garish lights of the *Royal Crown* slid off to one side, the ship seeming to preen itself like a fashion model on a revolving platform. And once again the ports of the good ship *Montecito* grew out of the black Pacific and the slow steady sweep of the searchlight turned around it like the beam of a lighthouse.

"I'm scared," I said suddenly. "I'm scared stiff."

Red throttled down the boat and let it slide up and down the swell as though the water moved underneath and the boat stayed in the same place. He turned his face and stared at me.

"I'm afraid of death and despair," I said. "Of dark water and drowned men's faces and skulls with empty eyesockets. I'm afraid of dying, of being nothing, of not finding a man named Brunette."

He chuckled. "You had me going for a minute. You sure give yourself a pep talk. Brunette might be any place. On either of the boats, at the club he owns, back east, Reno, in his slippers at home. That all you want?"

"I want a man named Malloy, a huge brute who got out of the Oregon State pen a while back after an eight-year stretch for bank robbery. He was hiding out in Bay City." I told him about it. I told him a great deal more than I intended to. It must have been his eyes.

At the end he thought and then spoke slowly and what he said had wisps of fog clinging to it, like the beads on a mustache. Maybe that made it seem wiser than it was, maybe not.

"Some of it makes sense," he said. "Some not. Some I wouldn't know about, some I would. If this Sonderborg was running a hideout and peddling reefers and sending boys out to heist jewels off rich ladies with a wild look in their eyes, it stands to reason that he had an in with the city government, but that don't mean they knew everything he did or that every cop on the force knew he had an in. Could be Blane did and Hemingway, as you call him, didn't. Blane's bad, the other guy is just tough cop, neither bad nor good, neither crooked nor honest, full of guts and just dumb enough, like me, to think being on the cops is a sensible way to make a living. This psychic fellow doesn't figure either way. He bought himself a line of protection in the best market, Bay City, and he used it when he had to. You never know what a guy like that is up to and so you never know what he has on his conscience or is afraid of. Could be he's human and fell for a customer once in a while. Them rich dames are easier to make than paper dolls. So my hunch about your stay in Sonderborg's place is simply that Blane knew Sonderborg would be scared when he found out who you were – and the story they told Sonderborg is probably what he told you, that they found you wandering with your head dizzy – and Sonderborg wouldn't know what to do with you and he would be afraid either to let you go or to knock you off, and after long enough Blane would drop around and raise the ante on him. That's all there was to that. It just happened they could use you and they did it. Blane might know about Malloy too. I wouldn't put it past him."

I listened and watched the slow sweep of the searchlight and the coming and going of the water taxi far over to the right.

"I know how these boys figure," Red said. "The trouble with cops is not that they're dumb or crooked or tough, but that they think just being a cop gives them a little something they didn't have before. Maybe it did once, but not any more. They're topped by too many smart minds. That brings us to Brunette. He don't run the town. He couldn't be bothered. He put up big money to elect a mayor so his water taxis wouldn't be bothered. If there was anything in particular he wanted, they would give it to him. Like a while ago one of his friends, a lawyer, was pinched for drunk driving felony and Brunette got the charge reduced to reckless driving. They changed the blotter to do it, and that's a felony too. Which gives you an idea. His racket is gambling and all rackets tie together these days. So he might handle reefers, or touch a percentage from some one of his workers he gave the business to. He might know Sonderborg and he might not. But the jewel heist is out. Figure the work these boys done for eight grand. It's a laugh to think Brunette would have anything to do with that."

"Yeah," I said. "There was a man murdered too – remember?"

"He didn't do that either, nor have it done. If Brunette had that done, you wouldn't have found any body. You never know what might be stitched into a guy's clothes. Why chance it? Look what I'm doing for you for twenty-five bucks. What would Brunette get done with the money *he* has to spend?"

"Would he have a man killed?"

Red thought for a moment. "He might. He probably has. But he's not a tough guy. These racketeers are a new type. We think about them the way we think about old time yeggs or needled-up punks. Big-mouthed police commissioners on the radio yell that they're all yellow rats, that they'll kill women and babies and howl for mercy if they see a police uniform. They ought to know better than to try to sell the public that stuff. There's yellow cops and there's yellow torpedoes – but damn few of either. And as for the top men, like Brunette – they didn't get there by murdering people. They got there by guts and brains – and they don't have the group courage the cops have either. But above all they're business men. What they do is for money. Just like other business men. Sometimes a guy gets badly in the way. Okay. Out. But they think plenty before they do it. What the hell am I giving a lecture for?"

"A man like Brunette wouldn't hide Malloy," I said. "After he had killed two people."

"No. Not unless there was some other reason than money. Want to go back?"

"No."

Red moved his hands on the wheel. The boat picked up speed. "Don't think I *like* these bastards," he said. "I hate their guts."

37

THE REVOLVING SEARCHLIGHT was a pale mist-ridden finger that barely skimmed the waves a hundred feet or so beyond the ship. It was probably more for show than anything else. Especially at this time in the evening. Anyone who had plans for hijacking the take on one of these gambling boats would need plenty of help and would pull the job about four in the morning, when the crowd was thinned down to a few bitter gamblers, and the crew were all dull with fatigue. Even then it would be a poor way to make money. It had been tried once.

A taxi curved to the landing stage, unloaded, went back shorewards. Red held his speedboat idling just beyond the sweep of the searchlight. If they lifted it a few feet, just for fun – but they didn't. It passed languidly and the dull water glowed with it and the speedboat slid across the line and closed in fast under the overhang, past the two huge scummy stern hawsers. We sidled up to the greasy plates of the hull as coyly as a hotel dick getting set to ease a hustler out of his lobby.

Double iron doors loomed high above us, and they looked too high to reach and too heavy to open even if we could reach them. The speedboat scuffed the *Montecito*'s ancient sides and the swell slapped loosely at the shell under our feet. A big shadow rose in the gloom at my side and a coiled rope slipped upwards through the air, slapped, caught, and the end ran down and splashed in water. Red fished it out with a boathook, pulled it tight and fastened the end to something on the engine cowling. There was just enough fog to make everything seem unreal. The wet air was as cold as the ashes of love.

Red leaned close to me and his breath tickled my ear. "She rides too high. Come a good blow and she'd wave her screws in the air. We got to climb those plates just the same."

"I can hardly wait," I said, shivering.

He put my hands on the wheel, turned it just as he wanted it, set the throttle, and told me to hold the boat just as she was. There was an iron ladder bolted close to the plates, curving with the hull, its rungs probably as slippery as a greased pole.

Going up it looked as tempting as climbing over the cornice of an office building. Red reached for it, after wiping his hands hard on his pants to get some tar on them. He hauled himself up noiselessly, without even a grunt, and his sneakers caught the metal rungs, and he braced his body out almost at right angles to get more traction.

The searchlight beam swept far outside us now. Light bounced off the water and seemed to make my face as obvious as a flare, but nothing happened. Then there was a dull creak of heavy hinges over my head. A faint ghost of yellowish light trickled out into the fog and died. The outline of one half of the loading port showed. It couldn't have been bolted from inside. I wondered why.

The whisper was a mere sound, without meaning. I left the wheel and started up. It was the hardest journey I ever made. It landed me panting and wheezing in a sour hold littered with packing boxes and barrels and coils of rope and clumps of rusted chain. Rats screamed in dark corners. The yellow light came from a narrow door on the far side.

Red put his lips against my ear. "From here we take a straight walk to the boiler room catwalk. They'll have steam in one auxiliary, because they don't have no Diesels on this piece of cheese. There will be probably one guy below. The crew doubles in brass up on the play decks, table men and spotters and waiters and so on. They all got to sign on as something that sounds like ship. From the boiler room I'll show you a ventilator with no grating in it. It goes to the boat deck and the boat deck is out of bounds. But it's all yours – while you live."

"You must have relatives on board," I said.

"Funnier things have happened. Will you come back fast?"

"I ought to make a good splash from the boat deck," I said, and got my wallet out. "I think this rates a little more money. Here. Handle the body as if it was your own."

"You don't owe me nothing more, pardner."

"I'm buying the trip back – even if I don't use it. Take the money before I bust out crying and wet your shirt."

"Need a little help up there?"

"All I need is a silver tongue and the one I have is like a lizard's back."

"Put your dough away," Red said. "You paid me for the trip back. I think you're scared." He took hold of my hand.

His was strong, hard, warm and slightly sticky. "I *know* you're scared," he whispered.

"I'll get over it," I said. "One way or another."

He turned away from me with a curious look I couldn't read in that light. I followed him among the cases and barrels, over the raised iron sill of the door, into a long dim passage with the ship smell. We came out of this on to a grilled steel platform, slick with oil, and went down a steel ladder that was hard to hold on to. The slow hiss of the oil burners filled the air now and blanketed all other sound. We turned towards the hiss through mountains of silent iron.

Around a corner we looked at a short dirty wop in a purple silk shirt who sat in a wired-together office chair, under a naked hanging light, and read the evening paper with the aid of a black forefinger and steel-rimmed spectacles that had probably belonged to his grandfather.

Red stepped behind him noiselessly. He said gently:

"Hi, Shorty. How's all the bambinos?"

The Italian opened his mouth with a click and threw a hand at the opening of his purple shirt. Red hit him on the angle of the jaw and caught him. He put him down on the floor gently and began to tear the purple shirt into strips.

"This is going to hurt him more than the poke on the button," Red said softly. "But the idea is a guy going up a ventilator ladder makes a lot of racket down below. Up above they won't hear a thing."

He bound and gagged the Italian neatly and folded his glasses and put them in a safe place and we went along to the ventilator that had no grating in it. I looked up and saw nothing but blackness.

"Good-bye," I said.

"Maybe you need a little help."

I shook myself like a wet dog. "I need a company of marines. But either I do it alone or I don't do it. So long."

"How long will you be?" His voice still sounded worried.

"An hour or less."

He stared at me and chewed his lip. Then he nodded. "Sometimes a guy has to," he said. "Drop by that bingo parlor, if you get time."

He walked away softly, took four steps, and came back. "That open loading port," he said. "That might buy you something. Use it." He went quickly.

38

COLD AIR RUSHED down the ventilator. It seemed a long way to the top. After three minutes that felt like an hour I poked my head out cautiously from the hornlike opening. Canvas-sheeted boats were gray blurs near by. Low voices muttered in the dark. The beam of the searchlight circled slowly. It came from a point still higher, probably a railed platform at the top of one of the stumpy masts. There would be a lad up there with a Tommy gun too, perhaps even a light Browning. Cold job, cold comfort when somebody left the loading port unbolted so nicely.

Distantly music throbbed like the phony bass of a cheap radio. Overhead a masthead light and through the higher layers of fog a few bitter stars stared down.

I climbed out of the ventilator, slipped my .38 from my shoulder clip and held it curled against my ribs, hiding it with my sleeve. I walked three silent steps and listened. Nothing happened. The muttering talk had stopped, but not on my account. I placed it now, between two lifeboats. And out of the night and the fog, as it mysteriously does, enough light gathered into one focus to shine on the dark hardness of a machine gun mounted on a high tripod and swung down over the rail. Two men stood near it, motionless, not smoking, and their voices began to mutter again, a quiet whisper that never became words.

I listened to the muttering too long. Another voice spoke clearly behind me.

"Sorry, guests are not allowed on the boat deck."

I turned, not too quickly, and looked at his hands. They were light blurs and empty.

I stepped sideways nodding and the end of a boat hid us. The man followed me gently, his shoes soundless on the damp deck.

"I guess I'm lost," I said.

"I guess you are." He had a youngish voice, not chewed out of marble. "But there's a door at the bottom of the companionway. It has a spring lock on it. It's a good lock. There used to be an open stairway with a chain and a brass sign. We found the livelier element would step over that."

He was talking a long time, either to be nice, or to be waiting. I didn't know which. I said: "Somebody must have left the door open."

The shadowed head nodded. It was lower than mine.

"You can see the spot that puts us in, though. If somebody did leave it open, the boss won't like it a nickel. If somebody didn't, we'd like to know how you got up here. I'm sure you get the idea."

"It seems a simple idea. Let's go down and talk to him about it."

"You come with a party?"

"A very nice party."

"You ought to have stayed with them."

"You know how it is – you turn your head and some other guy is buying her a drink."

He chuckled. Then he moved his chin slightly up and down.

I dropped and did a frogleap sideways and the swish of the blackjack was a long spent sigh in the quiet air. It was getting to be that every blackjack in the neighborhood swung at me automatically. The tall one swore.

I said: "Go ahead and be heroes."

I clicked the safety catch loudly.

415

Sometimes even a bad scene will rock the house. The tall one stood rooted, and I could see the blackjack swinging at his wrist. The one I had been talking to thought it over without any hurry.

"This won't buy you a thing," he said gravely. "You'll never get off the boat."

"I thought of that. Then I thought how little you'd care."

It was still a bum scene.

"You want what?" he said quietly.

"I have a loud gun," I said. "But it doesn't have to go off. I want to talk to Brunette."

"He went to San Diego on business."

"I'll talk to his stand-in."

"You're quite a lad," the nice one said. "We'll go down. You'll put the heater up before we go through the door."

"I'll put the heater up when I'm sure I'm going through the door."

He laughed lightly. "Go back to your post, Slim. I'll look into this."

He moved lazily in front of me and the tall one appeared to fade into the dark.

"Follow me, then."

We moved Indian file across the deck. We went down brassbound slippery steps. At the bottom was a thick door. He opened it and looked at the lock. He smiled, nodded, held the door for me and I stepped through, pocketing the gun.

The door closed and clicked behind us. He said:

"Quiet evening, so far."

There was a gilded arch in front of us and beyond it a gaming room, not very crowded. It looked much like any other gaming room. At the far end there was a short glass bar and some stools. In the middle a stairway going down and up this the music swelled and faded. I heard roulette wheels. A man was dealing faro to a single customer. There were not more than sixty people in the room. On the faro table there was a pile of yellowbacks that would start a bank. The player was an elderly white-haired man who looked politely attentive to the dealer, but no more.

Two quiet men in dinner jackets came through the archway sauntering, looking at nothing. That had to be expected. They strolled towards us and the short slender man with me waited for them. They were well beyond the arch before they let their hands find their side pockets, looking for cigarettes of course.

"From now on we have to have a little organization here," the short man said. "I don't think you'll mind?"

"You're Brunette," I said suddenly.

He shrugged. "Of course."

"You don't look so tough," I said.

"I hope not."

The two men in dinner jackets edged me gently.

"In here," Brunette said. "We can talk at ease."

He opened the door and they took me into dock.

The room was like a cabin and not like a cabin. Two brass lamps swung in gimbels hung above a dark desk that was not wood, possibly plastic. At the end were two bunks in grained wood. The lower of them was made up and on the top one were half a dozen stacks of phonograph record books. A big combination radio-phonograph stood in the corner. There was a red leather chesterfield, a red carpet, smoking stands, a tabouret with cigarettes and a decanter and glasses, a small bar sitting cattycorners at the opposite end from the bunks.

"Sit down," Brunette said and went around the desk. There were a lot of business-like papers on the desk, with columns of figures, done on a bookkeeping machine. He sat in a tall backed director's chair and tilted it a little and looked me over. Then he stood up again and stripped off his overcoat and scarf and tossed them to one side. He sat down again. He picked a pen up and tickled the lobe of one ear with it. He had a cat smile, but I like cats.

He was neither young nor old, neither fat nor thin. Spending a lot of time on or near the ocean had given him a good healthy complexion. His hair was nut-brown and waved naturally and waved still more at sea. His forehead was narrow and brainy and his eyes held a delicate menace. They were yellowish in color. He had nice hands, not babied to the point of insipidity, but well-kept. His dinner clothes were midnight blue, I judged, because they looked so black. I thought his pearl was a little too large, but that might have been jealousy.

He looked at me for quite a long time before he said: "He has a gun."

One of the velvety tough guys leaned against the middle of my spine with something that was probably not a fishing rod. Exploring hands removed the gun and looked for others.

"Anything else?" a voice asked.

Brunette shook his head. "Not now."

One of the gunners slid my automatic across the desk. Brunette put the pen down and picked up a letter opener and pushed the gun around gently on his blotter.

"Well," he said quietly, looking past my shoulder. "Do I have to explain what I want now?"

One of them went out quickly and shut the door. The other was so still he wasn't there. There was a long easy silence, broken by the distant hum of voices and the deep-toned music and somewhere down below a dull almost imperceptible throbbing.

"Drink?"

"Thanks."

The gorilla mixed a couple at the little bar. He didn't try to hide the glasses while he did it. He placed one on the side of the desk, on black glass scooters.

"Cigarette?"

"Thanks."

"Egyptian all right?"

"Sure."

We lit up. We drank. It tasted like good Scotch. The gorilla didn't drink.

"What I want —" I began.

"Excuse me, but that's rather unimportant, isn't it?"

The soft catlike smile and the lazy half-closing of the yellow eyes.

The door opened and the other one came back and with him was Mess-jacket, gangster mouth and all. He took one look at me and his face went oyster-white.

"He didn't get past me," he said swiftly, curling one end of his lips.

"He had a gun," Brunette said, pushing it with the letter opener. "This gun. He even pushed it into my back more or less, on the boat deck."

"Not past me, boss," Mess-jacket said just as swiftly.

Brunette raised his yellow eyes slightly and smiled at me. "Well?"

"Sweep him out," I said. "Squash him somewhere else."

"I can prove it by the taximan," Mess-jacket snarled.

"You've been off the stage since five-thirty?"

"Not a minute, boss."

"That's no answer. An empire can fall in a minute."

"Not a second, boss."

"But he can be had," I said, and laughed.

Mess-jacket took the smooth gliding step of a boxer and his fist lashed like a whip. It almost reached my temple. There was a dull thud. His fist seemed to melt in midair. He slumped sideways and clawed at a corner of the desk, then rolled on his back. It was nice to see somebody else get sapped for a change.

Brunette went on smiling at me.

"I hope you're not doing him an injustice," Brunette said. "There's still the matter of the door to the companionway."

"Accidentally open."

"Could you think of any other idea?"

"Not in such a crowd."

"I'll talk to you alone," Brunette said, not looking at anyone but me.

The gorilla lifted Mess-jacket by the armpits and dragged him across the cabin and his partner opened an inner door. They went through. The door closed.

"All right," Brunette said. "Who are you and what do you want?"

"I'm a private detective and I want to talk to a man named Moose Malloy."

"Show me you're a private dick."

I showed him. He tossed the wallet back across the desk. His wind-tanned lips continued to smile and the smile was getting stagy.

"I'm investigating a murder," I said. "The murder of a man named Marriott on the bluff near your Belvedere Club last Thursday night. This murder happens to be connected with another murder, of a woman, done by Malloy, an ex-con and bank robber and all-round tough guy."

He nodded. "I'm not asking you yet what it has to do with me. I assume you'll come to that. Suppose you tell me how you got on my boat?"

"I told you."

"It wasn't true," he said gently. "Marlowe is the name? It wasn't true, Marlowe. You know that. The kid down on the stage isn't lying. I pick my men carefully."

"You own a piece of Bay City," I said. "I don't know how big a piece, but enough for what you want. A man named Sonderborg has been running a hideout there. He has been running reefers and stickups and hiding hot boys. Naturally, he couldn't do that without connections. I don't think he could do it without you. Malloy was staying with him. Malloy has left. Malloy is about seven feet tall and hard to hide. I think he could hide nicely on a gambling boat."

"You're simple," Brunette said softly. "Supposing I wanted to hide him, why should I take the risk out here?" He sipped his drink. "After all I'm in another business. It's hard enough to keep a good taxi service running without a lot of trouble. The world is full of places a crook can hide. If he has money. Could you think of a better idea?"

"I could, but to hell with it."

"I can't do anything for you. So how did you get on the boat?"

"I don't care to say."

"I'm afraid I'll have to have you made to say, Marlowe." His teeth glinted in the light from the brass ship's lamps. "After all, it can be done."

"If I tell you, will you get word to Malloy?"

"What word?"

I reached for my wallet lying on the desk and drew a card from it and turned it over. I put the wallet away and got a pencil instead. I wrote five words on the back of the card and pushed it across the desk. Brunette took it and read what I had written on it. "It means nothing to me," he said.

"It will mean something to Malloy."

He leaned back and stared at me. "I don't make you out. You risk your hide to come out here and hand me a card to pass on to some thug I don't even know. There's no sense to it."

"There isn't if you don't know him."

"Why didn't you leave your gun ashore and come aboard the usual way?"

"I forgot the first time. Then I knew that toughie in the mess jacket would never let me on. Then I bumped into a fellow who knew another way."

His yellow eyes lighted as with a new flame. He smiled and said nothing.

"This other fellow is no crook but he's been on the beach with his ears open. You have a loading port that has been unbarred on the inside and you have a ventilator shaft out of which the grating has been removed. There's one man to knock over to get to the boat deck. You'd better check your crew list, Brunette."

He moved his lips softly, one over the other. He looked down at the card again. "Nobody named Malloy is on board this boat," he said. "But if you're telling the truth about that loading port, I'll buy."

"Go and look at it."

He still looked down. "If there's any way I can get word to Malloy, I will. I don't know why I bother."

"Take a look at that loading port."

He sat very still for a moment, then leaned forward and pushed the gun across the desk to me.

"The things I do," he mused, as if he was alone. "I run towns, I elect mayors, I corrupt police, I peddle dope, I hide out crooks, I heist old women strangled with pearls. What a lot of time I have." He laughed shortly. "What a lot of time."

I reached for my gun and tucked it back under my arm.

Brunette stood up. "I promise nothing," he said, eyeing me steadily. "But I believe you."

"Of course not."

"You took a long chance to hear so little."

"Yes."

"Well —" he made a meaningless gesture and then put his hand across the desk.

"Shake hands with a chump," he said softly.

I shook hands with him. His hand was small and firm and a little hot.

"You wouldn't tell me how you found out about this load-ing port?"

"I can't. But the man who told me is no crook."

"I could make you tell," he said, and immediately shook his head. "No. I believed you once. I'll believe you again. Sit still and have another drink."

He pushed a buzzer. The door at the back opened and one of the nice-tough guys came in.

"Stay here. Give him a drink, if he wants it. No rough stuff."

The torpedo sat down and smiled at me calmly. Brunette went quickly out of the office. I smoked. I finished my drink. The torpedo made me another. I finished that, and another cigarette.

Brunette came back and washed his hands over in the corner, then sat down at his desk again. He jerked his head at the torpedo. The torpedo went out silently.

The yellow eyes studied me. "You win, Marlowe. And I have one hundred and sixty-four men on my crew list. Well —" he shrugged. "You can go back by the taxi. Nobody will bother you. As to your message, I have a few contacts. I'll use them. Good night. I probably should say thanks. For the demonstration."

"Good night," I said, and stood up and went out.

There was a new man on the landing stage. I rode to shore on a different taxi. I went along to the bingo parlor and leaned against the wall in the crowd.

Red came along in a few minutes and leaned beside me against the wall.

"Easy, huh?" Red said softly, against the heavy clear voices of the table men calling the numbers.

"Thanks to you. He bought. He's worried."

Red looked this way and that and turned his lips a little more close to my ear. "Get your man?"

"No. But I'm hoping Brunette will find a way to get him a message."

Red turned his head and looked at the tables again. He yawned and straightened away from the wall. The beak-nosed man was in again. Red stepped over to him and said: "Hiya, Olson," and almost knocked the man off his feet pushing past him.

Olson looked after him sourly and straightened his hat. Then he spat viciously on the floor.

As soon as he had gone, I left the place and went along to the parking lot back towards the tracks where I had left my car.

I drove back to Hollywood and put the car away and went up to the apartment.

I took my shoes off and walked around in my socks feeling the floor with my toes. They would still get numb again once in a while.

Then I sat down on the side of the pulled-down bed and tried to figure time. It couldn't be done. It might take hours or days to find Malloy. He might never be found until the police got him. If they ever did – alive.

39

IT WAS ABOUT ten o'clock when I called the Grayle number in Bay City. I thought it would probably be too late to catch her, but it wasn't. I fought my way through a maid and the butler and finally heard her voice on the line. She sounded breezy and well-primed for the evening.

"I promised to call you," I said. "It's a little late, but I've had a lot to do."

"Another stand-up?" Her voice got cool.

"Perhaps not. Does your chauffeur work this late?"

"He works as late as I tell him to."

"How about dropping by to pick me up? I'll be getting squeezed into my commencement suit."

"Nice of you," she drawled. "Should I really bother?" Amthor had certainly done a wonderful job with her centers of speech – if anything had ever been wrong with them.

"I'd show you my etching."

"Just one etching?"

"It's just a single apartment."

"I heard they had such things," she drawled again, then changed her tone. "Don't act so hard to get. You have a lovely build, mister. And don't ever let anyone tell you different. Give me the address again."

I gave it to her and the apartment number. "The lobby door is locked," I said. "But I'll go down and slip the catch."

"That's fine," she said. "I won't have to bring my jimmy."

She hung up, leaving me with a curious feeling of having talked to somebody that didn't exist.

I went down to the lobby and slipped the catch and then took a shower and put my pajamas on and lay down on the bed. I could have slept for a week. I dragged myself up off the bed again and set the catch on the door, which I had forgotten to do, and walked through a deep hard snowdrift out to the kitchenette and laid out glasses and a bottle of liqueur Scotch I had been saving for a really high-class seduction.

I lay down on the bed again. "Pray," I said out loud. "There's nothing left but prayer."

I closed my eyes. The four walls of the room seemed to hold the throb of a boat, the still air seemed to drip with fog and rustle with sea wind. I smelled the rank sour smell of a disused hold. I smelled engine oil and saw a wop in a purple shirt reading under a naked light bulb with his grandfather's spectacles. I climbed and climbed up a ventilator shaft. I climbed the Himalayas and stepped out on top and guys with machine guns were all around me. I talked with a small and somehow very human yellow-eyed man who was a racketeer and probably worse. I thought of the giant with the red hair and the violet eyes, who was probably the nicest man I had ever met.

I stopped thinking. Lights moved behind my closed lids. I was lost in space. I was a gilt-edged sap come back from a vain adventure. I was a hundred dollar package of dynamite that went off with a noise like a pawnbroker looking at a dollar watch. I was a pink-headed bug crawling up the side of the City Hall.

I was asleep.

I woke slowly, unwillingly, and my eyes stared at reflected light on the ceiling from the lamp. Something moved gently in the room.

The movement was furtive and quiet and heavy. I listened to it. Then I turned my head slowly and looked at Moose Malloy. There were shadows and he moved in the shadows, as noiselessly as I had seen him once before. A gun in his hand had a dark oily business-like sheen. His hat was pushed back on his black curly hair and his nose sniffed, like the nose of a hunting dog.

He saw me open my eyes. He came softly over to the side of the bed and stood looking down at me.

"I got your note," he said. "I make the joint clean. I don't make no cops outside. If this is a plant, two guys goes out in baskets."

I rolled a little on the bed and he felt swiftly under the pillows. His face was still wide and pale and his deep-set eyes were still somehow gentle. He was wearing an overcoat tonight. It fitted him where it touched. It was burst out in one shoulder seam, probably just getting it on. It would be the largest size they had, but not large enough for Moose Malloy.

"I hoped you'd drop by," I said. "No copper knows anything about this. I just wanted to see you."

"Go on," he said.

He moved sideways to a table and put the gun down and dragged his overcoat off and sat down in my best easy chair. It creaked, but it held. He leaned back slowly and arranged the gun so that it was close to his right hand. He dug a pack of cigarettes out of his pocket and shook one loose and put it into his mouth without touching it with his fingers. A match flared on a thumbnail. The sharp smell of the smoke drifted across the room.

"You ain't sick or anything?" he said.

426

"Just resting. I had a hard day."

"Door was open. Expecting someone?"

"A dame."

He stared at me thoughtfully.

"Maybe she won't come," I said. "If she does, I'll stall her."

"What dame?"

"Oh, just a dame. If she comes, I'll get rid of her. I'd rather talk to you."

His very faint smile hardly moved his mouth. He puffed his cigarette awkwardly, as if it was too small for his fingers to hold with comfort.

"What made you think I was on the *Monty*?" he asked.

"A Bay City cop. It's a long story and too full of guessing."

"Bay City cops after me?"

"Would that bother you?"

He smiled the faint smile again. He shook his head slightly.

"You killed a woman," I said. "Jessie Florian. That was a mistake."

He thought. Then he nodded. "I'd drop that one," he said quietly.

"But that queered it," I said. "I'm not afraid of you. You're no killer. You didn't mean to kill her. The other one – over on Central – you could have squeezed out of. But not out of beating a woman's head on a bedpost until her brains were on her face."

"You take some awful chances, brother," he said softly.

"The way I've been handled," I said, "I don't know the difference any more. You didn't mean to kill her – did you?"

His eyes were restless. His head was cocked in a listening attitude.

"It's about time you learned your own strength," I said.

"It's too late," he said.

"You wanted her to tell you something," I said. "You took hold of her neck and shook her. She was already dead when you were banging her head against the bedpost."

He stared at me.

"I know what you wanted her to tell you," I said.

"Go ahead."

"There was a cop with me when she was found. I had to break clean."

"How clean?"

"Fairly clean," I said. "But not about tonight."

He stared at me. "Okay, how did you know I was on the *Monty*?" He had asked me that before. He seemed to have forgotten.

"I didn't. But the easiest way to get away would be by water. With the set-up they have in Bay City you could get out to one of the gambling boats. From there you could get clean away. With the right help."

"Laird Brunette is a nice guy," he said emptily. "So I've heard. I never even spoke to him."

"He got the message to you."

"Hell, there's a dozen grapevines that might help him to do that, pal. When do we do what you said on the card? I had a hunch you were leveling. I wouldn't take the chance to come here otherwise. Where do we go?"

He killed his cigarette and watched me. His shadow loomed against the wall, the shadow of a giant. He was so big he seemed unreal.

"What made you think I bumped Jessie Florian?" he asked suddenly.

"The spacing of the finger marks on her neck. The fact that you had something to get out of her, and that you are strong enough to kill people without meaning to."

"The johns tied me to it?"

"I don't know."

"What did I want out of her?"

"You thought she might know where Velma was."

He nodded silently and went on staring at me.

"But she didn't," I said. "Velma was too smart for her."

There was a light knocking at the door.

Malloy leaned forward a little and smiled and picked up his gun. Somebody tried the doorknob. Malloy stood up slowly and leaned forward in a crouch and listened. Then he looked back at me from looking at the door.

I sat up on the bed and put my feet on the floor and stood up. Malloy watched me silently, without a motion. I went over to the door.

"Who is it?" I asked with my lips to the panel.

It was her voice all right. "Open up, silly. It's the Duchess of Windsor."

"Just a second."

I looked back at Malloy. He was frowning. I went over close to him and said in a very low voice: "There's no other way out. Go in the dressing room behind the bed and wait. I'll get rid of her."

He listened and thought. His expression was unreadable. He was a man who had now very little to lose. He was a man who would never know fear. It was not built into even that giant frame. He nodded at last and picked up his hat and coat and moved silently around the bed and into the dressing room. The door closed, but did not shut tight.

I looked around for signs of him. Nothing but a cigarette butt that anybody might have smoked. I went to the room door and opened it. Malloy had set the catch again when he came in.

She stood there half smiling, in the highnecked white fox evening cloak she had told me about. Emerald pendants hung from her ears and almost buried themselves in the soft white fur. Her fingers were curled and soft on the small evening bag she carried.

The smile died off her face when she saw me. She looked me up and down. Her eyes were cold now.

"So it's like that," she said grimly. "Pajamas and dressing gown. To show me his lovely little etching. What a fool I am."

I stood aside and held the door. "It's not like that at all. I was getting dressed and a cop dropped in on me. He just left."

"Randall?"

I nodded. A lie with a nod is still a lie, but it's an easy lie. She hesitated a moment, then moved past me with a swirl of scented fur.

I shut the door. She walked slowly across the room, stared blankly at the wall, then turned quickly.

"Let's understand each other," she said. "I'm not this much of a pushover. I don't go for hall bedroom romance. There was a time in my life when I had too much of it. I like things done with an air."

"Will you have a drink before you go?" I was still leaning against the door, across the room from her.

"Am I going?"

"You gave me the impression you didn't like it here."

"I wanted to make a point. I have to be a little vulgar to make it. I'm not one of these promiscuous bitches. I can be had – but not just by reaching. Yes, I'll take a drink."

I went out into the kitchenette and mixed a couple of drinks with hands that were not too steady. I carried them in and handed her one.

There was no sound from the dressing room, not even a sound of breathing.

She took the glass and tasted it and looked across it at the far wall. "I don't like men to receive me in their pajamas," she said. "It's a funny thing. I liked you. I liked you a lot. But I could get over it. I have often got over such things."

I nodded and drank.

"Most men are just lousy animals," she said. "In fact it's a pretty lousy world, if you ask me."

"Money must help."

"You think it's going to when you haven't always had money. As a matter of fact it just makes new problems." She smiled curiously. "And you forget how hard the old problems were."

She got out a gold cigarette case from her bag and I went over and held a match for her. She blew a vague plume of smoke and watched it with half-shut eyes.

"Sit close to me," she said suddenly.

"Let's talk a little first."

"About what? Oh – my jade?"

"About murder."

Nothing changed in her face. She blew another plume of smoke, this time more carefully, more slowly. "It's a nasty subject. Do we have to?"

I shrugged.

"Lin Marriott was no saint," she said. "But I still don't want to talk about it."

She stared at me coolly for a long moment and then dipped her hand into her open bag for a handkerchief.

"Personally I don't think he was a finger man for a jewel mob, either," I said. "The police pretend that they think that, but they do a lot of pretending. I don't even think he was a blackmailer, in any real sense. Funny, isn't it?"

"Is it?" The voice was very, very cold now.

"Well, not really," I agreed and drank the rest of my drink. "It was awfully nice of you to come here, Mrs. Grayle. But we seem to have hit the wrong mood. I don't even, for example, think Marriott was killed by a gang. I don't think he was going to that canyon to buy a jade necklace. I don't even think a jade necklace was ever stolen. I think he went to that canyon to be murdered, although he thought he went there to help commit a murder. But Marriott was a very bad murderer."

She leaned forward a little and her smile became just a little glassy. Suddenly, without any real change in her, she ceased to be beautiful. She looked merely like a woman who would have been dangerous a hundred years ago, and twenty years ago daring, but who today was just Grade B Hollywood.

She said nothing, but her right hand was tapping the clasp of her bag.

"A very bad murderer," I said. "Like Shakespeare's Second Murderer in that scene in *King Richard III.* The fellow that had certain dregs of conscience, but still wanted the money, and in the end didn't do the job at all because he couldn't make up his mind. Such murderers are very dangerous. They have to be removed – sometimes with blackjacks."

She smiled. "And who was he about to murder, do you suppose?"

"Me."

"That must be very difficult to believe – that anyone would hate you that much. And you said my jade necklace was never stolen at all. Have you any proof of all this?"

"I didn't say I had. I said I thought these things."

"Then why be such a fool as to talk about them?"

"Proof," I said, "is always a relative thing. It's an overwhelming balance of probabilities. And that's a matter of how they strike you. There was a rather weak motive for murdering me – merely that I was trying to trace a former Central Avenue dive singer at the same time that a convict named Moose Malloy got out of jail and started to look for her too. Perhaps I was helping him find her. Obviously, it was possible to find her, or it wouldn't have been worth while to pretend to Marriott that I had to be killed and killed quickly. And obviously he wouldn't have believed it, if it wasn't so. But there was a much stronger motive for murdering Marriott, which he, out of vanity or love or greed or a mixture of all three, didn't evaluate. He was afraid, but not for himself. He was afraid of violence to which he was a part and for which he could be convicted. But on the other hand he was fighting for his meal ticket. So he took the chance."

I stopped. She nodded and said: "Very interesting. If one knows what you are talking about."

"And one does," I said.

We stared at each other. She had her right hand in her bag again now. I had a good idea what it held. But it hadn't started to come out yet. Every event takes time.

"Let's quit kidding," I said. "We're all alone here. Nothing either of us says has the slightest standing against what the other says. We cancel each other out. A girl who started in the gutter became the wife of a multimillionaire. On the way up a shabby old woman recognized her – probably heard her singing at the radio station and recognized the voice and went to see – and this old woman had to be kept quiet. But she was cheap, therefore she only knew a little. But the man who dealt with her and made her monthly payments and owned a trust deed on her home and could throw her into the gutter any time she got funny – that man knew it all. He was expensive. But that didn't matter either, as long as nobody else knew. But some day a tough guy named Moose Malloy was going to get out of jail and start finding things out about his former sweetie. Because the big sap loved her – and still does. That's what makes it funny, tragic-funny. And about that time a private dick starts nosing in also. So the weak link in the chain, Marriott, is no longer a luxury. He has become a menace. They'll get to him and they'll take him apart. He's that kind of lad. He melts under heat. So he was murdered before he could melt. With a blackjack. By you."

All she did was take her hand out of her bag, with a gun in it. All she did was point it at me and smile. All I did was nothing.

But that wasn't all that was done. Moose Malloy stepped out of the dressing room with the Colt .45 still looking like a toy in his big hairy paw.

He didn't look at me at all. He looked at Mrs. Lewin Lockridge Grayle. He leaned forward and his mouth smiled at her and he spoke to her softly.

"I thought I knew the voice," he said. "I listened to that voice for eight years – all I could remember of it. I kind of liked your hair red, though. Hiya, babe. Long time no see."

She turned the gun.

"Get away from me, you son of a bitch," she said.

He stopped dead and dropped the gun to his side. He was still a couple of feet from her. His breath labored.

"I never thought," he said quietly. "It just came to me out of the blue. *You* turned me in to the cops. *You*. Little Velma."

I threw a pillow, but it was too slow. She shot him five times in the stomach. The bullets made no more sound than fingers going into a glove.

Then she turned the gun and shot at me but it was empty. She dived for Malloy's gun on the floor. I didn't miss with the second pillow. I was around the bed and knocked her away before she got the pillow off her face. I picked the Colt up and went away around the bed again with it.

He was still standing, but he was swaying. His mouth was slack and his hands were fumbling at his body. He went slack at the knees and fell sideways on the bed, with his face down. His gasping breath filled the room.

I had the phone in my hand before she moved. Her eyes were a dead gray, like half-frozen water. She rushed for the door and I didn't try to stop her. She left the door wide, so when I had done phoning I went over and shut it. I turned his head a little on the bed, so he wouldn't smother. He was still alive, but after five in the stomach even a Moose Malloy doesn't live very long.

I went back to the phone and called Randall at his home. "Malloy," I said. "In my apartment. Shot five times in the stomach by Mrs. Grayle. I called the Receiving Hospital. She got away."

"So you had to play clever," was all he said and hung up quickly.

I went back to the bed. Malloy was on his knees beside the bed now, trying to get up, a great wad of bedclothes in one hand. His face poured sweat. His eyelids flickered slowly and the lobes of his ears were dark.

He was still on his knees and still trying to get up when the fast wagon got there. It took four men to get him on the stretcher.

434

"He has a slight chance – if they're .25's," the fast wagon doctor said just before he went out. "All depends what they hit inside. But he has a chance."

"He wouldn't want it," I said.

He didn't. He died in the night.

40

"YOU OUGHT TO have given a dinner party," Anne Riordan said looking at me across her tan figured rug. "Gleaming silver and crystal, bright crisp linen – if they're still using linen in the places where they give dinner parties – candlelight, the women in their best jewels and the men in white ties, the servants hovering discreetly with the wrapped bottles of wine, the cops looking a little uncomfortable in their hired evening clothes, as who the hell wouldn't, the suspects with their brittle smiles and restless hands, and you at the head of the long table telling all about it, little by little, with your charming light smile and a phony English accent like Philo Vance."

"Yeah," I said. "How about a little something to be holding in my hand while you go on being clever?"

She went out to her kitchen and rattled ice and came back with a couple of tall ones and sat down again.

"The liquor bills of your lady friends must be something fierce," she said and sipped.

"And suddenly the butler fainted," I said. "Only it wasn't the butler who did the murder. He just fainted to be cute."

I inhaled some of my drink. "It's not that kind of story," I said. "It's not lithe and clever. It's just dark and full of blood."

"So she got away?"

I nodded. "So far. She never went home. She must have had a little hideout where she could change her clothes and appearance. After all she lived in peril, like the sailors. She was alone when she came to see me. No chauffeur. She came in a small car and she left it a few dozen blocks away."

"They'll catch her – if they really try."

"Don't be like that. Wilde, the D.A., is on the level. I worked for him once. But if they catch her, what then? They're up against twenty million dollars and a lovely face and either Lee Farrell or Rennenkamp. It's going to be awfully hard to prove she killed Marriott. All they have is what looks like a heavy motive and her past life, if they can trace it. She probably has no record, or she wouldn't have played it this way."

"What about Malloy? If you had told me about him before, I'd have known who she was right away. By the way, how did *you* know? These two photos are not of the same woman."

"No. I doubt if even old lady Florian knew they had been switched on her. She looked kind of surprised when I showed the photo of Velma – the one that had Velma Valento written on it – in front of her nose. But she may have known. She may have just hid it with the idea of selling it to me later on. Knowing it was harmless, a photo of some other girl Marriott substituted."

"That's just guessing."

"It had to be that way. Just as when Marriott called me up and gave me a song and dance about a jewel ransom payoff it had to be because I had been to see Mrs. Florian asking about Velma. And when Marriott was killed, it had to be because he was the weak link in the chain. Mrs. Florian didn't even know Velma had become Mrs. Lewin Lockridge Grayle. She couldn't have. They bought her too cheap. Grayle says they went to Europe to be married and she was married under her real name. He won't tell where or when. He won't tell what her real name was. He won't tell where she is. I don't think he knows, but the cops don't believe that."

"Why won't he tell?" Anne Riordan cupped her chin on the backs of her laced fingers and stared at me with shadowed eyes.

"He's so crazy about her he doesn't care whose lap she sat in."

"I hope she enjoyed sitting in yours," Anne Riordan said acidly.

"She was playing me. She was a little afraid of me. She didn't want to kill me because it's bad business killing a man who is a sort of cop. But she probably would have tried in the end, just as she would have killed Jessie Florian, if Malloy hadn't saved her the trouble."

"I bet it's fun to be played by handsome blondes," Anne Riordan said. "Even if there is a little risk. As, I suppose, there usually is."

I didn't say anything.

"I suppose they can't do anything to her for killing Malloy, because he had a gun."

"No. Not with her pull."

The goldflecked eyes studied me solemnly. "Do you think she meant to kill Malloy?"

"She was afraid of him," I said. "She had turned him in eight years ago. He seemed to know that. But he wouldn't have hurt her. He was in love with her too. Yes, I think she meant to kill anybody she had to kill. She had a lot to fight for. But you can't keep that sort of thing up indefinitely. She took a shot at me in my apartment – but the gun was empty then. She ought to have killed me out on the bluff when she killed Marriott."

"He was in love with her," Anne said softly. "I mean Malloy. It didn't matter to him that she hadn't written to him in six years or ever gone to see him while he was in jail. It didn't matter to him that she had turned him in for a reward. He just bought some fine clothes and started to look for her the first thing when he got out. So she pumped five bullets into him, by way of saying hello. He had killed two people himself, but he was in love with her. What a world."

I finished my drink and got the thirsty look on my face again. She ignored it. She said:

437

"And she had to tell Grayle where she came from and he didn't care. He went away to marry her under another name and sold his radio station to break contact with anybody who might know her and he gave her everything that money can buy and she gave him – what?"

"That's hard to say." I shook the ice cubes at the bottom of my glass. That didn't get me anything either. "I suppose she gave him a sort of pride that he, a rather old man, could have a young and beautiful and dashing wife. He loved her. What the hell are we talking about it for? These things happen all the time. It didn't make any difference what she did or who she played around with or what she had once been. He loved her."

"Like Moose Malloy," Anne said quietly.

"Let's go riding along the water."

"You didn't tell me about Brunette or the cards that were in those reefers or Amthor or Dr. Sonderborg or that little clue that set you on the path of the great solution."

"I gave Mrs. Florian one of my cards. She put a wet glass on it. Such a card was in Marriott's pockets, wet glass mark and all. Marriott was not a messy man. That was a clue, of sorts. Once you suspected anything it was easy to find out other connections, such as that Marriott owned a trust deed on Mrs. Florian's home, just to keep her in line. As for Amthor, he's a bad hat. They picked him up in a New York hotel and they say he's an international con man. Scotland Yard has his prints, also Paris. How the hell they got all that since yesterday or the day before I don't know. These boys work fast when they feel like it. I think Randall has had this thing taped for days and was afraid I'd step on the tapes. But Amthor had nothing to do with killing anybody. Or with Sonderborg. They haven't found Sonderborg yet. They think he has a record too, but they're not sure until they get him. As for Brunette, you can't get anything on a guy like Brunette. They'll have him before the Grand Jury and he'll refuse to say anything, on his constitutional rights. He doesn't have to bother about his reputation. But there's a nice shakeup here in Bay City. The Chief has been canned and half the detectives have been reduced to acting patrolmen, and a very nice guy named Red Norgaard, who helped me get on the *Montecito*, has got his job back. The Mayor is doing all this, changing his pants hourly while the crisis lasts."

"Do you have to say things like that?"

"The Shakespearean touch. Let's go riding. After we've had another drink."

"You can have mine," Anne Riordan said, and got up and brought her untouched drink over to me. She stood in front of me holding it, her eyes wide and a little frightened.

"You're so marvelous," she said. "So brave, so determined and you work for so little money. Everybody bats you over the head and chokes you and smacks your jaw and fills you with morphine, but you just keep right on hitting between tackle and end until they're all worn out. What makes you so wonderful?"

"Go on," I growled. "Spill it."

Anne Riordan said thoughtfully: "I'd like to be kissed, damn you!"

41

IT TOOK OVER three months to find Velma. They wouldn't believe Grayle didn't know where she was and hadn't helped her get away. So every cop and newshawk in the country looked in all the places where money might be hiding her. And money wasn't hiding her at all. Although the way she hid was pretty obvious once it was found out.

One night a Baltimore detective with a camera eye as rare as a pink zebra wandered into a nightclub and listened to the band and looked at a handsome black-haired, black-browed torcher who could sing as if she meant it. Something in her face struck a chord and the chord went on vibrating.

He went back to Headquarters and got out the Wanted file and started through the pile of readers. When he came to the one he wanted he looked at it a long time. Then he straightened his straw hat on his head and went back to the nightclub and got hold of the manager. They went back to the dressing rooms behind the shell and the manager knocked on one of the doors. It wasn't locked. The dick pushed the manager aside and went in and locked it.

He must have smelled marihuana because she was smoking it, but he didn't pay any attention then. She was sitting in front of a triple mirror, studying the roots of her hair and eyebrows. They were her own eyebrows. The dick stepped across the room smiling and handed her the reader.

She must have looked at the face on the reader almost as long as the dick had down at Headquarters. There was a lot to think about while she was looking at it. The dick sat down and crossed his legs and lit a cigarette. He had a good eye, but he had over-specialized. He didn't know enough about women.

Finally she laughed a little and said: "You're a smart lad, copper. I thought I had a voice that would be remembered. A friend recognized me by it once, just hearing it on the radio. But I've been singing with this band for a month – twice a week on a network – and nobody gave it a thought."

"I never heard the voice," the dick said and went on smiling.

She said: "I suppose we can't make a deal on this. You know, there's a lot in it, if it's handled right."

"Not with me," the dick said. "Sorry."

"Let's go then," she said and stood up and grabbed up her bag and got her coat from a hanger. She went over to him holding the coat out so he could help her into it. He stood up and held it for her like a gentleman.

She turned and slipped a gun out of her bag and shot him three times through the coat he was holding.

She had two bullets left in the gun when they crashed the door. They got halfway across the room before she used them. She used them both, but the second shot must have been pure reflex. They caught her before she hit the floor, but her head was already hanging by a rag.

"The dick lived until the next day," Randall said, telling me about it. "He talked when he could. That's how we have the dope. I can't understand him being so careless, unless he really was thinking of letting her talk him into a deal of some kind. That would clutter up his mind. But I don't like to think that, of course."

I said I supposed that was so.

"Shot herself clean through the heart – twice," Randall said. "And I've heard experts on the stand say that's impossible, knowing all the time myself that it was. And you know something else?"

"What?"

"She was stupid to shoot that dick. We'd never have convicted her, not with her looks and money and the persecution story these high-priced guys would build up. Poor little girl from a dive climbs to be wife of rich man and the vultures that used to know her won't let her alone. That sort of thing. Hell, Rennenkamp would have half a dozen crummy old burlesque dames in court to sob that they'd blackmailed her for years, and in a way that you couldn't pin anything on them but the jury would go for it. She did a smart thing to run off on her own and leave Grayle out of it, but it would have been smarter to have come home when she was caught."

"Oh you believe now that she left Grayle out of it," I said.

He nodded. I said: "Do you think she had any particular reason for that?"

He stared at me. "I'll go for it, whatever it is."

"She was a killer," I said. "But so was Malloy. And *he* was a long way from being all rat. Maybe that Baltimore dick wasn't so pure as the record shows. Maybe she saw a chance – not to get away — she was tired of dodging by that time — but to give a break to the only man who had ever really given her one."

Randall stared at me with his mouth open and his eyes unconvinced.

"Hell, she didn't have to shoot a cop to do that," he said.

"I'm not saying she was a saint or even a halfway nice girl. Not ever. She wouldn't kill herself until she was cornered. But what she did and the way she did it, kept her from coming back here for trial. Think that over. And who would that trial hurt most? Who would be least able to bear it? And win, lose or draw, who would pay the biggest price for the show? An old man who had loved not wisely, but too well."

Randall said sharply: "That's just sentimental."

"Sure. It sounded like that when I said it. Probably all a mistake anyway. So long. Did my pink bug ever get back up here?"

He didn't know what I was talking about.

I rode down to the street floor and went out on the steps of the City Hall. It was a cool day and very clear. You could see a long way — but not as far as Velma had gone.

THE HIGH WINDOW

1

THE HOUSE WAS on Dresden Avenue in the Oak Noll section of Pasadena, a big solid cool-looking house with burgundy brick walls, a terra cotta tile roof, and a white stone trim. The front windows were leaded downstairs. Upstairs windows were of the cottage type and had a lot of rococo imitation stonework trimming around them.

From the front wall and its attendant flowering bushes a half acre or so of fine green lawn drifted in a gentle slope down to the street, passing on the way an enormous deodar around which it flowed like a cool green tide around a rock. The sidewalk and the parkway were both very wide and in the parkway were three white acacias that were worth seeing. There was a heavy scent of summer on the morning and everything that grew was perfectly still in the breathless air they get over there on what they call a nice cool day.

All I knew about the people was that they were a Mrs. Elizabeth Bright Murdock and family and that she wanted to hire a nice clean private detective who wouldn't drop cigar ashes on the floor and never carried more than one gun. And I knew she was the widow of an old coot with whiskers named Jasper Murdock who had made a lot of money helping out the community, and got his photograph in the Pasadena paper every year on his anniversary, with the years of his birth and death underneath, and the legend: *His Life Was His Service*.

I left my car on the street and walked over a few dozen stumble-stones set into the green lawn, and rang the bell in the brick portico under a peaked roof. A low red brick wall ran along the front of the house the short distance from the door to the edge of the driveway. At the end of the walk, on a concrete block, there was a little painted Negro in white riding breeches and a green jacket and a red cap. He was holding a whip, and there was an iron hitching ring in the block at his feet. He looked a little sad, as if he had been waiting there a long time and was getting discouraged. I went over and patted his head while I was waiting for somebody to come to the door.

After a while a middle-aged sourpuss in a maid's costume opened the front door about eight inches and gave me the beady eye.

"Philip Marlowe," I said. "Calling on Mrs. Murdock. By appointment."

The middle-aged sourpuss ground her teeth, snapped her eyes shut, snapped them open and said in one of those angular hardrock pioneer-type voices: "Which one?"

"Huh?"

"Which Mrs. Murdock?" she almost screamed at me.

"Mrs. Elizabeth Bright Murdock," I said. "I didn't know there was more than one."

"Well, there is," she snapped. "Got a card?"

She still had the door a scant eight inches open. She poked the end of her nose and a thin muscular hand into the opening. I got my wallet out and got one of the cards with just my name on it and put it in the hand. The hand and nose went in and the door slammed in my face.

I thought that maybe I ought to have gone to the back door. I went over and patted the little Negro on the head again.

"Brother," I said, "you and me both."

Time passed, quite a lot of time. I stuck a cigarette in my mouth but didn't light it. The Good Humor man went by in his little blue and white wagon, playing *Turkey in the Straw* on his music box. A large black and gold butterfly fishtailed in and landed on a hydrangea bush almost at my elbow, moved its wings slowly up and down a few times, then took off heavily and staggered away through the motionless hot scented air.

The front door came open again. The sourpuss said: "This way."

I went in. The room beyond was large and square and sunken and cool and had the restful atmosphere of a funeral chapel and something of the same smell. Tapestry on the blank roughened stucco walls, iron grilles imitating balconies outside high side windows, heavy carved chairs with plush seats and tapestry backs and tarnished gilt tassels hanging down their sides. At the back a stained-glass window about the size of a tennis court. Curtained french doors underneath it. An old musty, fusty, narrow-minded, clean and bitter room. It didn't look as if anybody ever sat in it or would ever want to. Marble-topped tables with crooked legs, gilt clocks, pieces of small statuary in two colors of marble. A lot of junk that would take a week to dust. A lot of money, and all wasted. Thirty years before, in the wealthy close-mouthed provincial town Pasadena then was, it must have seemed like quite a room.

We left it and went along a hallway and after a while the sourpuss opened a door and motioned me in.

"Mr. Marlowe," she said through the door in a nasty voice, and went away grinding her teeth.

2

IT WAS A small room looking out on the back garden. It had an ugly red and brown carpet and was furnished as an office. It contained what you would expect to find in a small office. A thin fragile-looking blondish girl in shell glasses sat behind a desk with a typewriter on a pulled-out leaf at her left. She had her hands poised on the keys, but she didn't have any paper in the machine. She watched me come into the room with the

447

stiff, half-silly expression of a self-conscious person posing for a snapshot. She had a clear soft voice, asking me to sit down.

"I am Miss Davis. Mrs. Murdock's secretary. She wanted me to ask you for a few references."

"References?"

"Certainly. References. Does that surprise you?"

I put my hat on her desk and the unlighted cigarette on the brim of the hat. "You mean she sent for me without knowing anything about me?"

Her lip trembled and she bit it. I didn't know whether she was scared or annoyed or just having trouble being cool and businesslike. But she didn't look happy.

"She got your name from the manager of a branch of the California-Security Bank. But he doesn't know you personally," she said.

"Get your pencil ready," I said.

She held it up and showed me that it was freshly sharpened and ready to go.

I said: "First off, one of the vice-presidents of that same bank. George S. Leake. He's in the main office. Then State Senator Huston Oglethorpe. He may be in Sacramento, or he may be at his office in the State Building in L.A. Then Sidney Dreyfus, Jr., of Dreyfus, Turner and Swayne, attorneys in the Title-Insurance Building. Got that?"

She wrote fast and easily. She nodded without looking up. The light danced on her blond hair.

"Oliver Fry of the Fry-Krantz Corporation, Oil Well Tools. They're over on East Ninth, in the industrial district. Then, if you would like a couple of cops, Bernard Ohls of the D.A.'s staff, and Detective-Lieutenant Carl Randall of the Central Homicide Bureau. You think maybe that would be enough?"

"Don't laugh at me," she said. "I'm only doing what I'm told."

"Better not call the last two, unless you know what the job is," I said. "I'm not laughing at you. Hot, isn't it?"

"It's not hot for Pasadena," she said, and hoisted her phone book up on the desk and went to work.

While she was looking up the numbers and telephoning hither and yon I looked her over. She was pale with a sort of natural paleness and she looked healthy enough. Her coarse-grained coppery blond hair was not ugly in itself, but it was drawn back so tightly over her narrow head that it almost lost the effect of being hair at all. Her eyebrows were thin and unusually straight and were darker than her hair, almost a chestnut color. Her nostrils had the whitish look of an anaemic person. Her chin was too small, too sharp and looked unstable. She wore no makeup except orange-red on her mouth and not much of that. Her eyes behind the glasses were very large, cobalt blue with big irises and a vague expression. Both lids were tight so that the eyes had a slightly oriental look, or as if the skin of her face was naturally so tight that it stretched her eyes at the corners. The whole face had a sort of off-key neurotic charm that only needed some clever make-up to be striking.

She wore a one-piece linen dress with short sleeves and no ornament of any kind. Her bare arms had down on them, and a few freckles.

I didn't pay much attention to what she said over the telephone. Whatever was said to her she wrote down in short-hand, with deft easy strokes of the pencil. When she was through she hung the phone book back on a hook and stood up and smoothed the linen dress down over her thighs and said:

"If you will just wait a few moments —" and went towards the door.

Halfway there she turned back and pushed a top drawer of her desk shut at the side. She went out. The door closed. There was silence. Outside the window bees buzzed. Far off I heard the whine of a vacuum cleaner. I picked the unlighted cigarette off my hat, put it in my mouth and stood up. I went around the desk and pulled open the drawer she had come back to shut.

It wasn't any of my business. I was just curious. It wasn't any of my business that she had a small Colt automatic in the drawer. I shut it and sat down again.

She was gone about four minutes. She opened the door and stayed at it and said: "Mrs. Murdock will see you now."

We went along some more hallway and she opened half of a double glass door and stood aside. I went in and the door was closed behind me.

It was so dark in there that at first I couldn't see anything but the outdoors light coming through thick bushes and screens. Then I saw that the room was a sort of sun porch that had been allowed to get completely overgrown outside. It was furnished with grass rugs and reed stuff. There was a reed chaise longue over by the window. It had a curved back and enough cushions to stuff an elephant and there was a woman leaning back on it with a wine glass in her hand. I could smell the thick scented alcoholic odor of the wine before I could see her properly. Then my eyes got used to the light and I could see her.

She had a lot of face and chin. She had pewter-colored hair set in a ruthless permanent, a hard beak and large moist eyes with the sympathetic expression of wet stones. There was lace at her throat, but it was the kind of throat that would have looked better in a football sweater. She wore a grayish silk dress. Her thick arms were bare and mottled. There were jet buttons in her ears. There was a low glass-topped table beside her and a bottle of port on the table. She sipped from the glass she was holding and looked at me over it and said nothing.

I stood there. She let me stand while she finished the port in her glass and put the glass down on the table and filled it again. Then she tapped her lips with a handkerchief. Then she spoke. Her voice had a hard baritone quality and sounded as if it didn't want any nonsense.

450

"Sit down, Mr. Marlowe. Please do not light that cigarette. I'm asthmatic."

I sat down in a reed rocker and tucked the still unlighted cigarette down behind the handkerchief in my outside pocket.

"I've never had any dealing with private detectives, Mr. Marlowe. I don't know anything about them. Your references seem satisfactory. What are your charges?"

"To do what, Mrs. Murdock?"

"It's a very confidential matter, naturally. Nothing to do with the police. If it had to do with the police, I should have called the police."

"I charge twenty-five dollars a day, Mrs. Murdock. And of course expenses."

"It seems high. You must make a great deal of money." She drank some more of her port. I don't like port in hot weather, but it's nice when they let you refuse it.

"No," I said. "It isn't. Of course you can get detective work done at any price – just like legal work. Or dental work. I'm not an organization. I'm just one man and I work at just one case at a time. I take risks, sometimes quite big risks, and I don't work all the time. No, I don't think twenty-five dollars a day is too much."

"I see. And what is the nature of the expenses?"

"Little things that come up here and there. You never know."

"I should prefer to know," she said acidly.

"You'll know," I said. "You'll get it all down in black and white. You'll have a chance to object, if you don't like it."

"And how much retainer would you expect?"

"A hundred dollars would hold me," I said.

"I should hope it would," she said and finished her port and poured the glass full again without even waiting to wipe her lips.

"From people in your position, Mrs. Murdock, I don't necessarily have to have a retainer."

"Mr. Marlowe," she said, "I'm a strong-minded woman. But don't let me scare you. Because if you can be scared by me, you won't be much use to me."

I nodded and let that one drift with the tide.

She laughed suddenly and then she belched. It was a nice light belch, nothing showy, and performed with easy unconcern. "My asthma," she said carelessly. "I drink this wine as medicine. That's why I'm not offering you any."

I swung a leg over my knee. I hoped that wouldn't hurt her asthma.

"Money," she said, "is not really important. A woman in my position is always overcharged and gets to expect it. I hope you will be worth your fee. Here is the situation. Something of considerable value has been stolen from me. I want it back, but I want more than that. I don't want anybody arrested. The thief happens to be a member of my family – by marriage."

She turned the wine glass with her thick fingers and smiled faintly in the dim light of the shadowed room. "My daughter-in-law," she said. "A charming girl – and tough as an oak board."

She looked at me with a sudden gleam in her eyes.

"I have a damn fool of a son," she said. "But I'm very fond of him. About a year ago he made an idiotic marriage, without my consent. This was foolish of him because he is quite incapable of earning a living and he has no money except what I give him, and I am not generous with money. The lady he chose, or who chose him, was a night club singer. Her name, appropriately enough, was Linda Conquest. They have lived here in this house. We didn't quarrel because I don't allow people to quarrel with me in my own house, but there has not been good feeling between us. I have paid their expenses, given each of them a car, made the lady a sufficient but not gaudy allowance for clothes and so on. No doubt she found the life rather dull. No doubt she found my son dull. I find him dull myself. At any rate she moved out, very abruptly, a week or so ago, without leaving a forwarding address or saying good-bye."

She coughed, fumbled for a handkerchief, and blew her nose.

"What was taken," she went on, "was a coin. A rare gold coin called a Brasher Doubloon. It was the pride of my husband's collection. I care nothing for such things, but he did. I have kept the collection intact since he died four years ago. It is upstairs, in a locked fireproof room, in a set of fireproof cases. It is insured, but I have not reported the loss yet. I don't want to, if I can help it. I'm quite sure Linda took it. The coin is said to be worth over ten thousand dollars. It's a mint specimen."

"But pretty hard to sell," I said.

"Perhaps. I don't know. I didn't miss the coin until yesterday. I should not have missed it then, as I never go near the collection, except that a man in Los Angeles named Morningstar called up, said he was a dealer, and was the Murdock Brasher, as he called it, for sale? My son happened to take the call. He said he didn't believe it was for sale, it never had been, but that if Mr. Morningstar would call some other time, he could probably talk to me. It was not convenient then, as I was resting. The man said he would do that. My son reported the conversation to Miss Davis, who reported it to me. I had her call the man back. I was faintly curious."

She sipped some more port, flopped her handkerchief about and grunted.

"Why were you curious, Mrs. Murdock?" I asked, just to be saying something.

"If the man was a dealer of any repute, he would know that the coin was not for sale. My husband, Jasper Murdock, provided in his will that no part of his collection might be sold, loaned or hypothecated during my lifetime. Nor removed

from this house, except in case of damage to the house neces-
sitating removal, and then only by action of the trustees. My
husband –" she smiled grimly – "seemed to feel that I ought
to have taken more interest in his little pieces of metal while
he was alive."

It was a nice day outside, the sun shining, the flowers blooming, the birds singing. Cars went by on the street with a distant
comfortable sound. In the dim room with the hardfaced
woman and the winy smell everything seemed a little unreal.
I tossed my foot up and down over my knee and waited.

"I spoke to Mr. Morningstar. His full name is Elisha
Morningstar and he has offices in the Belfont Building on
Ninth Street in downtown Los Angeles. I told him the
Murdock collection was not for sale, never had been, and, so
far as I was concerned, never would be, and that I was surprised that he didn't know that. He hemmed and hawed and
then asked me if he might examine the coin. I said certainly
not. He thanked me rather dryly and hung up. He sounded
like an old man. So I went upstairs to examine the coin
myself, something I had not done in a year. It was gone from
its place in one of the locked fireproof cases."

I said nothing. She refilled her glass and played a tattoo
with her thick fingers on the arm of the chaise longue. "What
I thought then you can probably guess."

I said: "The part about Mr. Morningstar, maybe. Somebody
had offered the coin to him for sale and he had known or suspected where it came from. The coin must be very rare."

"What they call a mint specimen is very rare indeed. Yes,
I had the same idea."

"How would it be stolen?" I asked.

"By anyone in this house, very easily. The keys are in my
bag, and my bag lies around here and there. It would be a very
simple matter to get hold of the keys long enough to unlock
a door and a cabinet and then return the keys. Difficult for an
outsider, but anybody in the house could have stolen it."

"I see. How do you establish that your daughter-in-law took it, Mrs. Murdock?"

"I don't – in a strictly evidential sense. But I'm quite sure of it. The servants are three women who have been here many, many years – long before I married Mr. Murdock, which was only seven years ago. The gardener never comes in the house. I have no chauffeur, because either my son or my secretary drives me. My son didn't take it, first because he is not the kind of fool that steals from his mother, and secondly, if he had taken it, he could easily have prevented me from speaking to the coin dealer, Morningstar. Miss Davis – ridiculous. Just not the type at all. Too mousy. No, Mr. Marlowe, Linda is the sort of lady who might do it just for spite, if nothing else. And you know what these nightclub people are."

"All sorts of people – like the rest of us," I said. "No signs of a burglar, I suppose? It would take a pretty smooth worker to lift just one valuable coin, so there wouldn't be. Maybe I had better look the room over, though."

She pushed her jaw at me and muscles in her neck made hard lumps. "I have just told you, Mr. Marlowe, that Mrs. Leslie Murdock, my daughter-in-law, took the Brasher Doubloon."

I stared at her and she stared back. Her eyes were as hard as the bricks in her front walk. I shrugged the stare off and said:

"Assuming that is so, Mrs. Murdock, just what do you want done?"

"In the first place I want the coin back. In the second place I want an uncontested divorce for my son. And I don't intend to buy it. I daresay you know how these things are arranged."

She finished the current instalment of port and laughed rudely.

"I may have heard," I said. "You say the lady left no forwarding address. Does that mean you have no idea at all where she went?"

"Exactly that."

"A disappearance then. Your son might have some ideas he hasn't passed along to you. I'll have to see him."

The big gray face hardened into even ruggeder lines. "My son knows nothing. He doesn't even know the doubloon has been stolen. I don't want him to know anything. When the time comes I'll handle him. Until then I want him left alone. He will do exactly what I want him to."

"He hasn't always," I said.

"His marriage," she said nastily, "was a momentary impulse. Afterwards he tried to act like a gentleman. I have no such scruples."

"It takes three days to have that kind of momentary impulse in California, Mrs. Murdock."

"Young man, do you want this job or don't you?"

"I want it if I'm told the facts and allowed to handle the case as I see fit. I don't want it if you're going to make a lot of rules and regulations for me to trip over."

She laughed harshly. "This is a delicate family matter, Mr. Marlowe. And it must be handled with delicacy."

"If you hire me, you'll get all the delicacy I have. If I don't have enough delicacy, maybe you'd better not hire me. For instance, I take it you don't want your daughter-in-law framed. I'm not delicate enough for that."

She turned the color of a cold boiled beet and opened her mouth to yell. Then she thought better of it, lifted her port glass and tucked away some more of her medicine.

"You'll do," she said dryly, "I wish I had met you two years ago, before he married her."

I didn't know exactly what this last meant, so I let it ride. She bent over sideways and fumbled with the key on a house telephone and growled into it when she was answered.

There were steps and the little copper-blonde came tripping into the room with her chin low, as if somebody might be going to take a swing at her.

"Make this man a check for two hundred and fifty dollars," the old dragon snarled at her. "And keep your mouth shut about it."

The little girl flushed all the way to her neck. "You know I never talk about your affairs, Mrs. Murdock," she bleated. "You know I don't. I wouldn't dream of it, I —"

She turned with her head down and ran out of the room. As she closed the door I looked out at her. Her little lip was trembling but her eyes were mad.

"I'll need a photo of the lady and some information," I said when the door was shut again.

"Look in the desk drawer." Her rings flashed in the dimness as her thick gray finger pointed.

I went over and opened the single drawer of the reed desk and took out the photo that lay all alone in the bottom of the drawer, face up, looking at me with cool dark eyes. I sat down again with the photo and looked it over. Dark hair parted loosely in the middle and drawn back loosely over a solid piece of forehead. A wide cool go-to-hell mouth with very kissable lips. Nice nose, not too small, not too large. Good bone all over the face. The expression of the face lacked something. Once the something might have been called breeding, but these days I didn't know what to call it. The face looked too wise and too guarded for its age. Too many passes had been made at it and it had grown a little too smart in dodging them. And behind this expression of wiseness there was the look of simplicity of the little girl who still believes in Santa Claus.

I nodded over the photo and slipped it into my pocket, thinking I was getting too much out of it to get out of a mere photo, and in a very poor light at that.

The door opened and the little girl in the linen dress came in with a three-decker check book and a fountain pen and made a desk of her arm for Mrs. Murdock to sign. She straightened up with a strained smile and Mrs. Murdock made a sharp gesture towards me and the little girl tore the check out and gave it to me. She hovered inside the door, waiting. Nothing was said to her, so she went out softly again and closed the door.

I shook the check dry, folded it and sat holding it. "What can you tell me about Linda?"

"Practically nothing. Before she married my son she shared an apartment with a girl named Lois Magic – charming names these people choose for themselves – who is an entertainer of some sort. They worked at a place called the Idle Valley Club, out Ventura Boulevard way. My son Leslie knows it far too well. I know nothing about Linda's family or origins. She said once she was born in Sioux Falls. I suppose she had parents. I was not interested enough to find out."

Like hell she wasn't. I could see her digging with both hands, digging hard, and getting herself a double handful of gravel.

"You don't know Miss Magic's address?"

"No. I never did know."

"Would your son be likely to know – or Miss Davis?"

"I'll ask my son when he comes in. I don't think so. You can ask Miss Davis. I'm sure she doesn't."

"I see. You don't know of any other friends of Linda's?"

"No."

"It's possible that your son is still in touch with her, Mrs. Murdock – without telling you."

She started to get purple again. I held my hand up and dragged a soothing smile over my face. "After all he has been married to her a year," I said. "He must know something about her."

"You leave my son out of this," she snarled.

I shrugged and made a disappointed sound with my lips. "Very well. She took her car, I suppose. The one you gave her?"

"A steel gray Mercury, 1940 model, a coupe. Miss Davis can give you the license number, if you want that. I don't know whether she took it."

"Would you know what money and clothes and jewels she had with her?"

"Not much money. She might have had a couple of hundred dollars, at most." A fat sneer made deep lines around her nose and mouth. "Unless of course she has found a new friend."

"There's that," I said. "Jewelry?"

"An emerald and diamond ring of no very great value, a platinum Longines watch with rubies in the mounting, a very good cloudy amber necklace which I was foolish enough to give her myself. It has a diamond clasp with twenty-six small diamonds in the shape of a playing card diamond. She had other things, of course. I never paid much attention to them. She dressed well but not strikingly. Thank God for a few small mercies."

She refilled her glass and drank and did some more of her semi-social belching.

"That's all you can tell me, Mrs. Murdock?"

"Isn't it enough?"

"Not nearly enough, but I'll have to be satisfied for the time being. If I find she did not steal the coin, that ends the investigation as far as I'm concerned. Correct?"

"We'll talk it over," she said roughly. "She stole it all right. And I don't intend to let her get away with it. Paste that in your hat, young man. And I hope you are even half as rough as you like to act, because these night club girls are apt to have some very nasty friends."

I was still holding the folded check by one corner down between my knees. I got my wallet out and put it away and stood up, reaching my hat off the floor.

"I like them nasty," I said. "The nasty ones have very simple minds. I'll report to you when there is anything to report, Mrs. Murdock. I think I'll tackle this coin dealer first. He sounds like a lead."

She let me get to the door before she growled at my back: "You don't like me very well, do you?"

I turned to grin back at her with my hand on the knob. "Does anybody?"

She threw her head back and opened her mouth wide and roared with laughter. In the middle of the laughter I opened the door and went out and shut the door on the rough mannish sound. I went back along the hall and knocked on the secretary's half open door, then pushed it open and looked in.

She had her arms folded on her desk and her face down on the folded arms. She was sobbing. She screwed her head around and looked up at me with tear-stained eyes. I shut the door and went over beside her and put an arm around her thin shoulders.

"Cheer up," I said. "You ought to feel sorry for her. She thinks she's tough and she's breaking her back trying to live up to it."

The little girl jumped erect, away from my arm. "Don't touch me," she said breathlessly. "Please. I never let men touch me. And don't say such awful things about Mrs. Murdock."

Her face was all pink and wet from tears. Without her glasses her eyes were very lovely.

I stuck my long-waiting cigarette into my mouth and lit it.

"I – I didn't mean to be rude," she snuffled. "But she does humiliate me so. And I only want to do my best for her." She snuffled some more and got a man's handkerchief out of her desk and shook it out and wiped her eyes with it. I saw on the hanging down corner the initials L.M. embroidered in purple. I stared at it and blew cigarette smoke towards the corner of the room, away from her hair. "Is there something you want?" she asked.

"I want the license number of Mrs. Leslie Murdock's car."

"It's 2X1111, a gray Mercury convertible, 1940 model."

"She told me it was a coupe."

"That's Mr. Leslie's car. They're the same make and year and color. Linda didn't take the car."

"Oh. What do you know about a Miss Lois Magic?"

"I only saw her once. She used to share an apartment with Linda. She came here with a Mr. – a Mr. Vannier."

"Who's he?"

She looked down at her desk. "I – she just came with him. I don't know him."

"Okay, what does Miss Lois Magic look like?"

"She's a tall handsome blonde. Very – very appealing."

"You mean sexy?"

"Well –" she blushed furiously, "in a nice well-bred sort of way, if you know what I mean."

"I know what you mean," I said, "but I never got anywhere with it."

"I can believe that," she said tartly.

"Know where Miss Magic lives?"

She shook her head, no. She folded the big handkerchief very carefully and put it in the drawer of her desk, the one where the gun was.

"You can swipe another one when that's dirty," I said.

She leaned back in her chair and put her small neat hands on her desk and looked at me levelly.

"I wouldn't carry that tough-guy manner too far, if I were you, Mr. Marlowe. Not with me, at any rate."

"No?"

"No. And I can't answer any more questions without specific instructions. My position here is very confidential."

"I'm not tough," I said. "Just virile."

She picked up a pencil and made a mark on a pad. She smiled faintly up at me, all composure again.

"Perhaps I don't like virile men," she said.

"You're a screwball," I said, "if ever I met one. Good-bye."

I went out of her office, shut the door firmly, and walked back along the empty halls through the big silent sunken funereal living room and out of the front door.

The sun danced on the warm lawn outside. I put my dark glasses on and went over and patted the little Negro on the head again.

"Brother, it's even worse than I expected," I told him.

The stumble-stones were hot through the soles of my shoes. I got into the car and started it and pulled away from the curb.

A small sand-colored coupe pulled away from the curb behind me. I didn't think anything of it. The man driving it wore a dark pork pie type straw hat with a gay print band and dark glasses were over his eyes, as over mine.

I drove back towards the city. A dozen blocks later at a traffic stop, the sand-colored coupe was still behind me. I shrugged and just for the fun of it circled a few blocks. The coupe held its position. I swung into a street lined with immense pepper trees, dragged my heap around in a fast U-turn and stopped against the curbing.

The coupe came carefully around the corner. The blond head under the cocoa straw hat with the tropical print band didn't even turn my way. The coupe sailed on and I drove back to the Arroyo Seco and on towards Hollywood. I looked carefully several times, but I didn't spot the coupe again.

3

I HAD AN office in the Cahuenga Building, sixth floor, two small rooms at the back. One I left open for a patient client to sit in, if I had a patient client. There was a buzzer on the door which I could switch on and off from my private thinking parlor.

I looked into the reception room. It was empty of everything but the smell of dust. I threw up another window, unlocked the communicating door and went into the room beyond. Three hard chairs and a swivel chair, flat desk with a glass top, five green filing cases, three of them full of nothing, a calendar and a framed license bond on the wall, a phone, a washbowl in a stained wood cupboard, a hatrack, a carpet that was just something on the floor, and two open windows with net curtains that puckered in and out like the lips of a toothless old man sleeping.

The same stuff I had had last year, and the year before that. Not beautiful, not gay, but better than a tent on the beach.

I hung my hat and coat on the hatrack, washed my face and hands in cold water, lit a cigarette and hoisted the phone book onto the desk. Elisha Morningstar was listed at 824 Belfont Building, 422 West Ninth Street. I wrote that down and the phone number that went with it and had my hand on the instrument when I remembered that I hadn't switched on the buzzer for the reception room. I reached over the side of the desk and clicked it on and caught it right in stride. Somebody had just opened the door of the outer office.

I turned my pad face down on the desk and went over to see who it was. It was a slim tall self-satisfied looking number in a tropical worsted suit of slate blue, black and white shoes, a dull ivory-colored shirt and a tie and display handkerchief the color of jacaranda bloom. He was holding a long black cigarette-holder in a peeled back white pigskin glove and he was wrinkling his nose at the dead magazines on the library table and the chairs and the rusty floor covering and the general air of not much money being made.

As I opened the communicating door he made a quarter turn and stared at me out of a pair of rather dreamy pale eyes set close to a narrow nose. His skin was sun-flushed, his reddish hair was brushed back hard over a narrow skull, and the thin line of his mustache was much redder than his hair.

He looked me over without haste and without much pleasure. He blew some smoke delicately and spoke through it with a faint sneer.

"You're Marlowe?"

I nodded.

"I'm a little disappointed," he said. "I rather expected something with dirty fingernails."

"Come inside," I said, "and you can be witty sitting down."

I held the door for him and he strolled past me flicking cigarette ash on the floor with the middle nail of his free hand. He sat down on the customer's side of the desk, took off the glove from his right hand and folded this with the other already off and laid them on the desk. He tapped the cigarette end out of the long black holder, prodded the coal with a match until it stopped smoking, fitted another cigarette and lit it with a broad mahogany-colored match. He leaned back in his chair with the smile of a bored aristocrat.

"All set?" I enquired. "Pulse and respiration normal? You wouldn't like a cold towel on your head or anything?"

He didn't curl his lip because it had been curled when he came in. "A private detective," he said. "I never met one. A shifty business, one gathers. Keyhole peeping, raking up scandal, that sort of thing."

"You here on business," I asked him, "or just slumming?"

His smile was as faint as a fat lady at a fireman's ball.

"The name is Murdock. That probably means a little something to you."

"You certainly made nice time over here," I said, and started to fill a pipe.

He watched me fill the pipe. He said slowly: "I understand my mother has employed you on a job of some sort. She has given you a check."

I finished filling the pipe, put a match to it, got it drawing and leaned back to blow smoke over my right shoulder towards the open window. I didn't say anything.

He leaned forward a little more and said earnestly: "I know being cagey is all part of your trade, but I am not guessing. A little worm told me, a simple garden worm, often trodden on, but still somehow surviving – like myself. I happened to be not far behind you. Does that help to clear things up?"

"Yeah," I said. "Supposing it made any difference to me."

"You are hired to find my wife, I gather."

I made a snorting sound and grinned at him over the pipe bowl.

"Marlowe," he said, even more earnestly, "I'll try hard, but I don't think I am going to like you."

"I'm screaming," I said. "With rage and pain."

"And if you will pardon a homely phrase, your tough guy act stinks."

"Coming from you, that's bitter."

He leaned back again and brooded at me with pale eyes. He fussed around in the chair, trying to get comfortable. A lot of people had tried to get comfortable in that chair. I ought to try it myself sometime. Maybe it was losing business for me.

"Why should my mother want Linda found?" he asked slowly. "She hated her guts. I mean my mother hated Linda's guts. Linda was quite decent to my mother. What do you think of her?"

"Your mother?"

"Of course. You haven't met Linda, have you?"

"That secretary of your mother's has her job hanging by a frayed thread. She talks out of turn."

He shook his head sharply. "Mother won't know. Anyhow, Mother couldn't do without Merle. She has to have somebody to bully. She might yell at her or even slap her face, but she couldn't do without her. What did you think of her?"

"Kind of cute – in an old world sort of way."

He frowned. "I mean Mother. Merle's just a simple little girl, I know."

"Your powers of observation startle me," I said.

He looked surprised. He almost forgot to fingernail the ash of his cigarette. But not quite. He was careful not to get any of it in the ashtray, however.

"About my mother," he said patiently.

"A grand old warhorse," I said. "A heart of gold, and the gold buried good and deep."

"But why does she want Linda found? I can't understand it. Spending money on it too. My mother hates to spend money. She thinks money is part of her skin. Why does she want Linda found?"

"Search me," I said. "Who said she did?"

"Why, you implied so. And Merle –"

"Merle's just romantic. She made it up. Hell, she blows her nose in a man's handkerchief. Probably one of yours."

He blushed. "That's silly. Look, Marlowe. Please, be reasonable and give me an idea what it's all about. I haven't much money, I'm afraid, but would a couple of hundred –"

"I ought to bop you," I said. "Besides I'm not supposed to talk to you. Orders."

"Why, for heaven's sake?"

"Don't ask me things I don't know. I can't tell you the answers. And don't ask me things I do know, because I won't tell you the answers. Where have you been all your life? If a man in my line of work is handed a job, does he go around answering questions about it to anyone that gets curious?"

"There must be a lot of electricity in the air," he said nastily, "for a man in your line of work to turn down two hundred dollars."

There was nothing in that for me either. I picked his broad mahogany match out of the tray and looked at it. It had thin yellow edges and there was white printing on it. ROSEMONT. H. RICHARDS '3 – the rest was burnt off. I doubled the match and squeezed the halves together and tossed it in the wastebasket.

"I love my wife," he said suddenly and showed me the hard white edges of his teeth. "A corny touch, but it's true."

"The Lombardos are still doing all right."

He kept his lips pulled back from his teeth and talked through them at me. "She doesn't love me. I know of no particular reason why she should. Things have been strained between us. She was used to a fast moving sort of life. With us, well, it has been pretty dull. We haven't quarreled. Linda's the cool type. But she hasn't really had a lot of fun being married to me."

"You're just too modest," I said.

His eyes glinted, but he kept his smooth manner pretty well in place.

"Not good, Marlowe. Not even fresh. Look, you have the air of a decent sort of guy. I know my mother is not putting out two hundred and fifty bucks just to be breezy. Maybe it's not Linda. Maybe it's something else. Maybe —" he stopped and then said this very slowly, watching my eyes, "maybe it's Morny."

"Maybe it is," I said cheerfully.

He picked his gloves up and slapped the desk with them and put them down again. "I'm in a spot there all right," he said. "But I didn't think she knew about it. Morny must have called her up. He promised not to."

This was easy. I said: "How much are you into him for?"

It wasn't so easy. He got suspicious again. "If he called her up, he would have told her. And she would have told you," he said thinly.

"Maybe it isn't Morny," I said, beginning to want a drink very badly. "Maybe the cook is with child by the iceman. But if it was Morny, how much?"

"Twelve thousand," he said, looking down and flushing.

"Threats?"

He nodded.

"Tell him to go fly a kite," I said. "What kind of lad is he? Tough?"

He looked up again, his face being brave. "I suppose he is. I suppose they all are. He used to be a screen heavy. Good looking in a flashy way, a chaser. But don't get any ideas. Linda just worked there, like the waiters and the band. And if you are looking for her, you'll have a hard time finding her."

I sneered at him politely.

"Why would I have a hard time finding her? She's not buried in the back yard, I hope."

He stood up with a flash of anger in his pale eyes. Standing there leaning over the desk a little he whipped his right hand up in a neat enough gesture and brought out a small automatic, about .25 caliber with a walnut grip. It looked like the brother of the one I had seen in the drawer of Merle's desk. The muzzle looked vicious enough pointing at me. I didn't move.

"If anybody tries to push Linda around, he'll have to push me around first," he said tightly.

"That oughtn't to be too hard. Better get more gun – unless you're just thinking of bees."

He put the little gun back in his inside pocket. He gave me a straight hard look and picked his gloves up and started for the door.

"It's a waste of time talking to you," he said. "All you do is crack wise."

I said: "Wait a minute," and got up and went around the desk. "It might be a good idea for you not to mention this interview to your mother, if only for the little girl's sake."

He nodded. "For the amount of information I got, it doesn't seem worth mentioning."

"That straight goods about your owing Morny twelve grand?"

He looked down, then up, then down again. He said: "Anybody who could get into Alex Morny for twelve grand would have to be a lot smarter than I am."

I was quite close to him. I said: "As a matter of fact I don't even think you are worried about your wife. I think you know where she is. She didn't run away from you at all. She just ran away from your mother."

He lifted his eyes and drew one glove on. He didn't say anything.

"Perhaps she'll get a job," I said. "And make enough money to support you."

He looked down at the floor again, turned his body to the right a little and the gloved fist made a tight unrelaxed arc through the air upwards. I moved my jaw out of the way and caught his wrist and pushed it slowly back against his chest, leaning on it. He slid a foot back on the floor and began to breathe hard. It was a slender wrist. My fingers went around it and met.

We stood there looking into each other's eyes. He was breathing like a drunk, his mouth open and his lips pulled back. Small round spots of bright red flamed on his cheeks. He tried to jerk his wrist away, but I put so much weight on him that he had to take another short step back to brace himself. Our faces were now only inches apart.

"How come your old man didn't leave you some money?" I sneered. "Or did you blow it all?"

He spoke between his teeth, still trying to jerk loose. "If it's any of your rotten business and you mean Jasper Murdock, he wasn't my father. He didn't like me and he didn't leave me a cent. My father was a man named Horace Bright who lost his money in the crash and jumped out of his office window."

"You milk easy," I said, "but you give pretty thin milk. I'm sorry for what I said about your wife supporting you. I just wanted to get your goat."

I dropped his wrist and stepped back. He still breathed hard and heavily. His eyes on mine were very angry, but he kept his voice down.

"Well, you got it. If you're satisfied, I'll be on my way."

"I was doing you a favor," I said. "A gun toter oughtn't to insult so easily. Better ditch it."

"That's my business," he said. "I'm sorry I took a swing at you. It probably wouldn't have hurt much, if it had connected."

"That's all right."

He opened the door and went on out. His steps died along the corridor. Another screwball. I tapped my teeth with a knuckle in time to the sound of his steps as long as I could hear them. Then I went back to the desk, looked at my pad, and lifted the phone.

4

AFTER THE BELL had rung three times at the other end of the line a light childish sort of girl's voice filtered itself through a hank of gum and said: "Good morning. Mr. Morningstar's office."

"Is the old gentleman in?"

"Who is calling, please?"

"Marlowe."

"Does he know you, Mr. Marlowe?"

"Ask him if he wants to buy any early American gold coins."

"Just a minute, please."

There was a pause suitable to an elderly party in an inner office having his attention called to the fact that somebody on the telephone wanted to talk to him. Then the phone clicked and a man spoke. He had a dry voice. You might even call it parched.

"This is Mr. Morningstar."

"I'm told you called Mrs. Murdock in Pasadena, Mr. Morningstar. About a certain coin."

"About a certain coin," he repeated. "Indeed. Well?"

"My understanding is that you wished to buy the coin in question from the Murdock collection."

"Indeed? And who are you, sir?"

"Philip Marlowe. A private detective. I'm working for Mrs. Murdock."

"Indeed," he said for the third time. He cleared his throat carefully. "And what did you wish to talk to me about, Mr. Marlowe?"

"About this coin."

"But I was informed it was not for sale."

"I still want to talk to you about it. In person."

"Do you mean she has changed her mind about selling?"

"No."

"Then I'm afraid I don't understand what you want, Mr. Marlowe. What have we to talk about?" He sounded sly now.

I took the ace out of my sleeve and played it with a languid grace. "The point is, Mr. Morningstar, that at the time you called up you already knew the coin wasn't for sale."

"Interesting," he said slowly. "How?"

"You're in the business, you couldn't help knowing. It's a matter of public record that the Murdock collection cannot be sold during Mrs. Murdock's lifetime."

"Ah," he said. "Ah." There was a silence. Then, "At three o'clock," he said, not sharp, but quick. "I shall be glad to see you here in my office. You probably know where it is. Will that suit you?"

"I'll be there," I said.

I hung up and lit my pipe again and sat there looking at the wall. My face was stiff with thought, or with something that made my face stiff. I took Linda Murdock's photo out of my pocket, stared at it for a while, decided that the face was pretty commonplace after all, locked the photo away in my desk. I picked Murdock's second match out of my ashtray and looked it over. The lettering on this one read: TOP ROW W. D. WRIGHT '36.

I dropped it back in the tray, wondering what made this important. Maybe it was a clue.

I got Mrs. Murdock's check out of my wallet, endorsed it, made out a deposit slip and a check for cash, got my bank book out of the desk, and folded the lot under a rubber band and put them in my pocket.

Lois Magic was not listed in the phone book.

I got the classified section up on the desk and made a list

of the half dozen theatrical agencies that showed in the largest type and called them. They all had bright cheerful voices and wanted to ask a lot of questions, but they either didn't know or didn't care to tell me anything about a Miss Lois Magic, said to be an entertainer.

I threw the list in the wastebasket and called Kenny Haste, a crime reporter on the *Chronicle*.

"What do you know about Alex Morny?" I asked him when we were through cracking wise at each other.

"Runs a plushy night club and gambling joint in Idle Valley, about two miles off the highway back towards the hills. Used to be in pictures. Lousy actor. Seems to have plenty of protection. I never heard of him shooting anybody on the public square at high noon. Or at any other time for that matter. But I wouldn't like to bet on it."

"Dangerous?"

"I'd say he might be, if necessary. All those boys have been to picture shows and know how night club bosses are supposed to act. He has a bodyguard who is quite a character. His name's Eddie Prue, he's about six feet five inches tall and thin as an honest alibi. He has a frozen eye, the result of a war wound."

"Is Morny dangerous to women?"

"Don't be Victorian, old top. Women don't call it danger."

"Do you know a girl named Lois Magic, said to be an entertainer? A tall gaudy blonde, I hear."

"No. Sounds as though I might like to."

"Don't be cute. Do you know anybody named Vannier? None of these people are in the phone book."

"Nope. But I could ask Gertie Arbogast, if you want to call back. He knows all the night club aristocrats. And heels."

"Thanks, Kenny. I'll do that. Half an hour?"

He said that would be fine, and we hung up. I locked the office and left.

At the end of the corridor, in the angle of the wall, a

youngish blond man in a brown suit and a cocoa-colored straw hat with a brown and yellow tropical print band was reading the evening paper with his back to the wall. As I passed him he yawned and tucked the paper under his arm and straightened up.

He got into the elevator with me. He could hardly keep his eyes open he was so tired. I went out on the street and walked a block to the bank to deposit my check and draw out a little folding money for expenses. From there I went to the Tigertail Lounge and sat in a shallow booth and drank a martini and ate a sandwich. The man in the brown suit posted himself at the end of the bar and drank coca colas and looked bored and piled pennies in front of him, carefully smoothing the edges. He had his dark glasses on again. That made him invisible.

I dragged my sandwich out as long as I could and then strolled back to the telephone booth at the inner end of the bar. The man in the brown suit turned his head quickly and then covered the motion by lifting his glass. I dialed the *Chronicle* office again.

"Okay," Kenny Haste said. "Gertie Arbogast says Morny married your gaudy blonde not very long ago. Lois Magic. He doesn't know Vannier. He says Morny bought a place out beyond Bel-Air, a white house on Stillwood Crescent Drive, about five blocks north of Sunset. Gertie says Morny took it over from a busted flush named Arthur Blake Popham who got caught in a mail fraud rap. Popham's initials are still on the gates. And probably on the toilet paper, Gertie says. He was that kind of a guy. That's all we seem to know."

"Nobody could ask more. Many thanks, Kenny."

I hung up, stepped out of the booth, met the dark glasses above the brown suit under the cocoa straw hat and watched them turn quickly away.

I spun around and went back through a swing door into the kitchen and through that to the alley and along the alley a quarter block to the back of the parking lot where I had put my car.

473

No sand-colored coupe succeeded in getting behind me as I drove off, in the general direction of Bel-Air.

5

STILLWOOD CRESCENT DRIVE curved leisurely north from Sunset Boulevard, well beyond the Bel-Air Country Club golf course. The road was lined with walled and fenced estates. Some had high walls, some had low walls, some had ornamental iron fences, some were a bit old-fashioned and got along with tall hedges. The street had no sidewalk. Nobody walked in that neighborhood, not even the mailman.

The afternoon was hot, but not hot like Pasadena. There was a drowsy smell of flowers and sun, a swishing of lawn sprinklers gentle behind hedges and walls, the clear ratchety sound of lawn mowers moving delicately over serene and confident lawns.

I drove up the hill slowly, looking for monograms on gates. Arthur Blake Popham was the name. ABP would be the initials. I found them almost at the top, gilt on a black shield, the gates folded back on a black composition driveway.

It was a glaring white house that had the air of being brand new, but the landscaping was well advanced. It was modest enough for the neighborhood, not more than fourteen rooms and probably only one swimming pool. Its wall was low, made of brick with the concrete all oozed out between and set that way and painted over white. On top of the wall a low iron railing painted black. The name A. P. Morny was stenciled on the large silver-colored mailbox at the service entrance.

I parked my crate on the street and walked up the black driveway to a side door of glittering white paint shot with patches of color from the stained glass canopy over it. I hammered on a large brass knocker. Back along the side of the house a chauffeur was washing off a Cadillac.

The door opened and a hard-eyed Filipino in a white coat curled his lip at me. I gave him a card.

"Mrs. Morny," I said.

He shut the door. Time passed, as it always does when I go calling. The swish of water on the Cadillac had a cool sound. The chauffeur was a little runt in breeches and leggings and a sweat-stained shirt. He looked like an overgrown jockey and he made the same kind of hissing noise as he worked on the car that a groom makes rubbing down a horse.

A red-throated hummingbird went into a scarlet bush beside the door, shook the long tubular blooms around a little, and zoomed off so fast he simply disappeared in the air.

The door opened, the Filipino poked my card at me. I didn't take it.

"What you want?"

It was a tight crackling voice, like someone tiptoeing across a lot of eggshells.

"Want to see Mrs. Morny."

"She not at home."

"Didn't you know that when I gave you the card?"

He opened his fingers and let the card flutter to the ground. He grinned, showing me a lot of cut-rate dental work.

"I know when she tell me."

He shut the door in my face, not gently.

I picked the card up and walked along the side of the house to where the chauffeur was squirting water on the Cadillac sedan and rubbing the dirt off with a big sponge. He had red rimmed eyes and a bang of corn-colored hair. A cigarette hung exhausted at the corner of his lower lip.

He gave me the quick side glance of a man who is minding his own business with difficulty. I said:

"Where's the boss?"

The cigarette jiggled in his mouth. The water went on swishing gently on the paint.

"Ask at the house, Jack."

"I done asked. They done shut the door in mah face."

"You're breaking my heart, Jack."

"How about Mrs. Morny?"

"Same answer, Jack. I just work here. Selling something?"

I held my card so that he could read it. It was a business card this time. He put the sponge down on the running board, and the hose on the cement. He stepped around the water to wipe his hands on a towel that hung at the side of the garage doors. He fished a match out of his pants, struck it and tilted his head back to light the dead butt that was stuck in his face.

His foxy little eyes flicked around this way and that and he moved behind the car, with a jerk of the head. I went over near him.

"How's the little old expense account?" he asked in a small careful voice.

"Fat with inactivity."

"For five I could start thinking."

"I wouldn't want to make it that tough for you."

"For ten I could sing like four canaries and a steel guitar."

"I don't like these plushy orchestrations," I said.

He cocked his head sideways. "Talk English, Jack."

"I don't want you to lose your job, son. All I want to know is whether Mrs. Morny is home. Does that rate more than a buck?"

"Don't worry about my job, Jack. I'm solid."

"With Morny – or somebody else?"

"You want that for the same buck?"

"Two bucks."

He eyed me over. "You ain't working for him, are you?"

"Sure."

"You're a liar."

"Sure."

"Gimme the two bucks," he snapped.

I gave him two dollars.

"She's in the backyard with a friend," he said. "A nice friend. You got a friend that don't work and a husband that works, you're all set, see?" he leered.

"You'll be all set in an irrigation ditch one of these days."

"Not me, Jack. I'm wise. I know how to play 'em. I monkeyed around these kind of people all my life."

He rubbed the two dollar bills between his palms, blew on them, folded them longways and wideways and tucked them in the watch pocket of his breeches.

"That was just the soup," he said. "Now for five more —"

A rather large blond cocker spaniel tore around the Cadillac, skidded a little on the wet concrete, took off neatly, hit me in the stomach and thighs with all four paws, licked my face, dropped to the ground, ran around my legs, sat down between them, let his tongue out all the way and started to pant.

I stepped over him and braced myself against the side of the car and got my handkerchief out.

A male voice called: "Here, Heathcliff. Here, Heathcliff." Steps sounded on a hard walk.

"That's Heathcliff," the chauffeur said sourly.

"Heathcliff?"

"Cripes, that's what they call the dog, Jack."

"*Wuthering Heights*?" I asked.

"Now you're double-talking again," he sneered. "Look out — company."

He picked up the sponge and the hose and went back to washing the car. I moved away from him. The cocker spaniel immediately moved between my legs again, almost tripping me.

"Here, Heathcliff," the male voice called out louder, and a man came into view through the opening of a latticed tunnel covered with climbing roses.

Tall, dark, with a clear olive skin, brilliant black eyes, gleaming white teeth. Sideburns. A narrow black mustache.

477

Sideburns too long, much too long. White shirt with embroidered initials on the pocket, white slacks, white shoes. A wrist watch that curved halfway around a lean dark wrist, held on by a gold chain. A yellow scarf around a bronzed slender neck.

He saw the dog squatted between my legs and didn't like it. He snapped long fingers and snapped a clear hard voice:

"Here, Heathcliff. Come here at once!"

The dog breathed hard and didn't move, except to lean a little closer to my right leg.

"Who are you?" the man asked, staring me down.

I held out my card. Olive fingers took the card. The dog quietly backed out from between my legs, edged around the front end of the car, and faded silently into the distance.

"Marlowe," the man said. "Marlowe, eh? What's this? A detective? What do you want?"

"Want to see Mrs. Morny."

He looked me up and down, brilliant black eyes sweeping slowly and the silky fringes of long eyelashes following them.

"Weren't you told she was not in?"

"Yeah, but I didn't believe it. Are you Mr. Morny?"

"No."

"That's Mr. Vannier," the chauffeur said behind my back, in the drawled, over-polite voice of deliberate insolence. "Mr. Vannier's a friend of the family. He comes here quite a lot."

Vannier looked past my shoulder, his eyes furious. The chauffeur came around the car and spit the cigarette stub out of his mouth with casual contempt.

"I told the shamus the boss wasn't here, Mr. Vannier."

"I see."

"I told him Mrs. Morny and you was here. Did I do wrong?"

Vannier said: "You could have minded your own business."

The chauffeur said: "I wonder why the hell I didn't think of that."

Vannier said: "Get out before I break your dirty little neck for you."

The chauffeur eyed him quietly and then went back into the gloom of the garage and started to whistle. Vannier moved his hot angry eyes over to me and snapped:

"You were told Mrs. Morny was not in, but it didn't take. Is that it? In other words the information failed to satisfy you."

"If we have to have other words," I said, "those might do."

"I see. Could you bring yourself to say what point you wish to discuss with Mrs. Morny?"

"I'd prefer to explain that to Mrs. Morny herself."

"The implication is that she doesn't care to see you."

Behind the car the chauffeur said: "Watch his right, Jack. It might have a knife in it."

Vannier's olive skin turned the color of dried seaweed. He turned on his heel and rapped at me in a stifled voice: "Follow me."

He went along the brick path under the tunnel of roses and through a white gate at the end. Beyond was a walled-in garden containing flower-beds crammed with showy annuals, a badminton court, a nice stretch of greensward, and a small tiled pool glittering angrily in the sun. Beside the pool there was a flagged space set with blue and white garden furniture, low tables with composition tops, reclining chairs with footrests and enormous cushions, and over all a blue and white umbrella as big as a small tent.

A long-limbed languorous type of showgirl blonde lay at her ease in one of the chairs, with her feet raised on a padded rest and a tall misted glass at her elbow, near a silver ice bucket and a Scotch bottle. She looked at us lazily as we came over the grass. From thirty feet away she looked like a lot of class. From ten feet away she looked like something made up to be seen from thirty feet away. Her mouth was too wide, her eyes were too blue, her makeup was too vivid, the thin arch of her eyebrows was almost fantastic in its curve and spread, and the mascara was so thick on her eyelashes that they looked like miniature iron railings.

She wore white duck slacks, blue and white open-toed sandals over bare feet and crimson lake toenails, a white silk blouse and a necklace of green stones that were not square cut emeralds. Her hair was as artificial as a night club lobby.

On the chair beside her there was a white straw garden hat with a brim the size of a spare tire and a white satin chin strap. On the brim of the hat lay a pair of green sun glasses with lenses the size of doughnuts.

Vannier marched over to her and snapped out: "You've got to can that nasty little red-eyed driver of yours, but quick. Otherwise I'm liable to break his neck any minute. I can't go near him without getting insulted."

The blonde coughed lightly, flicked a handkerchief around without doing anything with it, and said:

"Sit down and rest your sex appeal. Who's your friend?"

Vannier looked for my card, found he was holding it in his hand and threw it on her lap. She picked it up languidly, ran her eyes over it, ran them over me, sighed and tapped her teeth with her fingernails.

"Big, isn't he? Too much for you to handle, I guess."

Vannier looked at me nastily. "All right, get it over with, whatever it is."

"Do I talk to her?" I asked. "Or do I talk to you and have you put it in English?"

The blonde laughed. A silvery ripple of laughter that held the unspoiled naturalness of a bubble dance. A small tongue played roguishly along her lips.

Vannier sat down and lit a gold-tipped cigarette and I stood there looking at them.

I said: "I'm looking for a friend of yours, Mrs. Morny. I understand that she shared an apartment with you about a year ago. Her name is Linda Conquest."

Vannier flicked his eyes up, down, up, down. He turned his head and looked across the pool. The cocker spaniel named Heathcliff sat over there looking at us with the white of one eye.

Vannier snapped his fingers. "Here, Heathcliff! Here, Heathcliff! Come here, sir!"

The blonde said: "Shut up. The dog hates your guts. Give your vanity a rest, for heaven's sake."

Vannier snapped: "Don't talk like that to me."

The blonde giggled and petted his face with her eyes.

I said: "I'm looking for a girl named Linda Conquest, Mrs. Morny."

The blonde looked at me and said: "So you said. I was just thinking. I don't think I've seen her in six months. She got married."

"You haven't seen her in six months?"

"That's what I said, big boy. What do you want to know for?"

"Just a private enquiry I'm making."

"About what?"

"About a confidential matter," I said.

"Just think," the blonde said brightly. "He's making a private enquiry about a confidential matter. You hear that, Lou? Busting in on total strangers that don't want to see him is quite all right, though, isn't it, Lou? On account of he's making a private enquiry about a confidential matter."

"Then you don't know where she is, Mrs. Morny?"

"Didn't I say so?" Her voice rose a couple of notches.

"No. You said you didn't think you had seen her in six months. Not quite the same thing."

"Who told you I shared an apartment with her?" the blonde snapped.

"I never reveal a source of information, Mrs. Morny."

"Sweetheart, you're fussy enough to be a dance director. I should tell you everything, you should tell me nothing."

"The position is quite different," I said. "I'm a hired hand obeying instructions. The lady has no reason to hide out, has she?"

"Who's looking for her?"

"Her folks."

"Guess again. She doesn't have any folks."

"You must know her pretty well, if you know that," I said.

"Maybe I did once. That don't prove I do now."

"Okay," I said. "The answer is you know, but you won't tell."

"The answer," Vannier said suddenly, "is that you're not wanted here and the sooner you get out, the better we like it."

I kept on looking at Mrs. Morny. She winked at me and said to Vannier: "Don't get so hostile, darling. You have a lot of charm, but you have small bones. You're not built for the rough work. That right, big boy?"

I said: "I hadn't thought about it, Mrs. Morny. Do you think Mr. Morny could help me – or would?"

She shook her head. "How would I know? You could try. If he don't like you, he has guys around that can bounce you."

"I think you could tell me yourself, if you wanted to."

"How are you going to make me want to?" Her eyes were inviting.

"With all these people around," I said, "how can I?"

"That's a thought," she said, and sipped from her glass, watching me over it.

Vannier stood up very slowly. His face was white. He put his hand inside his shirt and said slowly, between his teeth: "Get out, mug. While you can still walk."

I looked at him in surprise. "Where's your refinement?" I asked him. "And don't tell me you wear a gun with your garden clothes."

The blonde laughed, showing a fine strong set of teeth. Vannier thrust his hand under his left arm inside the shirt and set his lips. His black eyes were sharp and blank at the same time, like a snake's eyes.

"You heard me," he said, almost softly. "And don't write me off too quick. I'd plug you as soon as I'd strike a match. And fix it afterwards."

I looked at the blonde. Her eyes were bright and her mouth looked sensual and eager, watching us.

I turned and walked away across the grass. About halfway across it I looked back at them. Vannier stood in exactly the same position, his hand inside his shirt. The blonde's eyes were still wide and her lips parted, but the shadow of the umbrella had dimmed her expression and at that distance it might have been either fear or pleased anticipation.

I went on over the grass, through the white gate and along the brick path under the rose arbor. I reached the end of it, turned, walked quietly back to the gate and took another look at them. I didn't know what there would be to see or what I cared about it when I saw it.

What I saw was Vannier practically sprawled on top of the blonde, kissing her.

I shook my head and went back along the walk.

The red-eyed chauffeur was still at work on the Cadillac. He had finished the wash job and was wiping off the glass and nickel with a large chamois. I went around and stood beside him.

"How you come out?" he asked me out of the side of his mouth.

"Badly. They tramped all over me," I said.

He nodded and went on making the hissing noise of a groom rubbing down a horse.

"You better watch your step. The guy's heeled," I said. "Or pretends to be."

The chauffeur laughed shortly. "Under that suit? Nix."

"Who is this guy Vannier? What does he do?"

The chauffeur straightened up, put the chamois over the sill of a window and wiped his hands on the towel that was now stuck in his waistband.

"Women, my guess would be," he said.

"Isn't it a bit dangerous – playing with this particular woman?"

"I'd say it was," he agreed. "Different guys got different ideas of danger. It would scare me."

"Where does he live?"

"Sherman Oaks. She goes over there. She'll go once too often."

"Ever run across a girl named Linda Conquest? Tall, dark, handsome, used to be a singer with a band?"

"For two bucks, Jack, you expect a lot of service."

"I could build it up to five."

He shook his head. "I don't know the party. Not by that name. All kinds of dames come here, mostly pretty flashy. I don't get introduced." He grinned.

I got my wallet out and put three ones in his little damp paw. I added a business card.

"I like small close-built men," I said. "They never seem to be afraid of anything. Come and see me some time."

"I might at that, Jack. Thanks. Linda Conquest, huh? I'll keep my ear flaps off."

"So long," I said. "The name?"

"They call me Shifty. I never knew why."

"So long, Shifty."

"So long. Gat under his arm – in them clothes? Not a chance."

"I don't know," I said. "He made the motion. I'm not hired to gunfight with strangers."

"Hell, that shirt he's wearing only got two buttons at the top. I noticed. Take him a week to pull a rod from under that." But he sounded faintly worried.

"I guess he was just bluffing," I agreed. "If you hear mention of Linda Conquest, I'll be glad to talk business with you."

"Okay, Jack."

I went back along the black driveway. He stood there scratching his chin.

6

I DROVE ALONG the block looking for a place to park so that I could run up to the office for a moment before going on downtown.

A chauffeur-driven Packard edged out from the curb in front of a cigar store about thirty feet from the entrance to my building. I slid into the space, locked the car and stepped out. It was only then that I noticed the car in front of which I had parked was a familiar-looking sand-colored coupe. It didn't have to be the same one. There were thousands of them. Nobody was in it. Nobody was near it that wore a cocoa straw hat with a brown and yellow band.

I went around to the street side and looked at the steering post. No license holder. I wrote the license plate number down on the back of an envelope, just in case, and went on into my building. He wasn't in the lobby, or in the corridor upstairs.

I went into the office, looked on the floor for mail, didn't find any, bought myself a short drink out of the office bottle and left. I didn't have any time to spare to get downtown before three o'clock.

The sand-colored coupe was still parked, still empty. I got into mine and started up and moved out into the traffic stream.

I was below Sunset on Vine before he picked me up. I kept on going, grinning, and wondering where he had hid. Perhaps in the car parked behind his own. I hadn't thought of that.

I drove south to Third and all the way downtown on Third. The sand-colored coupe kept half a block behind me all the way. I moved over to Seventh and Grand, parked near Seventh and Olive, stopped to buy cigarettes I didn't need, and then walked east along Seventh without looking behind me. At Spring I went into the Hotel Metropole, strolled over to the big horseshoe cigar counter to light one of my cigarettes and then sat down in one of the old brown leather chairs in the lobby.

A blond man in a brown suit, dark glasses and the now familiar hat came into the lobby and moved unobtrusively among the potted palms and the stucco arches to the cigar counter. He bought a package of cigarettes and broke it open standing there, using the time to lean his back against the counter and give the lobby the benefit of his eagle eye.

He picked up his change and went over and sat down with his back to a pillar. He tipped his hat down over his dark glasses and seemed to go to sleep with an unlighted cigarette between his lips.

I got up and wandered over and dropped into the chair beside him. I looked at him sideways. He didn't move. Seen at close quarters his face seemed young and pink and plump and the blond beard on his chin was very carelessly shaved. Behind the dark glasses his eyelashes flicked up and down rapidly. A hand on his knee tightened and pulled the cloth into wrinkles. There was a wart on his cheek just below the right eyelid.

I struck a match and held the flame to his cigarette. "Light?"

"Oh – thanks," he said, very surprised. He drew breath in until the cigarette tip glowed. I shook the match out, tossed it into the sand jar at my elbow and waited. He looked at me sideways several times before he spoke.

"Haven't I seen you somewhere before?"

"Over on Dresden Avenue in Pasadena. This morning."

I could see his cheeks get pinker than they had been. He sighed.

"I must be lousy," he said.

"Boy, you stink," I agreed.

486

"Maybe it's the hat," he said.

"The hat helps," I said. "But you don't really need it."

"It's a pretty tough dollar in this town," he said sadly. "You can't do it on foot, you ruin yourself with taxi fares if you use taxis, and if you use your own car, it's always where you can't get to it fast enough. You have to stay too close."

"But you don't have to climb in a guy's pocket," I said. "Did you want something with me or are you just practising?"

"I figured I'd find out if you were smart enough to be worth talking to."

"I'm very smart," I said. "It would be a shame not to talk to me."

He looked carefully around back of his chair and on both sides of where we were sitting and then drew a small, pigskin wallet out. He handed me a nice fresh card from it. It read: George Anson Phillips. Confidential Investigations. 212 Senger Building, 1924 North Wilcox Avenue, Hollywood. A Glenview telephone number. In the upper left-hand corner there was an open eye with an eyebrow arched in surprise and very long eyelashes.

"You can't do that," I said, pointing to the eye. "That's the Pinkertons'. You'll be stealing their business."

"Oh hell," he said, "what little I get wouldn't bother them."

I snapped the card on my fingernail and bit down hard on my teeth and slipped the card into my pocket.

"You want one of mine – or have you completed your file on me?"

"Oh, I know all about you," he said. "I was a deputy at Ventura the time you were working on the Gregson case."

Gregson was a con man from Oklahoma City who was followed all over the United States for two years by one of his victims until he got so jittery that he shot up a service station attendant who mistook him for an acquaintance. It seemed a long time ago to me.

I said: "Go on from there."

"I remembered your name when I saw it on your registration this A.M. So when I lost you on the way into town I just looked you up. I was going to come in and talk, but it would have been a violation of confidence. This way I kind of can't help myself."

Another screwball. That made three in one day, not counting Mrs. Murdock, who might turn out to be a screwball too.

I waited while he took his dark glasses off and polished them and put them on again and gave the neighborhood the once over again. Then he said:

"I figured we could maybe make a deal. Pool our resources, as they say. I saw the guy go into your office, so I figured he had hired you."

"You knew who he was?"

"I'm working on him," he said, and his voice sounded flat and discouraged. "And where I am getting is no place at all."

"What did he do to you?"

"Well, I'm working for his wife."

"Divorce?"

He looked all around him carefully and said in a small voice: "So she says. But I wonder."

"They both want one," I said. "Each trying to get something on the other. Comical, isn't it?"

"My end I don't like so well. A guy is tailing me around some of the time. A very tall guy with a funny eye. I shake him but after a while I see him again. A very tall guy. Like a lamp-post."

A very tall man with a funny eye. I smoked thoughtfully.

"Anything to do with you?" the blond man asked me a little anxiously.

I shook my head and threw my cigarette into the sand jar. "Never saw him that I know of." I looked at my strap watch. "We better get together and talk this thing over properly, but I can't do it now. I have an appointment."

"I'd like to," he said. "Very much."

"Let's then. My office, my apartment, or your office, or where?"

He scratched his badly shaved chin with a well-chewed thumbnail.

"My apartment," he said at last. "It's not in the phone book. Give me that card a minute."

He turned it over on his palm when I gave it to him and wrote slowly with a small metal pencil, moving his tongue along his lips. He was getting younger every minute. He didn't seem much more than twenty by now, but he had to be, because the Gregson case had been six years back.

He put his pencil away and handed me back the card. The address he had written on it was 204 Florence Apartments, 128 Court Street.

I looked at him curiously. "Court Street on Bunker Hill?"

He nodded, flushing all over his blond skin. "Not too good," he said quickly. "I haven't been in the chips lately. Do you mind?"

"No, why would I?"

I stood up and held a hand out. He shook it and dropped it and I pushed it down into my hip pocket and rubbed the palm against the handkerchief I had there. Looking at his face more closely I saw that there was a line of moisture across his upper lip and more of it along the side of his nose. It was not as hot as all that.

I started to move off and then I turned back to lean down close to his face and say: "Almost anybody can pull my leg, but just to make sure, she's a tall blonde with careless eyes, huh?"

"I wouldn't call them careless," he said.

I held my face together while I said: "And just between the two of us this divorce stuff is a lot of hooey. It's something else entirely, isn't it?"

"Yes," he said softly, "and something I don't like more every minute I think about it. Here."

He pulled something out of his pocket and dropped it into my hand. It was a flat key.

"No need for you to wait around in the hall, if I happen to be out. I have two of them. What time would you think you would come?"

"About four-thirty, the way it looks now. You sure you want to give me this key?"

"Why, we're in the same racket," he said, looking up at me innocently, or as innocently as he could look through a pair of dark glasses.

At the edge of the lobby I looked back. He sat there peacefully, with the half-smoked cigarette dead between his lips and the gaudy brown and yellow band on his hat looking as quiet as a cigarette ad on the back page of the Saturday Evening Post.

We were in the same racket. So I wouldn't chisel him. Just like that. I could have the key to his apartment and go in and make myself at home. I could wear his slippers and drink his liquor and lift up his carpet and count the thousand dollar bills under it. We were in the same racket.

7

THE BELFONT BUILDING was eight stories of nothing in particular that had got itself pinched off between a large green and chromium cut rate suit emporium and a three-story and basement garage that made a noise like lion cages at feeding time. The small dark narrow lobby was as dirty as a chicken yard. The building directory had a lot of vacant space on it. Only one of the names meant anything to me and I knew that one already. Opposite the directory a large sign tilted against the fake marble wall said: *Space for Renting Suitable for Cigar Stand. Apply Room 316.*

There were two open-grill elevators but only one seemed to be running and that not busy. An old man sat inside it slack-jawed and watery-eyed on a piece of folded burlap on top of a wooden stool. He looked as if he had been sitting there since the Civil War and had come out of that badly.

I got in with him and said eight, and he wrestled the doors shut and cranked his buggy and we dragged upwards lurching. The old man breathed hard, as if he was carrying the elevator on his back.

I got out at my floor and started along the hallway and behind me the old man leaned out of the car and blew his nose with his fingers into a carton full of floor sweepings.

Elisha Morningstar's office was at the back, opposite the firedoor. Two rooms, both lettered in flaked black paint on pebbled glass. *Elisha Morningstar. Numismatist.* The one farthest back said: *Entrance.*

I turned the knob and went into a small narrow room with two windows, a shabby little typewriter desk, closed, a number of wall cases of tarnished coins in tilted slots with yellowed typewritten labels under them, two brown filing cases at the back against the wall, no curtains at the windows, and a dust gray floor carpet so threadbare that you wouldn't notice the rips in it unless you tripped over one.

An inner wooden door was open at the back across from the filing cases, behind the little typewriter desk. Through the door came the small sounds a man makes when he isn't doing anything at all. Then the dry voice of Elisha Morningstar called out:

"Come in, please. Come in."

I went along and in. The inner office was just as small but had a lot more stuff in it. A green safe almost blocked off the front half. Beyond this a heavy old mahogany table against the entrance door held some dark books, some flabby old magazines, and a lot of dust. In the back wall a window was open a few inches, without effect on the musty smell. There was a hatrack with a greasy black felt hat on it. There were three long-legged tables with glass tops and more coins under the glass tops. There was a heavy dark leather-topped desk midway of the room. It had the usual desk stuff on it, and in addition a pair of jeweller's scales under a glass dome and two large nickel-framed magnifying glasses and a jeweller's eyepiece lying on a buff scratch pad, beside a cracked yellow silk handkerchief spotted with ink.

In the swivel chair at the desk sat an elderly party in a dark gray suit with high lapels and too many buttons down the front. He had some stringy white hair that grew long enough to tickle his ears. A pale gray bald patch loomed high up in the middle of it, like a rock above the timberline. Fuzz grew out of his ears, far enough to catch a moth.

He had sharp black eyes with a pair of pouches under each eye, brownish purple in color and traced with a network of wrinkles and veins. His cheeks were shiny and his short sharp nose looked as if it had hung over a lot of quick ones in its time. A Hoover collar which no decent laundry would have allowed on the premises nudged his Adam's apple and a black string tie poked a small hard knot out at the bottom of the collar, like a mouse getting ready to come out of a mousehole.

He said: "My young lady had to go to the dentist. You are Mr. Marlowe?"

I nodded.

"Pray, be seated." He waved a thin hand at the chair across the desk. I sat down. "You have some identification, I presume?"

I showed it to him. While he read it I smelled him from across the desk. He had a sort of dry musty smell, like a fairly clean Chinaman.

He placed my card face down on top of his desk and folded his hands on it. His sharp black eyes didn't miss anything in my face.

"Well, Mr. Marlowe, what can I do for you?"

"Tell me about the Brasher Doubloon."

"Ah, yes," he said. "The Brasher Doubloon. An interesting coin." He lifted his hands off the desk and made a steeple of the fingers, like an old time family lawyer getting set for a little tangled grammar. "In some ways the most interesting and valuable of all early American coins. As no doubt you know."

"What I don't know about early American coins you could almost crowd into the Rose Bowl."

"Is that so?" he said. "Is that so? Do you want me to tell you?"

"What I'm here for, Mr. Morningstar."

"It is a gold coin, roughly equivalent to a twenty-dollar gold piece, and about the size of a half dollar. Almost exactly. It was made for the State of New York in the year 1787. It was not minted. There were no mints until 1793, when the first mint was opened in Philadelphia. The Brasher Doubloon was coined probably by the pressure molding process and its maker was a private goldsmith named Ephraim Brasher, or Brashear. Where the name survives it is usually spelled Brashear, but not on the coin. I don't know why."

I got a cigarette into my mouth and lit it. I thought it might do something to the musty smell. "What's the pressure molding process?"

"The two halves of the mold were engraved in steel, in intaglio, of course. These halves were then mounted in lead. Gold blanks were pressed between them in a coin press. Then the edges were trimmed for weight and smoothed. The coin was not milled. There were no milling machines in 1787."

"Kind of a slow process," I said.

He nodded his peaked white head. "Quite. And, since the surface-hardening of steel without distortion could not be accomplished at that time, the dies wore and had to be remade from time to time. With consequent slight variations in design which would be visible under strong magnification. In fact it would be safe to say no two of the coins would be identical, judged by modern methods of microscopic examination. Am I clear?"

"Yeah," I said. "Up to a point. How many of these coins are there and what are they worth?"

He undid the steeple of fingers and put his hands back on the desk top and patted them gently up and down.

"I don't know how many there are. Nobody knows. A few hundred, a thousand, perhaps more. But of these very few indeed are uncirculated specimens in what is called mint condition. The value varies from a couple of thousand on up. I should say that at the present time, since the devaluation of the dollar, an uncirculated specimen, carefully handled by a reputable dealer, might easily bring ten thousand dollars, or even more. It would have to have a history, of course."

I said: "Ah," and let smoke out of my lungs slowly and waved it away with the flat of my hand, away from the old party across the desk from me. He looked like a non-smoker. "And without a history and not so carefully handled – how much?"

He shrugged. "There would be the implication that the coin was illegally acquired. Stolen, or obtained by fraud. Of course it might not be so. Rare coins do turn up in odd places at odd times. In old strong boxes, in the secret drawers of desks in old New England houses. Not often, I grant you. But it happens. I know of a very valuable coin that fell out of the stuffing of a horsehair sofa which was being restored by an antique dealer. The sofa had been in the same room in the same house in Fall River, Massachusetts, for ninety years. Nobody knew how the coin got there. But generally speaking, the implication of theft would be strong. Particularly in this part of the country."

He looked at the corner of the ceiling with an absent stare. I looked at him with a not so absent stare. He looked like a man who could be trusted with a secret – if it was his own secret.

He brought his eyes down to my level slowly and said: "Five dollars, please."

I said: "Huh?"

"Five dollars, please."

"What for?"

"Don't be absurd, Mr. Marlowe. Everything I have told you is available in the public library. In Fosdyke's Register, in particular. You choose to come here and take up my time relating it to you. For this my charge is five dollars."

"And suppose I don't pay it," I said.

He leaned back and closed his eyes. A very faint smile twitched at the corners of his lips. "You will pay it," he said.

I paid it. I took the five out of my wallet and got up to lean over the desk and spread it out right in front of him, carefully. I stroked the bill with my fingertips, as if it was a kitten.

"Five dollars, Mr. Morningstar," I said.

He opened his eyes and looked at the bill. He smiled.

"And now," I said, "let's talk about the Brasher Doubloon that somebody tried to sell you."

He opened his eyes a little wider. "Oh, did somebody try to sell me a Brasher Doubloon? Now why would they do that?"

"They needed the money," I said. "And they didn't want too many questions asked. They knew or found out that you were in the business and that the building where you had your office was a shabby dump where anything could happen. They knew your office was at the end of a corridor and that you were an elderly man who would probably not make any false moves – out of regard for your health."

"They seem to have known a great deal," Elisha Morningstar said dryly.

"They knew what they had to know in order to transact their business. Just like you and me. And none of it was hard to find out."

He stuck his little finger in his ear and worked it around and brought it out with a little dark wax on it. He wiped it off casually on his coat.

"And you assume all this from the mere fact that I called up Mrs. Murdock and asked if her Brasher Doubloon was for sale?"

"Sure. She had the same idea herself. It's reasonable. Like I said over the phone to you, you would know that coin was not for sale. If you knew anything about the business at all. And I can see that you do."

He bowed, about one inch. He didn't quite smile but he looked about as pleased as a man in a Hoover collar ever looks.

"You would be offered this coin for sale," I said, "in suspicious circumstances. You would want to buy it, if you could get it cheap and had the money to handle it. But you would want to know where it came from. And even if you were quite sure it was stolen, you could still buy it, if you could get it cheap enough."

"Oh, I could, could I?" He looked amused, but not in a large way.

"Sure you could – if you are a reputable dealer. I'll assume you are. By buying the coin – cheap – you would be protecting the owner or his insurance carrier from complete loss. They'd be glad to pay you back your outlay. It's done all the time."

"Then the Murdock Brasher has been stolen," he said abruptly.

"Don't quote me," I said. "It's a secret."

He almost picked his nose this time. He just caught himself. He picked a hair out of one nostril instead, with a quick jerk and a wince. He held it up and looked at it. Looking at me past it he said:

"And how much will your principal pay for the return of the coin?"

I leaned over the desk and gave him my shady leer. "One grand. What did you pay?"

"I think you are a very smart young man," he said. Then he screwed his face up and his chin wobbled and his chest began to bounce in and out and a sound came out of him like a convalescent rooster learning to crow again after a long illness.

He was laughing.

It stopped after a while. His face came all smooth again and his eyes opened, black and sharp and shrewd.

"Eight hundred dollars," he said. "Eight hundred dollars for an uncirculated specimen of the Brasher Doubloon." He chortled.

"Fine. Got it with you? That leaves you two hundred. Fair enough. A quick turnover, a reasonable profit and no trouble for anybody."

"It is not in my office," he said. "Do you take me for a fool?" He reached an ancient silver watch out of his vest on a black fob. He screwed up his eyes to look at it. "Let us say eleven in the morning," he said. "Come back with your money. The coin may or may not be here, but if I am satisfied with your behavior, I will arrange matters."

"That is satisfactory," I said, and stood up. "I have to get the money anyhow."

"Have it in used bills," he said almost dreamily. "Used twenties will do. An occasional fifty will do no harm."

I grinned and started for the door. Halfway there I turned around and went back to lean both hands on the desk and push my face over it.

"What did she look like?"

He looked blank.

"The girl that sold you the coin."

He looked blanker.

"Okay," I said. "It wasn't a girl. She had help. It was a man. What did the man look like?"

He pursed his lips and made another steeple with his fingers. "He was a middle-aged man, heavy set, about five feet seven inches tall and weighing around one hundred and seventy pounds. He said his name was Smith. He wore a blue suit, black shoes, a green tie and shirt, no hat. There was a brown bordered handkerchief in his outer pocket. His hair was dark brown sprinkled with gray. There was a bald patch about the size of a dollar on the crown of his head and a scar about two inches long running down the side of his jaw. On the left side, I think. Yes, on the left side."

"Not bad," I said. "What about the hole in his right sock?"

"I omitted to take his shoes off."

"Darn careless of you," I said.

He didn't say anything. We just stared at each other, half curious, half hostile, like new neighbors. Then suddenly he went into his laugh again.

The five dollar bill I had given him was still lying on his side of the desk. I flicked a hand across and took it.

"You won't want this now," I said. "Since we started talking in thousands."

He stopped laughing very suddenly. Then he shrugged.

"At eleven a.m.," he said. "And no tricks, Mr. Marlowe. Don't think I don't know how to protect myself."

"I hope you do," I said, "because what you are handling is dynamite."

I left him and tramped across the empty outer office and opened the door and let it shut, staying inside. There ought to be footsteps outside in the corridor, but his transom was closed and I hadn't made much noise coming on crepe rubber soles. I hoped he would remember that. I sneaked back across the threadbare carpet and edged in behind the door, between the door and the little closed typewriter desk. A kid trick, but once in a while it will work, especially after a lot of smart conversation, full of worldliness and sly wit. Like a sucker play in football. And if it didn't work this time, we would just be there sneering at each other again.

It worked. Nothing happened for a while except that a nose was blown. Then all by himself in there he went into his sick rooster laugh again. Then a throat was cleared. Then a swivel chair squeaked, and feet walked.

A dingy white head poked into the room, about two inches past the end of the door. It hung there suspended and I went

498

into a state of suspended animation. Then the head was drawn back and four unclean fingernails came around the edge of the door and pulled. The door closed, clicked, was shut. I started breathing again and put my ear to the wooden panel.

The swivel chair squeaked once more. The threshing sound of a telephone being dialed. I lunged across to the instrument on the little typewriter desk and lifted it. At the other end of the line the bell had started to ring. It rang six times. Then a man's voice said: "Yeah?"

"The Florence Apartments?"

"Yeah."

"I'd like to speak to Mr. Anson in Apartment two-o-four."

"Hold the wire. I'll see if he's in."

Mr. Morningstar and I held the wire. Noise came over it, the blaring sound of a loud radio broadcasting a baseball game. It was not close to the telephone, but it was noisy enough.

Then I could hear the hollow sound of steps coming nearer and the harsh rattle of the telephone receiver being picked up and the voice said:

"Not in. Any message?"

"I'll call later," Mr. Morningstar said.

I hung up fast and did a rapid glide across the floor to the entrance door and opened it very silently, like snow falling, and let it close the same way, taking its weight at the last moment, so that the click of the catch would not have been heard three feet away.

I breathed hard and tight going down the hall, listening to myself. I pushed the elevator button. Then I got out the card which Mr. George Anson Phillips had given me in the lobby of the Hotel Metropole. I didn't look at it in any real sense. I didn't have to look at it to recall that it referred to Apartment 204, Florence Apartments, 128 Court Street. I just stood there flicking it with a fingernail while the old elevator came heaving up in the shaft, straining like a gravel truck on a hairpin turn.

The time was three-fifty.

8

BUNKER HILL IS old town, lost town, shabby town, crook town. Once, very long ago, it was the choice residential district of the city, and there are still standing a few of the jigsaw Gothic mansions with wide porches and walls covered with round-end shingles and full corner bay windows with spindle turrets. They are all rooming houses now, their parquetry floors are scratched and worn through the once glossy finish and the wide sweeping staircases are dark with time and with cheap varnish laid on over generations of dirt. In the tall rooms haggard landladies bicker with shifty tenants. On the wide cool front porches, reaching their cracked shoes into the sun, and staring at nothing, sit the old men with faces like lost battles.

In and around the old houses there are flyblown restaurants and Italian fruitstands and cheap apartment houses and little candy stores where you can buy even nastier things than their candy. And there are ratty hotels where nobody except people named Smith and Jones sign the register and where the night clerk is half watchdog and half pander.

Out of the apartment houses come women who should be young but have faces like stale beer; men with pulled-down hats and quick eyes that look the street over behind the cupped hand that shields the match flame; worn intellectuals with cigarette coughs and no money in the bank; fly cops with granite faces and unwavering eyes; cokies and coke peddlers; people who look like nothing in particular and know it, and once in a while even men that actually go to work. But they come out early, when the wide cracked sidewalks are empty and still have dew on them.

I was earlier than four-thirty getting over there, but not much. I parked at the end of the street, where the funicular railway comes struggling up the yellow clay bank from Hill Street, and walked along Court Street to the Florence

Apartments. It was dark brick in front, three stories, the lower windows at sidewalk level and masked by rusted screens and dingy net curtains. The entrance door had a glass panel and enough of the name left to be read. I opened it and went down three brass bound steps into a hallway you could touch on both sides without stretching. Dim doors painted with numbers in dim paint. An alcove at the foot of the stairs with a pay telephone. A sign: *Manager, Apt. 106.* At the back of the hallway a screen door and in the alley beyond it four tall battered garbage pails in a line, with a dance of flies in the sunlit air above them.

I went up the stairs. The radio I had heard over the telephone was still blatting the baseball game. I read numbers and went up front. Apartment 204 was on the right side and the baseball game was right across the hall from it. I knocked, got no answer and knocked louder. Behind my back three Dodgers struck out against a welter of synthetic crowd noise. I knocked a third time and looked out of the front hall window while I felt in my pocket for the key George Anson Phillips had given me.

Across the street was an Italian funeral home, neat and quiet and reticent, white painted brick, flush with the sidewalk. Pietro Palermo Funeral Parlors. The thin green script of a neon sign lay across its facade, with a chaste air. A tall man in dark clothes came out of the front door and leaned against the white wall. He looked very handsome. He had dark skin and a handsome head of iron-gray hair brushed back from his forehead. He got out what looked at that distance to be a silver or platinum and black enamel cigarette case, opened it languidly with two long brown fingers and selected a gold-tipped cigarette. He put the case away and lit the cigarette with a pocket lighter that seemed to match the case. He put that away and folded his arms and stared at nothing with half closed eyes. From the tip of his motionless cigarette a thin wisp of smoke rose straight up past his face, as thin and straight as the smoke of a dying campfire at dawn.

Another batter struck out or flied out behind my back in the recreated ball game. I turned from watching the tall Italian, put the key into the door of Apartment 204 and went in.

A square room with a brown carpet, very little furniture and that not inviting. The wall bed with the usual distorting mirror faced me as I opened the door and made me look like a two-time loser sneaking home from a reefer party. There was a birchwood easy chair with some hard looking upholstery beside it in the form of a davenport. A table before the window held a lamp with a shirred paper shade. There was a door on either side of the bed.

The door to the left led into a small kitchenette with a brown woodstone sink and a three-burner stove and an old electric icebox that clicked and began to throb in torment just as I pushed the door open. On the woodstone drain board stood the remains of somebody's breakfast, mud at the bottom of a cup, a burnt crust of bread, crumbs on a board, a yellow slime of melted butter down the slope of a saucer, a smeared knife and a granite coffee pot that smelled like sacks in a hot barn.

I went back around the wall bed and through the other door. It gave on a short hallway with an open space for clothes and a built-in dresser. On the dresser was a comb and a black brush with a few blond hairs in its black bristles. Also a can of talcum, a small flashlight with a cracked lens, a pad of writing paper, a bank pen, a bottle of ink on a blotter, cigarettes and matches in a glass ashtray that contained half a dozen stubs.

In the drawers of the dresser were about what one suitcase would hold in the way of socks and underclothes and hand-kerchiefs. There was a dark gray suit on a hanger, not new but still good, and a pair of rather dusty black brogues on the floor under it.

I pushed the bathroom door. It opened about a foot and then stuck. My nose twitched and I could feel my lips stiffen and I smelled the harsh sharp bitter smell from beyond the door. I leaned against it. It gave a little, but came back, as though somebody was holding it against me. I poked my head through the opening.

The floor of the bathroom was too short for him, so his knees were poked up and hung outwards slackly and his head was pressed against the woodstone baseboard at the other end, not tilted up, but jammed tight. His brown suit was rumpled a little and his dark glasses stuck out of his breast pocket at an unsafe angle. As if that mattered. His right hand was thrown across his stomach, his left hand lay on the floor, palm up, the fingers curled a little. There was a blood-caked bruise on the right side of his head, in the blond hair. His open mouth was full of shiny crimson blood.

The door was stopped by his leg. I pushed hard and edged around it and got in. I bent down to push two fingers into the side of his neck against the big artery. No artery throbbed there, or even whispered. Nothing at all. The skin was icy. It couldn't have been icy. I just thought it was. I straightened up and leaned my back against the door and made hard fists in my pockets and smelled the cordite fumes. The baseball game was still going on, but through two closed doors it sounded remote.

I stood and looked down at him. Nothing in that, Marlowe, nothing at all. Nothing for you here, nothing. You didn't even know him. Get out, get out fast.

I pulled away from the door and pulled it open and went back through the hall into the living room. A face in the mirror looked at me. A strained, leering face. I turned away from it quickly and took out the flat key George Anson Phillips had given me and rubbed it between my moist palms and laid it down beside the lamp.

I smeared the doorknob opening the door and the outside knob closing the door. The Dodgers were ahead seven to three, the first half of the eighth. A lady who sounded well on with her drinking was singing Frankie and Johnny, the roundhouse version, in a voice that even whiskey had failed to improve. A deep man's voice growled at her to shut up and she kept on singing and there was a hard quick movement across the floor and a smack and a yelp and she stopped singing and the baseball game went right on.

I put the cigarette in my mouth and lit it and went back down the stairs and stood in the half dark of the hall angle looking at the little sign that read: *Manager, Apt. 106.*

I was a fool even to look at it. I looked at it for a long minute, biting the cigarette hard between my teeth.

I turned and walked down the hallway towards the back. A small enameled plate on a door said: *Manager.* I knocked on the door.

9

A CHAIR WAS pushed back, feet shuffled, the door opened.

"You the manager?"

"Yeah." It was the same voice I had heard over the telephone. Talking to Elisha Morningstar.

He held an empty smeared glass in his hand. It looked as if somebody had been keeping goldfish in it. He was a lanky man with carroty short hair growing down to a point on his forehead. He had a long narrow head packed with shabby cunning. Greenish eyes stared under orange eyebrows. His ears were large and might have flapped in a high wind. He had a long nose that would be into things. The whole face was a trained face, a face that would know how to keep a secret, a face that held the effortless composure of a corpse in the morgue.

He wore his vest open, no coat, a woven hair watchguard, and round blue sleeve garters with metal clasps.

I said: "Mr. Anson?"

"Two-o-four."

"He's not in."

"What should I do – lay an egg?"

"Neat," I said. "You have them all the time, or is this your birthday?"

"Beat it," he said. "Drift." He started to close the door. He opened it again to say: "Take the air. Scram. Push off." Having made his meaning clear he started to close the door again.

I leaned against the door. He leaned against it on his side. That brought our faces close together. "Five bucks," I said.

It rocked him. He opened the door very suddenly and I had to take a quick step forward in order not to butt his chin with my head.

"Come in," he said.

A living room with a wallbed, everything strictly to specifications, even to the shirred paper lampshade and the glass ashtray. This room was painted egg-yolk yellow. All it needed was a few fat black spiders painted on the yellow to be anybody's bilious attack.

"Sit down," he said, shutting the door.

I sat down. We looked at each other with the clear innocent eyes of a couple of used car salesmen.

"Beer?" he said.

"Thanks."

He opened two cans, filled the smeared glass he had been holding, and reached for another like it. I said I would drink out of the can. He handed me the can.

"A dime," he said.

I gave him a dime.

He dropped it into his vest and went on looking at me. He pulled a chair over and sat in it and spread his bony upjutting knees and let his empty hand droop between them.

"I ain't interested in your five bucks," he said.

"That's fine," I said. "I wasn't really thinking of giving it to you."

"A wisey," he said. "What gives? We run a nice respectable place here. No funny stuff gets pulled."

"Quiet too," I said. "Upstairs you could almost hear an eagle scream."

His smile was wide, about three quarters of an inch. "I don't amuse easy," he said.

"Just like Queen Victoria," I said.

"I don't get it."

"I don't expect miracles," I said. The meaningless talk had a sort of cold bracing effect on me, making a mood with a hard gritty edge.

I got my wallet out and selected a card from it. It wasn't my card. It read: *James B. Pollock, Reliance Indemnity Company, Field Agent.* I tried to remember what James B. Pollock looked like and where I had met him. I couldn't. I handed the carroty man the card.

He read it and scratched the end of his nose with one of the corners. "Wrong john?" he asked, keeping his green eyes plastered to my face.

"Jewelry," I said and waved a hand.

He thought this over. While he thought it over I tried to make up my mind whether it worried him at all. It didn't seem to.

"We get one once in a while," he conceded. "You can't help it. He didn't look like it to me, though. Soft looking."

"Maybe I got a bum steer." I said. I described George Anson Phillips to him, George Anson Phillips alive, in his brown suit and his dark glasses and his cocoa straw hat with the brown and yellow print band. I wondered what had happened to the hat. It hadn't been up there. He must have got rid of it, thinking it was too conspicuous. His blond head was almost, but not quite, as bad.

"That sound like him?"

The carroty man took his time making up his mind. Finally he nodded yes, green eyes watching me carefully, lean hard hand holding the card up to his mouth and running the card along his teeth like a stick along the palings of a picket fence.

"I didn't figure him for no crook," he said. "But hell, they come all sizes and shapes. Only been here a month. If he looked like a wrong gee, wouldn't have been here at all."

I did a good job of not laughing in his face. "What say we frisk the apartment while he's out?"

He shook his head. "Mr. Palermo wouldn't like it."

"Mr. Palermo?"

"He's the owner. Across the street. Owns the funeral parlors. Owns this building and a lot of other buildings. Practically owns the district, if you know what I mean." He gave me a twitch of the lip and a flutter of the right eyelid. "Gets the vote out. Not a guy to crowd."

"Well, while he's getting the vote out or playing with a stiff or whatever he's doing at the moment, let's go up and frisk the apartment."

"Don't get me sore at you," the carroty man said briefly.

"That would bother me like two per cent of nothing at all," I said. "Let's go up and frisk the apartment." I threw my empty beer can at the wastebasket and watched it bounce back and roll half way across the room.

The carroty man stood up suddenly and spread his feet apart and dusted his hands together and took hold of his lower lip with his teeth.

"You said something about five," he shrugged.

"That was hours ago," I said. "I thought better of it. Let's go up and frisk the apartment."

"Say that just once more —" his right hand slid towards his hip.

"If you're thinking of pulling a gun, Mr. Palermo wouldn't like it," I said.

"To hell with Mr. Palermo," he snarled, in a voice suddenly furious, out of a face suddenly charged with dark blood.

"Mr. Palermo will be glad to know that's how you feel about him," I said.

"Look," the carroty man said very slowly, dropping his hand to his side and leaning forward from the hips and pushing his face at me as hard as he could. "Look. I was sitting here having myself a beer or two. Maybe three. Maybe nine. What the hell? I wasn't bothering anybody. It was a nice day. It looked like it might be a nice evening – Then you come in." He waved a hand violently.

"Let's go up and frisk the apartment," I said.

He threw both fists forward in tight lumps. At the end of the motion he threw his hands wide open, straining the fingers as far as they would go. His nose twitched sharply.

"If it wasn't for the job," he said.

I opened my mouth. "Don't say it!" he yelled.

He put a hat on, but no coat, opened a drawer and took out a bunch of keys, walked past me to open the door and stood in it, jerking his chin at me. His face still looked a little wild.

We went out into the hall and along it and up the stairs. The ball game was over and dance music had taken its place. Very loud dance music. The carroty man selected one of his keys and put it in the lock of Apartment 204. Against the booming of the dance band behind us in the apartment across the way a woman's voice suddenly screamed hysterically.

The carroty man withdrew the key and bared his teeth at me. He walked across the narrow hallway and banged on the opposite door. He had to knock hard and long before any attention was paid. Then the door was jerked open and a sharp-faced blonde in scarlet slacks and a green pullover stared out with sultry eyes, one of which was puffed and the other had been socked several days ago. She also had a bruise on her throat and her hand held a tall cool glass of amber fluid.

"Pipe down, but soon," the carroty man said. "Too much racket. I don't aim to ask you again. Next time I call some law."

The girl looked back over her shoulder and screamed against the noise of the radio: "Hey, Del! The guy says to pipe down! You wanna sock him?"

A chair squeaked, the radio noise died abruptly and a thick bitter-eyed dark man appeared behind the blonde, yanked her out of the way with one hand and pushed his face at us. He needed a shave. He was wearing pants, street shoes and an undershirt.

He settled his feet in the doorway, whistled a little breath in through his nose and said:

"Buzz off. I just come in from lunch. I had a lousy lunch. I wouldn't want nobody to push muscle at me." He was very drunk, but in a hard practised sort of way.

The carroty man said: "You heard me, Mr. Hench. Dim that radio and stop the roughhouse in here. And make it sudden."

The man addressed as Hench said: "Listen, picklepuss —" and heaved forward with his right foot in a hard stamp.

The carroty man's left foot didn't wait to be stamped on. The lean body moved back quickly and the thrown bunch of keys hit the floor behind, and clanked against the door of Apartment 204. The carroty man's right hand made a sweeping movement and came up with a woven leather blackjack.

Hench said: "Yah!" and took two big handfuls of air in his two hairy hands, closed the hands into fists and swung hard at nothing.

The carroty man hit him on the top of his head and the girl screamed again and threw a glass of liquor in her boy friend's face. Whether because it was safe to do it now or because she made an honest mistake, I couldn't tell.

Hench turned blindly with his face dripping, stumbled and ran across the floor in a lurch that threatened to land him on his nose at every step. The bed was down and tumbled. Hench made the bed on one knee and plunged a hand under the pillow.

I said: "Look out – gun."

"I can fade that too," the carroty man said between his teeth and slid his right hand, empty now, under his open vest.

Hench was down on both knees. He came up on one and turned and there was a short black gun in his right hand and he was staring down at it, not holding it by the grip at all, holding it flat on his palm.

"Drop it!" the carroty man's voice said tightly and he went on into the room.

The blonde promptly jumped on his back and wound her long green arms around his neck, yelling lustily. The carroty man staggered and swore and waved his gun around.

"Get him, Del!" the blonde screamed. "Get him good!"

Hench, one hand on the bed and one foot on the floor, both knees doubled, right hand holding the black gun flat on his palm, eyes staring down at it, pushed himself slowly to his feet and growled deep in his throat:

"This ain't my gun."

I relieved the carroty man of the gun that was not doing him any good and stepped around him, leaving him to shake the blonde off his back as best he could. A door banged down the hallway and steps came along toward us.

I said: "Drop it, Hench."

He looked up at me, puzzled dark eyes suddenly sober.

"It ain't my gun," he said and held it out flat. "Mine's a Colt .32 – belly gun."

I took the gun off his hand. He made no effort to stop me. He sat down on the bed, rubbed the top of his head slowly, and screwed his face up in difficult thought. "Where the hell –" his voice trailed off and he shook his head and winced.

I sniffed the gun. It had been fired. I sprang the magazine out and counted the bullets through the small holes in the side. There were six. With one in the magazine, that made seven. The gun was a Colt .32, automatic, eight shot. It had been fired. If it had not been reloaded, one shot had been fired from it.

The carroty man had the blonde off his back now. He had thrown her into a chair and was wiping a scratch on his cheek. His green eyes were baleful.

"Better get some law," I said. "A shot has been fired from this gun and it's about time you found out there's a dead man in the apartment across the hall."

Hench looked up at me stupidly and said in a quiet, reasonable voice: "Brother, that simply ain't my gun."

The blonde sobbed in a rather theatrical manner and showed me an open mouth twisted with misery and ham acting. The carroty man went softly out of the door.

10

"SHOT IN THE throat with a medium caliber gun and a soft-nosed bullet," Detective-Lieutenant Jesse Breeze said. "A gun like this and bullets like is in here." He danced the gun on his hand, the gun Hence had said was not his gun. "Bullet ranged upwards and probably hit the back of the skull. Still inside his head. The man's dead about two hours. Hands and face cold, but body still warm. No rigor. Was sapped with something hard before being shot. Likely with a gun butt. All that mean anything to you boys and girls?"

The newspaper he was sitting on rustled. He took his hat off and mopped his face and the top of his almost bald head. A fringe of light colored hair around the crown was damp and dark with sweat. He put his hat back on, a flat-crowned panama, burned dark by the sun. Not this year's hat, and probably not last year's.

He was a big man, rather paunchy, wearing brown and white shoes and sloppy socks and white trousers with thin black stripes, an open neck shirt showing some ginger-colored hair at the top of his chest, and a rough sky-blue sports coat not wider at the shoulders than a two-car garage. He would be about fifty years old and the only thing about him that very much suggested cop was the calm, unwinking unwavering stare of his prominent pale blue eyes, a stare that had no thought of being rude, but that anybody but a cop would feel to be rude. Below his eyes across the top of his cheeks and the bridge of his nose there was a wide path of freckles, like a mine field on a war map.

We were sitting in Hench's apartment and the door was shut. Hench had his shirt on and he was absently tying a tie with thick blunt fingers that trembled. The girl was lying on the bed. She had a green wraparound thing twisted about her head, a purse by her side and a short squirrel coat across her feet. Her mouth was a little open and her face was drained and shocked.

Hench said thickly: "If the idea is the guy was shot with the gun under the pillow, okay. Seems like he might have been. It ain't my gun and nothing you boys can think up is going to make me say it's my gun."

"Assuming that to be so," Breeze said, "how come? Somebody swiped your gun and left this one. When, how, what kind of gun was yours?"

"We went out about three-thirty or so to get something to eat at the hashhouse around the corner," Hench said. "You can check that. We must have left the door unlocked. We were kind of hitting the bottle a little. I guess we were pretty noisy. We had the ball game going on the radio. I guess we shut it off when we went out. I'm not sure. You remember?" He looked at the girl lying white-faced and silent on the bed. "You remember, sweet?"

The girl didn't look at him or answer him.

"She's pooped," Hench said. "I had a gun, a Colt .32, same caliber as that, but a belly gun. A revolver, not an automatic. There's a piece broken off the rubber grip. A Jew named Morris gave it to me three four years ago. We worked together in a bar. I don't have no permit, but I don't carry the gun neither."

Breeze said: "Hitting the hooch like you birds been and having a gun under the pillow sooner or later somebody was going to get shot. You ought to know that."

"Hell, we didn't even know the guy," Hench said. His tie was tied now, very badly. He was cold sober and very shaky. He stood up and picked a coat off the end of the bed and put it on and sat down again. I watched his fingers tremble lighting a cigarette. "We don't know his name. We don't know anything about him. I see him maybe two three times in the hall, but he don't even speak to me. It's the same guy, I guess. I ain't even sure of that."

"It's the fellow that lived there," Breeze said. "Let me see now, this ball game is a studio re-broadcast, huh?"

"Goes on at three," Hench said. "Three to say four-thirty, or sometimes later. We went out about the last half the third. We was gone about an inning and a half, maybe two. Twenty minutes to half an hour. Not more."

"I guess he was shot just before you went out," Breeze said. "The radio would kill the noise of the gun near enough. You must of left your door unlocked. Or even open."

"Could be," Hench said wearily. "You remember, honey?"

Again the girl on the bed refused to answer him or even look at him.

Breeze said: "You left your door open or unlocked. The killer heard you go out. He got into your apartment, wanting to ditch his gun, saw the bed down, walked across and slipped his gun under the pillow, and then imagine his surprise. He found another gun there waiting for him. So he took it along. Now if he meant to ditch his gun, why not do it where he did his killing? Why take the risk of going into another apartment to do it? Why the fancy pants?"

I was sitting in the corner of the davenport by the window. I put in my nickel's worth, saying: "Suppose he had locked himself out of Phillips' apartment before he thought of ditching the gun? Suppose, coming out of the shock of his murder, he found himself in the hall still holding the murder gun. He would want to ditch it fast. Then if Hench's door was open and he had heard them go out along the hall —"

Breeze looked at me briefly and grunted: "I'm not saying it isn't so. I'm just considering." He turned his attention back to Hench. "So now, if this turns out to be the gun that killed Anson, we got to try and trace *your* gun. While we do that we got to have you and the young lady handy. You understand that, of course?"

Hench said: "You don't have any boys that can bounce me hard enough to make me tell it different."

"We can always try," Breeze said mildly. "And we might just as well get started."

He stood up, turned and swept the crumpled newspapers off the chair on to the floor. He went over to the door, then turned and stood looking at the girl on the bed. "You all right, sister, or should I call for a matron?"

The girl on the bed didn't answer him.

Hench said: "I need a drink. I need a drink bad."

"Not while I'm watching you," Breeze said and went out of the door.

Hench moved across the room and put the neck of a bottle into his mouth and gurgled liquor. He lowered the bottle, looked at what was left in it and went over to the girl. He pushed her shoulder.

"Wake up and have a drink," he growled at her.

The girl stared at the ceiling. She didn't answer him or show that she had heard him.

"Let her alone," I said. "Shock."

Hench finished what was in the bottle, put the empty bottle down carefully and looked at the girl again, then turned his back on her and stood frowning at the floor. "Jeeze, I wish I could remember better," he said under his breath.

Breeze came back into the room with a young fresh-faced plainclothes detective. "This is Lieutenant Spangler," he said. "He'll take you down. Get going, huh?"

Hench went back to the bed and shook the girl's shoulder. "Get on up, babe. We gotta take a ride."

The girl turned her eyes without turning her head, and looked at him slowly. She lifted her shoulders off the bed and put a hand under her and swung her legs over the side and stood up, stamping her right foot, as if it was numb.

"Tough, kid – but you know how it is," Hench said.

The girl put a hand to her mouth and bit the knuckle of her little finger, looking at him blankly. Then she swung the hand suddenly and hit him in the face as hard as she could. Then she half ran out of the door.

Hench didn't move a muscle for a long moment. There was a confused noise of men talking outside, a confused noise of cars down below in the street. Hench shrugged and cocked his heavy shoulders back and swept a slow look around the room, as if he didn't expect to see it again very soon, or at all. Then he went out past the young fresh-faced detective.

The detective went out. The door closed. The confused noise outside was dimmed a little and Breeze and I sat looking at each other heavily.

11

AFTER A WHILE Breeze got tired of looking at me and dug a cigar out of his pocket. He slit the cellophane band with a knife and trimmed the end of the cigar and lit it carefully, turning it around in the flame, and holding the burning match away from it while he stared thoughtfully at nothing and drew on the cigar and made sure it was burning the way he wanted it to burn.

Then he shook the match out very slowly and reached over to lay it on the sill of the open window. Then he looked at me some more.

"You and me," he said, "are going to get along."

"That's fine," I said.

"You don't think so," he said. "But we are. But not because I took any sudden fancy to you. It's the way I work. Everything in the clear. Everything sensible. Everything quiet. Not like that dame. That's the kind of dame that spends her life looking for trouble and when she finds it, it's the fault of the first guy she can get her fingernails into."

"He gave her a couple of shiners," I said. "That wouldn't make her love him too much."

"I can see," Breeze said, "that you know a lot about dames."

"Not knowing a lot about them has helped me in my business," I said. "I'm open-minded."

He nodded and examined the end of his cigar. He took a piece of paper out of his pocket and read from it. "Delmar B. Hench, 45, bartender, unemployed. Maybelle Masters, 26, dancer. That's all I know about them. I've got a hunch there ain't a lot more to know."

"You don't think he shot Anson?" I asked.

Breeze looked at me without pleasure. "Brother, I just got here." He took a card out of his pocket and read from that. "James B. Pollock, Reliance Indemnity Company, Field Agent. What's the idea?"

"In a neighborhood like this it's bad form to use your own name," I said. "Anson didn't either."

"What's the matter with the neighborhood?"

"Practically everything," I said.

"What I would like to know," Breeze said, "is what you know about the dead guy?"

"I told you already."

"Tell me again. People tell me so much stuff I get it all mixed up."

"I know what it says on his card, that his name is George Anson Phillips, that he claimed to be a private detective. He was outside my office when I went to lunch. He followed me downtown, into the lobby of the Hotel Metropole. I led him there. I spoke to him and he admitted he had been following me and said it was because he wanted to find out if I was smart enough to do business with. That's a lot of baloney, of course. He probably hadn't quite made up his mind what to do and was waiting for something to decide him. He was on a job – he said – he had got leery of and he wanted to join up with somebody, perhaps somebody with a little more experience than he had, if he had any at all. He didn't act as if he had."

Breeze said: "And the only reason he picked on you is that six years ago you worked on a case in Ventura while he was a deputy up there."

I said, "That's my story."

"But you don't have to get stuck with it," Breeze said calmly. "You can always give us a better one."

"It's good enough," I said. "I mean it's good enough in the sense that it's bad enough to be true."

He nodded his big slow head.

"What's your idea of all this?" he asked.

"Have you investigated Phillips' office address?"

He shook his head, no.

"My idea is you will find out he was hired because he was simple. He was hired to take this apartment here under a wrong name, and to do something that turned out to be not what he liked. He was scared. He wanted a friend, he wanted help. The fact that he picked me after so long a time and such little knowledge of me showed he didn't know many people in the detective business."

Breeze got his handkerchief out and mopped his head and face again. "But it don't begin to show why he had to follow you around like a lost pup instead of walking right up to your office door and in."

"No," I said, "it doesn't."

"Can you explain that?"

"No. Not really."

"Well, how would you try to explain it?"

"I've already explained it in the only way I know how. He was undecided whether to speak to me or not. He was waiting for something to decide him. I decided by speaking to him."

Breeze said: "That is a very simple explanation. It is so simple it stinks."

"You may be right," I said.

"And as the result of this little hotel lobby conversation this guy, a total stranger to you, asks you to his apartment and hands you his key. Because he wants to talk to you."

I said, "Yes."

"Why couldn't he talk to you then?"

"I had an appointment," I said.

"Business?"

I nodded.

"I see. What you working on?"

I shook my head and didn't answer.

"This is murder," Breeze said. "You're going to have to tell me."

I shook my head again. He flushed a little.

"Look," he said tightly, "you got to."

"I'm sorry, Breeze," I said. "But so far as things have gone, I'm not convinced of that."

"Of course you know I can throw you in the can as a material witness," he said casually.

"On what grounds?"

"On the grounds that you are the one who found the body, that you gave a false name to the manager here, and that you don't give a satisfactory account of your relations with the dead guy."

I said: "Are you going to do it?"

He smiled bleakly. "You got a lawyer?"

"I know several lawyers. I don't have a lawyer on a retainer basis."

"How many of the commissioners do you know personally?"

"None. That is, I've spoken to three of them, but they might not remember me."

"But you have good contacts, in the mayor's office and so on?"

"Tell me about them," I said. "I'd like to know."

"Look, buddy," he said earnestly, "you must got some friends somewhere. Surely."

"I've got a good friend in the Sheriff's office, but I'd rather leave him out of it."

He lifted his eyebrows. "Why? Maybe you're going to need friends. A good word from a cop we know to be right might go a long way."

"He's just a personal friend," I said. "I don't ride around on his back. If I get in trouble, it won't do him any good."

"How about the homicide bureau?"

"There's Randall," I said. "If he's still working out of Central Homicide. I had a little time with him on a case once. But he doesn't like me too well."

Breeze sighed and moved his feet on the floor, rustling the newspapers he had pushed down out of the chair.

"Is all this on the level – or are you just being smart? I mean about all the important guys you don't know?"

"It's on the level," I said. "But the way I am using it is smart."

"It ain't smart to say so right out."

"I think it is."

He put a big freckled hand over the whole lower part of his face and squeezed. When he took the hand away there were round red marks on his cheeks from the pressure of thumb and fingers. I watched the marks fade.

"Why don't you go on home and let a man work?" he asked crossly.

I got up and nodded and went towards the door. Breeze said to my back: "Gimme your home address."

I gave it to him. He wrote it down. "So long," he said drearily: "Don't leave town. We'll want a statement – maybe tonight."

I went out. There were two uniformed cops outside on the landing. The door across the way was open and a fingerprint man was still working inside. Downstairs I met two more cops in the hallway, one at each end of it. I didn't see the carroty manager. I went out the front door. There was an ambulance pulling away from the curb. A knot of people hung around on both sides of the street, not as many as would accumulate in some neighborhoods.

I pushed along the sidewalk. A man grabbed me by the arm and said: "What's the damage, Jack?"

I shook his arm off without speaking or looking at his face and went on down the street to where my car was.

12

IT WAS A quarter to seven when I let myself into the office and clicked the light on and picked a piece of paper off the floor. It was a notice from the Green Feather Messenger Service saying that a package was held awaiting my call and would be delivered upon request at any hour of the day or night. I put it on the desk, peeled my coat off and opened the windows. I got a half bottle of Old Taylor out of the deep drawer of the desk and drank a short drink, rolling it around on my tongue. Then I sat there holding the neck of the cool bottle and wondering how it would feel to be a homicide dick and find bodies lying around and not mind at all, not have to sneak out wiping doorknobs, not have to ponder how much I could tell without hurting a client and how little I could tell without too badly hurting myself. I decided I wouldn't like it.

I pulled the phone over and looked at the number on the slip and called it. They said my package could be sent right over. I said I would wait for it.

It was getting dark outside now. The rushing sound of the traffic had died a little and the air from the open window, not yet cool from the night, had that tired end-of-the-day smell of dust, automobile exhaust, sunlight rising from hot walls and sidewalks, the remote smell of food in a thousand restaurants, and perhaps, drifting down from the residential hills above Hollywood – if you had a nose like a hunting dog – a touch of that peculiar tomcat smell that eucalyptus trees give off in warm weather.

I sat there smoking. Ten minutes later the door was knocked on and I opened it to a boy in a uniform cap who took my signature and gave me a small square package, not more than two and a half inches wide, if that. I gave the boy a dime and listened to him whistling his way back to the elevators.

The label had my name and address printed on it in ink, in a quite fair imitation of typed letters, larger and thinner than pica. I cut the string that tied the label to the box and unwound the thin brown paper. Inside was a thin cheap cardboard box pasted over with brown paper and stamped *Made in Japan* with a rubber stamp. It would be the kind of box you would get in a Jap store to hold some small carved animal or a small piece of jade. The lid fitted down all the way and tightly. I pulled it off and saw tissue paper and cotton wool.

Separating these I was looking at a gold coin about the size of a half dollar, bright and shining as if it had just come from the mint.

The side facing me showed a spread eagle with a shield for a breast and the initials E.B. punched into the left wing. Around these was a circle of beading, between the beading and the smooth unmilled edge of the coin, the legend E PLURIBUS UNUM. At the bottom was the date 1787.

I turned the coin over on my palm. It was heavy and cold and my palm felt moist under it. The other side showed a sun rising or setting behind a sharp peak of mountain, then a double circle of what looked like oak leaves, then more Latin,

NOVA EBORACA COLUMBIA EXCELSIOR. At the bottom of this side, in smaller capitals, the name BRASHER.

I was looking at the Brasher Doubloon.

There was nothing else in the box or in the paper, nothing on the paper. The handwritten printing meant nothing to me. I didn't know anybody who used it.

I filled an empty tobacco pouch half full, wrapped the coin up in tissue paper, snapped a rubber band around it and tucked it into the tobacco in the pouch and put more in on top. I closed the zipper and put the pouch in my pocket. I locked the paper and string and box and label up in a filing cabinet, sat down again and dialed Elisha Morningstar's number on the phone. The bell rang eight times at the other end of the line. It was not answered. I hardly expected that. I hung up again, looked Elisha Morningstar up in the book and saw that he had no listing for a residence phone in Los Angeles or the outlying towns that were in the phone book.

I got a shoulder holster out of the desk and strapped it on and slipped a Colt .38 automatic into it, put on hat and coat, shut the windows again, put the whiskey away, clicked the lights off and had the office door unlatched when the phone rang.

The ringing bell had a sinister sound, for no reason of itself, but because of the ears to which it rang. I stood there braced and tense, lips tightly drawn back in a half grin. Beyond the closed window the neon lights glowed. The dead air didn't move. Outside the corridor was still. The bell rang in darkness, steady and strong.

I went back and leaned on the desk and answered. There was a click and a droning on the wire and beyond that nothing. I depressed the connection and stood there in the dark, leaning over, holding the phone with one hand and holding the flat riser on the pedestal down with the other. I didn't know what I was waiting for.

The phone rang again. I made a sound in my throat and put it to my ear again, not saying anything at all.

So we were there silent, both of us, miles apart maybe, each one holding a telephone and breathing and listening and hearing nothing, not even the breathing.

Then after what seemed a very long time there was the quiet remote whisper of a voice saying dimly, without any tone:

"Too bad for you, Marlowe."

Then the click again and the droning on the wire and I hung up and went back across the office and out.

13

I DROVE WEST on Sunset, fiddled around a few blocks without making up my mind whether anyone was trying to follow me, then parked near a drugstore and went into its phone booth. I dropped my nickel and asked the O-operator for a Pasadena number. She told me how much money to put in.

The voice which answered the phone was angular and cold. "Mrs. Murdock's residence."

"Philip Marlowe here. Mrs. Murdock, please."

I was told to wait. A soft but very clear voice said: "Mr. Marlowe? Mrs. Murdock is resting now. Can you tell me what it is?"

"You oughtn't to have told him."

"I – who – ?"

"That loopy guy whose handkerchief you cry into."

"How dare you?"

"That's fine," I said. "Now let me talk to Mrs. Murdock. I have to."

"Very well. I'll try." The soft clear voice went away and I waited a long wait. They would have to lift her up on the pillows and drag the port bottle out of her hard gray paw and feed her the telephone. A throat was cleared suddenly over the wire. It sounded like a freight train going through a tunnel.

"This is Mrs. Murdock."

"Could you identify the property we were talking about this morning, Mrs. Murdock? I mean could you pick it out from others just like it?"

"Well – are there others just like it?"

"There must be. Dozens, hundreds for all I know. Anyhow dozens. Of course I don't know where they are."

She coughed. "I don't really know much about it. I suppose I couldn't identify it then. But in the circumstances –"

"That's what I'm getting at, Mrs. Murdock. The identification would seem to depend on tracing the history of the article back to you. At least to be convincing."

"Yes. I suppose it would. Why? Do you know where it is?"

"Morningstar claims to have seen it. He says it was offered to him for sale – just as you suspected. He wouldn't buy. The seller was not a woman, he says. That doesn't mean a thing, because he gave me a detailed description of the party which was either made up or was a description of somebody he knew more than casually. So the seller may have been a woman."

"I see. It's not important now."

"Not important?"

"No. Have you anything else to report?"

"Another question to ask. Do you know a youngish blond fellow named George Anson Phillips? Rather heavy set, wearing a brown suit and a dark pork pie hat with a gay band. Wearing that today. Claimed to be a private detective."

"I do not. Why should I?"

"I don't know. He enters the picture somewhere. I think he was the one who tried to sell the article. Morningstar tried to call him up after I left. I snuck back into his office and overheard."

"You what?"

"I snuck."

"Please do not be witty, Mr. Marlowe. Anything else?"

"Yes, I agreed to pay Morningstar one thousand dollars for the return of the – the article. He said he could get it for eight hundred . . ."

"And where were you going to get the money, may I ask?"

"Well, I was just talking. This Morningstar is a downy bird. That's the kind of language he understands. And then again you might have wanted to pay it. I wouldn't want to persuade you. You could always go to the police. But if for any reason you didn't want to go to the police, it might be the only way you could get it back – buying it back."

I would probably have gone on like that for a long time, not knowing just what I was trying to say, if she hadn't stopped me with a noise like a seal barking.

"This is all very unnecessary now, Mr. Marlowe. I have decided to drop the matter. The coin has been returned to me."

"Hold the wire a minute," I said.

I put the phone down on the shelf and opened the booth door and stuck my head out, filling my chest with what they were using for air in the drugstore. Nobody was paying any attention to me. Up front the druggist, in a pale blue smock, was chatting across the cigar counter. The counter boy was polishing glasses at the fountain. Two girls in slacks were playing the pinball machine. A tall narrow party in a black shirt and a pale yellow scarf was fumbling magazines at the rack. He didn't look like a gunman.

I pulled the booth shut and picked up the phone and said: "A rat was gnawing my foot. It's all right now. You got it back, you said. Just like that. How?"

"I hope you are not too disappointed," she said in her uncompromising baritone. "The circumstances are a little difficult. I may decide to explain and I may not. You may call at the house tomorrow morning. Since I do not wish to proceed with the investigation, you will keep the retainer as payment in full."

"Let me get this straight," I said. "You actually got the coin back – not a promise of it, merely?"

"Certainly not. And I'm getting tired. So, if you –"

"One moment, Mrs. Murdock. It isn't going to be as simple as all that. Things have happened."

"In the morning you may tell me about them," she said sharply, and hung up.

I pushed out of the booth and lit a cigarette with thick awkward fingers. I went back along the store. The druggist was alone now. He was sharpening a pencil with a small knife, very intent, frowning.

"That's a nice sharp pencil you have there," I told him.

He looked up, surprised. The girls at the pinball machine looked at me, surprised. I went over and looked at myself in the mirror behind the counter. I looked surprised.

I sat down on one of the stools and said: "A double Scotch, straight."

The counter man looked surprised. "Sorry, this isn't a bar, sir. You can buy a bottle at the liquor counter."

"So it is," I said. "I mean, so it isn't. I've had a shock. I'm a little dazed. Give me a cup of coffee, weak, and a very thin ham sandwich on stale bread. No, I better not eat yet either. Good-bye."

I got down off the stool and walked to the door in a silence that was as loud as a ton of coal going down a chute. The man in the black shirt and yellow scarf was sneering at me over the New Republic.

"You ought to lay off that fluff and get your teeth into something solid, like a pulp magazine," I told him, just to be friendly.

I went on out. Behind me somebody said: "Hollywood's full of them."

14

THE WIND HAD risen and had a dry taut feeling, tossing the tops of trees, and making the swung arc light up the side street cast shadows like crawling lava. I turned the car and drove east again.

The hock shop was on Santa Monica, near Wilcox, a quiet old-fashioned little place, washed gently by the lapping waves of time. In the front window there was everything you could think of, from a set of trout flies in a thin wooden box to a portable organ, from a folding baby carriage to a portrait camera with a four-inch lens, from a mother-of-pearl lorgnette in a faded plush case to a Single Action Frontier Colt, .44 caliber, the model they still make for Western peace officers whose grandfathers taught them how to file the trigger and shoot by fanning the hammer back.

I went into the shop and a bell jangled over my head and somebody shuffled and blew his nose far at the back and steps came. An old Jew in a tall black skull cap came along behind the counter, smiling at me over cut out glasses.

I got my tobacco pouch out, got the Brasher Doubloon out of that and laid it on the counter. The window in front was clear glass and I felt naked. No paneled cubicles with hand-carved spittoons and doors that locked themselves as you closed them.

The Jew took the coin and lifted it on his hand. "Gold, is it? A gold hoarder you are maybe," he said, twinkling.

"Twenty-five dollars," I said. "The wife and the kiddies are hungry."

"Oi, that is terrible. Gold, it feels, by the weight. Only gold and maybe platinum it could be." He weighed it casually on a pair of small scales. "Gold it is," he said. "So ten dollars you are wanting?"

"Twenty-five dollars."

"For twenty-five dollars what would I do with it? Sell it, maybe? For fifteen dollars worth of gold is maybe in it. Okay. Fifteen dollars."

"You got a good safe?"

"Mister, in this business are the best safes money can buy. Nothing to worry about here. It is fifteen dollars, is it?"

"Make out the ticket."

He wrote it out partly with his pen and partly with his tongue. I gave my true name and address. Bristol Apartments, 1634 North Bristol Avenue, Hollywood.

"You are living in that district and you are borrowing fifteen dollars," the Jew said sadly, and tore off my half of the ticket and counted out the money.

I walked down to the corner drugstore and bought an envelope and borrowed a pen and mailed the pawnticket to myself.

I was hungry and hollow inside. I went over to Vine to eat, and after that I drove downtown again. The wind was still rising and it was drier than ever. The steering wheel had a gritty feeling under my fingers and the inside of my nostrils felt tight and drawn.

The lights were on here and there in the tall buildings. The green and chromium clothier's store on the corner of Ninth and Hill was a blaze of it. In the Belfont Building a few windows glowed here and there, but not many. The same old plowhorse sat in the elevator on his piece of folded burlap, looking straight in front of him, blank-eyed, almost gathered to history.

I said: "I don't suppose you know where I can get in touch with the building superintendent?"

He turned his head slowly and looked past my shoulder. "I hear how in Noo York they got elevators that just whiz. Go thirty floors at a time. High speed. That's in Noo York."

"The hell with New York," I said. "I like it here."

"Must take a good man to run them fast babies."

"Don't kid yourself, dad. All those cuties do is push buttons, say 'Good Morning, Mr. Whoosis,' and look at their beauty spots in the car mirror. Now you take a Model T job like this — it takes a man to run it. Satisfied?"

"I work twelve hours a day," he said. "And glad to get it."

"Don't let the union hear you."

"You know what the union can do?" I shook my head. He told me. Then he lowered his eyes until they almost looked at me. "Didn't I see you before somewhere?"

"About the building super," I said gently.

"Year ago he broke his glasses," the old man said. "I could of laughed. Almost did."

"Yes. Where could I get in touch with him this time of the evening?"

He looked at me a little more directly.

"Oh, the building super? He's home, ain't he?"

"Sure. Probably. Or gone to the pictures. But where is home? What's his name?"

"You want something?"

"Yes." I squeezed a fist in my pocket and tried to keep from yelling. "I want the address of one of the tenants. The tenant I want the address of isn't in the phone book – at his home. I mean where he lives when he's not in his office. You know, home." I took my hands out and made a shape in the air, writing the letters slowly, h o m e.

The old man said: "Which one?" It was so direct that it jarred me.

"Mr. Morningstar."

"He ain't home. Still in his office."

"Are you sure?"

"Sure I'm sure. I don't notice people much. But he's old like me and I notice him. He ain't been down yet."

I got into the car and said: "Eight."

He wrestled the doors shut and we ground our way up. He didn't look at me anymore. When the car stopped and I got out he didn't speak or look at me again. He just sat there blank-eyed, hunched on the burlap and the wooden stool. As I turned the angle of the corridor he was still sitting there. And the vague expression was back on his face.

At the end of the corridor two doors were alight. They were the only two in sight that were. I stopped outside to light a cigarette and listen, but I didn't hear any sound of activity. I opened the door marked *Entrance* and stepped into the narrow office with the small closed typewriter desk. The wooden door was still ajar. I walked along to it and knocked on the wood and said: "Mr. Morningstar."

No answer. Silence. Not even a sound of breathing. The hairs moved on the back of my neck. I stepped around the door. The ceiling light glowed down on the glass cover of the jeweller's scales, on the old polished wood around the leather desk top, down the side of the desk, on a square-toed, elastic-sided black shoe, with a white cotton sock above it.

The shoe was at the wrong angle, pointing to the corner of the ceiling. The rest of the leg was behind the corner of the big safe. I seemed to be wading through mud as I went on into the room.

He lay crumpled on his back. Very lonely, very dead.

The safe door was wide open and keys hung in the lock of the inner compartment. A metal drawer was pulled out. It was empty now. There may have been money in it once.

Nothing else in the room seemed to be different.

The old man's pockets had been pulled out, but I didn't touch him except to bend over and put the back of my hand against his livid, violet-colored face. It was like touching a frog's belly. Blood had oozed from the side of his forehead where he had been hit. But there was no powder smell on the air this time, and the violet color of his skin showed that he had died of a heart stoppage, due to shock and fear, probably. That didn't make it any less murder.

I left the lights burning, wiped the doorknobs, and walked down the fire stairs to the sixth floor. I read the names on the doors going along, for no reason at all. *H. R. Teager Dental Laboratories, L. Pridview, Public Accountant, Dalton and Rees Typewriting Service, Dr. E. J. Blaskowitz*, and underneath the name in small letters: *Chiropractic Physician*.

The elevator came growling up and the old man didn't look at me. His face was as empty as my brain.

I called the Receiving Hospital from the corner, giving no name.

15

THE CHESSMEN, RED and white bone, were lined up ready to go and had that sharp, competent and complicated look they always have at the beginning of a game. It was ten o'clock in the evening, I was home at the apartment, I had a pipe in my mouth, a drink at my elbow and nothing on my mind except two murders and the mystery of how Mrs. Elizabeth Bright Murdock had got her Brasher Doubloon back while I still had it in my pocket.

I opened a little paper-bound book of tournament games published in Leipzig, picked out a dashing-looking Queen's Gambit, moved the white pawn to Queen's four, and the bell rang at the door.

I stepped around the table and picked the Colt .38 off the drop leaf of the oak desk and went over to the door holding it down beside my right leg.

"Who is it?"

"Breeze."

I went back to the desk to lay the gun down again before I opened the door. Breeze stood there looking just as big and sloppy as ever, but a little more tired. The young, fresh-faced dick named Spangler was with him.

They rode me back into the room without seeming to and Spangler shut the door. His bright young eyes flicked this way and that while Breeze let his older and harder ones stay on my face for a long moment, then he walked around me to the davenport.

"Look around," he said out of the corner of his mouth.

Spangler left the door and crossed the room to the dinette, looked in there, recrossed and went into the hall. The bathroom door squeaked, his steps went farther along.

Breeze took his hat off and mopped his semi-bald dome. Doors opened and closed distantly. Closets. Spangler came back.

"Nobody here," he said.

Breeze nodded and sat down, placing his panama beside him.

Spangler saw the gun lying on the desk. He said: "Mind if I look?"

I said: "Phooey on both of you."

Spangler walked to the gun and held the muzzle to his nose, sniffing. He broke the magazine out, ejected the shell in the chamber, picked it up and pressed it into the magazine. He laid the magazine on the desk and held the gun so that light went into the open bottom of the breech. Holding it that way he squinted down the barrel.

"A little dust," he said. "Not much."

"What did you expect?" I said. "Rubies?"

He ignored me, looked at Breeze and added: "I'd say this gun has not been fired within twenty-four hours. I'm sure of it."

Breeze nodded and chewed his lip and explored my face with his eyes. Spangler put the gun together neatly and laid it aside and went and sat down. He put a cigarette between his lips and lit it and blew smoke contentedly.

"We know damn well it wasn't a long .38 anyway," he said. "One of those things will shoot through a wall. No chance of the slug staying inside a man's head."

"Just what are you guys talking about?" I asked.

Breeze said: "The usual thing in our business. Murder. Have a chair. Relax. I thought I heard voices in here. Maybe it was the next apartment."

"Maybe," I said.

"You always have a gun lying around on your desk?"

"Except when it's under my pillow," I said. "Or under my arm. Or in the drawer of the desk. Or somewhere I can't just remember where I happened to put it. That help you any?"

"We didn't come here to get tough, Marlowe."

"That's fine," I said. "So you prowl my apartment and handle my property without asking my permission. What do you do when you get tough – knock me down and kick me in the face?"

"Aw hell," he said and grinned. I grinned back. We all grinned. Then Breeze said: "Use your phone?"

I pointed to it. He dialed a number and talked to someone named Morrison, saying: "Breeze at –" He looked down at the base of the phone and read the number off – "Anytime now. Marlowe is the name that goes with it. Sure. Five or ten minutes is okay."

He hung up and went back to the davenport.

"I bet you can't guess why we're here."

"I'm always expecting the brothers to drop in," I said.

"Murder ain't funny, Marlowe."

"Who said it was?"

"Don't you kind of act as if it was?"

"I wasn't aware of it."

He looked at Spangler and shrugged. Then he looked at the floor. Then he lifted his eyes slowly, as if they were heavy, and looked at me again. I was sitting down by the chess table now.

"You play a lot of chess?" he asked, looking at the chessmen.

"Not a lot. Once in a while I fool around with a game here, thinking things out."

"Don't it take two guys to play chess?"

"I play over tournament games that have been recorded and published. There's a whole literature about chess. Once in a while I work out problems. They're not chess, properly speaking. What are we talking about chess for? Drink?"

"Not right now," Breeze said. "I talked to Randall about you. He remembers you very well, in connection with a case down at the beach." He moved his feet on the carpet, as if they were very tired. His solid old face was lined and gray with fatigue. "He said you wouldn't murder anybody. He says you are a nice guy, on the level."

"That was friendly of him," I said.

"He says you make good coffee and you get up kind of late in the mornings and are apt to run to a very bright line of chatter and that we should believe anything you say, provided we can check it by five independent witnesses."

"To hell with him," I said.

Breeze nodded exactly as though I had said just what he wanted me to say. He wasn't smiling and he wasn't tough, just a big solid man working at his job. Spangler had his head back on the chair and his eyes half closed and was watching the smoke from his cigarette.

"Randall says we should look out for you. He says you are not as smart as you think you are, but that you are a guy things happen to, and a guy like that could be a lot more trouble than a very smart guy. That's what he says, you understand. You look all right to me. I like everything in the clear. That's why I'm telling you."

I said it was nice of him.

The phone rang. I looked at Breeze, but he didn't move, so I reached for it and answered it. It was a girl's voice. I thought it was vaguely familiar, but I couldn't place it.

"Is this Mr. Philip Marlowe?"

"Yes."

"Mr. Marlowe, I'm in trouble, very great trouble. I want to see you very badly. When can I see you?"

I said: "You mean tonight? Who am I talking to?"

"My name is Gladys Crane. I live at the Hotel Normandy on Rampart. When can you —"

"You mean you want me to come over there tonight?" I asked, thinking about the voice, trying to place it.

"I —" The phone clicked and the line was dead. I sat there holding it, frowning at it, looking across it at Breeze. His face was quietly empty of interest.

"Some girl says she's in trouble," I said. "Connection broken." I held the plunger down on the base of the phone waiting for it to ring again. The two cops were completely silent and motionless. Too silent, too motionless.

The bell rang again and I let the plunger up and said: "You want to talk to Breeze, don't you?"

"Yeah." It was a man's voice and it sounded a little surprised.

"Go on, be tricky," I said, and got up from the chair and went out to the kitchen. I heard Breeze talking very briefly, then the sound of the phone being returned to the cradle.

I got a bottle of Four Roses out of the kitchen closet and three glasses. I got ice and ginger ale from the icebox and mixed three highballs and carried them in on a tray and sat the tray down on the cocktail table in front of the davenport where Breeze was sitting. I took two of the glasses, handed one to Spangler, and took the other to my chair.

Spangler held the glass uncertainly, pinching his lower lip between thumb and finger, looking at Breeze to see whether he would accept the drink.

Breeze looked at me very steadily. Then he sighed. Then he picked the glass up and tasted it and sighed again and shook his head sideways with a half smile; the way a man does when you give him a drink and he needs it very badly and it is just right and the first swallow is like a peek into a cleaner, sunnier, brighter world.

"I guess you catch on pretty fast, Mr. Marlowe," he said, and leaned back on the davenport completely relaxed. "I guess now we can do some business together."

"Not that way," I said.

"Huh?" He bent his eyebrows together. Spangler leaned forward in his chair and looked bright and attentive.

"Having stray broads call me up and give me a song and dance so you can say they said they recognized my voice somewhere sometime."

"The girl's name is Gladys Crane," Breeze said.

"So she told me. I never heard of her."

"Okay," Breeze said. "Okay." He showed me the flat of his freckled hand. "We're not trying to pull anything that's not legitimate. We only hope you ain't, either."

"Ain't either what?"

"Ain't either trying to pull anything not legitimate. Such as holding out on us."

"Just why shouldn't I hold out on you, if I feel like it?" I asked. "You're not paying my salary."

"Look, don't get tough, Marlowe."

"I'm not tough. I don't have any idea of being tough. I know enough about cops not to get tough with them. Go ahead and speak your piece and don't try to pull any more phonies like that telephone call."

"We're on a murder case," Breeze said. "We have to try to run it the best we can. You found the body. You had talked to the guy. He had asked you to come to his apartment. He gave you his key. You said you didn't know what he wanted to see you about. We figured that maybe with time to think back you could have remembered."

"In other words I was lying the first time," I said.

Breeze smiled a tired smile. "You been around enough to know that people always lie in murder cases."

"The trouble with that is how are you going to know when I stop lying?"

"When what you say begins to make sense, we'll be satisfied."

I looked at Spangler. He was leaning forward so far he was almost out of his chair. He looked as if he was going to jump. I couldn't think of any reason why he should jump, so I thought he must be excited. I looked back at Breeze. He was about as excited as a hole in the wall. He had one of his cellophane-wrapped cigars between his thick fingers and he was slitting the cellophane with a penknife. I watched him get the wrapping off and trim the cigar end with the blade and put the knife away, first wiping the blade carefully on his pants.

I watched him strike a wooden match and light the cigar carefully, turning it around in the flame, then hold the match away from the cigar, still burning, and draw on the cigar until he decided it was properly lighted. Then he shook the match out and laid it down beside the crumpled cellophane on the glass top of the cocktail table. Then he leaned back and pulled up one leg of his pants and smoked peacefully. Every motion had been exactly as it had been when he lit a cigar in Hench's apartment, and exactly as it always would be whenever he lit a cigar. He was that kind of man, and that made him danger-ous. Not as dangerous as a brilliant man, but much more dan-gerous than a quick excitable one like Spangler.

"I never saw Phillips before today," I said. "I don't count that he said he saw me up in Ventura once, because I don't remember him. I met him just the way I told you. He tailed me around and I braced him. He wanted to talk to me, he gave me his key, I went to his apartment, used the key to let myself in when he didn't answer – as he had told me to do. He was dead. The police were called and through a set of events or incidents that had nothing to do with me, a gun was found under Hench's pillow. A gun that had been fired. I told you this and it's true."

Breeze said: "When you found him you went down to the apartment manager, guy named Passmore, and got him to go up with you without telling him anybody was dead. You gave Passmore a phony card and talked about jewelry."

I nodded. "With people like Passmore and apartment houses like that one, it pays to be a little on the cagey side. I was interested in Phillips. I thought Passmore might tell me something about him, if he didn't know he was dead, that he wouldn't be likely to tell me, if he knew the cops were going to bounce in on him in a brief space of time. That's all there was to that."

Breeze drank a little of his drink and smoked a little of his cigar and said: "What I'd like to get in the clear is this.

Everything you just told us might be strictly the truth, and yet you might not be telling us the truth. If you get what I mean."

"Like what?" I asked, getting perfectly well what he meant.

He tapped on his knee and watched me with a quiet up from under look. Not hostile, not even suspicious. Just a quiet man doing his job.

"Like this. You're on a job. We don't know what it is. Phillips was playing at being a private dick. He was on a job. He tailed you around. How can we know, unless you tell us, that his job and your job don't tie in somewhere? And if they do, that's our business. Right?"

"That's one way to look at it," I said. "But it's not the only way, and it's not my way."

"Don't forget this is a murder case, Marlowe."

"I'm not. But don't you forget I've been around this town a long time, more than fifteen years. I've seen a lot of murder cases come and go. Some have been solved, some couldn't be solved, and some could have been solved that were not solved. And one or two or three of them have been solved wrong. Somebody was paid to take a rap, and the chances are it was known or strongly suspected. And winked at. But skip that. It happens, but not often. Consider a case like the Cassidy case. I guess you remember it, don't you?"

Breeze looked at his watch. "I'm tired," he said. "Let's forget the Cassidy case. Let's stick to the Phillips case."

I shook my head. "I'm going to make a point, and it's an important point. Just look at the Cassidy case. Cassidy was a very rich man, a multi-millionaire. He had a grown up son. One night the cops were called to his home and young Cassidy was on his back on the floor with blood all over his face and a bullet hole in the side of his head. His secretary was lying on *his* back in an adjoining bathroom, with his head against the second bathroom door, leading to a hall, and a cigarette burned out between the fingers of his left hand, just a short burned out stub that had scorched the skin between his fingers. A gun was lying by his right hand. He was shot in the head, not a contact wound. A lot of drinking had been done. Four hours had elapsed since the deaths and the family doctor had been there for three of them. Now, what did you do with the Cassidy case?"

Breeze sighed. "Murder and suicide during a drinking spree. The secretary went haywire and shot young Cassidy. I read it in the papers or something. Is that what you want me to say?"

"You read it in the papers," I said, "but it wasn't so. What's more you knew it wasn't so and the D.A. knew it wasn't so and the D.A.'s investigators were pulled off the case within a matter of hours. There was no inquest. But every crime reporter in town and every cop on every homicide detail knew it was Cassidy that did the shooting, that it was Cassidy that was crazy drunk, that it was the secretary who tried to handle him and couldn't and at last tried to get away from him, but wasn't quick enough. Cassidy's was a contact wound and the secretary's was not. The secretary was left-handed and he had a cigarette in his left hand when he was shot. Even if you are right-handed, you don't change a cigarette over to your other hand and shoot a man while casually holding the cigarette. They might do that on *Gang Busters*, but rich men's secretaries don't do it. And what were the family and the family doctor doing during the four hours they didn't call the cops? Fixing it so there would only be a superficial investigation. And why were no tests of the hands made for nitrates? Because you didn't want the truth. Cassidy was too big. But this was a murder case too, wasn't it?"

"The guys were both dead," Breeze said. "What the hell difference did it make who shot who?"

"Did you ever stop to think," I asked, "that Cassidy's secretary might have had a mother or a sister or a sweetheart – or all three? That they had their pride and their faith and their love for a kid who was made out to be a drunken paranoiac because his boss's father had a hundred million dollars?"

Breeze lifted his glass slowly and finished his drink slowly and put it down slowly and turned the glass slowly on the glass top of the cocktail table. Spangler sat rigid, all shining eyes and lips parted in a sort of rigid half smile.

Breeze said: "Make your point."

I said: "Until you guys own your own souls you don't own mine. Until you guys can be trusted every time and always, in all times and conditions, to seek the truth out and find it and let the chips fall where they may – until that time comes, I have a right to listen to my conscience, and protect my client the best way I can. Until I'm sure you won't do him more harm than you'll do the truth good. Or until I'm hauled before somebody that can make me talk."

Breeze said: "You sound to me just a little like a guy who is trying to hold his conscience down."

"Hell," I said. "Let's have another drink. And then you can tell me about that girl you had me talk to on the phone."

He grinned: "That was a dame that lives next door to Phillips. She heard a guy talking to him at the door one evening. She works days as an usherette. So we thought maybe she ought to hear your voice. Think nothing of it."

"What kind of voice was it?"

"Kind of a mean voice. She said she didn't like it."

"I guess that's what made you think of me," I said.

I picked up the three glasses and went out to the kitchen with them.

16

WHEN I GOT out there I had forgotten which glass was which, so I rinsed them all out and dried them and was starting to make more drinks when Spangler strolled out and stood just behind my shoulder.

"It's all right," I said. "I'm not using any cyanide this evening."

"Don't get too foxy with the old guy," he said quietly to the back of my neck. "He knows more angles than you think."

"Nice of you," I said.

"Say, I'd like to read up on that Cassidy case," he said. "Sounds interesting. Must have been before my time."

"It was a long time ago," I said. "And it never happened. I was just kidding." I put the glasses on the tray and carried them back into the living room and set them around. I took mine over to my chair behind the chess table.

"Another phony," I said. "Your sidekick sneaks out to the kitchen and gives me advice behind your back about how careful I ought to keep on account of the angles you know that I don't think you know. He has just the right face for it. Friendly and open and an easy blusher."

Spangler sat down on the edge of his chair and blushed. Breeze looked at him casually, without meaning.

"What did you find out about Phillips?" I asked.

"Yes," Breeze said. "Phillips. Well, George Anson Phillips is a kind of pathetic case. He thought he was a detective, but it looks as if he couldn't get anybody to agree with him. I talked to the sheriff at Ventura. He said George was a nice kind, maybe a little too nice to make a good cop, even if he had any brains. George did what they said and he would do it pretty well, provided they told him which foot to start on and how many steps to take which way and little things like that. But he didn't develop much, if you get what I mean. He was the sort of cop who would be likely to hang a pinch on a chicken thief, if he saw the guy steal the chicken and the guy fell down running away and hit his head on a post or something and knocked himself out. Otherwise it might get a little tough and George would have to go back to the office for instructions. Well, it wore the sheriff down after a while and he let George go."

Breeze drank some more of his drink and scratched his chin with a thumbnail like the blade of a shovel.

"After that George worked in a general store at Simi for a

man named Sutcliff. It was a credit business with little books for each customer and George would have trouble with the books. He would forget to write the stuff down or write it in the wrong book and some of the customers would straighten him out and some would let George forget. So Sutcliff thought maybe George would do better at something else, and George came to L.A. He had come into a little money, not much, but enough for him to get a license and put up a bond and get himself a piece of an office. I was over there. What he had was desk room with another guy who claims he is selling Christmas cards. Name of Marsh. If George had a customer, the arrangement was Marsh would go for a walk. Marsh says he didn't know where George lived and George didn't have any customers. That is, no business came into the office that Marsh knows about. But George put an ad in the paper and he might have got a customer out of that. I guess he did, because about a week ago Marsh found a note on his desk that George would be out of town for a few days. That's the last he heard of him. So George went over to Court Street and took an apartment under the name of Anson and got bumped off. And that's all we know about George so far. Kind of a pathetic case."

He looked at me with a level uncurious gaze and raised his glass to his lips.

"What about this ad?"

Breeze put the glass down and dug a thin piece of paper out of his wallet and put it down on the cocktail table. I went over and picked it up and read it. It said:

Why worry? Why be doubtful or confused? Why be gnawed by suspicion? Consult cool, careful, confidential, discreet investigator. George Anson Phillips. Glenview 9521.

I put it down on the glass again.

"It ain't any worse than lots of business personals," Breeze said. "It don't seem to be aimed at the carriage trade."

Spangler said: "The girl in the office wrote it for him. She said she could hardly keep from laughing, but George thought it was swell. The Hollywood Boulevard office of the *Chronicle*."

"You checked that fast," I said.

"We don't have any trouble getting information," Breeze said. "Except maybe from you."

"What about Hench?"

"Nothing about Hench. Him and the girl were having a liquor party. They would drink a little and sing a little and scrap a little and listen to the radio and go out to eat once in a while, when they thought of it. I guess it had been going on for days. Just as well we stopped it. The girl has two bad eyes. The next round Hench might have broken her neck. The world is full of bums like Hench – and his girl."

"What about the gun Hench said wasn't his?"

"It's the right gun. We don't have the slug yet, but we have the shell. It was under George's body and it checks. We had a couple more fired and comparisoned the ejector marks and the firing pin dents."

"You believe somebody planted it under Hench's pillow?"

"Sure. Why would Hench shoot Phillips? He didn't know him."

"How do you know that?"

"I know it," Breeze said, spreading his hands. "Look, there are things you know because you have them down in black and white. And there are things you know because they are reasonable and have to be so. You don't shoot somebody and then make a lot of racket calling attention to yourself, and all the time you have the gun under your pillow. The girl was with Hench all day. If Hench shot anybody, she would have some idea. She doesn't have any such idea. She would spill, if she had. What is Hench to her? A guy to play around with, no more. Look, forget Hench. The guy who did the shooting hears the loud radio and knows it will cover a shot. But all the same he saps Phillips and drags him into the bathroom and shuts the

543

door before he shoots him. He's not drunk. He's minding his own business, and careful. He goes out, shuts the bathroom door, the radio stops, Hench and the girl go out to eat. Just happens that way."

"How do you know the radio stopped?"

"I was told," Breeze said calmly. "Other people live in that dump. Take it the radio stopped and they went out. Not quiet. The killer steps out of the apartment and Hench's door is open. That must be because otherwise he wouldn't think anything about Hench's door."

"People don't leave their doors open in apartment houses. Especially in districts like that."

"Drunks do. Drunks are careless. Their minds don't focus well. And they only think of one thing at a time. The door was open – just a little maybe, but open. The killer went in and ditched his gun on the bed and found another gun there. He took that away, just to make it look worse for Hench."

"You can check the gun," I said.

"Hench's gun? We'll try to, but Hench says he doesn't know the number. If we find it, we might do something there. I doubt it. The gun we have we will try to check, but you know how those things are. You get just so far along and you think it is going to open up for you, and then the trail dies out cold. A dead end. Anything else you can think of that we might know that might be a help to you in your business?"

"I'm getting tired," I said. "My imagination isn't working very well."

"You were doing fine a while back," Breeze said. "On the Cassidy case."

I didn't say anything. I filled my pipe up again but it was too hot to light. I laid it on the edge of the table to cool off.

"It's God's truth," Breeze said slowly, "that I don't know what to make of you. I can't see you deliberately covering up on any murder. And neither can I see you knowing as little about all this as you pretend to know."

I didn't say anything, again.

Breeze leaned over to revolve his cigar butt in the tray until he had killed the fire. He finished his drink, put on his hat and stood up.

"How long you expect to stay dummied up?" he asked.

"I don't know."

"Let me help you out. I give you till tomorrow noon, a little better than twelve hours. I won't get my post mortem report before that anyway. I give you till then to talk things over with your party and decide to come clean."

"And after that?"

"After that I see the Captain of Detectives and tell him a private eye named Philip Marlowe is withholding information which I need in a murder investigation, or I'm pretty sure he is. And what about it? I figure he'll pull you in fast enough to singe your breeches."

I said: "Uh-huh. Did you go through Phillips' desk?"

"Sure. A very neat young feller. Nothing in it at all, except a little kind of diary. Nothing in that either, except about how he went to the beach or took some girl to the pictures and she didn't warm up much. Or how he sat in the office and no business come in. One time he got a little sore about his laundry and wrote a whole page. Mostly it was just three or four lines. There was only one thing about it. It was all done in a kind of printing."

I said: "Printing?"

"Yeah, printing in pen and ink. Not big block caps like people trying to disguise things. Just neat fast little printing as if the guy could write that way as fast and easy as any way."

"He didn't write like that on the card he gave me," I said.

Breeze thought about that for a moment. Then he nodded. "True. Maybe it was this way. There wasn't any name in the diary either, in the front. Maybe the printing was just a little game he played with himself."

545

"Like Pepys' shorthand," I said.

"What was that?"

"A diary a man wrote in a private shorthand, a long time ago."

Breeze looked at Spangler, who was standing up in front of his chair, tipping the last few drops of his glass.

"We better beat it," Breeze said. "This guy is warming up for another Cassidy case."

Spangler put his glass down and they both went over to the door. Breeze shuffled a foot and looked at me sideways, with his hand on the doorknob.

"You know any tall blondes?"

"I have to think," I said. "I hope so. How tall?"

"Just tall. I don't know how tall that is. Except that it would be tall to a guy who is tall himself. A wop named Palermo owns that apartment house on Court Street. We went across to see him in his funeral parlors. He owns them too. He says he saw a tall blonde come out of the apartment house about three-thirty. The manager, Passmore, don't place anybody in the joint that he would call a tall blonde. The wop says she was a looker. I give some weight to what he says because he gave us a good description of you. He didn't see this tall blonde go in, just saw her come out. She was wearing slacks and a sports jacket and a wrap-around. But she had light blonde hair and plenty of it under the wrap-around."

"Nothing comes to me," I said. "But I just remembered something else. I wrote the license number of Phillips' car down on the back of an envelope. That will give you his former address, probably. I'll get it."

They stood there while I went to get it out of my coat in the bedroom. I handed the piece of envelope to Breeze and he read what was on it and tucked it into his billfold.

"So you just thought of this, huh?"

"That's right."

"Well, well," he said. "Well, well."

The two of them went along the hallway towards the elevator, shaking their heads.

I shut the door and went back to my almost untasted second drink. It was flat. I carried it to the kitchen and hardened it up from the bottle and stood there holding it and looking out of the window at the eucalyptus trees tossing their limber tops against the bluish dark sky. The wind seemed to have risen again. It thumped at the north window and there was a heavy slow pounding noise on the wall of the building, like a thick wire banging the stucco between insulators.

I tasted my drink and wished I hadn't wasted the fresh whiskey on it. I poured it down the sink and got a fresh glass and drank some ice water.

Twelve hours to tie up a situation which I didn't even begin to understand. Either that or turn up a client and let the cops go to work on her and her whole family. Hire Marlowe and get your house full of law. Why worry? Why be doubtful and confused? Why be gnawed by suspicion? Consult cock-eyed, careless, clubfooted, dissipated investigator. Philip Marlowe, Glenview 7537. See me and you meet the best cops in town. Why despair? Why be lonely? Call Marlowe and watch the wagon come.

This didn't get me anywhere either. I went back to the living room and put a match to the pipe that had cooled off now on the edge of the chess table. I drew the smoke in slowly, but it still tasted like the smell of hot rubber. I put it away and stood in the middle of the floor pulling my lower lip out and letting it snap back against my teeth.

The telephone rang. I picked it up and growled into it.

"Marlowe?"

The voice was a harsh low whisper. It was a harsh low whisper I had heard before.

"All right," I said. "Talk it up whoever you are. Whose pocket have I got my hand in now?"

"Maybe you're a smart guy," the harsh whisper said. "Maybe you would like to do yourself some good."

"How much good?"

"Say about five C's worth of good."

"That's grand," I said. "Doing what?"

"Keeping your nose clean," the voice said. "Want to talk about it?"

"Where, when, and who to?"

"Idle Valley Club. Morny. Any time you get here."

"Who are you?"

A dim chuckle came over the wire. "Just ask at the gate for Eddie Prue."

The phone clicked dead. I hung it up.

It was near eleven-thirty when I backed my car out of the garage and drove towards Cahuenga Pass.

17

ABOUT TWENTY MILES north of the pass a wide boulevard with flowering moss in the parkways turned towards the foothills. It ran for five blocks and died – without a house in its entire length. From its end a curving asphalt road dove into the hills. This was Idle Valley.

Around the shoulder of the first hill there was a low white building with a tiled roof beside the road. It had a roofed porch and a floodlighted sign on it read: *Idle Valley Patrol*. Open gates were folded back on the shoulders of the road, in the middle of which a square white sign standing on its point said STOP in letters sprinkled with reflector buttons. Another floodlight blistered the space of road in front of the sign.

I stopped. A uniformed man with a star and a strapped-on gun in a woven leather holster looked at my car, then at a board on a post.

He came over to the car. "Good evening. I don't have your car. This is a private road. Visiting?"

"Going to the club."

"Which one?"

"Idle Valley Club."

"Eighty-seven Seventy-seven. That's what we call it here. You mean Mr. Morny's place?"

"Right."

"You're not a member, I guess."

"No."

"I have to check you in. To somebody who is a member or to somebody who lives in the valley. All private property here, you know."

"No gate crashers, huh?"

He smiled. "No gate crashers."

"The name is Philip Marlowe," I said. "Calling on Eddie Prue."

"Prue?"

"He's Mr. Morny's secretary. Or something."

"Just a minute, please."

He went to the door of the building, and spoke. Another uniformed man inside, plugged in on a PBX. A car came up behind me and honked. The clack of a typewriter came from the open door of the patrol office. The man who had spoken to me looked at the honking car and waved it in. It slid around me and scooted off into the dark, a green long open convertible sedan with three dizzy-looking dames in the front seat, all cigarettes and arched eyebrows and go-to-hell expressions. The car flashed around a curve and was gone.

The uniformed man came back to me and put a hand on the car door. "Okay, Mr. Marlowe. Check with the officer at the club, please. A mile ahead on your right. There's a lighted parking lot and the number on the wall. Just the number. Eighty-seven Seventy-seven. Check with the officer there, please."

I said: "Why would I do that?"

He was very calm, very polite, and very firm. "We have to

know exactly where you go. There's a great deal to protect in Idle Valley."

"Suppose I don't check with him?"

"You kidding me?" His voice hardened.

"No. I just wanted to know."

"A couple of cruisers would start looking for you."

"How many are you in the patrol?"

"Sorry," he said. "About a mile ahead on the right, Mr. Marlowe."

I looked at the gun strapped to his hip, the special badge pinned to his shirt. "And they call this a democracy," I said.

He looked behind him and then spat on the ground and put a hand on the sill of the car door. "Maybe you got company," he said. "I knew a fellow belonged to the John Reed Club. Over in Boyle Heights, it was."

"Tovarich," I said.

"The trouble with revolutions," he said, "is that they get in the hands of the wrong people."

"Check," I said.

"On the other hand," he said, "could they be any wronger than the bunch of rich phonies that live around here?"

"Maybe you'll be living in here yourself someday," I said.

He spat again. "I wouldn't live in here if they paid me fifty thousand a year and let me sleep in chiffon pajamas with a string of matched pink pearls around my neck."

"I'd hate to make you the offer," I said.

"You make me the offer any time," he said. "Day or night. Just make me the offer and see what it gets you."

"Well, I'll run along now and check with the officer of the club," I said.

"Tell him to go spit up his left pants leg," he said. "Tell him I said so."

"I'll do that," I said.

A car came up behind and honked. I drove on. Half a block

of dark limousine blew me off the road with its horn and went past me making a noise like dead leaves falling.

The wind was quiet out here and the valley moonlight was so sharp that the black shadows looked as if they had been cut with an engraving tool.

Around the curve the whole valley spread out before me. A thousand white houses built up and down the hills, ten thousand lighted windows and the stars hanging down over them politely, not getting too close, on account of the patrol.

The wall of the club building that faced the road was white and blank, with no entrance door, no windows on the lower floor. The number was small but bright in violet-colored neon. 8777. Nothing else. To the side, under rows of hooded, downward-shining lights, were even rows of cars, set out in the white lined slots on the smooth black asphalt. Attendants in crisp clean uniforms moved in the lights.

The road went around to the back. A deep concrete porch there, with an overhanging canopy of glass and chromium, but very dim lights. I got out of the car and received a check with the license number on it, carried it over to a small desk where a uniformed man sat and dumped it in front of him.

"Philip Marlowe," I said. "Visitor."

"Thank you, Mr. Marlowe." He wrote the name and number down, handed me back my check and picked up a telephone.

A Negro in a white linen double breasted guards uniform, gold epaulettes, a cap with a broad gold band, opened the door for me.

The lobby looked like a high-budget musical. A lot of light and glitter, a lot of scenery, a lot of clothes, a lot of sound, an all-star cast, and a plot with all the originality and drive of a split fingernail. Under the beautiful soft indirect lighting the walls seemed to go up forever and to be lost in soft lascivious stars that really twinkled. You could just manage to walk on the carpet without waders. At the back was a free-arched stairway with a chromium and white enamel gangway going up in wide shallow carpeted steps. At the entrance to the dining room a chubby captain of waiters stood negligently with a two-inch satin stripe on his pants and a bunch of gold-plated menus under his arm. He had the sort of face that can turn from a polite simper to cold-blooded fury almost without moving a muscle.

The bar entrance was to the left. It was dusky and quiet and a bartender moved mothlike against the faint glitter of piled glassware. A tall handsome blonde in a dress that looked like seawater sifted over with gold dust came out of the Ladies' Room touching up her lips and turned toward the arch, humming.

The sound of rhumba music came through the archway and she nodded her gold head in time to it, smiling. A short fat man with a red face and glittering eyes waited for her with a white wrap over his arm. He dug his thick fingers into her bare arm and leered up at her.

A check girl in peach-bloom Chinese pajamas came over to take my hat and disapprove of my clothes. She had eyes like strange sins.

A cigarette girl came down the gangway. She wore an egret plume in her hair, enough clothes to hide behind a toothpick, one of her long beautiful naked legs was silver, and one was gold. She had the utterly disdainful expression of a dame who makes her dates by long distance.

I went into the bar and sank into a leather bar seat packed with down. Glasses tinkled gently, lights glowed softly, there were quiet voices whispering of love, or ten per cent, or whatever they whisper about in a place like that.

A tall fine-looking man in a gray suit cut by an angel suddenly stood up from a small table by the wall and walked over to the bar and started to curse one of the barmen. He cursed him in a loud clear voice for a long minute, calling him about nine names that are not usually mentioned by tall fine-looking men in well cut gray suits. Everybody stopped talking and looked at him quietly. His voice cut through the muted rhumba music like a shovel through snow.

The barman stood perfectly still, looking at the man. The barman had curly hair and a clear warm skin and wide-set careful eyes. He didn't move or speak. The tall man stopped talking and stalked out of the bar. Everybody watched him out except the barman.

The barman moved slowly along the bar to the end where I sat and stood looking away from me, with nothing in his face but pallor. Then he turned to me and said:

"Yes, sir?"

"I want to talk to a fellow named Eddie Prue."

"So?"

"He works here," I said.

"Works here doing what?" His voice was perfectly level and as dry as dry sand.

"I understand he's the guy that walks behind the boss. If you know what I mean."

"Oh. Eddie Prue." He moved one lip slowly over the other and made small tight circles on the bar with his bar cloth. "Your name?"

"Marlowe."

"Marlowe. Drink while waiting?"

"A dry martini will do."

"A martini. Dry. Veddy, veddy dry."

"Okay."

"Will you eat it with a spoon or a knife and fork?"

"Cut it in strips," I said. "I'll just nibble it."

"On your way to school," he said. "Should I put the olive in a bag for you?"

"Sock me on the nose with it," I said. "If it will make you feel any better."

"Thank you, sir," he said. "A dry martini."

He took three steps away from me and then came back and leaned across the bar and said: "I made a mistake in a drink. The gentleman was telling me about it."

"I heard him."

"He was telling me about it as gentlemen tell you about things like that. As big shot directors like to point out to you your little errors. And you heard him."

"Yeah," I said, wondering how long this was going to go on.

"He made himself heard – the gentleman did. So I come over here and practically insult you."

"I got the idea," I said.

He held up one of his fingers and looked at it thoughtfully.

"Just like that," he said. "A perfect stranger."

"It's my big brown eyes," I said. "They have that gentle look."

"Thanks, chum," he said, and quietly went away.

I saw him talking into a phone at the end of the bar. Then I saw him working with a shaker. When he came back with the drink he was all right again.

18

I CARRIED THE drink over to a small table against the wall and sat down there and lit a cigarette. Five minutes went by. The music that was coming through the fret had changed in tempo without my noticing it. A girl was singing. She had a rich deep down around the ankles contralto that was pleasant to listen to. She was singing Dark Eyes and the band behind her seemed to be falling asleep.

There was a heavy round of applause and some whistling when she ended.

A man at the next table said to his girl: "They got Linda Conquest back with the band. I heard she got married to some rich guy in Pasadena, but it didn't take."

The girl said: "Nice voice. If you like female crooners."

I started to get up but a shadow fell across my table and a man was standing there.

A great long gallows of a man with a ravaged face and a haggard frozen right eye that had a clotted iris and the steady look of blindness. He was so tall that he had to stoop to put his hand on the back of the chair across the table from me. He stood there sizing me up without saying anything and I sat there sipping the last of my drink and listening to the contralto voice singing another song. The customers seemed to like corny music in there. Perhaps they were all tired out trying to be ahead of the minute in the place where they worked.

"I'm Prue," the man said in his harsh whisper.

"So I gathered. You want to talk to me, I want to talk to you, and I want to talk to the girl that just sang."

"Let's go."

There was a locked door at the back end of the bar. Prue unlocked it and held it for me and we went through that and up a flight of carpeted steps to the left. A long straight hallway with several closed doors. At the end of it a bright star cross-wired by the mesh of a screen. Prue knocked on a door near the screen and opened it and stood aside for me to pass him.

It was a cozy sort of office, not too large. There was a built-in upholstered corner seat by the french windows and a man in a white dinner jacket was standing with his back to the room, looking out. He had gray hair. There was a large black and chromium safe, some filing cases, a large globe in a stand, a small built-in bar, and the usual broad heavy executive desk with the usual high-backed padded leather chair behind it.

I looked at the ornaments on the desk. Everything standard and all copper. A copper lamp, pen set and pencil tray, a glass and copper ashtray with a copper elephant on the rim, a copper letter opener, a copper thermos bottle on a copper tray, copper corners on the blotter holder. There was a spray of almost copper-colored sweet peas in a copper vase.

It seemed like a lot of copper.

The man at the window turned around and showed me that he was going on fifty and had soft ash gray hair and plenty of it, and a heavy handsome face with nothing unusual about it except a short puckered scar in his left cheek that had almost the effect of a deep dimple. I remembered the dimple. I would have forgotten the man. I remembered that I had seen him in pictures a long time ago, at least ten years ago. I didn't remember the pictures or what they were about or what he did in them, but I remembered the dark heavy handsome face and the puckered scar. His hair had been dark then.

He walked over to his desk and sat down and picked up his letter opener and poked at the ball of his thumb with the point. He looked at me with no expression and said: "You're Marlowe?"

I nodded.

"Sit down." I sat down. Eddie Prue sat in a chair against the wall and tilted the front legs off the floor.

"I don't like peepers," Morny said.

I shrugged.

"I don't like them for a lot of reasons," he said. "I don't like them in any way or at any time. I don't like them when they bother my friends. I don't like them when they bust in on my wife."

I didn't say anything.

"I don't like them when they question my driver or when they get tough with my guests," he said.

I didn't say anything.

"In short," he said. "I just don't like them."

"I'm beginning to get what you mean," I said.

He flushed and his eyes glittered. "On the other hand," he said, "just at the moment I might have a use for you. It might pay you to play ball with me. It might be a good idea. It might pay you to keep your nose clean."

"How much might it pay me?" I asked.

"It might pay you in time and health."

"I seem to have heard this record somewhere," I said. "I just can't put a name to it."

He laid the letter opener down and swung open a door in the desk and got a cut glass decanter out. He poured liquid out of it in a glass and drank it and put the stopper back in the decanter and put the decanter back in the desk.

"In my business," he said, "tough boys come a dime a dozen. And would-be tough boys come a nickel a gross. Just mind your business and I'll mind my business and we won't have any trouble." He lit a cigarette. His hand shook a little.

I looked across the room at the tall man sitting tilted against the wall, like a loafer in a country store. He just sat there without motion, his long arms hanging, his lined gray face full of nothing.

"Somebody said something about some money," I said to Morny. "What's that for? I know what the bawling out is for. That's you trying to make yourself think you can scare me."

"Talk like that to me," Morny said, "and you are liable to be wearing lead buttons on your vest."

"Just think," I said. "Poor old Marlowe with lead buttons on his vest."

Eddie Prue made a dry sound in his throat that might have been a chuckle.

"And as for me minding my own business and not minding yours," I said, "it might be that my business and your business would get a little mixed up together. Through no fault of mine."

"It better not," Morny said. "In what way?" He lifted his eyes quickly and dropped them again.

"Well, for instance, your hard boy here calling me up on the phone and trying to scare me to death. And later in the evening calling me up and talking about five C's and how it would do me some good to drive out here and talk to you. And for instance that same hard boy or somebody who looks just like him – which is a little unlikely – following around after a fellow in my business who happened to get shot this afternoon, on Court Street on Bunker Hill."

Morny lifted his cigarette away from his lips and narrowed his eyes to look at the tip. Every motion, every gesture, right out of the catalogue.

"Who got shot?"

"A fellow named Phillips, a youngish blond kid. You wouldn't like him. He was a peeper." I described Phillips to him.

"I never heard of him," Morny said.

"And also for instance, a tall blonde who didn't live there was seen coming out of the apartment house just after he was killed," I said.

"What tall blonde?" His voice had changed a little. There was urgency in it.

"I don't know that. She was seen and the man who saw her could identify her, if he saw her again. Of course she need not have anything to do with Phillips."

"This man Phillips was a shamus?"

I nodded. "I told you that twice."

"Why was he killed and how?"

"He was sapped and shot in his apartment. We don't know why he was killed. If we knew that, we would likely know who killed him. It seems to be that kind of a situation."

"Who is 'we'?"

"The police and myself. I found him dead. So I had to stick around."

Prue let the front legs of his chair down on the carpet very quietly and looked at me. His good eye had a sleepy expression I didn't like.

Morny said: "You told the cops what?"

I said: "Very little. I gather from your opening remarks to me here that you know I am looking for Linda Conquest. Mrs. Leslie Murdock. I've found her. She's singing here.

I don't know why there should have been any secret about it. It seems to me that your wife or Mr. Vannier might have told me. But they didn't."

"What my wife would tell a peeper," Morny said, "you could put in a gnat's eye."

"No doubt she has her reasons," I said. "However that's not very important now. In fact it's not very important that I see Miss Conquest. Just the same I'd like to talk to her a little. If you don't mind."

"Suppose I mind," Morny said.

"I guess I would like to talk to her anyway," I said. I got a cigarette out of my pocket and rolled it around in my fingers and admired his thick and still-dark eyebrows. They had a fine shape, an elegant curve.

Prue chuckled. Morny looked at him and frowned and looked back at me, keeping the frown on his face.

"I asked you what you told the cops," he said.

"I told them as little as I could. This man Phillips asked me to come and see him. He implied he was too deep in a job he didn't like and needed help. When I got there he was dead. I told the police that. They didn't think it was quite the whole story. It probably isn't. I have until tomorrow noon to fill it out. So I'm trying to fill it out."

"You wasted your time coming here," Morny said.

"I got the idea that I was asked to come here."

"You can go to hell back any time you want to," Morny said. "Or you can do a little job for me – for five hundred dollars. Either way you leave Eddie and me out of any conversations you might have with the police."

"What's the nature of the job?"

"You were at my house this morning. You ought to have an idea."

"I don't do divorce business," I said.

His face turned white. "I love my wife," he said. "We've only been married eight months. I don't want any divorce.

559

She's a swell girl and she knows what time it is, as a rule. But I think she's playing with a wrong number at the moment."

"Wrong in what way?"

"I don't know. That's what I want found out."

"Let me get this straight," I said. "Are you hiring me on a job — or off a job I already have?"

Prue chuckled again against the wall.

Morny poured himself some more brandy and tossed it quickly down his throat. Color came back into his face. He didn't answer me.

"And let me get another thing straight," I said. "You don't mind your wife playing around, but you don't want her playing with somebody named Vannier. Is that it?"

"I trust her heart," he said slowly. "But I don't trust her judgment. Put it that way."

"And you want me to get something on this man Vannier?"

"I want to find out what he is up to."

"Oh. Is he up to something?"

"I think he is. I don't know what."

"You think he is — or you want to think he is?"

He stared at me levelly for a moment, then he pulled the middle drawer of his desk out, reached in and tossed a folded paper across to me. I picked it up and unfolded it. It was a carbon copy of a gray billhead. *Cal-Western Dental Supply Company*, and an address. The bill was for *30 lbs. Kerr's Crystobolite $15.75*, and *25 lbs. White's Albastone, $7.75*, plus tax. It was made out to *H. R. Teager, Will Call*, and stamped *Paid* with a rubber stamp. It was signed for in the corner: *L. G. Vannier*.

I put it down on the desk.

"That fell out of his pocket one night when he was here," Morny said. "About ten days ago. Eddie put one of his big feet on it and Vannier didn't notice he had dropped it."

I looked at Prue, then at Morny, then at my thumb. "Is this supposed to mean something to me?"

"I thought you were a smart detective. I figured you could find out."

I looked at the paper again, folded it and put it in my pocket. "I'm assuming you wouldn't give it to me unless it meant something," I said.

Morny went to the black and chromium safe against the wall and opened it. He came back with five new bills spread out in his fingers like a poker hand. He smoothed them edge to edge, riffled them lightly, and tossed them on the desk in front of me.

"There's your five C's," he said. "Take Vannier out of my wife's life and there will be the same again for you. I don't care how you do it and I don't want to know anything about how you do it. Just do it."

I poked at the crisp new bills with a hungry finger. Then I pushed them away. "You can pay me when – and if – I deliver," I said. "I'll take my payment tonight in a short interview with Miss Conquest."

Morny didn't touch the money. He lifted the square bottle and poured himself another drink. This time he poured one for me and pushed it across the desk.

"And as for this Phillips murder," I said, "Eddie here was following Phillips a little. You want to tell me why?"

"No."

"The trouble with a case like this is that the information might come from somebody else. When a murder gets into the papers you never know what will come out. If it does, you'll blame me."

He looked at me steadily and said: "I don't think so. I was a bit rough when you came in, but you shape up pretty good. I'll take a chance."

"Thanks," I said. "Would you mind telling me why you had Eddie call me up and give me the shakes?"

He looked down and tapped on the desk. "Linda's an old friend of mine. Young Murdock was out here this afternoon to see her. He told her you were working for old lady Murdock. She told me. I didn't know what the job was. You say you don't take divorce business, so it couldn't be that the old lady hired you to fix anything like that up." He raised his eyes on the last words and stared at me.

I stared back at him and waited.

"I guess I'm just a fellow who likes his friends," he said. "And doesn't want them bothered by dicks."

"Murdock owes you some money, doesn't he?"

He frowned. "I don't discuss things like that."

He finished his drink, nodded and stood up. "I'll send Linda up to talk to you. Pick your money up."

He went to the door and out. Eddie Prue unwound his long body and stood up and gave me a dim gray smile that meant nothing and wandered off after Morny.

I lit another cigarette and looked at the dental supply company's bill again. Something squirmed at the back of my mind, dimly. I walked to the window and stood looking out across the valley. A car was winding up a hill towards a big house with a tower that was half glass brick with light behind it. The headlights of the car moved across it and turned in toward a garage. The lights went out and the valley seemed darker.

It was very quiet and quite cool now. The dance band seemed to be somewhere under my feet. It was muffled, and the tune was indistinguishable.

Linda Conquest came in through the open door behind me and shut it and stood looking at me with a cold light in her eyes.

19

SHE LOOKED LIKE her photo and not like it. She had the wide cool mouth, the short nose, the wide cool eyes, the dark hair parted in the middle and the broad white line between the parting. She was wearing a white coat over her dress, with the collar turned up. She had her hands in the pockets of the coat and a cigarette in her mouth.

She looked older, her eyes were harder, and her lips seemed to have forgotten to smile. They would smile when she was singing, in that staged artificial smile. But in repose they were thin and tight and angry.

She moved over to the desk and stood looking down, as if counting the copper ornaments. She saw the cut glass decanter, took the stopper out, poured herself a drink and tossed it down with a quick flip of the wrist.

"You're a man named Marlowe?" she asked, looking at me. She put her hips against the end of the desk and crossed her ankles.

I said I was a man named Marlowe.

"By and large," she said, "I am quite sure I am not going to like you one damned little bit. So speak your piece and drift away."

"What I like about this place is everything runs so true to type," I said. "The cop on the gate, the shine on the door, the cigarette and check girls, the fat greasy sensual Jew with the tall stately bored showgirl, the well-dressed, drunk and horribly rude director cursing the barman, the silent guy with the gun, the night club owner with the soft gray hair and the B-picture mannerisms, and now you – the tall dark torcher with the negligent sneer, the husky voice, the hard-boiled vocabulary."

She said: "Is that so?" and fitted her cigarette between her lips and drew slowly on it. "And what about the wisecracking snooper with the last year's gags and the come-hither smile?"

"And what gives me the right to talk to you at all?" I said.

"I'll bite. What does?"

"She wants it back. Quickly. It has to be fast or there will be trouble."

"I thought −" she started to say and stopped cold. I watched her remove the sudden trace of interest from her face by monkeying with her cigarette and bending her face over it. "She wants what back, Mr. Marlowe?"

"The Brasher Doubloon."

She looked up at me and nodded, remembering − letting me see her remembering.

"Oh, the Brasher Doubloon."

"I bet you completely forgot it," I said.

"Well, no. I've seen it a number of times," she said. "She wants it back, you said. Do you mean she thinks I took it?"

"Yeah. Just that."

"She's a dirty old liar," Linda Conquest said.

"What you think doesn't make you a liar," I said. "It only sometimes makes you mistaken. Is she wrong?"

"Why would I take her silly old coin?"

"Well − it's worth a lot of money. She thinks you might need money. I gather she was not too generous."

She laughed, a tight sneering little laugh. "No," she said. "Mrs. Elizabeth Bright Murdock would not rate as very generous."

"Maybe you just took it for spite, kind of," I said hopefully.

"Maybe I ought to slap your face." She killed her cigarette in Morny's copper goldfish bowl, speared the crushed stub absently with the letter opener and dropped it into the wastebasket.

"Passing on from that to perhaps more important matters," I said, "will you give him a divorce?"

"For twenty-five grand," she said, not looking at me, "I should be glad to."

"You're not in love with the guy, huh?"

"You're breaking my heart, Marlowe."

"He's in love with you," I said. "After all you did marry him."

She looked at me lazily. "Mister, don't think I didn't pay for that mistake." She lit another cigarette. "But a girl has to live. And it isn't always as easy as it looks. And so a girl can make a mistake, marry the wrong guy and the wrong family, looking for something that isn't there. Security, or whatever."

"But not needing any love to do it," I said.

"I don't want to be too cynical, Marlowe. But you'd be surprised how many girls marry to find a home, especially girls whose arm muscles are all tired out fighting off the kind of optimists that come into these gin and glitter joints."

"You had a home and you gave it up."

"It got to be too dear. That port-sodden old fake made the bargain too tough. How do you like her for a client?"

"I've had worse."

She picked a shred of tobacco off her lip. "You notice what she's doing to that girl?"

"Merle? I noticed she bullied her."

"It isn't just that. She has her cutting out dolls. The girl had a shock of some kind and the old brute has used the effect of it to dominate the girl completely. In company she yells at her but in private she's apt to be stroking her hair and whispering in her ear. And the kid sort of shivers."

"I didn't quite get all that," I said.

"The kid's in love with Leslie, but she doesn't know it. Emotionally she's about ten years old. Something funny is going to happen in that family one of these days. I'm glad I won't be there."

I said: "You're a smart girl, Linda. And you're tough and you're wise. I suppose when you married him you thought you could get your hands on plenty."

She curled her lip. "I thought it would at least be a vacation. It wasn't even that. That's a smart ruthless woman, Marlowe. Whatever she's got you doing, it's not what she says. She's up to something. Watch your step."

"Would she kill a couple of men?"

She laughed.

"No kidding," I said. "A couple of men have been killed and one of them at least is connected with rare coins."

"I don't get it," she looked at me levelly. "Murdered, you mean?"

I nodded.

"You tell Morny all that?"

"About one of them."

"You tell the cops?"

"About one of them. The same one."

She moved her eyes over my face. We stared at each other. She looked a little pale, or just tired. I thought she had grown a little paler than before.

"You're making that up," she said between her teeth.

I grinned and nodded. She seemed to relax then.

"About the Brasher Doubloon?" I said. "You didn't take it. Okay. About the divorce, what?"

"That's none of your affair."

"I agree. Well, thanks for talking to me. Do you know a fellow named Vannier?"

"Yes." Her face froze hard now. "Not well. He's a friend of Lois."

"A very good friend."

"One of these days he's apt to turn out to be a small quiet funeral too."

"Hints," I said, "have sort of been thrown in that direction. There's something about the guy. Every time his name comes up the party freezes."

She stared at me and said nothing. I thought that an idea was stirring at the back of her eyes, but if so it didn't come out. She said quietly:

"Morny will sure as hell kill him, if he doesn't lay off Lois."

"Go on with you. Lois flops at the drop of a hat. Anybody can see that."

"Perhaps Alex is the one person who can't see it."

"Vannier hasn't anything to do with my job anyway. He has no connection with the Murdocks."

She lifted a corner of her lip at me and said: "No? Let me tell you something. No reason why I should. I'm just a great big open-hearted kid. Vannier knows Elizabeth Bright Murdock and well. He never came to the house but once while I was there, but he called on the phone plenty of times. I caught some of the calls. He always asked for Merle."

"Well – that's funny," I said. "Merle, huh?"

She bent to crush out her cigarette and again she speared the stub and dropped it into the wastebasket.

"I'm very tired," she said suddenly. "Please go away."

I stood there for a moment, looking at her and wondering. Then I said: "Good night and thanks. Good luck."

I went out and left her standing there with her hands in the pockets of the white coat, her head bent and her eyes looking at the floor.

It was two o'clock when I got back to Hollywood and put the car away and went upstairs to my apartment. The wind was all gone but the air still had that dryness and lightness of the desert. The air in the apartment was dead and Breeze's cigar butt had made it a little worse than dead. I opened windows and flushed the place through while I undressed and stripped the pockets of my suit.

Out of them with other things came the dental supply company's bill. It still looked like a bill to one H. R. Teager for 30 lbs. of crystobolite and 25 lbs. of albastone.

I dragged the phone book up on the desk in the living room and looked up Teager. Then the confused memory clicked into place. His address was 422 West Ninth Street. The address of the Belfont Building was 422 West Ninth Street.

H. R. Teager Dental Laboratories had been one of the names on doors on the sixth floor of the Belfont Building when I did my backstairs crawl away from the office of Elisha Morningstar.

But even the Pinkertons have to sleep, and Marlowe needed far, far more sleep than the Pinkertons. I went to bed.

20

IT WAS JUST as hot in Pasadena as the day before and the big dark red brick house on Dresden Avenue looked just as cool and the little painted Negro waiting by the hitching block looked just as sad. The same butterfly landed on the same hydrangea bush – or it looked like the same one – the same heavy scent of summer lay on the morning, and the same middle-aged sourpuss with the frontier voice opened to my ring.

She led me along the same hallways to the same sunless sunroom. In it Mrs. Elizabeth Bright Murdock sat in the same reed chaise-longue and as I came into the room she was pouring herself a slug from what looked like the same port bottle but was more probably a grandchild.

The maid shut the door, I sat down and put my hat on the floor, just like yesterday, and Mrs. Murdock gave me the same hard level stare and said:

"Well?"

"Things are bad," I said. "The cops are after me."

She looked as flustered as a side of beef. "Indeed. I thought you were more competent than that."

I brushed it off. "When I left here yesterday morning a man followed me in a coupe. I don't know what he was doing here or how he got here. I suppose he followed me here, but I feel doubtful about that. I shook him off, but he turned up again in the hall outside my office. He followed me again, so I invited him to explain why and he said he knew who I was and he needed help and asked me to come to his apartment on Bunker Hill and talk to him. I went, after I had seen Mr. Morningstar, and found the man shot to death on the floor of his bathroom."

Mrs. Murdock sipped a little port. Her hand might have shaken a little, but the light in the room was too dim for me to be sure. She cleared her throat.

"Go on."

"His name is George Anson Phillips. A young, blond fellow, rather dumb. He claimed to be a private detective."

"I never heard of him," Mrs. Murdock said coldly. "I never saw him to my knowledge and I don't know anything about him. Did you think I employed him to follow you?"

"I didn't know what to think. He talked about pooling our resources and he gave me the impression that he was working for some member of your family. He didn't say so in so many words."

"He wasn't. You can be quite definite on that." The baritone voice was as steady as a rock.

"I don't think you know quite as much about your family as you think you do, Mrs. Murdock."

"I know you have been questioning my son – contrary to my orders," she said coldly.

"I didn't question him. He questioned me. Or tried to."

"We'll go into that later," she said harshly. "What about this man you found shot? You are involved with the police on account of him?"

"Naturally. They want to know why he followed me, what I was working on, why he spoke to me, why he asked me to come to his apartment and why I went. But that is only the half of it."

She finished her port and poured herself another glass.

"How's your asthma?" I asked.

"Bad," she said. "Get on with your story."

"I saw Morningstar. I told you about that over the phone. He pretended not to have the Brasher Doubloon, but admitted it had been offered to him and said he could get it. As I told you. Then you told me it had been returned to you, so that was that."

I waited, thinking she would tell me some story about how the coin had been returned, but she just stared at me bleakly over the wine glass.

"So, as I had made a sort of arrangement with Mr. Morningstar to pay him a thousand dollars for the coin –"

"You had no authority to do anything like that," she barked.

I nodded, agreeing with her.

"Maybe I was kidding him a little," I said. "And I know I was kidding myself. Anyway after what you told me over the phone I tried to get in touch with him to tell him the deal was off. He's not in the phone book except at his office. I went to his office. This was quite late. The elevator man said he was still in his office. He was lying on his back on the floor, dead. Killed by a blow on the head and shock, apparently. Old men die easily. The blow might not have been intended to kill him. I called the Receiving Hospital, but didn't give my name."

"That was wise of you," she said.

"Was it? It was considerate of me, but I don't think I'd call it wise. I want to be nice, Mrs. Murdock. You understand that in your rough way, I hope. But two murders happened in a matter of hours and both the bodies were found by me. And both the victims were connected – in some manner – with your Brasher Doubloon."

"I don't understand. This other, younger man also?"

"Yes. Didn't I tell you over the phone? I thought I did." I wrinkled my brow, thinking back. I knew I had.

She said calmly: "It's possible. I wasn't paying a great deal of attention to what you said. You see, the doubloon had already been returned. And you sounded a little drunk."

"I wasn't drunk. I might have felt a little shock, but I wasn't drunk. You take all this very calmly."

"What do you want me to do?"

I took a deep breath. "I'm connected with one murder already, by having found the body and reported it. I may presently be connected with another, by having found the body and not reported it. Which is much more serious for me.

Even as far as it goes, I have until noon today to disclose the name of my client."

"That," she said, still much too calm for my taste, "would be a breach of confidence. You are not going to do that, I'm sure."

"I wish you'd leave that damn port alone and make some effort to understand the position," I snapped at her.

She looked vaguely surprised and pushed her glass away — about four inches away.

"This fellow Phillips," I said, "had a license as a private detective. How did I happen to find him dead? Because he followed me and I spoke to him and he asked me to come to his apartment. And when I got there he was dead. The police know all this. They may even believe it. But they don't believe the connection between Phillips and me is quite that much of a coincidence. They think there is a deeper connection between Phillips and me and they insist on knowing what I am doing, who I am working for. Is that clear?"

"You'll find a way out of all that," she said. "I expect it to cost me a little more money, of course."

I felt myself getting pinched around the nose. My mouth felt dry. I needed air. I took another deep breath and another dive into the tub of blubber that was sitting across the room from me on the reed chaise-longue, looking as unperturbed as a bank president refusing a loan.

"I'm working for you," I said, "now, this week, today. Next week I'll be working for somebody else, I hope. And the week after that for still somebody else. In order to do that I have to be on reasonably good terms with the police. They don't have to love me, but they have to be fairly sure I am not cheating on them. Assume Phillips knew nothing about the Brasher Doubloon. Assume, even, that he knew about it, but that his death had nothing to do with it. I still have to tell the cops what I know about him. And they have to question anybody they want to question. Can't you understand that?"

"Doesn't the law give you the right to protect a client?" she snapped. "If it doesn't, what is the use of anyone's hiring a detective?"

I got up and walked around my chair and sat down again. I leaned forward and took hold of my kneecaps and squeezed them until my knuckles glistened.

"The law, whatever it is, is a matter of give and take, Mrs. Murdock. Like most other things. Even if I had the legal right to stay clammed up – refuse to talk – and got away with it once, that would be the end of my business. I'd be a guy marked for trouble. One way or another they would get me. I value your business, Mrs. Murdock, but not enough to cut my throat for you and bleed in your lap."

She reached for her glass and emptied it.

"You seem to have made a nice mess of the whole thing," she said. "You didn't find my daughter-in-law and you didn't find my Brasher Doubloon. But you found a couple of dead men that I have nothing to do with and you have neatly arranged matters so that I must tell the police all my private and personal business in order to protect you from your own incompetence. That's what I see. If I am wrong, pray correct me."

She poured some more wine and gulped it too fast and went into a paroxysm of coughing. Her shaking hand slid the glass on to the table, slopping the wine. She threw herself forward in her seat and got purple in the face.

I jumped up and went over and landed one on her beefy back that would have shaken the City Hall.

She let out a long strangled wail and drew her breath in rackingly and stopped coughing. I pressed one of the keys on her dictaphone box and when somebody answered, metallic and loud, through the metal disk I said: "Bring Mrs. Murdock a glass of water, quick!" and then let the key up again.

I sat down again and watched her pull herself together. When her breath was coming evenly and without effort,

I said: "You're not tough. You just think you're tough. You been living too long with people that are scared of you. Wait'll you meet up with some law. Those boys are professionals. You're just a spoiled amateur."

The door opened and the maid came in with a pitcher of ice water and a glass. She put them down on the table and went out.

I poured Mrs. Murdock a glass of water and put it in her hand.

"Sip it, don't drink it. You won't like the taste of it, but it won't hurt you."

She sipped, then drank half of the glass, then put the glass down and wiped her lips.

"To think," she said raspingly, "that out of all the snoopers for hire I could have employed, I had to pick out a man who would bully me in my own home."

"That's not getting you anywhere either," I said. "We don't have a lot of time. What's our story to the police going to be?"

"The police mean nothing to me. Absolutely nothing. And if you give them my name, I shall regard it as a thoroughly disgusting breach of faith."

That put me back where we started.

"Murder changes everything, Mrs. Murdock. You can't dummy up on a murder case. We'll have to tell them why you employed me and what to do. They won't publish it in the papers, you know. That is, they won't if they believe it. They certainly won't believe you hired me to investigate Elisha Morningstar just because he called up and wanted to buy the doubloon. They may not find out that you couldn't have sold the coin, if you wanted to, because they might not think of that angle. But they won't believe you hired a private detective just to investigate a possible purchaser. Why should you?"

"That's my business, isn't it?"

"No. You can't fob the cops off that way. You have to satisfy them that you are being frank and open and have nothing to

573

hide. As long as they think you are hiding something they never let up. Give them a reasonable and plausible story and they go away cheerful. And the most reasonable and plausible story is always the truth. Any objection to telling it?"

"Every possible objection," she said. "But it doesn't seem to make much difference. Do we have to tell them that I suspected my daughter-in-law of stealing the coin and that I was wrong?"

"It would be better."

"And that it has been returned and how?"

"It would be better."

"That is going to humiliate me very much."

I shrugged.

"You're a callous brute," she said. "You're a cold-blooded fish. I don't like you. I deeply regret ever having met you."

"Mutual," I said.

She reached a thick finger to a key and barked into the talking box. "Merle. Ask my son to come in here at once. And I think you may as well come in with him."

She released the key, pressed her broad fingers together and let her hands drop heavily to her thighs. Her bleak eyes went up to the ceiling.

Her voice was quiet and sad saying: "My son took the coin, Mr. Marlowe. My son. My own son."

I didn't say anything. We sat there glaring at each other. In a couple of minutes they both came in and she barked at them to sit down.

21

LESLIE MURDOCK WAS wearing a greenish slack suit and his hair looked damp, as if he had just been taking a shower. He sat hunched forward, looking at the white buck shoes on his feet, and turning a ring on his finger. He didn't have his long black cigarette holder and he looked a little lonely without it.

574

Even his mustache seemed to droop a little more than it had in my office.

Merle Davis looked just the same as the day before. Probably she always looked the same. Her copper blond hair was dragged down just as tight, her shell-rimmed glasses looked just as large and empty, her eyes behind them just as vague. She was even wearing the same one-piece linen dress with short sleeves and no ornament of any kind, not even earrings.

I had the curious feeling of reliving something that had already happened.

Mrs. Murdock sipped her port and said quietly:

"All right, son. Tell Mr. Marlowe about the doubloon. I'm afraid he has to be told."

Murdock looked up at me quickly and then dropped his eyes again. His mouth twitched. When he spoke his voice had the toneless quality, a flat tired sound, like a man making a confession after an exhausting battle with his conscience.

"As I told you yesterday in your office I owe Morny a lot of money. Twelve thousand dollars. I denied it afterwards, but it's true. I do owe it. I didn't want mother to know. He was pressing me pretty hard for payment. I suppose I knew I would have to tell her in the end, but I was weak enough to want to put it off. I took the doubloon, using her keys one afternoon when she was asleep and Merle was out. I gave it to Morny and he agreed to hold it as security because I explained to him that he couldn't get anything like twelve thousand dollars for it unless he could give its history and show that it was legitimately in his possession."

He stopped talking and looked up at me to see how I was taking it. Mrs. Murdock had her eyes on my face, practically puttied there. The little girl was looking at Murdock with her lips parted and an expression of suffering on her face.

Murdock went on. "Morny gave me a receipt, in which he agreed to hold the coin as collateral and not to convert it without notice and demand. Something like that. I don't profess to know how legal it was. When this man Morningstar called up and asked about the coin I immediately became suspicious that Morny either was trying to sell it or that he was at least thinking of selling it and was trying to get a valuation on it from somebody who knew about rare coins. I was badly scared."

He looked up and made a sort of face at me. Maybe it was the face of somebody being badly scared. Then he took his handkerchief out and wiped his forehead and sat holding it between his hands.

"When Merle told me mother had employed a detective – Merle ought not to have told me, but mother has promised not to scold her for it –" He looked at his mother. The old warhorse clamped her jaws and looked grim. The little girl had her eyes still on his face and didn't seem to be very worried about the scolding. He went on: "– then I was sure she had missed the doubloon and had hired you on that account. I didn't really believe she had hired you to find Linda. I knew where Linda was all the time. I went to your office to see what I could find out. I didn't find out very much. I went to see Morny yesterday afternoon and told him about it. At first he laughed in my face, but when I told him that even my mother couldn't sell the coin without violating the terms of Jasper Murdock's will and that she would certainly set the police on him when I told her where the coin was, then he loosened up. He got up and went to the safe and got the coin out and handed it to me without a word. I gave him back his receipt and he tore it up. So I brought the coin home and told mother about it."

He stopped talking and wiped his face again. The little girl's eyes moved up and down with the motions of his hand.

In the silence that followed I said: "Did Morny threaten you?"

He shook his head. "He said he wanted his money and he needed it and I had better get busy and dig it up. But he wasn't threatening. He was very decent, really. In the circumstances."

"Where was this?"

"At the Idle Valley Club, in his private office."

"Was Eddie Prue there?"

The little girl tore her eyes away from his face and looked at me. Mrs. Murdock said thickly: "Who is Eddie Prue?"

"Morny's bodyguard," I said. "I didn't waste *all* my time yesterday, Mrs. Murdock." I looked at her son, waiting.

He said: "No, I didn't see him. I know him by sight, of course. You would only have to see him once to remember him. But he wasn't around yesterday."

I said: "Is that all?"

He looked at his mother. She said harshly: "Isn't it enough?"

"Maybe," I said. "Where is the coin now?"

"Where would you expect it to be?" she snapped.

I almost told her, just to see her jump. But I managed to hold it in. I said: "That seems to take care of that, then."

Mrs. Murdock said heavily: "Kiss your mother, son, and run along."

He got up dutifully and went over and kissed her on the forehead. She patted his hand. He went out of the room with his head down and quietly shut the door. I said to Merle: "I think you had better have him dictate that to you just the way he told it and make a copy of it and get him to sign it."

She looked startled. The old woman snarled:

"She certainly won't do anything of the sort. Go back to your work, Merle. I wanted you to hear this. But if I ever again catch you violating my confidence, you know what will happen."

The little girl stood up and smiled at her with shining eyes. "Oh yes, Mrs. Murdock. I never will. Never. You can trust me."

"I hope so," the old dragon growled. "Get out."

Merle went out softly.

Two big tears formed themselves in Mrs. Murdock's eyes and slowly made their way down the elephant hide of her cheeks, reached the corners of her fleshy nose and slid down her lip. She scrabbled around for a handkerchief, wiped them off and then wiped her eyes. She put the handkerchief away, reached for her wine and said placidly:

"I'm very fond of my son, Mr. Marlowe. Very fond. This grieves me deeply. Do you think he will have to tell this story to the police?"

"I hope not," I said. "He'd have a hell of a time getting them to believe it."

Her mouth snapped open and her teeth glinted at me in the dim light. She closed her lips and pressed them tight, scowling at me with her head lowered.

"Just what do you mean by that?" she snapped.

"Just what I said. The story doesn't ring true. It has a fabricated, over-simple sound. Did he make it up himself or did you think it up and teach it to him?"

"Mr. Marlowe," she said in a deadly voice, "you are treading on very thin ice."

I waved a hand. "Aren't we all? All right, suppose it's true. Morny will deny it, and we'll be right back where we started. Morny will have to deny it, because otherwise it would tie him to a couple of murders."

"Is there anything so unlikely about that being the exact situation?" she blared.

"Why would Morny, a man with backing, protection and some influence, tie himself to a couple of small murders in order to avoid tying himself to something trifling, like selling a pledge? It doesn't make sense to me."

She stared, saying nothing. I grinned at her, because for the first time she was going to like something I said.

"I found your daughter-in-law, Mrs. Murdock. It's a little strange to me that your son, who seems so well under your control, didn't tell you where she was."

"I didn't ask him," she said in a curiously quiet voice, for her.

"She's back where she started, singing with the band at the Idle Valley Club. I talked to her. She's a pretty hard sort of girl in a way. She doesn't like you very well. I don't find it impossible to think that she took the coin all right, partly from spite. And I find it slightly less impossible to believe that Leslie knew it or found it out and cooked up that yarn to protect her. He says he's very much in love with her."

She smiled. It wasn't a beautiful smile, being on slightly the wrong kind of face. But it was a smile.

"Yes," she said gently. "Yes. Poor Leslie. He would do just that. And in that case —" she stopped and her smile widened until it was almost ecstatic, "in that case my dear daughter-in-law may be involved in murder."

I watched her enjoying the idea for a quarter of a minute. "And you'd just love that," I said.

She nodded, still smiling, getting the idea she liked before she got the rudeness in my voice. Then her face stiffened and her lips came together hard. Between them and her teeth she said:

"I don't like your tone. I don't like your tone at all."

"I don't blame you," I said. "I don't like it myself. I don't like anything. I don't like this house or you or the air of repression in the joint, or the squeezed down face of the little girl or that twerp of a son you have, or this case or the truth I'm not told about it and the lies I am told about it and —"

She started yelling then, noise out of a splotched furious face, eyes tossing with fury, sharp with hate:

"Get out! Get out of this house at once! Don't delay one instant! Get out!"

I stood up and reached my hat off the carpet and said: "I'll be glad to."

I gave her a sort of a tired leer and picked my way to the door and opened it and went out. I shut it quietly, holding the knob with a stiff hand and clicking the lock gently into place.

For no reason at all.

22

STEPS GIBBERED ALONG after me and my name was called and I kept on going until I was in the middle of the living room. Then I stopped and turned and let her catch up with me, out of breath, her eyes trying to pop through her glasses and her shining copper-blond hair catching funny little lights from the high windows.

"Mr. Marlowe? Please! Please don't go away. She wants you. She really does!"

"I'll be darned. You've got Sub-deb Bright on your mouth this morning. Looks all right too."

She grabbed my sleeve. "Please!"

"The hell with her," I said. "Tell her to jump in the lake. Marlowe can get sore too. Tell her to jump in two lakes, if one won't hold her. Not clever, but quick."

I looked down at the hand on my sleeve and patted it. She drew it away swiftly and her eyes looked shocked.

"Please, Mr. Marlowe. She's in trouble. She needs you."

"I'm in trouble too," I growled. "I'm up to my ear flaps in trouble. What are you crying about?"

"Oh, I'm really very fond of her. I know she's rough and blustery, but her heart is pure gold."

"To hell with her heart too," I said. "I don't expect to get intimate enough with her for that to make any difference. She's a fat-faced old liar. I've had enough of her. I think she's in trouble all right, but I'm not in the excavating business. I have to get told things."

"Oh, I'm sure if you would only be patient –"

I put my arm around her shoulders, without thinking. She jumped about three feet and her eyes blazed with panic.

We stood there staring at each other, making breath noises, me with my mouth open as it too frequently is, she with her lips pressed tight and her little pale nostrils quivering. Her face was as pale as the unhandy makeup would let it be.

"Look," I said slowly, "did something happen to you when you were a little girl?"

She nodded, very quickly.

"A man scared you or something like that?"

She nodded again. She took her lower lip between her little white teeth.

"And you've been like this ever since?"

She just stood there, looking white.

"Look," I said, "I won't do anything to you that will scare you. Not ever."

Her eyes melted with tears.

"If I touched you," I said, "it was just like touching a chair or a door. It didn't mean anything. Is that clear?"

"Yes." She got a word out at last. Panic still twitched in the depths of her eyes, behind the tears. "Yes."

"That takes care of me," I said. "I'm all adjusted. Nothing to worry about in me any more. Now take Leslie. He has his mind on other things. You know he's all right – in the way we mean. Right?"

"Oh, yes," she said. "Yes, indeed." Leslie was aces. With her. With me he was a handful of bird gravel.

"Now take the old wine barrel," I said. "She's rough and she's tough and she thinks she can eat walls and spit bricks, and she bawls you out, but she's fundamentally decent to you, isn't she?"

"Oh, she is, Mr. Marlowe. I was trying to tell you –"

"Sure. Now why don't you get over it? Is he still around – this other one that hurt you?"

She put her hand to her mouth and gnawed the fleshy part at the base of the thumb, looking at me over it, as if it was a balcony.

"He's dead," she said. "He fell out of a – out of a – a window."

I stopped her with my big right hand. "Oh, that guy. I heard about him. Forget it, can't you?"

"No," she said, shaking her head seriously behind the hand. "I can't. I can't seem to forget it at all. Mrs. Murdock is always telling me to forget it. She talks to me for the longest times telling me to forget it. But I just can't."

"It would be a darn sight better," I snarled, "if she would keep her fat mouth shut about it for the longest times. She just keeps it alive."

She looked surprised and rather hurt at that. "Oh, that isn't all," she said. "I was his secretary. She was his wife. He was her first husband. Naturally she doesn't forget it either. How could she?"

I scratched my ear. That seemed sort of non-committal. There was nothing much in her expression now except that I didn't really think she realized that I was there. I was a voice coming out of somewhere, but rather impersonal. Almost a voice in her own head.

Then I had one of my funny and often unreliable hunches. "Look," I said, "is there someone you meet that has that effect on you? Some one person more than another?"

She looked all around the room. I looked with her. Nobody was under a chair or peeking at us through a door or a window.

"Why do I have to tell you?" she breathed.

"You don't. It's just how you feel about it."

"Will you promise not to tell anybody — anybody in the whole world, not even Mrs. Murdock?"

"Her last of all," I said. "I promise."

She opened her mouth and put a funny little confiding smile on her face, and then it went wrong. Her throat froze up. She made a croaking noise. Her teeth actually rattled.

I wanted to give her a good hard squeeze but I was afraid to touch her. We stood. Nothing happened. We stood. I was about as much use as a hummingbird's spare egg would have been.

Then she turned and ran. I heard her steps going along the hall. I heard a door close.

I went after her along the hall and reached the door. She was sobbing behind it. I stood there and listened to the sobbing.

There was nothing I could do about it. I wondered if there was anything anybody could do about it.

I went back to the glass porch and knocked on the door and opened it and put my head in. Mrs. Murdock sat just as I had left her. She didn't seem to have moved at all.

"Who's scaring the life out of that little girl?" I asked her.

"Get out of my house," she said between her fat lips.

I didn't move. Then she laughed at me hoarsely.

"Do you regard yourself as a clever man, Mr. Marlowe?"

"Well, I'm not dripping with it," I said.

"Suppose you find out for yourself."

"At your expense?"

She shrugged her heavy shoulders. "Possibly. It depends. Who knows?"

"You haven't bought a thing," I said. "I'm still going to have to talk to the police."

"I haven't bought anything," she said, "and I haven't paid for anything. Except the return of the coin. I'm satisfied to accept that for the money I have already given you. Now go away. You bore me. Unspeakably."

I shut the door and went back. No sobbing behind the door. Very still. I went on.

I let myself out of the house. I stood there, listening to the sunshine burn the grass. A car started up in back and a gray Mercury came drifting along the drive at the side of the house. Mr. Leslie Murdock was driving it. When he saw me he stopped.

He got out of the car and walked quickly over to me. He was nicely dressed; cream colored gabardine now, all fresh clothes, slacks, black and white shoes, with polished black toes, a sport coat of very small black and white check, black and white handkerchief, cream shirt, no tie. He had a pair of green sun glasses on his nose.

He stood close to me and said in a low timid sort of voice: "I guess you think I'm an awful heel."

"On account of that story you told about the doubloon?"

"Yes."

"That didn't affect my way of thinking about you in the least," I said.

"Well —"

"Just what do you want me to say?"

He moved his smoothly tailored shoulders in a deprecatory shrug. His silly little reddish brown mustache glittered in the sun.

"I suppose I like to be liked," he said.

"I'm sorry, Murdock. I like your being that devoted to your wife. If that's what it is."

"Oh. Didn't you think I was telling the truth? I mean, did you think I was saying all that just to protect her?"

"There was that possibility."

"I see." He put a cigarette into the long black holder, which he took from behind his display handkerchief. "Well — I guess I can take it that you don't like me." The dim movement of his eyes was visible behind the green lenses, fish moving in a deep pool.

"It's a silly subject," I said. "And damned unimportant. To both of us."

He put a match to the cigarette and inhaled. "I see," he said quietly. "Pardon me for being crude enough to bring it up."

He turned on his heel and walked back to his car and got in. I watched him drive away before I moved. Then I went over and patted the little painted Negro boy on the head a couple of times before I left.

"Son," I said to him, "you're the only person around this house that's not nuts."

23

THE POLICE LOUDSPEAKER box on the wall grunted and a voice said: "KGPL. Testing." A click and it went dead.

Detective-Lieutenant Jesse Breeze stretched his arms high in the air and yawned and said: "Couple of hours late, ain't you?"

I said: "Yes. But I left a message for you that I would be. I had to go to the dentist."

"Sit down."

He had a small littered desk across one corner of the room. He sat in the angle behind it, with a tall bare window to his left and a wall with a large calendar about eye height to his right. The days that had gone down to dust were crossed off carefully in soft black pencil, so that Breeze glancing at the calendar always knew exactly what day it was.

Spangler was sitting sideways at a smaller and much neater desk. It had a green blotter and an onyx pen set and a small brass calendar and an abalone shell full of ashes and matches and cigarette stubs. Spangler was flipping a handful of bank pens at the felt back of a seat cushion on end against the wall, like a Mexican knife thrower flipping knives at a target. He wasn't getting anywhere with it. The pens refused to stick.

The room had that remote, heartless, not quite dirty, not quite clean, not quite human smell that such rooms always have. Give a police department a brand new building and in three months all its rooms will smell like that. There must be something symbolic in it.

A New York police reporter wrote once that when you pass in beyond the green lights of a precinct station you pass clear out of this world, into a place beyond the law.

I sat down. Breeze got a cellophane-wrapped cigar out of his pocket and the routine with it started. I watched it detail by detail, unvarying, precise. He drew in smoke, shook his match out, laid it gently in the black glass ashtray, and said: "Hi, Spangler."

Spangler turned his head and Breeze turned his head. They grinned at each other. Breeze poked the cigar at me.

"Watch him sweat," he said.

Spangler had to move his feet to turn far enough around to watch me sweat. If I was sweating, I didn't know it.

"You boys are as cute as a couple of lost golf balls," I said. "How in the world do you do it?"

"Skip the wisecracks," Breeze said. "Had a busy little morning?"

"Fair," I said.

He was still grinning. Spangler was still grinning. Whatever it was Breeze was tasting he hated to swallow it.

Finally he cleared his throat, straightened his big freckled face out, turned his head enough so that he was not looking at me but could still see me and said in a vague empty sort of voice:

"Hench confessed."

Spangler swung clear around to look at me. He leaned forward on the edge of his chair and his lips were parted in an ecstatic half smile that was almost indecent.

I said: "What did you use on him – a pickax?"

"Nope."

They were both silent, staring at me.

"A wop," Breeze said.

"A what?"

"Boy, are you glad?" Breeze said.

"You are going to tell me or are you just going to sit there looking fat and complacent and watch me being glad?"

"We like to watch a guy being glad," Breeze said. "We don't often get a chance."

I put a cigarette in my mouth and jiggled it up and down.

"We used a wop on him," Breeze said. "A wop named Palermo."

"Oh. You know something?"

"What?" Breeze asked.

"I just thought of what is the matter with policemen's dialogue."

"What?"

"They think every line is a punch line."

"And every pinch is a good pinch," Breeze said calmly. "You want to know – or you want to just crack wise?"

"I want to know."

"Was like this, then. Hench was drunk. I mean he was drunk deep inside, not just on the surface. Screwy drunk. He'd been living on it for weeks. He'd practically quit eating and sleeping. Just liquor. He'd got to the point where liquor wasn't making him drunk, it was keeping him sober. It was the last hold he had on the real world. When a guy gets like that and you take his liquor away and don't give him anything to hold him down, he's a lost cuckoo."

I didn't say anything. Spangler still had the same erotic leer on his young face. Breeze tapped the side of his cigar and no ash fell off and he put it back in his mouth and went on.

"He's a psycho case, but we don't want any psycho case made out of our pinch. We make that clear. We want a guy that don't have any psycho record."

"I thought you were sure Hench was innocent."

Breeze nodded vaguely. "That was last night. Or maybe I was kidding a little. Anyway in the night, bang, Hench is bugs. So they drag him over to the hospital ward and shoot him full of hop. The jail doc does. That's between you and me. No hop in the record. Get the idea?"

"All too clearly," I said.

"Yeah." He looked vaguely suspicious of the remark, but he was too full of his subject to waste time on it. "Well, this a.m. he is fine. Hop still working, the guy is pale but peaceful. We go see him. How you doing, kid? Anything you need?

Any little thing at all? Be glad to get it for you. They treating you nice in here? You know the line."

"I do," I said. "I know the line."

Spangler licked his lips in a nasty way.

"So after a while he opens his trap just enough to say 'Palermo.' Palermo is the name of the wop across the street that owns the funeral home and the apartment house and stuff. You remember? Yeah, you remember. On account of he said something about a tall blonde. All hooey. Them wops got tall blondes on the brain. In sets of twelve. But this Palermo is important. I asked around. He gets the vote out up there. He's a guy that can't be pushed around. Well, I don't aim to push him around. I say to Hench, 'You mean Palermo's a friend of yours?' He says, 'Get Palermo.' So we come back here to the hutch and phone Palermo and Palermo says he will be right down. Okay. He is here very soon. We talk like this: Hench wants to see you, Mr. Palermo. I wouldn't know why. He's a poor guy, Palermo says. A nice guy. I think he's okay. He wanta see me, that'sa fine. I see him. I see him alone. Without any coppers. I say, Okay, Mr. Palermo, and we go over to the hospital ward and Palermo talks to Hench and nobody listens. After a while Palermo comes out and he says, Okay, copper. He make the confess. I pay the lawyer, maybe. I like the poor guy. Just like that. He goes away."

I didn't say anything. There was a pause. The loudspeaker on the wall put out a bulletin and Breeze cocked his head and listened to ten or twelve words and then ignored it.

"So we go in with a steno and Hench gives us the dope. Phillips made a pass at Hench's girl. That was day before yesterday, out in the hall. Hench was in the room and he saw it, but Phillips got into his apartment and shut the door before Hench could get out. But Hench was sore. He socked the girl in the eye. But that didn't satisfy him. He got to brooding, the way a drunk will brood. He says to himself, that guy can't make a pass at my girl. I'm the boy that will give him something to remember me by. So he keeps an eye open for

Phillips. Yesterday afternoon he sees Phillips go into his apartment. He tells the girl to go for a walk. She don't want to go for a walk, so Hench socks her in the other eye. She goes for a walk. Hench knocks on Phillips' door and Phillips opens it. Hench is a little surprised at that, but I told him Phillips was expecting you. Anyway the door opens and Hench goes in and tells Phillips how he feels and what he is going to do and Phillips is scared and pulls a gun. Hench hits him with a sap. Phillips falls down and Hench ain't satisfied. You hit a guy with a sap and he falls down and what have you? No satisfaction, no revenge. Hench picks the gun off the floor and he is very drunk there being dissatisfied and Phillips grabs for his ankle. Hench doesn't know why he did what he did then. He's all fuzzy in the head. He drags Phillips into the bathroom and gives him the business with his own gun. You like it?"

"I love it," I said. "But what is the satisfaction in it for Hench?"

"Well, you know how a drunk is. Anyway he gives him the business. Well it ain't Hench's gun, you see, but he can't make a suicide out of it. There wouldn't be any satisfaction for him in that. So Hench takes the gun away and puts it under his pillow and takes his own gun out and ditches it. He won't tell us where. Probably passes it to some tough guy in the neighborhood. Then he finds the girl and they eat."

"That was a lovely touch," I said. "Putting the gun under his pillow. I'd never in the world have thought of that."

Breeze leaned back in his chair and looked at the ceiling. Spangler, the big part of the entertainment over, swung around in his chair and picked up a couple of bank pens and threw one at the cushion.

"Look at it this way," Breeze said. "What was the effect of that stunt? Look how Hench did it. He was drunk, but he was smart. He found that gun and showed it before Phillips was found dead. First we get the idea that a gun is under Hench's pillow that killed a guy – been fired anyway – and then we get the stiff. We believed Hench's story. It seemed reasonable. Why would we think any man would be such a sap as to do what Hench did? It doesn't make any sense. So we believed somebody put the gun under Hench's pillow and took Hench's gun away and ditched it. And suppose Hench ditched the death gun instead of his own, would he have been any better off? Things being what they were we would be bound to suspect him. And that way he wouldn't have started our minds thinking any particular way about him. The way he did he got us thinking he was a harmless drunk that went out and left his door open and somebody ditched a gun on him."

He waited, with his mouth a little open and the cigar in front of it, held up by a hard freckled hand and his pale blue eyes full of dim satisfaction.

"Well," I said, "if he was going to confess anyway, it wouldn't have made very much difference. Will he cop a plea?"

"Sure. I think so. I figure Palermo could get him off with manslaughter. Naturally I'm not sure."

"Why would Palermo want to get him off with anything?"

"He kind of likes Hench. And Palermo is a guy we can't push around."

I said: "I see." I stood up. Spangler looked at me sideways along glistening eyes. "What about the girl?"

"Won't say a word. She's smart. We can't do anything to her. Nice neat little job all around. You wouldn't kick, would you? Whatever your business is, it's still your business. Get me?"

"And the girl is a tall blonde," I said. "Not of the freshest, but still a tall blonde. Although only one. Maybe Palermo doesn't mind."

"Hell, I never thought of that," Breeze said. He thought about it and shook it off. "Nothing in that, Marlowe. Not enough class."

"Cleaned up and sober, you never can tell," I said. "Class is a thing that has a way of dissolving rapidly in alcohol. That all you want with me?"

"Guess so." He slanted the cigar up and aimed it at my eye. "Not that I wouldn't like to hear your story. But I don't figure I have an absolute right to insist on it the way things are."

"That's white of you, Breeze," I said. "And you too, Spangler. A lot of the good things in life to both of you."

They watched me go out, both with their mouths a little open.

I rode down to the big marble lobby and went and got my car out of the official parking lot.

24

MR. PIETRO PALERMO was sitting in a room which, except for a mahogany roll-top desk, a sacred triptych in gilt frames and a large ebony and ivory crucifixion, looked exactly like a Victorian parlor. It contained a horseshoe sofa and chairs with carved mahogany frames and antimacassars of fine lace. There was an ormolu clock on the gray green marble mantel, a grandfather clock ticking lazily in the corner, and some wax flowers under a glass dome on an oval table with a marble top and curved elegant legs. The carpet was thick and full of gentle sprays of flowers. There was even a cabinet for bric-a-brac and there was plenty of bric-a-brac in it, little cups in fine china, little figurines in glass and porcelain, odds and ends of ivory and dark rosewood, painted saucers, an early American set of swan salt cellars, stuff like that.

Long lace curtains hung across the windows, but the room faced south and there was plenty of light. Across the street I could see the windows of the apartment where George Anson Phillips had been killed. The street between was sunny and silent.

The tall Italian with the dark skin and the handsome head of iron gray hair read my card and said:

"I got business in twelve minutes. What you want, Meester Marlowe?"

"I'm the man that found the dead man across the street yesterday. He was a friend of mine."

His cold black eyes looked me over silently. "That'sa not what you tell Luke."

"Luke?"

"He manage the joint for me."

"I don't talk much to strangers, Mr. Palermo."

"That'sa good. You talk to me, huh?"

"You're a man of standing, an important man. I can talk to you. You saw me yesterday. You described me to the police. Very accurately, they said."

"Si. I see much," he said without emotion.

"You saw a tall blonde woman come out of there yesterday."

He studied me. "Not yesterday. Wasa two three days ago. I tell the coppers yesterday." He snapped his long dark fingers. "The coppers, bah!"

"Did you see any strangers yesterday, Mr. Palermo?"

"Is back way in and out," he said. "Is stair from second floor also." He looked at his wrist watch.

"Nothing there then," I said. "This morning you saw Hench."

He lifted his eyes and ran them lazily over my face. "The coppers tell you that, huh?"

"They told me you got Hench to confess. They said he was a friend of yours. How good a friend they didn't know, of course."

"Hench make the confess, huh?" He smiled, a sudden brilliant smile.

"Only Hench didn't do the killing," I said.

"No?"

"No."

"That'sa interesting. Go on, Meester Marlowe."

"The confession is a lot of baloney. You got him to make it for some reason of your own."

He stood up and went to the door and called out: "Tony."

592

He sat down again. A short tough-looking wop came into the room, looked at me and sat down against the wall in a straight chair.

"Tony, thees man a Meester Marlowe. Look, take the card."

Tony came to get the card and sat down with it. "You look at thees man very good, Tony. Not forget him, huh?"

Tony said: "Leave it to me, Mr. Palermo."

Palermo said: "Was a friend to you, huh? A good friend, huh?"

"Yes."

"That'sa bad. Yeah. That'sa bad. I tell you something. A man's friend is a man's friend. So I tell you. But you don' tell anybody else. Not the damn coppers, huh?"

"No."

"That'sa promise, Meester Marlowe. That'sa something not to forget. You not forget?"

"I won't forget."

"Tony, he not forget you. Get the idea?"

"I gave you my word. What you tell me is between us here."

"That'sa fine. Okay. I come of large family. Many sisters and brothers. One brother very bad. Almost so bad as Tony."

Tony grinned.

"Okay, thees brother live very quiet. Across the street. Gotta move. Okay, the coppers fill the joint up. Not so good. Ask too many questions. Not good for business, not good for thees bad brother. You get the idea?"

"Yes," I said. "I get the idea."

"Okay, thees Hench no good, but poor guy, drunk, no job. Pay no rent, but I got lotsa money. So I say, Look, Hench, you make the confess. You sick man. Two three weeks sick. You go into court. I have a lawyer for you. You say to hell with the confess. I was drunk. The damn coppers are stuck. The judge he turn you loose and you come back to me and I take care of you. Okay? So Hench say okay, make the confess. That'sa all."

I said: "And after two or three weeks the bad brother is a long way from here and the trail is cold and the cops will likely just write the Phillips killing off as unsolved. Is that it?"

"Si." He smiled again. A brilliant warm smile, like the kiss of death.

"That takes care of Hench, Mr. Palermo," I said. "But it doesn't help me much about my friend."

He shook his head and looked at his watch again. I stood up. Tony stood up. He wasn't going to do anything, but it's better to be standing up. You move faster.

"The trouble with you birds," I said, "is you make mystery of nothing. You have to give the password before you bite a piece of bread. If I went down to headquarters and told the boys everything you have told me, they would laugh in my face. And I would be laughing with them."

"Tony don't laugh much," Palermo said.

"The earth is full of people who don't laugh much, Mr. Palermo," I said. "You ought to know. You put a lot of them where they are."

"Is my business," he said, shrugging enormously.

"I'll keep my promise," I said. "But in case you should get to doubting that, don't try to make any business for yourself out of me. Because in my part of town I'm a pretty good man and if the business got made out of Tony instead, it would be strictly on the house. No profit."

Palermo laughed. "That'sa good," he said. "Tony. One funeral – on the house. Okay."

He stood up and held his hand out, a fine strong warm hand.

25

IN THE LOBBY of the Belfont Building, in the single elevator that had light in it, on the piece of folded burlap, the same watery-eyed relic sat motionless, giving his imitation of the forgotten man. I got in with him and said: "Six."

The elevator lurched into motion and pounded its way upstairs. It stopped at six, I got out, and the old man leaned out of the car to spit and said in a dull voice:

"What's cookin'?"

I turned around all in one piece, like a dummy on a revolving platform. I stared at him.

He said: "You got a gray suit on today."

"So I have," I said. "Yes."

"Looks nice," he said. "I like the blue you was wearing yesterday too."

"Go on," I said. "Give out."

"You rode up to eight," he said. "Twice. Second time was late. You got back on at six. Shortly after that the boys in blue came bustlin' in."

"Any of them up there now?"

He shook his head. His face was like a vacant lot. "I ain't told them anything," he said. "Too late to mention it now. They'd eat my ass off."

I said: "Why?"

"Why I ain't told them? The hell with them. You talked to me civil. Damn few people do that. Hell, I know you didn't have nothing to do with that killing."

"I played you wrong," I said. "Very wrong." I got a card out and gave it to him. He fished a pair of metal-framed glasses out of his pocket, perched them on his nose and held the card a foot away from them. He read it slowly, moving his lips, looked at me over the glasses, handed me back the card.

"Better keep it," he said. "Case I get careless and drop it. Mighty interestin' life yours, I guess."

"Yes and no. What was the name?"

"Grandy. Just call me Pop. Who killed him?"

"I don't know. Did you notice anybody going up there or coming down — anybody that seemed out of place in this building, or strange to you?"

"I don't notice much," he said. "I just happened to notice you."

"A tall blonde, for instance, or a tall slender man with sideburns, about thirty-five years old."

"Nope."

"Everybody going up or down about then would ride in your car."

He nodded his worn head. "'Less they used the fire stairs. They come out in the alley, bar-lock door. Party would have to come in this way, but there's stairs back of the elevator to the second floor. From there they can get to the fire stairs. Nothing to it."

I nodded. "Mr. Grandy, could you use a five dollar bill – not as a bribe in any sense, but as a token of esteem from a sincere friend?"

"Son, I could use a five dollar bill so rough Abe Lincoln's whiskers would be all lathered up with sweat."

I gave him one. I looked at it before I passed it over. It was Lincoln on the five, all right.

He tucked it small and put it away deep in his pocket. "That's right nice of you," he said. "I hope to hell you didn't think I was fishin'."

I shook my head and went along the corridor, reading the names again. *Dr. E. J. Blaskowitz, Chiropractic Physician. Dalton and Rees, Typewriting Service. L. Pridview, Public Accountant.* Four blank doors. *Moss Mailing Company.* Two more blank doors. *H. R. Teager, Dental Laboratories.* In the same relative position as the Morningstar office two floors above, but the rooms were cut up differently. Teager had only one door and there was more wall space in between his door and the next one.

The knob didn't turn. I knocked. There was no answer. I knocked harder, with the same result. I went back to the elevator. It was still at the sixth floor. Pop Grandy watched me come as if he had never seen me before.

"Know anything about H. R. Teager?" I asked him.

He thought. "Heavy-set, oldish, sloppy clothes, dirty fingernails, like mine. Come to think I didn't see him in today."

"Do you think the super would let me into his office to look around?"

"Pretty nosey, the super is. I wouldn't recommend it."

He turned his head very slowly and looked up the side of the car. Over his head on a big metal ring a key was hanging. A pass-key. Pop Grandy turned his head back to normal position, stood up off his stool and said: "Right now I gotta go to the can."

He went. When the door had closed behind him I took the key off the cage wall and went back along to the office of H. R. Teager, unlocked it and went in.

Inside was a small windowless anteroom on the furnishings of which a great deal of expense had been spared. Two chairs, a smoking stand from a cut rate drugstore, a standing lamp from the basement of some borax emporium, a flat stained wood table with some old picture magazines on it. The door closed behind me on the door closer and the place went dark except for what little light came through the pebbled glass panel. I pulled the chain switch of the lamp and went over to the inner door in a wall that cut across the room. It was marked: *H. R. Teager. Private*. It was not locked.

Inside it there was a square office with two uncurtained east windows and very dusty sills. There was a swivel chair and two straight chairs, both plain hard stained wood, and there was a squarish flat-topped desk. There was nothing on the top of it except an old blotter and a cheap pen set and a round glass ashtray with cigar ash in it. The drawers of the desk contained some dusty paper linings, a few wire clips, rubber bands, worn down pencils, pens, rusty pen points, used blotters, four uncanceled two-cent stamps, and some printed letterheads, envelopes and bill forms.

The wire paper basket was full of junk. I almost wasted ten minutes going through it rather carefully. At the end of that time I knew what I was pretty sure of already: that H. R. Teager carried on a small business as a dental technician doing laboratory work for a number of dentists in unprosperous sections of the city, the kind of dentists who have shabby offices on second floor walk-ups over stores, who lack both the skill and the equipment to do their own laboratory work, and who like to send it out to men like themselves, rather than to the big efficient hardboiled laboratories who wouldn't give them any credit.

I did find one thing. Teager's home address at 1354B Toberman Street on the receipted part of a gas bill.

I straightened up, dumped the stuff back into the basket and went over to the wooden door marked *Laboratory*. It had a new Yale lock on it and the pass-key didn't fit it. That was that. I switched off the lamp in the outer office and left.

The elevator was downstairs again. I rang for it and when it came up I sidled in around Pop Grandy, hiding the key, and hung it up over his head. The ring tinkled against the cage. He grinned.

"He's gone," I said. "Must have left last night. Must have been carrying a lot of stuff. His desk is cleaned out."

Pop Grandy nodded. "Carried two suitcases. I wouldn't notice that, though. Most always does carry a suitcase. I figure he picks up and delivers his work."

"Work such as what?" I asked as the car growled down. Just to be saying something.

"Such as makin' teeth that don't fit," Pop Grandy said. "For poor old bastards like me."

"You wouldn't notice," I said, as the doors struggled open on the lobby. "You wouldn't notice the color of a hummingbird's eye at fifty feet. Not much you wouldn't."

He grinned. "What's he done?"

"I'm going over to his house and find out," I said. "I think most likely he's taken a cruise to nowhere."

"I'd shift places with him," Pop Grandy said. "Even if he only got to Frisco and got pinched there, I'd shift places with him."

26

TOBERMAN STREET. A wide dusty street, off Pico. No. 1354B was an upstairs flat, south, in a yellow and white frame building. The entrance door was on the porch, beside another marked 1352B. The entrances to the downstairs flats were at right angles, facing each other across the width of the porch. I kept on ringing the bell, even after I was sure that nobody would answer it. In a neighborhood like that there is always an expert window-peeker.

Sure enough the door of 1354A was pulled open and a small bright-eyed woman looked out at me. Her dark hair had been washed and waved and was an intricate mass of bobby pins.

"You want Mrs. Teager?" she shrilled.

"Mr. or Mrs."

"They gone away last night on their vacation. They loaded up and gone away late. They had me stop the milk and the paper. They didn't have much time. Kind of sudden, it was."

"Thanks. What kind of car do they drive?"

The heartrending dialogue of some love serial came out of the room behind her and hit me in the face like a wet dishtowel.

The bright-eyed woman said: "You a friend of theirs?" In her voice, suspicion was as thick as the ham in her radio.

"Never mind," I said in a tough voice. "All we want is our money. Lots of ways to find out what car they were driving."

The woman cocked her head, listening. "That's Beula May," she told me with a sad smile. "She won't go to the dance with Doctor Myers. I was scared she wouldn't."

"Aw hell," I said, and went back to my car and drove on home to Hollywood.

The office was empty. I unlocked my inner room and threw the windows up and sat down.

Another day drawing to its end, the air dull and tired, the heavy growl of homing traffic on the boulevard, and Marlowe in his office nibbling a drink and sorting the day's mail. Four ads; two bills; a handsome colored postcard from a hotel in Santa Rosa where I had stayed for four days last year, working on a case; a long, badly typed letter from a man named Peabody in Sausalito, the general and slightly cloudy drift of which was that a sample of the handwriting of a suspected person would, when exposed to the searching Peabody examination, reveal the inner emotional characteristics of the individual, classified according to both the Freudian and Jung systems.

There was a stamped addressed envelope inside. As I tore the stamp off and threw the letter and envelope away I had a vision of a pathetic old rooster in long hair, black felt hat and black bow tie, rocking on a rickety porch in front of a lettered window, with the smell of ham hocks and cabbage coming out of the door at his elbow.

I sighed, retrieved the envelope, wrote its name and address on a fresh one, folded a dollar bill into a sheet of paper and wrote on it: "This is positively the last contribution." I signed my name, sealed the envelope, stuck a stamp on it and poured another drink.

I filled and lit my pipe and sat there smoking. Nobody came in, nobody called, nothing happened, nobody cared whether I died or went to El Paso.

Little by little the roar of the traffic quieted down. The sky lost its glare. Over in the west it would be red. An early neon light showed a block away, diagonally over roofs. The ventilator churned dully in the wall of the coffee shop down in the alley. A truck filled and backed and growled its way out on to the boulevard.

Finally the telephone rang. I answered it and the voice said: "Mr. Marlowe? This is Mr. Shaw. At the Bristol."

"Yes, Mr. Shaw. How are you?"

"I'm very well thanks, Mr. Marlowe. I hope you are the same. There's a young lady here asking to be let into your apartment. I don't know why."

"Me neither, Mr. Shaw. I didn't order anything like that. Does she give a name?"

"Oh yes. Quite. Her name is Davis. Miss Merle Davis. She is – what shall I say? – quite verging on the hysterical."

"Let her in," I said, rapidly. "I'll be there in ten minutes. She's the secretary of a client. It's a business matter entirely."

"Quite. Oh yes. Shall I – er – remain with her?"

"Whatever you think," I said and hung up.

Passing the open door of the wash cabinet I saw a stiff excited face in the glass.

27

AS I TURNED the key in my door and opened it Shaw was already standing up from the davenport. He was a tall man with glasses and a high domed bald head that made his ears look as if they had slipped down on his head. He had the fixed smile of polite idiocy on his face.

The girl sat in my easy chair behind the chess table. She wasn't doing anything, just sitting there.

"Ah, there you are, Mr. Marlowe," Shaw chirped. "Yes. Quite. Miss Davis and I have been having such an interesting little conversation. I was telling her I originally came from England. She hasn't – er – told me where she came from." He was halfway to the door saying this.

"Very kind of you, Mr. Shaw," I said.

"Not at all," he chirped. "Not at all. I'll just run along now. My dinner, possibly –"

"It's very nice of you," I said, "I appreciate it."

He nodded and was gone. The unnatural brightness of his smile seemed to linger in the air after the door closed, like the smile of the Cheshire Cat.

I said: "Hello, there."

She said: "Hello." Her voice was quite calm, quite serious. She was wearing a brownish linen coat and skirt, a broad-brimmed low-crowned straw hat with a brown velvet band that exactly matched the color of her shoes and the leather trimming on the edges of her linen envelope bag. The hat was tilted rather daringly, for her. She was not wearing her glasses.

Except for her face she would have looked all right. In the first place her eyes were quite mad. There was white showing all around the iris and they had a sort of fixed look. When they moved the movement was so stiff that you could almost hear something creak. Her mouth was in a tight line at the corners, but the middle part of her upper lip kept lifting off her teeth, upwards and outwards as if fine threads attached to the edge of the lip were pulling it. It would go up so far that it didn't seem possible, and then the entire lower part of her face would go into a spasm and when the spasm was over her mouth would be tight shut, and then the process would slowly start all over again. In addition to this there was something wrong with her neck, so that very slowly her head was drawn around to the left about forty-five degrees. It would stop there, her neck would twitch, and her head would slide back the way it had come.

The combination of these two movements, taken with the immobility of her body, the tight-clasped hands in her lap, and the fixed stare of her eyes, was enough to start anybody's nerves backfiring.

There was a can of tobacco on the desk, between which and her chair was the chess table with the chessmen in their box. I got the pipe out of my pocket and went over to fill it at the can of tobacco. That put me just on the other side of the chess table from her. Her bag was lying on the edge of the table, in front of her and a little to one side. She jumped a little when I went over there, but after that she was just like before. She even made an effort to smile.

I filled the pipe and struck a paper match and lit it and stood there holding the match after I had blown it out.

"You're not wearing your glasses," I said.

She spoke. Her voice was quiet, composed. "Oh, I only wear them around the house and for reading. They're in my bag."

"You're in the house now," I said. "You ought to be wearing them."

I reached casually for the bag. She didn't move. She didn't watch my hands. Her eyes were on my face. I turned my body a little as I opened the bag. I fished the glass case out and slid it across the table.

"Put them on," I said.

"Oh, yes, I'll put them on," she said. "But I'll have to take my hat off, I think . . ."

"Yes, take your hat off," I said.

She took her hat off and held it on her knees. Then she remembered about the glasses and forgot about the hat. The hat fell on the floor while she reached for the glasses. She put them on. That helped her appearance a lot, I thought.

While she was doing this I got the gun out of her bag and slid it into my hip pocket. I didn't think she saw me. It looked like the same Colt .25 automatic with the walnut grip that I had seen in the top right-hand drawer of her desk the day before.

I went back to the davenport and sat down and said: "Well, here we are. What do we do now? Are you hungry?"

"I've been over to Mr. Vannier's house," she said.

"Oh."

"He lives in Sherman Oaks. At the end of Escamillo Drive. At the very end."

"Quite, probably," I said without meaning, and tried to blow a smoke ring, but didn't make it. A nerve in my cheek was trying to twang like a wire. I didn't like it.

"Yes," she said in her composed voice, with her upper lip still doing the hoist and flop movement and her chin still swinging around at anchor and back again. "It's very quiet

603

there. Mr. Vannier has been living there three years now. Before that he lived up in the Hollywood hills, on Diamond Street. Another man lived with him there, but they didn't get along very well, Mr. Vannier said."

"I feel as if I could understand that too," I said. "How long have you known Mr. Vannier?"

"I've known him eight years. I haven't known him very well. I have had to take him a – a parcel now and then. He liked to have me bring it myself."

I tried again with a smoke ring. Nope.

"Of course," she said, "I never liked him very well. I was afraid he would – I was afraid he –"

"But he didn't," I said.

For the first time her face got a human natural expression – surprise.

"No," she said. "He didn't. That is, he didn't really. But he had his pajamas on."

"Taking it easy," I said. "Lying around all afternoon with his pajamas on. Well, some guys have all the luck, don't they?"

"Well you have to know something," she said seriously. "Something that makes people pay you money. Mrs. Murdock has been wonderful to me, hasn't she?"

"She certainly has," I said. "How much were you taking him today?"

"Only five hundred dollars. Mrs. Murdock said that was all she could spare, and she couldn't really spare that. She said it would have to stop. It couldn't go on. Mr. Vannier would always promise to stop, but he never did."

"It's a way they have," I said.

"So there was only one thing to do. I've known that for years, really. It was all my fault and Mrs. Murdock has been so wonderful to me. It couldn't make me any worse than I was already, could it?"

I put my hand up and rubbed my cheek hard, to quiet the nerve. She forgot that I hadn't answered her and went on again.

"So I did it," she said. "He was there in his pajamas, with a glass beside him. He was leering at me. He didn't even get up to let me in. But there was a key in the front door. Somebody had left a key there. It was – it was –" her voice jammed in her throat.

"It was a key in the front door," I said. "So you were able to get in."

"Yes." She nodded and almost smiled again. "There wasn't anything to it, really. I don't even remember hearing the noise. But there must have been a noise, of course. Quite a loud noise."

"I suppose so," I said.

"I went over quite close to him, so I couldn't miss," she said.

"And what did Mr. Vannier do?"

"He didn't do anything at all. He just leered, sort of. Well, that's all there is to it. I didn't like to go back to Mrs. Murdock and make any more trouble for her. And for Leslie." Her voice hushed on the name, and hung suspended, and a little shiver rippled over her body. "So I came here," she said. "And when you didn't answer the bell, I found the office and asked the manager to let me in and wait for you. I knew you would know what to do."

"And what did you touch in the house while you were there?" I asked. "Can you remember at all? I mean, besides the front door. Did you just go in at the door and come out without touching anything in the house?"

She thought and her face stopped moving. "Oh, I remember one thing," she said. "I put the light out. Before I left. It was a lamp. One of these lamps that shine upwards, with big bulbs. I put that out."

I nodded and smiled at her. Marlowe, one smile, cheerful.

"What time was this – how long ago?"

"Oh just before I came over here. I drove. I had Mrs. Murdock's car. The one you asked about yesterday. I forgot to

605

tell you that she didn't take it when she went away. Or did I? No, I remember now I did tell you."

"Let's see," I said. "Half an hour to drive here anyway. You've been here close to an hour. That would be about five-thirty when you left Mr. Vannier's house. And you put the light off."

"That's right." She nodded again, quite brightly. Pleased at remembering. "I put the light out."

"Would you care for a drink?" I asked her.

"Oh, no." She shook her head quite vigorously. "I never drink anything at all."

"Would you mind if I had one?"

"Certainly not. Why should I?"

I stood up, gave her a studying look. Her lip was still going up and her head was still going around, but I thought not so far. It was like a rhythm which is dying down.

It was difficult to know how far to go with this. It might be that the more she talked, the better. Nobody knows very much about the time of absorption of a shock.

I said: "Where is your home?"

"Why – I live with Mrs. Murdock. In Pasadena."

"I mean, your real home. Where your folks are."

"My parents live in Wichita," she said. "But I don't go there – ever. I write once in a while, but I haven't seen them for years."

"What does your father do?"

"He has a dog and cat hospital. He's a veterinarian. I hope they won't have to know. They didn't about the other time. Mrs. Murdock kept it from everybody."

"Maybe they won't have to know," I said. "I'll get my drink."

I went out around the back of her chair to the kitchen and poured it and I made it a drink that was a drink. I put it down in a lump and took the little gun off my hip and saw that the safety was on. I smelled the muzzle, broke out the magazine.

606

There was a shell in the chamber, but it was one of those guns that won't fire when the magazine is out. I held it so that I could look into the breech. The shell in there was the wrong size and was crooked against the breech block. It looked like a .32. The shells in the magazine were the right size, .25's. I fitted the gun together again and went back to the living room.

I hadn't heard a sound. She had just slid forward in a pile in front of the chair, on top of her nice hat. She was as cold as a mackerel.

I spread her out a little and took her glasses off and made sure she hadn't swallowed her tongue. I wedged my folded handkerchief into the corner of her mouth so that she wouldn't bite her tongue when she came out of it. I went to the phone and called Carl Moss.

"Phil Marlowe, Doc. Any more patients or are you through?"

"All through," he said. "Leaving. Trouble?"

"I'm home," I said. "Four-o-eight Bristol Apartments, if you don't remember. I've got a girl here who has pulled a faint. I'm not afraid of the faint, I'm afraid she may be nuts when she comes out of it."

"Don't give her any liquor," he said. "I'm on my way."

I hung up and knelt down beside her. I began to rub her temples. She opened her eyes. The lip started to lift. I pulled the handkerchief out of her mouth. She looked up at me and said: "I've been over to Mr. Vannier's house. He lives in Sherman Oaks. I –"

"Do you mind if I lift you up and put you on the davenport? You know me – Marlowe, the big boob that goes around asking all the wrong questions."

"Hello," she said.

I lifted her. She went stiff on me, but she didn't say anything. I put her on the davenport and tucked her skirt down over her legs and put a pillow under her head and picked her hat up. It was as flat as a flounder. I did what I could to straighten it out and laid it aside on the desk.

She watched me sideways, doing this.

"Did you call the police?" she asked softly.

"Not yet," I said. "I've been too busy."

She looked surprised. I wasn't quite sure, but I thought she looked a little hurt, too.

I opened up her bag and turned my back to her to slip the gun back into it. While I was doing that I took a look at what else was in the bag. The usual oddments, a couple of handkerchiefs, lipstick, a silver and red enamel compact with powder in it, a couple of tissues, a purse with some hard money and a few dollar bills, no cigarettes, no matches, no tickets to the theater.

I pulled open the zipper pocket at the back. That held her driver's license and a flat packet of bills, ten fifties. I riffled them. None of them brand new. Tucked into the rubber band that held them was a folded paper. I took it out and opened it and read it. It was neatly typewritten, dated that day. It was a common receipt form and it would, when signed, acknowledge the receipt of $500. "Payment on Account."

It didn't seem as if it would ever be signed now. I slipped money and receipt into my pocket. I closed the bag and looked over at the davenport.

She was looking at the ceiling and doing that with her face again. I went into my bedroom and got a blanket to throw over her.

Then I went to the kitchen for another drink.

28

DR. CARL MOSS was a big burly Jew with a Hitler mustache, pop eyes and the calmness of a glacier. He put his hat and bag in a chair and went over and stood looking down at the girl on the davenport inscrutably.

"I'm Dr. Moss," he said. "How are you?"

She said: "Aren't you the police?"

He bent down and felt her pulse and then stood there watching her breathing. "Where does it hurt, Miss —"

"Davis," I said. "Miss Merle Davis."

"Miss Davis."

"Nothing hurts me," she said, staring up at him. "I — I don't even know why I'm lying here like this. I thought you were the police. You see, I killed a man."

"Well, that's a normal human impulse," he said. "I've killed dozens." He didn't smile.

She lifted her lip and moved her head around for him.

"You know you don't have to do that," he said, quite gently. "You feel a twitch of the nerves here and there and you proceed to build it up and dramatize it. You can control it, if you want to."

"Can I?" she whispered.

"If you want to," he said. "You don't have to. It doesn't make any difference to me either way. Nothing pains at all, eh?"

"No." She shook her head.

He patted her shoulder and walked out to the kitchen. I went after him. He leaned his hips against the sink and gave me a cool stare. "What's the story?"

"She's the secretary of a client. A Mrs. Murdock in Pasadena. The client is rather a brute. About eight years ago a man made a hard pass at Merle. How hard I don't know. Then — I don't mean immediately — but around that time he fell out of a window or jumped. Since then she can't have a man touch her — not in the most casual way, I mean."

"Uh-huh." His pop eyes continued to read my face. "Does she think he jumped out of the window on her account?"

"I don't know. Mrs. Murdock is the man's widow. She married again and her second husband is dead too. Merle has stayed with her. The old woman treats her like a rough parent treats a naughty child."

609

"I see. Regressive."

"What's that?"

"Emotional shock, and the subconscious attempt to escape back to childhood. If Mrs. Murdock scolds her a good deal, but not too much, that would increase the tendency. Identification of childhood subordination with childhood protection."

"Do we have to go into that stuff?" I growled.

He grinned at me calmly. "Look, pal. The girl's obviously a neurotic. It's partly induced and partly deliberate. I mean to say that she really enjoys a lot of it. Even if she doesn't realize that she enjoys it. However, that's not of immediate importance. What's this about killing a man?"

"A man named Vannier who lives in Sherman Oaks. There seems to be some blackmail angle. Merle had to take him his money, from time to time. She was afraid of him. I've seen the guy. A nasty type. She went over there this afternoon and she says she shot him."

"Why?"

"She says she didn't like the way he leered at her."

"Shot him with what?"

"She had a gun in her bag. Don't ask me why. I don't know. But if she shot him, it wasn't with that. The gun's got a wrong cartridge in the breech. It can't be fired as it is. Also it hasn't been fired."

"This is too deep for me," he said. "I'm just a doctor. What did you want me to do with her?"

"Also," I said, ignoring the question, "she said the lamp was turned on and it was about five-thirty of a nice summery afternoon. And the guy was wearing his sleeping suit and there was a key in the lock of the front door. And he didn't get up to let her in. He just sort of sat there sort of leering."

He nodded and said: "Oh." He pushed a cigarette between his heavy lips and lit it. "If you expect me to tell you whether she really thinks she shot him, I can't do it. From your description I gather that the man is shot. That so?"

"Brother, I haven't been there. But that much seems pretty clear."

"If she thinks she shot him and isn't just acting – and God, how these types do act! – that indicates it was not a new idea to her. You say she carried a gun. So perhaps it wasn't. She may have a guilt complex. Wants to be punished, wants to expiate some real or imaginary crime. Again I ask what do you want me to do with her? She's not sick, she's not loony."

"She's not going back to Pasadena."

"Oh." He looked at me curiously. "Any family?"

"In Wichita. Father's a vet. I'll call him, but she'll have to stay here tonight."

"I don't know about that. Does she trust you enough to spend the night in your apartment?"

"She came here of her own free will, and not socially. So I guess she does."

He shrugged and fingered the sidewall of his coarse black mustache. "Well, I'll give her some nembutal and we'll put her to bed. And you can walk the floor wrestling with your conscience."

"I have to go out," I said. "I have to go over there and see what has happened. And she can't stay here alone. And no man, not even a doctor is going to put her to bed. Get a nurse. I'll sleep somewhere else."

"Phil Marlowe," he said. "The shop-soiled Galahad. Okay. I'll stick around until the nurse comes."

He went back into the living room and telephoned the Nurses' Registry. Then he telephoned his wife. While he was telephoning, Merle sat up on the davenport and clasped her hands primly in her lap.

"I don't see why the lamp was on," she said. "It wasn't dark in the house at all. Not that dark."

I said: "What's your dad's first name?"

"Dr. Wilbur Davis. Why?"

"Wouldn't you like something to eat?"

At the telephone Carl Moss said to me: "Tomorrow will do for that. This is probably just a lull." He finished his call, hung up, went to his bag and came back with a couple of yellow capsules in his hand on a fragment of cotton. He got a glass of water, handed her the capsules and said: "Swallow."

"I'm not sick, am I?" she said, looking up at him.

"Swallow, my child, swallow."

She took them and put them in her mouth and took the glass of water and drank.

I put my hat on and left.

On the way down in the elevator I remembered that there hadn't been any keys in her bag, so I stopped at the lobby floor and went out through the lobby to the Bristol Avenue side. The car was not hard to find. It was parked crookedly about two feet from the curb. It was a gray Mercury convertible and its license number was 2X1111. I remembered that this was the number of Linda Murdock's car.

A leather keyholder hung in the lock. I got into the car, started the engine, saw that there was plenty of gas, and drove it away. It was a nice eager little car. Over Cahuenga Pass it had the wings of a bird.

29

ESCAMILLO DRIVE MADE three jogs in four blocks, for no reason that I could see. It was very narrow, averaged about five houses to a block and was overhung by a section of shaggy brown foothill on which nothing lived at this season except sage and manzanita. In its fifth and last block, Escamillo Drive did a neat little curve to the left, hit the base of the hill hard, and died without a whimper. In this last block were three houses, two on the opposite entering corners, one at the dead end. This was Vannier's. My spotlight showed the key still in the door.

It was a narrow English type bungalow with a high roof,

leaded front windows, a garage to the side, and a trailer parked beside the garage. The early moon lay quietly on its small lawn. A large oak tree grew almost on the front porch. There was no light in the house now, none visible from the front at least.

From the lay of the land a light in the living room in the daytime did not seem utterly improbable. It would be a dark house except in the morning. As a love nest the place had its points, but as a residence for a blackmailer I didn't give it very high marks. Sudden death can come to you anywhere, but Vannier had made it too easy.

I turned into his driveway, backed to get myself pointed out of the dead end, and then drove down to the corner and parked there. I walked back in the street because there was no sidewalk. The front door was made of iron-bound oak planks, beveled where they joined. There was a thumb latch instead of a knob. The head of the flat key projected from the lock. I rang the bell, and it rang with that remote sound of a bell ringing at night in an empty house. I walked around the oak tree and poked the light of my pencil flash between the leaves of the garage door. There was a car in there. I went back around the house and looked at a small flowerless yard, walled in by a low wall of field-stone. Three more oak trees, a table and a couple of all metal chairs under one of them. A rubbish burner at the back. I shone my light into the trailer before I went back to the front. There didn't seem to be anybody in the trailer. Its door was locked.

I opened the front door, leaving the key in the lock. I wasn't going to work any dipsy-doodle in this place. What ever was, was. I just wanted to make sure. I felt around on the wall inside the door for a light switch, found one and tilted it up. Pale flame bulbs in pairs in wall brackets went on all around the room, showing me the big lamp Merle had spoken of, as well as other things. I went over to switch the lamp on, then back to switch the wall light off. The lamp had a big bulb inverted in a porcelain glass bowl. You could get three different intensities of light. I clicked the button switch around until I had all there was.

The room ran from front to back, with a door at the back and an arch up front to the right. Inside that was a small dining room. Curtains were half drawn across the arch, heavy pale green brocade curtains, far from new. The fireplace was in the middle of the left wall, bookshelves opposite and on both sides of it, not built in. Two davenports angled across the corners of the room and there was one gold chair, one pink chair, one brown chair, one brown and gold jacquard chair with footstool.

Yellow pajama legs were on the footstool, bare ankles, feet in dark green morocco leather slippers. My eyes ran up from the feet, slowly, carefully. A dark green figured silk robe, tied with a tasseled belt. Open above the belt showing a monogram on the pocket of the pajamas. A handkerchief neat in the pocket, two stiff points of white linen. A yellow neck, the face turned sideways, pointed at a mirror on the wall. I walked around and looked in the mirror. The face leered all right.

The left arm and hand lay between a knee and the side of the chair, the right arm hung outside the chair, the ends of the fingers touching the rug. Touching also the butt of a small revolver, about .32 caliber, a belly gun, with practically no barrel. The right side of the face was against the back of the chair, but the right shoulder was dark brown with blood and there was some on the right sleeve. Also on the chair. A lot of it on the chair.

I didn't think his head had taken that position naturally. Some sensitive soul had not liked the right side of it.

I lifted my foot and gently pushed the footstool sideways a few inches. The heels of the slippers moved reluctantly over the jacquard surface, not with it. The man was as stiff as a board. So I reached down and touched his ankle. Ice was never half as cold.

On a table at his right elbow was half of a dead drink, an

ashtray full of butts and ash. Three of the butts had lipstick on them. Bright Chinese red lipstick. What a blonde would use.

There was another ashtray beside another chair. Matches in it and a lot of ash, but no stubs.

On the air of the room a rather heavy perfume struggled with the smell of death, and lost. Although defeated, it was still there.

I poked through the rest of the house, putting lights on and off. Two bedrooms, one furnished in light wood, one in red maple. The light one seemed to be a spare. A nice bathroom with tan and mulberry tiling and a stall shower with a glass door. The kitchen was small. There were a lot of bottles on the sink. Lots of bottles, lots of glass, lots of fingerprints, lots of evidence. Or not, as the case may be.

I went back to the living room and stood in the middle of the floor breathing with my mouth as far as possible and wondering what the score would be when I turned this one in. Turn this one in and report that I was the fellow who had found Morningstar and run away. The score would be low, very low. Marlowe, three murders. Marlowe practically knee-deep in dead men. And no reasonable, logical, friendly account of himself whatsoever. But that wasn't the worst of it. The minute I opened up I would cease to be a free agent. I would be through with doing whatever it was I was doing and with finding out whatever it was I was finding out.

Carl Moss might be willing to protect Merle with the mantle of Aesculapius, up to a point. Or he might think it would do her more good in the long run to get it all off her chest, whatever it was.

I wandered back to the jacquard chair and set my teeth and grabbed enough of his hair to pull the head away from the chair back. The bullet had gone in at the temple. The set-up could be for suicide. But people like Louis Vannier do not commit suicide. A blackmailer, even a scared blackmailer, has a sense of power, and loves it.

I let the head go back where it wanted to go and leaned down to scrub my hand on the nap of the rug. Leaning down I saw the corner of a picture frame under the lower shelf of the table at Vannier's elbow. I went around and reached for it with a handkerchief.

The glass was cracked across. It had fallen off the wall. I could see the small nail. I could make a guess how it had happened. Somebody standing at Vannier's right, even leaning over him, somebody he knew and had no fear of, had suddenly pulled a gun and shot him in the right temple. And then, startled by the blood or the recoil of the shot, the killer had jumped back against the wall and knocked the picture down. It had landed on a corner and jumped under the table. And the killer had been too careful to touch it, or too scared.

I looked at it. It was a small picture, not interesting at all. A guy in doublet and hose, with lace at his sleeve ends, and one of those round puffy velvet hats with a feather, leaning far out of a window and apparently calling out to somebody downstairs. Downstairs not being in the picture. It was a color reproduction of something that had never been needed in the first place.

I looked around the room. There were other pictures, a couple of rather nice water colors, some engravings – very old-fashioned this year, engravings, or are they? Half a dozen in all. Well, perhaps the guy liked the picture, so what? A man leaning out of a high window. A long time ago.

I looked at Vannier. He wouldn't help me at all. A man leaning out of a high window, a long time ago.

The touch of the idea at first was so light that I almost missed it and passed on. A touch of a feather, hardly that. The touch of a snowflake. A high window, a man leaning out – a long time ago.

It snapped in place. It was so hot it sizzled. Out of a high window a long time ago – eight years ago – a man leaning – too far – a man falling – to his death. A man named Horace Bright.

"Mr. Vannier," I said with a little touch of admiration, "you played that rather neatly."

I turned the picture over. On the back dates and amounts of money were written. Dates over almost eight years, amounts mostly of $500, a few $750's, two for $1000. There was a running total in small figures. It was $11,100. Mr. Vannier had not received the latest payment. He had been dead when it arrived. It was not a lot of money, spread over eight years. Mr. Vannier's customer had bargained hard.

The cardboard back was fastened into the frame with steel victrola needles. Two of them had fallen out. I worked the cardboard loose and tore it a little getting it loose. There was a white envelope between the back and the picture. Sealed, blank. I tore it open. It contained two square photographs and a negative. The photos were just the same. They showed a man leaning far out of a window with his mouth open yelling. His hands were on the brick edges of the window frame. There was a woman's face behind his shoulder.

He was a thinnish dark-haired man. His face was not very clear, nor the face of the woman behind him. He was leaning out of a window and yelling or calling out.

There I was holding the photograph and looking at it. And so far as I could see it didn't mean a thing. I knew it had to. I just didn't know why. But I kept on looking at it. And in a little while something was wrong. It was a very small thing, but it was vital. The position of the man's hands, lined against the corner of the wall where it was cut out to make the window frame. The hands were not holding anything, they were not touching anything. It was the inside of his wrists that lined against the angle of the bricks. The hands were in air.

The man was not leaning. He was falling.

I put the stuff back in the envelope and folded the cardboard back and stuffed that into my pocket also. I hid frame, glass and picture in the linen closet under towels.

All this had taken too long. A car stopped outside the house. Feet came up the walk.

I dodged behind the curtains in the archway.

30

THE FRONT DOOR opened and then quietly closed.

There was a silence, hanging in the air like a man's breath in frosty air, and then a thick scream, ending in a wail of despair.

Then a man's voice, tight with fury, saying: "Not bad, not good. Try again."

The woman's voice said: "My God, it's Louis! He's dead!"

The man's voice said: "I may be wrong, but I still think it stinks."

"My God! He's dead, Alex. Do something – for God's sake – *do* something!"

"Yeah," the hard tight voice of Alex Morny said. "I ought to. I ought to make you look just like him. With blood and everything. I ought to make you just as dead, just as cold, just as rotten. No, I don't have to do that. You're that already. Just as rotten. Eight months married and cheating on me with a piece of merchandise like that. My God! What did I ever think of to put in with a chippy like you?"

He was almost yelling at the end of it.

The woman made another wailing noise.

"Quit stalling," Morny said bitterly. "What do you think I brought you over here for? You're not kidding anybody. You've been watched for weeks. You were here last night. I've been here already today. I've seen what there is to see. Your lipstick on cigarettes, your glass that you drank out of. I can see you now, sitting on the arm of his chair, rubbing his greasy hair, and then feeding him a slug while he was still purring. Why?"

"Oh, Alex – darling – don't say such awful things."

"Early Lillian Gish," Morny said. "Very early Lillian Gish. Skip the agony, toots. I have to know how to handle this. What the hell you think I'm here for? I don't give one little flash in hell about you any more. Not any more, toots, not any more, my precious darling angel blonde man-killer. But I do care about myself and my reputation and my business. For instance, did you wipe the gun off?"

Silence. Then the sound of a blow. The woman wailed. She was hurt, terribly hurt. Hurt in the depths of her soul. She made it rather good.

"Look, angel," Morny snarled. "Don't feed me the ham. I've been in pictures. I'm a connoisseur of ham. Skip it. You're going to tell me how this was done if I have to drag you around the room by your hair. Now – did you wipe off the gun?"

Suddenly she laughed. An unnatural laugh, but clear and with a nice tinkle to it. Then she stopped laughing, just as suddenly.

Her voice said: "Yes."

"And the glass you were using?"

"Yes." Very quiet now, very cool.

"And you put his prints on the gun?"

"Yes."

He thought in the silence. "Probably won't fool them," he said. "It's almost impossible to get a dead man's prints on a gun in a convincing way. However. What else did you wipe off?"

"N-nothing. Oh Alex. Please don't be so brutal."

"Stop it. *Stop it!* Show me how you did it, how you were standing, how you held the gun."

She didn't move.

"Never mind about the prints," Morny said. "I'll put better ones on. Much better ones."

She moved slowly across the opening of the curtains and I saw her. She was wearing pale green gabardine slacks, a fawn-colored leisure jacket with stitching on it, a scarlet turban with a gold snake in it. Her face was smeared with tears.

619

"Pick it up," Morny yelled at her. "Show me!"

She bent beside the chair and came up with the gun in her hand and her teeth bared. She pointed the gun across the opening in the curtains, towards the space of room where the door was.

Morny didn't move, didn't make a sound.

The blonde's hand began to shake and the gun did a queer up and down dance in the air. Her mouth trembled and her arm fell.

"I can't do it," she breathed. "I ought to shoot you, but I can't."

The hand opened and the gun thudded to the floor.

Morny went swiftly past the break in the curtains, pushed her out of the way and with his foot pushed the gun back to about where it had been.

"You couldn't do it," he said thickly. "You couldn't do it. Now watch."

He whipped a handkerchief out and bent to pick the gun up again. He pressed something and the gate fell open. He reached his right hand into his pocket and rolled a cartridge in his fingers, moving his fingertips on the metal, pushed the cartridge into a cylinder. He repeated the performance four times more, snapped the gate shut, then opened it and spun it a little to set it in a certain spot. He placed the gun down on the floor, withdrew his hand and handkerchief and straightened up.

"You couldn't shoot me," he sneered, "because there was nothing in the gun but one empty shell. Now it's loaded again. The cylinders are in the right place. One shot has been fired. And your fingerprints are on the gun."

The blonde was very still, looking at him with haggard eyes.

"I forgot to tell you," he said softly, "*I* wiped the gun off. I thought it would be so much nicer to be *sure* your prints were on it. I was pretty sure they were – but I felt as if I would like to be *quite* sure. Get it?"

The girl said quietly: "You're going to turn me in?"

His back was towards me. Dark clothes. Felt hat pulled low. So I couldn't see his face. But I could just about see the leer with which he said:

"Yes, angel, I am going to turn you in."

"I see," she said, and looked at him levelly. There was a sudden grave dignity in her over-emphasized chorus girl's face.

"I'm going to turn you in, angel," he said slowly, spacing his words as if he enjoyed his act. "Some people are going to be sorry for me and some people are going to laugh at me. But it's not going to do my business any harm. Not a bit of harm. That's one nice thing about a business like mine. A little notoriety won't hurt it at all."

"So I'm just publicity value to you, now," she said. "Apart, of course, from the danger that you might have been suspected yourself."

"Just so," he said. "Just so."

"How about my motive?" she asked, still calm, still level-eyed and so gravely contemptuous that he didn't get the expression at all.

"I don't know," he said. "I don't care. You were up to something with him. Eddie tailed you downtown to a street on Bunker Hill where you met a blond guy in a brown suit. You gave him something. Eddie dropped you and tailed the guy to an apartment house near there. He tried to tail him some more, but he had a hunch the guy spotted him, and he had to drop it. I don't know what it was all about. I know one thing, though. In that apartment house a young guy named Phillips was shot yesterday. Would you know anything about that, my sweet?"

The blonde said: "I wouldn't know anything about it. I don't know anybody named Phillips and strangely enough I didn't just run up and shoot anybody out of sheer girlish fun."

"But you shot Vannier, my dear," Morny said almost gently.

"Oh yes," she drawled. "Of course. We were wondering what my motive was. You get it figured out yet?"

"You can work that out with the johns," he snapped. "Call it a lovers' quarrel. Call it anything you like."

"Perhaps," she said, "when he was drunk he looked just a little like you. Perhaps that was the motive."

He said: "Ah," and sucked his breath in.

"Better looking," she said. "Younger, with less belly. But with the same goddamned self-satisfied smirk."

"Ah," Morny said, and he was suffering.

"Would that do?" she asked him softly.

He stepped forward and swung a fist. It caught her on the side of the face and she went down and sat on the floor, a long leg straight out in front of her, one hand to her jaw, her very blue eyes looking up at him.

"Maybe you oughtn't to have done that," she said. "Maybe I won't go through with it, now."

"You'll go through with it, all right. You won't have any choice. You'll get off easy enough. Christ, I know that. With your looks. But you'll go through with it, angel. Your finger-prints are on that gun."

She got to her feet slowly, still with the hand to her jaw.

Then she smiled. "I knew he was dead," she said. "That is my key in the door. I'm quite willing to go downtown and say I shot him. But don't lay your smooth white paw on me again – if you want my story. Yes. I'm quite willing to go to the cops. I'll feel a lot safer with them than I feel with you."

Morny turned and I saw the hard white leer of his face and the scar dimple in his cheek twitching. He walked past the opening in the curtains. The front door opened again. The blonde stood still a moment, looked back over her shoulder at the corpse, shuddered slightly, and passed out of my line of vision.

The door closed. Steps on the walk. Then car doors opening and closing. The motor throbbed, and the car went away.

31

AFTER A LONG time I moved out from my hiding place and stood looking around the living room again. I went over and picked the gun up and wiped it off very carefully and put it down again. I picked the three rouge-stained cigarette stubs out of the tray on the table and carried them into the bathroom and flushed them down the toilet. Then I looked around for the second glass with her fingerprints on it. There wasn't any second glass. The one that was half full of a dead drink I took to the kitchen and rinsed out and wiped on a dish towel.

Then the nasty part. I kneeled on the rug by his chair and picked up the gun and reached for the trailing bone-stiff hand. The prints would not be good, but they would be prints and they would not be Lois Morny's. The gun had a checked rubber grip, with a piece broken off on the left side below the screw. No prints on that. An index print on the right side of the barrel, two fingers on the trigger guard, a thumb print on the flat piece on the left side, behind the chambers. Good enough.

I took one more look around the living room.

I put the lamp down to a lower light. It still glared too much on the dead yellow face. I opened the front door, pulled the key out and wiped it off and pushed it back into the lock. I shut the door and wiped the thumblatch off and went my way down the block to the Mercury.

I drove back to Hollywood and locked the car up and started along the sidewalk past the other parked cars to the entrance of the Bristol.

A harsh whisper spoke to me out of darkness, out of a car. It spoke my name. Eddie Prue's long blank face hung somewhere up near the roof of a small Packard, behind its wheel. He was alone in it. I leaned on the door of the car and looked in at him.

"How you making out, shamus?"

I tossed a match down and blew smoke at his face. I said: "Who dropped that dental supply company's bill you gave me last night? Vannier, or somebody else?"

"Vannier."

"What was I supposed to do with it – guess the life history of a man named Teager?"

"I don't go for dumb guys," Eddie Prue said.

I said: "Why would he have it in his pocket to drop? And if he did drop it, why wouldn't you just hand it back to him? In other words, seeing that I'm a dumb guy, explain to me why a bill for dental supplies should get anybody all excited and start trying to hire private detectives. Especially gents like Alex Morny, who don't like private detectives."

"Morny's a good head," Eddie Prue said coldly.

"He's the fellow for whom they coined the phrase, 'as ignorant as an actor.' "

"Skip that. Don't you know what they use that dental stuff for?"

"Yeah. I found out. They use albastone for making molds of teeth and cavities. It's very hard, very fine grain and retains any amount of fine detail. The other stuff, crystobolite, is used to cook out the wax in an invested wax model. It's used because it stands a great deal of heat without distortion. Tell me you don't know what I'm talking about."

"I guess you know how they make gold inlays," Eddie Prue said. "I guess you do, huh?"

"I spent two of my hours learning today. I'm an expert. What does it get me?"

He was silent for a little while, and then he said: "You ever read the paper?"

"Once in a while."

"It couldn't be you read where an old guy named Morningstar was bumped off in the Belfont Building on Ninth Street, just two floors above where this H. R. Teager had his office. It couldn't be you read that, could it?"

I didn't answer him. He looked at me for a moment longer, then he put his hand forward to the dash and pushed the starter button. The motor of his car caught and he started to ease in the clutch.

"Nobody could be as dumb as you act," he said softly. "Nobody ain't. Good night to you."

The car moved away from the curb and drifted down the hill towards Franklin. I was grinning into the distance as it disappeared.

I went up to the apartment and unlocked the door and pushed it open a few inches and then knocked gently. There was movement in the room. The door was pulled open by a strong-looking girl with a black stripe on the cap of her white nurse's uniform.

"I'm Marlowe. I live here."

"Come in, Mr. Marlowe. Dr. Moss told me."

I shut the door quietly and we spoke in low voices. "How is she?" I asked.

"She's asleep. She was already drowsy when I got here. I'm Miss Lymington. I don't know very much about her except that her temperature is normal and her pulse still rather fast, but going down. A mental disturbance, I gather."

"She found a man murdered," I said. "It shot her full of holes. Is she hard enough asleep so that I could go in and get a few things to take to the hotel?"

"Oh, yes. If you're quiet. She probably won't wake. If she does, it won't matter."

I went over and put some money on the desk. "There's coffee and bacon and eggs and bread and tomato juice and oranges and liquor here," I said. "Anything else you'll have to phone for."

"I've already investigated your supplies," she said, smiling. "We have all we need until after breakfast tomorrow. Is she going to stay here?"

"That's up to Dr. Moss. I think she'll be going home as soon as she is fit for it. Home being quite a long way off, in Wichita."

"I'm only a nurse," she said. "But I don't think there is anything the matter with her that a good night's sleep won't cure."

"A good night's sleep and a change of company," I said, but that didn't mean anything to Miss Lymington.

I went along the hallway and peeked into the bedroom. They had put a pair of my pajamas on her. She lay almost on her back with one arm outside the bedclothes. The sleeve of the pajama coat was turned up six inches or more. The small hand below the end of the sleeve was in a tight fist. Her face looked drawn and white and quite peaceful. I poked about in the closet and got a suitcase and put some junk in it. As I started back out I looked at Merle again. Her eyes opened and looked straight up at the ceiling. Then they moved just enough to see me and a faint little smile tugged at the corners of her lips.

"Hello." It was a weak spent little voice, a voice that knew its owner was in bed and had a nurse and everything.

"Hello."

I went around near her and stood looking down, with my polished smile on my clear-cut features.

"I'm all right," she whispered. "I'm fine. Aren't I?"

"Sure."

"Is this your bed I'm in?"

"That's all right. It won't bite you."

"I'm not afraid," she said. A hand came sliding towards me and lay palm up, waiting to be held. I held it. "I'm not afraid of you. No woman would ever be afraid of you, would she?"

"Coming from you," I said, "I guess that's meant to be a compliment."

Her eyes smiled, then got grave again. "I lied to you," she said softly. "I – I didn't shoot anybody."

"I know. I was over there. Forget it. Don't think about it."

"People are always telling you to forget unpleasant things.

But you never do. It's so kind of silly to tell you to, I mean."

"Okay," I said, pretending to be hurt. "I'm silly. How about making some more sleep?"

She turned her head until she was looking into my eyes. I sat on the edge of the bed, holding her hand.

"Will the police come here?" she asked.

"No. And try not to be disappointed."

She frowned. "You must think I'm an awful fool."

"Well – maybe."

A couple of tears formed in her eyes and slid out at the corners and rolled gently down her cheeks.

"Does Mrs. Murdock know where I am?"

"Not yet. I'm going over and tell her."

"Will you have to tell her – everything?"

"Yeah, why not?"

She turned the head away from me. "She'll understand," her voice said softly. "She knows the awful thing I did eight years ago. The frightful terrible thing."

"Sure," I said. "That's why she's been paying Vannier money all this time."

"Oh dear," she said, and brought her other hand out from under the bedclothes and pulled away the one I was holding so that she could squeeze them tightly together. "I wish you hadn't had to know that. I wish you hadn't. Nobody ever knew but Mrs. Murdock. My parents never knew. I wish you hadn't."

The nurse came in at the door and looked at me severely.

"I don't think she ought to be talking like this, Mr. Marlowe. I think you should leave now."

"Look, Miss Lymington, I've known this little girl two days. You've only known her two hours. This is doing her a lot of good."

"It might bring on another – er – spasm," she said severely, avoiding my eyes.

"Well, if she has to have it, isn't it better for her to have it now, while you're here, and get it over with? Go on out to the kitchen and buy yourself a drink."

"I never drink on duty," she said coldly. "Besides somebody might smell my breath."

"You're working for me now. All my employees are required to get liquored up from time to time. Besides, if you had a good dinner and were to eat a couple of the Chasers in the kitchen cabinet, nobody would smell your breath."

She gave me a quick grin and went back out of the room. Merle had been listening to this as if it was a frivolous interruption to a very serious play. Rather annoyed.

"I want to tell you all about it," she said breathlessly. "I –"

I reached over and put a paw over her two locked hands. "Skip it. I know. Marlowe knows everything – except how to make a decent living. It doesn't amount to beans. Now you're going back to sleep and tomorrow I'm going to take you on the way back to Wichita – to visit your parents. At Mrs. Murdock's expense."

"Why, that's wonderful of her," she cried, her eyes opening wide and shining. "But she's always been wonderful to me."

I got up off the bed. "She's a wonderful woman," I said, grinning down at her. "Wonderful. I'm going over there now and we're going to have a perfectly lovely little talk over the teacups. And if you don't go to sleep right now, I won't let you confess to any more murders."

"You're horrid," she said. "I don't like you." She turned her head away and put her arms back under the bedclothes and shut her eyes.

I went towards the door. At the door I swung around and looked back quickly. She had one eye open, watching me. I gave her a leer and it snapped shut in a hurry.

I went back to the living room, gave Miss Lymington what was left of my leer, and went out with my suitcase.

I drove over to Santa Monica Boulevard. The hockshop was still open. The old Jew in the tall black skull cap seemed surprised that I was able to redeem my pledge so soon. I told him that was the way it was in Hollywood.

He got the envelope out of the safe and tore it open and took my money and pawnticket and slipped the shining gold coin out on his palm.

"So valuable this is I am hating to give it back to you," he said. "The workmanship, you understand, the workmanship, is beautiful."

"And the gold in it must be worth all of twenty dollars," I said.

He shrugged and smiled and I put the coin in my pocket and said goodnight to him.

32

THE MOONLIGHT LAY like a white sheet on the front lawn except under the deodar where there was the thick darkness of black velvet. Lights in two lower windows were lit and in one upstairs room visible from the front. I walked across the stumble-stones and rang the bell.

I didn't look at the little painted Negro by the hitching block. I didn't pat his head tonight. The joke seemed to have worn thin.

A white-haired, red-faced woman I hadn't seen before opened the door and I said: "I'm Philip Marlowe. I'd like to see Mrs. Murdock. Mrs. Elizabeth Murdock."

She looked doubtful. "I think she's gone to bed," she said. "I don't think you can see her."

"It's only nine o'clock."

"Mrs. Murdock goes to bed early." She started to close the door.

She was a nice old thing and I hated to give the door the heavy shoulder. I just leaned against it.

"It's about Miss Davis," I said. "It's important. Could you tell her that?"

"I'll see."

I stepped back and let her shut the door.

A mockingbird sang in a dark tree nearby. A car tore down the street much too fast and skidded around the next corner. The thin shreds of a girl's laughter came back along the dark street as if the car had spilled them out in its rush.

The door opened after a while and the woman said: "You can come in."

I followed her across the big empty entrance room. A single dim light burned in one lamp, hardly reaching to the opposite wall. The place was too still, and the air needed freshening. We went along the hall to the end and up a flight of stairs with a carved handrail and newel post. Another hall at the top, a door open towards the back.

I was shown in at the open door and the door was closed behind me. It was a big sitting room with a lot of chintz, a blue and silver wallpaper, a couch, a blue carpet and french windows open on a balcony. There was an awning over the balcony.

Mrs. Murdock was sitting in a padded wing chair with a card table in front of her. She was wearing a quilted robe and her hair looked a little fluffed out. She was playing solitaire. She had the pack in her left hand and she put a card down and moved another one before she looked up at me.

Then she said: "Well?"

I went over by the card table and looked down at the game. It was Canfield.

"Merle's at my apartment," I said. "She threw an ingbing."

Without looking up she said: "And just what is an ingbing, Mr. Marlowe?"

She moved another card, then two more quickly.

"A case of the vapors, they used to call it," I said. "Ever catch yourself cheating at that game?"

"It's no fun if you cheat," she said gruffly. "And very little if you don't. What's this about Merle? She has never stayed out like this before. I was getting worried about her."

630

I pulled a slipper chair over and sat down across the table from her. It put me too low down. I got up and got a better chair and sat in that.

"No need to worry about her," I said. "I got a doctor and a nurse. She's asleep. She was over to see Vannier."

She laid the pack of cards down and folded her big gray hands on the edge of the table and looked at me solidly.

"Mr. Marlowe," she said, "you and I had better have something out. I made a mistake calling you in the first place. That was my dislike of being played for a sucker, as you would say, by a hardboiled little animal like Linda. But it would have been much better, if I had not raised the point at all. The loss of the doubloon would have been much easier to bear than you are. Even if I had never got it back."

"But you did get it back," I said.

She nodded. Her eyes stayed on my face. "Yes. I got it back. You heard how."

"I didn't believe it."

"Neither did I," she said calmly. "My fool of a son was simply taking the blame for Linda. An attitude I find childish."

"You have a sort of knack," I said, "of getting yourselves surrounded with people who take such attitudes."

She picked her cards up again and reached down to put a black ten on a red jack, both cards that were already in the layout. Then she reached sideways to a small heavy table on which was her port. She drank some, put the glass down and gave me a hard level stare.

"I have a feeling that you are going to be insolent, Mr. Marlowe."

I shook my head. "Not insolent. Just frank. I haven't done so badly for you, Mrs. Murdock. You did get the doubloon back. I kept the police away from you — so far. I didn't do anything on the divorce, but I found Linda — your son knew where she was all the time — and I don't think you'll have any trouble with her. She knows she made a mistake marrying Leslie. However, if you don't think you got value —"

She made a humph noise and played another card. She got the ace of diamonds up to the top line. "The ace of clubs is buried, darn it. I'm not going to get it out in time."

"Kind of slide it out," I said, "when you're not looking."

"Hadn't you better," she said very quietly, "get on with telling me about Merle? And don't gloat too much, if you have found out a few family secrets, Mr. Marlowe."

"I'm not gloating about anything. You sent Merle to Vannier's place this afternoon, with five hundred dollars."

"And if I did?" She poured some of her port and sipped, eyeing me steadily over the glass.

"When did he ask for it?"

"Yesterday. I couldn't get it out of the bank until today. What happened?"

"Vannier's been blackmailing you for about eight years, hasn't he? On account of something that happened on April 26th, 1933?"

A sort of panic twitched in the depths of her eyes, but very far back, very dim, and somehow as though it had been there for a long time and had just peeped out at me for a second.

"Merle told me a few things," I said. "Your son told me how his father died. I looked up the records and the papers today. Accidental death. There had been an accident in the street under his office and a lot of people were craning out of windows. He just craned out too far. There was some talk of suicide because he was broke and had fifty thousand life insurance for his family. But the coroner was nice and slid past that."

"Well?" she said. It was a cold hard voice, neither a croak nor a gasp. A cold hard utterly composed voice.

"Merle was Horace Bright's secretary. A queer little girl in a way, overtimid, not sophisticated, a little girl mentality, likes to dramatize herself, very old-fashioned ideas about men, all that sort of thing. I figure he got high one time and made a pass at her and scared her out of her socks."

"Yes?" Another cold hard monosyllable prodding me like a gun barrel.

"She brooded and got a little murderous inside. She got a chance and passed right back at him. While he was leaning out of a window. Anything in it?"

"Speak plainly, Mr. Marlowe. I can stand plain talk."

"Good grief, how plain do you want it? She pushed her employer out of a window. Murdered him, in two words. And got away with it. With your help."

She looked down at the left hand clenched over her cards. She nodded. Her chin moved a short inch, down, up.

"Did Vannier have any evidence?" I asked. "Or did he just happen to see what happened and put the bite on you and you paid him a little now and then to avoid scandal – and because you were really very fond of Merle?"

She played another card before she answered me. Steady as a rock.

"He talked about a photograph," she said. "But I never believed it. He couldn't have taken one. And if he had taken one, he would have shown it to me – sooner or later."

I said: "No, I don't think so. It would have been a very fluky shot, even if he happened to have the camera in his hand, on account of the doings down below in the street. But I can see he might not have dared to show it. You're a pretty hard woman, in some ways. He might have been afraid you would have him taken care of. I mean that's how it might look to him, a crook. How much have you paid him?"

"That's none –" she started to say, then stopped and shrugged her big shoulders. A powerful woman, strong, rugged, ruthless and able to take it. She thought. "Eleven thousand one hundred dollars, not counting the five hundred I sent him this afternoon."

"Ah. It was pretty darn nice of you, Mrs. Murdock. Considering everything."

633

She moved a hand vaguely, made another shrug. "It was my husband's fault," she said. "He was drunk, vile. I don't think he really hurt her, but, as you say, he frightened her out of her wits. I – I can't blame her too much. She has blamed herself enough all these years."

"She had to take the money to Vannier in person?"

"That was her idea of penance. A strange penance."

I nodded. "I guess that would be in character. Later you married Jasper Murdock and you kept Merle with you and took care of her. Anybody else know?"

"Nobody. Only Vannier. Surely he wouldn't tell anybody."

"No. I hardly think so. Well, it's all over now. Vannier is through."

She lifted her eyes slowly and gave me a long level gaze. Her gray head was a rock on top of a hill. She put the cards down at last and clasped her hands tightly on the edge of the table. The knuckles glistened.

I said: "Merle came to my apartment when I was out. She asked the manager to let her in. He phoned me and I said yes. I got over there quickly. She told me she had shot Vannier."

Her breath was a faint swift whisper in the stillness of the room.

"She had a gun in her bag, God knows why. Some idea of protecting herself against men, I suppose. But somebody – Leslie, I should guess – had fixed it to be harmless by jamming a wrong size cartridge in the breech. She told me she had killed Vannier and fainted. I got a doctor friend of mine. I went over to Vannier's house. There was a key in the door. He was dead in a chair, long dead, cold, stiff. Dead long before Merle went there. She didn't shoot him. Her telling me that was just drama. The doctor explained it after a fashion, but I won't bore you with it. I guess you understand all right."

She said: "Yes. I think I understand. And now?"

"She's in bed, in my apartment. There's a nurse there.

I phoned Merle's father long distance. He wants her to come home. That all right with you?"

She just stared.

"He doesn't know anything," I said quickly. "Not this or the other time. I'm sure of that. He just wants her to come home. I thought I'd take her. It seems to be my responsibility now. I'll need that last five hundred that Vannier didn't get – for expenses."

"And how much more?" she asked brutally.

"Don't say that. You know better."

"Who killed Vannier?"

"Looks like he committed suicide. A gun at his right hand. Temple contact wound. Morny and his wife were there while I was. I hid. Morny's trying to pin it on his wife. She was playing games with Vannier. So she probably thinks he did it, or had it done. But it shapes up like suicide. The cops will be there by now. I don't know what they will make of it. We just have to sit tight and wait it out."

"Men like Vannier," she said grimly, "don't commit suicide."

"That's like saying girls like Merle don't push people out of windows. It doesn't mean anything."

We stared at each other, with that inner hostility that had been there from the first. After a moment I pushed my chair back and went over to the french windows. I opened the screen and stepped out on to the porch. The night was all around, soft and quiet. The white moonlight was cold and clear, like the justice we dream of but don't find.

The trees down below cast heavy shadows under the moon. In the middle of the garden there was a sort of garden within a garden. I caught the glint of an ornamental pool. A lawn swing beside it. Somebody was lying in the lawn swing and a cigarette tip glowed as I looked down.

I went back into the room. Mrs. Murdock was playing solitaire again. I went over to the table and looked down.

"You got the ace of clubs out," I said.

635

"I cheated," she said without looking up.

"There was one thing I wanted to ask you," I said. "This doubloon business is still cloudy, on account of a couple of murders which don't seem to make sense now that you have the coin back. What I wondered was if there was anything about the Murdock Brasher that might identify it to an expert – to a man like old Morningstar."

She thought, sitting still, not looking up. "Yes. There might be. The coinmaker's initials, E. B., are on the left wing of the eagle. Usually, I'm told, they are on the right wing. That's the only thing I can think of."

I said: "I think that might be enough. You did actually get the coin back, didn't you? I mean that wasn't just something said to stop my ferreting around?"

She looked up swiftly and then down. "It's in the strong room at this moment. If you can find my son, he will show it to you."

"Well, I'll say good night. Please have Merle's clothes packed and sent to my apartment in the morning."

Her head snapped up again and her eyes glared. "You're pretty high-handed about all this, young man."

"Have them packed," I said. "And send them. You don't need Merle any more – now that Vannier is dead."

Our eyes locked hard and held locked for a long moment. A queer stiff smile moved the corners of her lips. Then her head went down and her right hand took the top card off the pack held in her left hand and turned it and her eyes looked at it and she added it to the pile of unplayed cards below the layout, and then turned the next card, quietly, calmly, in a hand as steady as a stone pier in a light breeze.

I went across the room and out, closed the door softly, went along the hall, down the stairs, along the lower hall past the sun room and Merle's little office, and out into the cheerless stuffy unused living room that made me feel like an embalmed corpse just to be in it.

636

The french doors at the back opened and Leslie Murdock stepped in and stopped, staring at me.

33

HIS SLACK SUIT was rumpled and also his hair. His little reddish mustache looked just as ineffectual as ever. The shadows under his eyes were almost pits.

He was carrying his long black cigarette holder, empty, and tapping it against the heel of his left hand as he stood not liking me, not wanting to meet me, not wanting to talk to me.

"Good evening," he said stiffly. "Leaving?"

"Not quite yet. I want to talk to you."

"I don't think we have anything to talk about. And I'm tired of talking."

"Oh yes we have. A man named Vannier."

"Vannier? I hardly know the man. I've seen him around. What I know I don't like."

"You know him a little better than that," I said.

He came forward into the room and sat down in one of the I-dare-you-to-sit-in-me chairs and leaned forward to cup his chin in his left hand and look at the floor.

"All right," he said wearily. "Get on with it. I have a feeling you are going to be very brilliant. Remorseless flow of logic and intuition and all that rot. Just like a detective in a book."

"Sure. Taking the evidence piece by piece, putting it all together in a neat pattern, sneaking in an odd bit I had on my hip here and there, analyzing the motives and characters and making them out to be quite different from what anybody — or I myself for that matter — thought them to be up to this golden moment — and finally making a sort of world-weary pounce on the least promising suspect."

He lifted his eyes and almost smiled. "Who thereupon turns as pale as paper, froths at the mouth, and pulls a gun out of his right ear."

I sat down near him and got a cigarette out. "That's right. We ought to play it together sometime. You got a gun?"

"Not with me. I have one. You know that."

"Have it with you last night when you called on Vannier?"

He shrugged and bared his teeth. "Oh. Did I call on Vannier last night?"

"I think so. Deduction. You smoke Benson and Hedges Virginia cigarettes. They leave a firm ash that keeps its shape. An ashtray at his house had enough of those little gray rolls to account for at least two cigarettes. But no stubs in the tray. Because you smoke them in a holder and a stub from a holder looks different. So you removed the stubs. Like it?"

"No." His voice was quiet. He looked down at the floor again.

"That's an example of deduction. A bad one. For there might not have been any stubs, but if there had been and they had been removed, it might have been because they had lip-stick on them. Of a certain shade that would at least indicate the coloring of the smoker. And your wife has a quaint habit of throwing her stubs into the wastebasket."

"Leave Linda out of this," he said coldly.

"Your mother still thinks Linda took the doubloon and that your story about taking it to give to Alex Morny was just a cover-up to protect her."

"I said leave Linda out of it." The tapping of the black holder against his teeth had a sharp quick sound, like a telegraph key.

"I'm willing to," I said. "But I didn't believe your story for a different reason. This." I took the doubloon out and held it on my hand under his eyes.

He stared at it tightly. His mouth set.

"This morning when you were telling your story this was hocked on Santa Monica Boulevard for safekeeping. It was sent to me by a would-be detective named George Phillips. A simple sort of fellow who allowed himself to get into a bad spot through poor judgment and over-eagerness for a job. A thickset blond fellow in a brown suit, wearing dark glasses and a rather gay hat. Driving a sand-colored Pontiac, almost new. You might have seen him hanging about in the hall outside my office yesterday morning. He had been following me around and before that he might have been following you around."

He looked genuinely surprised. "Why would he do that?"

I lit my cigarette and dropped the match in a jade ashtray that looked as if it had never been used as an ashtray.

"I said he might have. I'm not sure he did. He might have just been watching this house. He picked me up here and I don't think he followed me here." I still had the coin on my hand. I looked down at it, turned it over by tossing it, looked at the initials E. B. stamped into the left wing, and put it away. "He might have been watching the house because he had been hired to peddle a rare coin to an old coin dealer named Morningstar. And the old coin dealer somehow suspected where the coin came from, and told Phillips, or hinted to him, that the coin was stolen. Incidentally, he was wrong about that. If your Brasher Doubloon is really at this moment upstairs, then the coin Phillips was hired to peddle was not a stolen coin. It was a counterfeit."

His shoulders gave a quick little jerk, as if he was cold. Otherwise he didn't move or change position.

"I'm afraid it's getting to be one of those long stories after all," I said, rather gently. "I'm sorry. I'd better organize it a little better. It's not a pretty story, because it has two murders in it, maybe three. A man named Vannier and a man named Teager had an idea. Teager is a dental technician in the Belfont Building, old Morningstar's building. The idea was to counterfeit a rare and valuable gold coin, not too rare to be marketable, but rare enough to be worth a lot of money. The method they thought of was about what a dental technician uses to make a gold inlay. Requiring the same materials, the same apparatus, the same skills. That is, to reproduce a model exactly, in gold, by making a matrix in a hard white fine cement called albastone, then making a replica of the model in that matrix in molding wax, complete in the finest detail, then investing the wax, as they call it, in another kind of cement called crystobolite, which has the property of standing great heat without distortion. A small opening is left from the wax to outside by attaching a steel pin which is withdrawn when the cement sets. Then the crystobolite casting is cooked over a flame until the wax boils out through this small opening, leaving a hollow mold of the original model. This is clamped against a crucible on a centrifuge and molten gold is shot into it by centrifugal force from the crucible. Then the crystobolite, still hot, is held under cold water and it disintegrates, leaving the gold core with a gold pin attached, representing the small opening. That is trimmed off, the casting is cleaned in acid and polished and you have, in this case, a brand new Brasher Doubloon, made of solid gold and exactly the same as the original. You get the idea?"

He nodded and moved a hand wearily across his head.

"The amount of skill this would take," I went on, "would be just what a dental technician would have. The process would be of no use for a current coinage, if we had a gold coinage, because the material and labor would cost more than the coin would be worth. But for a gold coin that was valuable through being rare, it would fit fine. So that's what they did. But they had to have a model. That's where you came in. You took the doubloon all right, but not to give to Morny. You took it to give to Vannier. Right?"

He stared at the floor and didn't speak.

"Loosen up," I said. "In the circumstances it's nothing very awful. I suppose he promised you money, because you needed it to pay off gambling debts and your mother is close. But he had a stronger hold over you than that."

He looked up quickly then, his face very white, a kind of horror in his eyes.

"How did you know that?" he almost whispered.

"I found out. Some I was told, some I researched, some I guessed. I'll get to that later. Now Vannier and his pal have made a doubloon and they want to try it out. They wanted to know their merchandise would stand up under inspection by a man supposed to know rare coins. So Vannier had the idea of hiring a sucker and getting him to try to sell the counterfeit to old Morningstar, cheap enough so the old guy would think it was stolen. They picked George Phillips for their sucker, through a silly ad he was running in the paper for business. I think Lois Morny was Vannier's contact with Phillips, at first anyway. I don't think she was in the racket. She was seen to give Phillips a small package. This package may have contained the doubloon Phillips was to try to sell. But when he showed it to old Morningstar he ran into a snag. The old man knew his coin collections and his rare coins. He probably thought the coin was genuine enough – it would take a lot of testing to show it wasn't – but the way the maker's initials were stamped on the coin was unusual and suggested to him that the coin might be the Murdock Brasher. He called up here and tried to find out. That made your mother suspicious and the coin was found to be missing and she suspected Linda, whom she hates, and hired me to get it back and put the squeeze on Linda for a divorce, without alimony."

"I don't want a divorce," Murdock said hotly. "I never had any such idea. She had no right –" he stopped and made a despairing gesture and a kind of sobbing sound.

"Okay, I know that. Well, old Morningstar threw a scare into Phillips, who wasn't crooked, just dumb. He managed to get Phillips' phone number out of him. I heard the old man call that number, eavesdropping in his office after he thought I had left. I had just offered to buy the doubloon back for a thousand dollars and Morningstar had taken up the offer, thinking he could get the coin from Phillips, make himself some money and everything lovely. Meantime Phillips was watching this house, perhaps to see if any cops were coming and going. He saw me, saw my car, got my name off the registration and it just happened he knew who I was.

"He followed me around trying to make up his mind to ask me for help until I braced him in a downtown hotel and he mumbled about knowing me from a case in Ventura when he was a deputy up there, and about being in a spot he didn't like and about being followed around by a tall guy with a funny eye. That was Eddie Prue, Morny's sidewinder. Morny knew his wife was playing games with Vannier and had her shadowed. Prue saw her make contact with Phillips near where he lived on Court Street, Bunker Hill, and then followed Phillips until he thought Phillips had spotted him, which he had. And Prue, or somebody working for Morny, may have seen me go to Phillips' apartment on Court Street. Because he tried to scare me over the phone and later asked me to come and see Morny."

I got rid of my cigarette stub in the jade ashtray, looked at the bleak unhappy face of the man sitting opposite me, and plowed on. It was heavy going, and the sound of my voice was beginning to sicken me.

"Now we come back to you. When Merle told you your mother had hired a dick, that threw a scare into *you*. You figured she had missed the doubloon and you came steaming up to my office and tried to pump me. Very debonair, very sarcastic at first, very solicitous for your wife, but very worried. I don't know what you think you found out, but you got in touch with Vannier. You now had to get the coin back to your mother in a hurry, with some kind of story. You met Vannier somewhere and he gave you a doubloon. Chances are it's another counterfeit. He would be likely to hang on to the real one. Now Vannier sees his racket in danger of blowing up before it gets started. Morningstar has called your mother and

I have been hired. Morningstar has spotted something. Vannier goes down to Phillips' apartment, sneaks in the back way, and has it out with Phillips, trying to find out where he stands.

"Phillips doesn't tell him he has already sent the counterfeit doubloon to me, addressing it in a kind of printing afterwards found in a diary in his office. I infer that from the fact Vannier didn't try to get it back from me. I don't know what Phillips told Vannier, of course, but the chances are he told him the job was crooked, that he knew where the coin came from, and that he was going to the police or to Mrs. Murdock. And Vannier pulled a gun, knocked him on the head and shot him. He searched him and the apartment and didn't find the doubloon. So he went to Morningstar. Morningstar didn't have the counterfeit doubloon either, but Vannier probably thought he had. He cracked the old man's skull with a gun butt and went through his safe, perhaps found some money, perhaps found nothing, at any rate left the appearance of a stickup behind him. Then Mr. Vannier breezed on home, still rather annoyed because he hadn't found the doubloon, but with the satisfaction of a good afternoon's work under his vest. A couple of nice neat murders. That left you."

34

MURDOCK FLICKED a strained look at me, then his eyes went to the black cigarette holder he still had clenched in his hand. He tucked it in his shirt pocket, stood up suddenly, ground the heels of his hands together and sat down again. He got a handkerchief out and mopped his face.

"Why me?" he asked in a thick strained voice.

"You knew too much. Perhaps you knew about Phillips, perhaps not. Depends how deep you were in it. But you knew about Morningstar. The scheme had gone wrong and Morningstar had been murdered. Vannier couldn't just sit back and hope you wouldn't hear about that. He had to shut your mouth, very, very tight. But he didn't have to kill you to do it. In fact killing you would be a bad move. It would break his hold on your mother. She's a cold ruthless grasping woman, but hurting you would make a wildcat of her. She wouldn't care what happened."

Murdock lifted his eyes. He tried to make them blank with astonishment. He only made them dull and shocked.

"My mother — what —?"

"Don't kid me any more than you have to," I said. "I'm tired to death of being kidded by the Murdock family. Merle came to my apartment this evening. She's there now. She had been over to Vannier's house to bring him some money. Blackmail money. Money that had been paid to him off and on for eight years. I know why."

He didn't move. His hands were rigid with strain on his knees. His eyes had almost disappeared into the back of his head. They were doomed eyes.

"Merle found Vannier dead. She came to me and said she had killed him. Let's not go into why she thinks she ought to confess to other people's murders. I went over there and he had been dead since last night. He was as stiff as a wax dummy. There was a gun lying on the floor by his right hand. It was a gun I had heard described, a gun that belonged to a man named Hench, in an apartment across the hall from Phillips' apartment. Somebody ditched the gun that killed Phillips and took Hench's gun. Hench and his girl were drunk and left their apartment open. It's not proved that it was Hench's gun, but it will be. If it is Hench's gun, and Vannier committed suicide, it ties Vannier to the death of Phillips. Lois Morny also ties him to Phillips, in another way. If Vannier didn't commit suicide — and I don't believe he did — it might still tie him to Phillips. Or it might tie somebody else to Phillips, somebody who also killed Vannier. There are reasons why I don't like that idea."

Murdock's head came up. He said: "No?" in a suddenly clear voice. There was a new expression on his face, something bright and shining and at the same time just a little silly. The expression of a weak man being proud.

I said: "I think you killed Vannier."

He didn't move and the bright shining expression stayed on his face.

"You went over there last night. He sent for you. He told you he was in a jam and that if the law caught up with him, he would see that you were in the jam with him. Didn't he say something like that?"

"Yes," Murdock said quietly. "Something exactly like that. He was drunk and a bit high and he seemed to have a sense of power. He gloated, almost. He said if they got him in the gas chamber, I would be sitting right beside him. But that wasn't all he said."

"No. He didn't want to sit in the gas chamber and he didn't at the time see any very good reason why he should, if you kept your mouth good and tight. So he played his trump card. His first hold on you, what made you take the doubloon and give it to him, even if he did promise you money as well, was something about Merle and your father. I know about it. Your mother told me what little I hadn't put together already. That was his first hold and it was pretty strong. Because it would let you justify yourself. But last night he wanted something still stronger. So he told you the truth and said he had proof."

He shivered, but the light clear proud look managed to stay on his face.

"I pulled a gun on him," he said, almost in a happy voice. "After all she is my mother."

"Nobody can take that away from you."

He stood up, very straight, very tall. "I went over to the chair he sat in and reached down and put the gun against his face. He had a gun in the pocket of his robe. He tried to get it, but he didn't get it in time. I took it away from him. I put my gun back in my pocket. I put the muzzle of the other gun against the side of his head and told him I would kill him, if he didn't produce his proof and give it to me. He began to sweat and babble that he was just kidding me. I clicked back the hammer on the gun to scare him some more."

He stopped and held a hand out in front of him. The hand shook but as he stared down at it it got steady. He dropped it to his side and looked me in the eye.

"The gun must have been filed or had a very light action. It went off. I jumped back against the wall and knocked a picture down. I jumped from surprise that the gun went off, but it kept the blood off me. I wiped the gun off and put his fingers around it and then put it down on the floor close to his hand. He was dead at once. He hardly bled except the first spurt. It was an accident."

"Why spoil it?" I half sneered. "Why not make it a nice clean honest murder?"

"That's what happened. I can't prove it, of course. But I think I might have killed him anyway. What about the police?"

I stood up and shrugged my shoulders. I felt tired, spent, drawn out and sapped. My throat was sore from yapping and my brain ached from trying to keep my thoughts orderly.

"I don't know about the police," I said. "They and I are not very good friends, on account of they think I am holding out on them. And God knows they are right. They may get to you. If you weren't seen, if you didn't leave any fingerprints around, and even if you did, if they don't have any other reason to suspect you and get your fingerprints to check, then they may never think of you. If they find out about the doubloon and that it was the Murdock Brasher, I don't know where you stand. It all depends on how well you stand up to them."

"Except for mother's sake," he said, "I don't very much care. I've always been a flop."

"And on the other hand," I said, ignoring the feeble talk, "if the gun really has a very light action and you get a good lawyer and tell an honest story and so on, no jury will convict you. Juries don't like blackmailers."

"That's too bad," he said. "Because I am not in a position to use that defense. I don't know anything about blackmail. Vannier showed me where I could make some money, and I needed it badly."

I said: "Uh-huh. If they get you where you need the black-mail dope, you'll use it all right. Your old lady will make you. If it's her neck or yours, she'll spill."

"It's horrible," he said. "Horrible to say that."

"You were lucky about that gun. All the people we know have been playing with it, wiping prints off and putting them on. I even put a set on myself just to be fashionable. It's tricky when the hand is stiff. But I had to do it. Morny was over there having his wife put hers on. He thinks she killed Vannier, so she probably thinks he did."

He just stared at me. I chewed my lip. It felt as stiff as a piece of glass.

"Well, I guess I'll just be running along now," I said.

"You mean you are going to let me get away with it?" His voice was getting a little supercilious again.

"I'm not going to turn you in, if that's what you mean. Beyond that I guarantee nothing. If I'm involved in it, I'll have to face up to the situation. There's no question of morality involved. I'm not a cop nor a common informer nor an officer of the court. You say it was an accident. Okay, it was an accident. I wasn't a witness. I haven't any proof either way. I've been working for your mother and whatever right to my silence that gives her, she can have. I don't like her, I don't like you, I don't like this house. I didn't particularly like your wife. But I like Merle. She's kind of silly and morbid, but she's kind of sweet too. And I know what has been done to her in this damn family for the past eight years. And I know she didn't

647

push anybody out of any window. Does that explain matters?"

He gobbled, but nothing came that was coherent.

"I'm taking Merle home," I said. "I asked your mother to send her clothes to my apartment in the morning. In case she kind of forgets, being busy with her solitaire game, would you see that that is done?"

He nodded dumbly. Then he said in a queer small voice: "You are going – just like that? I haven't – I haven't even thanked you. A man I hardly know, taking risks for me – I don't know what to say."

"I'm going the way I always go," I said. "With an airy smile and a quick flip of the wrist. And with a deep and heartfelt hope that I won't be seeing you in the fish bowl. Good night."

I turned my back on him and went to the door and out. I shut the door with a quiet firm click of the lock. A nice smooth exit, in spite of all the nastiness. For the last time I went over and patted the little painted Negro on the head and then walked across the long lawn by the moon-drenched shrubs and the deodar tree to the street and my car.

I drove back to Hollywood, bought a pint of good liquor, checked in at the Plaza, and sat on the side of the bed staring at my feet and lapping the whiskey out of the bottle.

Just like any common bedroom drunk.

When I had enough of it to make my brain fuzzy enough to stop thinking, I undressed and got into bed and after a while, but not soon enough, I went to sleep.

35

IT WAS THREE o'clock in the afternoon and there were five pieces of luggage inside the apartment door, side by side on the carpet. There was my yellow cowhide, well scraped on both sides from being pushed around in the boots of cars. There were two nice pieces of airplane luggage both marked L.M. There was an old black imitation walrus thing marked M.D. and there was one of these little leatherette overnight cases which you can buy in drugstores for a dollar forty-nine.

Dr. Carl Moss had just gone out of the door cursing me because he had kept his afternoon class of hypochondriacs waiting. The sweetish smell of his Fatima poisoned the air for me. I was turning over in what was left of my mind what he had said when I asked him how long it would take Merle to get well.

"It depends what you mean by well. She'll always be high on nerves and low on animal emotion. She'll always breathe thin air and smell snow. She'd have made a perfect nun. The religious dream, with its narrowness, its stylized emotions and its grim purity, would have been a perfect release for her. As it is she will probably turn out to be one of these acid-faced virgins that sit behind little desks in public libraries and stamp dates in books."

"She's not that bad," I had said, but he had just grinned at me with his wise Jew face and gone out of the door. "And besides how do you know they are virgins?" I added to the closed door, but that didn't get me any farther.

I lit a cigarette and wandered over to the window and after a while she came through the doorway from the bedroom part of the apartment and stood there looking at me with her eyes dark-ringed and a pale composed little face without any makeup except on the lips.

"Put some rouge on your cheeks," I told her. "You look like the snow maiden after a hard night with the fishing fleet."

So she went back and put some rouge on her cheeks. When she came back again she looked at the luggage and said softly: "Leslie lent me two of his suitcases."

I said: "Yeah," and looked her over. She looked very nice. She had a pair of long-waisted rust-colored slacks on, and Bata shoes and a brown and white print shirt and an orange scarf. She didn't have her glasses on. Her large clear cobalt eyes

649

had a slightly dopey look, but not more than you would expect. Her hair was dragged down tight, but I couldn't do anything much about that.

"I've been a terrible nuisance," she said. "I'm terribly sorry."

"Nonsense. I talked to your father and mother both. They're tickled to death. They've only seen you twice in over eight years and they feel as if they had almost lost you."

"I'll love seeing them for a while," she said, looking down at the carpet. "It's very kind of Mrs. Murdock to let me go. She's never been able to spare me for long." She moved her legs as if she wondered what to do with them in slacks, although they were her slacks and she must have had to face the problem before. She finally put her knees close together and clasped her hands on top of them.

"Any little talking we might have to do," I said, "or anything you might want to say to me, let's get it over with now. Because I'm not driving halfway across the United States with a nervous breakdown in the seat beside me."

She bit a knuckle and sneaked a couple of quick looks at me around the side of the knuckle. "Last night —" she said, and stopped and colored.

"Let's use a little of the old acid," I said. "Last night you told me you killed Vannier and then you told me you didn't. I know you didn't. That's settled."

She dropped the knuckle, looked at me levelly, quiet, composed and the hands on her knees now not straining at all.

"Vannier was dead a long time before you got there. You went there to give him some money for Mrs. Murdock."

"No — for me," she said. "Although of course it was Mrs. Murdock's money. I owe her more than I'll ever be able to repay. Of course she doesn't give me much salary, but that would hardly —"

I said roughly: "Her not giving you much salary is a characteristic touch and your owing her more than you can ever repay is more truth than poetry. It would take the Yankee outfield with two bats each to give her what she has coming from you. However, that's unimportant now. Vannier committed suicide because he had got caught out in a crooked job. That's flat and final. The way you behaved was more or less an act. You got a severe nervous shock seeing his leering dead face in a mirror and that shock merged into another one a long time ago and you just dramatized it in your screwy little way."

She looked at me shyly and nodded her copper-blond head, as if in agreement.

"And you didn't push Horace Bright out of any window," I said.

Her face jumped then and turned startlingly pale. "I – I –" her hand went to her mouth and stayed there and her shocked eyes looked at me over it.

"I wouldn't be doing this," I said, "if Dr. Moss hadn't said it would be all right and we might as well hand it to you now. I think maybe you think you killed Horace Bright. You had a motive and an opportunity and just for a second I think you might have had the impulse to take advantage of the opportunity. But it wouldn't be in your nature. At the last minute you would hold back. But at that last minute probably something snapped and you pulled a faint. He did actually fall, of course, but you were not the one that pushed him."

I held it a moment and watched the hand drop down again to join the other one and the two of them twine together and pull hard on each other.

"You were made to think you had pushed him," I said. "It was done with care, deliberation and the sort of quiet ruthlessness you only find in a certain kind of woman dealing with another woman. You wouldn't think of jealousy to look at Mrs. Murdock now – but if that was a motive, she had it. She had a better one – fifty thousand dollars' life insurance – all that was left from a ruined fortune. She had the strange wild possessive love for her son such women have. She's cold, bitter, unscrupulous and she used you without mercy or pity, as insurance, in case Vannier ever blew his top. You were just a scapegoat to her. If you want to come out of this pallid sub-emotional life you have been living, you have got to realize and believe what I am telling you. I know it's tough."

"It's utterly impossible," she said quietly, looking at the bridge of my nose, "Mrs. Murdock has been wonderful to me always. It's true I never remembered very well – but you shouldn't say such awful things about people."

I got out the white envelope that had been in the back of Vannier's picture. Two prints in it and a negative. I stood in front of her and put a print on her lap.

"Okay, look at it. Vannier took it from across the street."

She looked at it. "Why that's Mr. Bright," she said. "It's not a very good picture, is it? And that's Mrs. Murdock – Mrs. Bright she was then – right behind him. Mr. Bright looks mad." She looked up at me with a sort of mild curiosity.

"If he looks mad there," I said, "you ought to have seen him a few seconds later, when he bounced."

"When he what?"

"Look," I said, and there was a kind of desperation in my voice now, "that is a snapshot of Mrs. Elizabeth Bright Murdock giving her first husband the heave out of his office window. He's falling. Look at the position of his hands. He's screaming with fear. She is behind him and her face is hard with rage – or something. Don't you get it at all? This is what Vannier has had for proof all these years. The Murdocks never saw it, never really believed it existed. But it did. I found it last night, by a fluke of the same sort that was involved in the taking of the picture. Which is a fair sort of justice. Do you begin to understand?"

She looked at the photo again and laid it aside. "Mrs. Murdock has always been lovely to me," she said.

"She made you the goat," I said, in the quietly strained voice of a stage manager at a bad rehearsal. "She's a smart tough patient woman. She knows her complexes. She'll even spend a dollar to keep a dollar, which is what few of her type will do. I hand it to her. I'd like to hand it to her with an elephant gun, but my polite breeding restrains me."

"Well," she said, "that's that." And I could see she had heard one word in three and hadn't believed what she had heard. "You must never show this to Mrs. Murdock. It would upset her terribly."

I got up and took the photo out of her hand and tore it into small pieces and dropped them in the wastebasket.

"Maybe you'll be sorry I did that," I told her, not telling her I had another and the negative. "Maybe some night — three months — three years from now — you will wake up in the night and realize I have been telling you the truth. And maybe then you will wish you could look at that photograph again. And maybe I am wrong about this too. Maybe you would be very disappointed to find out you hadn't really killed anybody. That's fine. Either way it's fine. Now we are going downstairs and get in my car and we are going to drive to Wichita to visit your parents. And I don't think you are going back to Mrs. Murdock, but it may well be that I am wrong about that too. But we are not going to talk about this any more. Not any more."

"I haven't any money," she said.

"You have five hundred dollars that Mrs. Murdock sent you. I have it in my pocket."

"That's really awfully kind of her," she said.

"Oh hell and fireflies," I said and went out to the kitchen and gobbled a quick drink, before we started. It didn't do me any good. It just made me want to climb up the wall and gnaw my way across the ceiling.

36

I WAS GONE ten days. Merle's parents were vague kind patient people living in an old frame house in a quiet shady street. They cried when I told them as much of the story as I thought they should know. They said they were glad to have her back and they would take good care of her and they blamed themselves a lot, and I let them do it.

When I left Merle was wearing a bungalow apron and rolling pie crust. She came to the door wiping her hands on the apron and kissed me on the mouth and began to cry and ran back into the house, leaving the doorway empty until her mother came into the space with a broad homey smile on her face to watch me drive away.

I had a funny feeling as I saw the house disappear, as though I had written a poem and it was very good and I had lost it and would never remember it again.

I called Lieutenant Breeze when I got back and went down to ask him how the Phillips case was coming. They had cracked it very neatly, with the right mixture of brains and luck you always have to have. The Mornys never went to the police after all, but somebody called and told about a shot in Vannier's house and hung up quickly. The fingerprint man didn't like the prints on the gun too well, so they checked Vannier's hand for powder nitrates. When they found them they decided it was suicide after all. Then a dick named Lackey working out of Central Homicide thought to work on the gun a little and he found that a description of it had been distributed, and a gun like it was wanted in connection with the Phillips killing. Hench identified it, but better than that they found a half print of his thumb on the side of the trigger, which, not ordinarily being pulled back, had not been wiped off completely.

With that much in hand and a better set of Vannier's prints

than I could make they went over Phillips' apartment again and also over Hench's. They found Vannier's left hand on Hench's bed and one of his fingers on the underside of the toilet flush lever in Phillips' place. Then they got to work in the neighborhood with photographs of Vannier and proved he had been along the alley twice and on a side street at least three times. Curiously, nobody in the apartment house had seen him, or would admit it.

All they lacked now was a motive. Teager obligingly gave them that by getting himself pinched in Salt Lake City trying to peddle a Brasher Doubloon to a coin dealer who thought it was genuine but stolen. He had a dozen of them at his hotel, and one of them turned out to be genuine. He told them the whole story and showed a minute mark that he had used to identify the genuine coin. He didn't know where Vannier got it and they never found out because there was enough in the papers to make the owner come forward, if it had been stolen. And the owner never did. And the police didn't care any more about Vannier once they were convinced he had done murder. They left it at suicide, although they had a few doubts.

They let Teager go after a while, because they didn't think he had any idea of murder being done and all they had on him was attempted fraud. He had bought the gold legally and counterfeiting an obsolete New York State coin didn't come under the federal counterfeiting laws. Utah refused to bother with him.

They never believed Hench's confession. Breeze said he just used it for a squeeze on me, in case I was holding out. He knew I couldn't keep quiet if I had proof that Hench was innocent. It didn't do Hench any good either. They put him in the lineup and pinned five liquor store holdups on him and a wop named Gaetano Prisco, in one of which a man was shot dead. I never heard whether Prisco was a relative of Palermo's, but they never caught him anyway.

"Like it?" Breeze asked me, when he had told me all this, or all that had then happened.

"Two points not clear," I said. "Why did Teager run away and why did Phillips live on Court Street under a phony name?"

"Teager ran away because the elevator man told him old Morningstar had been murdered and he smelled a hookup. Phillips was using the name of Anson because the finance company was after his car and he was practically broke and getting desperate. That explains why a nice young boob like him could get roped in to something that must have looked shady from the start."

I nodded and agreed that could be so.

Breeze walked to his door with me. He put a hard hand on my shoulder and squeezed.

"Remember that Cassidy case you were howling about to Spangler and me that night in your apartment?"

"Yes."

"You told Spangler there wasn't any Cassidy case. There was – under another name. I worked on it."

He took his hand off my shoulder and opened the door for me and grinned straight into my eyes.

"On account of the Cassidy case," he said, "and the way it made me feel, I sometimes give a guy a break he could perhaps not really deserve. A little something paid back out of the dirty millions to a working stiff – like me – or like you. Be good."

It was night. I went home and put my old house clothes on and set the chessmen out and mixed a drink and played over another Capablanca. It went fifty-nine moves. Beautiful cold remorseless chess, almost creepy in its silent implacability.

When it was done I listened at the open window for a while and smelled the night. Then I carried my glass out to the kitchen and rinsed it and filled it with ice water and stood at the sink sipping it and looking at my face in the mirror.

"You and Capablanca," I said.